DEFIANCE OF THE FALL
BOOK SIX

aethonbooks.com

DEFIANCE OF THE FALL 6
©2022 JF BRINK/THEFIRSTDEFIER

This book is protected under the copyright laws of the United States of America. No part of this publication may be reproduced, stored in a retrieval system, or transmitted, in any form or by any means, without the prior permission in writing of the publisher, nor be otherwise circulated in any form of binding or cover other than that in which it is published and without a similar condition including this condition being imposed on the subsequent purchaser. Any reproduction or unauthorized use of the material or artwork contained herein is prohibited without the express written permission of the authors.

Aethon Books supports the right to free expression and the value of copyright. The purpose of copyright is to encourage writers and artists to produce the creative works that enrich our culture.

The scanning, uploading, and distribution of this book without permission is a theft of the author's intellectual property. If you would like to use material from the book (other than for review purposes), please contact editor@aethonbooks.com. Thank you for your support of the author's rights.

Aethon Books
www.aethonbooks.com

Print and eBook formatting by Steve Beaulieu. Artwork provided by Fernando Granea.

Published by Aethon Books LLC.

Aethon Books is not responsible for websites (or their content) that are not owned by the publisher.

This book is a work of fiction. Names, characters, places, and incidents are the product of the author's imagination or are used fictitiously. Any resemblance to actual events, locales, or persons, living or dead is coincidental.

All rights reserved.

ALSO IN SERIES

DEFIANCE OF THE FALL

BOOK ONE

BOOK TWO

BOOK THREE

BOOK FOUR

BOOK FIVE

BOOK SIX

BOOK SEVEN

Want to discuss our books with other readers and even the authors like J.F. Brink (TheFirstDefier), Shirtaloon, Zogarth, Cale Plamann, Noret Flood (Puddles4263) and so many more?

Join our Discord server today and be a part of the Aethon community.

1
CHALLENGE

The aquamarine, almost green, luster from the miasmic sky shone through the small windows by the ceiling of the warehouse, a reminder they were still in the heart of the Undead Incursion. However, Zac's worries about hidden dangers in the Dead Zone were thrown into the back of his mind upon hearing the news.

The Mystic Realm Ogras visited before their trip to the Tower of Eternity was actually a research base, one focusing on bloodlines? And escaped test subjects were likely ancestors to some families on earth? Zac had just lamented that using the Bloodline Marrow he got for stopping the Undead Empire's realignment would be a bit wasteful on its own, and now this opportunity presented itself?

What if he could find something to bring out the most of the marrow and guarantee that his bloodline could awaken?

"Perhaps we can find things to strengthen the people of Port Atwood," Kenzie exclaimed, echoing Zac's thoughts. "There might be bloodline manuals or elixirs stashed inside the Mystic Realm. Perhaps even things to open hidden nodes."

"There are also werewolves and god knows what else in there, according to Ogras," Zac said to calm his sister down before he turned to Triv. "Do you have any proof of this theory?"

"Young master, I don't. But we are quite good judges of the quality of bodies, and as far as we can tell, the inhabitants of this planet aren't natural," Triv said.

"That's impossible, though. We have mapped our evolution for millions of years," Zac countered, the words of his mother's projection echoing in the back of his head.

According to her, she had been surprised to find Earth inhabited at all when she arrived.

"Yes, this planet has a natural seed of life, but many Heritages do not belong here," Triv conceded. "I personally believe that some accident happened inside that Mystic Realm a few thousand years ago. The owners left, and a group of test subjects managed to break free and ended up on this planet."

Zac quickly understood what would happen next if what the ghost said was true. Those escapees would find themselves on an unintegrated planet utterly devoid of Cosmic Energy. They would be like castaways, unable to become stronger and unable to leave. Their children wouldn't have any chance to become cultivators, but their bloodlines would still be passed on.

Was this the source of Billy's golden blood? And was it perhaps even the source of his own bloodline? He had figured that it came from his mother, but perhaps that was completely wrong. Perhaps his [Void Heart] came from someone who had fled the Mystic Realm thousands of years ago.

"What kind of experiments do you think would take place in such a hidden base?" Zac asked.

"We believed it was related to some boundless faction; they're always up to something. Perhaps they wanted to create a new bloodline suited to their needs, using other bloodlines as a base. Perhaps they wanted to evolve bloodlines and sell the results to wealthy families. It is impossible to tell without gaining access to the research data," the ghost said.

"The undead incursion was after the Mystic Realm as well, and so are the cultists," Kenzie added.

"I know." Zac nodded.

Void's Disciple had said as much when they met, and the invaders had pretty much confirmed it by sailing toward his Mystic Realm entrance even after failing their attack on Port Atwood. He still didn't know what was so alluring about that place, but it considering that even the top factions were so interested, its value probably exceeded a whole newly integrated world like Earth.

"Well, did you know that the Church of Everlasting Dao already controls three different portals that all lead to our Mystic Realm?" Kenzie said. "According to Triv, at least."

"How come you're so talkative all of a sudden?" Zac asked skeptically. "You almost exploded the last time I tried to have you divulge some minor secrets."

"This matter regarding bloodlines was a welcome surprise, but it's not related to the goal of the Undead Empire," Triv explained, this time taking a spiritual hit.

"So you were after something else," Zac said.

"Yes," the ghost croaked, further wounding himself.

"What was it?" Zac muttered curiously, but he hurriedly corrected himself when he saw that Triv was starting to shake and expand. "Wait, don't answer that!"

He was still extremely curious about what could elicit such a response. Two major factions and the Dominators were all gunning toward that item, yet he was somehow still kept out of the loop.

"Julia might be able to find out more," Kenzie said, seemingly reading his thoughts.

"What? Julia?" Zac repeated with confusion. "How would that be possible?"

The former government official had simply stayed on the island since jumping onto the teleporter with him, sometimes assisting with diplomatic issues with the Marshall Clan. How would she know something that he didn't about the Mystic Realm?

"The New World Government actually performed an all-out assault on one of the cultists' bases and killed one of their generals. That's how they got access to the Mystic Realm and started the 'Ark World' project," Kenzie explained. "They should have found out a few things if they're taking such drastic measures."

"The one time that little faction showed some spine," the ghost muttered from the side. "The humans of this planet are wholly unimpressive. If it weren't for young master and the many bloodlines running around, then this world would be completely worthless."

"So you're saying I should send out Julia as a spy? I doubt she will be able to return to her position after all these months," Zac said, ignoring the ghost.

"She should still have some contacts who would want to make a connection with you, especially now that the undead incursion is dealt with," Kenzie explained.

"I'll talk with her when we get back." Zac nodded before he turned to the ghost.

However, Zac couldn't help but feel himself being dragged against his will once more as he thought about the Mystic Realm, just like when the System had placed him in front of the two Remnants. It seemed like he really didn't have a choice but to explore its depths this time either. All his enemies would be there, and it was related to his family. The Mystic Realm was his best bet at figuring out whether Leandra was a friend or a foe.

And now it might even help him with his constitution?

His having some sort of bloodline was pretty much confirmed from getting the odd hidden node **[Void Heart]**. If it was based on some previous captive, then there might actually be more information and even a manual waiting for him inside the Mystic Realm. After all, he wanted to maintain his above-average power, and opening additional hidden nodes was one of the best available methods in the E-grade.

Just like the F-grade was the best opportunity to farm titles, the E-grade was the best opportunity to open up nodes that might benefit him for the rest of his life. Every grade was like that, as far as Zac understood. He wasn't sure about how the higher grades worked, but it seemed like D-grade was the only rank where you could perfect your Cultivator Core.

"What else do you know about the Mystic Realm?" Zac asked Triv.

"Not much," the ghost said, but he hurriedly explained after getting a glare from Zac. "The scant intelligence we had was based on spying on the cultists and capturing a few of their warriors. We were focused on the realignment. As long as it succeeded, the planet would be ours, including the Mystic Realm."

Zac asked a few more questions, but he soon realized there was not much else that the butler could divulge between lack of firsthand information and the compulsions. Hopefully, he'd be able to gain more information through Julia. Of course, by this point, he could probably just fly over to New Washington and demand answers from Thomas Fischer.

Seeing that the teleporter was up and running was a relief, but there was one more thing Zac wanted to take care of before he left this place.

"Take me to the residence Mhal used before I killed him," Zac said as he turned to Triv.

"It was you?" Triv blurted with surprise as he led the way. "We figured it was the Monks."

Zac only shrugged in response as he ushered the ghost out of the warehouse. The fortress was only so big, and they soon reached a structure, or at least the ruins of one. The aboveground manor had been completely destroyed from the battle, but the ghost informed him that there was a large underground compound as well after it activated some sort of ocular skill.

A quick search led him to a reinforced steel hatch in the ground. A physical barrier was no match for Zac, who simply ripped the thick metal plate off its hinges. However, he immediately regretted his action, as a rancid odor rose from the dark hole. It was so bad that he nearly swapped over to his Draugr form to avoid keeling over.

"What is this stench?" Zac blanched.

"Mhal performed quite a few experiments in his spare time. I believe he was trying to find a suitable upgrade for his current constitution. Corpselords are usually like that, obsessed with their bodies. Better to discard the body entirely, if you ask me. You become a bit weaker, but you only need to focus on one type of improvement," Triv said as he looked down at the tunnel with some disdain.

"I found a notebook on his body after I defeated him. He brought something valuable to this place, something that he hid from you and the Lich King. He was instructed by his clan to experiment on this planet, away from prying eyes," Zac said. "I need to find it."

"He did?" Triv said with surprise. "He never struck me or Lord Adriel as the clever type, but rather a brute. But perhaps that was exactly what he wanted."

Zac quickly found the source of the stench as he walked down a set of stairs. Three dank holding cells were filled with dismembered bodies in various states of decay. There were a handful of Zombies as well, who desperately charged at the bars when they sensed him. Zac made short work of them all before he threw out a massive amount of corpse-destroying powder.

It alleviated the smell a bit, but Zac still worked at maximum efficiency to look for the hidden Draugr samples. Triv was flying straight through walls and the ground in search of hidden compartments as well, eager to prove his worth.

"Young master, over here," Triv said a while later as he rose from the floor. "How curious, I couldn't sense anything at all until I hit a barrier. It really seems like this little vassal force was keeping a lot of secrets. Are they planning a rebellion?"

"That doesn't have anything to do with you, remember?" Zac snorted as he walked over. "You're an earthling now."

"Of course, of course." The ghost hurriedly nodded. "But the young master should know that returning to the embrace of the empire is the only way for a pure-blood Draugr to realize his full potential."

"How do you know I'm pure-blood?" Zac asked with some curiosity as he started digging up the ground.

"I cannot be certain, but your bloodline is certainly a lot stronger than anything I've encountered before. And it feels… old. That's how it feels with the ancient clans of the Heartlands, I'm told," the ghost hesitantly said. "If I may, why cling to your human form at all if you have the chance to discard it? You even have the opportunity to awaken without losing your sense of self, something that is usually extremely difficult to achieve."

"Well, being human doesn't seem so glamorous to you, perhaps, but I like it," Zac muttered, his eyes trained on the box he had unearthed.

Zac hesitated about what to do for a few seconds as he looked down at the pitch-black container. He could sense that this truly was what he was looking for, as there was a slight resonance between his Specialty Core and the box. But what now? Were the samples of his bloodline any use to him any longer?

He eventually stashed away the box without opening it, much to

Triv's disappointment. Zac was afraid that there were traps in the chest itself that would break the samples inside. Who knew, they might become useful for upgrading his Specialty Core in the future. He had the System to help him out for the first evolution, but next time, he might not be so lucky.

There was nothing else of interest in the chamber, and Zac quickly returned to the surface, the stale air feeling like a fresh gust after that rancid environment. If there had been any lingering feelings of pity for the Corpselord's clan before due to the letter he read, then that pity had been utterly quashed after seeing the aftermath of Mhal's experimentation.

In either case, there was not much left to do in the Dead Zone, and Zac prepared to get going. However, he realized that the ghost presented a problem as he returned to his sister's side.

"Is there any way you can hide?" Zac asked as he turned to the ghost, who kept pace two steps behind. "I can't be bringing you around in the open. I already have enough people talking behind my back from working with the demons."

"Here," the ghost said as he produced a small black tower no larger than three centimeters in height. "I can stay inside this as long as young master doesn't put it into a Spatial Treasure. With your permission, I'll rest for a few days, as my soul is wounded. If you need me, just call by nudging the mark in your mind."

Zac nodded, and the ghost disappeared the next moment as the small tower started giving off a weak aquamarine light. Zac curiously looked at the thing, but he couldn't figure out if it was a Spatial Treasure or if the ghost could actually shrink itself to such a diminutive size.

"I don't understand why you don't just kill that thing," Ogras muttered with disgust as he stepped out of the shadows. "Nothing good will come from keeping that one."

"I'll destroy any Karmic Ties he might carry later," Zac said. "I have the lamp now."

"Karmic Ties is just one of the many dangers in the Multiverse." Ogras shrugged. "Another one is consorting with the unliving. It usually ends with you joining them."

"A bit late for that," Zac snorted, which elicited a laugh from Kenzie as she fiddled with her new inscription tool.

"One of you are playing with ghosts, the other with Technocrat toys. You two siblings are truly testing the limits," the demon muttered. "You'd better pray the Ruthless Heavens don't take you up on your challenge."

2
EVENINGTIDE

Zac rolled his eyes at the demon's slightly ominous comment, but he did somewhat agree. The two of them were playing a dangerous game, him with the Remnants and Kenzie with Jeeves. Such powerful items really shouldn't be in the hands of piddling low-grade cultivators, and it would only drag them into trouble with the System.

But there wasn't much he could do about it right now, apart from growing stronger to tackle whatever came their way.

"Are you done here?" Zac asked instead.

"I managed to dig out some of the intelligence crystals from the place you indicated, but most of them were ruined. Also, I can't read them," the demon said as he threw one over to Zac.

He tried to activate it as well, but his Cosmic Energy was rebuffed. Even worse, some cracks spread across its surface, prompting Zac to hurriedly retract his energy.

"I'll try as an undead later," Zac said as he placed Triv's tower in a pocket. "If we're done here, then you can call over our people. I'll leave as soon as we can confirm the situation on the other side. Send this to Port Atwood, please."

He quickly imprinted a few instructions onto a crystal and handed it to his sister. Kenzie grabbed it before she poured hundreds of Nexus Crystals out on the ground in a circle around the teleportation array. She looked a bit hesitant about what to do next, but Ogras seemed to understand her thoughts.

"Here," Ogras said and threw a scaled leg from some unknown beast onto the array. "Harvested it during the climb. It tasted like wet fur anyway."

Kenzie nodded and placed the crystal on top of the leg, and the next moment, the two items flashed away.

"We're returning to Port Atwood?" Joanna asked as they waited for a response on the other side.

"I want that tree, but I need to see what's happened with the ship heading for Mystic Island. I'll go back if there's still a chance to protect our teleporter," Zac said after some consideration. "If not, I'll simply fly and get the tree. I'll be able to observe the Dead Zone that way as well."

Ten minutes later, a group of soldiers emerged from the teleporter, including a suntanned Ilvere.

"You did it," Ilvere said with a grin as he looked around at the ruins. "Must have been some battle. I wish I were here to kick these damn Zombies off the planet as well. What about Alea's...?"

Zac sighed as he saw the demon general's downcast expression. Zac had made sure that only a few core members knew about Alea's situation, but the two remaining demon generals were among the group of people he felt should be aware of what was going on. The normal demons would only think that she had been killed by the invaders when they assaulted the island.

"I ripped him apart with her chains," Zac simply said.

"Good!" Ilvere roared. "Then her soul can be at peace no matter what happens next."

"What's going on with the boat?" Zac asked, eager to change the subject.

"We failed." Ilvere sighed. "Those ships are so slow, but it suddenly spat out a smaller vessel that shot toward the Mystic Island with a speed that eclipsed our ships. Worse yet, they managed to break the tunnel just by detonating something on the shore. We currently have around a hundred people trapped inside the Mystic Realm. We managed to sink the large warship in retaliation."

"At least our people are safe," Zac said as he turned to his sister. "Can you see what you can do?"

"Sure." Kenzie nodded.

Since there wasn't much he could do now that the spatial tunnel was already broken, he decided to go fetch the mutated tree instead. Ilvere would lead the squad of soldiers to search for the core of the Dead Zone, while simultaneously taking away all the Unholy Beacons that were still standing.

After all, they still hadn't found any natural resources in the area. All the other incursions had been placed near some valuable resources of Earth, so it stood to reason that it should be the same here. Of course, there was the possibility that the perk of the Undead Empire was getting placed in an extremely population-dense area, as corpses were the most valuable resource to them.

Seeing his army get to work with practiced ease let him bring out his flying treasure without worry, but he was surprised to see Ogras jumping on top as well.

"I have nothing to do, so I figure I'll come along for the ride." The demon shrugged with a grin. "What if you suddenly pass out again and fall into a horde of Zombies?"

"The company is always welcome." Zac slowly nodded.

"I'm curious if you can actually gain something from the tree. You're a mortal, but you keep getting insights left and right. I want to figure out if there's something I've missed. Just look at that giant. Sometimes there's genius hidden within a haze of stupidity." The demon smiled.

"Well, thank you," Zac snorted as he turned to Joanna, who had also joined him on the leaf.

"I'm just here to help you steer in case you need to relax," Joanna explained.

Emily and the rest of the Valkyries would return to Port Atwood with Kenzie. They weren't as high-leveled, and they had stayed long enough in such a Miasma-dense area. Any longer and it might have adverse effects.

The trio soon set off, and the atmosphere was a lot more relaxed as they returned toward the outer reaches of the Dead Zone. Zac took Joanna up on the offer to steer so that he could focus on recuperation, whereas Ogras took out a jug of some liquor and drank as he gazed out across the horizon.

Zac got a bit bored after an hour and joined Ogras for a drink instead.

"By the way, I found out some more about the Eveningtide Asura after you left the Base Town," Ogras said as he handed Zac a jug. "Figured it might be useful, as some see you as the second coming of that guy after your display of erecting a netherblasted Corpse Tree right in front of the Tower entrance."

"A what?" Joanna asked from the side.

"And?" Zac coughed with some embarrassment, ignoring the question. "Is that good news or bad news?"

"Hard to say. Unattached elites cropping out of nowhere is always a cause for concern. It will usually result in multiple forces getting destroyed before a balance is restored," the demon said.

"But that rarely happens to the peak forces because of their hidden reserves. The attacker would have to overpower an ancient empire, and that's easier said than done. So they have grown complacent," Ogras continued.

Zac nodded in agreement. If it had been before he visited the Base Town, he would have believed it wasn't too hard for a powerhouse to take out a slightly weaker force, but he had experienced just how desperate things became upon his exiting the Tower. And that was only a few hundred warriors with limitations on what sort of items they could bring to the special dimensions.

What about the biggest forces? They would be able to bring out billions of warriors and an almost inexhaustible number of treasures to defend themselves. Taking them out as a lone powerhouse would be almost impossible.

"But then the Eveningtide Asura came along." Ogras smiled. "And now there's you."

"Just who is that guy, and what did he do?" Zac asked.

Zac had repeatedly been compared to that man since he had conquered the eighth floor, so it was a bit interesting to hear what kind of man the so-called Asura was.

"He utterly annihilated a fifth of the peak forces in this sector," Ogras said with gleaming eyes. "Killed them to the last man. Trillions of lives lost; even a C-grade continent was grievously wounded to the point it decreased in grade. A murderous lunatic, it sounds like."

"Why would he do something like that?" Zac said with shock.

No wonder so many seemed so leery about him after the fight outside the Tower. The problem was whether the forces of the Multiverse would want to stomp him out before he grew powerful, or whether they would instead try to nurture a good relationship. Some obviously tried the latter, such as Boje and Pretty, but that didn't necessarily represent the intentions of their ancestors.

"To resolve grudges. Those who died had tried to hunt him down when he was younger. They wanted to get their hands on his treasures before he grew powerful, and he was almost killed dozens of times. He barely managed to slip away each time, until he finally disappeared for one hundred thousand years," Ogras said. "Then he finally came back, as a Peak C-grade Monarch. Blood flowed like rivers for five hundred years before he was satisfied and left our sector for good."

"Wait, just Peak C-grade? Did he manage to do all that without even breaking into the B-grade? How is that possible? Don't all the peak forces have Peak C-grade Monarchs hidden in seclusion?" Zac asked incredulously. "With the help of their arrays, they should be able to defend even against someone like that."

"I actually learned something interesting regarding that," Ogras snorted. "Our sector is a bit generous, or rather boastful, when it comes to assigning grades to forces."

"What?" Zac asked with confusion.

"There are probably less than ten High C-grade Monarchs in the whole sector," Ogras said, drawing a surprised exclamation from both Joanna and Zac. "Some say even less than five. And not a single Peak C-grade warrior unless they are hiding their strength for some reason. The reason that Dravorak Dynasty is so famous right now is that they have one of the few confirmed High C-grade Monarchs."

"What?" Zac said. "Are you messing with me? What about all the peak C-grade forces?"

"Having a pseudo C-grade Monarch makes a force C-grade. Having a true C-grade Monarch, no matter how weak, makes the force Middle C-grade. Having an elite Early C-grade or a weak Mid C-grade makes the force a High C-grade force. Finally, forces with at least Mid-grade C-grade warriors and strong foundations are called the Peak C-grade forces of the Zecia Sector," Ogras snorted.

Zac was about to refute the man, but he suddenly remembered Anzonil. His force was regarded as a weak D-grade force simply because he had formed a Pseudo Core. It sounded like the same was possible with whatever was required to move into the C-grade, and a remote sector like Zecia considered that good enough.

It also explained why Catheya's master seemingly held such a level of esteem in the Undead Kingdom. Perhaps it wasn't only the fact that he came from the Heartlands, but also that he simply was stronger than anyone else in the whole sector. No wonder that Catheya could decapitate forty people without anyone lifting a finger to retaliate.

It didn't make a big difference for Zac as things were, but it did actually lessen the pressure he felt somewhat. It meant that if he managed to reach at least Early C-grade in the future, then there was probably no force in the whole sector that would dare mess with him or Earth. He had thought he would have to reach High C-grade for that effect.

Of course, the revelation also indicated that there might be something lacking in the Zecia Sector as a whole if no one was able to reach Peak C-grade. Perhaps it was resources, or perhaps the cultivation techniques. In either case, it was bad news for him. If not even the most talented cultivators could reach Peak C-grade, how would he, a talentless mortal, do it?

Of course, he was way early in worrying about the C-grade. But it was worth remembering, as it meant that following the "standard" elite route of Zecia would have an end point that was even lower than that of his master, Yrial. He would have to go above and beyond somehow, and it was clearly possible if the Eveningtide Asura had managed to break through.

"Is he still alive?" Zac asked curiously. "The Asura?"

"No idea." Ogras shrugged. "This happened something like a million years ago. Perhaps not even the ancient bastards from the strongest forces were alive back then. There were rumors that he had offended some terrifying force on the outside a few hundred thousand years ago, and after that, he hasn't been heard of. Sounds like someone who loved getting himself in trouble, and perhaps his luck ran out. Also, considering how many mortals he killed in his quest for vengeance, he might have been punished by the Ruthless Heavens."

The atmosphere on the leaf became a bit subdued as they looked out across the landscape. Zac prayed that things wouldn't play out as they had with the Eveningtide Asura. It also confirmed the importance of keeping anything valuable with you hidden, at least until you were strong enough to defend yourself.

However, his mood soon lightened again as they closed in on their target: the mutated tree that was somehow generating life through death. Joanna set them down next to the tree, and Zac walked up to it once more. However, no matter what he did, he found himself unable to push his Dao any further, and he couldn't make any inroads on his skill quests either.

He was forced to give up after five hours, but he still felt that the tree held some secrets worth exploring. He took out a large barrel and filled it with dirt before he gingerly cut three branches and placed them inside. He also inserted a couple of Miasma Crystals into the soil after some consideration.

He hadn't gained much from the last set of saplings he took, but that might be because of him having placed them into his Cosmos Sack. He had long forgotten to replant them, which had turned them into worthless sticks in his bag. But now that he was planning on building a death-attuned cultivation cave, he would have a proper home ready for them.

They set out a minute later, and they actually reached the edge of the Dead Zone a bit faster than expected. However, they soon realized that it wasn't because of their speed, but rather because the Dead Zone seemed to be shrinking. It was a huge relief to see the world naturally heal itself so quickly, and it felt like a good indicator that it hadn't been damaged beyond repair.

But that didn't mean that the undead threat was completely dealt with, as they saw massive swathes of Zombies lumbering around as they flew closer to the battlefield he had seen in his crystal. Some of them seemed to be heading toward the core of the Dead Zone, whereas others trailed off toward inhabited lands.

It would take a lot of work to deal with the hundreds of millions of undead.

Some were already working on it, though, and Zac was surprised to see the battle was still raging. It wasn't an all-out battle, as the humans mostly seemed to fight in an effort to corral the Zombies away from the area with human settlements. However, the horde still looked extremely rowdy. Some drifted back toward the Dead Zone, but most seemed intent on feasting on the living.

Zac looked inward to check the status of his body. The node had mostly stabilized by now, and while the pathways were still a bit messy, he had started to work on redrawing them over the past day. He still had a long way to go, but he felt he had made enough progress to comfortably dish out a couple of fractal edges.

"I'll help them out a bit," Zac said as he jumped down from the leaf, hurtling toward the Zombies like a human cannonball.

3
PLANS AND SCHEMES

"How is it?" Gregor asked with a cough, and his mouth was filled with the taste of iron, reminding him of his internal injuries.

A decent number of wounds covered his body from ceaseless fighting over the past two days, and the two newly gained scimitars in his hands felt as heavy as mountains. But there was not much else to do. The Zombie bastards had gone crazy out of nowhere, and it only became worse when that shudder had gone through the planet.

But the pain was intermixed with a sweet sense of bliss, as that shudder had indicated the continued survival of Earth. That man had really done it. One man and a small support staff charging into the core of the Dead Zone to kill the Lich King, and somehow living to tell the tale.

If only the other undead bastards could take the hint and throw in the towel as well.

"We won't be able to hold much longer." Lararia frowned as she looked out over the front lines. "I think our best bet is fighting a battle of retreat, leading them away from our sector."

"Some of these bastards will still ignore us and do whatever they want," Oksana muttered. "Our scouts are indicating that packs of Zombies are appearing all over the place, causing havoc."

"What about Enigma?" Gregor asked.

"We can't find him," Lararia said with worry. "He took his squad to search for the general, but we've lost contact."

"Well, let's hope he's just held up," Gregor mumbled. "Our faction will need – wait, is that him?"

The other councilors followed his gaze, and their eyes immediately lit up. It wasn't their unsociable strongman, who essentially lived out in the battlefields, but rather an emerald leaf that pushed through the clear blue sky.

The others didn't have time to comment before someone jumped out from the flying treasure, falling straight toward the sea of Zombies like a meteor. A terrifying impact erupted the next second as a coruscating wave of rock and mud spread out like a tsunami, swallowing hundreds of Zombies in an instant.

A massive plume of sand rose to the sky from the impact and obscured their vision. Gregor barely had time to register the series of events as an enormous blade ripped the dust apart as it shot out with terrifying momentum.

It was at least fifty meters long, and the Zombies were cut apart as though they were made of paper. Were these the same wretched creatures that caused their soldiers so much trouble with their sturdy bodies? A shocking corridor of destruction ripped forward, leaving not a single body intact. Gregor had to rapidly blink a couple of times as he stared at the edge's advance, as it almost felt like his eyes were cut by just looking at the skill.

Gregor himself and many of the councilors had tried to take advantage of the thick density of Zombies in a similar fashion, utilizing their area skills to cause as much damage as possible. However, the Zombies were just too tough. Each Zombie drained their attacks, like they sucked up some of the energy like sponges, causing the skills to fizzle after a dozen kills or so.

However, Lord Atwood's attack seemed to face no such impediments. It kept flying until they destabilized well over a hundred meters away from him. Was it a difference of Dao? The fractal blade that cut through the horde like butter had a greenish tint, the color giving the attack a distinct power.

They had already guessed that Lord Atwood had surpassed the stage of Dao Seeds, and this seemed to be a confirmation of it.

However, it quickly became apparent that the enormous blade was no ultimate strike, as Lord Atwood seemingly was able to keep conjuring them at will. One, two, three blades followed suit in short order, each reaping their own set of the unliving as Lord Atwood moved with impossible speed within the horde. Each blade took out thousands of the clumped-together bastards.

"So many of them dead in an instant," Oksana muttered with disbelief written all over her face. "Is this the power of the E-grade?"

"No way," Lararia said with a shake of her head, her tail nervously flitting back and forth from watching the bloody display. "If that was the case, then the general would have singlehandedly decimated our army. This is Lord Atwood's personal power."

"Shit, didn't he just fight the Lich King yesterday? And now he's already back at full power?" Gregor sputtered with disbelief. "Is that man unstoppable?"

Each step moved Lord Atwood fifty meters forward and resulted in another gory wave of destruction, and a primordial fear gripped Gregor's heart as he looked at the carnage. They could sense his immense aura even all the way from where they stood, and Gregor felt like a helpless hare gazing at an apex predator.

An eruption of darkness suddenly swallowed another section of the Zombie horde, and the undead fell by the hundreds. Gregor looked at the spectacle with confusion until he suddenly noticed the horned demon emerging out of the shadows to decimate everything in his surroundings, only to disappear a moment later.

He kept moving the battlefield through teleportation, like a grim reaper toying with the mindless undead. Gregor had thought Lord Atwood to be an outlier after he'd essentially dealt with the Fire Golem incursion singlehandedly, but it looked like he had extremely capable followers as well.

"Enigma isn't even a match to the right-hand man," Lararia muttered, echoing his thoughts. "We'd probably need the whole council to secure a kill. Provided that this is the limits of that man's power."

"Don't speak such unlucky words. What if they hear us?" Oksana said with a frown. "Besides, they are our saviors."

"Should we join them?" Gregor ventured after a while.

"No point," a new voice said, and they saw Romal walk over, his bloody shovel slung across his back. "We might just get in the way. Let's hold the line and deal with stragglers until they're done."

The other councilors nodded in agreement, and they spent the next hour dealing with the scraps while the two monsters kept wreaking havoc. Joanna, the spear warrior following Lord Atwood, joined them early on and confirmed the destruction of the undead incursion.

The demon joined them half an hour later, appearing in their midst without notice. However, Lord Atwood kept mowing down Zombies for over two hours, methodically decimating the undead. Every three seconds, the air would shudder as he released a massive fractal edge, and he would move toward the next group without bothering to look at the results.

Gregor had already turned numb to that man's actions, but he couldn't help but wonder just how much Cosmic Energy that man had used by this point. He almost felt a bit thankful when it looked like the Lord Atwood had finally reached his limit, proving there were some checks and balances in the universe as he walked over toward their army.

A tremendous pressure radiated from his body, but Gregor was surprised to feel a refreshing aura coming from it as well. The Zombies clearly didn't share his sentiments as they fled for their lives, desperately moving out of the Dao Field as he walked toward the council's army.

Releasing the aura essentially ended the battle, and over a hundred thousand warriors silently watched the approach of a single bloodied man. Even Gregor felt mesmerized as he looked at Lord Atwood's approach, as he drew quite the picture with the suns setting behind his back.

The bestial axe in his hand glistened in the sunlight as dark blood dripped from the teeth fastened to its axe-head. However, the white flowing robes he wore were unmarred by even a speck of dust, proving that he hadn't even been close to becoming injured during the fight.

However, the most gripping things were his eyes. It felt like they contained a boundless power that made Gregor shudder from hundreds of meters away. His very existence was cause for pressure, and it looked like the army felt the same as a wide passage in the ranks opened up without any order. It wasn't surprising, of course.

Who'd dare to block a man who had just mowed down millions of Zombies?

Lord Atwood soon appeared in front of them and nodded as he stashed away his weapon.

"Have you found any clues about the general who was leading this horde?" he simply asked.

"Ah – ehm, no," Gregor said, quickly finding his bearings. "I'm afraid not. The horde suddenly turned chaotic and rowdy without warning two days ago; we believe it might have been because the general fled. Enigma set out to find him with a group of elites, but we haven't heard any news."

Lord Atwood nodded with a sigh.

"Well, the portal is closed, and the Dead Zone is shrinking. We'll be able to smoke him out sooner or later. Contact Port Atwood if you hear anything," he said.

"Of course." Gregor nodded.

"Where's the closest teleporter?" Lord Atwood asked.

"An hour by foot in that direction," Romal said with a weak voice as he pointed westward.

"Thank you for your hard work," Lord Atwood said as he jumped back onto his flying treasure. "But remember, this isn't over. There are still multiple dangers threatening Earth, so don't let down your guards. I will hold an auction in a few weeks; there will be a lot of items that will be helpful for the elites of our world. You should come."

"Port Atwood next?" the mysterious demon asked, but Lord Atwood shook his head.

"No, there's someone I need to talk to first," Lord Atwood said with a shake of his head.

"Who?" the demon asked with surprise.

"Verana," Zac simply answered as he nodded for his bodyguard to start flying. "I need some answers."

A bloodthirsty laugh echoed out across the area as the demon joined him on the leaf, leaving a subdued group of councilors behind. Only when the trio had turned into a small spot on the horizon did

Gregor remember to breathe, and he realized his back was completely drenched in sweat.

"Imagine if we actually had gone with the original plan to fight that monster." Gregor wryly smiled. "We'd be skeletons tossed into some corner of the Underworld by now."

And more importantly, he felt very happy that he wasn't related to that Verana character, going by the fire in Lord Atwood's eyes.

A subdued silence lingered in the large conference room, with no one of the ten-odd people present wanting to be the first one to speak up. Thomas wasn't in any hurry either, so he slowly looked out across the room of representatives to get a sense of their thoughts.

The power dynamic of the New World Government had slowly changed with democracy giving way to hegemony, but such was the natural result in a world like theirs. However, Thomas knew all too well that his current position was nowhere near as stable as that of Super Brother-Man, Zachary Atwood.

He was unable to completely subdue the other factions of the government with his strength alone, so he was still forced to accede to the will of the many in some scenarios. It did bog down his plans a bit, but he could only blame himself for being lacking in talent.

"It's closed, and the array has been turned off," Francis Girardot finally muttered as he looked over at Thomas.

Thomas slowly nodded in confirmation, but he didn't speak up just yet. Zachary Atwood had made his move after all, and he was curious to see what the others had to say about it. His biggest worry right now was that the other members would start flocking to his rising star, abandoning the arduously crafted plans of theirs.

"Is this good news or bad news?" Johana, the Russian representative, asked.

"It is obviously good news to have one less threat to worry about," Asano said from the other side of the table. "The question is whether it changes our plans."

Multiple heads slowly turned toward Thomas sitting at the short end of the table. Asano's words had a clear implication. What can you provide that Super Brother-Man can't?

"This doesn't change our plans," Thomas finally said. "Zachary's defeating the Undead Empire is not wholly unexpected. The undead were powerful, but ultimately limited by the rules of the System. The real threat to Earth is not. The threat of the Redeemer remains. We will proceed with the Ark World Project."

Murmurs of agreement went around the table, though a few faces looked troubled.

"What about bringing Zachary Atwood into the plan?" a councilor ventured. "It would greatly improve our chances to seize the item."

"Absolutely not," Thomas Fischer said without hesitation. "Remember the uses of the Dimensional Seed? We want it to create a safe haven for our people. But what would Zachary Atwood use it for?"

"The C-grade," Asano muttered thoughtfully.

"Exactly. All our intelligence indicates that he only cares about the safety of his sister. He even left his whole army to fend for themselves for weeks against the undead. He mysteriously disappeared for a month while humans died by the millions. He will no doubt save the seed to break through in the future," Thomas said without missing a beat.

"But he's facing the same threat as us. The master of the Dominators," another representative muttered. "Surely he can be convin–"

"We already possess two tokens that would take us off-world," Thomas cut him off. "There is no way that Zachary Atwood doesn't have at least as many. He can always cut and run, bringing his closest people with him after having looted all the treasures of Earth."

The representatives slowly nodded in agreement, clearly seeing the problem as well.

"Besides, it's not like we're hopeless," Thomas added with a smile. "I'm happy to announce that Silverfox and I have finally managed to broker an agreement with the True Sky Faction of the Ark World. Zachary Atwood is strong, but can he contend with their High E-grade ancestors?"

4
REGRET

Verana sat by a flowerbed in her garden, absentmindedly stroking Lulu's soft fur as the beast slept in her lap while cradling a Beast Crystal. A sense of impending doom had filled her heart the entire day, and she finally knew it was time for a reckoning the moment Lys hurried into her room with worry in her eyes. Not that her maid needed to explain what was going on, as she had already received the prompt.

Zachary Atwood had arrived.

The humans under her employ had already divulged his evolution and explosive gain in levels over the past days, and the fact that their surroundings weren't drowned in Miasma was proof enough of what had transpired. The young master of the Brindevalt had sent a message as well five hours ago, confirming her hunch. The Undead Empire had been thrown off this baby world, making Zachary Atwood its de facto leader.

This should normally have been a joyous occasion, but she had messed up. She had been frozen in hesitation about the implications of offending the undead and the Church of the Everlasting Dao, until the point that they lost connection through the teleporter. Now Zac was back, and his thoughts about the actions of the Tal-Eladar were known only to himself.

Why had she hesitated back then? It was not like either of those forces were on good terms with the Tal-Eladar. In fact, it was the opposite, with the higher-tiered tribes having joined more than one excursion to curtail the expansion of the Undead Kingdoms.

She finally understood the weight of command that her grandmother had tried teaching her about, but now it might be too late. Her mind ran a mile a minute as she tried to figure out the optimal path to take from here on out. There was a palpable pressure on her, as the course of the meeting might decide whether she and her people would survive the day.

Because one thing was clear. If Super Brother-Man had arrived with the intent to kill, then there was nothing she could do. He had taken out almost a dozen forces stronger than theirs, and even the undead weren't a match to him. She still couldn't believe it, as she had seen him in action on multiple occasions.

But it was hard to argue with the facts placed in front of her.

She finally concluded that her best course of action was to feign ignorance, that she had been preparing her forces to assist when Port Atwood was under attack, but the arrays had suddenly disappeared just when they were about to set out. So she adorned a welcoming smile when the human and his annoying companion stepped into her garden.

Verana gasped as she felt a terrifying pressure spread out through her backyard. Zachary Atwood was clearly making his stance known, and the few attendants were forced to flee from the immense pressure as the flora was pushed to the ground. Even Verana felt the strain, and Lulu whined in her lap as she was startled awake, her little muscles growing taut.

There was no longer any confusion about how Zachary Atwood had defeated the undead after feeling this terrorizing aura. It was almost incomprehensible how much he had grown since they last met. Verana already knew that he had gone off-world for some opportunity, but just what kind of encounter could utterly transform someone to this degree? She still maintained the smile, wanting to make it feel like nothing was amiss.

However, that smile turned extremely forced when she heard Zac's first words.

"I thought you would have left for the Brindevalt Clan by now."

Zac looked at the frozen smile of Verana with a snort before he sat down opposite her.

"I am not sure what you've heard, but I assure you that the Tir'Emarel family has upheld their part of the agreement without any deviance," Verana said after a second. "We have not divulged any information about you to the Brindevalt. I feared the worst had happened to you when we lost contact, and we sought out an ally."

"You know, I wondered what made you so willing to stay behind on a planet invaded by not only the undead but also the insane cultists," Zac said, freely speaking his thoughts. "It turns out you had an escape route from the beginning."

"Can't trust the pointy-ears; they are only true to their beasts," Ogras snorted from the side, drawing an angered look from Verana.

"I can understand how it looks, but I hope that you can understand my predicament. I wanted to assist, but I also had orders from my family to not offend any powerful forces while I was cut off from the clan. By the time I found the resolve to go against my family's wishes, we had lost connection to Port Atwood," Verana explained. "Also, I believe the Brindevalt can become a great asset as well. They are–"

"You can send a message to your friends," Zac cut her off. "I am heading back to consolidate my gains. But I will head out and slaughter every invading force that remains on Earth the moment I'm done. They'd better be gone within the week unless they're ready to face me in battle."

Zac stood up, not caring that Verana's smiling face had turned into an emotionless mask, her eyes the only thing that betrayed the churning emotions within.

"I'll uphold my bargain; you are welcome to stay as a trading partner. However, since you're unwilling to fight for this planet's survival, then you can forget about taking part in its resources. I will see any expansion from the Tal-Eladar as an act of war, and I will act swiftly in response," Zac said as he walked out without another word.

He had said what needed to be said, and he was in no mood to stay any longer. His wholesale slaughter of the Zombie horde had tired him out, and he just wanted to sleep for a few hours. Ogras stood up as well, but he didn't immediately join Zac as he left. Instead, he turned toward Verana with a grin.

"What?" she snorted with annoyance after Zac had left the garden. "Don't pretend a calculating coward like you would have acted any different when faced with such a situation."

"I may be a coward, but I at least have a nose for opportunity. You've just pissed off the first person to reach the ninth floor of the Tower of Eternity in a million years," Ogras said, his grin almost splitting his face apart. "You'd better pray that the tribal elders of your Race don't sacrifice your whole clan, as a form of appeasement to the second coming of the Eveningtide Asura."

"WHAT?!" Verana exclaimed with shock, but she quickly calmed down. "Another lie from a demon's poisonous tongue."

However, Ogras noticed that the Beast Master was not as calm as she let on, and he decided to twist the knife a bit.

"Believe what you will. Would I bother lying about something like this? The news will sooner or later spread across the whole sector, and the natives will bring back news over the coming years. You'll see. Silly girl, you stayed on this little planet for its opportunities, but you let it all slip through your fingers." Ogras laughed as he flashed away, effortlessly avoiding an infuriated swipe by Verana.

He appeared right at the exit of the garden and looked back at Verana, who stood rooted in place with a stormy expression. One of them looked physically ill, and the other looked like he had just won the lottery.

"What were you doing?" Zac asked when Ogras appeared by his side again.

"Rubbing some salt in the wound." The demon snickered. "Never forget to kick your enemies when they are down."

"What do you think they'll do?" Zac asked, ignoring the comment.

"The potential of a trade route like this is too valuable to simply give up, especially now that you've proven your worth," Ogras slowly said. "They will definitely leave at least some people here. Not that I think that they can simply leave as they want through someone else's incursion. There should be a massive cost to that. I didn't even know it was possible. At best, the girl and a few of her elites will be able to escape this planet, leaving the rest behind. Doesn't really matter now, does it? You have gained many superior allies since we met these bastards."

Zac nodded in agreement. If things fell through with the Tir'E-marel Clan, then there would be a hundred stronger factions that would probably be more than willing to trade with him after the System's shroud was lifted. Provided he didn't become a pariah of the sector, of course.

The Tal-Eladar kept a wide berth around them as they walked through the town, and they soon reached the teleportation array. They appeared in Port Atwood a bout of darkness later, and the two let out a collective sigh of relief. He had seen the others step through just fine, but almost getting ripped to shreds while stuck mid-teleportation had left a small seed of fear in Zac's heart.

He just wanted to run home and sleep, but there was one thing that couldn't wait.

"You want to see your girlfriend?" Zac asked after having nodded at the soldiers standing guard at the teleportation tree.

"What? Who?" Ogras blurted and took a step back.

"Emma MacHale," Zac snorted.

"Oh, her?" Ogras muttered. "What a waste. Why are you seeing her?"

"I need to speak with Julia," Zac explained. "I want information from the New World Government."

"Why not just go over and lop off a couple of heads before demanding answers?" Ogras asked. "The amount of scheming and bad-mouthing coming from those cretins would have gotten them all killed long ago back home."

"I might disband them, or I might not." Zac shrugged. "I haven't decided yet. There should be quite a few turncoats who are willing to offer intelligence though, so I'll have Julia work a bit in the meantime."

The two soon found themselves at the sprawling mansion that Emma had demanded as remuneration for getting "kidnapped." They found the two sitting outside, with Emma reading some scripts while Julia cultivated.

"What are the two of you doing here?" Emma said with a raised brow. "Questions about same-sex relationships? The two of you finally tying the knot?"

"That bore wouldn't be able to land me in a thousand years." Ogras laughed as he snatched the bottle of wine next to Emma. "He's here for your little lover."

"What's going on?" Julia said as she opened her eyes.

"Are you interested in some work?" Zac asked as he looked down at the former government official.

It turned out that the answer was a resounding yes, and Julia almost ran out of the mansion before Zac had explained the situation in full. Staying still for months on end on an isolated island was clearly fraying her nerves.

They eventually decided that Julia would go to Westfort, bringing two bodyguards with her upon Emma's insistence. As for her next step, that would depend on what she found out in the town. She seemed to have the matter in hand, so Zac left after giving her a deadline of a week. If she couldn't find out anything by then, he would have to take some more drastic measures.

"What will you do next?" Ogras asked after the two left the mansion.

"I need to recuperate." Zac sighed. "Cracking open a node caused more trouble than expected. It's really a pain to be a mortal."

"Yes, you're one unlucky bastard," Ogras muttered, his voice dripping with sarcasm as he flashed away.

Zac smiled with a shake of his head as he looked the shadows disperse before he set out as well. He didn't immediately head toward his private compound, but rather toward the sick bay. His mind had been muddled from the situation with Alea last time, so he wanted to properly talk with Thea and Billy.

Thea, in particular, had been on his mind a lot over the past few days, and it wasn't just because of the vision he saw during his Heart Tribulation. They had grown quite close during their travels in the Hunt, but after returning to Earth, their relationship had grown a bit stiff and almost distant.

They both were saddled with the responsibilities of their factions and the looming threats facing Earth, but he also knew he himself was to blame. The visions in the Heart Tribulation were twisted and made worse than how things really were, but they did point to an undeniable truth.

He had closed off his heart and ignored troubling social interactions as he focused on getting stronger, even if there weren't really any need to. Saving Earth was obviously priority one, but that didn't mean he couldn't put in some effort with the people around him.

However, it turned out that both Billy and Thea had recovered enough to return to their respective factions by the time Zac had made it back to Port Atwood. He still wanted to talk, but his condition was really a bit troublesome. So in lieu of a personal meeting, he could only send Thea a letter for now and try to clear the air a bit.

After that, Zac made his way to his compound and found that his sister had left a note of her own. She had already left for Mystic Island by teleporting to the closest island. The teleporter on Mystic Island itself was apparently blocked by spatial turbulence, probably due to whatever the cultists had done to close the tunnel.

Since there was nothing else to do, he finally let himself rest for a bit, and he drifted off before his head even touched the pillow. He only woke a full six hours later, feeling a lot better compared to before.

Seeing that no one was looking for him, Zac took the opportunity to start redrawing his pathways again. A map of the extremely intricate lines had thankfully been imprinted in his mind when he evolved, so there was no guesswork involved. However, the process was anything but simple just because he knew how things were supposed to look.

He slowly carved the extremely thin pathways with the help of his Cosmic Energy, but he was repeatedly forced to stop and redraw the lines. The slightest deviation would ruin everything, and he kept slipping up, forcing him to start over. Minutes turned to hours, but when he finally paused, he realized that he had just redrawn a centimeter's length, even though it felt like kilometers of interwoven lines.

This was going to be a lot of work.

5
PATHWAYS

Zac grunted as he got to his feet after having finished his recuperation for the night. One week had passed since the events in the Dead Zone, and he had finally restored the pathways in his leg to optimal condition. It had also given him some time to take it easy and regain a sense of stability. Having first rushed through the levels in the Tower of Eternity, only to be thrown into a hectic battle against the Undead Empire, had taken its mental toll.

Redrawing the pathways had felt like a chore the first days, but he quickly realized the benefits of doing so. One of his weaknesses was a lack of familiarity with the patterns and fractals that made up pathways and skill fractals alike, but he was slowly shoring up that weakness while redrawing his fractals. He had generally considered them magic veins until now, pumping Cosmic Energy instead of blood. Now he realized that was a reductionist way to look at it.

The pathways created an extremely intricate network of thousands of fine energy routes that actually worked together to transform the Cosmic Energy he used. You could say that raw Cosmic Energy entered his pathways from his cells, where it was stored until he would form a Cultivation Core.

That Cosmic Energy wasn't in tune with his class, but the energy was split apart into thousands of minuscule streams through the pathways. When the streams eventually recombined in the skill fractals, the energy had transformed a bit. The previously raw Cosmic Energy had been forced to all stay on the same wavelength. Zac guessed that the pathways also did the same with Cosmic Energy that was absorbed through cultivation, though he couldn't test that for himself.

He hadn't been completely certain why the pathways between classes were so different before, but this was the most likely explanation. It was not only about fitting with the skills but rather forming a specific type of Cosmic Energy. It didn't quite go as far as giving the energy an attunement, but perhaps that was exactly what would happen at higher grades.

Having spent most of his waking time redrawing these pathways had given Zac a newfound understanding not only of the fractals but also about his class. He still lacked a theoretical foundation, but he felt that his understanding would perhaps even eclipse that of most cultivators by the time he reached peak E-grade.

Furthermore, his week of introspection had not only given him a better understanding of the pathways - he had also gained a better understanding of what the nodes actually did. If the pathway was a pattern of pipes that helped remold his Cosmic Energy, then the spinning whirlwinds of the nodes were essentially self-sustaining repeaters that sped up the process.

He still couldn't figure out exactly how his hidden node fit into this system just yet, but he hoped he'd be able to find out more when exploring the Mystic Realm in the future.

Seeing as he had essentially been holed up in his courtyard since returning, Zac decided to take a stroll through Port Atwood. Most things were pretty much the same as usual, but there was an extraordinarily large number of Tal-Eladar and their beast companions walking the streets. Zac knew that these were only the ones on a break as well, with most of them working on the surroundings of Port Atwood and Azh'Rodum.

Verana had quickly made her stance known as she appeared in Port Atwood just a few hours after Zac, bringing with her most of her noncombat class clansmen. They had quickly gotten to work rebuilding broken parts of the town, replanting burnt-down trees, and even expanding the town with new structures.

The leader herself had spent a lot of time in Atwood Academy, teaching the kids what she knew about beast rearing and cultivation, even bringing a couple of litters of infant beasts. Zac had half-expected her to flee with the Brindevalt Clan, but she clearly felt there was more value to stay on, even with the cooling relations with Zac.

Zac obviously didn't really buy into this PR campaign, but he also wouldn't say no to free labor.

As for the Brindevalt, they were long gone. The few remaining incursions had all closed their doors and returned to wherever they came from by now, apart from the cultists. The Brindevalts had even sent a batch of resources and their congratulations through Verana before leaving, while setting things up so that taking over their domain would go smoothly.

Verana was most likely the reason for their congeniality, as the others had simply slunk away in the night after looting everything they could. They probably understood that the natives would come for them next, even if they had fought against the Zombie hordes together.

Or perhaps they had heard about Zac's existence and his deeds inside the Tower and had decisively left.

He still had no idea exactly what kinds of waves his emergence had created. He was still a small shrimp, but he had done something that hadn't been accomplished for a million years. No still living cultivator in the whole Zecia Sector had reached his level in the Tower of Eternity, at least not to his knowledge.

Zac had asked Calrin to try to buy some reports of what was going on, but he still hadn't heard anything from the Sky Gnome. It wasn't that surprising though, as less than ten days had passed since he left the Base Town. With Calrin's limited network, it might take some more time before they got hold of the news.

But that very same uncertainty made him unsure about his next steps. One of the first orders he had sent out to his people after returning was to look for places with high numbers of E-grade beasts. Mystic Island was the best place in the archipelago, but much of its core had been cleansed of beasts to secure the base camp by the spatial tunnel.

Unfortunately, there weren't a lot of other good options. He had essentially outleveled Earth, making it extremely hard for him to advance. He had gotten his hands on quite a few Teleportation Tokens by now, allowing him to go to a lot of interesting places. He alone had tokens from Galau, Pretty, Boje, and Catheya. But that was just the tip of the iceberg.

Ogras had received over a hundred tokens from all kinds of forces during the time he stayed behind in the Base Town. Zac essentially had access to every major empire in the Zecia Sector except a few xenophobic and racially uniform ones. Unfortunately, it turned out that all the tokens he had gathered were useless at the moment.

The Nexus Hub was still inert, most likely because the cultists were still on the loose.

That meant he was stuck on Earth for the time being, unable to whizz off to some off-world hunting grounds to grind out a couple of levels. His predicament had also made him understand why the Dominators had barely gained any levels apart from the boost from the Hunt. It simply wasn't possible on Earth.

Zac's aimless wandering soon led him to the Academy, and he entered after having thought of something he had put off until now. He found Alyn sitting on the veranda of her house like many times before, and he sat down next to her.

"A cup of tea?" Alyn asked as she looked over with a smile.

"No, thank you," Zac said. "A lot to do today."

"Be careful, or you will get addicted to the stress," Alyn said. "It's okay to take a break sometimes. In fact, it's advisable. It allows your Dao and your path to harmonize with the real you, the one that isn't forced into one desperate situation after another."

"I will hopefully have time for that when I've closed the final incursion." Zac smiled, though he honestly wasn't so sure.

"Have you found their whereabouts by now?" she asked. "They've killed quite a few of our people through their two visits to this island."

"Not yet." Zac sighed. "I've been busy, but I have my people looking into it. We'll probably hear back soon."

"Good." Alyn nodded. "You are nurturing the heart of an emperor. Let others deal with the little things while you focus on your cultivation."

"Got any tips?" Zac smiled again, feeling a bit reminiscent of the days the two had spent in the Nexus Crystal mine while Zac was working on ridding his body of his Cosmic Water dependency.

Life had felt a lot simpler back then.

"What tips can I give you?" Alyn shook her head. "My teachings are meant to bring the most out of the talentless cultivators, turning them into contributing cogs in the machine. Neither I nor Clan Azh'Rezak knew anything about raising true elites. If we did, we wouldn't have been a clan that could barely be considered nobility. You will have to find your own path, or find a better teacher."

"No worries, I've come to enjoy the feeling of searching for answers of my own as well. On another note, can you call back any students who participated in the Dao Funnel last month, in case they are out training? Not a single one can be missing," Zac said.

"What's going on?" Alyn said, a small frown adorning her face.

Zac was about to explain, but he froze for a second and instead took out the Lantern. He infused some energy into it, and he suddenly felt a connection to the thing as a ghastly white flame lit up behind the glass.

The two were doused in the spectral shine, and Zac was suddenly covered in ribbons in all kinds of colors. A few were pretty thick, but most were as thin as a strand of hair. Alyn also had a few bonds, most of them stretching out in various directions of the town. There were also two that rose straight into the sky, but Zac was relieved to see that they looked completely different than those of the Great Redeemer.

They rather had the same red color as the demon incursion had had while it was still active, making Zac believe they were rather Karmic Links to some family or friends back on her home planet.

Satisfied that there was no hidden problem with Alyn, he quickly turned off the Lantern, unwilling to spend any more life force than needed. He had actually seen a gray hair when his hair started to grow out the other day, a reminder of how much life force he had already lost because of the Shard of Creation.

He would gain it back many times over when he reached D-grade Race, but it was still pretty disconcerting to see, considering his life span should be over five hundred years by this point.

"I need to do this with everyone who was there," Zac said. "It turns out the Redeemer guy is actually a member of a C-grade clan of Karmic Cultivators. This thing will root out hidden dangers. Keep this to yourself."

The truth about Voridis A'Heliophos, or rather the Great

Redeemer, was still not disseminated among even the core of Port Atwood. No one present really knew too much about the abilities and limits of a Karmic Clan, so they kept it on the safe side. The fewer who knew any real details, the smaller the risk of inadvertently forming any Karmic Links.

"I understand. I will arrange things properly." Alyn nodded as she took out a crystal. "When do you need them gathered?"

"Make it three days from now," Zac said as he stood up. "A few of the soldiers are out to sea right now, I think."

Since he couldn't scan for Karmic threats right now, he could only focus on one of his other projects while he waited for Julia to return. A small smile tugged at Zac's mouth when remembering the former government employee's excitement to get some responsibilities. She had lived a quiet life while her partner had worked on Ogras' movie along with a few PR gigs across the archipelago, and she seemed bored out of her mind.

Ogras had said that it was suspicious how eager she was to go talk with some unknown people at the New World Government, but Zac didn't believe she was a spy. There were no doubt spies on the island, judging from how the invaders seemed to have known about the general situation, but Julia wasn't a prime suspect.

She had been restricted to a far greater degree compared to others to avoid this very situation, so it was more likely that she just wanted to do something productive. Besides, she seemed to have gotten extremely complicated feelings for the New World Government since hearing Emma's stories. The suspect was likely someone else.

Not that it really mattered any longer. The undead were dealt with, and the zealots were next, and any planning or scheming of the New World Government was redundant in the face of pure power. Besides, they seemed more invested in their "Ark Project" than world domination by now, even after the undead threat had been dealt with.

Zac was soon back in his private area, and he stepped onto his personal teleporter. The next moment, he appeared in a small, nondescript cave. It looked like any other place among the subterranean tunnels of his mountain range, apart from being illuminated by Luminous Pearls rather than the luminescent moss.

But it was anything but normal.

Zac started walking toward an empty wall, but when he passed an almost invisible layer, the surroundings changed, and he was inundated in dense waves of energies. The hair on his arms stood up as he was simultaneously buffeted by both life and death.

It looked like his cultivation cave was finally up and running.

6
CULTIVATION CAVE

Zac had finally set up a private cultivation area for his Draugr side and soul cultivation, or rather his sister and Triv had. They had completely transformed the cave system around the original cultivation cave, and it would barely be recognizable by this point. He felt bad about constantly having his sister work on one array project after another, but he had no one else to turn to.

The demons were completely incompetent in that regard, and the Creators couldn't help with this project. The Sky Gnomes had helped with a portion of it, but they were only allowed to help install arrays that were bought through them. Triv was a welcome addition, though.

The ghost was just acceptable in his skill of placing arrays, but he had shown a surprising insight and attunement to natural energy flows, a genuine feng shui master. That knowledge allowed Kenzie to take advantage of the rich energies in the cave to a much higher degree, drastically increasing the efficacy of the formations.

Between that and Kenzie's unnaturally high precision in array placement, they had managed to make amazing progress in one short week. He would have to hire a genuine Array Master to improve things even further, but those kinds of services weren't available in the Town Shop. It was a restriction put in place by the System to prevent people from having too easy access to means of empowerment. It wanted people to struggle, after all.

There were a lot of buildings he could purchase from the store, but they were almost all services that were geared toward various types of convenience. He had, for example, purchased a bank to go with the Merit Store in the square of the town, though there were pretty strict limits on how much you could deposit. Not by the bankers themselves, but by the System.

Zac had already deposited his maximum allowance as an Early E-grade warrior, 1 billion Nexus Coins, which would be directly handed over to his sister in case he died. It would be just a small portion of his full wealth, but he couldn't be certain what would happen if he got himself killed. The people of Earth might turn on Kenzie because of greed, but she could just use one of his Teleportation Tokens and withdraw the money on some other world instead.

The cave Zac stood in right now was simply the entrance rather than the real cultivation area, as Triv had insisted that a teleportation array would cause too much spatial turbulence. Besides, Kenzie would be able to teleport here now without inadvertently disturbing him mid-cultivation. The shudder he had felt as he stepped forward was a simple illusion and containment array, hiding the real entrance and stopping the dense energies from escaping.

The tunnel had changed a lot since he visited the last time. Before, it had been filled with subterranean plants such as the mushrooms and glowing moss, creating a magical passage into the hidden cultivation chambers. But now it was like the tunnel had been split in two, each side representing either life or death.

The left side of the tunnel still looked very much the same, but the right side had turned dour and colorless as an ashy haze emerged from the rock wall itself. Some of the plants had already died off, whereas others were barely hanging on. New growth had started to emerge, mainly a pitch-black moss that had supplanted the luminescent one.

It was an odd feeling walking in the middle of the tunnel, with half his body feeling the vigorous life coming from the lotus, while the other side was drenched in the cold grip of death. This was obviously not an accidental design, but rather meticulously planned. However, the miraculous environment was nothing compared to the cave he entered next.

It was a perfectly circular cavern that had actually been turned into a small forest, with the domed ceiling reaching almost fifty meters in the air. Half the chamber was filled with death-attuned trees that had been brought over from the core of the Dead Zone, and the other half were trees that had grown in the secluded valley.

It was Triv's idea to plant the trees here, based on Zac's preferences. Some liked to cultivate in austere chambers without any distracting components, whereas others liked to be surrounded by things that made them peaceful. Zac had chosen this type of environment, as this was how he usually had meditated since the beginning, sitting in the forest by his campsite.

In the middle of the cave was a large glade, with a prayer mat placed perfectly aligned to be in the center. There were two more mats in the chamber, though Zac couldn't see them from his current vantage. They were placed at central locations in the respective attunement of the cave. The area around the left mat would be full of life-attuned energies, whereas the other one would be surrounded by Miasma.

The trees might seem haphazardly planted, but that was anything but the truth. This was the work of Triv, who had meticulously aligned every tree to form the embryo of a natural formation. The formation itself wasn't anything special, but it filled a very important purpose. It would gather the energies in the room and have them naturally flow toward the prayer mat in the center.

If he sat down on that mat, he would be able to see two passageways perfectly opposite each other, one to the left and another to the right. The left one would lead to his original cultivation cave, where the life-attuned lotus still resided in the pool of Cosmic Water. Dense waves of purest life force entered his subterranean forest from that side, but it met an opposing force coming from the other.

The right door led to a completely new chamber that had been dug into the mountain, and it was a smaller and modified version of the array they had found beneath the undead fortress. In the center of the chamber was the Seed of Undeath, surrounded by the very same pillars as before.

However, the pillars didn't blast Miasma toward the World Core any longer, but rather extracted it from the seed to push it toward the central cave.

There was also a hidden room beneath it filled with Unholy

Beacons. They took the Cosmic Energy that the Nexus Vein emitted and transformed it into Miasma that fed the Seed of Undeath and its array. Together with a couple of shielding arrays that kept the Death Attunement from spreading out, it formed a hidden ecosystem of death in the heart of the mountain.

Zac heard some rustling on the life-attuned side of the forest, and he walked over to see his sister scrutinizing a large stone pillar. It was embedded into the ground just outside the glade on the life-attuned half of the forest. It did look a bit like the pillars that now stood in the Death Chamber, but they were actually Array Flags that Kenzie had created herself.

Normally, such a flag would just be a few decimeters long, but she was still unable to make them as small as the small sticks he had bought from the System.

"How does it look?" Zac asked as he walked over.

"It should work as intended. I've compared it with the disks you gave me. I've also recreated similar pillars on the other side of the cave." Kenzie smiled.

"Why?" Zac asked curiously. "Was there something wrong with the Array Disks?"

The array that Kenzie was working on wasn't something related to energy flow, but it was something much more pressing. It was the array to practice his Soul Strengthening Manual. The Remnants were still very docile in his mind, but he hadn't forgotten just how dangerous they could be. It felt like a miracle that he was still standing after the events in the Tower, and he needed to be proactive in dealing with them.

The Remnants were still extremely weak, but they were slowly but surely regaining their strength. Most of the energy they gained still entered his soul and his body to strengthen them, but a part of it remained. For example, he was pretty certain that he would be able to conjure a bronze flash by this point just based on the amount of energy contained in the markings covering his soul.

Part of him wanted to just exhaust the energies that had gathered up 'til now to avoid any danger, but part of him was reluctant to waste his hidden ace. Who knew when he would need to be able to blast something with a ball of pure destruction?

"No, they were honestly better than what I created. But I can't create Array Disks, and the arrays would become lopsided if one was a small disk and the other half a forest in size," Kenzie said, looking a bit embarrassed. "I talked with Triv, and he believed that it might cause the death-attuned energies to push into the life cave too much."

"That's fine," Zac said. "Thank you for your help, and sorry I keep asking you to do stuff like this."

"I'm not in a hurry to reach the E-grade, and I don't care about ladder positions or stuff like that." Kenzie shrugged. "This way, I can at least help you and help protect Earth."

The two walked around the cave for a bit longer while Kenzie made a final inspection of the pillars.

"It good to go. I won't disturb you any longer," Kenzie said as she packed up her things. "Good luck with this stuff."

"Thank you," Zac said as he walked over to the mat placed on the right side of the cave.

Dense clouds of Miasma slowly swirled around it, somewhat reminding Zac of how it looked in his opened nodes. The mat itself was actually a corner of the one he had looted from the dragon cave.

Calrin had identified it to be made from extremely valuable materials that aided in cultivation, with the inner pieces holding the most value. It had been cut into almost a hundred pieces and refashioned into a set of mats, with the inner mats going to the core warriors of Port Atwood, with the rest being put in the Merit Exchange.

Zac took a deep breath before he sat down. It was finally time for him to start working on his **[Nine Reincarnations Manual]**.

The cultivation method for the first Reincarnation of the **[Nine Reincarnations Manual]** was quite simple. There was not much he needed to do except alternate between using the Death Array aptly called **[Death Soul Array]** and the counterpart that Kenzie had just finished setting up, the **[Life Soul Array]**.

There were some ways that one could improve the efficacy of the two arrays. The manual mentioned cultivating in life- and death-attuned cultivation caves, for example, and there were also a few treasures listed that could help speed up the process. However, Zac had only taken the most basic steps with the help so far by relying on the attunements generated by the lotus and the seed respectively.

But it was entirely possible that he would start using more expensive methods to boost the cave even further. Triv was quite adept in improving the atmosphere this way, though his knowledge was mostly limited to death attunements so far. But the ghost was already studiously working on expanding his knowledge of life-attuned measures to be more of service.

Honestly, Zac was becoming more and more pleased with his decision to keep the ghost around. Triv had already proven an extremely valuable asset in the construction of this cave, and he had all sorts of ideas to improve the state of Port Atwood in general. Most of the changes would be pretty expensive to enact, but Zac wasn't too worried about cost at the moment. Now that the undead threat was dealt with, his force had started to focus on expansion rather than war, and his income increased every day.

There was still the zealots and the Dominators to deal with, but they weren't a threat that required his whole force. He himself and perhaps a small strike squad would be all that he needed for those two threats, whereas the endless number of Zombies had required the cooperation of the whole world.

Zac went over the cultivation method in his mind, still keeping his human form. He wanted to get the hang of things before he started to experiment with swapping Races for the cultivation.

A low hum echoed across the glade as Zac activated the array, and it felt like the Miasma around him stirred. His skin prickled as well, and he quickly started to become a bit uncomfortable. However, he ignored the impulses to turn into a Draugr as he infused the array with some spiritual energy.

The moment his mind made a connection with the array, he felt a weak but constant drain on his mind as the array absorbed more and more of his Mental Energy. It wasn't a problem in the beginning, but he started to feel a bit queasy after half an hour had passed. He even started to wonder if there was something wrong with the array.

However, just as he was about to abort the experiment, a surge of energy rose from the array, and he felt a powerful stream enter his mind. It was his own Mental Energy, but it was tinged with death this time. Zac nodded in satisfaction and kept going, and the array had completed a circulation after roughly forty-five minutes.

Zac kept going according to the manual, seeing that the array worked as intended. He slowly completed one revolution after another, and his soul became a bit ghastlier every time. The two Remnants even woke up from their slumber for a few seconds, but they quickly calmed down again for some unknown reason. Perhaps they knew that whatever Zac was doing wasn't a threat to their existence.

Only after nine full revolutions was the first half of the cultivation session complete. His mind was completely permeated by death by now, and he almost felt like a ghost. The Miasma around him no longer felt uncomfortable, but rather inviting to the point that Zac almost thought he had changed to his Draugr constitution subconsciously.

It even felt so good that he was inclined to lie down and take a nap in the soothing mists. However, he immediately snapped out of it as he walked over to the other side of the forest. The usually soothing life-attuned energies that had turned the greenery even lusher felt like scorching gusts that threatened to blister his skin, but Zac ignored the illusion as he sat down on the second prayer mat.

Another revolution began, but this time, his Mental Energy brought back some warmth after it had passed through the array. He completed the nine revolutions once more, and only then did he feel like he was back to his normal self. Zac stood up from his mat and stretched before he checked on his gains.

And truthfully, they weren't all that great.

7
DIVIDE

A lot of work for little benefit. That was Zac's first impression of the results from completing a full cycle of the [Nine Reincarnations Manual].

His soul was in very good condition, all things considered, and it looked like it had turned a smidgeon more condensed. However, Zac had spent almost fourteen hours in this session, and the results felt a bit lackluster for such an investment. He started to understand why so few warriors chose to spend time on a Soul Strengthening Manual.

But he didn't have a choice.

The two Remnants would wake up sooner or later, and he needed to empower his soul before then. He needed to be the one in charge, a fact that had become even more apparent after seeing the name of the Arcane class he was presented. He didn't just want to be a vessel; he needed to be the controller.

But it was undeniable that there was a problem with the time expenditure. He couldn't waste fourteen hours a day on this array; he needed to gather Cosmic Energy to crack open nodes, ponder on the Daos, and work on his Race Evolution as well, besides all the other stuff that required his attention in Port Atwood.

The situation wasn't hopeless. This was just a trial run in unoptimized conditions, and he was hopeful that he would be able to expedite the speed of each revolution. If he could decrease each Revolution from forty-five to fifteen minutes with the help of his unique constitution, he would suddenly only need to spend four and a half hours a day on soul cultivation, which was far more acceptable.

Zac already had ideas on how to improve efficiency. The two arrays were essentially dialysis machines for his Mental Energy. It sucked the energy out and ran it across the arrays, where some impurities were shed while some attuned energies were infused. Each revolution would increase the attunement until his soul was stuffed, at which point he swapped arrays.

The clash between life-attuned energies and death-attuned energies at the second set of revolutions seemed to strengthen his soul without really hurting it as well, and he had a feeling that this controlled clash was one of the interesting aspects that set this method apart from other Soul Strengthening Manuals.

The other was obviously the transformative impact when enough cycles had taken place to form a "Reincarnation."

Another small benefit came from his [Void Heart]. It had actually absorbed some of the dense energies in the cave and pushed it into the next node to break open, this one located in his right leg instead. It wasn't a huge amount, but it also wasn't negligible. If he also managed to get his hands on a better version of the [Mother-Daughter Array], the benefits would be quite noticeable over time.

Zac also felt pretty relieved that the nodes in early E-grade seemed to be located in his extremities. A lot of nodes were located in his torso, neck, and head, and they were the cause for a lot of sleepless nights. Those around his heart and organs could always be cracked open in his undead form, but others felt extremely dangerous. What if he accidentally decapitated himself when he cracked open a node in his throat?

He needed to find a way to contain the damage from node-breaking to only his spirit body somehow, leaving his flesh intact. Either that or become sturdy enough that a node explosion couldn't harm him. Zac wasn't all that worried, as a lot of E-grade mortals had passed this hurdle before him. He just needed to find out how they did it.

Part of Zac wanted to sit down again and start tinkering with the process, for example, trying to perform a revolution while changing his Race. There was no time to experiment with improving the process right now. The Manual said that he could only do one revolution a day. Any more would just needlessly tax his soul without any benefits.

He walked over to the central glade instead and looked down at the small tree that grew there.

It was the very same branch he had brought from the Dead Zone, the tree that encompassed both life and death. He had planted it right at the delimitation of the two attunements, which meant that half of its branches were drenched in death while the other half enjoyed the sweet succor of life. He hoped to study what changes that brought to the mutated tree, and perhaps even gain some insights from the process.

A second branch was placed in the life-attuned side, with a final one being steeped in Miasma. He wanted to see how the saplings adapted to the different environments. The branch shouldn't have any problems surviving being replanted in the area teeming with Miasma, as that would be the same conditions it had had in the Dead Zone.

But what about being placed in a place already teeming with life? Would it double up on producing vibrant energies, becoming a beacon of verdure? Or would it perhaps swap over and start creating Miasma? Zac couldn't wait to find out. Of course, something like this wouldn't change in a day or two.

Not much had happened in the few days since the tree was replanted, but Zac was relieved to see that it was doing just fine. There were no signs of wilting or that it hadn't taken to the earth, and after infusing it a bit with the Fragment of the Bodhi, he could confirm that roots had already taken hold.

A glance with [Cosmic Gaze] showed that the tree was still mostly attuned to death, which wasn't a surprise, considering where it grew up. However, life was slowly gaining a foothold in the branches, and it didn't seem impossible that it would reach a true equilibrium in the future.

Zac nodded with satisfaction before he sat down on the central mat. It was already getting late, and Zac wasn't in the mood to leave this place for the day. Many people would still be awake all the way until 2 or 3 a.m. now that they only needed a few hours of sleep, but old habits died hard. You couldn't just pop in at someone's place at 11 p.m.

He instead focused his attention on Fragment of the Bodhi. Zac hoped to gain some sort of insight by sitting in an area where life was in a constant struggle against death. The battle with the Lich King, unfortunately, hadn't provided any real inspiration, and the only thing he could do now was to grind at it until it was time to face the last threats to Earth.

That was not to say that his experience in the Dead Zone was without any benefits. His battle of attrition with the Head Priest, where his Bodhi-infused branch managed to overpower the scorching flames, had resonated with him. Following that, it was his meditation in front of the mutated tree.

The two together had pushed him forward, and it felt like he was on the cusp of crystallizing some sort of breakthrough. But it still needed more time or some sort of breakthrough.

He needed to make the best of the time, as he actually sensed that the Origin Dao was slowly starting to dissipate. It wasn't like it was a rapid decline, but the peak had clearly been met. What would follow would be a gradual dissipation of the Origin Dao until Earth was indistinguishable from any other world of the Zecia Sector.

It was a bit surprising the decline was happening so fast; the snippets of information on the subject indicated that it could stay for well over a decade. As things looked now, the Origin Dao would run out in a year or two. One possibility was that there actually were more Dao Funnels like the one Salvation had carried on Earth.

If the Great Redeemer really was planning to harvest the Origin Dao of the planet, then it also made sense that he would leave more than one funnel behind to collect it for him. That way he would only need to pick up the Funnels upon arrival before he did whatever the Fulcrum plan entailed.

Another possibility was that the Realignment Array had caused some irredeemable damage to Earth even if it was shut off in time. It still was anyone's guess whether the seemingly endless swathe of death around the undead incursion would ever heal completely, but the damage was perhaps also done to a more fundamental level.

In either case, the time of rapid growth for Earth's population was coming to an end as quickly as it had begun, and most cultivators of Port Atwood had been instructed to focus on the Dao rather than leveling to make the most of it. Anyone could reach Peak F-grade in a few years with the right support system, but gaining and evolving a Dao Seed was something else entirely.

It was by far the most common reason for people not being able to evolve. People simply didn't have the affinities or opportunities to form a seed on their own. A large number of the citizens of Earth might never form a Dao Seed if they didn't seize this opportunity.

The scenes of his recent battles flashed through his mind as he occasionally looked over at the branch that was able to perform such a miraculous transformation. He even thought back to the original vision with the cherry tree, where the blessed tree had created a magical realm beneath its branches.

The canopy had turned into a perfect barrier that took on the heat and the desolation from the badlands outside and fed it into its Buddhist kingdom inside. It was just like how the branch in front of him took the Miasma of the area and turned it into life.

However, the transformation process was just one part of the miracle. The other was to form and protect the core of life that was allowed to grow powerful without outside interference. The seed would be weak at the beginning, and only through protection would it be able to grow. Otherwise, it would be like a candle in the wind.

"Isolation. Creation through protection," Zac muttered, and his mind shuddered as he felt a resonance from the Dao.

Zac followed the instinct and kept searching for answers, various scenes flashing before his eyes as they slowly congealed into something new. It all began with the vision in the Tower. The general had been allowed to grow into his potential only due to the stele shielding him from the outside worlds for millennia, which echoed his current thoughts.

The hours passed until something finally congealed in Zac's mind. A surge of warmth spread from his mind to every corner of his body as the Fragment of the Bodhi evolved into middle stage. He felt more powerful than ever, but he held off on checking his gains, as his intuition told him that he wasn't done. There was more to gain.

Zac stood up, pushed forward by an intangible momentum, and he swiped his right hand through the air as though his hand were a bladed weapon. A shudder spread forward, as the swing actually was infused with the Fragment of the Bodhi. However, the energies in the air didn't turn chaotic from the action, but rather the opposite.

The whole air around the central glade was one big conflict zone between life and death, where Miasma and divine energy fought for supremacy. At some places, the Miasma had encroached a bit on the other side, whereas life had managed to gain a small foothold in places on the death-attuned side.

However, the moment Zac swung his palm, the fighting stopped, and a clean line of demarcation could be seen. The Miasma spread to an invisible line but didn't move an inch further. Order had been brought to the area, and life was split from death.

This was thanks to Zac's latest insight into the Fragment of the Bodhi, and he marveled at the scene until the effects of the swing dissipated, causing the thousand small conflicts to once again erupt all over the glade. But it had been enough to reach his goal, and Zac opened his Quest screen to check it out.

[Rapturous Divide (Class): Split Life and Death. Reward: Rapturous Divide Skill (1/1) COMPLETE]

A fractal appeared the next moment, taking a spot on his left arm, essentially mirroring the fractal for **[Nature's Punishment]** on his right. The fractal looked a lot different, forming two completely separate lines that didn't have one single fractal that connected each side. The only fractal until now that had even been a little bit similar was **[Cyclic Strike]**, though these fractals were a lot more intricate.

Zac's heartbeat sped up with excitement, but he restrained himself from immediately busting out the skill. Who knew what effect the skill would have; he'd get lambasted by his sister if he accidentally tore apart the arrays she had spent so much time and energy to set up.

Zac instead only turned his sight inward, to try to get a sense of what kind of skill **[Rapturous Divide]** was, but there were no clues he could glean at all from the new pattern. However, he did notice that the two lines looked far more intricate compared to his previous skills, like it was an embroidery using extremely fine silk threads compared to the coarse rope of the F-grade skills.

He marveled at the fractal for a while before he eventually retracted his sight. He also wanted to see his attribute gains, so he opened his status screen to see the boost he got from his upgraded fragment.

Name: Zachary Atwood
Level: 81
Class: [E-Epic] Edge of Arcadia
Race: [E] Human
Alignment: [Earth] Port Atwood – Lord

Titles: [...] Tower of Eternity – 8th Floor, Heaven's Triumvirate, Fated, Peak Power, Sovereign-select
Limited Titles: Frontrunner, Tower of Eternity Sector All-Star – 14th
Dao: Fragment of the Axe – Middle, Fragment of the Coffin – Middle, Fragment of the Bodhi – Middle
Core: [E] Duplicity

Strength: 2,090 [Increase: 91%. Efficiency: 199%]
Dexterity: 992 [Increase: 65%. Efficiency: 170%]
Endurance: 2,229 [Increase: 99%. Efficiency: 199%]
Vitality: 1,476 [Increase: 89%. Efficiency: 199%]
Intelligence: 545 [Increase: 65%. Efficiency: 170%]
Wisdom: 911 [Increase: 70%. Efficiency: 170%]
Luck: 340 [Increase: 91%. Efficiency: 179%]

Free Points: 0
Nexus Coins: [F] 5,919,241,817
Fragment of the Bodhi (Middle): All attributes +20, Endurance +140, Vitality +160, Intelligence +30, Wisdom +80, Effectiveness of Vitality +10%.

He had made shocking progress in one night, though the two breakthroughs were related. However, Zac knew he couldn't rest on his laurels as things stood. Some things had gone above expectations, but he was still struggling in other departments.

Perhaps he should have realized that his unique situation with dual Races would cause complications when upgrading them.

8
BEASTCRAFTING

Miasma spread out through Zac's body as he activated his Specialty Core. He walked over to the death-attuned side once more and took out a large tub that he filled with water before he threw in a dozen E-grade Miasma Crystals. Next were a handful of stalks of Netherbloom, along with various other herbs that he had found in the Cosmos Sack left on the body of Adriel.

It was time to work on his Race once more.

He had already used up the **[Fruit of Rebirth]** the moment he returned to Port Atwood, and the great progress Zac had made on his racial upgrade allowed him to realize a somewhat surprising aspect of his body. His nodes were the same between his Races, but his actual Races were separate.

Zac had somewhat figured that his racial grade would be shared between his two sides, as he only had one body and because his two classes shared the same node system. However, that wasn't the case. He could clearly feel that his human side was on the cusp of evolving into D-grade, whereas his undead side barely had improved at all.

That was starting to become an extremely urgent issue now that his third Dao Fragment had evolved. Even worse, the insight had been partly based on protection, which had caused the Fragment to boost Endurance more than expected. One more breakthrough and he might actually hit the attribute limit on his undead side.

Of course, Zac had already tried to remedy the situation by eating the remaining Racial Upgrade Pills he'd bought at the Base Town auctions, but he had almost killed himself doing so. It turned out his Draugr side was extremely picky, and the pills that humans would use were essentially poison to him.

Triv was no use either. He could barely confirm that the undead used various methods of improving Races. For example, they created incense sticks using herbs, where the composition depended on what Race the original body was. There were also the standard medicinal baths, according to Triv, but his helpfulness ended there.

The ghost was unable to divulge a single mixture, as his commandments apparently regarded that as betraying the Undead Empire. However, the ghost didn't have any issues at all mixing up a medicinal bath following a recipe that Zac provided, proving there were loopholes to the limitations. Unfortunately, the same issue arose with the normal medicinal baths; they didn't work on his undead side either.

Zac had no idea what would happen if he passed the attribute cap as things stood. Would both his classes lose out on points? Or would his Draugr side alone take the hit? Zac really wasn't willing to find out, and he was doing everything he could to stave off that ever happening.

He had no idea how things came to this. He had specifically asked about Race upgrades while visiting the Undead Kingdom inside the Tower of Eternity, but he'd heard no clues about his current predicament. He had been afraid that he would need a Lich to help him upgrade his Race to D-grade, as they were responsible for giving Revenants sapience, but that thankfully wasn't the case.

They had assured him that cultivation and treasures would work just fine, but the care package they had provided him with hadn't contained anything to improve his constitution. Perhaps they expected his "master" or elders to have prepared far superior materials for him already and felt it would almost be an insult to give him their scraps.

The freezing bath he had concocted was just a stopgap measure, as he was all out of ideas. The dense death-attuned waters along with random herbs from Adriel's Cosmos Sack did help a bit, but properly preparing a medicinal bath was far more complicated than what he was haphazardly throwing together. It required precise measurements of the different herbs, and they needed to be processed and added in a certain manner.

Using it as he did was essentially wasting over 95% of the efficacy, and he would run out of herbs long before he upgraded his Race at this pace. He was rapidly burning money for very little gain. The [Void Heart] was no use for upgrading his Race either, but rather the opposite. It just stole some of the energies of the medicinal baths and fed it into the node in his leg, leaving a bunch of impurities in his bloodstream.

He did get small amounts of refined energies from the Shard of Creation, but he had no idea if that mysterious energy actually helped with his Race, or if it had some other sort of effect on his body.

He had already sent Valkyries and demons to look for manuals or clues in the ruins of his newly acquired death fort, but he didn't hold out much hope. Zac knew he most likely already was in possession of the recipes anyway, locked away inside the crystals of the Lich King. But those were still out of his reach, as even the old Sky Gnome had failed in cracking their protections no matter what he or his little pet tried.

He felt as though he was falling into the same old predicament as last time. He had managed to improve his constitution a small bit, but he didn't know how much his attribute cap had increased as a result. His Strength had already passed his Endurance by now, and it felt like the tragedy of the F-grade cap could take place again at any moment.

But he also knew he needed to keep pushing himself forward. Inevitability was level 111 by now, and Void's Disciple was level 108. Zac still believed that the older Zhix warrior was a far larger threat compared to the unhinged maniac he'd battled during the Hunt. Zac was confident in dealing with Inevitability if they met again today, but he was far less certain about the Dominator Leader.

He had given Zac an extremely oppressive and mysterious feeling when they met, and Zac had no clue exactly what skills he had. The Zhix hordes had no idea either; everyone who had seen Void's Disciple in action had been killed. He was like a murderous ghost that moved back and forth across the hives.

Zac knew that catching him was impossible, even though he still coordinated with the Zhix armies to track his movements. He had somehow opened up a rift in space and walked straight through it when they met, and the Lich King had indicated that Void's Disciple actually had gained the Dao of Space. How was he supposed to catch someone like that?

Even if Zac found him and started fighting, he could still just slink away if he started losing.

The best solution was taking him on inside the Mystic Realm, and Julia would hopefully return with good news today. Until then, he needed to do what he could to improve his power, even if it meant him wasting mountains of precious herbs.

Zac only stepped out of the vat two hours later, after which he swapped back to his human form. A knife appeared in his right hand as he cut a deep wound across his forearm. Ice-cold blood spurted out for a few seconds until his extreme Vitality closed the wound, but Zac repeated the process a few times to release well over two liters of blood.

His makeshift medicine baths did have some effect on his Draugr Race, but it also came with a huge amount of impurities that the **[Void Heart]** puked out into his bloodstream. Just one bath meant he would have to bleed himself a few more times over the coming day, and there were also the impurities from the soul-strengthening session to deal with.

The lackluster results of his racial upgrade had somewhat put a damper on the excitement of upgrading his Dao Fragment, and Zac sighed with annoyance as he left his cultivation cave. He teleported back to his compound, but he didn't head over to his courtyard. Instead, he left the small number of mansions behind and entered the wilderness.

He walked for two minutes until he appeared in a secluded spot hidden deep in his private forest. It was actually a place that held some significance to him; it was the very spot where he'd woken up after the integration.

However, the small glade was completely unrecognizable by now, with its bloodroot and cardinals replaced with a sanguine pond with a diameter of five meters. The pond of dragon blood put even him under pressure, and Zac even felt that he could even hear distant roars. The pressure no doubt came from the dragon's bloodline, as it felt similar to the pressure that he had felt during his fight with the primordial beast.

The pond had shrunk a bit since his last visit. Zac was both surprised and expectant as that was the third time. He topped the pond off with more dragon blood from one of his vats, realizing he would run out in a week if things kept up like this. However, he had no direct usage for the blood anyway, and he felt it was best used like this.

He also threw in a few more Beast Crystals for good measure, as he couldn't sense the unique energy fluctuations from the previous ones he'd thrown in. He didn't know if he was simply wasting money, but Verun seemed to like them any time it got close to one. A sense of anticipation gripped Zac's heart as he looked at the large crystal sticking out of the middle of the pond.

It was the latest transformation of [Verun's Bite]. The Spirit Tool had been pushed hard in the latest fights against the Lich King and the elites of the Tower of Eternity. He honestly wasn't confident that the weapon would be able to keep up for the coming fights, and this was his best bet unless he actually chose to swap it out for a new axe.

That was why he'd chosen to feed it the Dragon Core the moment he returned to Port Atwood, though he still kept the Bloodline Marrow for himself. The weapon had turned into a crystal like the previous time it underwent significant changes, but it had still sent out a mental plea for more dragon blood.

It looked like Verun needed a while longer before the evolution was complete, which was a shame, as Zac was extremely eager to see the result. He hoped that the primordial bloodline of the dragon along with the Beast Crystals would cause some equivalent of a bloodline evolution of Verun.

It didn't really work like that for normal Spirit Tools as far as he knew, but it was possible for Beastcrafted weapons, according to Triv. Bloodline evolutions were obviously a pretty impressive boost to the potential power such Spirit Tools could exhibit, but Beastcrafted weapons had downsides as well.

First of all, their upgrade ceiling was generally low to start with. Secondly, they were a lot pickier about upgrade components compared to normal weapons, and two seemingly identical weapons could have completely different requirements. The latter in particular was a big reason why pretty much all the weapons he had seen at the Base Town were made from metals, wood, or crystal.

They were simpler to evolve, and the upgrade paths were generally a lot clearer. No one wanted to risk being stuck with a weapon that couldn't evolve any longer, forcing them to get a new weapon instead. One's weapon was a huge component of your combat prowess, after all, and it was impossible to immediately exhibit one's full strength after changing weapons.

But Zac didn't really have either desire or the ability to swap out his axe to a better one, and his eyes were locked on the pupa as he conjured all kinds of possibilities in his mind. Zac only spent a couple of minutes by the pond before he got ready to leave, but a crack echoed out across the glade just as he turned away.

Zac's eyes lit up in anticipation as the red crystal crumbled bit by bit, slowly showcasing the weapon hidden within. A sudden shockwave blasted the crystal to pieces, and an enormous shape appeared by the pool as the blood was sucked into the weapon.

It was Verun, which still looked like an oversized ancestor of a hyena, apart from its massively oversized maw and multiple sets of eyes. Zac had almost thought it would turn into a half-dragon or something after eating the core, but its changes were a lot more subtle than that. Its fur had turned from a dusty brown to a glossy black, with red highlights covering its body.

It almost looked like it had scales, but a second glance showed that it was just a pattern. It had also grown a thick mane that ran from its head all the way down to its short tail, somewhat reminding Zac of the spikes of the black dragon he'd fought. Its claws had changed as well, turning bigger and darker.

Its whole image had turned more refined, without losing its aura of lethality. There was a sense of sharpness and danger to it, like it was a true predator that didn't only use its brawn to take down its enemies.

Finally, there were streams of energy that circulated around each of its four legs, and a glance with [Cosmic Gaze] displayed two swirls just above its paws, both with a different color. The first one had a sanguine hue, which wasn't surprising, as its favorite food had always been blood. The other one was a bit more surprising, though.

The second swirl was steely gray and felt pretty similar to his

Fragment of the Axe, though the Heaviness was swapped out by something else. Force maybe? In either case, it thankfully wasn't fire-related, something Zac had worried would happen from ingesting a Dragon Core.

Dragon flames were obviously powerful, but not something that suited Zac's current path. So the fact that the addition felt element neutral was a relief. The massive beast looked down at Zac from the other side of the pool, happiness radiating through their mental bond. It raised its head and let out a primal roar the next moment. The terrifying cry was powerful enough to cause the closest trees to shake, and even Zac had to take a step back from the volume.

Birds screeched in panic in the distance, and Zac wouldn't be surprised if the whole settlement heard the roar. It felt like the Verun wanted the whole world to know there was a new alpha in town.

9
JAMMERS

Volume was not the only thing extraordinary with Verun's roar as dozens of trees suddenly exploded, utterly ripped to shreds. It almost looked like Verun had torn them apart with its mouth, but Zac guessed it had been the sound waves.

The Tool Spirit leaped over the now-emptied pond and butted Zac's chest once before it dissipated into a stream of energy that entered the axe that now was embedded in the ground of the dried-out pool. Zac jumped down and ripped it out, but he almost lost his balance from how heavy it was.

The axe had always been on the heavier side, and he would never have been able to wield **[Verun's Bite]** before the integration. But its weight had increased by over ten times from absorbing the Dragon Core and evolving, and that wasn't the only thing that had changed. Its overall design was the same as before, but the handle was now pitch-black to match Verun's fur.

More importantly, a third rune had lit up, meaning another skill or function should have been unlocked from the upgrade.

The axe-head itself had slightly changed as well. It had turned even bigger, with its edge gaining over five centimeters in length. The bone it was made from felt sturdier as well, and the edge was sharp enough to easily draw blood on even his durable skin. There were also thin red lines running across the bone, almost looking like cracks in the material.

However, Zac didn't feel any weakness or damage when holding the weapon, and he guessed the new pattern was just mirroring the red streaks in Verun's fur. He jumped up from the pond and swung it around a bit, and deep growls echoed out as it split the air apart.

He had initially worried that the increased weight would make it feel unwieldy, but it was actually the opposite. The weapon felt far sturdier, and it resonated better with his Dao. It felt like every swing contained a gigantic and undeniable force, like a mountain was crashing down where he swung his weapon. But he put away the weapon after a while and started to walk back toward his courtyard.

Between his Dao Epiphany and working on his Race, morning had already come, so Zac just planned on resting for an hour or two before starting his next day. However, he noticed a drone zooming about outside the entrance to his courtyard as he returned. Kenzie had painted it red to be more easily spotted as well.

It was no longer a surveillance drone, but more of a flying butler to his sister, who sent it on all kinds of errands. She, or rather Jeeves, had even equipped it with speaking capabilities, though Zac had made sure that it wasn't an actual AI.

[Julia has returned.] The consciously mechanical voice of the drone spoke up.

"Is Kenzie home?" Zac asked.

[Yes. The mistress is working on her arrays.]

"I'm coming over; there's something we need to talk about." Zac sighed.

Seeing how his sister was becoming increasingly comfortable with using Technocrat tech, he knew he couldn't hold off any longer. He needed to tell his sister about his visions of his mother. What if she kept going like this, and one day connected to the Digital World of the Machine God Faction? Who knew what kinds of alarms that would trigger?

Earth already had enough to deal with without dragging a full-blown Technocrat armada to the Zecia Sector.

Zac soon arrived at her mansion, or rather the series of towering structures that his sister had erected. Only the smallest of the houses, a rusting one-story house with a large garden, was her residence. The other buildings were workshops for her experiments, Technocrat technology and arrays alike.

He found her tinkering with a human-sized onyx stone in the middle of one of the workshops, surrounded by protective arrays. Zac's brows rose in alarm when he saw the series of formations, as it felt like her experiments were far more dangerous than she had let on. Kenzie looked over when he entered the workroom, and she finished up whatever inscriptions she was adding to the block with the tool she'd gotten from the quest last week.

"Good timing. I've made a breakthrough with these jamming arrays. I think we can actually use them when we're finished. They should work as long as you activate it in your Draugr form," Kenzie said but frowned when she saw Zac's expression. "What's wrong? You look so serious. Didn't the soul-boosting array work?"

"The array worked great. I just need to figure out some way to make my soul cultivation faster," Zac said as he walked over and poked a defensive shield. "What's with these shields? You're not risking your life for this, are you?"

"It's a precaution so I don't blow up his building, but I'm not in any danger. Jeeves will notice if it starts destabilizing, so I can run away with time to spare," Kenzie said. "By the way, what was that roar earlier? It almost made me ruin this thing."

"Just remember to be careful. These things come from pretty damn dangerous factions." Zac sighed. "The roar was Verun; it finally finished absorbing all the materials."

"It sounded pretty powerful." Kenzie smiled.

"Let's hope it will be enough to deal with the Dominators," Zac said as he looked closer at the jamming array. "Will these things be as effective as when the undead used them?"

"They should work the same." Kenzie nodded. "Just put Miasma Crystals into the sockets and everything within a day's march will be blocked out. But we still need to finish some modifications to circumvent the restrictions on these things, and that will turn them into consumable items. They'll only work for a handful of times before they break down."

"How many?" Zac asked.

"Probably more than ten, but no more than twenty," Kenzie hesitantly said.

"That's plenty," Zac said with a sigh of relief.

These things would come in handy over the following month, and it was something his force sorely lacked. Because Earth was about to be plunged into a civil war, and this would give them the advantage they needed. The war wasn't against the New World Government, but against a far more dangerous enemy: the Dominators.

The Zhix hordes had cleanly split into two camps by now, either gathering behind the Anointed or the Dominators. Now that the undead threat was dealt with, the tensions had risen to an unprecedented degree. The followers of the Dominators needed to be rooted out, but the efforts of the other Zhix had proven futile since the integration took place.

Their previous methods of dealing with the Dominators and their followers had been crude but effective. They had sent wave after wave of soldiers after their target, drowning them in a sea of relentless violence. The Dominators ran out of Cosmic Energy sooner or later, at which point they were slaughtered.

The Zhix were still more than willing to sacrifice themselves to root out the final vestiges of corruption in their bloodline, especially now that they knew of the source. But the emergence of teleportation arrays had turned their efforts useless. The War Council of the Zhix had already contacted Port Atwood in search of a solution, and he would meet up with them in a week, provided he didn't need to change his plans due to Julia.

These jamming devices would allow him to trap the Zhix hives who had defected, and with the help of the Zhix hordes take out anyone who might have formed a Karmic Link with the Great Redeemer.

Zac didn't feel it was enough to locate the leading Dominators to secure Earth. His instincts told him the Dominators were using these traitors as a backup. Void's Disciple had been slowly converting hives to join their side over the past year, and mercilessly slaughtering some of the staunchest detractors.

There had to be a purpose to this, and the most likely reason Zac and Ogras could fathom was to form a Karmic Link. The Great

Redeemer would perhaps be able to find Earth as long as there were enough followers spread across the planet, even if the main perpetrators were already killed.

Or perhaps it wasn't about backup plans, but about boosting the signal. The Karmic Link between the Great Redeemer and the Dominators couldn't be too strong, as they hadn't even met in person. Voridis had visited the Zhix planet thousands of years ago, and the link should have weakened by now. But what if there were tens of millions of insectoids praising his name? It might give him all the clues he needed to find Earth.

It would also explain why both the Dominators and the Medhin Clan were so intent on taking over the planet, apart from avoiding the incursions spawning. The more who were under his banner, the easier the planet would be to find.

He needed to deal with the traitors as soon as possible, and these jammers were the key to fighting them.

"So what's up?" Kenzie said, dragging him out of his thoughts. "Scarlet said you needed to talk?"

"It's about Mom. There's something I haven't told you." Zac sighed before he started recounting his visions.

This time, he held nothing back, retelling both his visions of their mother and the words Leandra had spoken. He connected that with what he had learned so far about Firmament's Edge and added his own analysis of the situation. He knew it would probably upset his sister, but she needed to know that their mom might be an extremely dangerous character and as large a threat to them as the Great Redeemer.

"You really met Mom?" Kenzie said with a low voice. "Why didn't you get me? Then I would at least have been able to hear her voice, even if it was just a projection."

"I didn't dare let Jeeves close to her, even if it was just an AI," Zac explained. "Something about the way she talked felt unsettling."

"Jeeves said that no one but me can access him," Kenzie said with a downcast voice.

"Would he really know if that was true?" Zac countered. "Can he really know more about any hidden functions than his creator?"

The two kept going back and forth for a while longer. Kenzie initially refused to believe that their mother might wish them harm. The fact that she might even have been used as a test subject seemed to be too much to even consider, and from the rapidly changing expressions on her face, she didn't seem to hear the answers she was looking for from Jeeves either.

"In any case, we don't know which version was the true one. Perhaps both were false. But if Leandra really is a top-tier warrior of the Technocrat Faction, just her appearance might plunge the whole planet into a storm of blood. Simply getting close to the Technocrat incursion gave me a quest to kill them all," Zac said. "We can't deal with the battle between the System and the Technocrats for the time being, and Jeeves seems to be right at the heart of the conflict."

"I know." Kenzie sighed. "You might be right. It's definitely suspicious she only called Jeeves an assistant. Jeeves definitely isn't like other Technocrat technology. He doesn't follow any rules these things do. In a way, he seems capable of breaking the fundamental rules of cultivation altogether."

"For now, see if you can figure out a way to hide Jeeves' location. The stronger he grows, the easier he might be to find. I doubt Technocrats would use Karma to find him, but rather some sort of hidden bug or connection through the Soul World," Zac said.

"I'll see what I can do," Kenzie said with a slightly hollow voice.

"I'm sorry I didn't have any better news to give you." Zac sighed.

"That's okay. We're still better off than most people on Earth," Kenzie said. "Besides, we might find the truth when we start looking into the Mystic Realm in earnest. Who knows, it might even be one of the labs where they researched Jeeves. Even if some other force took it over later, they still left a lot of the infrastructure intact, according to Ogras. There might be records that only Jeeves can access."

"That's what I'm thinking as well. There is no rush to find Leandra. We will both be able to live thousands of years. We can slowly figure out the truth without risking our lives or the lives of everyone on Earth." Zac nodded. "Perhaps Julia will have some good news as well."

"That's true," Kenzie said, her eyes lighting up a bit again. "I told her that you'd meet her at 7 a.m. in the government building."

"Thank you," Zac said as he stood up. "Will you be okay?"

"I'll be fine," Kenzie said.

Zac felt a sense of heaviness as he walked back to his courtyard. Things had gone pretty much as expected, and he could only pray that would be the end of his sister's attempts at looking for their mother in the short run. But he honestly didn't feel completely secure, and he made a note to look into whether it was possible to block out the Technocrat's Soul World, like a multiversal Wi-Fi blocker.

There was still a few hours before the arranged time, so he just took a short nap before he started consolidating his latest gains, getting a feel of his upgraded Dao Fragment. The insight mostly felt defensive in nature, which Zac was pretty happy with. His defensive capabilities were starting to slip now that he got so little Endurance, but this would push him a step further.

He was also surprised to find out that the insight actually had changed his Dao Field by quite a bit.

10
ARTIFACT

It was now extremely clear how big the improved Dao Field was, as it formed an almost perfect bubble around him, spreading for up to two hundred meters. It looked like he used a defensive treasure, though his Dao Field was more transparent.

It even had a direct defensive capability, as Zac noticed that a few falling leaves were rebuffed and pushed to the side. He didn't expect the Dao Field to protect him against ultimate strikes or anything, but who knew how strong such a field could become as he progressed.

His other Dao Fields were a lot more diffuse, with his Dao Field of the Axe being a pretty much invisible field full of razor blades. Zac found it interesting how they started to move apart in how they looked, and it made him curious about how things would work at the higher grades. The time quickly passed as he meditated, and it was soon enough time to get going.

Zac walked over to the enormous government building, and he couldn't help but notice that the sprawling structure had grown in size in between every time he visited. This time, another wing had been added, built in an interesting mix of human and demon architecture that was a blend of living wood and glass.

The building was full of people even though it was still early. Zac walked over to the desk and was soon led to a secluded meeting room overlooking the square, guided by an extremely flustered office clerk he didn't recognize. He guessed it was someone who had been transferred to Port Atwood recently from one of the satellite towns in the archipelago.

It still felt a bit odd to see strangers on his island, as he still somewhat considered Port Atwood the desolate place where he had spent months alone with the demons. Even when new people finally started arriving, it was still in small numbers, and he could place every single face. But the last months had seen an explosion in population, though everyone was thoroughly screened by Adran and Abby.

Julia had already arrived, gazing at the town below through the large window with a cup of coffee in her hands.

"One of the things I like about our new lives." Zac smiled as he sat down at the conference table, pouring himself a cup. "Spiritual coffee beans."

"Now if everything didn't want to kill us, then we would have been golden," Julia responded with a wry smile as she turned toward him.

"So? What did you learn?" Zac asked.

"It's a mess," Julia said, looking completely crestfallen. "The New World Government is beyond salvation. The cultist shape-shifters have infiltrated extremely deep, but a core section led by Thomas Fischer has actually taken up with the Dominators. A lot of the cultists were purged soon after, but I don't know if they got them all or how they were exposed."

"If we could buy that **[Origin Array]** to root out any aliens, then so can they." Zac shrugged. "Did you find out anything else about the cultists?"

"Not much, honestly. It feels like the shape-shifters have gone to huge lengths to obfuscate anything tangible about their origins," Julia said as she took out a tablet. "However, I did manage to find the location of both the government's spatial tunnel, along with the location of another entrance currently held by the Church of Everlasting Dao."

"Good." Zac nodded with relief. "I may have to enter from somewhere else in the future unless the spatial turbulence around ours dies down."

"You should know that at least the government's entrance is booby-trapped," Julia said. "Officially, it was to protect everyone in case they needed to flee the undead, but it would work just as well against you. There are also strict checks to get inside. The whole entrance is a fortress; anyone coming by foot will be attacked without pardon."

"Pretty careful," Zac muttered. "Well, it makes sense. They're essentially the weakest group around. I still don't understand how they expect things to work out in their favor. They're only around because no one can be bothered with wiping them out."

"Well, I actually learned quite a few things about the Mystic Realm, in case you want to move on from the subject of the invaders," Julia said.

Zac tapped the table in thought.

"What do you think?" he finally asked. "You haven't been with the government for a while, but you were still a part of the upper management during a time when the infiltration most likely had already started. The shape-shifters must have come from somewhere."

"I have a theory, but I am unable to confirm it," Julia slowly said.

Zac didn't say anything, only indicated for her to keep talking.

"The government secured a handful of hunting grounds for our soldiers during the early stages of the integration, even before you appeared," Julia began. "We had found one place in particular, just one week's travel from Main Paris, one of the larger secondary hubs of the government. Better yet, the route to get there was pretty safe, which was key, as we still hadn't set up too many teleportation arrays. The cost of mass teleportation was also something we had trouble affording.

"We sent soldiers to Main Paris through arrays and then put them on cargo planes or convoys. Some would return directly to New Washington by teleportation array later, but others would stay there. There was constant traffic both the old way and through teleporters, and infiltrators could easily have used Main Paris as the point of ingress," Julia said as she showed Main Paris on a map.

"Main Paris is located in the middle of Pangea," Zac muttered. "They would have been able to travel to most major towns of Earth within a month or two even if they traveled by foot. Such a trip would be suicide for most humans, but it shouldn't have been too difficult for the Church."

"Exactly." Julia nodded.

"So you think the incursion is in this forest?" Zac asked.

"Probably not. We should have found it if that was the case," Julia said with a shake of her head. "The training ground was a medium-sized forest full of Derriers, a pack animal from the Ishiate world. They are quite aggressive, but not very powerful, and there's a lot of them. Makes for perfect target practice. The forest was blocked to the north and west by an inhospitable mountain range and a massive saltwater lake to the east. We came from the south. It created an enclosed area that allowed the Derriers to multiply freely.

"We mapped the forest easily, but we never managed to get past the mountain range due to extremely aggressive birds that lived there. They were hunting Derriers as well, so our soldiers mostly stayed at the southern side of the forest. But if the invaders could find a path through the mountain…" she continued.

"So they might be on the other side." Zac nodded in understanding.

"Exactly. The area on the other side of that mountain range is one of the twelve yet uncharted territories of Pangea, and my best guess of their whereabouts," she explained.

"Sounds like our best bet," Zac agreed. "I will go there to check things out as soon as I've prepared everything I need."

"Be careful; those birds in the mountain are extremely territorial. They even ripped apart a couple of our fighter jets that we sent to scout things out," Julia said.

"The more powerful they are, the better." Zac shrugged. "I could use the experience. What have you found out about the Mystic Realm? Have you found what everyone's after?"

"Thomas is keeping a lot of details close to the vest. But it's impossible to keep everything secret in this big an operation, so my contacts and I have managed to piece together some things," Julia said. "The fact that there are a lot of people who wish that they joined you instead of New Washington made my job a lot easier as well."

Zac wryly smiled in response, but he honestly wasn't all that interested in taking on a bunch of flaky diplomats from the New World Government. Especially not after hearing the disgusting stories from Emma MacHale and seeing how they'd mismanaged his hometown.

"Thomas Fisher seems to believe there is some sort of dimensional artifact inside the Mystic Realm that will save them not only from the cultists and Dominators, but even the Great Redeemer himself. It's this item that every force is after," Julia said, dragging Zac out of his thoughts.

"Dimensional artifact?" Zac repeated with confusion. "What's that?"

"No idea. But from what I gathered, it seems to be still growing in the depths of the realm. Thomas is moving a lot of his resources into the Mystic Realm, and many of the elite squads never leave any longer. Even Thomas only exits for a few hours at a time. I believe…" Julia said, gathering her thoughts.

"Yes?" Zac asked.

"It is because of this dimensional artifact. The moment it's uncovered, it will temporarily destabilize the Mystic Realm, cutting off the entrances. That's why everyone's missing. The Dominators, the cultists, the New World Government. No one wants to be caught outside. That's at least the conclusion I and my contacts reached," Julia said.

"Do you have any timeline for when that would happen?" Zac asked with worry.

If it really was true, then he needed to get going quicker than he anticipated. He absolutely couldn't be locked outside if both the incursion leader and the Dominators were inside the Mystic Realm. Not only would that leave the most powerful invaders unchecked, but it would also make it impossible to kill the Dominators.

He didn't know whether the Great Redeemer could find Earth while the Dominators were inside the Mystic Realm, but he didn't want to risk it. What if Void's Disciple managed to lock the Mystic Realm down completely and simply stayed there until Voridis appeared?

"We couldn't find an exact date, but you should have at least a month. I got a hold of various orders to the military and a few departments. There are multiple projects related to the Ark World that have a delivery deadline of thirty-six days from now. I think the government is confident of the entrances being open until then, while the elites are already standing by in case something unexpected happens," Julia said.

"Thirty-six days," Zac muttered. "A month."

It wasn't a lot, but it was better than nothing. In fact, it might even be for the best to deal with this matter as quickly as possible. However, he knew that the number of power-ups he would be able to gain in such a short time was limited.

"What makes the government think they can actually compete for that item?" Zac asked next, which was the most burning question in his mind. "I could simply fly over to their entrance and snatch it if I wanted to, and I bet the Dominators could do the same."

"You shouldn't underestimate them," Julia said. "They control most of the old world's weaponry. Thousands of missiles and other types of explosives."

Zac made a noncommittal shrug, not feeling too threatened by something like that any longer. He would be able to push them all away with a few swings of his axe, or just move out of the way with [Loamwalker]. Or just block them with some defensive skills.

"You also shouldn't take their entrance unless you have to. They've already made it clear that multiple people can set off the booby trap at the entrance. Stealing the entrance and jumping inside would be suicidal," Julia said.

Zac grunted with annoyance, but he had to admit it was a pretty good deterrent. He'd almost died the last time he entered a booby-trapped teleporter, after all. If it weren't for his sister adding a safety measure, he would have been ripped apart instead of thrown out over the ocean. But would that method really work in a spatial tunnel to a Mystic Realm?

Where would he be thrown out if he exited mid-transportation? The void of space?

"More importantly, they have apparently brokered an agreement with some of the forces inside the Mystic Realm," Julia added, dragging Zac out of his thoughts. "They are currently advertising it, how they have allied with multiple powerful E-grade warriors."

"They have? What do the aliens get out of that deal?" Zac said skeptically.

"Freedom. Getting out of the Mystic Realm when this is all done," Julia said.

Zac frowned when he heard her explanation. Joining up with a bunch of strangers who were far more powerful was a recipe for disaster, something that Catheya had driven home during their talk. The government obviously had some way to restrain them, as Earth wasn't already crawling with escapees.

Ogras had mentioned the extremely strong security measures in the research base; perhaps the government had managed to use those checkpoints to their advantage. Still. It only took one mistake to release the floodgates, at which point any agreement would be null and void. Why would a bunch of powerful E-grade warriors bother following the orders of Thomas Fisher and the useless diplomats?

"Wait, forces plural?" Zac asked, but he suddenly remembered Ogras' description of his visit to the Mystic Realm.

He had met two Peak F-grade warriors fighting to the death, meaning they might come from opposing factions.

"There are at least four forces in the Mystic Realm, each trapped inside and in control of their own section of the research base," Julia explained, opening a rough sketch on her tablet. "It's apparently shockingly large, like a country. No one has access to the core region of the base, as I've understood it. But the restrictions are weakening inside for some reason, and everyone is looking for a path to the dimensional artifact."

Zac looked down at the sketch that looked like a hexagonal star, his eyes drawn to the X marked in the center of the map – the location of this mysterious treasure that had all the factions in a tizzy. An artifact that could deal with even the Great Redeemer?

He couldn't let that fall into the hands of anyone else.

11
CLEANSE

Zac already knew there were some natives living inside the Mystic Realm since long ago, but the situation that Julia described had exceeded his expectations.

"Do you know the strength of the aliens?" Zac asked with some worry.

"The intelligence said High E-grade, but it's hard to know what that means," Julia said.

Zac nodded in agreement. Just level alone was an imprecise measurement of someone's power. For example, the dragon he had fought in the Tower of Eternity was likely only Early E-grade, but extremely powerful due to its Race and bloodline. Meanwhile, there were Mid-E Grade warriors by this point who were essentially no threat to Zac.

With his recent gains, he felt confident in dealing with some High E-grade warriors as well, though that would depend on whether they had any unique advantages of their own. Ogras said that the energy inside the Mystic Realm was pretty sparse, and perhaps it was hard to ponder on the Dao as well.

However, the base had most likely been used to research bloodlines once upon a time, meaning every force should have one or multiple powerful bloodlines to boost their combat power. Besides, the E-grade warriors he had fought up until now were mostly newly ascended, whereas those in the Mystic Realm might be thousands of years old.

What if he met someone who had polished their skills for millennia while spending centuries on opening each and every one of their Inherited hidden nodes? The leaders might even be stronger than the Dominators.

"The vast majority of the construct is unpopulated, as far as I heard, and the government is currently busy exploring the sections that the natives are locked out of. There are even large forests full of monsters," Julia added.

"There are forests? Like real outside forests?" Zac asked with surprise. "Is there a world outside this star-shaped structure?"

"No, it's still inside, with walls all around. I have no idea if there's anything outside," Julia said with a shake of her head. "The government's entrance has ended up in one of these forests, but it is vastly different compared to the one you describe in the information package you gave me."

"Different how?"

"The forest is massive, roughly half the size of this island, I reckon. And it is full of powerful beasts at Peak F-grade," Julia said. "The government can only use their entrance at certain times of day when the beasts sleep, and rush to an entrance they have secured. Perhaps the builders of the research base were breeding the beasts once, but they have definitely gone feral by now."

Zac nodded in understanding, and his heart still sped up a bit.

A bunch of powerful beasts? Wasn't that exactly what he was looking for? These ones were just F-grade and mostly useless to Zac, but perhaps there were similar forests full of Early E-grade beasts further inside the realm?

"There is all kinds of information on this tablet," Julia said as she handed it over. "But it is mostly about the government's latest movement and the situation on Earth. The government has barely scratched the surface of the Mystic Realm, and I think you would have to go for yourself to get a real understanding of that place."

"Thank you. Good job," Zac said as he stood up.

It looked like the real showdown with the Dominators would take place in a month or two. He wasn't confident in being able to lock down Void's Disciple even with the jamming arrays, but the situation inside the Mystic Realm would likely force them into each other's crosshairs.

The only time Void's Disciple had lost his cool was when Zac threatened to take the item inside the Mystic Realm. Snatching that item would force the Dominators to come to him rather than him trying to find them, which was the best solution he could think of right now. It was no doubt crucial to the Great Redeemer, and it beat having to scour every Zhix hive on the planet.

The biggest flaw of the plan would be the delay. Voridis might reach Earth's universe at any moment, and there really wasn't any backup plan if that happened. It would be every man for himself. The only relief was the impressive number of Teleportation Tokens he had amassed in the Base Town. It would allow everyone close to him to leave Earth, as long as he closed down the cultist incursion first.

Of course, that only went for something like two hundred people.

"Ah, one more thing," Julia said as Zac was about to leave.

"Yes?" Zac asked with confusion.

"I want a job," Julia said. "A permanent one."

"Oh?" Zac asked as he stopped in his tracks. "What do you have in mind?"

"Alea was in charge of law and order for a while, until she wasn't," Julia said, drawing a frown from Zac. "Security is still high in Port Atwood with your existence as a deterrence, but things are more chaotic in your other settlements. You are still maintaining control thanks to your armies, but we need civil law enforcement as well. I want to help build such a section."

Zac slowly mulled it over for a few seconds without giving a direct response. He had honestly dropped a ball regarding this, but he could absolutely understand if normal noncombat classes and the weaker citizens felt unsafe if there was no one around to keep law and order.

But the whole concept of law enforcement was a bit tricky in their new world as well. It was easier said than done keeping a population in check when anyone could gain superpowers. Perhaps there was some service he could purchase as more options became available in the Town Shop?

"I'll talk it over with a few others before making a decision," Zac said after a while. "But it sounds like a good idea."

He had a lot to think about, so he sent a message to his sister as he left that he needed to consolidate his gains before he retreated to his cultivation cave. He started up the second cycle of the [**Nine Reincarnations Manual**] since he felt he might as well be productive while sitting around, and he decided to try the array as a Draugr this time.

He didn't change much, apart from starting at the life-attuned side of the array. His mind was soon filled with life, and the life-attuned energies no longer felt like poison to his undead body. Seeing that things seemed to work just fine, he started circulating the manual by rote while he went over his meeting with Julia.

The array didn't take too much of his concentration while it was active, and he could even look through the tablet while his Mental Energy was drained and infused with attunement. Most of it was reports of movements of the various forces of Earth just like she said, which wasn't really something Zac cared about.

There were some minor conflicts brewing between the council and the New World Governments, according to the intelligence, and Zac was actually a bit surprised at how unified the council stayed even after returning to the surface. None of the thirteen councilors had joined any of their racial factions as far as Zac could tell, instead choosing to stay with their former group.

In either case, squabbles between local forces wasn't really something that Zac wanted to get involved in, as long as they didn't involve his people or hurt innocents. Some internal strife might even toughen them up, which would prepare the earthlings for when the planet was properly integrated into the Multiverse in the future.

Zac was more interested in the more pressing issues: the Dominators, the cultists, and the Mystic Realm. He was trying to figure out the best approach, one that would allow him to rid the world of lingering threats with the highest success rate.

He eventually decided against assaulting either of the two tunnels that Julia had located. He was curious about the pocket realm since he still hadn't been able to explore its mysteries, but it felt like a safer route to reopen their own entrance. Kenzie had already made some preliminary measurements that were positive.

The cultists had detonated a massive bomb on the shores of Mystic Island, but they were forced to do it far from the tunnel itself. So it had only destabilized rather than broken down completely. Right now they were still waiting out the spatial turbulence, but it would gradually calm down over the following weeks. They might even be able to add some stabilizing arrays or treasures to the tunnel, which would force it open early if necessary.

More preparations were needed for the war against the traitor Zhix as well, which left the cultist incursion. Closing the incursion next felt like the most optimal route. It might leave some cultists spread all across Earth, but they could methodically be purged with the help of **[Origin Arrays]** over the following hundred years.

Closing the incursion would come with a lot of benefits as well. Earth was still in a "trial" phase as things stood, and some parts of the System were still locked away from them. Closing the incursion would allow him to purchase more structures, and it would probably activate his Nexus Hub.

Succeeding in proving your worth to the System by booting out all invaders also came with direct benefits, according to Abby, though what kind of benefits differed since the System was always trying out new methods of integration. For example, the ladder system was something that neither Abby nor Ogras had heard of before.

Dealing with the cultists sooner rather than later was the best option as well. He had almost killed the Head Priest, and only a week had passed since then. He might still be severely weakened from barely escaping **[Fate's Obduracy]**, allowing Zac to strike while the iron was hot.

The bird mountain was also pretty interesting from Julia's description. There was a critical lack of good grinding spots, but those birds sounded pretty formidable if they could even take down airplanes soon after the integration.

The hours passed as Zac finished his second day of soul cultivation, and the results were identical to when he'd cultivated as a human. He was about to work on his Draugr Race next, but his communication crystal suddenly shook, delivering the message he had been waiting for.

The time to scan everyone for lingering Karmic threats was finally here, and Zac teleported over to the Atwood Academy. A Valkyrie informed him that everyone was already waiting, so he flashed over to the Dao House.

He noticed a few Tal-Eladar standing in the distance, looking at the Dao House with thoughtful faces. They had probably figured out some things about it after staying at the Academy for a few days, but he only nodded at them before entering. The thirty-odd people were already gathered in the inner chambers of the Dao House, and they all looked over when Zac arrived.

Even Ogras had emerged from his bout of secluded cultivation, though Zac could sense that he still hadn't evolved.

Zac nodded at the familiar faces before he glanced at the wall. He was surprised to feel that he still could sense a small echo of the Dao in the walls themselves, imprinted from when they'd cracked open the funnel. If people kept pondering on the Dao inside this place over the years, it might become a real treasure even though it was made from normal materials, kind of like the cherry tree in his vision.

The mysterious grooves covering the Dao House weren't the only interesting change. He spotted Sap Trang standing with two of the Valkyries. Zac barely recognized him, as his hair had turned completely black over the past week. Having taken medicinal baths for months had improved the old fisherman's constitution tremendously, but the latest improvement was far more drastic than anything up 'til now.

"Long time no see." Zac smiled as he walked over to Sap Trang. "How do you feel?"

"Better than I have in decades," Sap Trang said with a toothy smile. "That compound you sent over has worked wonders. It felt like it helped me absorb the medicinal baths better as well. I talked with little Alyn earlier, and she believes my odds of evolving my constitution have improved by a lot. You don't happen to have some more? Not for me, but the other elderly in the town."

"I'm glad it worked," Zac said with a smile. "I'm afraid I don't have much of that stuff left over to help the others, but I'll see if we can buy some through the Consortium. We'll catch up later."

It was truly great news that things were looking up for the old fisherman. He was essentially the first human member of his force, and he had proven himself over and over. It would have been a real shame if he passed away from old age just as the doors to nigh immortality had opened themselves to the people of Earth.

The compound that Sap Trang mentioned was simply some Longevity Pearls that had been ground down by the Sky Gnomes, together with a few dried herbs that were there to stop the efficacy from immediately dissipating. The short remaining life span of the old fisherman was one of the biggest hindrances to evolving his Race, and Zac wanted to see if the pearls could help with that situation.

To put it a bit bluntly, it was also an experiment that would benefit Zac. He had wasted a lot of life force during his climb, and similar situations might arise in the future as well, as long as the Shard was stuck in his head.

Seeing the effect of longevity treasures on Mr. Trang was a way for him to prepare for the future.

12
A CLEAN BREAK

Zac had tried the compound on himself as well, but the efficacy was extremely limited in his case. He didn't believe it was because of his constitution or anything like that, but simply because he was already E-grade Race. He would probably have to get his hands on better pearls. These longevity treasures were something he'd picked up on the second level of the Tower, after all, so they weren't some supreme treasures.

Of course, there was also the possibility that the life force sucked clean by the Shard was gone forever, but Zac wouldn't take that for a given until he had tried to remedy the situation with better materials. Even if that was the case, it wasn't the end of the world, as long as he reached D-grade and restocked on a few millennia of additional life span.

In fact, he felt it was a possibility that his life span was already longer than most people's, as he'd had to evolve his Race twice. Wasn't it more than fair that he got twice as much life force from the double upgrades?

The discussions in the room had died down as soon as Zac arrived, and he quickly realized what was going through their heads, going by their expressions.

"I'm sorry to disappoint you all, but this is not another opportunity." Zac smiled as he looked around at the hopeful faces. "We are just making sure that there are no lingering side effects to our earlier experiment. You don't need to do anything; just stand still while we do our thing."

With that, Zac took out the **[Lantern of Fate]** and activated it, illuminating the whole inner chamber and the participants in an ethereal light. Hundreds of strands appeared in the room, with Zac singlehandedly being the source of almost half of them. The others couldn't see anything except the spooky light from the lantern, but Zac could quickly figure out what was going on, as each strand emitted a unique aura.

"How is it?" Ogras asked as he walked over, and Zac sighed in response.

Most of the lines attached to the people in the room weren't anything special, mostly leading toward various directions in Port Atwood. Zac and most of the demons also had additional strands pointing toward the sky, with the demons having blood-red lines that pointed toward the same direction.

Zac and Ogras had an additional mix of different colors, no doubt representing the connections they had made in the Tower of Eternity. However, there was a group of people who all had an ashy-gray strand that pointed toward the sky, people who really shouldn't have any connection to anyone outside Earth.

It looked like the gift of Origin Dao came with a price after all.

"What do we do now? How does that thing work?" Ogras asked from the side with a low volume. "Should we...?"

"No," Zac said with a shake of his head, but he still took out **[Verun's Bite]**. "The lamp has a solution."

The changed appearance of the axe drew a whistle from Ogras and appreciative looks from the demons, who could easily understand that the Spirit Tool had become even more powerful. Zac didn't simply swing at the ribbons, but instead, he opened a small compartment on the lamp, exposing a small reservoir of oil.

This part was just as important as the lamp itself since seeing the Karmic lines was just half the battle. The second part was cutting them, and a normal weapon wouldn't be able to accomplish that. The best would be things like the dagger that the Abbot had given him back then, but it had broken apart after one usage.

However, the lamp wasn't a top-tier treasure without reason, and it came with a solution that even he could use.

"I only have a little bit of this," Zac said as he smeared some of the oil across the edge of his axe. "Let's hope we won't have to use this thing too much."

He did have the second treasure of the Undead Kingdom as well, the item of erasure. However, he wanted to save that for the Dominators and their items since they should have a much stronger Karmic connection to the Redeemer compared to these weak ribbons.

The students of Atwood Academy recoiled in fear as Zac suddenly appeared in front of them, but he didn't dare explain what was going on in case that would ruin their preparations. He moved as quickly as he could and swung his axe at the closest gray ribbon with such speed that the young girl in front of him couldn't even react.

Ogras was just one step behind, though he simply moved the girl away from the others in case something went wrong. Groans echoed across the hall as one person after another coughed up a mouthful of blood and fell unconscious until less than twenty people remained standing. Most of the students were among the unconscious, but one demon and a few of the Valkyries had been affected as well, along with Sap Trang.

Zac wasn't surprised by the group of unconscious people. They were essentially the same group as those who had been accosted by those ghosts when he cracked open the funnel. He felt that these people were a bit pitiful, not only reaping the smallest rewards from the funnel but also getting all of the drawbacks.

The rest stood rooted in place, not completely understanding what was going on. They had only seen Zac starting to swing his axe in the air like a lunatic while one person after another collapsed onto the floor. They looked warily at Zac and Ogras, but they breathed out in relief when they saw Zac put the lamp away.

"Take them to the infirmary," Ogras said to the demons who stood by before he walked Zac away from the others. "We should do this again at a later date to make sure it worked. Can't be too careful with that old bastard."

"We'll do a second scan before we enter the Mystic Realm." Zac nodded in agreement before he properly looked up and down at the demon. "You still haven't evolved? What's going on?"

"It's the netherblasted shadow-beast." Ogras sighed after making sure no one else was within earshot. "The bastard has complicated things for me. I heard from your sister about the Mystic Realm. I really need to go into seclusion if I want a shot at evolving before then. Can you deal with the rest yourself?"

Zac thought it over, and he eventually nodded.

"I'll head out to find the cultists next," Zac said. "They are different from the Undead Empire. I should be able to deal with it alone."

"Their defenses seem a lot simpler; just kill everything in the surroundings. But be careful. Don't forget how crazy they are. That's how I got my arm replaced by this bastard," Ogras said as he knocked the metal cast on his arm.

"I know." Zac sighed. "I'll go alone. I'm not sure I'd be able to protect others from their fire if they start exploding themselves."

"Well, your past year has led to this moment," Ogras snorted. "Some zealot fire shouldn't be able to take out the unkillable cockroach."

"Thank you for the vote of confidence." Zac grinned at the demon, who melded into the shadows the next moment.

Zac left as well after having made sure that everyone was alive and stable, and headed over to Thayer Consortium to pick up some items he had ordered. While he was there, he also asked Calrin to look into blocking Technocrat tech, though he didn't hold too much hope of him finding anything useful.

He also asked them to start preparing for the auction. He still hadn't decided whether he should hold it before or after he dealt with the Mystic Realm, but he leaned toward the latter. No point in empowering outsiders just before the showdown that would decide Earth's future. It might come back to bite him in the ass.

He returned to his compound next and found Emily having dinner with his sister.

"I'm heading out to deal with the cultists," Zac said to the two. "Be careful while I'm gone."

"Already? You need me to call the shield squad?" Kenzie asked.

"No, I'm going alone this time," Zac said with a shake of his head, ignoring the pout coming from Emily's side.

Since Ogras had gone into seclusion to prepare for his breakthrough, he didn't feel comfortable bringing Emily and the others. He had mostly brought them last time because of the high stakes of the undead incursion, but it was different now. If things went according to plan, he would find a half-abandoned incursion base, as most of the cultists were busy exploring the Mystic Realm.

He would either close it down or flee with the help of the emerald leaf, allowing him to try again later. There was no point in risking the lives of his people in such a scenario.

In fact, he felt that anyone except Ogras might turn out to be a liability, where Zac would have to split his attention between protecting others and taking out the invaders. The Valkyries had made tremendous gains over the past months, but they still weren't ready to tackle people like the cultists head-on.

Meanwhile, he felt confident that his recent gain in power was enough to close the incursion. After all, he had managed to defeat the Head Priest once already in a head-on collision, and that was before his Dao upgrade and while being weakened from the node opening. He was in tip-top shape right now, and he even had a charge from the Splinter as a backup in case things turned really dire.

"Fine." Kenzie sighed. "But be careful. They seem pretty insane, but they are an ancient faction. They must have some things to rely on after being able to avoid getting eradicated after making enemies left and right."

Zac talked with his sister and Emily a bit longer before he walked over to his teleportation house. He changed his appearance with **[Thousand Faces]** before he entered, as he didn't want his movements to be tracked. His vision turned black for a minute before he appeared in Westfort.

The teleportation station was bustling with activity, and over a hundred warriors were coming and going. The small British town was quickly becoming a proper world hub, though Zac believed that they hadn't managed to upgrade the town through the System just yet.

He showed an ID given to him by Thea at the security checkpoint, and he was quickly escorted to a secured area without another word. A somewhat familiar face hurried over the next moment, and Zac remembered he was one of the intelligence officers of the Marshall Clan.

"Lord Atwood," the officer said with a small bow, "what brings you here today?"

"Is Thea around?" he asked after some thought.

He had received a letter in response to his own already, but he still wanted to talk to her face-to-face. He wasn't running against the clock right now, and it wouldn't change anything if he arrived at Main Paris an hour later.

"She and Mr. Trask Jr. are currently in the library. Would you like for us to arrange transportation?" the officer asked, and Zac soon found himself sitting in the back of a town car with tinted windows.

All the defensive perimeters around the Old Homestead opened up without issue, and he was quickly led to the shell-like tower. His appearance reverted back to normal as he stepped through the door, and he found Thea sitting on the sofa where he'd read about Galvarion a few months back. Billy was dozing off next to her, his snores likely blocked out by an array.

However, he woke up as Zac approached, and waved at him with a big grin.

"How are you two feeling?" Zac smiled as he sat down on a sofa opposite them.

"Haha, Billy is good," the giant said as he waved his meaty arms with enough force to create a gust, which earned him a slap from one of Big Blue's tentacles. "Stupid fish."

Zac wondered if the two would erupt in battle, but Thea smoothly distracted Billy by taking out a grilled turkey leg, as though she had done this dance many times before.

"That's good to hear," Zac said as he looked over at Thea. "And how are you?"

"I'm not too bad," Thea said with a small smile. "I'm no worse than I've been for most of the past year. It doesn't feel like the System ever lets you completely rest up."

"About earlier, I—" Zac hesitated, but he stopped when Thea placed her hand on his.

"You don't have to keep beating yourself up, or desperately try to fix everything," Thea said. "If anything, I think I owe you an apology. I was furious when you disappeared. But I only considered things from my perspective. It was unfair of me to demand you risk your life before you felt confident of success."

"Well, my sister seems to believe I have problems communicating clearly, so I'm partly to blame as well," Zac said with a wry smile.

"We're all just scrambling to make do here. No one is expecting you to be perfect. The fact that you're trying your hardest is more than enough. And if you need me, I'm here for you. In a way, our situation is similar – we've both become guardians of those around us. So we should learn from and support each other as we figure this all out."

"Alright." Zac smiled. "Thank you."

"We're the ones who should thank you for all you've done," Thea said with a smile. "Now, what brought you here today?"

"Well, I have some news."

Zac quickly recounted what he had found out from Julia regarding the Mystic Realm, though Billy quickly zoned out until he mentioned the large number of powerful beasts. He immediately wanted to head out for some thwonking, but Zac and Thea managed to calm him down.

"So what do you want to do?" Thea asked after a while. "Are you heading in now?"

"I'm completely healed up now," Zac slowly said. "So I am thinking I'll hit the cultists first. That way I'll both gain a new entrance while also cutting off their escape route. We can slowly flush them out afterward. Those lunatics don't deserve any leniency. Besides, that way we can limit the spread of information about Earth."

"They probably have already sent back information about the Mystic Realm. I think that's what prompted the extra investment," Thea countered.

"Still," Zac said.

Another reason he wanted to close the incursion was to free himself up to use both his classes while battling the invaders without risking the news reaching the Church. However, he wasn't really willing to discuss that matter in front of Big Blue and Billy. He didn't believe that Billy would betray him, but the giant didn't really have any filters and might blurt it out at an inopportune time.

"Do you need help with the cultists?" Thea asked, changing the subject.

"Billy want to help as well!" the giant roared. "Stupid fire-lizards burned Billy's clothes."

"Just focus on recuperation." Zac smiled. "It will be all hands on deck in the Mystic Realm later."

"We're mostly better. Billy and I have already talked about it. If you don't need help with the incursion, can we enter the inheritance while you are away?"

13
BIRDS

"You want to enter right now? You sure you don't want to wait?" Zac asked with surprise. "You might die, you know. As I told you in the letter, the masters of the inheritances all seem to be eccentric characters. Why not wait until you've reached level 75?"

Zac had decided to give them each a shot at an inheritance as thanks for protecting Port Atwood while he was away. Their efforts had slowed down the approach of the invaders by hours, which was the whole reason he could complete the climb without worries.

He didn't know what he would have done if he'd suddenly gotten the prompt of the invasion while he was inside the Tower, but he most likely would have left early. He would have lost out on so much if that had happened, including the Shard of Creation.

Not only that, but the two had completely missed out on the quest for defeating the undead incursion because of their wounds. Thea and Billy should have been two of the highest contributors in the battle against the undead except himself and the Abbot, but they never got the quest as they had been stuck in sickbeds on his island.

Giving them each a shot at an inheritance along with some of the things he had gotten during the climb was the least he could do as thanks. The inheritances were limited, so any spot he gave out might mean that some descendant of his missed out in the future. But he figured that he would be powerful enough to be able to provide even better things to his grandchildren if it ever came to that.

Better to use the inheritances now while they still could provide a lot of value.

So Zac wasn't surprised to hear Thea bring it up, but he was a bit confused that she already wanted to take the trial. They knew they only had one chance, so he had assumed that the two would wait until they reached Peak F-grade. After all, that came with a set of power-ups, such as titles, bonus attributes, and skills.

"We're sure." Thea nodded. "We can't keep playing it safe. I feel we're not powerful enough to help out as we are. We won't be able to reach level 75 in thirty-six days; there's just no way. We'll enter in a day or two after I've confirmed a few things here."

"Billy wants the Titan," Billy said from the side. "Billy doesn't know why, but it feels familiar…?"

"It does?" Zac asked with interest.

Was it perhaps his bloodline calling to him?

"Billy thinks he dreamt being a big giant that was called a Titan?" Billy muttered with a frown. "Can't remember…"

"Well, I think it suits you," Zac said. "I've seen the statue of the master of the Titan inheritance. He looks just as strong as you, so you should be able to get things that make you stronger as well."

The Titan felt like the given choice for Billy, though Zac also felt that the Undying Fiend might be able to provide Billy with means of shoring up his lacking defenses. The inheritances were ultimately a matter of compatibility rather than what people needed, and Billy was definitely the most compatible with the Titan inheritance.

"Good!" Billy fervently nodded. "Billy has slept too much. Last fight hurt. Billy needs to get better at thwonkin'."

"What about you?" Zac asked as he turned to Thea.

"I'll take the Blade Emperor if that's okay," Thea said after a few seconds.

Zac nodded, feeling inwardly relieved. There wasn't really any standout in Port Atwood who could benefit from that inheritance. The only one of the core combatants using a sword was Sap Trang, but he wasn't really a swordmaster, but instead a water mage or beast tamer. Besides, Zac also had the Heritage for the Blade Emperor, which probably contained half of the value that the old master left behind.

"What kind of test was there?" Thea asked. "Is it based on strength or suitability?"

"Suitability," Zac said after some hesitation. "It got a bit dangerous for me because I kind of cheated a bit, and Ogras was only in danger because the master he chose was a lunatic. The trials should be achievable by normal talented people, as they were meant as gifts for the descendants of Brazla, the towers' creator."

"Good," Thea said with some relief.

"I'm not sure how long I'll be gone this time while looking for the cultists. Just have my sister lead you in if I'm not around. Oh, the Tool Spirit is slightly insane as well, so don't try to anger it. It might mess with your trial out of spite," Zac said, drawing an even stare from Thea.

"Anything else...?" she asked.

"No, that's it," Zac said with a shake of his head. "Or, well, just compliment it a bit, and it might make your lives easier. I need some help from your family with the teleporters, but I'll just grab someone from your intelligence office."

"Good luck," Thea said as she quickly scribbled a letter. "What we can do is limited, but don't be afraid to ask for help if you need it. I don't think anyone over at the Intelligence Bureau will cause any trouble for you, but take this letter just in case."

"Thank you." Zac nodded as he stood up. "I will see you guys later."

"I was very happy to receive your letter," Thea said just as Zac walked away.

"Then I'll write some more." Zac smiled before he left.

From there, Zac walked over to the building that housed the intelligence department of the Marshall Clan. Charles Marshall soon met up with him, and Zac inwardly laughed when he saw Charles peek at the shadows with some worry. The demon had apparently left quite an impression during his last visit to the bureau.

"Ogras isn't here," Zac said with a smile. "I need to be teleported to Main Paris without anyone finding out."

"Main Paris...?" Charles repeated with a calculating look. "You're not...?"

"I'm not planning on taking out the New World Government," Zac snorted as he handed him Thea's letter. "At least not yet. I am looking for the base of operations of the cultists. You don't happen to know anything else?"

Charles' eyes lit up, and he quickly took out a stack of documents. He provided a rundown of their findings, and much of it was similar to what Julia had said. The old spy had singled out three possible locations, one of which was the same uncharted territory as Julia had pointed out.

A second one was in the middle of a vast marshland that spread out to the south of the heartlands of Pangea. There were some settlements there, but only at the edge. The place was swarming with hostile wildlife, the worst of which being the millions of oversized mosquitoes that could suck a person dry in a second.

The high humidity of the area had turned the core of the swamp essentially uncharted as well, which was why Charles believed that an incursion could hide there without notice. The pillars weren't lighthouses that could be seen from tens of miles, after all, and Zac had only spotted the undead one through the Miasmic haze when he was almost upon it.

The final spot was a remote area to the far north, an inhospitable world of ice north of even the most distant of settlements. It was the least likely place in Charles' opinion, but he had scribbled a note that said that they might like the hostile environment to temper themselves since they were fire attributed.

Zac went over the documents as Charles read Thea's letter, and Zac felt some relief that it probably wouldn't take too long to deal with the cultists. He personally felt the northern location was a long shot, which meant he only needed two trips to find his target. The fact that both Julia and Charles had landed on the same spot was a good indicator, as both had access to vast, but different, intelligence networks.

"Inheritance," Charles muttered from the side. "May I ask if this is a real inheritance like the ones described in our library?"

"It is. A Peak D-grade inheritance. I have a few of them, and I gave Thea one slot. Keep this to yourself, though." Zac nodded.

"Certainly, though I need to share it with Henry. May I ask if there is danger?" the thin old man asked with worry.

It was easy to forget that this kindly old man was a ruthless assassin who had murdered a family member for breaking the family rules, rather than a doting grandpa worrying for Thea's safety.

"Some. She can give up if it gets too hard." Zac shrugged. "I'll take a look at the place near Main Paris first. Do you have a method to take me there?"

"You appeared in Westfort with a disguise. Are you able to take on specific faces with your skill?" Charles asked.

"I can, but it doesn't hold up to scrutiny too well." Zac nodded.

"That's fine," Charles said as he started tapping on a tablet before he handed it over.

"This is an informant of mine who has access to Main Paris. If that doesn't work, we also control a remote town roughly half a day's flight from the city. It's up to you which you want to utilize," the old man said.

Zac eventually decided to forgo his plan of going through Main Paris in his search for the cultist incursion. After seeing the location of the Marshall-controlled town on the map, he felt it would only delay him a couple of hours. There were a lot more mountains to cross going from that direction, but it didn't matter to Zac, who had a flying treasure.

This way he was less likely to tip off any infiltrators hiding in Main Paris, or being spotted when flying above a trafficked route.

"I'll go through the smaller town," Zac said as he stood up. "One more thing. The remaining invaders gained the ability to use teleporters the moment their incursion was closed. You might want to increase security going forward. Who knows what a bunch of zealots trapped on Earth will do."

"We have been preparing for this for some time." Charles nodded. "We'll slowly ramp up our measures over the next days to not cause any alarm."

Zac nodded in agreement, and things from there went quite smoothly. Zac was led by a nondescript family member of the Marshall Clan to the village called Peyraud. It was apparently a small French town with less than a thousand citizens that had turned into a minor stronghold.

It had survived until now because it was just outside the hunting range of the mutated birds of the mountain range. The ferocious flocks hunted everything else, which had scared off any stronger beasts from the area.

Of course, Zac knew that this place would be overrun in a year at most, like most places that only survived thanks to a lack of natural predators. The birds would sooner or later evolve, which in turn would increase their appetite and hunting grounds. These villagers were lucky enough that they at least had managed to get a teleporter, allowing them to flee before they got gobbled up.

Zac didn't jump onto his flying treasure but rather kept running through a dense forest for an hour until he was far away from any human activity. Only then did he take out the emerald leaf and set off for the vast mountain range. He quickly understood why people hadn't ventured past the mountains until now. They were simply enormous.

Something this big was hard to properly gauge, but he guessed that they were a match to the Himalayan mountain ranges of old Earth. However, these mountains were made from an almost pristine white rock, making Zac believe they came from one of the other planets.

The second reason why people avoided the mountains soon presented itself as well, as hundreds of small spots rose from a mountain peak as Zac approached. The distant spots quickly grew in size until Zac realized that some of the incoming birds were just enormous. There were some with a wingspan of just a couple of meters, but the larger ones looked like they could snatch up a fighter jet in their claws.

Zac didn't want to get embroiled in an aerial battle at this juncture, so he urged the leaf to take evasive maneuvers. But the mutated eagles had no problem matching his speed as they intercepted. A piercing cry suddenly exploded in his ears with enough power to make him dizzy, but he quickly righted himself just in time to see a bird bursting forward with shocking speed.

It seemed like the bird had activated some inherent skill, as it appeared right in front of him in almost an instant. A light flashed among the clouds as Verun was unleashed, and a rain of blood followed as the eagle was chopped in two. The bloodthirsty bird had been on the threshold of reaching the E-grade, but it was cut apart like paper in the face of the upgraded Spirit Tool.

More importantly, the weapon actually emitted a primordial aura that made the eagles stop in their tracks. It allowed him to increase the distance as the flying treasure was pushed to its limits. However, their territorial instincts soon won over their primal fear of the aura the axe emitted, and they swooped toward Zac like kamikaze pilots.

Zac could only sigh in annoyance as he started pushing Cosmic Energy toward **[Chop]**, but he suddenly stopped himself and moved the energy toward the fractal on his left arm instead. He still hadn't tested **[Rapturous Divide]**, but wasn't this the perfect opportunity? He was still just at the edge of the mountain range, far from the supposed location of the incursion.

However, as he pushed Cosmic Energy into the fractal, he realized a problem; the skill refused to activate.

14
THE ABYSS AND ARCADIA

The massive eagles soared ever closer, but Zac didn't panic as he opened his skill menu while fleeing from the flock. He had already looked at the description, but he wanted to use it as a clue to what might be the problem.

[E] Rapturous Divide – Proficiency: Early. Between the Abyss and Arcadia is an endless chasm. Upgradeable.

The [E] in front of the skill was unique, as the other skills were without any tag. However, that wasn't important right now, but rather finding out why he couldn't use the skill. His eyes bored into the text like he was trying to see any hidden truths behind it, and his mind furiously worked to put together the clues so far.

"Split life and death... the Abyss and Arcadia," Zac muttered with a frown as he tried to understand the fractal, and something suddenly clicked.

He quickly pushed Cosmic Energy into **[Chop]** as well, and a terrifyingly large fractal blade grew out from **[Verun's Bite]**. He was still only able to maintain a stable edge that was around ten meters, whereas anything larger would start to destabilize after a few seconds.

However, a change quickly spread out through the blade as a powerful twinned surge of energy shot into the fractal edge from his left arm. The shaky blade immediately stabilized before it started to transform. The blade grew even larger and more robust as a new set of overlapping fractals covered its length, one golden and one black.

Zac felt a completely new connection to the blade like it was part of himself, and he finally understood what his new skill would do. He infused the edge with the Fragment of the Coffin before swinging it in a wide horizontal arc toward the hundreds of enormous eagles that were still bearing down on him.

The evasive maneuvers while he tried to figure out his skills had incited bloodlust in the flock, and their eyes shone with a sinister light as they flapped their wings with enough force to cause a storm. The fractal edge didn't shoot toward the beasts like how [Chop] usually worked, but it remained attached to his axe while a black wave instead came flooding out from it.

The wave was extremely swift, and it covered a large number of the eagles before they even had a chance to react.

There was no scene of carnage that followed the swing. A few eagles screamed in pain as they were assaulted by the corrosive components of the Fragment of the Coffin, but there was no blood raining on the mountain walls this time. The eagles were instead shrouded in darkness, like Zac had thrown a can of black paint rather than a ferocious attack at them.

The odd scene wasn't surprising to Zac – he knew he had only completed the first half going by how the fractal edge had turned pure golden by this point. The air screamed as he swung his axe once more, and another wave shot out, this one looking like a wave of sunlight breaking through the clouds. The fractal edge remained attached to **[Verun's Bite]**, but it crumbled shortly after the second wave had left it.

The golden wave passed through the flock of birds as well, and a shocking change occurred. A clear line ran straight across the flock, with the upper side only holding the golden sheen, and the lower side drenched in darkness. It reminded Zac of his bout of inspiration inside his cultivation cave, where he split the two conflicting energies apart.

This was on a far grander scale, though.

The odd scene only lasted for an instant before the horizon cracked, the dividing line between gold and black turning into a crack in space itself. Two opposite shockwaves spread out, one toward the sky and one toward the ground. Hundreds of birds fell apart midflight, looking like they had been cut apart by a laser.

The two shockwaves caused a cascading halo to emerge on the horizon, and Zac froze in awe as he looked at the spectacle. The golden wave had turned into what looked like a massive sunset that spread for over a hundred meters. Even more amazing, Zac felt like he could hear Buddhist hymns coming from a paradise he could barely discern through the golden haze.

The golden sun was matched by a black opposite, the two halves forming an almost perfect circle. The hair on Zac's arms stood on end as he turned his attention to the darker half, feeling like he was looking at the netherworld itself. Distant wails of lost souls rattled in his mind, and Zac felt like someone or something was staring back at him from within the darkness.

The effect only lasted for a few seconds before it dissipated, leaving the sky clear of any aggressive birds. The attack hadn't hit every eagle, but it looked like a couple of them had been swallowed by the half-suns, not even leaving a corpse like their bisected brethren. Zac nodded in appreciation as he kept flying, thankful he had done this test on the outer side of the mountain range.

[Rapturous Divide] was a lot flashier than he had expected, and he could only pray that no lizardmen scouts were hiding in this remote part of the mountain range. Of course, he knew that he had pushed the skill hard, and he realized now that he didn't actually need to use a hundred-meter blade to create it.

He could have activated the skill by adding a small half-meter edge over [Verun's Bite] as well, which would allow him to use the skill in a one-on-one melee battle.

The skill took advantage of the opposing natures of life and death. The two were each other's opposites, and this fact was utilized to create a divide in space itself. It was a high-concept empowerment that would turn most defenses useless, just like a spatial tear would. If he'd had this skill when fighting the Battleroach King or the dragon, he wouldn't have been so hard-pressed to wound them.

Such a divide might not completely be what he looked for when it came to his insights to his cultivation path, but Zac felt it didn't matter too much. It was just a single skill. Not every action he took needed to be an echo of his insights. It was still based on life and death, which was better than most of his other skills, proving that his new class was moving in the right direction.

Zac looked inward for a second, and he was somewhat disappointed to see that he had lost connection to the skill fractal, just like when his other skills were on cooldown. It looked like he wouldn't be able to shoot out a rapid barrage of space-splitting life-and-death waves. Then again, that wasn't really on the table in any case, as that single strike had cost him almost 10 percent of his total Cosmic Energy reserves.

At least it didn't seem to be a long cooldown skill like **[Deforestation]**, which could only be used every twelve hours or so. He kept a close eye on the fractal as he flew between the mountain peaks, and soon confirmed that **[Rapturous Divide]** could be used again after three minutes.

Three minutes wasn't bad, but not great either. Most intense fights felt quite long, but they were usually over in less time than that. It would still be a great addition in prolonged battles, providing a repeatable destructive boost to just shooting out an infinite number of fractal edges. However, he still didn't use the skill on the next group of predatory birds that assaulted him, and instead opted to take them out with **[Chop]**.

The pack of eagles that Zac had annihilated earlier wasn't the only one, but most likely a single roost out of the hundreds, perhaps thousands, in the mountain range. His flight through the towering peaks quickly turned into an endless battle, where the skyline was covered by frenzied birds defending their mountain.

Most of the birds were F-grade, but the occasional Early E-grade alpha appeared as well. The feathers of the evolved birds were like steel, partly absorbing the strikes of a normal **[Chop]** even though **[Verun's Bite]** had been upgraded. Zac realized that this wasn't the fault of his Spirit Tool, but rather the skill itself.

The skill had definitely become stronger with the upgrade of the axe, but the effect was only partial. It seemed like a simple F-grade skill wouldn't be able to keep up with the upgrades of an E-grade axe. He sighed in disappointment when he realized that his main skill would peter out into obsolescence sooner or later.

However, the skill was still useful, not only as a delivery method for his E-grade skill, but on its own. The skill itself might not be able to outright kill these powerful birds, but it was another matter entirely when he infused the blades with the Fragment of the Axe. One silver flash after another lit up the pristine mountain peaks as desolate cries resounded, each wail marking the end of a king of the sky.

An ever-increasing amount of energy surged toward the turbid node in his left leg, and Zac realized that he would be able to burst open a node in a day or two if he kept going like this. However, Zac slowly started to look for some way to get out of this situation. It felt like no matter how many beasts he killed, there were still more and more that appeared in the skyline all around him.

It did allow him to get acquainted with his new skill, though, and now and then, a group of birds would be split apart as the white mountain wall was lit up in golden splendor. He quickly figured out that his maximum limit of the skill was a 150-meter spatial tear, while he actually realized there was a lower limit as well at 75 centimeters.

The cost of the activation wasn't quite linear. Just activating the skill was the cause of over half of the energy expenditure, while the length of the tear added an almost linear expenditure.

The strength of the attack was based on the length of the tear as well, with the shorter tear unleashing a more intense wave of destruction. However, the shortest tear was at best twice as strong as the largest one, meaning that the maxed-out divide wasn't all that weak compared to the one-on-one strike.

The hours passed, and Zac couldn't take it any longer. He was starting to tire even when fighting while holding a D-grade Nexus Crystal for energy restoration. He flew into a narrow canyon and jumped off the leaf mid-flight, immediately taking out an Illusion Array Disk the moment he landed. He shot forward a few hundred meters with the help of **[Loamwalker]** the next second, hiding inside a cave.

A sleeping bear yowled in surprise at the unwelcome intruder, but it was quickly cut in two before it could warn the frenzied eagles that flew back and forth outside. Their screeches caused the walls of the cave to shake as their feathers carved deep grooves in the mountain walls, but they couldn't find the target no matter how hard they looked.

They finally left after taking out their frustrations on a group of poor mountain goats who failed to blend in with the white rocks, allowing Zac to breathe out. He wasn't really worried about being overrun by the bloodthirsty birds, but rather that he was causing too big a ruckus. He had passed most of the mountain range by now, and he was closing in on the uncharted territory on the other side.

Thousands of eagles clumping around a foreign object in the sky while screeching at the top of their lungs would probably be spotted from miles away, and he wanted to retain at least some of the element of surprise. The birds were gone, but Zac still didn't move out, and instead sat down to recuperate his lost Cosmic Energy for a few hours.

Only when he was completely topped off again did he move out. This time, he didn't take out his flying treasure, but instead tried to stay as inconspicuous as possible between the mountains. There was pretty much not a single beast barring his path down in the canyon, which wasn't surprising considering what lived on the mountaintops. It allowed Zac to make good speed, and he reached the end of the mountain range just an hour later.

And what met his eyes was an endless primordial jungle.

15
JUNGLE

It turned out that on the other side of the expansive mountain range was a basin, a vast depression in the landscape. It looked like something left behind by a meteor millions of years ago, and it almost felt like he had entered a different climate zone, as warm winds wafted onto his face. The humidity had gained a huge spike on this side of the mountains, like all the moisture was trapped in the basin.

That wasn't surprising, as a series of enormous waterfalls could be spotted to the west, no doubt stemming from the inland sea Julia had mentioned before. He would have turned completely clammy in seconds if it weren't for his improved constitution. Judging by how healthy the enormous plant life looked, there was no doubt a lot of rain as well, perhaps as the clouds would get stopped by the mountains.

Zac still couldn't spot any incursion pillar, but he had a good feeling about this place. First of all, the energy was quite dense in the area. The second reason was simple as well; there were a lot of fire-attuned energies in the air even though there was so much humidity. Zac first thought there might be a Fire Crystal mine beneath the ground, but he soon found the real source of the energies.

He could barely discern a volcano in the distance, standing roughly in the middle of the basin. It was pretty far away, and he guessed that it would take half a day getting there on foot even if he kept a high pace. Smoke rose from the top, proving it was active, and it looked like it was continuously releasing energies out into the forest around it.

It really looked like a pretty good starting spot for a force like the Church of the Everlasting Dao. A volcano in an energy-dense valley was probably a treasure trove for a fire-based force. Better yet, the humidity had created a large amount of low-hanging clouds that limited his vision. It wasn't nearly as dense as the clouds of Miasma in the Dead Zone, but it would do just fine in hiding an incursion pillar if you were far away.

Especially if the cultists helped improve the effect somehow.

The volcano spread small amounts of fire energies across the whole jungle, but when Zac activated **[Cosmic Gaze]**, there was an odd sight. The whole jungle lit up in a dim red glow from his special sight, but the volcano itself was utterly devoid of energy. Something close to the volcano was either hiding the energies or absorbing them.

The clammy haze thankfully allowed Zac some protection as he took out his flying treasure once more. He honestly would have preferred to travel by foot, but he had a mission to complete. His desire wasn't about safety or stealth, but something more primal. It felt like the forest was calling out to him somehow.

It wasn't as strong as when he had come close to great natural treasures like the cherry or the Tree of Ascension, but the feeling was similar. It felt like the forest itself had gained a semblance of spirituality that resonated with his body, or perhaps more accurately his class. He felt like he would be able to progress both his nature-based skills and his Dao in this place a lot more efficiently than even staying in his cultivation cave.

Progressing skills wasn't necessarily about energy density, but rather about opportunity and insight. So secluded cultivation might be good to improve some aspects of his strength, but skills were not one of them. A few of his skills, like **[Forester's Constitution]** and **[Loamwalker]**, were still stuck at Late proficiency, and this might be a good place to practice those skills.

Of course, Zac knew that would have to wait until he dealt with the cultists, so he set off on top of his flying treasure, heading straight for the volcano.

He kept a much lower altitude than normal this time, staying close to the treetops in hopes of blending in with the enormous leaves of the tree crowns. A roar suddenly echoed out across the area as a five-meter panther jumped up straight at him, but Zac killed it with one swift swing. Its carcass joined the mountain of high-grade meat in his Cosmos Sack before even a second had passed as Zac whizzed past the area.

It was no wonder that the desolate mountain range could support so many birds, the jungle below was simply littered with beasts. Everything from ten-meter snakes to insects as large as dogs tried to strike at him as Zac sped through their domains, and the area was drenched in a constant clamor of thousands of different animal calls.

The beasts unfortunately weren't very powerful even though many of them were quite large. The birds might have already hunted anything that could be a threat to them, or perhaps it was the cultists' doing if this indeed was their hidden base of operations. It was even possible that the stronger beasts were smart enough to figure out that he wasn't some tasty morsel drifting around on a wayward leaf.

A streak of flames suddenly shot toward him out of nowhere, forcing Zac to quickly swivel out of the way. It pushed past him toward the skies and only ran out of steam after having flown hundreds of meters. Zac first thought there was some beast spewing fire at him, but he quickly spotted an inconspicuous tower among the tall palms, colored so that it would blend in with the surroundings.

Another fireball soared just past him, and Zac felt the familiar aura of the zealots from the golden flames. Zac shot out a [Chop], and the tower crumbled, its defensive shield utterly incapable of withstanding a middle-grade fragment. He was quite happy that he had probably found the right place, but it would take him half an hour before he reached the volcano even if he pushed the leaf to its limits.

There was no way he would be able to launch a surprise strike at the cultists any longer, but there was only so much you could prepare in thirty minutes. They should still be unable to utilize any teleportation arrays, making it impossible for them to recall any forces from the Mystic Realm. Unless their incursion had spawned right on top of one of the entrances, they wouldn't be able to return in time.

Zac quickly scoured the surroundings, and he soon realized there actually was a neat perimeter of similar towers forming a circle around the volcano. Zac felt that these things weren't meant to deal with cultivators, but instead to scare off the flocks of birds. They would be almost useless to deal with forces on the ground with the thick foliage blocking their fireballs.

If that was the case, it might still take some time before they realized something was wrong, but Zac wouldn't hold his breath. The cultists were crazy, but not stupid. They should be fully aware that he was coming for them sooner or later, as they were the last invaders remaining on Earth.

Deep thuds echoed out from his chest as his heart started beating rapidly in anticipation of the upcoming battle, but Zac took a few calming breaths to steady himself as he started to fly toward the volcano again. He quickly realized that the various sounds of the jungle were steadily growing few and far between, like the beasts knew better than to stay close to the mountain in the middle of the jungle.

Zac kept his eye peeled for any hints of the incursion, and his eyes lit up when he saw a shimmering glow as he started to make his way around the volcano. He had figured that the pillar would either have to be inside the volcano itself or hidden behind it, and it looked like it was the latter.

A minute later, the whole pillar was on full display, rising into the clouds right behind the plumes of smoke coming from the volcano. The cultists were full-fledged lunatics, but Zac had to admit they had a flair for architecture. The back of the mountain was lit up with splashes of gold and red, and grand temples and mansions built from the pristine white stones seemed to compete with each other in how elaborate their designs were.

The incursion pillar started right at the foot of the mountain, while the town itself was comprised of an ascending series of tiered structures running halfway up the volcano. It did look a bit odd, as the most important structure was essentially located furthest out, while it was the temples that took the best spots at the highest positions of the mountain.

The buildings only reached halfway up the volcano, after which they abruptly stopped. Above that was only one thing: a gargantuan rune of three lines. The three simple wavy lines were the insignia of the Church of Everlasting Dao, and the huge rune emitted a pressure that Zac could even feel from the distance. The lines apparently represented the Heavens, the System, and the Dao: their concept of divinity.

The scene reminded Zac of the consecrated mountain that Abbot Everlasting Peace had lived on, where prayer and conviction had brought forth a true power. It was a reminder of how contradictory a force the Church of Everlasting Dao was. Triv had talked about them at great length over the past week, seemingly taking real pleasure in causing trouble for the enemies of the Undead Empire.

It was more correct to call the Church of Everlasting Dao two entwined forces rather than one single unit, with one being the fanatics and the other the body merchants.

Some considered the fanatics as just a front, but the gilded rune was a stark reminder that there were quite a few members who wholeheartedly believed in the Divinity of the System. Mount Everlasting Peace had been consecrated over a thousand years to gain spirituality upon the integration, but this mountain was coming close to emitting the same holiness after just a year.

The confusing layout of the town itself made Zac a bit unsure of how to proceed. Normally, he would bash through a wall and defeat the armies, and finally corral the remaining enemies toward the Incursion pillar. But the Nexus Hub was already within his reach unless the open-aired temple surrounding the red-and-gold pillar contained some hidden safeguards.

It felt a bit too simple. Abby had already explained the rules of taking over towns, and it worked the same with incursions. If he walked over and claimed the Nexus Hub, a quest would start where the invaders had a short time window to rebuff him before their invasion ended by default. That was why the incursion leaders seldom left their base of operations.

Seeing the pillar unguarded like this made him feel there was some sort of trap, which was only reinforced by the fact that he hadn't spotted a single person so far. The whole town looked abandoned, like they had already fled before he arrived. However, there was no way that a force like the Church of the Everlasting Dao would simply pack up and leave without a fight.

Besides, there was no prompt from the system that the incursion had failed, which meant that the Head Priest was still around somewhere. Zac activated [**Cosmic Gaze**] to see if any suspicious energy movements surrounded the Nexus Hub, but the pillar itself drowned out any potential clues. It almost blinded him from how much energies it contained, and he was forced to look away.

Indecision gnawed at him for a few seconds, but he eventually made his decision and shot toward the largest temple, a resplendent structure placed right beneath the enormous rune. It was a massive construction with spires well over a hundred meters high, each of them holding a radiant fire.

In fact, every single building had a golden fire burning at the roof, though the ones at the main temple were quite a bit larger than the others. Zac chose to target the temple because those spires reminded him of the array towers at the undead fortress. He could always claim the Nexus Hub after destroying the temples and the gargantuan rune, which would hopefully preempt any booby traps the cultists had left for him.

The leaf made a detour around the pillar before it made a beeline for the temple, and there was finally some activity from the cultists' side. A hundred warriors streamed out of the gates of the temple, seemingly readying for battle. Just a hundred warriors wouldn't even slow Zac for more than a few seconds, but he still activated [**Nature's Barrier**].

Zac felt that there was no way that this was all these guys had prepared, and his suspicions were quickly proven right as hundreds of fiery globes moved to intercept him. It was the braziers on top of the houses all along the mountainside that rose into the air, creating a beautiful spectacle.

The air screamed as Zac whizzed back and forth, dodging the incendiary attacks. But there were just too many of them. One projectile after another slammed into the leaves he had conjured, setting them on fire. It quickly turned Zac's whole vision into a golden inferno. He lost a steady stream of energy just to keep the initial salvo at bay.

The emerald shield surrounding the flying treasure was still holding out just fine, but Zac knew it was just a matter of time before a breach happened. The emerald leaf didn't seem to be made for anything but travel. There were no offensive arrays; just a decent set of defensive options. It wouldn't hold for too long against a barrage of this magnitude.

Zac infused the leaf with the Fragment of the Bodhi, and it blasted toward the town with regained momentum. The intensity of the barrage just increased as he closed in on the temple, but he finally was close enough for his purposes. A hundred-meter fractal blade reached toward the sky as Zac raised **[Verun's Bite]**, preparing for a vertical swing.

Two streams of opposing forces crawled up along the blade, reinforcing it and allowing it to grow another fifty percent as it was colored in gold and black. The flying treasure stopped in its tracks a few hundred meters away from the temple, and Zac pushed as much of his Fragment of the Coffin as he could into the towering blade.

It felt like the world split apart as the blade swung down, unleashing a wave of unadulterated darkness toward the temple and the top of the volcano itself. The attack passed through the barrage of golden flames like they weren't even there before it covered the radiant temple in a desolate gloom.

It was time to send these cultists to a true paradise.

16
FANATICISM

The zealots seemed enraged rather than wounded after being drenched in the darkness of **[Rapturous Divide]**. It was like they took it as a personal affront that he had shrouded their temple and part of their holy rune in darkness.

They all started emitting flames that actually seemed to counteract the darkness, and Zac's eyes widened in surprise when he saw that even the temple itself seemed capable of resisting the effect of his skill. Nothing like this had happened when he fought the massive eagles before, but they were just dumb birds, after all.

It was naïve to think that there was no way to counteract his newly acquired skill, and Zac knew he couldn't waste any time. He had already tested this before. The separate clouds didn't hold any individual power; they were only useful if they worked together. If the cultists managed to destroy the first wave before he managed to release the second one, the skill would have been wasted.

He hurriedly swung his golden blade in a second arc, the fractal edge crumbling into motes of light as a second wave shot out, this one reinforced by the Fragment of the Bodhi.

A few cultists welcomed the golden wave as they peppered Zac with a barrage of flame-based attacks, but most seemed to understand that something was wrong. They used movement skills to get out of the way, clearly treasuring their lives higher than the well-being of their temple. Zac didn't care about that, as his main goal wasn't some weak foot soldiers.

Zac looked at the golden wave flying toward the mountain with anticipation as he conjured another set of leaves from [**Nature's Barrier**] to block out the attacks that still tried to bring him out of the sky. However, there was still a sense of unease lingering in the back of his mind. The problem wasn't that he felt pressure from the large number of attacks, but rather that it all felt extremely haphazard for such a powerful force.

A few simple fireball arrays and a hundred soldiers from a force that was a scourge known across the whole Multiverse? He had taken out far more than that during the invasion of Port Atwood, and everything indicated that there should be thousands of cultists remaining on Earth. What was going on?

Zac's first instinct when he saw how empty the town was that this place actually wasn't the incursion, but instead one of their bases. It was hard to argue with the incursion pillar in red and gold that rose into the sky behind him.

Did the cultists perhaps conduct multiple simultaneous invasions on Earth, allowing them to discard all pillars but one? Their go-to method was to simply snatch the incursion opportunity from other forces as far as he could tell, and perhaps they sometimes doubled up by mistake.

All that would have to wait as the golden wave pushed into the temple shrouded in darkness, causing the whole mountain to rumble. Screams of fury and grief echoed across the mountainside as the whole temple was cleanly split into two, and the opposing shockwaves toppled the four spires in one go.

Zac only managed to glimpse the opulent decor of the temple before it was utterly reduced to rubble, and a cascading wave of destruction followed in its wake as massive pieces of white boulders and raw rocks started falling down the side of the volcano, smashing everything in their path. It started to look like a mountain slide that kept growing in severity, and even Zac was a bit shocked by how effective his attack was.

Of course, his success was aided by the fact that the temple itself was unaided by any defensive arrays apart from the natural aura that had seemed to resist the darkness of his first wave. Zac figured that the swing wouldn't have been anywhere near as effective against the undead fortress and its sturdy formations.

The large rune remained, and Zac started to launch a series of fractal edges at it, all infused with the Fragment of the Axe. A few zealots tried everything within their power to stop him, but they were like flies to Zac, who stood far up in the air, launching his punishment upon the lands like a god of death.

His hunch about the rune was quickly proven right, as it was far better protected against strikes compared to the rest of the buildings. A fiery aura burst out from the three wavy lines and rebuffed the fractal blades, turning them into cinders before they could bite into the engraving itself.

Zac wasn't discouraged, and his arm turned into a blur that rapidly launched blade after blade without exhaustion. What he was doing was high sacrilege judging by how pissed off the zealots down on the ground appeared. One had actually burst into flames and exploded out of sheer anger, and Zac figured that if this couldn't draw out the Head Priest, then nothing would.

He still moved about in random patterns in the sky as he whittled down the energy of the rune, afraid that the zealots were setting up a death beam or something similar. However, he was completely left to his own devices, apart from the occasional fireball coming from the few still-standing houses of the mountainside.

Blind faith ultimately wasn't an opponent to a sharp edge, and the three lines finally ran out of their mysterious energy, allowing Zac to turn the whole section of the volcano into a broken mess full of jagged scars. The rune was replaced with a hundred cracks in less than thirty seconds, and part of the wall even collapsed into the center of the volcano, allowing a stream of magma to escape the volcano and crawl down toward the incursion pillar.

The scene made Zac's brows furrow, as he had no idea what would happen if the Nexus Hub was swallowed by magma. Would the incursion end, or would he become unable to claim the crystal? He looked around to get an indication of what was going on from the remaining invaders, but they weren't much help. Most of them had simply slumped down on the ground with tears running down their faces, looking at the destruction with despair.

Zac felt a small sense of relief, as they looked utterly incapable of mounting any sort of trap. Had they really given up on this place? Didn't they care about going back home, instead focusing all their resources on the Mystic Realm? However, Zac eventually noticed something off: a group of nine cultists in high-quality robes who shot toward the incursion pillar with impressive speed.

He hadn't seen them before as far as he could tell, meaning they perhaps had been waiting for some opportunity to strike. Zac hesitated what to do as he saw their escape, but he felt he finally couldn't wait any longer as he saw the cultists take out nine fiery crystals larger than themselves. They looked a lot like the Nexus Hub itself, except for the weak fire-attuned energies they emitted. The cultists wasted no time before they started inserting them into a set of grooves in the open-air temple that encircled the incursion.

Were they summoning someone? Or something?

Nothing good would come from letting the leaders complete their ritual, and Zac shot forward in an instant, putting away the leaf in midair as he soared toward the pillar. A few of the cultists tried to impede his trajectory, some even sacrificing themselves by blowing up. But Zac was unstoppable as he slammed into the ground right next to the pillar. He destroyed the closest Fire Crystal with a swing of his axe, simultaneously killing the priest who fiddled with it.

He quickly transformed **[Love's Bond]** into its shield form before the swing even finished its trajectory, expecting a massive eruption of flames to swallow him when the crystal cracked. However, nothing of the sort happened. A bunch of shards flew in all directions, accompanied by some fiery dust that spread out like a small cloud. Zac made sure not to inhale it, even though he didn't sense any danger from the stuff.

A sense of unease grew as the remaining eight priests seemed to work on inscribing the crystals even faster. Zac pushed his speed to the limit, moving like a tornado in a circle around the incursion. The eight priests and their pillars were destroyed in short order, allowing Zac to finally breathe out in relief.

The creeping sense of danger only increased rather than subsided, and Zac quickly jumped up on the roof of the temple to get a better vantage.

A second group of cultists he hadn't sensed at all until now had somehow emerged among the rubble, but none of them cared about Zac in the slightest. They instead knelt toward the mountain peak, or perhaps toward the rune that Zac had destroyed. Zac didn't understand what they were doing, but the scene filled him with a sinking feeling.

This was all too shady, and he would rather retreat for a bit and reassess the situation than stay for whatever these guys had planned. He ignored the Nexus Hub that hovered just fifty meters away, afraid that touching it was the key to their trap. Zac instead took out his flying treasure once more. However, his eyes widened in alarm when he infused it with his mental command, as the emerald leaf was utterly unresponsive.

It felt like he was standing on some random palm leaf snatched from the jungle rather than a treasure inscribed and empowered by some unknown master from a greater sector than Zecia. He tried swapping the crystals that were already provided as a power source, but it didn't improve the situation at all.

Zac could pretty much confirm that something was wrong now, and he started running for his life. But he only managed to activate **[Loamwalker]** once, barely getting a hundred meters away from the incursion toward the jungle, before the ground started heaving to the point that he was thrown off his feet and unable to regain his footing.

Some fear finally started to set in, and he tried to scramble toward the comparable safety of the jungle. But an apocalyptic explosion erupted behind him, forcing him to look back. The whole sky had been replaced by fire and molten rock as the volcano exploded. Not erupted, but literally exploded.

Pieces of the volcano as large as skyscrapers flew through the air as though they were weightless, soaring toward the distant edges of the basin. Only the foot of the mountain remained, releasing an endless amount of lava. A tremendous shockwave slammed into him before he even had a chance to erect any defenses, and Zac coughed out a mouthful of blood as he felt some of his bones were broken.

If he was in such bad shape this far away from the epicenter, then there was no need to talk about the cultists who had knelt in prayer. They were either ashes or meat paste by now, swallowed by the blast.

Zac didn't know whether he should feel lucky that the eruption had contained such force that no rocks were falling anywhere near the volcano, but he quickly understood that he had bigger problems, as the rumbles beneath him just kept increasing in intensity. Just the vibrations alone would probably have killed a weaker cultivator, and even Zac felt his wounds worsen by the second.

But even that wasn't the scariest thing going on right now. It was the three golden waves that slowly rose from within the lava, carried upward by a pillar of golden flames. An intense wave of divinity, far eclipsing that of the simple inscription on the wall, radiated from the enormous insignia. Even Zac felt tears running down his face from just gazing at it - looking at the three lines truly felt like gazing upon God himself.

If God was an entity of endless fury and destruction.

Zac's mind shook as his danger sense screamed bloody murder. Just a minute ago, he had felt like a god of slaughter as he dismantled the rune and half the town from the safety of his leaf, but he realized how valuable that feeling had been. He was not a god; he could barely be considered an ant compared to the real powers of the universe.

The golden insignia finally stabilized up in the sky, drowning the whole basin in its golden splendor. At least the rumblings had subsided somewhat, allowing Zac to get back on his feet. There was no hesitation in his mind as he activated **[Loamwalker]** to get the hell away from there.

However, he only managed to flee less than a hundred meters before a scorching pain enveloped him, prompting him to fall over once more. He shot out a series of fractal edges in each direction while his eyes wildly looked for the source of the threat, but he only cut through empty air. His harried mind scrambled to figure out what was going on, and he quickly figured out the reason for the pain.

It was that dust he had been covered in earlier, the innocuous substance that had been released from the crystals. A moment ago, it had felt like just some golden sand that had covered him as he destroyed the Array Crystals, but it wasn't so innocuous any longer. It now radiated a restrictive force that made it look like he was on fire.

Even worse, the flames also formed an intangible bond that ran between his body and the temple behind him, like a leash made of energy. It connected him to the cloud of golden sand that was still spread around the broken crystals like a fetter. Or perhaps it was more apt to say that the light was connected to the incursion itself, as he saw that the flames had merged with the energy pillar itself.

He had been tricked.

17
SIGIL

Zac finally understood why the cultists had acted so weirdly until now. A few of them had simply been sacrificial pawns for Zac to kill in hopes that it would make him lower his guard. The cultists utilized the fact that everyone thought of them as insane zealots with no regard for their lives. They were ruthless against others, but perhaps even more so against themselves.

But the real method to deal with him was obviously not the meager defense in front of the main temple, and the inscription in the mountain wall was probably just a red herring as well. The real threat was brooding inside the lava itself, its presence obscured by the huge rune and the natural fire-attuned energies of the volcano itself.

That only left the issue of the nine Flame Crystals. Zac had thought back to the invasion of Port Atwood when he saw them setting up their "array." The invaders had set up a very similar constellation back then to summon the set of meteors. Nine clergymen had set themselves ablaze in a circle around him, just like these ones planted the crystals in a circle around the incursion pillar.

Were the actions back on the island all a sacrifice to trick him into destroying those crystals?

The utter lack of powerful arrays had also made him lower his guard somewhat after he had destroyed everything that looked like a threat. But the golden insignia in the sky radiated a terrifying pressure, even eclipsing the force of Adriel's blast that had been powered by four array towers.

Figuring out how they had actually managed to create the massive avatar in the sky obviously wasn't as important as getting the hell out of here though. He activated [Cosmic Gaze] to get a hint of how the burning fetters worked, and it was mostly fire-attuned, as expected. There was also that other odd energy mixed within: the energy of conviction.

The golden fetter seemed to be held together by the faith of these zealots, and Zac long knew their conviction was as strong as it could get. Zac growled with frustration as he tried cutting the bindings apart, but [Verun's Bite] just flew straight through the flames without affecting it at all. Infusing the blade with his Dao Fragments didn't make a lick of difference either; it was even more intangible than the ghosts he had fought until now.

He tried to ignore the pain and keep running away next, and he was soon screaming at the top of his lungs as he stretched the flames to their limits. He was hoping to snap the fetter with brute force, but the pain quickly became too much to bear even for him, forcing him to move back toward the incursion pillar once more.

A bell suddenly echoed across the basin, a clear gong that seemed to reach the depths of his soul. It obviously came from the rune in the sky, like it was announcing the descent of the divine. A few cracks echoed out from his body, and he coughed out another mouthful of blood, just in time to see a waterfall of fire fall out of the sky.

The flames came out of the insignia itself, and it felt like time itself slowed down as they slowly made their way toward the ground. Zac's danger sense was once again screaming at him to get away, and one glance was enough to realize that the fire that was currently moving toward him was far more dangerous than normal flames.

It was once more that power of conviction that made the flames almost seem holy, and Zac started to understand what was going on.

The zealots had probably prayed toward the rune on the volcano since they arrived, constantly reinforcing it with the power of their conviction. The rune in turn had taken that energy and infused the golden insignia that now hung in the sky. Who knew what the end goal of this thing was, if Zac had not shown up to ruin their plans.

Set the whole world on fire?

Knowing the cultists, it wasn't such a far-fetched idea. The body snatchers would capture the high-value corpses of Earth, after which the fanatics would torch the whole planet, leaving no evidence or lingering threats behind.

Zac's mind churned as he tried to figure out a way out of the situation, and he could eventually only come up with one solution. Space split apart above him as he ran toward the incursion, once more jumping on top of the roof closest to the pillar itself.

The wooden hand of **[Nature's Punishment]** rose toward the sky, but Zac frowned when he felt the hand being rebuffed as it tried to ascend after a certain height. The three lines hummed as they released a radiant light, and Zac found himself unable to place the skill above the insignia, like it was some sacrilege that went against the order of the Heavens themselves.

It dashed his idea of drowning the burning sigil in a deluge of water.

With his first plan ruined, he could only move to his backup plan, and he instead activated the hand where it was. The enormous emerald fractal lit up in the sky, and a torrent of water started pouring out. However, the water didn't target the insignia itself, but rather the golden flames it spewed out. He could at least deal with the flames even if he couldn't take out the root cause just yet.

A massive explosion threw Zac off the roof again as the water of **[Nature's Punishment]** was instantly turned into steam the moment it came in contact with the holy flames. The same happened to the streams that missed the flames and instead fell on the lava below, but the reaction at least managed to slow the lava's advance toward his location.

Pain racked Zac's body, but he made sure to keep the skill going as he scrambled back on his feet, pushing **[Nature's Punishment]** to its limits as he infused it with the Fragment of the Bodhi. There was thankfully no lack of water with such an enormous lake nearby, and enough liquid to submerge a city block burst out of the fractal.

Zac breathed out in relief, as he could quickly make out that the descending sea of golden flames had been stopped in its tracks, whittled down by the incessant outpouring of water. However, that didn't mean that he had won, but that he had entered a competition of endurance of which skill would run out of steam first.

If it was just a cultivator on the other side, then Zac would have been confident in outlasting them without breaking a sweat, but he quickly came to realize that he was dealing with something else entirely as the seconds passed. Sweat started streaming down his whole body from the heat and exertion, and he felt that he wouldn't be able to keep the skill going for much longer.

It wasn't an issue of Cosmic Energy, but simply that there was a limit to how long the skill could function. Thankfully, he could sense that the energy that the golden lines radiated had been expended by more than half, meaning it wasn't some infallible item that drew power from the heavens or something.

Only five seconds remained on [Nature's Punishment], and he made his choice as he pushed the golden hand to readjust itself somewhat. The emerald fractal that came with the skill was pretty much fixed after having been activated, but he could tilt it a little bit, which allowed him to change the direction of the stream of water.

He didn't try to catch a larger part of the wave of flames that kept raining down from the insignia, but rather the opposite. The water instead shot straight toward the incursion pillar and himself. Zac steadied himself as a wall of water slammed into him, completely drenching him as it tried to carry him away toward the jungle.

However, Zac quickly stomped his feet into the ground with enough force to lodge himself in the rock while doing the same with a fractal blade from [Chop]. He wouldn't have loved anything more than being carried far from this place, but the water was unfortunately unable to douse the fiery bonds that kept him in place. The incursion pillar rebuffed the water without any effort, and it looked like the pillar empowered the bond.

He was afraid that he would accidentally kill himself if he pushed himself too far, so he had to stick around. [Nature's Punishment] finally ended, and Zac saw that his efforts at least had allowed him to quell the threat of the magma flowing out from the remains of the volcano. It had already cooled into odd layers of stone that formed a towering wall where the city once stood.

The insignia was still going strong, and Zac scrambled to figure out what to do next. The flames weren't especially fast, but they would still reach him in just a few seconds. Wasting no time, he rushed into the incursion pillar itself. A strong rebounding force was emitted from the Nexus Hub, but he had no problem pushing through.

He quickly reached the center of the pillar, and he swung his axe with all the force he could muster.

A golden shield that Zac recognized all too well appeared in front of his edge just as it was about to bite into the large crystal, and Zac sighed when he realized that the System prevented him from destroying the crystal itself. He'd hoped he would be able to free himself from the burning bond that way, but it looked like it would be impossible. However, that didn't mean that there was no reaction to his attack, as a prompt appeared in front of him.

[Nexus Hub Capture Activated. Hold for 1 hour to conquer.]

Zac quickly read the screen before he waved it away. It wouldn't help him against the incoming sea of flames, but it did sound like there wouldn't be any grace period for the invaders if he completed the capture. How would they use his Nexus Hub to return home when they were enemies?

But before that, Zac needed to survive the incoming flames, and he looked up with consternation. He eventually decided against unleashing **[Deforestation]** in hopes of destroying the rune, wanting to save it just in case. It was still possible that the Head Priest and his remaining generals were hiding in the vicinity somewhere, waiting for him to be weakened enough by the insignia before they struck a killing blow.

He needed to save his most powerful ace just in case.

The bronze flash would probably do the trick, but he had no way to get up there with his flying treasure being blocked out somehow. There was something else, though. Zac sighed as he took out the rusty sword, and discordant wails immediately assaulted his ears.

Using the cursed sword so soon after activating it last time came with very real risks, according to Catheya. A weapon like this fed on its victims, and it was evidenced by how he already heard the voices even before unsheathing the weapon. He would normally use some restraining method on a weapon like this, or starve it out to weaken it before he used it again.

Zac didn't have the luxury of waiting around, as the golden insignia seemed more than capable of spewing out its unceasing flames for a while longer. His whole body was racked with pain as he drew the blade, unleashing the half-moon toward the three lines in the sky. It steadily started to grow as it picked up speed, seemingly eager to attack the energy-rich rune in the sky.

A handful of tendrils emerged from the weapon and latched on to Zac's arm as well, making it look like the sword was fusing with his body. A mysterious energy burrowed into his arm and headed straight for his head the next moment, effortlessly evading his attempts to block it out with **[Mental Fortress]**.

Extremely intrusive voices boomed in his mind, blocking out any coherent thought. Zac's eyes widened in fear as he saw more and more tendrils reaching out from the weapon, and his whole arm was covered in an instant. He wanted to stow away the weapon, but he knew he needed to hold on, as putting it away would cancel the attack in the sky.

A deep, resounding heartbeat suddenly quelled the voices, and Zac felt like his heart turned into a black hole that swallowed the invading energies whole. More and more energy entered his hidden node, and more was dragged out from the sword itself. Zac sensed fear from the weapon just before the sword detached itself from his arm and turned inert.

The half-moon, thankfully, wasn't affected by the struggle on the ground, and it effortlessly cut through the sea of flames in the sky, heading straight for the divine rune. It created a corridor free of fire for a brief second before the sea closed in on itself as it passed by. It seemed unable to actually absorb the flames, but the flames also seemed unable to deter its progression.

Finally, it reached its maximum size just as it slammed into the rune. There was no clear winner and no explosion of wild energies, only a stalemate that emitted a steadily increasing pressure. Zac knew things wouldn't end well no matter what the outcome was, judging by the ominous buildup, and he quickly tried to activate one of his defensive treasures.

Something was wrong. Zac infused one talisman after another with Cosmic Energy, but they only shuddered a bit before dimming again. The restriction on the area didn't only apply to his flying leaf, it looked like. **[Love's Bond]** was unable to activate its skills either, though he could thankfully swap between its different forms.

An explosion finally rocked the area, and the thick haze from the evaporated water was pushed away, exposing three golden lines and no silver half-moon. Even the cursed sword had been unable to take out the divine symbol, it appeared. However, Zac soon noticed that the rune wasn't completely unscathed.

Not only had it lost its radiant luster, but there was even a small tear on one of the golden lines. The crack quickly spread, like a piece of ice that was slowly breaking apart. The scene should have been good news, but Zac's hair still stood on end while his danger sense only screamed louder and louder. Looking up at the enormous rune made him feel like he was standing in front of a dam that was slowly bursting.

That rune had contained terrifying amounts of flames. What would happen when it finally broke apart?

He couldn't help but think back to Ogras' words of warning, of how the cultists always seemed to default to blowing everything up when it looked like they would fail. Miasma started coursing through his body as his eyes turned pitch-black. He couldn't flee, and breaking the rune didn't seem to have helped all too much. He would need to endure the final blast, and that would require his other class.

Ogras and his big mouth.

18

HOLY FIRE

Zac didn't have time to curse the demon for his ominous foreshadowing. Something terrifying was brewing, and he needed to do something. He started setting up his layers of defenses, not holding anything back for potential enemies. Everything except him was long dead in the area, killed by either the explosion, the magma, or the concussive explosions that had rocked the whole core of the basin.

The cage of **[Profane Seal]** sprang up around him, forming an outer layer of protection. Zac normally used the skill as a means of caging his enemies, but it was just as good at defending from the outside. It was also one of the skills that hadn't worsened in compatibility at all since gaining the Fetters of Desolation class. Between the chains and the entrapment, it looked like it was right up the new class's alley.

The cage encapsulated the incursion as well even when he shrank it to the smallest size possible, and Zac was both surprised and relieved to see that the energy-dense pillar didn't cause a clash with his skill. The pillar that almost blinded him with its intense fire-attuned energies shone straight through the fractal dome of his skill like it was just an illusion.

Zac had no idea how that worked, but he had no time to look into it, as the flames were almost upon him.

A huge amount of Miasma left his body the next moment as a hundred skeletons materialized. They didn't stay around inside the cage, but instead, they ran out as Zac opened the back gate of [Profane Seal] before closing it again. The skeletons didn't stop there, but they kept running into the jungle, only stopping hundreds of meters away when he couldn't control them any further away.

They weren't there to defend against the incoming flames, but rather act as damage substitutes. They would hopefully work as sentries as well in case there actually were cultists hiding in the jungle. He didn't share vision with the things, but he did have a vague sense of the life force around them. He would also feel it if they were destroyed by something, giving him an early warning that way.

The skeletons barely made it out in time as the holy flames finally descended upon the cage. He was inundated in not only a blazing heat, but also a pressure that he could feel on a spiritual level. But the shield held, though Zac knew that the golden flames were not the true threat. The real danger was the damaged insignia in the sky.

The enormous rune hadn't completely cracked yet, but Zac could see in the fiery sky that it wasn't long for this world. There was a deep cut in the middle of it now, where the half-moon blade had struck it. Hairline cracks spread all across its surface as well, and an intense light radiated out from the cracks, proving there was still a lot of untamed energies trapped inside.

Zac still didn't feel safe after seeing the ominous portents in the sky, and the black armor spread out across his body as [Love's Bond] took its defensive form. He might not be able to activate [Death's Embrace] as things stood, but he could still use the shield-shaped coffin to summon [Immutable Bulwark].

He also tried activating a few backup defensive talismans just in case, but they still didn't work, just like everything else. There was nothing else he could activate, so he finally started digging a hole into the ground, hoping to use the earth itself as an insulating layer against the flames. It had worked against Salvation, so he hoped it would work once more.

Unfortunately, Zac only managed to rip a ten-meter hole before an earthshattering snap in the sky released a waves of pressure, almost destroying the outer cage in an instant. The sturdy gates and Miasmic towers were reduced to decrepit ruins, and the aquamarine fractals had almost turned invisible from the flames. There was no more time, so

Zac jumped into the hole and punched the wall to bury himself. Finally, he put his bulwark as a last layer to block out the flames.

[Profane Seal] completely crumbled the next moment just as a shocking aura was released above him. Zac couldn't see what was going on because of having burrowed down, but it almost felt like a celestial had descended upon the basin. A marvelous aura drenched the whole jungle, and Zac felt his mind going blank.

The Lord was calling him, so what was he doing underground? He needed to welcome His arrival and offer obeisance. Zac slowly got up to his feet, but his whole body suddenly froze as he was startled awake.

What the hell was that?

One more second and he would have deactivated his defensive shield and welcomed the holy flames from above. His mind had thankfully been hardened by constant life-and-death struggles and competing with the Splinter, allowing him to snap out of it before it was too late. More importantly, he still had [Indomitable] to fall back on. It was far stronger than [Mental Fortress], and it had managed to rebuff the false thoughts after just a second, even though the skill was still Middle proficiency.

It was just in time too, as the flames slammed into the bulwark the next second, incinerating the shallow layers of dirt above.

The Miasmic shield from [Immutable Bulwark] was mostly opaque, but it still allowed him to somewhat see the fiery hellscape above. The flames were no longer golden, but rather replaced by a milky white. The holy aura in the flames was multiple times stronger than what he'd felt before, no doubt containing the essence of the rune in the sky.

His heartstrings tugged again as he saw the pristine flames, and part of him just wanted to open his arms and take it on. He didn't completely lose himself this time after already having realized the threat of the flames. However, it did make him wonder. Were the zealots perhaps not quite as pious as advertised, but forcibly converted?

Zac's pitch-black eyes were illuminated by the flames as he thought of the possibilities. What if the Church of Everlasting Dao had formed some sort of ingenious cultivation system? They turned cultivators into zealots with the holy flames, and the zealots kept empowering the flames with their conviction. It formed a self-perpetuating source of power that could swallow everything in its surroundings.

Things quickly took a turn for the worse, stopping Zac from entertaining any other stray thoughts. The flames steadily ate away at the floor itself until he was standing in a deep crater, assaulted by flames from every direction.

His bulwark was able to rebuff the flames, but it couldn't cover him from all sides, so the flames finally reached his last line of defense, the black armor of [Vanguard of Undeath]. His whole body was awash with pain the next moment as the flames glommed onto him. Zac tried to at least keep the flames outside, but they were like burrowing parasites that found their way inside through the tiniest cracks and weaknesses in his defenses.

Sizzling sounds escaped from within his armor as he was getting cremated alive. He screamed at the top of his lungs, but his cries were drowned out by the roaring flames. Rolling around on the ground did nothing, and the bulwark had essentially become useless by this point. All he could see was white, and all he could feel was agony.

Even his mind was assaulted by the insidious whispers of the holy flames, trying to make him stop resisting with the help of [Vanguard of Undeath] and [Undying Legion]. He was currently infusing the black armor with the Fragment of the Coffin, while his body itself fought the flames with the Fragment of the Bodhi. He also released a steady stream of Miasma from his pores, which helped combat the flames as well.

He also got one surge of vitality after another as a handful of skeleton warriors crumbled every second or so. He felt that if he stopped any one of these things, he would actually die, so he could only keep going while ignoring the calls from within the fire. Zac rapidly worked his way through the hundred-odd summons, at which point he only was able to rely on himself.

Every second felt like an hour, but he finally felt the flames starting to weaken. Or was he just so badly burned that he couldn't really tell any longer? A deep thud suddenly shook the ground, and Zac glanced toward the source of the sound with bleary eyes, only to see a golden pillar stab into the ground just fifty meters away from him.

The sigil had finally broken down and was falling apart.

Zac didn't have time to celebrate, as the surroundings suddenly started to darken, and he looked up in horror only to see an enormous golden pillar falling straight toward him. His legs didn't really listen to him, so Zac barely had time to resummon his bulwark before it slammed into him like a mountain. The pressure from the slam transferred into his body, and Zac once more felt the cracking of broken bones.

The thing was just way too heavy to throw off, and Zac was forced to activate [Unholy Strike] to just angle his bulwark and have it thump down next to him, causing a minor earthquake. A series of tremendous shockwaves followed, and the area was soon covered in the remnants of the broken sigil.

The fall of the insignia also meant the end of the white-hot flames, but the remnants of the sea of golden fire still covered the area. The golden flames only felt like a sunburn after having withstood the condensed version, and Zac slowly made his way toward the Nexus Hub.

Without the sigil in the sky, the sea of golden flames had lost its source, and it died down soon after. There was one annoying fire remaining: the fetters binding him to the incursion pillar. Zac was shocked to see that the fetter still held. Just what was that golden dust made of to be able to withstand just about everything and keep him in place?

Thankfully, the only capability of the odd flame was to prevent him from leaving, which was fine with Zac. He wasn't planning on going anywhere while the pillar was still active, so he simply sat down in the middle of the crater and popped a healing pill into his mouth.

Only when things had calmed down did he realize just how bad his state was. He had nine broken bones and multiple wounded organs. Even worse, most of his body was covered in severe burns from the flames. If he had been a weaker human, he would likely have died from the shock alone. Even with his impressive Endurance and Vitality, it still felt like his skin was on fire, and the salves in his possession were only limited in their efficacy.

His wretched state wasn't the only surprise, though.

There was a lot of energy in his body, slowly swirling around his hidden node. Zac hadn't noticed earlier due to the pain, but it looked like his **[Void Heart]** had been busy while he withstood the flames, and a massive amount of power had accumulated. Even better, it looked like energy extracted with his hidden node stayed within his body longer without dissipating compared to the energy that came from kills.

It was good news, as he didn't want to repeat the mistake from the undead incursion. What if he broke open his next node, only for the Head Priest to jump out of the woodwork once more? Then again, he had already done some research to avoid something like that happening again, and he had actually learned a few tricks thanks to Triv.

The ghost had been utterly astounded to find out that Zac actually was a mortal, and he even insisted that a pureblood Draugr couldn't be one. It also made him a lot more adamant about having Zac "return" to the Empire Heartlands to seize his so-called birthright. Triv was sure that Zac would be able to cultivate as long as he found a proper Draugr master.

Zac wasn't so sure, though, even if his undead side was of the noble Race. He had a feeling that his utter lack of cultivation ability was related to his constitution and not something a better master could solve.

But after the ghost had calmed down, he actually taught Zac a pretty nifty trick. Being an incorporeal creature, Triv had really marvelous control of his energy. He taught Zac a simple method to use his own Miasma or Cosmic Energy to "trap" external energy.

Triv used it as a defensive measure, but it worked for Zac as well in preventing energy loss. It was far from foolproof, but it did prolong the duration he could keep the energy he gained from kills by a large margin.

Cultivators could apparently just use their own cultivation manuals for a far superior result, with some being able to store the energy for weeks if need be. Zac was nowhere near that, but he could at least keep 80% of any energy he gained for over an hour. It was enough for his purposes, as it would give him ample time to get to safety in case he wanted to try breaking open a node.

It was also enough to wait out the Nexus Hub this time, and the golden pillar finally winked out of existence, and Zac sighed in relief when his bindings disappeared as well.

During this whole time, he had kept an eye out for any movement, but the area was utterly desolate. Neither **[Cosmic Gaze]** nor his augmented Draugr vision had seen a lick of activity, essentially proving that the cultists had given up on this place.

With the incursion being closed as well, there was not much reason for the cultists to return either. Zac guessed they were either running toward the Mystic Realm or hiding in some desolate corner of Earth right now. With no threat appearing, Zac decided to try bursting open the node in his leg. He was in a wretched state, but not to the point that he needed bed rest.

He would need to rest up in either case after this fight, so he might as well take the opportunity to push his cultivation along. That way he could heal everything together without wasting time. But just as he was about to take control of the energy circling his heart, a series of prompts appeared, making him stop in his tracks.

[Congratulations. Integration Trial succeeded. Calculating Grade.]

[Grade awarded: A. Contribution Rank: #1. Grade awarded increased to S.]

19

THE NEXT STEP

"Shit, why is it so hard to get one's hands on some tokens? Or some other way to activate that big-ass crystal inland?" Smaug muttered in annoyance as he paced back and forth in his home-prison in Port Atwood.

Who would have thought that he would be put under house arrest and tasked with coming up with moneymaking schemes by that little blue devil? He had just tried to get a better understanding of the resources available to his new boss, and this was the thanks he got?

"Ai, the Heavens are truly jealous of talent. To think I would be turned prisoner because I wanted to help out," Smaug lamented as he paced back and forth.

"What are you talking about, prisoner? You can still walk around in this neighborhood without getting impaled by those Amazons." Rima giggled. "And you wouldn't be in this predicament if you hadn't tried to infiltrate that shipyard. You knew that place was off-limits."

"I had to take the shot, stupid. That place is extremely suspicious, even more so than the repository," Smaug snorted. "Those muscleheads are busy now, and I need to get some things done before that man realizes how open-ended his orders were."

That was the good point of Lord Atwood; he wasn't a hands-on boss. He had told him to head to Port Atwood and listen to the little blue bastard. But it turned out that secondhand commands weren't actually binding under his contract. He had pretended that the little imp's order to stay in the neighborhood was binding, but it was anything but.

He could leave anytime. Lord Atwood only told him to go here and listen, not that he couldn't leave.

"Don't you have any decency?" Rima said with disdain. "Instead of thinking of ways of enriching yourself, you could actually do what was asked of you."

"Would me having decency help Earth survive this shitstorm?" Smaug countered. "No, right? So I might as well prepare for the off chance we survive, or more likely if things go south here. What about you? How goes it with the sister? Do they have a way off this cursed rock?"

"She's never around," Rima muttered. "And besides, I don't want to get closer to Mackenzie for you, useless brother. She is the sister of Lord Atwood and a good friend of Ogras Azh'Rezak. She's even close to that manly demon general."

"What would those three want with a useless brat?" Smaug snorted. "What do you bring to the table to those kinds of people?"

"Why would I need to be strong to become someone's wife?" Rima said with a roll of her eyes.

"Don't get too attached," Smaug muttered. "This planet's future is limited even if the great Lord Atwood manages to deal with the most immediate mess. I've found out a few things. Even if we survive all this, we'll just turn into some backwater planet at the edge of the universe, a place where even the birds won't shit."

"This again." Rima sighed.

"I am telling you. Our aim should be getting to some real human metropolis! There will be opportunities for advancement for me. And for you? Won't there be real geniuses to marry? People with family trees millions of years old and pockets as deep as the Mariana Trench," Smaug said, his eyes glistening.

"Besides–" Smaug continued, but he was stopped in his tracks by a series of prompts that appeared in front of him.

He had actually done it. That wooden block had taken out the cultists.

"You see!" Rima said with glee. "He really is a prince charming. He's done more for this world than the rest of us combined. Perhaps he even has some time to settle down now. He's been single for a while now."

"I've seen it before. That man has become an addict already – an addict to becoming stronger," Smaug muttered absentmindedly as he closed the screen that told him his rating was a measly D-grade. "He won't be looking for romance anytime soon."

Rima snorted in response, but Smaug wasn't interested in having this debate once more. He was more interested in going through his licensed wares. He already knew that there were limitations to the items he could purchase because of the ongoing invasions, and his eyes glimmered when he saw two of the latest additions that had appeared now that the war was over.

[Goblin Honor – Temporarily ignore a contract erected by someone at Level 100 or below.]

[Stumpbugle Talisman – Teleport to Stumpbugle Headquarters for career opportunities!]

Going to a place called "Stumpbugle" wasn't really what he had in mind when he said he would strike out in a real metropolis, and he had no desire to meet the inventors of the weird treasures that were available for purchase. But it was also an undeniable fact that Earth was on the brink of destruction, even if they had dealt with the incursion.

The weaker threat was gone, but what about that old monster who could appear at a moment's notice?

Those Zombie bastards had clearly known how to block teleportation arrays, so a Peak D-grade cultivator was probably able to do the same with just a wave of his arm. What if the whole planet got jammed the moment he arrived? Wouldn't that mean that he and Rima would be stuck here until they were turned into some sort of cultivation resource? Was he willing to bet everything on Zachary Atwood prevailing against those odds?

He wasn't.

The vast cloud of dust in a hidden pocket of space outside the Zecia Sector shuddered as it started spinning and condensing. Only by coming close would one be able to realize that these weren't particles of ice drifting about in space, but rather tens of millions of intricate machines lying dormant, soaking up the energies of the nearby irregularity.

The machines soon congealed into a person, a woman freely floating about in the vast beyond. Her amber eyes opened for the first time in decades as she looked around with some confusion. It was too early. She thoughtfully opened a screen to see what had dragged her out of the reverie.

Had something happened to the project?

She quickly learned she had been awoken due to her talisman activating from scenario 18, and she sighed in relief. Tens of thousands of screens appeared in front of her, taking up thousands of square meters in front of her. All kinds of readings and snippets flittered across the screens with terrifying speed for a second before they dissolved to dust and returned to her body again.

"Hm? How curious. He was actually able to evolve with his cursed constitution? Were our assumptions back then wrong, or did we miss something?" Leandra muttered as she thoughtfully looked at the vast star in front of her. "Is it another ploy by the Cursed Heavens?"

In either case, it was good news. Her daughter should be safe with such a powerful protector now that the planet had withstood the Integration Trial. Her suggestions should remain in their depths, helping them stay alive even without her assistance. She really wanted to rush back, but she knew that she had to be careful. She was in a better state than before, but only two short decades had passed – it wasn't enough.

A lot of sacrifices had been made to come this far; she couldn't ruin the efforts of her ancestors by being hasty.

There was also the oddity of someone using one of her backdoor keys on a merchant's vessel at the edge of integrated space. Had one of the children been sent on a mission by the Cursed Heavens? Such a quest was obviously not an accident, and annoyance flared up in her heart at the thought of her flesh and blood being manipulated to turn against her by that damned broken AI.

A slight pressure in her forehead dragged her out of her thoughts, and she quickly activated defensive measures to evade the tracking attempt on her soul.

"They still haven't given up," Leandra muttered as she once more dissolved into motes that spread across space.

The last thing to dissolve was the two amber eyes radiating an unshakeable conviction.

"There will be a reckoning one day. Those who moved against our family will all pay the price, even the Heavens themselves."

"Do you have it?" A'Feris asked, not without some interest as far as Io could tell.

He was glad to see some fire within the eyes of his old friend. Io knew his own limits had long been reached, but A'Feris still had a small chance to go even further. However, he was losing his momentum, the most dangerous thing to lose in cultivation apart from one's life.

Perhaps this Zac Piker was the key.

The more he gathered, the more he felt like this little demon was just what A'Feris needed. The young axe-man's penchant for drawing ire from both his contemporaries and the Boundless Heavens itself almost seemed unmatched.

"I have it here," Io said, and one scene after another appeared.

It showed the utter destruction of a grand mansion by a square, and a bloodied man walking out of the rubble, holding a head in his hand. A young demonling appeared next to him, and they fled to a teleporter, harried by hundreds of attacks.

It showed a hazy outline of how the Tower of Eternity changed into one of the Primordial Steles, and how it infected the minds of the children gathered in front of it. Finally, it culminated in a heated battle where one stood against many but prevailed.

"The Stele of Conflict?" A'Feris snorted. "The Zecia Sector will become hectic as the ripples of war spread out from this enclosed dimension. That thing is like a mindplague."

"Conflicts will engulf the sector, and heroes will emerge from the flames." Io nodded.

"Axe, sharpness, heaviness. Corpse? No, putrefaction? Interesting," A'Feris muttered, his eyes glistening as he looked on. "And echoes of the Sukhavati? Greedy boy."

"It might look greedy, but what if it works out?" Io said. "He is clearly on his way to forming a path of supremacy. With some guidance–"

"It's not that easy to walk the edge between Life and Death. Even our friends in the Sangha have to compromise," A'Feris sighed with a shake of his head. "He is too discordant right now. He is grasping for everything, trying to encompass the universe. It is an extremely unstable and dangerous state. Me or someone else stepping in now would only impede his path. He needs to form his own understanding and be the one to make the sacrifices."

"So you're not taking him in after all?" Io asked. "Such a rare seedling, and with your path…"

"I didn't say that." A'Feris smiled. "I just said that it is too early now. He seems to have a few interesting challenges ahead. Let him deal with them by himself. If he can emerge alive, he might be able to create a workable path from the experience. It's not too late to join a proper force by that point and benefit from some structured guidance. Have any of the old bastards claimed him?"

"Not at the moment," Io said. "Perhaps they are thinking in the same way."

"Are you saying I'm becoming like the old geezers?" A'Feris snorted. "I'm still pretty young for someone at my stage, you know."

Io smiled and shook his head before his eye turned back to the screen.

"He reminds me of you. I watched your struggle against the Foradine Covenant back on the Verokh Continent just like this. I hope he can become another pillar of our sect some day in the future," Io said with reminiscence in his eyes.

"I was a lot more dashing, no doubt." A'Feris laughed. "But I agree.

There is potential in him, and he's a gamble worthy to take. Well, unless he goes and does something stupid like joining the unorthodox. He's a progenitor, right? We'll go pick him up after the shroud has been lifted. The quarantine should have been lifted by then as well. It was just an image of the Stele, after all, rather than the real thing."

A sigh escaped from Uld's lips as he kept infusing the altar with power. The fires danced in his eyes, but his gaze was locked on the unmoving form of Arkensau. Who knew that this bastard possessed something as valuable as a **[Heaven's Intervention]**?

If not for that, then he would have been interring the body and preparing it for sale. But now he was stuck nurturing this idiot back to health, while the Sovereign-select ran rampant across the planet. And now he was stuck here on this desolate rock.

"Orders from above, for your eyes only," Trovad said as his eyes turned to the altar. "Arrived just hours before the gate was closed. How is Inquisitor Arkensau?"

"With Heaven's blessing, he will be fine within a week or two. The seed burns strong within him," Uld said as he accepted the golden-inlaid crystal.

Uld touched the crystal with the sigil in his mind, and a mix of exhaustion and relief washed through him as the strict voice of Archbishop Vantes echoed in his mind.

Be wary of the local called Super Brother-Man. We believe him to have appeared in the Tower of Eternity recently, causing a storm and conquering the eighth floor. The Church has never feared other forces of this remote sector, but caution is warranted.

The Dimensional Seed is of utmost importance, far eclipsing the value of any bodies. This mission will replace all the original goals. Keep the inquisitors in check; leave no weaknesses. Acquire the seed and lock yourselves away in the Mystic Realm. We will be able to find you after the shroud of the Heavens has been lifted. Your reward for a completed mission will far eclipse the cost of a hundred years.

Failure will likewise come at a great cost.

A wave of exhaustion buffeted his mind, but there was nothing Uld could do. The orders had been given, so he could only comply.

"How did it go? Did the Sovereign-select fall?" Uld asked.

"Not even he should have survived the judgment," Trovad said with conviction. "We will know for sure in a day. The glory of the Heavens still lingers, blocking our sight, but the recordings should arrive shortly."

20
S-GRADE

"He did it!" Kenzie smiled, her clenched fists finally relaxing in her lap.

"It's amazing," Lyla said from the side. "It's finally over. Maybe we can finally start living our lives again."

"There are still some things that need to be done." Kenzie smiled, though the smile felt a bit strained.

"Like what?" Lyla asked with confusion.

Lyla had stayed with Kenzie in her courtyard to help take her mind off the fact that Zac was risking his life against the cultists. She had instead asked far and wide about the various arrays and contraptions. It was a welcome distraction, and Kenzie had freely told her about the various arrays she was working on.

But all things must come to an end sooner or later. Her hesitation had already cost too much.

"Dealing with the traitors and the spies on the island, for example," she said with a steady voice, her eyes boring into Lyla's.

Kenzie had known for a while. She had known that Lyla was the one feeding intelligence back to the mainland through an ingenious array that was no doubt provided by the cultist infiltrators of the New World Government. It was because of her that so many had died, and she was the reason the cultists had learned of the entrance to the Mystic Realm.

Zac had saved her life, but she had returned the favor with malice, increasing the risk to him and everyone else in Port Atwood. Lyla had almost cut off their access to something their mother had left behind as well, which was unforgivable by itself.

Lyla only looked at her with incomprehension for a second until her form fell apart, her body replaced by a clay dummy. However, how could Kenzie not be prepared for something like this? She had seen Lyla use this very skill to survive multiple times during the Tutorial and their expeditions in the Dead Zone.

Her garden was like a fortress with layers and layers of arrays. They were originally meant to keep the area safe in case of a mishap with her experiments, but they worked just as well for trapping a level 36 cultivator. Not even her brother would be able to sense the slightest fluctuation, even if he passed by right outside.

Lyla had learned to almost perfectly blend with the earth, but Kenzie had already managed to push her Seed of Loam to Peak mastery. Together with Jeeves, it was effortless to pinpoint her location. Kenzie slightly circulated her Cosmic Energy, and an earth pillar rose from the ground, unearthing a horrified Lyla.

"Wait, they have my parents! I had no choice–" Lyla cried, but it was too late.

A Dao-empowered flame swallowed her whole, and no substitution or movement skill would save her from the Seed of Tinder. A shrill scream emerged from her throat, but it was almost instantly cut short by a wind-blade that decapitated her. The headless corpse was turned into ashes in less than a minute, and a wave of Kenzie's hand spread the ashes in the garden.

Lyla had almost been as powerful as herself back during the Tutorial, but those days were long gone. She had stopped pushing herself since arriving at Port Atwood, spending most days not even cultivating at all. In contrast, Jeeves had gone from stalling Kenzie's progress with all the energy it needed to fully awaken, to completely rehauling her cultivation. Killing Lyla was completely effortless.

Some confusion and guilt appeared in Kenzie's auburn eyes, but a red flash appeared in their depths, and she gradually regained her composure.

"You're right, I need to harden myself." Kenzie sighed before she looked down at the scorched spot on the grass. "I'm sorry. But those who move against the family will have to pay the price."

Zac's eyes lit up upon seeing the prompts. It looked very similar to when he had completed the Incursion Master quest, where he had gained the Dao Repository. He obviously wasn't surprised at being placed first in the contribution tally, but the grade was something new.

He had only heard of A-grade before, and this was something even above that. Did that mean there were S-grade cultivators as well? Zac had asked around about what the limit of cultivation was, but he had never got a real answer. The people of the Zecia Sector didn't even know what the B-grade entailed, let alone anything above that.

The next moment, an even better prompt appeared.

[Distributing Rewards]

[Additional Reward: Limited Title Slots +1. Frontrunner Title Permanence.]

Zac whistled in surprise upon seeing the reward, or rather tried to whistle with his badly burnt lips. This was pretty huge. He had essentially received not one, but two additional Limited Title slots in one go. This was just what he needed to maintain his attribute lead against the elite cultivators of the sector.

He might not get double the attributes per level any longer, but having five Limited Title slots should allow him to stay ahead of even the greatest elites of the sector. Of course, that still required him to actually find some opportunities that provided a title.

The title permanence was a welcome surprise as well, but it made him think of something. Zac quickly tried to open the ladder screen, only to find that nothing happened. Zac grimaced in annoyance when he realized the System had finished its ladder experiment.

This could both be seen as good news and bad news. It was good news in the sense that no one beneath D-grade would be able to find out his level any longer thanks to his bracer. Every single step he had taken until now had been monitored by millions of people, but now he was suddenly free. However, the change came with detriments as well.

He could no longer find any information about the Dominators either, though he didn't expect them to gain a bunch of levels out of nowhere. But more importantly, he wouldn't be able to keep tabs on his force and make sure everything was alright. Just opening the screen and looking at the familiar names during his Tower climb had been a huge source of comfort, but he wouldn't be able to do so any longer while traveling the Zecia Sector in the future.

There were life-monitoring treasures to buy that would provide a similar function, and Zac added it to the ever-growing list of things that Calrin needed to get for him. But he also realized that the odds of actually getting something useful from the Sky Gnome might have increased now that the incursions were gone and some restrictions were removed.

It was also somewhat of a relief that the title rewards didn't provide immediate attributes, as he still wasn't sure how much his home-made Draugr baths had increased his attribute cap. Zac quickly opened his title screen to be sure nothing had changed.

Name: Zachary Atwood
Level: 81
Class: [E-Epic] Fetters of Desolation
Race: [E] Draugr
Alignment: [Earth] Port Atwood – Lord

Titles: [...] Fated, Peak Power, Sovereign-select, Frontrunner, Apex Progenitor
Limited Titles: Tower of Eternity Sector All-Star – 14th
Dao: Fragment of the Axe – Middle, Fragment of the Coffin – Middle, Fragment of the Bodhi – Middle
Core: [E] Duplicity

Strength: 2,090 [Increase: 91%. Efficiency: 218%]
Dexterity: 992 [Increase: 65%. Efficiency: 187%]
Endurance: 2,083 [Increase: 86%. Efficiency: 218%]

Vitality: 1,375 [Increase: 76%. Efficiency: 218%]
Intelligence: 545 [Increase: 65%. Efficiency: 187%]
Wisdom: 911 [Increase: 70%. Efficiency: 187%]
Luck: 340 [Increase: 91%. Efficiency: 197%]

Free Points: 0
Nexus Coins: [F] 5,919,187,601

Zac sighed in relief when he saw that his attributes were still the same, but he did notice a few differences after looking around through his screens. The first of all was the update of the titles, with Frontrunner having moved to the permanent bracket. But he had also gained a new title, which honestly wasn't too surprising.

[Apex Progenitor: Pass the World Integration Trial with S-grade. Reward: Effect of Attributes +10%]

It was a real top-tier title, only being rivaled by his Tower climb and Apex Hunter titles so far, giving a whopping 10% efficiency in every attribute. It had actually pushed him past 200% efficiency on his main attributes, meaning that he was more than twice as strong as his attributes indicated.

Efficiency was pretty much impossible to discern even with high-quality spying skills, from what Zac had learned, so even if someone managed to glean his attributes, they might only set themselves up for disaster. They would see Zac having 2,000 Strength, only for him to burst out with the power of more than double a second later.

He was also happy to see that he had finally taken some steps forward with his undead skills, with **[Indomitable]** reaching Late proficiency, and both his ultimate skills having reached Middle proficiency. He was still lagging behind compared to his human class, but it was a step in the right direction.

The fit of his skills, especially **[Undying Legion]** and **[Indomitable]**, had worsened in compatibility since evolving, but they were still useful. They might turn into components of skill fusions for his new class in the future, but they would have to reach Peak proficiency first for that to work.

There were also a lot of additions to his Town Shop, mainly defensive arrays that looked far more powerful than anything he had been able to purchase before. However, they were still limited by his power, with the strongest arrays being marked as "Early E-grade." That didn't really come as a surprise.

The System would never let people buy too powerful defenses, as that would drastically lessen the amount of conflict in the Multiverse.

It was still a big upgrade to his weak Town Protection Array, and Zac looked through the options for a few seconds until he suddenly froze in realization. The System called the Limited Title boost an additional reward. If that was the addition, then where were the original rewards?

The greed for loot quickly overcame the weariness in his body, and he scoured the whole crater for treasures. There was nothing apart from smoking-hot soil and an inert Nexus Hub in the hole he found himself in. Glee was slowly replaced with confusion as he looked around. What was going on?

Was the reward once again related to his town? The phrasing of the prompts was extremely familiar to the way the System had spoken when he received the Dao Repository, so Abby might have gotten the rewards back home. Last time, the Stargazer had held it back so that he would be able to choose where to place the reward, so there might be a similar situation waiting for him.

Zac bought a teleportation array, but this time, he didn't make it public. Zac kept it to himself like the array in his private area. If the teleporter was open, a group of Valkyries and demons would step through to this place a few minutes later, and Zac wasn't comfortable leaving them here in case the cultists returned.

He soon found himself back in his compound, somewhat relieved that there were no signs of his sister. It allowed him to hobble over to his courtyard and close the arrays without causing any worry with his wretched appearance. There were no rewards in his home either, but he still held off on his urge to visit the Stargazer.

There was no way he wouldn't cause a panic if he entered the government building looking like a mix of a Zombie and a rotisserie chicken, but more importantly, he still had a node to break open. He had been interrupted by the prompt just as he was about to break it open, and the rewards had allowed him to slow down and think clearly. There was no point in staying in a burning crater to open a node when he had free access to his home.

The accumulated energy in his chest was running a bit low because of the delay, so Zac ate one of his node-breaking pills while channeling the remains from the **[Void Heart]** to his leg. He also ate an anesthetic pill to block out the pain of his broken bones and burned skin. The pain wasn't to the point that he was immobilized, but he was afraid that it would mess with his concentration breaking open the node.

He only got something like 20% of the efficacy of the node-breaking pill, but it was enough to tide him over along with the energies ripped from his cursed sword and the holy flames. A small explosion echoed out in the isolated courtyard after around ten minutes, and a splatter of black ichor stained the ground.

Zac suddenly remembered learning about a medical factoid before the integration, of how some women naturally forget the excruciating pain of childbirth. It was apparently an evolutionary measure so that people wouldn't shy away from having more children. The reason for remembering such a random tidbit was obviously that he must have blocked out just how painful breaking open the last node was.

His pain-relief pill had worked wonders against the burns, but it was utterly incapable of dealing with the agony of getting his pathways blasted open. Waves of pain crashed into his mind, and he helplessly fell back on the ground, unable to move in the slightest. He ate another healing pill as he grabbed a Miasma Crystal in each hand, his eyes closed to block out the world.

Only an hour later was he able to get up again, but he had to admit that his state was a lot better than last time.

Recuperating instead of entering a life-and-death battle right after breaking open a node had not surprisingly helped him minimize the damage from the node-breaking. He would still need to redraw the section of the pathways around the node, this time in his Draugr form. But he felt stable enough that he could get up again without falling unconscious like he did last time.

He soon left his courtyard, but he still didn't enter the town. He instead returned to the burnt-out crater he just came from, relieved to see that it was still devoid of cultists. He finally made the teleporter public as he gazed at the massive golden pillars that were deeply embedded in the ground. Just how had the zealots gotten their hands on this much gold?

And how much was it worth?

21
ADAPTABILITY

The broken pieces of the enormous sigil still radiated some heat even after over an hour had passed, but it wasn't to the point that Zac felt it was dangerous any longer. He walked closer to it to see if it actually was just normal gold, and he finally realized a pattern covered its surface. It almost looked like Damascus steel but in gold and white, and the white formed what looked like hazy patterns.

It clearly wasn't inscribed, but it rather looked more like something that had naturally grown over time. However, the patterns didn't contain anywhere near the amount of meaning and power as the grooves he had seen on the Stele during the vision in the Tower of Eternity. It almost felt like the patterns hadn't really finished forming just yet.

It made Zac unsure whether it actually was a normal metal that was in the process of being enhanced by the fire-attuned energies and prayer, or if it was some alloy the cultists were creating inside the volcano. Zac shook his head and instead made his way up the crater, feeling that it would have to be a mystery for someone else to solve. He had enough on his plate as it was.

His deathly gaze roved across the smoldering mountainside and the jungles for a couple of minutes, but he couldn't sense the slightest hint of life. Had every single cultist died after all? Not that it mattered too much, as there obviously hadn't been anyone of import at the base when he arrived. Just a skeleton crew that would set about the chain reaction that almost got him killed.

They were obviously ready to completely abandon the incursion.

Zac sighed as he understood the implication. He had hoped to be done with the zealots in one swift move with this final fight, at least dealing with the Head Priest and his bishops. But they were probably all still around, waiting to cause trouble at a moment's notice. It was a bit of a shame there was not a single cultist to catch and interrogate, but they probably would rather blow themselves up than answer any questions.

Their actions were still a bit perplexing, though. Why would they do something like this rather than just cutting their losses and returning home, just like the other invaders? Was the Mystic Realm really that important to them, or rather the dimensional artifact inside? It looked like they bet everything on that item and the fact that he wouldn't be able to hunt them down over the next century.

He would need to visit the Mystic Realm entrance to make sure, but Zac guessed that he would be met by a closed entrance impossible to open from outside. If he put himself in their shoes, their best course of action would be to hide inside the Mystic Realm for a hundred years, at which point he would try to contact his superiors to pick them up.

Preferably while snatching the dimensional artifact.

A hundred years might be a long time to someone like himself, but to the elders of the Church of the Everlasting Dao, it was nothing. Waiting a bit longer for the results would probably not matter all that much to them. Not everyone was strapped for time like the Great Redeemer. It meant that yet another old monster probably had set his sights on Earth and its resources.

He would either get the dimensional artifact or try to hunt them down, as the Church didn't feel like the kind of people who would drop something like this. However, Zac couldn't really muster any urgency from the realization, as it honestly didn't feel like it changed much by this point. There were already a bunch of old monsters bearing down on the planet, including his mother. What was one more?

Zac sighed as he sat down on the ground, his form once more

turning back to human. A wave of pain radiated through his body as it came alive, and he quickly ate another healing pill as he kept watch over the area. But there was not much to guard against, as everything was completely burned and leveled.

The soothing energy of the Fragment of the Bodhi also spread through his body, helping out with restoring his tissue. There was still a stubborn energy hiding in the wounds, rabidly resisting both his pills and his Dao. It looked like some special energy had been infused into the blast, and he would have to slowly grind it down.

As he looked down at the crater, he felt that the near-death experience had brought home an important lesson. There were all sorts of amazing treasures and arrays in the world, but nothing was impervious. Treasures could fail at any time, and he could only trust his own body in the end.

A buzz behind him told him that the teleporter had activated, and he turned around to see a vanguard group of demons carefully emerging inside the crater. Ilvere stood at the front, and he looked around with wide eyes before he spotted Zac sitting above. He quickly jumped up, and he gave a start when he saw Zac's wretched appearance.

"Don't you look like shit?" Ilvere laughed as he took out a large vat from his Cosmos Sack. "Something to drink? You look like you need one. I made it myself, with some help from that barkeep."

Zac wryly smiled as he took a swig from the demonic homebrew, and he immediately became thankful that his gullet was reinforced by his high Endurance. The vile concoction tasted like paint thinner, but it actually managed to give him a slight buzz. He wouldn't be surprised if a single mouthful would kill a normal human.

"What happened here?" the demon asked as he looked around at the destruction. "It looks like a natural disaster rather than a battlefield. No bodies. They sacrificed themselves?"

"There was almost no one here." Zac sighed as he recounted what had happened.

"So the lunatics are here to stay," Ilvere muttered with a grimace, echoing Zac's own thoughts. "I hoped we'd be done with them after their two invasions. Like fleas, these ones. Got to take them all out before they start to fester."

"Well, that's why I have you guys, right?" Zac snorted.

"Well, whatever. What do you want us to do?" Ilvere asked.

"Just the usual." Zac grunted as he got back on his feet. "Stay close to this area. I think the valuable resource was the volcano, but I'm not sure if they broke it. What do you think about those golden things?"

Ilvere grunted in thought before his massive weapon shot out with extreme momentum, slamming into one of the huge slabs of metal not far from where Zac sat. A deep gong echoed out across the area, and Ilvere even had to take a step back from the power inside the sound wave. Zac felt a bit impacted as well, but not to the point that he was hurt.

A small mark was left on the slab, but it didn't even look dented from the attack. The metal ball, on the other hand, looked like it had been put over a fire, radiating some heat that forced Ilvere to spin it in the air until it cooled down again.

"Probably won't be able to maintain its original function, but it's definitely good stuff. Perhaps we can reforge it into weapons and armor with flame attunement?" Ilvere muttered. "You have that mine in the underworld as well. If you can figure out a way to fuse the two resources, you might even be able to make something valuable enough to export through the blue one's Mercantile License."

Zac's eyes lit up at the prospect. He still hadn't been able to use Calrin's consortium for interplanetary trades, as the fees were too high to justify selling stuff like the ant carapace armors. But what if he could make a bunch of attuned weaponry? Fire had always been a popular Dao and cultivation path due to its offensive nature.

Armor providing flame resistance would be a huge asset against fire-based forces like the Church of Everlasting Dao or the flame golems of the Underworld, and flame-attuned weaponry would no doubt sell like hotcakes.

"Harvesting those things has the highest priority, then. Don't bother scouring the jungle. It's full of beasts, and it would take the whole army to canvass it," Zac said.

Zac gave it a thought and bought a set of defensive arrays as well for the area around his newly acquired ruins. He usually didn't bother with that in the beginning, but he didn't want to risk the lives of his people in case some suicidal zealot was waiting for an opportunity in the vast jungle.

"Everyone returns together later, and everyone gets tested," Zac added. "Both with the Origin Array and the root."

"Understood," Ilvere agreed. "We'll make sure not to bring any of those bastards back to the island."

Zac nodded and stepped through the teleporter the next moment, appearing in the public teleportation station. He was surprised to find Joanna waiting there for him, and she walked over with brisk steps.

"Welcome back. The Administrator is looking for you," Joanna said with a smile. "You really did it. You actually saved Earth, like a real-life action hero."

"I don't think that action heroes look like this after winning." Zac smiled. "And there are still a lot of bad guys around."

"You know, it's okay to celebrate taking a step in the right direction," Joanna said as she walked next to him. "If you only focus on what's wrong, you'll always feel stressed out."

"I know." Zac smiled. "One step at a time. By the way, have Billy and Thea come here while I was gone?"

"Not to my knowledge," Joanna said. "Is there something wrong?"

"No, it's nothing," Zac said with a shake of his head.

Zac had somewhat expected the two to claim their inheritances by now, but perhaps they weren't quite ready just yet. Then again, he had closed the incursion a bit faster than expected, taking less than a day to get the job done. They would probably come over within the week unless their reward for surviving the integration allowed them to gain another boost before the trial.

Joanna followed him over toward the government building, and Zac heard she had gained a rating of C by the System, with most of the Valkyries having gained a D. C was apparently the highest of anyone in Port Atwood, though Joanna hadn't asked his sister, as she was busy with her experiments.

Most of the townspeople got an F or E, which didn't surprise Zac, seeing as how the System was so biased in favor of the elites. It also turned out that only those with C or higher gained rewards and a title. Zac guessed that getting to live another day was the only gift those with worse ratings got.

However, the situation was a bit baffling to Zac.

"What do you think the System graded you on?" Zac asked with some confusion. "A rating of D seems pretty bad for how many incursions you guys helped me close. Not even Thea has closed as many as you did."

"I don't think it's just that," Joanna said with a shake of her head. "It has only been an hour, but I've started to get a small understanding of the situation after asking around. A part of the grade was definitely achievements, Dao, and level, which isn't a surprise. But I also think a big part of it was adaptability."

"Adaptability?" Zac muttered.

"Ryan, for example, got a D-grade like the Valkyries, even though he hasn't closed a single incursion. He did, however, quickly adapt after coming here, and now he's one of the most successful people on the island," Joanna said. "But both Ryan and us Valkyries didn't really excel in the beginning. We only got where we are because of you, so we didn't get too impressive grades."

Zac slowly nodded, feeling it made sense. The incursions and the integration was a massive trial, and the System was probably only interested in helping those who were able to embrace their new reality and make the most of it. Besides, not only those like him or Thea were of value to the System. People like Smaug and Henry Marshall should probably have pretty decent ratings as well, as they excelled in what they set out to do.

There was a palpable celebratory atmosphere in the town as the two walked toward the government building. People were out on the street with big smiles on their faces, and Zac was surprised to see that some had even raised the flag of Port Atwood on their storefronts or from their porches.

Zac had already hidden his identity with a hooded robe, mostly because he was a bit embarrassed about his crispy appearance. Joanna wanted him to hold some sort of speech to rouse the citizens, but Zac was far too tired for something like that. He only wanted to get his rewards, then rest up for a day or two.

They soon reached their destination, and Zac walked up to Abby's private floor in one of the wings after issuing a set of orders for Joanna to start preparing the Valkyries for the Mystic Realm. He entered after a knock and found Abby hovering in the middle of a bunch of screens. She closed them and turned toward him, and Zac was surprised to see that she had grown since last time.

The diameter of the floating eyeball must have increased by 20 to 30 percent, and her shimmering eye looked even more magical compared to before. It seemed like his Administrator had reached E-grade or at least evolved her Race.

Another new addition was a golem standing in the corner of the room, an intimidating construct of polished stone that reached almost three meters into the air. One of its arms was just a long spike, and the other formed a shield. It didn't move in the slightest when Zac entered, but Zac still felt a vague pressure from it, meaning it should probably have the combat strength of an Early E-grade cultivator.

Had the Stargazer bought herself a bodyguard?

"It's been a while." Zac smiled as he sat down on a free seat.

"Well, you've been busy," Abby said as her shimmering eye turned toward him. "I'm guessing you're here about the reward?"

"So there is one after all?" Zac said, his eyes lighting up in anticipation.

"Yes, three, actually," Abby said.

22

INCENTIVES FOR EXPLORATION

"There are three rewards? What are they?" Zac asked with anticipation.

"You could say one is for you, one is for Port Atwood, and one is for Earth. The first is a pretty interesting mobile array called the [**Spatial Convergence Array**]. It is a two-part array that has two functions, the first of which will allow you to teleport to Port Atwood from almost anywhere in the whole sector once every decade," Abby said.

"What? Can't I already do that as a world leader?" Zac asked with disappointment. "And without the wait time."

"Well, it's not quite that simple. Nexus Hubs require upgrades. You might need to do multiple jumps to return if the hubs you use are too low quality. Each jump is a risk of entering a hostile environment," Abby said. "Besides, from what I've heard, your identity has become a bit sensitive in your sector."

"So?" Zac asked, still feeling a bit peeved.

"What if your identity gets exposed while traveling? The first thing a City Lord would do is deactivate the teleportation arrays, trapping you in place," Abby said. "Not much you can do about that apart from either taking over the town or fleeing to some other force in hopes of using their teleportation array.

"This bangle could help you circumvent this, making you far harder to pin down. You could be stuck on a desolate planet or in the void of space itself. As long as you're not in a Mystic Realm, you can just activate this treasure and get sent home as soon as you've infused enough energy," Abby explained.

Zac whistled in understanding. It did indeed sound convenient. It would allow him to venture out to improve himself with greater peace of mind. The cultists joining hands with the undead had reminded him how exposed his people were while he wasn't around. There was a limit of what one could do with the Town Shop against a powerful enemy, after all.

Once a decade was a very long cooldown, but it was enough in case of an emergency. Things usually moved pretty slowly in the Multiverse. With people's life spans being in the millennia, it was unlikely that Earth would be attacked multiple times within a decade when things had stabilized.

"It is an extremely convenient array and a valuable lifeline for someone who is planning on traveling the Multiverse. Any outlaw or wandering cultivator would kill for something like this. You would almost become as hard to trap as a Karmic or Spatial Cultivator," Abby said. "The escape measure has various good functions as well, such as countermeasures to spatial lockdowns and tampering."

"What about the other function?" Zac asked.

"It allows you to erect a temporary teleportation array lasting a few minutes, even out in the wilderness," Abby said. "You need the materials for it, though, and it has a downside. It's expensive. Very expensive."

"How expensive?" Zac asked with some worry.

"Five times the standard rate," Abby said.

"Doesn't that make it useless?" Zac blanched.

The reason that almost no one below the D-grade would travel between worlds was the cost of teleportation. It wasn't like weaker cultivators didn't want to travel to Mystic Realms to gain titles and experience, but they simply couldn't afford it. Just the fees alone could ruin even a wealthy scion.

Zac was extremely wealthy for a self-made cultivator at his level, but just the prospect of teleporting to the Allbright Empire or some of the other cultivation spots he had in mind was a source of some dread.

Paying five times that price would put him in the poorhouse. It was like taking a helicopter to go buy groceries.

"It's a bit extravagant, but it is a good option to have. It doesn't have the cooldown like the escape function of the [Spatial Convergence Array], meaning you never need to worry about being stranded on some desolate planet," Abby said. "Remember, you might not have the resources of the established factions right now, but you will only grow wealthier as you and your settlement progress. Eventually, the costs of intra-sector teleportation won't matter at all to you."

"Well, I'm still far from that stage." Zac smiled. "Is the escape function as expensive?"

"No, that function is free. You don't even need a teleportation array," Abby explained. "Just activate the bangle and off you go. You only need to set up the beacon somewhere here on the island first. Truthfully, I have never heard of such an item before. I don't think it's possible without the active help of the System."

Zac decided he would put the beacon in his cultivation cave, and had Abby make the arrangements. With the layers of arrays, that place had become even more fortified than his compound, and he could empower the protections even further with the new arrays available in the store.

More importantly, only his sister, Abby, and Triv knew the exact location of that place, making the risk of sabotage lower. The [Spatial Convergence Array] was pretty amazing all in all and something that he didn't even know he needed until now.

Even if the instant escape function was used up, he would still be able to construct a mobile teleportation array. It did mean that he would need to walk around with more Nexus Coins than he anticipated, but the auction should take care of his lack of funds soon enough. Zac wondered what this thing could be worth, and he opened his Town Shop menu to see if it was available there.

"You don't need to look. This definitely isn't something available in the Town Shop, no matter how much of the inventory you unlock. It only contains base arrays. In fact, you shouldn't rely on those arrays too much. There are extremely effective Array Breakers readily available in the Multiverse for every single array in the shop." The Stargazer snickered.

"What?" Zac exclaimed. "So they're useless?"

"Well, no. They might be useless against invasions of advanced enemies who have done their research about your defenses, but they work just fine against weaker foes and beasts. It's not like anyone on Earth can get their hands on those kinds of siege tools right now," Abby explained.

Zac sighed in relief, but he was still worried about the future. It felt like he was buying a door lock that everyone had a master key for. It wasn't like forces like the Underworld Council and the New World Government were the enemies he was worried about, but rather the more advanced forces that might make their way to Earth in the future in search of his secrets and wealth.

That was years away, though, and he would have ample time to construct individualized defensive arrays. Kenzie might even be able to adjust the store-bought ones so that they wouldn't be so easy to break open with standardized solutions.

"Worrying me for nothing," Zac snorted. "What about the second reward?"

"Nothing as exciting, but still something of use to you. It's an upgradeable puppet army," Abby said. "They can both defend your lands autonomously, or you can control them with an adept Array Master. Your sister could use them instead of those cursed items she seems to like."

"How strong are they?" Zac asked.

"There are one thousand soldiers, each equivalent to Early E-grade, with three leaders at Middle E-grade. And when I say Middle E-grade, I mean elites, not cannon fodder. They should be able to keep most forces of Earth at bay for the foreseeable future," the Stargazer explained. "I haven't summoned them all yet, as you need to pick a spawn zone."

"Is that one of them behind me?" Zac asked as he pointed at the unmoving golem standing in the corner.

"Just so. I took one out to make sure I understood the reward. But now that you mention it, an Administrator without any guards is highly irregular," Abby said.

"Just keep it." Zac snorted before he considered what he could do with an additional army. "Can I bring them to the Mystic Realm?"

Pure power wouldn't cut it in the Mystic Realm, judging by what he'd heard so far. Half the battle would be exploring the research base to find the dimensional artifact, while securing his base from the other factions. That was an endeavor that was manpower intensive, and he would feel much better about sending a bunch of puppets into the depths of the Research Lab rather than the Valkyries and his soldiers.

"No, you can consider them a defensive structure. You can send them out by themselves, though they work best in squads under the three leaders," Abby explained, dashing his hopes.

"How big an area can they guard autonomously?" Zac asked with some disappointment.

"An island of this size wouldn't be an issue," Abby said without hesitation.

Zac asked a few more questions until he understood the function of the puppet army properly. He eventually decided to keep two of the armies in Port Atwood while sending the last one to Mystic Island to protect against any further sabotage. He could change the composition in the future, allowing him to protect the settlements that were more important to Port Atwood.

"You said they're upgradeable? How do I upgrade them?" Zac probed.

"You will have to ask the golems over at the shipyard. The System has connected the puppet army to them, which is good news for you. Any upgrade they do will be of a much higher quality than a standardized solution," Abby said. "Not only that, but upgrades will be completely free of charge. That alone is worth a fortune – you can't imagine what autonomous D-grade guardians cost. The only caveat is their grade will be linked to yours."

Zac's eyes lit up when he heard the Creators would not only be in charge of upgrading them, but that it would be free. By the looks of it, the captain golems would be one stage above him, meaning he'd get his hands on D-grade puppets when he reached the peak of the E-grade. As long as he maintained his level lead on Earth, Port Atwood would remain impenetrable.

They might turn out pretty weird after Karunthel got his spider-hands on the puppets, but their offensive capabilities would probably be extremely impressive. He had to head over there later, in either case, to see about the possibilities of upgrading the shipyard.

"One item that will freely allow me to return to Earth, another that will allow me to protect the town while I'm gone? Do you think the System is sending me a message?" Zac said as a joke after instructing Abby where to set up the puppet armies, but he was surprised to see that the Stargazer agreed without hesitation.

"Of course it is," Abby said as matter of course. "The System wants you to become stronger, but this planet is holding you back. The best route for you to become a powerhouse is to spread your wings, so I wouldn't be surprised that the System calculated the most pertinent rewards to help you become stronger were those that allowed you to leave. And if this doesn't convince you, there's still the third reward."

"What's that?" Zac asked curiously.

"Remember how I said Nexus Hubs need to be upgraded?" the Stargazer asked, getting an affirmative nod from Zac. "Well, that doesn't apply to you any longer. The System has upgraded yours to the limit of the Sector, saving you thousands of years of work. You have the same kind of access as ancient empires now."

"Really?"

"Normally, you start out with a Nexus Hub that can teleport you to neighboring planets at most. From there, you need to gradually expand its radius with quests and improving your empire. It's not a task that can be rushed unless the System itself helps you cheat," Abby sighed.

"How does that help me right now?" Zac asked.

"Well, at the moment, not much. You only have teleportation tokens after all, and those work with any hub," the Stargazer said. "But it has immense uses in the long term. Now, as long as you gain access to a faraway teleportation network, you can use it from earth without making multiple jumps.

"If Port Atwood enters an alliance with another empire, your population can freely teleport there with this upgrade. Trade, mobility, opportunities – this upgrade provides it all. And it is all tied to you personally, which means you have become the de-facto leader of Earth."

Zac was not sure if he believed Abby's theory of the System

wanting him to go out and explore, but the gifts were indeed exactly what he needed. The **[Spatial Convergence Array]** was especially valuable in the short run, as it would allow himself and his companions to escape certain death in many situations. The other two seemed to be more of long-term rewards like the shipyard, but that didn't mean the bangle would become useless anytime soon. It would be a lifesaver all the way until he reached C-grade and started traveling beyond the Zecia Sector.

Since he was already there, he asked the Stargazer to update him on the state of things, but he quickly felt himself being submerged in a sea of data he didn't understand. Abby quickly caught on and slowed down and finally stopped narrating altogether.

"Remember, this is not your old reality. The day-to-day running of a force isn't something the leader bothers with. Are the elders of mighty clans or sects busying themselves each day with diplomatic issues and crop yields? No, they are cultivating. You don't have a younger generation to deal with this for you, but you do have me and many other promising administrators," Abby said.

Zac knew that was true. The patriarch or sect leaders were never the most powerful people of a force, but something that could be considered middle management. They were powerful enough to command respect, but they only ran the day-to-day operations. The real decision-makers were the elders who either traveled the sector for opportunities or were perennially secluded in cultivation in hopes of breaking through.

That wasn't to say that those positions were useless. The sect leader did have access to most of the resources of the force, and they were in a far better position to break through in the future. Most of the grand elders of a clan had probably been clan leaders for a couple of millennia once upon a time.

This was probably also why Abby was pushing for Zac to be such a hands-off boss. She had clearly evolved since they met last time, no doubt benefitting from having almost free rein when running his force. He would have to put in some checks and balances eventually, but some pilfering of public resources was pretty much bound to happen.

Of course, there were limits to everything.

"How are criminals dealt with today?" Zac asked out of the blue.

"Thrown out of your sphere of influence or killed, depending on the severity of their crime. You don't have a dungeon at the moment, though you might want to consider building one. They are usually an effective deterrent against criminals," Abby said. "Your army is keeping the law at the moment."

"Julia wants to set up a proper law enforcement section for Port Atwood. What do you think about that?" Zac asked.

"Most sects and clans have some sort of law enforcement to keep the rabble in check," Abby said with a bob. "How they deal with transgressions varies wildly between forces. That girl seems capable enough, but she would need someone more powerful to help enforce the laws. The leader of the Law Enforcement Hall of a sect is usually one of the strongest cultivators around. They have to be."

Zac nodded in agreement. Just Julia wouldn't be enough. His first choice would be Ilvere, but he was already in charge of the army. But on further thought, Zac felt Janos might be a pretty decent choice. He didn't speak much, but he was as powerful as Ilvere while having a skill set extremely suited for incapacitating without killing.

He left the government building soon after and made his way back to his courtyard. The festivities in the town had only grown during his talk with Abby, but he was too tired to join in on the excitement. He found a drone mentioning that Kenzie had left for Mystic Island to work on the tunnel there. It was for the best with the cultists acting as they did.

The chance of him being able to steal one of their entrances felt slim at best, especially after the New World Government already had done so once. So he instead spent the next day in rest, working on restoring his body. The worst of his burns were healed by that point, making him look like a boiled lobster instead of a grilled chicken.

The wound from breaking open his node was healing nicely as well, though Zac had only just started redrawing his pathway. Zac guessed he would need another week or so to return to 100%, but that didn't mean he needed to sit around in his courtyard. There were a lot of things he could do, some of which he had put off for too long already.

Zac somberly left his courtyard and walked over to the teleportation array. He took a deep breath before he stepped onto the array, and he appeared at the top of a small hill covered in flowers a few seconds later. It was his first time coming to this specific island, the only prison of his archipelago.

The secluded island where Hannah and David lived.

23
PEACE

The island might be the only place where Zac held a captive, but it looked like a paradise rather than a dungeon. A vibrant array of colors spread across the hill, as flowers covered almost every inch apart from a small path. It wasn't wildflowers, but rather a meticulously arranged garden that stretched from the teleportation array down into a field below.

If that was all, it wouldn't have been too surprising, as getting flowers to bloom was infinitely easier now that there was Cosmic Energy in the atmosphere. What actually surprised Zac was that the flowers seemed to contain a hint of the Dao, and together managed to form an elusive Dao Field.

Zac couldn't tell what it was, as it was just a weak hint at the moment, but if given time, it might grow into something impressive. He slowly walked along the path, spreading out his own Dao of the Bodhi to get a sense of what was going on.

"From what I've heard about you, I would have thought that your aura would turn my flowers into dust rather than fill them with happiness." A voice drifted over from a tree to the side, causing Zac's heart to lurch. "But your Dao almost feels like that of a farmer's. Or perhaps of a forest elf?"

Part of Zac's reaction was because he recognized the voice, but part of it was that Zac actually hadn't sensed David at all as he sat beneath the poplar at the edge of the forest. He had utterly blended in with the surroundings, causing Zac's senses to pretty much register him as another shrub or something.

Zac still felt some nervousness as memories of the meeting with David during his tribulation flashed through his mind. However, it was a completely different David who sat beneath the tree and enjoyed the rays of sun that managed to make their way through the thick foliage.

David wasn't disfigured, for one. He still had a series of scars, but they were only thin white lines on healthy suntanned skin, much like the ones Zac had had before he evolved his Race to E-grade. There was also no hatred or blame in his eyes, but rather an almost eerie tranquility.

Zac wondered just what had happened to the boisterous man during his months on this island. Or had the previously energetic personality already died from being captured by the cultist? Or perhaps it had already happened during the Tutorial when Izzie died?

There was only one way to find out what went through his head, so Zac deactivated his Dao and walked over with a smile.

"It's called the Dao of the Bodhi, and it comes from the Seed of Trees and the Seed of Sanctuary," he explained, not hiding anything. "I actually have a class related to nature, though I focus more on fighting."

"That explains it," David said as he handed Zac a fruit from a basket next to him. "Taste it. I grew these myself."

Zac looked down at the fruit that looked like a red plum before he took a bite, mostly out of courtesy. A sweet taste almost exploded in his mouth, making Zac wolf down the rest of the fruit in a second.

"This might be one of the most delicious things I've ever eaten," Zac said with wide eyes, not exaggerating at all.

The fruit wasn't quite as tasty as the Fruit of Ascension, but the plum wasn't actually a spiritual fruit. It contained a weak hint of Cosmic Energy, but so did everything else in this day and age. The taste must have come from something else, like how it had been nurtured by David.

"It's my first harvest." David smiled as he handed Zac another one. "Months of work for twenty-nine plums. The next harvest will be bigger, and I believe the fruits will be even tastier."

Zac ate the second one with a lot more reserve, but he actually stopped halfway through. It was nice sitting here like this under the rustling trees while gazing at the fields of flowers, but it was not why he came here.

"I'm sorry." Zac sighed. "I'm sorry about you getting captured because of me. I'm sorry about putting off visiting for so long."

"You shouldn't carry the blame for the deeds of others," David said with a shake of his head. "And I know you have your hands full. We're all just scraping by here in the apocalypse. At least now I've found my path, and I am at peace."

"You know, I have a few islands that specialize in farming, and a spot on the main continent that has Spiritual Soil. You're welcome to head over there if you want if you need seeds or to just experiment with various ideas," Zac offered.

"Perhaps I will one day. But I feel I still have a lot to gain by staying on this island. Besides, I don't want to leave Hannah here all alone." David smiled. "Both Izzie and Tyler passed away during the Tutorial, so there's only the two of us still alive of the old gang. There's no point in going back to Greenworth either. We have to stick together."

Zac didn't take offense that David didn't include him in his list of "the gang." He had just met Hannah a few months before the integration, whereas the four of them had been friends since the first grade. As for him not going back to Greenworth, it was no surprise.

Port Atwood had long since gotten a pretty good overview of who was alive and who was dead or missing around the world thanks to their cooperation with the Marshall Clan. It had already been confirmed that both of David's parents had passed away during the first chaotic month, while his big brother and cousin had passed away in the very same Tutorial that Kenzie was part of.

There was nothing really connecting him to their old hometown any longer, just like how it was with Zac.

It was the same for most people of Port Atwood. With only a tenth of the population of Earth surviving the integration, most had lost their whole families. A few lucky ones had been able to help their households move to Port Atwood or another city under his control, but most were left alone in this new reality of theirs.

It was a cause for concern, as quite a few people were suffering from depression and post-traumatic stress on the island. The few therapists on the island had their hands full, and there were all sorts of support groups for those who had trouble acclimatizing.

At the same time, there was undeniably something about cultivation that changed you to your core. Perhaps it was the increase in Intelligence or Wisdom that made your mind stronger, or perhaps it was the effect of their ruthless reality, but a surprising number of people were able to bear the mental strain just fine. They kept moving forward while the people around them were dying left and right.

Zac himself was a prime example of that. Someone who had gone through so much bloodshed and near-death experiences over the past years should be a broken mess by now. But he honestly felt fine, apart from exhaustion that could be felt all the way to his bones. Even the fact that his ex-girlfriend had tried to murder him just a few short months ago barely registered on his mind.

"How is she?" Zac asked.

"Not bad. Not great. She doesn't like this island as much as I do. But I guess she agrees that it beats prison," David said with a wry smile. "We... are dating."

"That's good." Zac only nodded in response, not surprised in the slightest.

The two of them shared a deep history, and they had survived the Tutorial and everything else together. Besides, something was almost bound to happen with only two people marooned on an island with just the occasional visitor there to drop off supplies. It was either start dating or turn on each other.

"It's she who planted these flowers around the array, though I made the pattern. I think she sees the arrays as the door to her cell, and she wanted to hide it in beauty."

"Do you blame me for sending her here?" Zac asked.

"No." David smiled as he looked across his fields. "She was under the influence of that infiltrator, but she was ultimately exploited because there was a character flaw to exploit. Luckily, you survived, or she would have been a real sinner of Earth."

Zac sighed as he looked out across the flowers, not sure what to say next.

"Come, let me show you what I've done so far," David finally said as he stood up, and Zac was relieved to see him walking with neither a limp nor needing some sort of cane as he had in the vision.

The two toured the fields and the pruned forest that David spent his days tending, mostly talking about things of lesser import. Zac described some of the Races and odd things he had encountered during his visit to the Tower of Eternity, and David spoke about his life on the island and his insights into the various plants he cared for.

The longer they spent together, the more Zac felt that David reminded him of someone else: Abbot Everlasting Peace. Not in their manner of speech, but some sort of mental tranquility that made them attuned to their surroundings.

However, Zac didn't feel that David had become one with the universe and taken the first step on the path of Karma or Samsara, but rather that he had become one with nature. Zac was the one with a mid-tier Nature-aspected Dao Fragment, yet it felt like David was the one who was more in tune with the plants around them.

Zac even asked David about it, but he didn't have any real answer. He only felt that it was a natural result of persistence and being wholehearted in his desire to grow and connect with the plants. David said that he believed that everything had a soul, or at least the potential for birthing one, in this new reality of theirs.

There was an important truth in there, something that Zac felt might one day become extremely important in his own cultivation. The matter of sincerity toward the Dao, something that he felt that he was currently lacking a bit. He had made amazing gains in his understanding of the Dao over the past year, but he wouldn't say that he was sincere in his interest.

He had worked so hard on the Daos in order to get stronger rather than having a desire to delve deeper into the mysteries of the universe. He honestly didn't care all too much about trees or coffins, but rather the power the fragments represented.

But that might become a bottleneck that kept him back in the future. He was just scraping by, reliant on treasures and lucky opportunities to shore up his weakness. Zac knew he would need to find some sort of common ground with his Daos sooner or later, and he believed that taking a cue from David was an important first step.

He slowly released his Dao Field once more, but he let energy naturally seep out of his body as he tried to connect with the fields around him. And he had to admit that David was onto something. It felt like many of the trees were living, and the energy inside them responded to the touch of his Dao.

"You see," David said with a smile, somehow understanding what was going on.

Their stroll soon took them to a small hill by the sea some distance from the teleporter. On top of it stood a beautiful farmhouse surrounded by flowers. It almost looked like something out of a fairy tale, with the glistening sea and rustling plants creating an extremely soothing atmosphere.

However, Zac wasn't able to completely immerse himself in the beauty, as his eyes were trained on something else; his former girlfriend, who was currently tending to a small patch outside one of the windows of the house. She wore a simple dress that somewhat reminded Zac of the Amish, but there were lines of fractals lining the hem.

Zac guessed that it was something that his sister had sent over, as he doubted that the demons would be so accommodating. Hannah looked up when she heard them approaching, a small smile on her face. However, the smile froze on her face when she saw Zac standing next to David. Zac only looked back at her, surprised at how calm he felt inside.

The same couldn't be said for Hannah, as she hurried back inside the building with her head hanging low. The door slammed shut, leaving the two of them outside. Zac was a bit surprised by the violent reaction, though he guessed she might be afraid that he was coming here for revenge.

"I'm sorry." David sighed. "I guess she's not ready to face you just yet."

"It's fine. We can talk another day," Zac said with a shake of his head. "Tell her that I don't carry any resentment for what happened."

It was true that Zac didn't mind not being able to talk things through with his ex. He had mostly come here for David rather than Hannah, as he was a victim while she was ultimately a perpetrator. Seeing that she looked fine was enough for him, as it allowed him to erase the image that had built up in his mind since the Heart Tribulation.

Zac was just about to leave, but David suddenly spoke up after some hesitation.

"Wait, before you go. Hannah wrote you this some time ago, but she never sent it out," he said as he took out a sealed envelope from his Cosmos Sack. "I think she would regret it if you just left like this."

Zac accepted the letter, and a movement in the periphery caught his eye. It was Hannah, who looked at them from the second story of the small house. Their eyes met once more before Hannah sighed and shook her head. She receded further into the room, while Zac turned toward the teleportation array without another word. He felt a sense of serenity, but also some lament as he walked through the fields, the beauty of the island barely registering in his mind.

Peace because he'd finally faced a fear that had been buried deep in his heart, and sadness because it felt like yet one more of his scant few connections to the past had been lost.

24

UPGRADING THE SHIPYARD

Zac looked down at the letter in his hand as he walked the last stretch toward the array, but he didn't open it just yet. He didn't want to ruin the state he was in right now, and he took one last look at the world David had built for himself and Hannah.

David had said something that stuck with him as they walked along the fields. He said that the world had become extremely terrifying, but it had also become far more beautiful. David had chosen to focus on the latter, which was what had turned this island into such an amazing place.

It was true. With the Dao unlocked, the world had fundamentally changed, like a bleak tapestry having been given color and meaning. Wasn't the quest for meaning something that so many struggled with before the integration? Searching for an understanding of the universe and what their place was.

Now it was actually possible.

Over the past year, he had just run from one goal to another, desperately clawing himself forward in his pursuit of power. But that wasn't any way to live. He would eventually crash and burn if things continued this way, or he would at least end up with a shaky understanding of the world around him. It wasn't that he needed to ignore all the things that needed to be done, but he also needed to find some joy in his life.

This was the mindset he needed to remember, along with the

sincerity he needed to nurture as he kept working on his Dao Fragments.

Eventually, he reached the patch of flowers surrounding the teleportation array, at which point his attention finally returned to the letter. He took a deep breath of the enticing mix of aromas before he opened it up, his eyes scanning the three paragraphs inside.

A minute passed before a small smile spread on his face, and Zac released a pent-up sigh as he released a burst of Cosmic Energy. The letter was reduced to ashes as a series of arrays were added to the island. It would take a decently strong E-grade beast a lot of effort to break through the barriers, and Zac would be alerted no matter where on Earth he was.

He had faced the demon in his heart, and Hannah had said her piece. Now their paths had truly diverged, and their Karma was severed, as Abbot Everlasting Peace would have called it. The teleportation array hummed to life, and Zac was gone the next moment.

Zac didn't return to his compound but rather decided to tour his domain for a bit. Visiting Abby had reminded him how long it had been since he had seen the day-to-day operations of his force, and now was as good a time as any to check things out.

He visited the farming islands first, but he was surprised to see that the scale actually hadn't increased over the past months. Zac asked a foreman what was going on, and learned that most of the herb production had been moved to either his own island or the large Spirit Soil Fields on the main continent.

The old farming island was mainly used for growing high-quality crops for the people of Port Atwood now, rather than Spiritual Herbs for cultivation.

It was a step in the right direction in Zac's mind, as it showed that people were not only thinking of surviving and getting stronger. People were no longer living day to day, and didn't just plant what would grow the fastest. They were instead growing rice and all kinds of vegetables to improve their quality of life, while simultaneously providing them with greater profit.

He could see the same energy in the towns that were studded along the archipelago, though some of the verve no doubt came from the fact that the incursions had finally been closed. A massive harbor had sprung up in Refugee Harbor unbeknownst to him, and he could spot dozens of boats sailing out on the sea, likely to catch fish or search for valuable herbs underwater.

All kinds of shops had cropped up as well, real businesses started by people. Strong-looking warriors walked down the streets as well, seemingly returning from monster-hunting ventures. Most of them carried the insignia of Port Atwood, meaning they were part of his army, whereas others looked like free cultivators.

Zac felt that it really wasn't a coincidence that humans littered the Multiverse. They were resilient creatures that could adapt so quickly to such a drastic change in their lives. Or perhaps that was too generous a conclusion. With only around 10% of all humans remaining, one might rather say that those unable to adapt had long perished.

In either case, it felt extremely gratifying to walk through the bustling streets, his real identity hidden with **[Thousand Faces]**. He had already arranged a secondary set of credentials with Adran, a Port Atwood inspector, which gave him blanket access without having to expose his true identity.

He soon continued from the local cluster of towns to the various alien towns he had snatched out of the hands of the invaders. Here, he quickly realized that most of them were little more than outposts that would be hard-pressed to do much more than act as scouts for any threats. He had multiple mines and fields standing empty, with no personnel there to extract the resources.

Port Atwood needed more people. That was the biggest takeaway Zac got after making the rounds. Thankfully, he shouldn't be as hard-pressed to attract talents as when he'd had to sell himself with the help of Sap Trang in the market of New Washington. There should be millions of people willing to relocate to one of his towns.

He finally made a series of jumps that took him to the small outpost at the edge of the uninhabited continent. It had grown to a proper town by now, and Zac saw quite a few Molemen walking the streets. He found the local mayor, a human administrator who worked under Adran, to find out what was going on.

It turned out that Westbound Harbor had turned into a central trade hub in the short time since it was established. It still wasn't possible to freely travel back and forth between the two continents, as there were still the cultists roaming about. Of course, it was not solely a security issue, but also a financial one.

There were still enormous untapped resources in the underworld that were almost worthless to its inhabitants, while they lacked some things that existed in abundance on Pangea. It would be foolish not to take advantage of this opportunity, so Port Atwood allowed people to travel here from the underworld to trade with their own merchants.

These merchants would then head over to the other continent to unload the inventory before returning once more. It was exceedingly lucrative, but Zac snorted when he saw how nervous the mayor started to become the more Zac asked about the situation. A short interrogation later had netted Zac over 200 million Nexus Coins that the administrator had gathered through bribes and skimming Port Atwood's coffers.

It wasn't that much compared to the fortune Zac controlled at the moment, but it was still shocking how much one single person had managed to take for himself in just a few months thanks to the lack of oversight. He really needed to set up a proper organization to take care of issues like this.

The mayor obviously couldn't stay on, so Zac released his aura in the government building, which alerted all the nearby guards. A squad of demons appeared a few seconds later, but they visibly relaxed when they saw it was Zac who had appeared rather than some dangerous threat.

"This guy has proven a bit greedy. Have someone new take over. Remind the next mayor about the value of moderation," Zac said to the guards, who nodded as they sneered at the despondent administrator.

Zac also asked the guards on duty about whether they had found anything of interest on the continent, but there was nothing at all for at least four days' travel inland. There were just endless dunes. However, initial estimations put the continent at at least half the size of Pangea, which meant there was ample room for multiple climate zones.

Someday, he would travel further inland, assisted by his flying treasure, but not today. He had some breathing room before he needed to enter the Mystic Realm, but not to the point that he could map such a massive place. He instead returned to his courtyard before he started walking toward the Creator Shipyard.

This was one of the things Zac had looked forward to since getting the Iliex Shipyard as a reward, though upgrading the shipyard had gone down in priority somewhat since he got his hands on his flying treasure. Equipping his army with proper flying treasures would be a huge boon for his force in general, as long as he could stomach the price.

Zac soon arrived at the shipyard and headed straight into the Liaison's office. Rahm stood behind a reception, like he had been expecting Zac's arrival. Of course, knowing this particular Creator, it was just as possible that he had simply stood there without moving for a couple of days.

"Lord Atwood, congratulations on your evolution," Rahm said with his usual staid expression.

"Thank you." Zac smiled. "Is Foreman Karunthel here?"

"About time you came to visit," a rumbling voice snorted as Karunthel emerged from the depths of the building. "Didn't you evolve almost two weeks ago?"

"I'm sorry. There's just too much for me to do," Zac said with a wry smile. "You don't happen to have a clone technique that can allow me to get more stuff done?"

"Takes a certain aptitude to make the most of clones, and I'm not too sure you have that kind of aptitude, you little brat." Karunthel laughed, not seeming all that miffed about being forgotten.

"Well, it was just a joke," Zac coughed, though he couldn't help but feel irritated about the low evaluation.

It really felt like he would have to work a bit on his image. Everyone seemed to think that he was just an unkillable brute swinging his axe around. Certainly, it was mostly true, but he still wanted to be known for more than just that.

"Are you here about upgrading our facilities, Lord Atwood?" Rahm asked, conveniently giving Zac an opening for the real reason he came.

"Yes, exactly." Zac nodded. "You said I could upgrade the shipyard after I evolved. Is the process automatic, or do I need to pay a price…?"

"Not so fast, kiddo. I am supposed to come up with some sort of quest for you before we can release the good items," Karunthel mused.

"We already have instruct–" Rahm tried to interject, but he was silenced by a wave of one of Karunthel's legs.

"How about this. Being stuck on this desolate rock is causing delays to my experiments. I am lacking some materials that I cannot get my hands on here. Bring me what I require and we'll process the upgrade for you," the foreman decided.

"This is not–"

"This is not an unreasonable request indeed, *thank you, Rahm*, I know," Karunthel said as a dense aura spread out throughout the lobby.

Only then was Zac reminded that the spider golem in front of him was no doubt a D-grade being, and not an Early D-grade warrior either. His aura was far beyond that of the Technocrat captain that almost got him killed, and Zac could barely breathe in front of the suffocating pressure. Rahm didn't look affected at all, keeping his neutral expression.

However, he seemed to relent to the demands of his boss, as he only sighed and took a step back.

"That's better." Karunthel smiled as the pressure disappeared. "Here, get me these things. It might be a bit challenging to gather them all, but I'll add something extra as a reward."

"Get you what?" Zac asked, but he soon understood what Karunthel was talking about as a quest prompt appeared in front of him.

Materials for Karunthel (Unique, Limited): Acquire 100 Kilograms of [Urgarat Flakes], 1 kilogram of [Realm Locus], 1 living [Ferric Worldeater], 1 [Daemonic Manastone]. Reward: Upgrade Iliex Shipyard to Early D-grade. 1 Custom-Designed Early D-grade Vessel. (0/4)

Zac read through the quest, his mouth turning a bit upward, as he felt like he had just gotten a standard fetch quest from an MMO game. The problem was that he didn't recognize a single one of the materials. The last two seemed to be pretty rare, as they only needed one of each.

The demons might have some clues about the last one, but the third item seemed exceedingly troublesome.

"How am I supposed to catch something that eats worlds?" Zac asked with a grimace.

"They're not as dangerous as it sounds." Karunthel laughed. "Well, not the young ones anyway."

"Where can I get these things?" Zac asked, hoping to get a running start on the quest.

"Sorry, can't give any clues. Finding the items is half the challenge," Karunthel said, his smile widening even further.

Zac couldn't help but feel that the Creator foreman was messing with him a bit, but there wasn't much he could do about it. He would have to inquire with someone more knowledgeable, like Brazla or Calrin. The quest seemed daunting, but Zac didn't care. He was more interested in the rewards right now.

"What's this reward at the end?" Zac asked with anticipation.

"It's a reward for completing the quest. We'll be able to provide a flagship vessel for your force, and I'll be in charge of it myself since you're helping me out," Karunthel explained. "It'll have to be based on a Creator model, but I'll modify it to your specifications."

"D-grade vessel. A Cosmic Vessel?" Zac said, his gaze shifting to the sky through a window.

"Don't get your hopes up too high, brat," the foreman snorted. "I only make good things, but it is still an Early D-grade vessel. You will not be able to explore the whole sector in that thing, its speed is too slow. But you will be able to travel between planets in whatever faction this planet ends up in in the future."

"What about the customization?" Zac asked.

"The reward has a set budget," Rahm said. "It cannot excel at everything for the quoted price."

"You could skimp out on the spatial arrays and focus only on offensive capabilities, turning it into a slow-moving mobile fortress. Or you could do the opposite, making a scout vessel that can reach further into the cosmos," the foreman added. "Just figure out what you want to use the thing for, and I'll whip up something nice."

"That's perfect." Zac smiled. "Oh, and I got some puppets?"

"I noticed," Karunthel said with a wide smile. "These things are not our area of expertise, but don't worry. The work will be up-to-par. They'll come over for upgrades on their own any time you break through a minor stage. However, the reward will only last you until Peak D-grade. We will not be able to turn them into Monarch Puppets."

"Peak D-grade?" Zac whistled. "That's still amazing."

"Well, don't get ahead of yourself, brat," Karunthel grinned. "You'll have to reach that stage yourself before the puppets can get there."

"I guess I'll have to keep working on my levels, then."

25
NONLETHAL LETHALITY

A keening cry echoed out across the jungle as Zac swung his axe in one lightning-quick motion, his abyssal eyes keeping track of the streams of life inside the target. However, the massive boar didn't fall apart into two gory slabs from the swing as one might expect, but it rather just seemed enraged.

A deep cut had appeared on its flank, and while it was freely bleeding down on the forest floor, it was far from a grievous wound. With the high Vitality of an E-grade beast, the wound would soon enough heal by itself without any intervention.

"Kill through a nonlethal cut," Zac muttered as he dodged the boar's charge.

He had been walking around the jungles surrounding the former volcano over the past five days, fighting for a couple of hours while spending the rest on cultivation in his cave. He knew that any potential progress before the Mystic Realm closed its doors was limited, and he tried to make the most of it until Kenzie managed to crack open the tunnel.

The most obvious solution he could think of was gaining **[Blighted Cut]**, a skill that would hopefully improve his offensive capabilities in his undead form. He needed a mainstay skill in the vein of **[Chop]**, and this might just be it. Walking around in nature like this would also allow him to bond with nature, for lack of a better word, trying to incorporate the lessons he'd learned from visiting David.

But completing the quest was proving more difficult than expected, though he was making decent inroads. The wound in the boar's side had already turned a sickly dark color, and the beast shook from the pain.

This effect solely came about from infusing his blade with the Fragment of the Coffin, as this was the only method he could think of to complete the quest. He had already tried killing an evolved beast the same way he'd killed Vul, the barghest alpha, all those months ago. He had inflicted a shallow wound that blinded a panther before tricking it into impaling itself on a sharpened log that he had prepared.

He had technically killed it with a single nonlethal cut that time, but the System wasn't impressed. That meant that his initial guess was more likely, that he needed to use his Dao to kill the beast. Considering his class, the most likely suspect was obviously Fragment of the Coffin, and the boar was just the latest experiment.

The wound had already been inflicted, so he didn't swing again. Zac strained his mind to connect to the wound instead, trying to impose his will upon it. It actually worked, and the wound kept getting worse instead of closing itself.

This was a method he had devised after discussing the Dao with his sister. He had already come to terms with the fact that his control over the Dao was pretty bad, and he probably wasn't going to form any Dao Arrays like those Catheya described anytime soon. But he had also realized that there were more ways to make the most of his Mental Energy than just using fine control.

Kenzie had told him of the various ways she used her Dao infusion when fighting. Jeeves had taught her various ways that she could maximize the efficiency of her Cosmic Energy and Dao, doing as much damage as possible for as low a cost as possible. For example, when she shot the fireballs that seemed to bounce from head to head between her targets, it wasn't the skill's work.

Her skill was just a normal fireball, as basic as they came, but it changed with the help of her Seed of Tinder. It only managed to bounce around like that because she controlled her Seed of Tinder to move toward the next target from a distance, and the skill kind of just followed along if she controlled things just right.

Zac never used the Dao like that when it came to [Chop], for example. He just crammed a bunch of Mental Energy into the fractal edge before he launched it at his enemies. But he understood now that he didn't actually need to disconnect his soul from the strike immediately, though it did free up his concentration for other things.

That was what he was doing now with the strike against the boar. He was trying to use the corrosive elements of the Fragment of the Coffin to worsen the condition of the beast, turning a nonlethal strike lethal. He urged his mental energies festering in the wound to spread toward its heart, to enter the bloodstream, to fight off the natural resistance of the animal. Anything that could kill it.

But he suddenly felt a pang in his mind, and the connection was broken. It was the natural resistance of an evolved being that booted the foreign intruder, and Zac knew that the wound would start to close if he didn't do anything.

The attempt was a failure, but Zac still didn't feel disappointed.

He had managed to hold the connection longer than his last attempt, and at a greater distance as well. He was quickly understanding that it wasn't really a matter of control or skill, but it was more akin to learning to use a limb you didn't know you had. A bit more and he would get there.

Then again, Zac understood that maintaining the Dao inside his enemy was only part of the requirements to complete the quest for **[Blighted Cut]**. There was also the issue of causing enough damage, which was as much an issue of understanding his Dao and his target as it was about maintaining its effectiveness.

His first attempt had simply been to keep the wound festering as long as possible in hopes that the beast would succumb that way. However, he quickly learned that maintaining a status quo wasn't enough, and it was a losing battle. The Mental Energy infused into his strike was only so strong, and it would be slowly whittled down by the natural defenses of his target.

So he couldn't just run out the clock, but he needed to proactively push his skill forward. This was where his own limitations came in, as he simply wasn't able to turn the Dao into fine strands that burrowed toward his intended targets like some sort of designer poison. He could only push it in the general direction, just like he pushed the chaotic clouds of energy forward during his Dao Discourse.

Zac was surprised how big an impact this simple action had. The previously shallow cut had quickly turned into serious festering wounds that would ail the beast even after his Mental Energy had been routed.

The boar roared in pain and anger as it charged Zac once more, but a chain shot out from his back and punched a large hole in its forehead. There was not much point in practicing on the same target over and over, as the beasts quickly learned to resist his attempts.

That was fine, as there was no lack of beasts in the enormous forest, and Zac guessed that hundreds broke through to E-grade every day right now. With the cultists gone and the defensive towers destroyed, the only threat to the beasts was the flock of birds from the mountains.

It felt like Earth in general was fast reaching a tipping point, where millions of Peak F-grade beasts would break the shackles of their inferior bloodlines and take the next step on the path of cultivation. The beasts had always been a step ahead of the cultivators since the integration, and the humans were fast approaching Peak F-grade as well.

That was great news for Zac, though killing level 76 beasts wasn't all that beneficial for his cultivation either. At least it provided him with a seemingly endless supply of targets to practice both his Dao and his control over [Love's Bond].

Any Spirit Tool created by the [Divine Investiture Array] was supposed to be a perfect fit for his needs and something that would be able to follow him in his cultivation until the end. He needed to become better at using it and not only relying on his axe.

Doing so would not only improve his overall strength, as using both his Spirit Tools at the same time wasn't a problem, but it might even give him a greater understanding of both his classes and his cultivation path.

It was probably the best he could do for Alea as well. Just hanging around his neck day after day wouldn't challenge her spirit. Spirit Tools grew and were refined through battle, and only through being used could they bring out their full potential.

The boar fell to the ground with a thud, but Zac didn't bother harvesting the meat since it was tainted by him. He only extracted the two tusks, as they might be of use to the craftsmen on Port Atwood, before he shot out a chain that latched on to a tree in the distance. The beast was left where it was, its meat turning into a feast for the other beasts in the region.

The trees flashed past Zac with a dizzying blur as the chains pulled him forward with extreme momentum. He almost felt like a certain superhero as he flew through the forest toward the domain of the next E-grade beast he had marked for target practice.

Using the chains as a mode of transportation was something he had already dabbled with since fighting the dragon, and he was quickly becoming more accustomed to it. With [Love's Bond], he could also use real and extremely sturdy chains rather than the flimsy spectral ones that the cultist Bishop had effortlessly cut apart with his flames.

He still wasn't as fast as when he walked with the help of [Loamwalker], but it was still a huge improvement for his Draugr side, which was previously a slow-moving tank. It looked a bit embarrassing, though, like he was being dragged around through the jungle like a ragdoll. Then again, he had long discarded any semblance of cultivator's dignity in favor of pragmatism, so this was nothing to him.

Zac kept working on his coordination and his strikes like this over the next two days, slowly making progress in how much damage he was causing with a "nonlethal" strike. Better yet, he would no doubt be able to apply these insights to his other Daos and his other class in the future.

Most of his time was still spent in the cultivation cave, sitting inside his Soul Strengthening Arrays while going over his insights. The array pretty much ran on its own by now with how used Zac was getting to the feeling, and he could both ponder on the Dao and work on repairing his pathways while cycling his Mental Energy.

It was a bit like working while being severely sleep-deprived though since the array was siphoning his Mental Energy. He made quite a few mistakes and was forced to redraw the pathways many times, though it was still a lot more efficient to multitask than just sit around waiting for the array to finish.

Another interesting thing he had learned about the array was that he was actually making better progress when swapping his Race in the middle. However, the benefits only appeared when he sat as a Draugr in the life-attuned side and as a human in the death-attuned.

It was like the stark contrasts helped reinforce the effect of the array, which resulted in a larger number of clashes and his soul getting strengthened and purified to a higher degree. One full cultivation procedure still took around ten hours even when using E-grade crystals to power the array, but the improvement he saw while swapping his Races was double a normal circulation.

That meant that he was almost three times as efficient compared to his first try, getting twenty-eight hours' worth of cultivation done in just ten hours. There were probably even greater gains to be had in the future as well, though Zac guessed any future improvements wouldn't come quite as easily.

He had ordered a couple of D-grade attuned crystals from the Sky Gnome to see the effect, but the cost of that was a bit extravagant even for him. It would have to provide a huge benefit to motivate spending over 100 million Nexus Coins every day. For now, he made do with just E-grade crystals, as he was still mostly focusing on short-term benefits and upgrading his skills.

Zac was currently fighting some sort of mutated cat that was as big as a rhino. It looked extremely cute even with its size, with two enormous eyes that stared straight into his. The beast suddenly turned into a blur, and Zac barely had time to block a furious swipe toward his throat by using the flat side of his axe.

The beast unsurprisingly excelled at Dexterity, and Zac tried multiple times to inflict it with a wound without success. It was like trying to hit a cloud, where the cat was just a blur. It was almost as bad as when he'd fought Faceless #9 back in the Tower, though the cat didn't have that man's lethality.

It wouldn't have been hard to kill the thing with the help of **[Deathwish]**, but that wasn't his goal. He instead activated **[Vanguard of Undeath]** and grew to a towering behemoth almost reaching four meters. The transformation added around half a meter to his height after reaching Middle proficiency, while also increasing the thickness of the plating of his Miasmic armor.

More importantly, it increased the power of his taunting effect, and the cat suddenly rammed straight into him by mistake when it tried to pass him by. Zac took the opportunity and delivered a shallow cut in its side, eliciting a pained yowl from the beast. It scrambled out of the way as Zac stood rooted to the ground, keeping his focus on the skill.

Zac pushed the Mental Energy further into its body, like an army performing a blitz to attack its enemy unaware. The natural defenses of the beast were quickly roused, but Zac was like a steamroller as he pushed his energy toward its organs.

This was the one.

2 6
BLIGHTED CUT

The enormous feline had become utterly enraged by Zac's attack, and it even seemed that the shallow wound had emboldened it, making it think that was the limit of Zac's capabilities. It shot forward over and over, its claws trying to rip through his armor. However, the cat couldn't get through the thick plating, allowing Zac to completely focus on his quest.

His abyssal eyes were trained on the nimble form, his eyes clearly seeing the vibrant life force rousing in the beast's body to combat the virulence of his strike. It was like witnessing the clash between white blood cells and a virus with his own eyes. However, he was actually able to impact the battle with his mind.

A small headache throbbed in his head as he pushed his concentration to the max, and it look like a surge of death stormed toward the innards of the beast. The cat stumbled on the ground, thrashing in pain from the invasion. Zac felt adrenaline in his body spike, but he still kept his eyes peeled on the animal.

There was some hesitation in Zac's heart about subjecting such a stunning animal to such cruel treatment. However, Zac quickly pushed those discordant thoughts out of his mind, as he knew that this thing was anything but a docile house pet. He had seen carcasses of almost a hundred animals at the edge of this thing's domain.

Their bodies had been utterly mutilated before they were left to rot. The cat seemed to enjoy hunting and torturing animals for sport, even when it didn't require food. This, along with the fact that it was at least level 85, was why Zac had marked it for death the moment he started trying to complete his quest in earnest.

Most of the kills until now had been for training, whereas Zac saved the beasts that met the requirements of his quest for when he felt he had made enough progress to try for the quest again. He'd found this animal three days ago, and he would immediately have executed it if he hadn't needed some more practice first.

The surprising cruelty that this cat exhibited toward its prey wasn't something unique for this specific E-grade beast, though it was a bit more excessive than most. Beasts seemed to grow more ruthless and aggressive as they evolved, with even herbivores gaining a thirst for blood.

Things on Earth would probably be a bit chaotic over the coming years. A second wave of bloodshed would assault Earth's settlements with bloodthirsty beasts trying to take everyone out through starting beast tides like the ones that the System sometimes conjured as a quest. The forces who had survived until now thanks to not having any close-by incursions to worry about would probably fall by the wayside, while powerful warriors would emerge from the surviving towns.

Things would only calm down when D-grade beast kings emerged, as they were intelligent enough not to mindlessly attack human settlements. They instead set up their kingdoms deep in unclaimed territories, where no humans would dare enter. Even better, they kept their subjects in check, lessening the number of beast tides.

Of course, when the Beast Kings made their move, the result would be far more devastating than any unorganized tide.

Only at that point could Earth be considered to have been fully integrated, when the energy infusion of the planet was finished, and a balance between Races, forces, and beasts had been reached.

For now, there could be no peace with the animals. If Zac didn't take out this beast now, then it would probably target the people who moved to the town next to the volcano. It had already been determined that the volcano itself was a unique natural treasure that produced something that Calrin called an Earth-Fire, a spiritual flame that was extremely beneficial for craftsmen.

Blacksmiths in particular would be able to both increase the quality and quantity of their crafts with the help of the volcano, and it was no coincidence that the zealots had nurtured the massive insignia inside the magma itself. If Zac could set up a bunch of smithies here, then it was just a matter of time before someone like the Craftsman Brazla would emerge within his sphere of influence.

So all potential threats to this area had to die for the future of his force.

Zac pushed his energy more and more, though it felt just as frustrating as during the Dao Discourse. It was like he was trying to move the clouds with his bare hands, and it was slow and arduous work. However, the cat had entered a frenzy from the pain, discarding its survival instincts in favor of taking Zac down with it.

Sparks flew across the area as the beast slammed into his armor over and over, and trees toppled as the air itself was split apart from its attempts to tear him apart. Some puncture wounds even started to appear across Zac's body as the beast managed to bite through his sturdy armor, but Zac didn't care as he did everything in his power to boost the corruption.

Finally, he succeeded in what he had tried so many times before. The corrosive energy managed to take hold in the cat's heart, and its heartbeat rapidly started getting erratic before the whole organ ruptured. The beast yowled at the top of its lungs from the pain before its survival instincts finally overrode its bloodlust.

It tried to flee into the jungle, but it had lost its coordination, as many of its muscles had turned into a rotten mess by now. A deep thud echoed across the jungle before Zac felt a surge of Cosmic Energy. However, he wasn't happy with the result, as the stupid thing had actually gored itself on the trunk of a tree it had felled earlier.

Zac quickly opened his quest screen and sighed in relief when he could confirm that the quest actually had been completed even with the abrupt end to the cat's life. He guessed the System passed him because the thing was just a walking corpse with its heart being ruined, and there was no way it would survive even a minute longer.

He wouldn't look in the mouth of a gift horse, and Zac smiled with anticipation as a fractal appeared on his left forearm.

[Blighted Cut] actually took the exact same spot as [**Rapturous**

Divide], though the skill fractal itself obviously looked completely different. He activated it since he was in a perfect spot to try it out, and he was surprised to find that it was a toggled skill just like **[Deathwish]** or his mental defense skills.

A small but constant stream of energy entered the skill fractal, and he looked around to see what the skill did. He didn't feel stronger at all, and no avatar appeared to fight for him. But he soon heard a corrosive sizzling on the ground, and he found that his axe was slowly dripping a gray liquid that seemed to seep out of the weapon itself.

The scene made him worried for Verun, as the Tool Spirit had shown some apprehension about some of his skills before. However, there were no complaints from the Spirit Tool at all, meaning it wasn't hurt or uncomfortable. In fact, the same was true for when he used **[Vanguard of Undeath]**.

He had been forced to use another weapon before to conjure the massive black bardiche, but after Verun had swallowed the Dragon Core, it had no problem stomaching the corrosive and deathly elements of his skills.

Eager to try the effect of the liquid, Zac quickly walked over to the closest tree and simply pushed the edge toward the bark. The sizzling sound of corrosion quickly emerged from the point of contact, but that was the least of what happened. Ashy-gray tendrils spread across the tree with impressive speed, and it only took four seconds before the tree fell apart.

Only a minute later, the tree was a rotten mess on the ground, with almost nothing remaining intact. Zac wasn't done there, and he transformed **[Love's Bond]** to its backpack form, and four chains emerged like snakes. Zac suddenly felt his Miasmic consumption increasing by a large degree, and he wasn't surprised as he looked at his other Spirit Tool.

The whole coffin had gained a temporary upgrade, just like how Verun had grown into a bardiche. **[Love's Bond]** still looked like a coffin, but instead of being child-sized, it turned into a rugged box that reached almost three meters tall. It was a lot wider as well, and it completely blocked his whole back like a turtle shell.

Zac had already tried it out before, and he knew that a similar effect would happen when he used the weapon in its shield form. The difference wasn't as startling there, as **[Love's Bond]** was able to adjust its size to match his increased stature by itself. It only gained another protective layer from **[Vanguard of Undeath]**.

The increase in Miasmic consumption obviously didn't come about from this change, but rather that he had activated **[Blighted Cut]**. Each of the chains was dripping with the corrosive liquid all along their length, though the links themselves weren't hurt in the slightest. Each of the chains already contained a hint of corruption, but even Zac felt some trepidation when he looked at the chains now.

Even he would probably be in some danger if an enemy came at him with this kind of setup.

Just attacking a tree was obviously not enough to get a proper gauge of the limits of his new skill, and he spent the next hour like a god of death in the jungle. Anything he targeted was turned into rotting goop before he moved on. It utterly ruined the bodies of the beasts, meaning Zac probably shouldn't use it when hunting for valuable body parts.

Zac had first thought he had gained a supercharged version of his Fragment of the Coffin, but he quickly learned that wasn't the case. He couldn't combine **[Blighted Cut]** with skills like **[Deathwish]**, **[Profane Seal]** or **[Winds of Decay]**, though it was fine together with **[Vanguard of Undeath]** and **[Unholy Strike]**.

The skill provided him with a way to deal real damage while skills like **[Deathwish]** and **[Profane Seal]** restrained his enemies.

As for the lethality of the skill, it went without mention. Nothing under E-grade could withstand a single strike, even when he didn't empower the corrosion even further with the Fragment of the Coffin. A simple scrape when lashing out with **[Love's Bond]** was enough to condemn them to a bout of excruciating pain before they died.

The only animal that survived more than half a minute was the massive rhinoceros Zac was currently fighting, but that wasn't because of it having some sort of immunity to his skill. He had caught it with two chains of **[Love's Bond]**, keeping it in place. It had tried to run the moment it saw Zac, but it was currently utterly unable to move.

Zac had just attacked anything he came across until now, but he wanted to see the effect of the skill while just restraining an enemy. Zac quickly realized that the effect was clearly worse when he didn't draw blood. There was still a sizzling sound across the rhino's thick hide, but it didn't immediately turn into a pile of rotting meat. It meant that the skill acted more like a venom than an acid, which had an important distinction.

However, that wasn't the real surprise, as Zac felt a startling feedback from the skill the moment the beast was caught. Zac followed his instincts and infused the skill with more Miasma, and his eyes widened when three blades of the corrosive liquid appeared out of nowhere around the rhino, each shooting into the beast from a different direction before it had a chance to react.

They each hit the animal simultaneously, and Zac gaped when he saw that the animal didn't even have time to cry out in pain before it had turned into a black pool of goop on the ground. The blades had not only cut the animal apart into six pieces, but they had infused every piece with a terrifying amount of corrosive liquid.

The blades had appeared for less than a second before they were gone, and Zac barely had time to see them. However, he still had goosebumps on his arms from the terrifying aura they emitted. It felt like just a graze from those things could kill just about anything.

It was a truly sinister skill. Not only did it continuously inflict enemies with a shocking virulence, it even had some sort of execution that only worked when the target was trapped. Perhaps it was a hint of what the future held for his Fetters of Desolation class. Zac quickly looked inward at the skill fractal, and he wasn't surprised that the skill went on cooldown after activating the final strike. Not even the passive effect worked any longer, meaning Zac would have to be careful about using the execution preemptively in the future.

The skill itself wasn't as flashy as [**Rapturous Divide**], but Zac was still very happy with the result. It was extremely lethal, which shored up one of his weaknesses in his current class. He was lacking in offense, which turned every match into a drawn-out slugfest. Between his coffin and his new skill, he would probably be able to take out E-grade enemies even faster as a Draugr compared to as a human.

His human form was still superior to his Draugr side in large-scale combat, as he didn't have any way to properly attack large hordes with [**Blighted Cut**]. The situation was fine with him, as he had always felt it a good idea to allow each class to have its own specialty apart from just being based on different elements.

Zac had finally reached his goal of completing his class quest, but he still didn't leave the jungle. He had spent the last ten days almost solely as a Draugr, but he had some things to do here in his human form as well. He had already felt that spending some time in this jungle as a human might benefit some of his skills, and that idea had only become stronger after meeting David.

So Zac swapped over to his Edge of Arcadia class and started clearing out a perimeter around the volcano. However, he only had time to battle for less than thirty minutes before someone tried to contact him through his communication crystal.

"Are you free? Thea and Billy are here; they need your help," Joanna said through the crystal.

27
WAR COUNCIL

"What? Are Thea and Billy okay?" Zac asked with worry.

"They're fine. They arrived a while ago, and tried to enter the inheritance. But the Tool Spirit is blocking them, and not even your sister could change its mind," Joanna explained. "He's also being a bit… like himself."

Zac groaned and took out his flying treasure, quickly returning to the volcano. Joanna was waiting for him there, and they teleported to his private courtyard, as it was closest to the Towers of Myriad Dao. However, he barely had time to exit the teleportation house before he saw a herculean form appear in front of the Dao Repository.

It was Billy, who must have evolved his skill. He was almost as tall as some of the smaller towers, reaching roughly fifteen meters into the air. His club looked like something used to smash mountains, the skull on its end having a diameter of at least five meters. Worry gripped Zac's heart as he activated [**Loamwalker**], leaving Joanna behind.

Had the Tool Spirit annoyed Billy to the point that he was gearing up to destroy the whole Dao Repository?

It wasn't that he was worried about the repository itself. It was probably a Peak D-grade Spirit Tool and nothing that Billy would be able to destroy no matter how much he wanted to. He was more worried about the retaliation from an insane Tool Spirit. There were D-grade golems inside, from what he had gathered, meant to be the challenge to open up the higher floors.

What if Brazla released them upon the town as punishment?

"HAHA, BILLY WINS!" A booming roar echoed across half of Port Atwood as Billy jumped high into the air while stretching his weapon toward the sky.

Between the jump and the length of the club, they reached a bit higher than the tallest towers, and the whole square shook when the giant landed again.

"Stupid golden ghost thinks he can be bigg–"

Billy didn't get any further before Brazla's towering form appeared in full splendor above the Towers of Myriad Dao, accompanied by his signature golden radiance. The avatar was well over a hundred meters tall, and it looked down upon Billy and Port Atwood like a god standing in judgment.

"An ant dreaming of matching the sky," a rumbling voice echoed out across the area, and Zac's eyes widened when he saw that Brazla was about to blast Billy with one of his lightning bolts.

"WAIT!" Zac roared as he appeared in front of the towering giant. "Calm down. What is going on here?!"

Billy looked down with surprise, and he started to shrink again after throwing Brazla a glare.

"Golden boy said Billy and Thea were small, so Billy proved him wrong. He still needs a good thwonkin'," the giant snorted.

Zac wryly smiled before he turned to Thea, who had appeared close by as well.

"You weren't lying about the Tool Spirit," she said, a few veins popping out on her forehead. "He makes Big Blue feel like a true gentleman."

"I know," Zac said with some resignation. "What's the problem here?"

"These two talentless ants tried to enter the trial without adult supervision," a haughty voice echoed out from the gates as the massive head in the sky disappeared.

The gates swung open the next moment, and Brazla, along with an exasperated Kenzie walked out.

"I already told you Thea and Billy would come to take the trial, and you said that you didn't care." Zac sighed. "What's changed?"

"That was before I saw what kind of wretched beings you wanted to waste the Great Brazla's gifts upon. Why don't I just send two pigs into the inheritances that my creator so arduously gathered? The effect will be the same," Brazla snorted as his back bent further and further back until the Tool Spirit was almost looking straight up into the sky.

Zac inwardly groaned when he saw that Brazla was in his most haughty mode today for some reason. He only took that insane power pose when he started to refer to himself in third person and his annoyance factor maxed out. Zac knew he could probably force the thing to make way if he wanted, but he was afraid that Brazla would mess with the trials if he did something like that.

Simultaneously, he could feel killing intent leaking from Thea, and Billy's brows were crunching together until they almost formed a unibrow.

"How can anyone enter the eyes of the Great Brazla?" Kenzie cajoled from the side. "We are just scraping by on this desolate rock, trying to glean a fraction of the wisdom from the Great Sage. Surely the Great Brazla wouldn't hold back on this little bit of wisdom? I am sure my brother would improve your surroundings as a thank-you for your magnanimity."

The Tool Spirit froze, and he slowly returned to a normal standing position, his eyes slowly turning toward Zac.

"What do you want me to build?" Zac sighed.

"The Great Brazla has noticed your little spectral servant scurrying about lately, moving trees and planting flowers. His efforts are barely passable, and this great sage will allow him to create a natural spirit-gathering formation around this domicile," Brazla said as though he were doing Zac a favor.

"You want a Spirit Gathering Array?" Zac said in confusion. "Why?"

Brazla might have acted like a cultivator, but he couldn't actually cultivate. Increasing the density of the Cosmic Energy in his surroundings wouldn't help him in the slightest, and it would just make the direct area around the repository slightly worse, as the energy had to come from somewhere. However, he immediately regretted his question when he saw the Tool Spirit gearing up for some insane tirade.

"Never mind. A Natural Spirit Array, right? I'll have Triv set one up as soon as he returns from his mission," Zac said. "So, they can enter now?"

"Fine, though the Great Brazla still feels that his gifts are wasted on these two. At least the little bird," Brazla lamented. "The dumb brute seems to have found the resting place of his ancestor, so it might be a bit more apropos. Well, the Great Brazla is a gracious master and an even more gracious host. Enter, and witness a glimpse of greatness."

"Wow," Thea said as she passed through the gates, and Zac inwardly sighed again when he saw she was still fuming.

"I'm sorry, Billy," Zac said to Billy, who still glared at Brazla. "He is a bit mean, but you can be the bigger man here and let it go."

"Mama always said to forgive those who don't know better," the giant said with a snort as he entered as well. "So Billy will forgive the stupid ghost."

"You look better," Kenzie commented from the side. "I heard from Ilvere you looked a bit–"

"Disgusting," Brazla cut in. "You should understand it reflects poorly upon the Great Brazla if you walk around town looking like a burnt piece of dung. Have you no shame? At least you waited to heal up before you dared present yourself in front of me."

"Well, if you unlocked the E-grade skills, I wouldn't be in such a wretched state after every battle," Zac snorted.

"You're welcome to try the trial if you're tired of living," Brazla said with disinterest as he conjured a mirror, blocking him from seeing Zac. "That's better."

Zac rolled his eyes as he looked away. He really wanted to access the skills locked away in the repository, but he wasn't ready. The trial to open up the second floor was to defeat at least one Half-Step D-grade Golem, meaning someone at the same level as Anzonil, the Array Master he'd met during the Hunt.

If it were just a Peak E-grade Golem, then he would probably have tried his luck, as he was somewhat confident in taking it out as long as he went all out. However, the D-grade was a quantitative leap that far surpassed that between F- and E-grade, and he didn't want to burn his chance. He only had one shot at the trial, and if he failed, then he would have to wait for one of his subjects to get the job done.

Certainly, a Half-Step D-grade Golem was ultimately not a true D-grade golem, but it should still be far more powerful than a Peak E-grade warrior. Zac was currently hoping to reach the point where he could challenge the trial before he left Earth to continue his cultivation so that he could arm himself with a few additional skills.

But for now, he would have to make do with the things that were already unlocked.

Thea stood in the distance, gazing up at the enormous statue of the Blade Emperor. His face was obscured by a wide-brimmed hat, but her focus was rather on the large blade that was stabbed into the ground in front of him. It radiated a terrifying sharpness, eclipsing the insights of Zac's own Dao even though it was just a statue. Of course, the sharpness was hollow without true meaning, just like everything else in this place.

The Marshall scion clearly wasn't in any mood to stay here, as she flashed away after taking a few calming breaths.

"STUPID STATUE MAN! I'LL THWONK YOU THIS TI–" a roar suddenly echoed out through the hall.

Zac turned toward the source of the commotion, only to see Billy flying toward the head of the statue depicting the Titan. However, Billy was thankfully swallowed by the inheritance teleporter mid-flight before he could do any damage.

"What in the world…" Kenzie muttered from the side, and Zac started to wonder if he had made a mistake letting Billy enter that place.

"Can you see what's going on inside their trials?" Zac asked as he turned back toward the Tool Spirit.

"Perhaps I do; perhaps I don't. The Heavens' secrets are not so easily divulged," Brazla said, trying to adopt a mysterious air, but only came off as condescending.

"Well, can you tell me about the Blade Emperor and the Titan? What kind of people were they?" Zac asked.

"The Titan was a dumb brute who kept causing trouble. He came to my master to have him forge a set of defensive treasures," Brazla said. "The small mountain of muscles you brought should do just fine."

Zac sighed in relief, as he felt like Billy and that guy would be two peas in a pod. Besides, someone like that would probably not have a convoluted trial. His relief only lasted until a weird smile spread across Brazla's face.

"As for the Blade Emperor… A lunatic who married his sword," Brazla snorted before he shot Zac a mocking glance. "Be careful you don't end up like him. He was a friend of my master and a talented swordsman, but he died a laughingstock, and his wife was sold at an auction soon after."

Zac coughed and didn't deign to comment on the Spirit Tool's snide remark, and he walked out before the Tool Spirit had time to make any more remarks about Alea.

Since Zac was back in Port Atwood, he felt that he might as well head over to the Soul Strengthening Array for the day, waiting for the two to come out. He had spent the better part of a day inside, though their trials could take anything from a few hours to a few days. It was up to whatever the creator of the inheritance had decided, and Brazla wasn't any help there.

However, Kenzie held him back before he had a chance to walk away.

"Wait. I was about to call you anyway," Kenzie said.

"What's wrong?" Zac asked as he stopped in his tracks.

"Nothing. We just got a message from Nonet before. They asked if you could join the Zhix War Council for a meeting tomorrow?" she asked.

"Of course. Are the jammers completed?" Zac asked.

"They're up and running since a few days ago." Kenzie nodded and took out the three black pillars. "Do you want to prepare the armies?"

"Have the elite squads get ready," Zac said after some thought. "We shouldn't need the whole army for these fights. We'll only target one hive at a time, and there's no lack of Zhix warriors who can make up the numbers."

Kenzie nodded in understanding as Zac put away the jamming arrays. He had almost forgotten about the matter of the Zhix due to his hectic schedule over the past weeks. But it looked like he had run out of time to play around in the jungle. It was a bit of a shame, but he still had accomplished his main goal over there, and he could work on his skills in other places as well.

However, he didn't know how long he would be gone after joining the Zhix war chariot, so he needed to finish up with his other tasks here in Port Atwood first.

"Oh, and Calrin said he found something you were looking for," Kenzie added.

"Really? Already?" Zac said, and he immediately changed his plans.

He had visited Calrin about the Shipyard Upgrade quest just a week ago, and things had looked a bit bleak at first outlook. Even the knowledgeable Sky Gnome had only heard of half of the required materials, and they were the two most common ones.

But had the little gnome suddenly come through for them and actually gathered the items ahead of schedule? It should either be that or he had finally unsealed and cleansed the hundreds of Cosmos Sacks Zac had claimed after the battle outside the Tower of Eternity.

In either case, he was about to gain a windfall, and his steps got quicker and quicker as he walked toward the Thayer Consortium.

28

SINCERITY

What an asshole.

She knew that Zac had warned her of this Brazla, but she was still fuming after the encounter. However, she knew that part of the reason she got so angry was that the words of the Tool Spirit were getting to her a bit. The image she had nurtured of herself had been cracking over the past weeks.

Waking up in the Tutorial had been horrifying, but also exhilarating. Her life had lacked any drive and goals before, with everything she could dream of readily handed to her. But she suddenly found herself at the edge of life and death, and she had *excelled*. The pixies had called her a once-a-millennium genius, and her performance compared to the other Tutorial takers echoed that remark.

She even had the [Apex Trainee] title to prove it. Not a single human on Earth had performed better than she had. But was that enough?

Zachary Atwood had initially crushed her confidence with his monstrous power, but she had eventually come to terms with the fact that some people were just beyond comprehension. However, her genius' halo kept taking one hit after another as the months passed. There was Inevitability, who could only make her feel despair, then the undead, and finally, the cultists.

She had pushed herself beyond her limits, but it wasn't enough.

Were the pixies just humoring her? Or was the title of a millennial genius on a godforsaken planet just worthless? So hearing Brazla utterly disregard her like that had dug at those insecurities, and those insecurities had turned to anger. However, that anger was quickly exchanged with vigilance as she appeared in the inheritance trial.

Just what had happened here?

It looked like she had arrived in a compound where a battle had just taken place. She stood in a massive courtyard full of training equipment, but the hundreds of dead bodies were a clear indication that something had gone terribly wrong if this was just an exercise. The corpses were fresh, and the pools of blood still hadn't dried out. However, there were no sounds of fighting anywhere, meaning that the battle was over.

It had obviously been a one-sided slaughter as well, as every single corpse wore the same type of robes. It was likely a sword sect, judging by the weapons in their hands and the insignia covering their backs. She stood frozen for a couple of seconds until she gritted her teeth and walked over to the closest corpse.

This was a test, and she couldn't show any weakness. Wasn't part of the reason she decided to undergo this trial early to shake off her weaknesses, both mental and physical, and regain her momentum? A little bit of carnage was nothing special any longer.

Thea turned over the corpse and inspected the wounds, and she could immediately confirm that she had been killed with one extremely precise cut. Half her throat and her jugular were cut, and an extremely sharp energy emanated from the wound. A stabbing pain prickled her eyes just looking at the wound, and she hurriedly looked away to avoid being injured.

Suddenly, a hidden killing intent assaulted her senses, and she didn't hesitate to shoot out **[Petalstorm]** preemptively. However, she only saw a flash of light as her weapon was intercepted and thrown back to her side.

"A hidden blade," a tired voice drifted over. "Who are you? You are not a conjuration by my demons, but you are definitely not one of that bastard's descendants either."

Thea naturally understood whom the voice belonged to, but she still didn't dare to move over. That killing intent hadn't been fake. However, she at least spotted the source of the voice, sitting with his back toward one of the few still-standing sections of a building.

"I am Thea Marshall. I am not sure what has happened to the original creator of the Towers of Myriad Dao. It was awarded by the System to a friend of mine, and he gave me the opportunity to come here," Thea said, not hiding anything.

"Towers of Myriad Dao," the man snorted. "That's Brazla alright. So that old goat croaked before he could sire any descendants. A shame, but that's what you get when looking for love in the wrong places. No wonder that insufferable Tool Spirit has had the guts to break into my sanctum."

Thea didn't know how to respond to that, and the man seemed content to let the silence stretch out. She cursed her lacking conversational abilities, but the silence at least let her observe the cultivator in front of her. It was a humanoid male, but his skin had a yellowish tint while his eyes were amber with a thin slit, like those of an alligator.

His build was quite slender, but he still felt extremely muscular. It almost looked like his forearms were covered in steel wires. As impressive as his physique was, her eyes couldn't help but turn to the massive sword in his grip. Or it would perhaps be more apt to say that he cradled it like it was his only source of comfort, with both his legs and arms entwining the blade in an embrace.

Thea's mouth opened and closed a few times, and she was unsure what would happen next. Zac hadn't really explained what would happen inside, true to his laconic self. He'd just said that there would be a trial to pass, but it was up to the masters to design those trials.

"I am hoping to lear–" Thea finally said, but she was cut off as the swordsman suddenly appeared three meters away from her, the large sword in his hand.

"Live or die," he simply said as he lazily swung his sword.

It looked like the Blade Emperor was barely putting any effort into the swing, but it felt like the whole universe was splitting apart to Thea as the sword approached. Her instincts were screaming at her to retreat, to activate her life-saving skill. However, a sense of stubbornness bloomed in her heart.

This was a test. She knew it. This was the kind of pressure that guy had endured over and over as he pushed forward, and conquering those obstacles was what had allowed him to push far beyond anyone else on Earth. She couldn't keep dancing around, balancing progress with the burdens of her family.

She wouldn't retreat any longer; she didn't want to be left behind. She wanted to walk forward with confidence as well. Thea sent out a mental command, causing [Petalstorm] to return to its original form, a slender rapier just over a meter long. She rarely used this form any longer due to the convenience of it splitting apart, but a bunch of miniature blades wouldn't cut it here.

The blade-master didn't use any skill in his swing, so she wouldn't either. She instead infused her Daos and her conviction into the strike as she met blade with blade, putting it all on the line. It felt like she was trying to keep the whole universe at bay, and her arms were instantly covered with cuts.

But she held on, refusing to relent to the strike. She wouldn't give in even if she was turned into ribbons.

"Rare class... Tempest Blade..." the Blade Emperor muttered as he looked at her, not sharing her plight in the slightest. "Passable technique... Above average Strength... Decent control of your Dao... However..."

The monumental pressure disappeared the next moment, and her own swing was simultaneously canceled. Thea's hands were shaking from the experience, feeling that she had just narrowly escaped death. This was a true D-grade Hegemon, completely different from anything she had encountered before.

Just a thoughtless swing contained the truth of the sword itself, making her Dao Braiding look like a child's plaything. Her emotions were in turmoil as well from the Blade Emperor's comments. Her confidence had soared after hearing one positive comment after another, but that "however" had felt like a cold shower.

Was she just a nobody after all?

"Is there something wrong?" Thea asked, her heart beating furiously. "I am willing to learn and improve."

This was the most powerful being she had met thus far, even if it was just a fragment of an old cultivator. Any insight he could provide would probably be worth more than a dozen battles or spending years in her library.

"Why did you come to me if you mess about with the elements? I am the Blade Emperor, not the Wind Emperor. My path is one of purity," he said as his aura exploded, and Thea was forced a step back from the pressure. "What is your goal? Where does your heart lie?"

Her eyes widened as his aura towered toward the sky, but what really startled her was its shape. His aura was actually a perfect copy of his sword, though thousands of times larger. Could an aura actually take a shape like that? He was truly the Blade Emperor.

"I-I just want to become stronger. I want to hit faster, kill my enemies before they can kill me or my family. I want to become more powerful to stand at the peak. I don't want to be a nobody," Thea said, the words pouring out of her mouth as she bared her inner thoughts. "I attained the Seed of Gale during the Tutorial and incorporated it in my blade. Was that a mistake? I heard I could fuse it with my Seed of Sharpness into a speed-based Fragment of the Sword."

The Blade Emperor didn't immediately answer, but his eyes bored into hers. Even his pupils felt like two swords under his aura, but she shoved away any hesitation as she stared back with steely eyes.

"Well, you are passable, I guess. You can call me Irei, and this is Silene," he said as he caressed his sword, and the terrifying pressure disappeared the next moment.

"What? Just like that?" Thea said with wide eyes before she had time to correct herself. "I mean–"

She lost her train of thought mid-sentence as she noticed that the surroundings had changed, the battlefield replaced with a run-down courtyard located deep in some mountain range.

"I didn't leave many things in this inheritance, but the things I left all hold tremendous value," the Blade Emperor said with a solemn expression.

Six blades rose out of the ground the next moment before they lined up in the air in front of her. Thea's eyes lit up when she saw the exquisite weapons. Each of them emitted both spirituality and power that far eclipsed her **[Petalstorm]**.

They exuded quality, and when Thea prodded the weapons, she even felt a sense of spirituality in every single one. She had already learned that her own weapon was barely of passable grade, with neither an attunement nor any spirituality. Its future would be limited, and she had already started looking for ways to acquire something better.

This was exactly why she had chosen this inheritance: the chance to gain a weapon that could stay with her as she took the next step on her path of cultivation.

"Children, come out," Irei said, and Thea's eyes widened when six projections emerged.

She couldn't believe that every single one of the six weapons had such spirituality that their Tool Spirit could emerge, though they were just small, hazy projections. She believed she had a decent understanding of Spirit Tools thanks to Big Blue, and these swords should only be Early E-grade. It meant that their potential was even greater than she had anticipated.

However, she didn't quite understand what Irei meant by children, as they looked nothing of the sort. For example, the largest sword, a massive two-hander that reeked of bloodlust, conjured what looked like a small devil. Another Tool Spirit looked like a feline predator that would probably turn into the apex predator in any forest it was placed in.

There was even one that just looked just like the sword itself, though its colors were inverted. She quickly realized that there was a correlation between the spirits and their weapons like they embodied the way the weapon was meant to be used. Her eyes moved back and forth between the six Spirit Tools, and she tried to understand which one was the best for her path.

"You can choose to leave here with one of my children, or you can choose to leave empty-handed. It is up to you," Irei said as he looked at the hovering swords, and Thea felt there was true love in his eyes as he looked at each one of them.

She soon enough discarded three weapons that were clearly incompatible with her class and fighting style, and also the odd inverted Tool Spirit. Both of the two remaining ones looked quite strong, especially one that had a Tool Spirit that looked like a gemstone with a trapped lightning bolt. The other weapon looked a lot more nondescript.

It was a thin and slightly curved scimitar made from an elegant blue metal that would blend into the sky. Its Tool Spirit was a fluffy cloud that continuously changed between a small thundercloud and an innocuous ball of cotton. The weapon didn't look as intricate as the crystalline weapon, and the Tool Spirit was probably the least imposing one.

However, her eyes kept coming back to it, and she felt some sort of connection to it.

"You've chosen Aigale, I see, or [Storm's Break] as the original creator called it. It seems you understand yourself well enough; only Aigale and Naral, to a lesser degree, are suitable for you," Irei said as the other weapons disappeared. "She is my eighty-fourth adopted child, and she gained incipient spirit after we witnessed a storm of such ferocity that a D-grade force was killed to the last man. Aigale is meant to dance among the clouds and strike without warning like a sudden clap of thunder."

The other swords disappeared, and Thea eagerly grabbed the scimitar and cut a small wound on her hand to bind the Spirit Tool to herself. However, the moment she felt a sense of connection to [Storm's Break], she also found herself trapped in a storm of extremely sharp energies. She looked over at the Blade Emperor, but he only had eyes for his own weapon.

"I have fulfilled my bargain with that old bastard, but our business is yet not done. Seeing a woman with a fickle heart brings up some bad memories," the Blade Emperor muttered as a terrifying killing intent started leaking from his body.

"Fickle heart?" Thea said, some anger blossoming in her heart even when she felt herself being under tremendous pressure from the sword energies around her. "I've never messed around with anyone's feelings."

"Not toward men. Toward your weapon, your true companion," the Blade Emperor grunted with disdain. "What if you treat my daughter in the same manner as that little thing you are so ready to discard? Wouldn't she lead a miserable existence if that was the case?"

"What do you want me to do?!" Thea screamed as she was left with a dozen deep gashes in just seconds.

She tried using her Dexterity to dodge the spiritual blades, but they were simply everywhere. Forcing her way out was impossible as well, as the intensity of the blades just increased as she tried to exit the sphere. She would perish long before getting out.

"Prove your sincerity toward the sword. That is the only way for a weakling like you to leave my Blade Domain," the Blade Emperor said. "Become one with the sword or die. It is up to you."

29
CLUES

Had the Sky Gnome actually managed to get his hands on one of the four materials required for the Shipyard Upgrade? If it actually was the case, then it would most likely be the first one, the **[Urgarat Flakes]**. It was a very rare form of metal, but it was not nearly as rare as the other things Karunthel had asked for.

As to why the metal was so rare, it was because it was not a natural element you could find in a mine, but rather something produced when a certain stone beast evolved to D-grade. The beast was called an **[Urgarat Crawler]**, and it was a creature that only lived on certain earth- or metal-attuned planets.

When it was ready to form its Beast Core and evolve to D-grade, it first created a thick cocoon from the materials it found in the ground. These materials were in turn transformed by the heavy Dao fluctuations that were released from its evolution. One of the most common mutations was the **[Urgarat Flakes]**, an extremely sturdy alloy.

It was, in other words, something you could only stumble upon by chance. You might be able to keep the crawlers as domesticated animals, but the value of the materials didn't make up for the cost of nurturing a beast all the way to the D-grade, so no one wasted their time on such an unprofitable venture.

The Sky Gnome did find the second material, the **[Realm Locus]**, in one of his large encyclopedias as well, though the information was limited. It was an organic gemstone that grew in places with a lot of spatial activity. That meant that they were mostly found inside Mystic Realms, and they contained a small amount of sealed space-time.

The gnome guessed that Karunthel wanted the gem in order to improve some spatial array for either a weapon or space flight. However, the supply of [Realm Locus] was even worse than that of [Urgarat Flakes], and the demand was a lot higher, as things with Spatial Attunement had a lot of uses.

There were barely any Nexus Crystals attuned with the Dao of Space in the Zecia Sector either, so people had to make do with other materials. The [Realm Locus] was one of the few Spatial Materials available that was stable enough to be used in crafting, making it highly desirable.

Things only got worse from there, as Calrin couldn't make heads or tails of the last two materials, and they were forced to send an inquiry to an intelligence agency in the end. That could probably only mean that they were even harder to acquire.

The quest that had seemed easy enough to complete at first glance had quickly turned into an arduous task, and the Sky Gnome had already indicated that Zac would most likely need to find most of the materials himself. That obviously couldn't be done on Earth, but rather required him to travel to places where there was a chance of the items appearing.

Now, just a week later, Calrin was already calling for him, and Zac couldn't help but get his hopes up. There were just four materials he needed to find, after all, so getting just one was a huge step in the right direction. Of course, it was more likely that he had simply gotten the intelligence reports back than the materials themselves.

Zac wanted to find out what was going on as quickly as possible, but he still found himself stopping to admire the fundamental transformation the consortium had undergone since arriving at Earth. The huge compound had looked like a condemned city block where not even beggars would stay before, but now domineering structures stood in front with opulent mansions hiding in the back.

There were also four shops now instead of one, each focusing on their respective wares.

The largest one sold armor and weaponry, most of it made by Port Atwood craftsmen themselves, and the second store contained miscellaneous tools for cultivators along with day-to-day items. There was everything from crude talismans to Cosmos Sacks to all sorts of tools required by noncombat classes.

The next store was natural treasures, where you could buy herbs and pills, along with a limited supply of Nexus Crystals. The store also bought most sorts of herbs as well, and from what Zac heard, they actually bought more than they sold. They also sold some foodstuffs in the store, though most foods were still sold in the open square by the farmers themselves.

The final store was the smallest one, but also the most exclusive. Only VIP clients of the consortium could enter, and it was the place with the most valuable items of every type. This was the store that Zac entered, and he was quickly shown to the highest floor by one of the clerks. Calrin appeared a minute later, sporting a dapper suit that no doubt was made from Spiritual Materials.

The somewhat impoverished image of the Sky Gnome was long gone, replaced by a man looking like a titan of industry. Of course, the effect was pretty limited with his diminutive size.

"Have you found one of the materials?" Zac asked without preamble.

"Alas, no." Calrin sighed. "Though I believe I will receive word from the intelligence agency soon enough."

"So why did you call me here?" Zac sighed as he sat down.

"You've put in quite a few orders with me apart from the four materials, remember?" Calrin smiled as he took out a crystal. "I called you about this."

Zac accepted the crystal with some confusion and infused it with some energy.

A long list of materials appeared, followed by an in-depth guide on how to create a powder that should be applied to one's body.

"[**Bone-Forging Dust**]?" Zac read aloud with confusion before he looked up at the Sky Gnome. "What is this stuff?"

"It's a Race-improvement formula, see how the materials differ from anything else you've seen?" Calrin explained.

Zac took a second look at the materials, and something suddenly dawned on him. Not a single one of the items was a herb. It was all bones from ferocious beasts, stones, or metals. It was extremely different from the medicinal baths that the people of Port Atwood were using, as those were almost exclusively using various herbs that they grew in the Spiritual Soil.

"It's unfortunately not a recipe for the undead. Those things are just impossible to buy, it seems." Calrin sighed. "But I came across this recipe when I tried to come up with a solution for you. I believe your problems might occur because your dead body clashes with the life- and nature-attunement in the plants of a medicinal bath. But what if there's nothing like that in the mixture?"

"So you think I won't have the same reaction with this new recipe." Zac nodded in understanding.

"Even better, you possessed more than half the materials after killing beasts in all four directions, including the most annoying component to get," Calrin said before he produced a long, shimmering horn. "And I have already acquired the rest."

It was the [Star Ox Horn] that Zac had left with Calrin long ago in hopes of finding some use for it. Back then, it was one of the most valuable things in his possession, but it had quickly been thrown aside for actually precious treasures like the [Pathfinder Oracle Eye] and the [Divine Investiture Array].

He had honestly forgotten about it, but it turned out it was doubly lucky he hadn't sold the opportunity to Average for a measly 1 billion Nexus Coins. It also wasn't too surprising that the horn was used for a recipe like this, as Calrin had already found out that the item was related to evolutions. Zac felt that the gnome's idea was feasible, and it was definitely worth trying.

The worst thing that could happen was that he slightly poisoned himself once more, but he was already used to that.

"You should know this, though. The only reason I managed to buy a full recipe on the cheap was that it is not too impressive. It is just one notch better than the dirt-cheap concoctions we are preparing for your army, but its cost is well over a hundredfold," Calrin said. "And it is supposed to hurt pretty bad. So bad that it's actually possible to gain a few points in Endurance from using it."

"It's worth some pain if I can get the benefits from it. As for cost, it shouldn't matter either. How are we looking? Is everything unsealed and uncursed or whatever?" Zac asked.

He had waited a long time now to get a proper look at the small mountain of items he had absconded with after his massacre outside the Tower of Eternity. He had done one preliminary check just before heading over to the undead incursion, but he had handed over the rest of the sacks that he and Ogras had collected to the Sky Gnomes later.

The demon probably still held on to some of the benefits he had siphoned off the various scions while Zac met with Catheya, but most of the loot was in the Cosmos Sacks and Spatial Rings they had taken off the bodies of the victims. However, he worried about hidden threats such as Karmic Links or even booby traps, something that was apparently not too uncommon, so he had hired Calrin and his ilk to cleanse them.

Truthfully, utilizing Karmic Links wasn't all that common in the Multiverse, and it was more likely for a cultivator to plant a bomb as a final act of revenge on their killer. First of all, karmic links were easy to break, with even Zac being able to break the links of a D-grade Karmic Cultivator. Stronger warriors could break, or at least obscure, that kind of weak link even without the help of treasures.

Secondly, normal cultivators couldn't utilize a Karmic Link to hunt down someone on the other side of the sector. It would take someone with a deep understanding like Voridis A'Heliophos or his clan members to actually make use of them, or powerful forces ready to spend the money to hire a Karmic Cultivator.

Another issue apart from traps was the seals that covered a large number of the more valuable items, anti-theft devices that were put in place to disallow outsiders to steal the secrets of their clan.

"Almost all of the cultivation crystals containing manuals and skills are beyond our capabilities to crack, but that is usually how it goes," Calrin said with a shake of his head. "They are always guarded the hardest. However, seventeen of the manuals are public manuals that are commonly known in the Multiverse, and those weren't sealed or were only using standard seals. The best of them is **[Warrior's Heart]**. It's an unattuned manual that can only take you to Peak E-grade if you're lucky, but the bonus to combat power and recovery is impressive."

"It's meant for armies?" Zac asked, naturally understanding the use of the manual.

"Exactly. It's made for armies using traditional weaponry. I've heard that it is a simplification of a much better manual, but I don't know if that's true. In either case, it is very popular in the Zecia Sector, and you've gathered four versions of it," the Sky Gnome said.

"Four versions of the same manual?" Zac asked with confusion.

"Some forces modify manuals to better suit their inheritance or what weapons they enjoy. Others manage to make some adjustments to increase the power output or recovery by some degree," Calrin explained. "Like most things, you can classify a manual from being from Low to Peak quality. The original manual is a Mid E-grade cultivation manual, but I'd say that one of the versions you got is almost High Grade. It must have belonged to a pretty powerful clan who exerted a lot of effort in improving it before."

"What do you recommend doing with manuals like that?" Zac asked.

"Sell the worse duplicates; keep one or two of the best ones for yourself," Calrin said. "You could either sell them through me or wait for the auction you're planning on holding. I would say you stand to gain more by selling them here on Earth. There should be a lack of manuals of this kind on Earth, while they are ultimately very common in the Multiverse. Besides, that way, you would know what manuals your competition is cultivating."

"We'll add them to the auction, then," Zac agreed. "What about the rest?"

"It's too much to go over one by one," Calrin said with an avaricious glint in his eyes as he took out another crystal. "We created a tally for you. Incidentally, the cost of unsealing all these treasures landed at 1 billion Nexus Coins."

30
NEPOTISM

Billy looked around curiously, but he frowned when there was nothing but fog everywhere. Still, Billy remembered Zac's words. This magic statue was dangerous. Of course, Billy was smart enough to understand that without Zac telling him. The statue was able to grow in size so much that Billy could fit inside without a problem, so how could it be normal?

Zac was just trying to help, so Billy wouldn't point out his friend's silly mistake. Billy was more confused why the statue in Zac's house made Billy so annoyed. It was almost as handsome as Billy himself, so he should like it.

Billy couldn't figure it out, so he just gripped **[Bonker]** even harder as he walked forward. Finally, there was a change in the fog as a smaller statue appeared, standing just a bit taller than Billy himself. Billy frowned at the sight, and something about this statue man was really annoying Billy after all. It felt like the statue was really asking for a beating.

"Welcome, descendant. I am Thrak, the Titan. Prove your worthi–" a loud voice shouted from the stone, but it didn't get any further before **[Bonker]** slammed into its head, utterly reducing the whole statue into rubble.

"Stupid stone, trying to talk like a person," Billy said with a snort, anger smoldering in his chest.

Wait, why was Billy angry? Something about the talking stone had made Billy extremely annoyed, but he couldn't remember why. Had Mama warned him of talking statues before? No, that wasn't it. Billy looked down at the broken stone for a few seconds before he shrugged and kept walking.

If Mama hadn't mentioned it, and he couldn't remember, then it couldn't be too important.

Still, the hidden space within the big statue started to annoy Billy. Zac had said that there would be a lot of good things inside, but there were just crazy stones and mist. He kept trying to remember Zac's other ideas, but Billy had been busy looking at the big octopus when he talked. It was a lot bigger than the ones he had seen at the aquarium, and it even had more arms.

Mama said that a lot of people thought octopuses were really yummy, but Billy had never tasted it. He wondered what Big Blue tasted like. Billy bet it tasted real good since it had so many arms. He couldn't help but drool a bit as he thought about it. Perhaps he should ask Thea if she could give Billy an arm? Big Blue already had so many.

An hour passed, and Billy finally gave up on finding the treasure. Perhaps it was buried under the ground, but it was too hard to dig in, even for Billy. He took out a bed from his Magic Pouch and lay down, and thunderous snores soon echoed across the inheritance site.

"You're back," Statue Man said.

"Ah! Billy remembers now!" Billy roared in anger. "You're the one who sent the talking stone to trick me! You're the one who stole Billy's good things!"

He furiously ran toward the statue, and **[Bonker]** ripped through the air as it shot against Statue Man's head. **[Bonker]**'s bubbly skull was stopped by the shield, meaning that Billy wouldn't be able to destroy Statue Man today either.

"Calm down. I haven't done anything to steal your good things. In fact, I've been trying to give you good things for months now," the statue said, like Billy didn't know that Statue Man was a trickster.

But in this case, it seemed like it was telling the truth. Billy was smart, so he could tell when people were lying.

"Oh, it wasn't you?" Billy said with confusion. "Why didn't you say so, trying to confuse Billy. Stupid."

"Anyway." Statue Man sighed. "What's going on? What talking stone? Why do I sense a familiar aura from where you are sleeping?"

Billy considered whether he should tell Statue Man or not, but he eventually decided he could use some help. Billy had been lost in the mist for too long, and he was starting to get bored. Perhaps the Statue Man could help him figure out how to dig for treasure in the hard ground. Or perhaps he was even friends with the other Statue Man.

"Billy's friend had another Statue Man, and he let Billy go inside to look for treasures. But Billy couldn't find any treasure anyway. Statues are all bad," Billy said.

Statue Man was a bit stupid as usual, needing Billy to repeat himself multiple times before he understood what Billy was talking about. But he eventually understood.

"So you're inside a trial created by a descendant of our clan? Small world; no wonder it felt familiar. The bloodline is weak and impure, but it has undergone a real awakening," Statue Man muttered. "This is good. I can only provide you with theory through this realm, but this half-blood child might be able to help you take the first steps with your bloodline."

"Billy has told you, Billy is human. Billy doesn't need any blood either. Billy's body is full of it," Billy snorted.

"Never mind, then," the statue said. "But what about treasures? There is a lot of treasure outside, but you won't be able to find it without help. So let me help you find some treasure, ok?"

"How?" Billy asked skeptically. "Billy knows you can't get out. Billy won't draw the thing outside to let you free."

"How about this?" the statue said. "This time when you wake up, you will remember me for one hour. If you shout 'Statue Man, help me!' I'll be able to come out and help you, but only for ten seconds. Any more than that might hurt me and the place where you are."

"How does Billy know you're not lying?" Billy said skeptically.

"I swear on my mother that what I said just now was true," the statue said solemnly.

"Good! Billy will trust you this time!" Billy said with a big smile.

However, Billy knew now that Statue Man was a liar. He never swore on his mama when it came to drawing that thing outside. Billy had actually considered drawing it before, but now he definitely wouldn't. Some statues are just too stupid.

"But first, explain to me how the trial works," the statue said, drawing Billy out of his thoughts.

"Billy doesn't know. Billy only saw a talking stone. It was annoying, so it got thwonked." Billy shrugged. "Then nothing happened."

"The inheritance trial seems to have been pretty poorly crafted to allow such a situation to occur without any fallbacks," the statue muttered. "Well, just call for me outside, and I'll find the guy with the treasure for you."

Billy woke up a bit later, and he actually remembered Statue Man this time, just like he said. However, he didn't immediately call for him, but rather looked around for a while longer. Billy didn't want to call that guy unless he had to. However, there really was just mist everywhere, and Billy finally gave up.

"STUPID STATUE MAN, COME HELP ME!" Billy roared, and a terrifying pressure spread out the next moment.

Billy's eyes widened in shock as he looked for the threat. However, he was afraid that [Bonker] wouldn't be able to help him right now. Not even that old spear guy during the Hunt was as scary as this. He felt a bunch of bad feelings in his chest, just like those days he'd had to protect Mama from Papa when his mouth smelled funny.

Why had Billy cast the spell to let Statue Man out? Was it actually he who was the stupid one?

"IN THE NAME OF THE EASTERN MOUNTAIN, HELP THIS CHILD," a thunderous voice suddenly echoed out across the area, causing the whole world to shake and most of the mist to disappear.

The terrifying pressure was gone the next moment, and Billy could breathe out in relief. Statue Man really didn't lie this time and went back inside Billy's dreams.

"Ah? The Eastern Mountain?" a startled voice answered from nowhere the next second, though Billy felt it was a lot weaker than the earlier voice.

Wait, what earlier voice?

Billy frowned with confusion, feeling like he had forgotten something again. Whatever, he had finally solved the riddle, as the mist was going away, opening a tunnel to somewhere that shone with light. A wide smile spread across Billy's face as he hurried along, and he could already see himself decked in treasure, looking rich enough to make even the golden ghost jealous.

No stupid trial could trick Billy for too long.

However, Billy stopped in his tracks with confusion when he realized he was standing on a cliff on top of a mountain. He quickly looked back, but the mist was gone, and the flat place he had walked around in for so long was no longer there. This really was a mysterious statue to hold a whole mountain and magic mist.

"Welcome," a deep voice said, and Billy looked toward the source of the voice with vigilance, but he breathed out in relief when he saw that it wasn't another stone, but a man who actually looked a lot like Billy himself.

"Hello! I am Billy. Do you have treasures to give out?" Billy said as he walked over with quick steps.

"I do." The man grinned. "A lot of good ones. Are you really a descendant of Brazla? You look much more handsome than him. Almost as handsome as Thrak himself."

"Brazla? Who is that?" Billy said with confusion. "Billy came here because Billy's friend has a house full of large statues. Zac said that if Billy jumped into the Titan statue, then Billy would get a bunch of good things."

"Haha, that greedy bastard kicked the bucket!" Thrak roared with laughter, and the whole mountain shook with his laughter. "That's what you get for tricking Thrak!"

Billy didn't say anything and only looked at the muscular man with suspicion. He seemed a bit stupid; could he really have good treasure?

"Who was it who spoke earlier? Are you really someone from Eastern Mountain?" Thrak asked with almost burning eyes, and Billy started to feel a bit uncomfortable.

It was a bit troublesome to be the world's most handsome boy, even if it made him happy when Mama complimented him.

"Ah? Why do you keep asking Billy weird stuff? Billy was lost in the mist; then Billy fell asleep. Suddenly, I found you after I woke up." Billy shrugged as he took a step away.

"Interesting. I can still feel that aura on you, so I definitely didn't dream it," Thrak rumbled. "Well, whatever. I'll help like the great ancestor asked, but rules are rules. Do you want my treasures?"

Billy hurriedly nodded in agreement, his eyes scanning the mountain for good places to start digging.

"Only someone strong can get the treasures of Thrak. It's a rule. Prove you're strong by bashing that rock," Thrak said as he pointed next to Billy.

Billy looked over with confusion, and he saw that there was a round rock just twenty meters away. It was over ten meters tall too, and Billy didn't understand how he had missed it earlier.

"I just need to thwonk the stone?" Billy said skeptically. "Can Billy use [Bonker]?"

"Its name is Bonker?" Thrak laughed. "Good name!"

"It called itself something else, but it was stupid, so Billy renamed it." Billy shrugged.

"Sure, you can use your club. Just turn that ball into small stones, and I'll give you treasures." Thrak smiled.

Billy shrugged in confusion, but he still walked over to the stone. He had thwonked a lot bigger things than this stone, so it didn't really feel like a challenge to break it. He still took the mission seriously, so he walked over and swung at the stone with a lot of power, and the impact caused a shockwave to spread out all around them.

However, the rock was completely fine.

"Tsk, you're pretty weak, huh?" the man said from behind, which ignited a fire in Billy's chest.

Billy glared back before he looked over at the stupid rock again, and this time, he activated [Disintegrator], which gave the club a huge destructive power. This was the skill Billy had used to break apart that golden ship earlier. Surely it should work on a rock? Billy even infused the Seed of Expansion in the strike.

The air around [Bonker] started shaking as popping sounds echoed out across the mountain, and Billy bashed the stone with everything he had. A huge explosion erupted, as the air around the stone was sucked into a ball the size of a marble before it exploded with the force of a missile. This eruption repeated six times, each explosion larger than the ones before, and even Billy was thrown away twenty meters from the shockwaves.

Six times was just one worse than Billy's record, and he victoriously looked up at his work. Billy's eyes almost popped out of their sockets when he saw that the rock didn't so much as move from the attack, and it only had a small mark where he hit it. The ground around it was turned into sand like expected, but the ball was fine.

What kind of super stone was this?

Thrak didn't say anything this time, but Billy blushed a bit when he heard a snicker from the side. No holding back anymore. Billy got back up on his feet, and he grew one meter every step he took toward the stone. Power coursed through his veins, and he suddenly felt connected to the whole mountain beneath him.

He now realized what he had missed. The Dao of Expansion wasn't right. **[Bonker]** rose into the air, and it suddenly turned heavier as it was imbued with the Dao of Boulder, and Billy swung down with everything in his body as he activated another skill. The mountain shook, and the ball finally cracked.

"Good! Good seedling! I understand why the Eastern Mountain is interested in you!" Thrak roared from the side.

"So will you give Billy treasures now?" Billy panted.

"Of course. But before that. How about you stay with Thrak for a few days and learn a thing or two?" The man smiled.

"What can you teach Billy? No offense, but you seem a bit stupid," Billy said skeptically.

"Haha, I am stupid, but that doesn't matter because I am strong." Thrak laughed as he thumped his chest.

He suddenly started growing, and Billy's eyes widened when he saw Thrak using the same trick as himself. However, he was a bit different from Billy. Billy got golden hair when growing for some reason, but this guy's hair stayed brown. He was a lot better at growing than Billy, and Billy gaped when the man became as big as the mountain they stood on.

What was this?! One fart from him and his town Billyville would be blown away.

"See? Pretty strong, right?" Thrak laughed, and his voice alone caused the whole mountain to shake.

Thrak shrank again after flexing his muscles for a bit, and he was soon enough just a bit taller than Billy again.

"Now let Thrak teach you how to bash without getting bashed. It took Thrak a lot of effort to figure this out, so listen well."

31
LOOT

"What? ONE BILLION for some unsealing?" Zac almost roared as some killing intent started leaking from his body.

"Most of it was the cost of materials. Unsealing is akin to array breaking, and we had to spend a lot to get the work done. Just the best version of [Warrior's Heart] cost us almost 45 million to unseal, in addition to time and manpower spent. The whole process of unsealing this many treasures required half the clan to work arduously through the week, including our elders and children," Calrin said with a sorrowful visage.

"It was quite an ordeal; come look how gaunt the young ones have become from the stress," Calrin said with a deep sigh, clearly getting ready to summon a bunch of gnome kids once more to tug at Zac's heartstrings.

"Alright, alright," Zac snorted. "No need to parade the children around again. One billion it is, but you'd better not have unsealed a bunch of garbage and expect me to pay."

"Just a pittance for a man such as yourself," Calrin said with a smile. "Don't be too surprised when you hear this, but the total value of the treasures in the Cosmos Sacks reached almost 100 billion Nexus Coins."

"So you took a flat 1% fee?" Zac said, the quoted value of his treasures quickly calming him down.

Zac had actually expected it to be a lot lower after seeing how few treasures there were in the mentalist's Spatial Ring. People wouldn't be bringing items meant for the E-grade into the Tower, but rather leave it with their clans, and F-grade items along with their equipment could only be so valuable.

However, he was happy to be wrong this time.

He had felt a bit like a pauper after [Love's Bond] had swallowed most of his net worth, and much of the remainder had been swallowed by [Verun's Bite]. He still had a few billion Nexus Coins, but it no longer felt like a mountain of wealth, especially not after having visited the Base Town. The elites there could throw out over 100 billion Nexus Coins without batting an eye, and all the Peak treasures were far out of his price range.

"Indeed, where else can you get such a low fee for work of this nature? Only for friends and family," Calrin said with righteousness.

Zac snorted when he saw the Sky Gnome's expression, but he knew that Calrin was telling the truth. One percent wasn't a very high fee for this kind of work. Identifying items cost 5% at the General Store that the System provided to all Town Lords, and they could only identify pretty common items. One percent to not only identify, but also tally and unseal was a great deal.

"Well, whatever," Zac said as he turned his attention toward the crystal with the list of items.

A list materialized as he infused some energy into it, and his eyes widened as one line after another appeared, listing an untold number of treasures. The scions of the clans of the Zecia Sector had really come prepared when dealing with the Tower.

"We've consolidated items of the same category into the same list item, as there are simply too many of some items," Calrin explained. "For example, both [Second Wind Pill] and [Surging Vitality Pill] are E-grade healing pills of the same quality, so they are both listed as such. And you have 2,348 of those kinds of pills."

Zac nodded in understanding, and he saw that the list clumped items together by category and quality. For example, there were 84 Low-quality swords, and 12 Peak-quality swords among the weaponry. However, there were actually 643 High-quality Swords, which obviously stood out compared to the other qualities.

"Why are there so many High-quality Swords?" Zac asked with confusion. "Was someone carrying around hundreds of them?"

"Most of them are of the same make, unattuned shortswords with matching inscriptions. I am guessing that the previous owner was either planning on selling some weapons that their clan had produced, or was able to use the swords in some sort of weapon array," Calrin said.

"Weapon array?" Zac asked with interest.

"A mix of a swordmaster and an Array Master. It is neither a common nor an uncommon path. Rather than just controlling one weapon, you would control hundreds of them like a swarm. Some C-grade Monarchs command millions. You can even set up arrays to unleash powerful attacks or just overwhelm the enemies with numbers," Calrin explained. "But it puts a great demand on control and your soul can't be too weak, so it's not suitable for everyone."

Zac nodded in understanding. He had encountered that sort of fighter before; it was just that he didn't know the name for it. One of the incursion masters had used flying needles to attack him from every imaginable angle. There was also the poison master at the start of the eighth floor who had attacked with a flying swarm of daggers.

Even a few of the visions he had seen when reaching Peak mastery of [Axe Mastery] had used sets of flying axes.

Of course, swords were just one type of weapon he had gathered, and Zac realized he had gotten almost ten thousand weapons from his trip to the Base Town, most of them Medium- and High-quality E-grade weapons. This was far more than he had anticipated, as there were just a few hundred people he killed. He had picked up a couple of dozen weapons during his climb as well, but nothing that would explain this number.

These were all normal weapons forged with E-grade materials, but they weren't Spirit Tools. Calrin's explanation seemed pretty likely, that some of these collections of gear were meant for resale. A lot of people used the Tower of Eternity as an opportunity to make money, as it was a way to circumvent the fees for trading through the Mercantile System.

This was even further evidenced by the mountains of raw materials. There were over fifty thousand E-grade attuned crystals altogether, making up roughly a fifth of the total value of the loot. They had probably been brought from attuned worlds where there was a massive surplus of certain crystals, intended to trade for other ones that were more valuable back home.

It was the same with there being large stocks of over a hundred different materials and herbs, many of them extremely useful for Port Atwood. All of them were just Peak F-grade or E-grade materials, but that was just what Port Atwood needed right now to successfully upgrade from an F-grade force to a legitimate E-grade force.

Finally, there was the list of "big-ticket items" at the end, and Zac looked through them one by one.

There was first of all ninety-two Spirit Tools, though most of them were the bog-standard fare that might not even make it into an auction. At least a quarter of those who managed to get a ticket to the Tower of Eternity would already have gotten their hands on a Spirit Tool, and it was mostly the stronger people of the Base Town who had assaulted him at the end.

Of course, there were still a lot of people who might have the wealth or background to own a Spirit Tool but hadn't found a fitting one. Ogras was a prime example of this, as his spear was just a High-quality E-grade weapon without any spirituality.

However, there were some good Spirit Tools among those he had acquired too, and two of the Spirit Tools were actually marked as Peak quality by Calrin. The Sky Gnome assigned two types of grades on each weapon: rank and quality. For example, one of the Peak-quality Spirit Tools was Early E-grade, whereas the other one was Peak-quality Peak F-grade.

That meant that they were both good enough to have been put in the last section of the auctions that Zac had attended, with the former probably being something that would be saved for one of the bigger monthly auctions.

The quality assessment by the Sky Gnomes was a mix of attunement, craftsmanship, and upgrade potential. **[Verun's Bite]** would no doubt have been assessed as Low-quality when he got it, but Calrin said it was either High- or Peak-quality by now. He was unsure, though, as Zac had taken an unorthodox path in upgrading it by feeding it a bunch of uncommon treasures.

Who knew what the stone he fed Verun was, and who knew what effect a bunch of dragon blood and a Dragon Core would have? But it had definitely improved the weapon at a fundamental level, and not just evolved it to a higher grade. The bones that created the axe-head looked completely different from how it did before, and its potential had probably shot through the roof.

Just the fact that Verun already had enough spirituality to actually leave the weapon and take form meant that reaching D-grade would probably just require him finding the right set of materials. There shouldn't be any bottlenecks to mention.

Zac didn't really care about the lower quality Spirit Tools, and he guessed that some would be sold during the auction while others would enter the merit exchange. But the two Peak-quality Spirit Tools were essentially strategic resources that he wanted to assign himself. They were a bit troubling, as he didn't have a clear candidate in mind.

The F-grade one was a bestial claw, perhaps something that could be used by a pugilist. It actually came from one of the leaders of the attack, but he hadn't even taken it out during the fight, as he had been busy maintaining that Six Directions Array or whatever it was called. It was a bit sad; the man got killed by the cursed blade's half-moon before he even had a chance to display his ultimate skills.

The highest-graded Spirit Tool was actually a cauldron, and according to Calrin, it could both be used for alchemy and fighting. It was much higher in quality compared to the cauldron he had gifted to his sister, and it was likely the most valuable Spirit Tool on Port Atwood apart from [Love's Bond].

His first idea was to give it to his sister as well, but he eventually decided against it. Kenzie had only shown a fleeting interest in alchemy, and it felt like a waste to give something this valuable away as though it were a toy. He would keep it for himself for now and rent it out in case his force managed to nurture a talented Alchemist in the future.

That would bind him or her to his force, as a good cauldron was extremely important to progress in alchemy, just like a proper weapon was required to bring out your greatest potential in battle.

The origin of the cauldron was a bit baffling, though. Zac's first assumption was that he had killed someone from the Zethaya Clan, but he felt that he would have been informed some way or another if that was the case. It didn't come from one of the five leaders of the assault either, but one of the nameless faces in the mob. Calrin had found the cauldron inside a normal Cosmos Sack along with over ten thousand pills of middling quality.

Calrin guessed that it was the defining treasure of a weaker or declining alchemy clan, and the elders had lent it to whoever had entered the Tower of Eternity. The scion would probably just use the cauldron to smash through the earlier floors of the Tower before he focused on his alchemy and selling pills, but he had probably been caught up in the madness that his projection elicited.

Zac had been shocked to hear from Ogras that the projection of the Stele had turned everyone almost mad, and it had somewhat lowered the anger he had felt over the incident. He remembered feeling extremely confused that a bunch of weaklings dared to risk their lives fighting him even after he reached the ninth floor, but it turned out that the System had essentially shoved a berserker pill down everyone's throats.

Or perhaps it was the Stele itself. It was based on war or conflict, after all, and the power of its impartment might just have been too high. Perhaps all ninth-floor apparitions had that kind of effect.

In either case, Spirit Tools were obviously not the only high-value items in the Cosmos Sacks. There was one item on the list that was a natural treasure similar to the **[Evolution Fruit]** he'd gotten from Yrial, though it was a shimmering liquid stored in a large crystal vial. Zac was a bit tempted to drink it himself, but he felt it was a bit unnecessary.

It probably wouldn't work on his Draugr side judging by its name, **[Water of Exuberance]**, and it felt like a waste to use it on his human side. His human side had almost reached D-grade Race already thanks to the **[Evolution Fruit]**, and he could just complete the final step by taking normal medicinal baths.

It would better serve someone on his force, perhaps Sap Trang now that his odds of evolving seemed to have improved.

32

ATTUNEMENT

There were also over a dozen Peak-quality talismans that were a mix of defensive and offensive among the most valuable treasures, but Zac realized that their craftsmanship paled compared to the ones he had looted from the mentalist. They would still work as backups to his somewhat depleted reserves, and he could give out a few more to his core fighters.

But he wasn't personally very interested in talismans of that tier any longer, feeling that his recent attribute gain had made him outgrow these items to a certain degree. After all, a Peak E-grade talisman contained roughly the power of an average Peak E-grade warrior, and he was nearing that point as is.

There were a few items he was extremely keen on keeping for himself.

The first of them was a consumable talisman as well, called **[Zephyr's Charge]**. It was a Peak-quality speed imbuement treasure, if he understood the explanation correctly, and it would essentially give him wings and increase his speed for a few minutes. It would be perfect in case he needed to flee or run down a fleeing enemy, especially in his Draugr form that lacked dependable mobility options.

The second was a handful of **[Spatial Displacement Talismans]**, a treasure that would instantaneously move him to a random spot within a kilometer. It was an amazing treasure to escape certain doom scenarios, provided that space wasn't locked down. For example, if he'd had a treasure like this when the Hayner Clan patriarch had tried to drop a meteor on his head, then he wouldn't have had to leave the floor so early. He could just have teleported out of the hole and hunted down that treasure.

Finally, there was something called a [Blood Nucleus], a rare treasure related to bloodline awakenings. It was the most valuable item of them all, and Calrin had priced it at 20 billion Nexus Coins. That might not seem like a terrifying amount after having possessed something like the [Divine Investiture Array], but it was still something that Zac would never have been able to afford if he tried to purchase it during an auction.

He figured that the [Blood Nucleus] would go perfect together with the marrow he got for himself from the previous quest. The only reason he didn't cram both of them down his throat right now was that he needed some sort of understanding of his supposed bloodline before trying to wake it up.

There were many items that Zac didn't recognize either, but judging by the value that Calrin had assigned, they were rare treasures that warriors most likely had brought to the Base Town to sell. These kinds of treasures weren't useful to Zac, but that didn't mean that they would sell them for Nexus Coins.

Almost all forces in the Multiverse were constantly operating under a lack of resources, and there were always thousands of plans or undertakings on hold due to missing certain ingredients. Top forces like the Dravorak Dynasty might not struggle like this due to their power and vast connections, but Zac had already encountered the problem of lacking materials from the Creator quest.

There were a million ways he could gain more Nexus Coins, so selling precious resources instead of holding on to them for a rainy day was just stupid. This was unfortunately how most forces reasoned, which only worsened the availability of rare items.

Calrin also provided his recommendations of what to keep, what to save for the auction, what to put in the merit exchange, and so on. Zac mostly went with the Sky Gnome's arrangements, apart from making some minor adjustments.

It wasn't that the Sky Gnome suddenly had turned a new leaf and become a decent and honest merchant, but he had kept his greed under check since Zac had returned from the Tower of Eternity. Part of it was probably because of Zac's amazing performance, while part of it was that Calrin knew he was on thin ice after the trouble the ring he'd gifted Zac caused.

Zac felt like he had just won the lottery as he left the Thayer Consortium, even though there was only one "supreme" treasure like the [Blood Nucleus]. Calrin's estimate was around 100 billion, but that was going by Zecia Sector prices. They believed they could make even more as long as they were smart about what items to put in the auction for the native forces.

The elites of Earth were flush with cash at the moment, and they needed to exploit that.

Every force was hunting the hundreds of millions of Zombies for everything they were worth at the moment, wanting to capitalize on this onetime opportunity. The undead were like headless chickens with the Lich King gone, and they had essentially turned into walking bags of wealth to the cultivators of Earth, just like how it was during the beginning of the integration.

Not only did people gain clean-up quests by the System, but the Zombies gave a good amount of both Cosmic Energy and Nexus Coins. Add to that the Miasma Cores that formed in the elite Zombies' heads, and it was so lucrative that people were still forgoing sleep even two weeks later. Even the Underworld Council only undertook a cursory search for Enigma, who was still missing, while they focused on enriching themselves.

At the same time, there was almost nothing for the earthlings to spend their money on. The general stores provided by the System only sold bare essentials and the lowest grades of weaponry, and there weren't a lot of other options for them. Starlight, the Ishiate elite, apparently possessed a limited Mercantile License and had some wares to sell. But his influence was limited thanks to pushback from Calrin and the Marshall Clan, who were aiming to set up their own business empire.

The Marshalls themselves had kept a low profile until now, perhaps partly because they already knew about his auction. Zac had mentioned it to Thea, who no doubt had informed her grandfather as well. Perhaps they were ready to roll out their businesses already but held themselves back out of respect for him.

Either case was good for Zac, as it meant that people were more likely to spend their hard-earned money in Port Atwood. He could almost see the mountain of wealth in front of his eyes as he teleported back to his cultivation cave.

When he arrived in the hidden cave, he looked over at the array that looked similar to the teleportation array, though the inscriptions were a lot denser. It was the "homing point" of the **[Spatial Convergence Array]**, the location where he would arrive in case he was forced to use the escape function.

The other part was a thin bracelet that was hidden beneath the sturdy bracer he got from Greatest. He kept the bracer on at all times, and he figured it might be able to hide the **[Spatial Convergence Array]** from any discerning eyes. It seemed to be one of the most valuable things in his possession, though not quite at the level of things like the **[Pathfinder Eye]** or the **[Divine Investiture Array]**.

Then again, it was hard to put a price on survival. There was simply no supply of an item like the **[Spatial Array Gate]** in the Zecia Sector, though there were a lot of other escape measures around. For example, there was the skill that Thea possessed, and whatever the Head Priest used to turn into a stream of flames that had allowed him to escape the Dead Zone. There were even the weaker teleportation talismans he had gained just now.

"My Lord, welcome back." A voice drifted out from the rocks themselves as Triv emerged.

"It's been a while. I was almost starting to fear that you had managed to escape your contract," Zac said with a small smile. "Did you find anything interesting?"

The ghost had been gone for over a week, as Zac had sent him on a mission after he finished helping Kenzie set up the cultivation caves. The ghost was a noncombat class, but his incorporeal form also made him a qualified scout by default. So Zac sent the ghost out to explore the depths of his island, to see if there was anything interesting or valuable in the vicinity of the root of the Nexus Vein.

"Even if I managed to break the Contract of Servitude, I would still surely stay with the young master," Triv hurriedly exclaimed, eliciting a snort from Zac.

But honestly, it wasn't impossible that the ghost was telling the truth. Just like Calrin hugged onto his legs because of the potential he represented, so could Triv. A completely purebred Draugr of an ancient bloodline was unheard of in a remote sector like Zecia. The few Draugr clans around were apparently just mixed-blood clans that would just barely be considered Draugr by Heartland standards.

Following Zac was Triv's ticket to the Empire Heartlands in the future, as Triv was still certain that Zac would end up there sooner or later. Zac probably would, provided that he ever reached C-grade or higher. By that time, Earth should already be safe, and the Zecia Sector wouldn't be able to provide him with a proper environment.

Triv had mentioned a common saying during one of his campaigns to recruit Zac to the dark side. The ghost said that there were four requirements to cultivation: wealth, companionship, method, and environment. Not one could be lacking if one wanted to reach the peak.

Wealth was the most important, and that went double for someone like Zac, who was just a mortal. To cultivate was to burn money, and it only got exponentially worse. In the beginning, he could cultivate and gain levels with just a couple of Nexus Crystals that were barely worth anything, but now he was contemplating buying attuned D-grade crystals for hundreds of millions just for some small advancements to his soul.

It was no coincidence that almost all C-grade Monarchs had sprawling factions even if they tied the Monarchs down– they needed the manpower to generate enough wealth for their cultivation.

Second was companionship, but it didn't refer to girlfriends or even Dao Companions. It meant that no one could reach the peak alone. You needed a master to teach you, friends you could trust your back to, a support system that could take care of things that were distracting you from your cultivation.

Method was partly referring to a cultivation manual, but it also incorporated things such as inheritances, Heritages, Dao Impartments, and even hunting grounds. Some insights would have to come from within, but there was no need to reinvent the wheel at every turn. Taking advantage of the wisdom and knowledge of others would allow you to make faster progress without any detriment.

The last requirement was environment, and this one was why Triv believed Zac would end up in the Empire Heartlands sooner or later. It wasn't without reason that B-grade cultivators never appeared in the Zecia Sector. The environment simply didn't allow for it. No crops would grow if the soil was barren. Zac needed to go to the more prosperous sectors of the Multiverse if he wanted to progress beyond a certain stage.

In fact, moving as soon as possible was the optimal choice from a cultivation standpoint. Earth was just a desolate rock by most standards, and staying here would no doubt delay his cultivation speed.

"It is quite odd," Triv said, dragging Zac back to the present. "There are some Divine Crystals growing close to the source of the Nexus Vein. This can happen spontaneously, but it is far more likely on life- or nature-aspected planets. When the world becomes attuned, so do most of the neutral veins."

"So the World Core's upgrade was gaining an attunement after all?" Zac said with excitement.

This was something that had stumped him and everyone else over the past two weeks. The world was supposed to have upgraded its core because he had defeated the undead incursion. There was even that pulse that spread across the whole planet. However, after the pulse, there was no follow-up at all.

The density of energy was pretty much the same as before, still slowly climbing as the world continued its gradual integration. No new Nexus Veins or treasures were sprouting up from the ground either, and no attuned energies could be found. Most had simply assumed that it would take more time for the world to adapt to the reward, but it looked like the clues were finally starting to appear.

"Well, that's the thing. I also sensed weak hints of Miasma close to the vein," Triv said with hesitation. "Though I don't believe the vein is turning death attuned."

"What? Did you do something?" Zac said with a frown.

"I swear on the empire, I didn't do anything! It could be an effect of the realignment array being shut off at the last minute. Either that, or…" the ghost said, drifting off at the end.

"Or what?" Zac asked.

"Or the planet has gained a multi-attunement," Triv said.

"You mean the planet might both have life and death attunements?" Zac said, his eyes lighting up.

Wouldn't that mean that the planet was turning into a cultivation haven for himself?

"I wouldn't be so quick to celebrate if that was the case." Triv sighed. "It might not be a good thing."

Zac couldn't stop himself from audibly groaning when he saw the scrunched-up visage of the ghost. What now?

33
DUST AND BONES

"How can a planet having multiple attunements not be good? It sounds extremely good," Zac asked with a frown.

"In some cases, certainly. Worlds with Wood and Water attunements are supremely valuable among Herbalists, for example. One such planet might be worth as much as a thousand normal worlds of the same grade, as they can grow unique plants that require both attunements to thrive. However, such planets appearing is thanks to the two elements harmonizing well with each other," Triv explained.

Zac understood what the ghost was driving at. Was the World Core going to explode from the clashing elements of life and death? Attunements didn't get much more mismatched than life and death. They were each other's opposites, and they would constantly clash. His own cultivation chamber was proof of that.

"So what would happen with such a world?" Zac asked with some trepidation. "Will the World Core be in trouble?"

"I have never heard of a life and death planet before," Triv admitted. "I don't think there's much use for one, with young master being the exception. The empire wouldn't want their planets tainted with life, and death attunement would make large sections unsuitable for the living. Perhaps it would be able to birth unique treasures, but that's beyond my knowledge."

"So what is the worst-case scenario?" Zac sighed.

"The World Core might crumble from the opposing attunements, which would turn the planet into a desolate rock devoid of energy. Or it could cause the whole planet to completely fall apart," Triv said.

Zac closed his eyes, a wave of exhaustion hitting him almost like a sledgehammer. Was there yet another thing for him to worry about now? There was already enough on his plate, and now he had to prevent the planet from going up in smoke on top of everything else?

"It might not happen," Triv quickly said when he saw Zac's reaction. "I am not an expert on the subject, but there are multiple outcomes. Sometimes one attunement can overpower the other and turn it into a single-attunement planet. It is also possible that the planet finds some sort of equilibrium, turning it into an extremely rare existence in the cosmos. In fact, I believe this is the most likely scenario."

"Why? What did you find?" Zac asked eagerly, like a man gripping hold of a life buoy.

Zac would take any clue that indicated that the world wasn't actually ending.

"Well, didn't young master mention that the World Core upgrade was part of a quest reward that encompassed the whole planet? It would make no sense that the System would provide a detriment as a reward," Triv said.

Zac quickly nodded in agreement. It was true. The System was pretty annoying, and its gifts often felt a bit backhanded. Being stuck with annoying Tool Spirits like Brazla and Big Blue was ample proof of that. However, they were undeniably rewards. It made no sense that the System would leave the world worse off than before as a reward.

However, it didn't hurt to make sure.

"Is there anything I can do to decrease the risk of anything bad happening?" Zac sighed.

"Our empire can easily realign a planet, as you know, and many living forces possess similar capabilities. Perhaps there are some arrays to stabilize the process of giving a planet attunement?" Triv ventured, but he didn't seem very sure. "In either case, with the speed things are progressing, it will probably take decades before the attunement is finished, so we have ample time to prepare. There are only small hints right next to the Nexus Vein. I might even have seen things incorrectly."

"Well, that's good, I guess. Wait, your first instinct was that the planet would blow up because of the dual attunement? What about me? Am I in any danger?" Zac asked.

"I honestly don't know how young master is still alive." The ghost coughed. "Life and death shouldn't intermingle. It is one of the most basic rules of the Undead Empire. But at the same time, everything is possible. I am just a poor ghost; my understanding of the truths of the Heavens is shallow at best."

"Have you ever heard of undead cultivating life-attuned classes or Daos?" Zac asked.

"No, never. It is almost impossible. Our affinities with those types of Daos are essentially nonexistent. Why would you spend centuries on attaining a life-aspected Dao Seed when you can gain a death-aspected one in a few months?" the ghost said, looking disgusted at the mere thought.

The ghost shuddered the next second, meaning that this line of questioning wasn't permitted by the restrictions engraved on his soul, so Zac could only drop it.

"Well, I guess I will have to figure things out myself." Zac sighed before he produced the body-refining recipe he just got from Calrin. "Do you think this will work on me?"

The ghost scanned the guide, his eyes widening in incredulity.

"It looks like something you would use on a beast companion to refine its constitution," he hesitantly said. "I'm not sure. It might work? I don't see anything that would directly clash with you at least. But a pureblood Draugr using some sort of beast powder... The Heavens will weep."

"I'm sure the Heavens will be fine," Zac snorted as he handed the ghost the materials required for the dust. "I'll go cultivate for a bit. Are you able to prepare the [Bone-Forging Dust]?"

"Certainly, young master," the ghost said as he took the Cosmos Sack. "The process is quite similar to grinding the materials used for making incense sticks, and I have ample experience in this regard. There will not be any issues."

Zac nodded in thanks, and the ghost disappeared into the wall the next moment.

It was quite an impressive skill the specter had, being able to freely pass through walls. He could even bring inanimate objects with him, making him an excellent scout or assassin. It sort of felt like a bit of a waste for such a special existence to become a butler.

Unfortunately, his abilities didn't work with the living, which ruined Zac's idea to have the ghost take him to the depths of the Mystic Realm, ignoring all the barriers and walls. He couldn't send Triv by himself either, as that was a death sentence for a noncombat class.

Zac walked into his cultivation cave and started up the Soul Strengthening Array. His mind was slowly drained, and he let his thoughts drift for a bit. Between grinding his skill and going over the list of treasures, his mind was a bit exhausted, and he was too tired to ponder on the Dao while cultivating his soul.

He even dozed off a bit and was only awakened when the revolution finished and he felt a surge of Mental Energy entering his mind. Every time he completed a revolution, he couldn't help but marvel at his soul. It wasn't really growing all that much bigger from the revolutions, but it felt like his soul was getting polished each time.

More importantly, it also seemed like the revolutions helped deal with the Splinter to some regard. He never felt the surges of murderousness like he did before any longer, even though the Splinter had regained a decent amount of its strength by now. It was still restrained by the Shard, but it wasn't in a completely half-dead state any longer.

The two Remnants were still interlocked and unmoving inside the improved cage, but the amount of cleansed energies that were seeping out was gradually increasing without him feeling any negative effects from it. His mind had gained a few boosts during the climb, but it couldn't completely explain his balanced state of mind.

The small improvements that came from the array couldn't be the reason for his tranquil state either. His soul was definitely a bit stronger, but soul strengthening was a slow grind and not something that gave instant results. It was more likely that the spiritual dialysis also helped with the hidden corruption from the Splinter, either by design or by chance.

If that was true, it was a huge boon, though it also meant that skipping cultivation sessions would harm his mental state.

Zac finished up the session after ten hours as usual before he walked over to the inner cave that housed the **[Seed of Undeath]**. He found his ghost butler cultivating by silently hovering in the air, and there was a supersized pestle by its side. Inside was a silvery compound, no doubt the **[Bone-Forging Dust]** the ghost had prepared for him.

"Young master, it is all done according to the specifications," the ghost said as he woke up. "There should be enough for eight to ten applications."

Zac nodded in understanding, though he felt a bit disappointed. The powder had roughly the same effect as the medicinal baths according to Calrin, and ten medicinal baths on the road to D-grade would just scratch the surface. It should be able to increase his attribute limits by a few hundred points, which was the most pressing matter.

"And the pain," the ghost hesitantly added.

"I know," Zac said as he sat down and disrobed. "Not much of a choice right now. Help me apply it."

The ghost nodded, and a stream of the silvery powder rose from the pitch-black mortar, controlled by the ghost's Miasmic tendrils.

Zac sat motionless for over a minute, waiting with a mix of fear and anticipation for the dust to start working. However, he started to worry about the dust not working after all, which would mean that he had wasted over 300 million Nexus Coins. Thankfully, his fears soon abated as he started to feel some warmth covering his whole body.

"It seems to be working," Zac said with excitement to Triv, who waited upon him to the side, but the smile on his face quickly turned crooked as the warmth turned to pain.

First, it just felt like an itch he couldn't scratch, but that was just the appetizer. It seemed as though the powder was slowly getting absorbed through the skin, and the pain just kept getting worse as more and more of the powder entered his pores. The itch turned into a stabbing pain after ten minutes, and after another ten minutes, he felt like he was on fire.

The slowly mounting degree of agony was torture by itself, as Zac still didn't know where the limits lay. There were no timeframes indicated in the crystal either, meaning he had no idea how long the torment would last. He could only try to keep his mind stabilized and bear with it, while not even using his Daos to counteract the powder.

Doing so would no doubt counteract the effect, and it would be the same if his [**Void Heart**] activated. Even he couldn't stop himself from shuddering as the pain suddenly spiked to a level he previously thought was impossible.

"My Lord, are you okay?" Triv worriedly asked.

"Ow... My bones," Zac spat through gritted teeth as veins danced all across his body.

He didn't trust himself to open his mouth again, afraid that he would start screaming at the top of his lungs. The powder had just entered his bones, and it felt like some sort of parasite was gnawing at him, slowly breaking down his body from the inside. It was beyond painful, and it almost made him look back at the ordeal with the cultists with longing.

Zac quickly realized what the powder was doing. It was continuously breaking down his body parts, especially his bones, before forcibly mending them, each time leaving them slightly stronger. It was a bit like his Soul Strengthening Array, which utilized the clashes between life and death to strengthen his soul, though the powder was far more crude and brutal.

"All the powder has entered your body by now," the ghost suddenly said. "Young master just needs to bear it a bit longer."

Zac stiffly nodded, no longer able to speak. He didn't know how long he sat in the death-attuned sanctum until the pain finally abated, and he took a deep ragged breath even though there actually wasn't any need for oxygen in his current form. He slowly put on his robes once more, but his hands didn't really listen to his commands.

"Let me, young master," the ghost said and hurriedly dressed Zac.

"Thank you," Zac said with a hoarse voice. "How long did this take?"

"Around forty minutes," Triv said.

"Forty minutes?!" Zac exclaimed, his voice cracking. "It felt like days."

Zac shakily threw a healing pill into his mouth, though he knew that he wasn't really hurt. The soothing stream of energy that spread through his body helped him stabilize himself a bit at least, but he still needed over thirty minutes before he felt ready to stand up.

"What does young master want to do with the rest of the powder?" Triv asked.

"I'll take it." Zac sighed.

"If I may, if you just–"

"Enough," Zac said, not in any mood to hear about how great the Undead Empire was and how this all was unnecessary. "When can I use this next time?"

"Three days." The ghost sighed. "Your body will need to rest and recuperate for three days."

"Fine." Zac nodded. "By the way, ready yourself for war. You will need to come with me and activate the jamming arrays, perhaps as soon as today. I could do it, but I don't want to expose my identity."

"I would love to, but I can't," Triv said, clearly relieved. "Those arrays can't be activated by just anyone. There are restrictions in place."

"We've removed them," Zac said. "Anyone wielding Miasma can activate them now."

"What?! Impossible!" the ghost said with shock. "There's no way we would leave such a weakness that it could be used against us… Hm?"

"You figured it out?" Zac snorted. "It might be impossible for the living to take control of those things, but it's not like the protections against other undead are as strong. But don't worry. You just need to activate the array, then hide while we do the fighting."

"It's my pleasure to assist," the ghost said, clearly devoid of any sort of pleasure.

"Oh, and that insane Tool Spirit at my Dao Repository wants a Natural Spirit Gathering Array because he thinks he's a cultivator; can you start thinking about how such a thing would look? It needs to be pretty too, or he'll probably start shooting lightning bolts at people," Zac added.

"Naturally." Triv nodded. "Anything else?"

"No, that's it," Zac said as he left. "Pretty calm day for Port Atwood."

34

CRUSADE

Zac returned to his compound and visited his sister for a bit before turning in for the night. Neither Billy nor Thea had returned from their trials just yet, according to Kenzie, which hopefully was a good thing. It might mean they'd managed to get opportunities similar to himself, where he got an additional trial that increased the time that the trial took.

Ogras' inheritance had passed quicker, only taking him a few hours. The demon hadn't divulged everything that had happened; it did seem like his haul wasn't all too impressive apart from the weird creature he was bonded with. Zac guessed his encounter was similar to Zac's if he only defeated the golem and simply got some contribution points to shop for.

The harrowing experience of using the [**Bone-Forging Dust**] left him utterly unable to find the tranquility to ponder on the Dao, especially not with his bones still throbbing painfully. His mind was far too muddled to go over any plans for the war with the Zhix traitors as well, so he just fell on top of his bed and entered a dreamless slumber.

He woke up the next day expecting to be met with a wave of pain, but he was surprised to notice that he felt fine. In fact, better than fine. The pain was completely washed away, and his body felt like he had just spent the last hour stretching and limbering up. He didn't know if it was thanks to his high Vitality or if it was just how the powder worked, but he felt a lot lighter as he walked toward the teleporter.

He had already gotten all the pertinent details yesterday from Kenzie, and his destination appeared on his teleportation screen.

Zac cracked his neck before he stepped into the teleporter, ready to withstand an assault at a moment's notice. He was expected by the Zhix War Council, but you never knew what that meant. There might be a hundred Anointed on the other side of the teleporter, waiting to welcome him with their massive fists, for all he knew.

Or even worse, a banquet full of all the disgusting things Ibtep had tried to feed him before.

He appeared in a dark cave the next moment, with ten Zhix warriors standing guard. Two of them shot toward him without hesitation, their short spears aiming for his vitals the moment he materialized. Zac didn't panic at all and simply materialized the crude club he had used against the Zhix before.

Two hollow bonks later and the two attacking warriors lay sprawled out on the ground at the other side of the room.

"Strength to your hive," Zac said. "I am Zachary Atwood. I am expected."

The still-standing Zhix didn't answer with anything but a bow, and two of them stepped off and led him through an intricate series of tunnels, ignoring their unconscious brethren. Zac looked at the surroundings with interest, as this was the first time he had actually been inside a Zhix hive. He had always meant to revisit his local hive to meet with Nonet, but there was always some fire or another he had to put out.

Zac had always pictured something a bit like a mix of an Ayn hive and the town caves he had visited, but he realized he had severely underestimated the love for architecture among the Zhix. It would be fairer to compare the Zhix hive with a dwarven subterranean city. There was extraordinary attention to detail, no matter whether you looked at the intricately tiled floor or the engraved patterns adorning the walls.

Unfortunately, it seemed like he was walking in a restricted part of the complex structure, as he saw almost no Zhix warriors while they proceeded deeper into the hive, and there were no buildings or rooms to give an insight into how they lived day to day. It was clear they walked further into the earth, into the heart of the hive.

It only took them a few minutes to reach their goal, a large chamber with no point of interest apart from a massive set of doors. In front of it, a familiar figure stood waiting, and Zac walked over with a smile. Zac looked at Ibtep with interest, feeling that the past months had transformed them from a harmless oddball to a warrior emitting a solid aura. Zac could still discern the inquisitive light in their eyes, the thing that somewhat set them apart from most other insectoids.

The two hadn't actually seen each other since they'd split ways at Marshall Manor. Ibtep had been in one long deployment against the undead hordes, both working as a liaison due to their knowledge of humans, and as a scout. Zac had felt a bit bad that this guy hadn't been there to join in the opportunity of the Dao Funnel, but it felt like they had improved tremendously even without it.

"Greetings, Lord Atwood," Ibtep said with a bow, almost toppling over due to the weight of the oversized backpack that they still carried around. "Care for a snack? They are quite delicious, and they can calm a warrior's mind, readying you for combat."

They produced a small jar the next moment, and Zac blanched when he saw it contained a few extraordinarily fatty larvae. It looked like some of the Zhix's odd customs remained, and it made him worry about what came next.

"No, thank you," Zac said with a somewhat forced smile. "It's good to see you're okay. How is Nonet?"

"Nonet has fought valiantly for Hive Kundevi and Port Atwood, and our hive can now join the council," Ibtep said with pride before they slightly deflated again. "Of course, Lord Atwood might be a part of that reason."

"Are the others already here?" Zac asked.

"Yes, they are waiting on the other side of this door. I cannot follow inside; it is not my place," Ibtep explained.

Zac nodded as he looked up at the towering gates once more. They reached over ten meters into the air and were covered in a painstakingly detailed mural that depicted various battles. It was a vivid reminder that the Zhix wasn't just a barbaric tribe of insectoids, but an ancient society with thousands of years of history.

"Your people actually managed to open these things before the integration?" Zac asked as he looked up at the enormous doors.

"Just the greatest of the Anointed," Ibtep said with a shake of their head. "Normal warriors would never be able to step through these gates. It requires both renown and enough power to actually open the doors."

Zac only smiled as he put his hands against the doors and pushed. There was some resistance, but they soundlessly opened and let him inside. He was still inwardly shocked when he realized just how much power was required to open these things. There was no way that anyone beneath level 40 or 50 would be able to open these doors, proving just how powerful the Zhix Anointed had been even before the integration.

It was ultimately not a challenge for an E-grade warrior, and Zac effortlessly entered the inner chambers, where over thirty Anointed stood around a table, with another ten normal Zhix warriors standing by at the side. The smaller Zhix obviously weren't as powerful as the hulking spiritual leaders of their race, but Zac could sense that every single one of them was quite strong. He wouldn't be surprised if they all were between level 65 and 75.

The group of Anointed turned toward him as he entered, silently gazing down at him like giants looking down at a small critter. Zac wryly smiled and wondered if this was how it felt to be a Sky Gnome. Zac was about to greet the group, but he inwardly groaned when he felt the aura of one of the largest Anointed blast across the chamber as they started walking toward him.

It looked like Zhix traditions were still going strong.

Zac even started to wonder if there was any limit to how big these guys could grow. Normal Zhix were slightly shorter than male humans on average, with weaker anointed like Nonet reaching a bit over three meters. Herat, the Anointed he'd met during the Hunt, was another half meter taller than that, but he was far from the largest one in this place.

There were three Anointed in particular that towered above the others, each of them well over four meters tall. The largest one was probably approaching five meters. Zac barely reached their thighs, like a young child next to their parents. And it was one of these three behemoths that had decided to test his mettle as they flashed forward and swung a huge fist toward his chest.

It felt like the fist grew to the size of a mountain, but Zac realized it was just an illusion brought on by the dense killing intent carried within. This hulking Anointed had no doubt been steeped in battle the past months to accumulate such a terrifying aura. It was not only aura – the fist was still as large as his whole torso, and Zac was afraid he'd shoot out like a bullet when he got hit.

The fist accompanied by that dense aura was pretty intimidating, but Zac was no slouch either. A boundless killing intent spread throughout the whole chamber, almost turning into a palpable haze from how thick it was. A few of the attendants even fell down on their knees before they forced themselves back on their feet with embarrassment.

Zac didn't care about the normal Zhix, but he instead readied his body to receive the strike. He stomped down into the ground to lodge himself in place as he leaned forward. He could only pray that his bones were completely healed from using the **[Bone-Forging Dust]** yesterday, as this would probably hurt. At least it couldn't be too bad, as his danger sense barely acted up.

A deep clap of thunder echoed out across the hall as the Zhix's fist slammed into Zac's chest. Even digging his legs into the solid stone tiles wasn't enough, and Zac was pushed back over twenty meters from the furious momentum. It felt like someone had swung a wrecking ball into him, and Zac actually had to stop himself from grunting in pain.

The Zhix warrior clearly had almost 800 or 900 Strength, and it also had a Dexterity that was almost on par, increasing the speed and destructiveness of the strike. There was even a hint of a high-tiered Dao Seed in the fist, but Zac knew they hadn't actually infused their strike. This was just a normal attack to test his might.

He looked with surprise at the towering Anointed. Had they found a way to move forward and evolve? From what Zac understood, the rite of Anointment came at a cost, cutting off their path of advancement. But these were not attributes that a normal F-grade warrior should have, at least not without a huge number of special opportunities that he doubted the Anointed would possess.

"You are wondering how I could bring forth such strength, human Warmaster?" The huge Zhix laughed, their booming voice causing ripples in the air. "I have entered the crusade. I will fight for another year or so; then I will join the ancestors. This will be the final war, and my final gift to my hive."

Zac's eyes widened in understanding, once more shocked at the conviction these people carried. He didn't know the specifics, but it seemed as though the Anointed knew of some technique for trading their life span for power. It didn't seem to be directly burning life force, as Zac had seen that enough times to recognize the unique aura it radiated.

"So I guess it's time for me to reciprocate?" Zac said as he fully unleashed his aura.

The whole cave shuddered, and it only got worse as Zac started moving toward the enormous insectoid.

"Wait, Warmaster," the Anointed hurriedly said as they took a step back. "If there is one thing we have learned over the past year, it is that our hives cannot only rely on the old teachings to survive. We must also adapt and move forward. There is no need for you to carry on with that archaic tradition; let us instead talk about the looming threat."

The other Anointed hurriedly nodded as well, immediately launching into a discussion while pointedly looking away from Zac and his rapidly dwindling momentum. Zac speechlessly looked on with his fist still in the air.

So I just ate your fist for nothing? Zac thought as he looked at the shameless Zhix with mixed feelings.

"I am Rhubat. Strength to your hive. Nonet said you might be able to provide a tactic that would expedite our crusade?" the shameless Zhix said.

"Is this room secure?" Zac asked with a sigh, finally dropping the subject.

"Everyone who has not yet entered the crusade, leave this room," Rhubat said without hesitation, and a small group of Anointed along with the group of normal Zhix warriors left the chambers.

However, almost all the Anointed stayed, including Nonet, who stood to the side, looking almost like a child next to some of their larger colleagues. However, Zac noted that Nonet must have grown by something like thirty centimeters since he had seen the hive leader last time.

"You too?" Zac asked with a frown as he looked over in Nonet's direction.

"The Anointed exist to serve the hives. The crusade is our highest order. This is the final crusade, after which the Zhix will be eradicated or have no need for the Anointed any longer. Our era is coming to an end," Nonet said, and the other Anointed nodded in agreement.

35
BATTLEPLANS

Zac sighed when he heard Nonet's declaration, but he could understand the sentiment. The Anointed were terrifyingly powerful beings who had act as spiritual leaders and protectors of the Zhix for millennia, but that could only continue for so long. The world would soon pass them by while they were stuck at the F-grade. A random warrior would be able to kill them with a simple swing in a decade or two.

Such a transference in power would undoubtedly affect their positions as leaders as well, especially as their purpose of existence would fade into memory with the fall of the Dominators. Instead, they wanted to go out on their own terms, fulfilling the mission they had carried for over a thousand years.

"What about Hive Kundevi?" Zac asked.

"We have made arrangements for our elders and strongest warriors to take over after we've fulfilled our purpose," another Zhix explained, and one Anointed after another added a snippet of information.

Zac listened to their explanation, and it sounded like the Zhix would set up governance with two major pillars, the clergy and the army. One would provide spiritual guidance and be in charge of running the noncombat side of things, while the army would nurture the next generation of warriors and protect the hives.

The true elites would still be interred into some sort of templar order, making sure there was a balance in power between the two factions.

As for their reproduction, it turned out that Anointed weren't actually needed for that. From how Ibtep had explained it back then, it sounded like the Anointed were like hive queens that made it possible for Zhix eggs to be fertilized, but it wasn't the whole story. They were simply the "alphas" of the hive, but the alpha didn't necessarily need to be Anointed.

It had always simply been like that until now, as they were so much more powerful than anyone else in the hives.

"We hope you will be able to watch over the children in the future. This new world is hectic and confusing, but you humans seem quite able to adapt," Nonet added after the group had explained the future path of the Zhix.

Zac finally understood why the large Zhix had taken the time to explain things in such detail. They would be gone in a year, and he was the greatest threat to their population apart from the Dominators. He could definitely eradicate the Zhix if he put his mind to it.

"I'll do my best," Zac said with a nod and, after some thought, added some more reassurance. "I believe my force has become so successful because I welcomed people from all the Races. It has allowed me to advance much further than other factions. I will make sure that none of the Races will get pushed out in the future."

Of course, both Zac and the Zhix understood that promise was provided that no one stepped out of line. Zac didn't really have an active interest in the governance of the new planet, but he definitely wasn't some sort of pacifist. He wouldn't mind making examples out of some factions if people started causing trouble for him.

"That's all we ask," Rhubat said.

With that out of the way, they dove into discussing the details of the crusade. Zac took out one of the jammers from his Cosmos Sack and briefly explained how it worked. He was a bit fuzzy on the limitations of the array, though, to give himself some leeway. He didn't believe anyone here was a traitor, but better safe than sorry.

"My army can set out at any time," Zac said. "And I am sure the Human Council would join if I ask as well. We just need to leave some to keep whittling down the Zombies."

"Thank you, but there is no need. It is the Zhix who have brought this threat onto this world, so it will fall onto the Zhix to solve it," another one of the three enormous Anointed said with a shake of their head. "It is better your kind deal with the remaining unliving before they spread across the planet like the corruption they are."

"With your ability to stop the traitors from fleeing, there will be no need for massive armies," another Anointed added. "Just enough to take out one hive at a time. An army assisted by a coalition of us Anointed will be more than enough."

"Fine." Zac slowly nodded.

Zac was honestly somewhat relieved that his army wouldn't have to get their hands dirtied once again. The war was a good opportunity for them to gain battle experience against a strong opponent that wasn't brain-dead like the Zombies, but it would definitely lead to casualties. The Zhix were more like the demons than humans in one regard.

Their culture was steeped in battle, and the integration only added to their power. And there were a lot of them. His army had many elites, but there were too few of them. Meanwhile, the Zhix warfare doctrine was essentially based around taking down more powerful warriors by grinding them down with a ceaseless wave of violence.

"But I still need to come with. The items that can block out teleporters and communication must be activated by the unliving, so I need to bring my undead servant," Zac said, and added a short explanation after seeing the odd stares. "I captured it from the incursion for information."

Zac also felt that he needed to be present in case the real Dominators showed up. That way, he might be able to avoid a wholesale slaughter of his allies. Zac might not be fully confident in killing them without sounding them out first, but he was confident in both being able to slow them down and getting away in one piece.

After all, there would be a need for manpower in the Mystic Realm, and this group of Anointed might be the best allies he could get his hands on. They were as powerful as Early E-grade warriors, and they had ample combat experience. Bringing these guys would help him even out the odds against the other factions.

Besides, Zac guessed that they would have to enter the Mystic

Realm anyway if they wanted to finish their crusade. Void's Disciple had no doubt already brought in some hives to help him look for the dimensional treasure. He couldn't do everything himself. And there were only so many hives that this group could ambush before the Dominators realized something was wrong.

"That is fine. We need the assistance of humans for another matter," Rhubat added. "Teleportation. Our hives were not placed too close together in this new world, and many hives have been destroyed already from the war. If we used our own network, then we would have to spend months on foot."

The enormous table lit up the next moment, and Zac's eyes widened when he saw it was a surprisingly detailed map of Pangea. There were a lot of indistinct sections, including most of the unmapped zones on his own tablet. But a lot of it was properly filled in with what seemed to be even greater detail than the maps produced by the Marshall Clan.

"This is something Vanexis was gifted by the System," Rhubat explained, nodding to the other five-meter Anointed who had spoken earlier, as they took out a small metal ball from their Cosmos Sack. "As long as a warrior travels with a ball like this in their possession, then everything around them will be recorded and added to the map. We have thousands of these balls."

Zac whistled with surprise as he looked down at the map again. The Zhix had truly been busy going by how much distance they had covered to map out these places.

"There are twenty-eight hives we have marked," Rhubat said. "All of them are within two hours' travel."

"Only twenty-eight hives?" Zac asked with surprise.

Twenty-eight cities were nothing to the human population, even after the integration, so it sounded like a really low number if the Zhix had actually defected to the Dominators.

"Don't underestimate these hives. The Dominators have gathered their subjects into massive hives far eclipsing any structures from our old world. Their numbers are almost on par with our hundreds of remaining hives," Vanexis rumbled. "Each of them holds over a hundred thousand warriors along with millions of normal Zhix."

Zac nodded in understanding when he heard the explanation, and he tried to understand the motivation for the Dominators to concentrate their followers like this. Was it just out of convenience, or did it have to do with Karma? Was the effect of faith more pronounced when one's followers gathered together rather than having them spread across the planet?

It was undeniably how cults worked, where groups of people secluded themselves from the rest of the world. This closed system shut out any dissenting voices, which led to a deeper and deeper indoctrination.

"We will need the help of another human force for this," Zac said as he looked at the map. "I don't have access to that many teleporters."

"Do you still have multiple factions within your species? We thought the human towns were all under you?" Rhubat asked with confusion. "I have seen the strength of the other human elites. How can they challenge your rule?"

Zac didn't understand the question at first, but it turned out that the Zhix had already changed their structure so that there were only two forces among their people: the Council of the Anointed and the Dominators. All Anointed-run hives were accessible for all the Zhix, whereas they were obviously shut out from their enemies' teleporters.

It was extremely different from humans, who not only had a handful of major factions like Port Atwood and the New World Government, but also dozens of midsized forces, though most of the midsized forces were kind of under the umbrella of the Marshall Clan by now. There were even hundreds, perhaps thousands, of towns that weren't really aligned with any of the forces, but rather free bases that had survived some way or another.

"I have been busy throwing out all the invaders of our planet until now," Zac said. "I guess humans are a bit more individualistic as well. We didn't really get along before the integration either. I probably won't meddle with the human forces unless necessary. But I can fetch a guide to open the portals for us without a problem."

The group went over the details for some time, but the idea was quite simple. Zac would enter a human-controlled town ahead of the army together with a squadron of Zhix scouts, and they would rush to the hive and get ready to activate the jammers. The army would enter after a short interval, and Zac would activate the jammers the moment the last of the Zhix army had passed through the teleporter.

Activating the jammer before the army had actually arrived at the hive might warn the traitor Zhix, but they were afraid that the elites would flee through the teleporter the moment they spotted an incoming army. The elites might still try to flee by foot, but the scouts would hopefully be able to spot them this way.

As for the battle itself, it sounded straightforward enough. The Anointed would act as wall breakers and crush all resistance, while the normal Zhix warriors would back them up. In case one of the Dominators showed up, they would take them down even if they had to sacrifice tens of thousands of lives.

"How long do you need to prepare, Warmaster?" Rhubat finally asked, surprising Zac a bit.

"I only need to pick up my ghost and a guide," Zac said after some thought. "It's dependent on how quickly you can gather your armies."

"The armies and the other Anointed are standing ready. Our movements are no doubt being watched, so we need to move quickly from this point on. We want to take out as many of these hives as possible before they adapt," Rhubat said as killing intent started to leak from its body. "If we can take down five of the hives before the rest gather, then we are confident in emerging victorious even if Void's Disciple shows up."

"Remember, not even the humans can know where we are going," Nonet added.

"I know." Zac nodded.

It was already known that there were humans co-operating with the Dominators, and they would have to move randomly to avoid being exposed and ambushed. There was no point in messing around, so Zac soon exited the secluded chambers. Ibtep was still waiting for him outside, and the scout joined him as they returned to Port Atwood.

However, Zac didn't even have time to call the ghost before he sensed strong fluctuations over at the Dao Repository.

"Wait here," Zac groaned in exasperation as he rushed over.

Thankfully, it turned out that it wasn't Brazla who was causing trouble. The square outside the repository was completely tranquil, and neither lightning bolts nor a massive face was hovering above it.

The fluctuations only grew in power, and Zac felt they came from inside the towers themselves.

Zac quickly entered the Towers of Myriad Dao, and he quickly spotted the source of the commotion, the statue of the Blade Emperor.

"The girl is coming out," Brazla said as he descended from a golden cloud floating around near the ceiling.

"Did she pass?" Zac asked as his eyes returned to the statue.

"She did, if barely," the Tool Spirit snorted as he turned two disdainful eyes toward the array in the same direction. "Though I'm not so sure she will have the guts to take on the following challenge in the E-grade."

36
INTENT

Zac looked over at the Tool Spirit with surprise. This time, Brazla was dressed like a scholar, and he held a golden abacus in his hands instead of some sort of oversized weaponry. There was also a sense of calmness in his eyes like he had transcended the mortal plane or was beyond mundane worries.

Of course, it was just Brazla playing the part, but it was far preferable to the domineering and arrogant persona he had when pretending to be a cultivator. In fact, Kenzie had already told him that Brazla was usually easier to deal with when he was dressed as a noncombat class. If you saw him wielding some sort of weaponry, you were usually better off throwing out a few compliments and trying again tomorrow.

Thea appeared the next moment, and Zac's eyes widened in shock when he saw her appearance. Brazla wasn't kidding around when he said that Thea had barely passed. She was unconscious, and she looked beyond wretched. Her clothes were in tatters, and her whole body was completely drenched in blood. Just a few stripes of her hair remained, hanging in clumps held together by coagulated blood.

The only thing that looked completely intact was a blue sword that hummed with power. It was gripped in Thea's right hand with such force that her knuckles were white. Zac wondered if this was the invisible weapon she usually wielded, or if it was something she had gained inside the inheritance.

This was not the time to worry about the details, and Zac unhesitantly rushed over as he took out one of his better healing pills. However, his mind actually screamed of danger the moment he reached her side.

"Wai–" Zac shouted as he jumped backward, but it was too late as an extremely sharp energy shot out of one of her wounds and flew toward him, cutting open a shallow wound on his right arm.

He had been utterly incapable of stopping that attack, and his usually impervious skin was cut like butter. If Zac had reacted any slower, he might actually have lost his arm. The odd energy thankfully didn't try again but rather returned and entered Thea's body once more, causing a small shudder.

Zac barely felt any pain at all from the small cut, but a burning pain bloomed a second later. He looked down at the wound with surprise, and he found that it was an extremely clean wound, even exceeding the sharpness of the cuts he formed with [Rapturous Divide]. Was this the power of the Fragment of the Sword, or was this something else entirely?

Because that small energy didn't simply feel like a Dao.

"Such profound Dao Intent," Brazla muttered. "That strand of consciousness has actually made progress on his path."

"The Blade Emperor did this?" Zac asked. "And what is Dao Intent?"

"That girl is not adept enough in the Dao to form such a pure strand of Sword Intent. It can only come from Irei. It's really a shame," Brazla said, unfortunately ignoring the second question.

Only then did Thea wake up, and she looked around with some confusion before she realized where she was.

"Hey, catch this," Zac said before throwing the pill to Thea, who swallowed it before she once again closed her eyes to focus on her recuperation. Zac sighed in relief when he saw Thea was fine before he turned back to the Tool Spirit. "What's a shame?"

"Irei," Brazla said as he looked up at the statue. "He was destined to become a C-grade Monarch, but he fell to his demons in the end. Do you know why the Blade Emperor is the only one who left a complete Heritage in addition to an inheritance?"

"Because he was a friend of your creator?" Zac asked, not hesitating to take advantage of the fact that Brazla was in one of his rare sharing moods today.

"True, but that's not the reason. It's here because of his obsession with the sword and creating a family. He adopted one sword child after another after marrying his main weapon, and he poured obscene amounts of wealth into them to awaken their spirits. When he ran out of money, he turned to my master, who helped him evolve the swords in return for the Heritage," Brazla said. "If he had used even a third of all that wealth on himself, he would have broken past his bottleneck without a doubt. He is the second most talented person of the seven."

"So what happened?" Zac asked.

"Mental disorder brought by betrayal. It turned into a heart demon that was the source of his obsession with gathering swords," Brazla said with a shake of his head. "Remember his fate well. You mundane beings are not meant to grasp at Heaven's secrets. To cultivate is to go against the Heavens, and it is not done without shedding your humanity. As the millennia pass, you will come to realize that you no longer recognize the person who stares back at you through the mirror."

Thea opened her eyes and listened to Brazla with a serious expression, and Zac felt a sense of heaviness as well. It was true. How could someone keep their humanity as the eons passed and almost everyone they had ever known had long turned to dust? The reasons for struggling to become more powerful might no longer matter, and you were suddenly just a walking nuclear weapon devoid of purpose.

"Thankfully, the Great Brazla is not limited by such trifles, as he is endless and eternal," Brazla said as he drifted away with a snort.

"Are you okay?" Zac asked, shaking off Brazla's ominous portents.

"I'll be fine. I haven't completely absorbed the sword energies. Did the Tool Spirit call it Sword Intent just now? And where is Billy?" Thea croaked.

"Billy is still inside," Zac said before looking at Thea with interest. "He called it both a Dao Intent and a Sword Intent. Are you able to share how it's created?"

That small amount of energy had been extremely powerful, and Zac was hoping to form something similar for himself. After all, if there was Sword Intent, then there should surely be Axe Intent as well.

If he could add that power to his strikes, then he would probably be able to fight one-tier-stronger enemies without breaking a sweat.

"It seems to be something that comes after a Dao Field," Thea hesitantly said as she started smearing her vast number of scars with some ointment. "The Blade Emperor was able to materialize real objects with it. He trapped me in a cage of Dao Intent swords, and I had to use my own Dao Field to get out. I'm not sure if it's even possible to create naturally in my rank. You might be able to do it."

"You vastly overestimate my skills," Zac said with a weak smile. "I can hit things pretty hard, but manipulation like that... That's another story."

"Well, it seems to work for you." Thea smiled in return. "I don't think there's only one route to getting stronger. It's more about finding what's suitable for you."

"I think you're right. So, how do you still have the energy?" Zac asked before he remembered how rude it was to pry into other's cultivation secrets. "Sorry, it's fine if you don't want to tell."

"It's okay. I was imparted with a small amount of Sword Intent to guide me on the path of the sword. I think I might be able to use it sort of like a mother dough for my own strikes too, as long as I don't overuse it," Thea said after some thought. "We could spar a bit if you want."

"It sounds like a good idea, but it will have to wait. The war against the Dominators is starting right now." Zac sighed.

"I'll come along," she said as she got up and started walking toward the exit, though her steps were shaky.

"Are you crazy?" Zac said as he rushed over to stabilize her. "You're covered in wounds; go rest. We do need someone from the Marshalls to take us around, but I'll grab one of your cousins."

"No, I'm going. I'm not staying behind any longer," Thea said with determination. "I'm moving forward as well."

"You... Fine." Zac sighed. "Our job is only ancillary anyway. I won't fight either; I'll just help with the jammers. This is the Zhix's war, and they don't want us to step in unless absolutely necessary."

"Fine," Thea said as she wobbled out of the Dao Repository.

"Are you really...?" Zac couldn't help but interject again, but he was quickly shut up by another glare.

Zac was about to call Triv as well, but he actually appeared from between two bushes and shot toward them.

"My Lord," Triv said, but his greeting turned into a scream as Thea unhesitantly drew her blade in one fluid motion aimed at slaughter. "Ai!"

"He's my butler," Zac shouted in alarm, and he barely had time to block the swing with Verun, narrowly preventing Triv from getting cut in two.

Normally, a sword swing wouldn't matter to a ghost, but Zac sensed a shadow of that terrifyingly sharp energy inside the weapon. He still wasn't completely clear how it was made, but it would definitely be able to harm the ghost since it was related to the Dao.

"I'm sorry," Thea said as she sheathed her weapon before she gave Zac an odd look. "You have a ghost butler?"

"This is why young master shouldn't consort with the living. Violent and lowly creatures." Triv sighed as he retreated some distance from Thea.

"Triv is quite knowledgeable about all kinds of things, and he helps me sorting out the day-to-day." Zac shrugged.

Zac hesitated for a bit before he also told Thea about Triv's early findings.

"A life and death planet," Thea slowly said before she sighed. "This will be a detriment to most of us."

"Well, as I said, it's not sure it will come to happen," Zac said as he scratched his chin, feeling a bit guilty.

There was no way it was a coincidence that the planet got such a weird attunement. Zac was the main contributor to the quest, dealing with the Lich King, the elite army, and two and a half of the generals himself. The planet probably got its attunements to match his, as the System wanted to gift him a suitable cultivation environment. The fact that it screwed over the rest of the planet wasn't something that the elitist System would care about.

"It might not be too bad for normal humans either. A lot of people lived quite well at the edge of the Dead Zone, living outside and hunting inside. As long as we can concentrate the attunements in certain spots, we can maintain that sort of balance," Zac added after a bit, trying to find some positives in the situation. "And both life and death are powerful attunements. Powerful healers and Black Mages might emerge from Earth in the future."

Undead might not be able to deal with life attunements, but humans didn't have the same limitations. Having a high affinity to Death was extremely unlikely, but people could still go down that path without too much going against them. Assassins, Necromancers, Black Mages. A death-attuned planet would help nurture all those kinds of powerful existences.

"That might be true. Even if half the world turns into a Dead Zone, there will still be plenty of room to live on." Thea slowly nodded as she walked toward the teleporter. "Well, that's an issue for later. Let's go."

"You might want to change clothes first." Zac coughed, which drew a snicker from Triv.

Only then did Thea look down at the rags she wore over her bloodied body, and her hand moved up to her almost-bald head. She stiffly nodded without a word, and Zac hurriedly led her to his sister's mansion, where she could shower and change.

She only emerged thirty minutes later, but the transformation was almost shocking. Her hair had been regrown and her clothes changed, but the sword scars remained all over her body, angry red lines that seemed to refuse to disappear. The wound on Zac's arm was actually in a similar state, though he felt it would close in a few hours.

That still was a pretty long time for an errant spurt of energy, just a fragment of whatever Thea carried inside her body. Zac could actually sense that very same power in her eyes, as her piercing blue eyes had gained an undeniable sharpness to them. It looked both dangerous and mesmerizing, and Zac found himself almost lost in that deep blue.

The only thing that he couldn't ascertain was whether that energy was something beneficial or yet another risky venture like his own Remnants. The trio soon returned to the teleporter where Ibtep still was waiting, and Zac turned to the ghost.

"You'd better enter your house for now. We'll be traveling with the Zhix for a while. The Anointed seem to really hate the undead."

"Those things," Triv muttered with a mix of disgust and incredulity, clearly understanding whom Zac was talking about. "Not natural."

"A being wrought from purest corruption shouldn't talk of what is natural," Ibtep said with a snort as it gave the ghost a look of askance.

Triv didn't respond and only flew into the pagoda in Zac's sleeve and disappeared. The trio activated the teleporter the next moment and found themselves surrounded by dozens of Anointed who stood ready. The teleporter they appeared in was a different one than the array he'd entered through last time.

They were in an unfathomably large underground chamber, and Zac spotted a vast army behind the towering priests. There were hundreds of thousands of Zhix standing ready and armed to their teeth, every one of them radiating palpable killing intent. The whole chamber felt like a pressure cooker from the accumulated aura, and it felt claustrophobic even though it was over twenty meters to the ceiling.

"We're ready to go," Zac said after making sure he wouldn't get sucker-punched again. "Where do you want to teleport first?"

"We want to take out the first hives as quickly as possible, which will hopefully help us trap more of them before they devise some sort of retaliation," Rhubat said as he turned to Thea, who was clearly affected by the extremely dense killing intent. "Please take us to the town called Lübeck, pathfinder."

37
WAR MACHINE

"I'm no–" Thea was about to interject, but she just shrugged and accepted her new title in the end.

Zac only smiled wryly as he stepped into the teleporter with Thea, the squad of ten Zhix scouts and Ibtep following close behind.

It looked like the town didn't get a lot of visitors, as the guards reeled with shock when their group stepped out of the teleporter. The reclusive Marshall scion wasn't immediately recognized, but the small German town exploded with activity when the guards realized who they were.

The mayor, a shockingly rotund middle-aged lady, came rushing over with such momentum that she almost looked like a spherical blur.

"Our armies are passing through here," Thea said without preamble when the breathless mayor appeared. "More Zhix will come. A lot more. Tell your people to stand down. And close the gates to make sure our presence isn't leaked."

Zac nodded when he saw the mayor give a rapid series of orders into a walkie-talkie without hesitation. Bringing a big shot like Thea rather than some random guide was already proving to be the right choice. He needed to hold up his part of the bargain, so he turned to the group of scouts, who all seemed fully focused on the mission.

"We'll go on ahead," Zac said as he took out his leaf. "Can you stay here and make sure there's no trouble?"

"Sure." Thea nodded. "I'll catch up with the army."

The group of scouts stepped onto the leaf after some explaining, and the group of twelve shot out toward the enemy hive. They stayed close to the ground to avoid being spotted, though Zhix surveillance was seldom performed aboveground. They rather built scouting chutes designed to catch the vibrations from the surface, sending the signals back to the hives as an early warning.

It only took them thirty minutes to reach their destination, a dense crop of forest on the opposite side of the hive. Zac figured that the array of Lübeck should be unaffected when activating the jammer at this position, though the thing hadn't been through enough testing to ascertain its exact limits. This would be a learning experience for him as well.

The leaf stopped just above the ground, and the group of scouts nodded at Zac before they spread out through the forest, soundlessly moving between the trees like ghosts. Only Ibtep stayed behind in case they were needed to communicate with the Zhix army. Zac stepped down from the flying treasure as well and took out a concealment array disk to avoid being spotted.

He took out the jamming array next, while also prodding the sigil in his mind that connected him to his butler. The small pagoda floated out from his sleeve a second later, after which the ghost appeared.

"My Lord," Triv said with a bow as he looked around.

"Convenient," Ibtep muttered from the side, its eyes trained on the small pagoda. "Is it the same magic as that of the Ayn hive in your base? If the Zhix could use this sort of magic on our hives…"

"I'm not sure," Zac said. "I think only ghosts can live in this pagoda. But the Ayn hive might be possible to mimic? Not sure how much use it would be, though."

"Imagine, one Zhix could carry a whole hive in their pocket, tens of thousands of warriors pouring out when attacked," Ibtep muttered.

"I think it would be a bit uncomfortable to stay in someone's pocket all day. Imagine the shaking," Zac countered, which made Ibtep nod thoughtfully.

"This item is not made for the living," Triv said as he shot Ibtep a cool glance. "There are many ways to create portable worlds, but all of them are beyond your means."

"Some further thinking is required on this matter," Ibtep only murmured, their eyes clearly spinning with ideas.

Zac shrugged and turned back toward the jamming array. The thing was pretty much idiotproof thanks to his sister, so he only needed to place it down on the ground and insert fifty E-grade Miasma Crystals. He started to get to work, and Triv soon floated over to look at the jammer with interest.

The preparations were soon finished, and Zac performed a cursory inspection before he sent a message to Thea to start calling over the Zhix. His job was essentially done by now, and he only needed to make sure no one messed with the jammer.

"The modifications are crude, but they can't hide the amazing ideas they were built upon. To think that it would be possible to rework the array this way. The person who did this is definitely a genius," Triv muttered before he turned to Zac. "It's your sister, isn't it? She has a unique talent when it comes to understanding and modifying energy paths."

Zac thought for a second before he nodded in affirmation. It wasn't like it was a big secret, especially not after Kenzie had helped Triv create his cultivation cave.

"You might want to consider sending her to one of the powerful craftsmen sects in the sector," the ghost said. "It comes with some restrictions, but she will get proper guidance, and she can return home as a resident Array Master after having reached a certain level."

"Why would a sect be generous enough to train people before letting them go?" Zac asked with skepticism. "That would be like watering someone else's fields."

"They take a tax. If your sister returns to your force, you will have to pay a fee based on her attainments, part of which would go to the sect as remuneration for the training," Triv said. "It is mostly just academies and craftsmen sects that do things this way, though. Joining a combat-focused sect is generally a more permanent decision."

"Pay a fee? For life?" Zac asked with a frown.

"No, until enough benefits have been provided," Triv said. "She can also work off that debt herself as a roaming cultivator or by staying inside the sect."

"So you essentially become an indentured worker until you can free yourself?" Zac sighed. "Doesn't sound like a good place to send Kenzie."

"It might sound harsh, but such are the rules of the universe. No one will go out of their way and share their arduously accumulated Heritage for no return. Just working off the debt over a few centuries isn't too bad. It will help you improve on your craft, and there is no lack of applicants to such places. The best ones require both great connections and heaven-sent talents," Triv said.

Kenzie's future was something Zac often thought about, but it was ultimately up to her what path she wanted to take. She would need to find some environment that suited her unique gifts, and Zac knew that place wasn't by his side. He needed mountains of enemies to cut his way through in order to progress, but she seemed far better suited to orthodox cultivation.

Jeeves was able to improve both her class and her skills, and Kenzie also made tremendous progress by just cultivating inside his cultivation cave. She might be able to make huge gains if she entered some of those ancient places and gobbled up and improved all the great manuals and skills for herself. Just the thought made him both a bit excited and jealous.

"What about me?" Zac asked. "Aren't there some good opportunities for me like that as well?"

"Well... perhaps," Triv said hesitantly. "Young master might be better off joining an army or a mercenary band and fighting at the borders."

The borders in this case were referring to the space outside the properly integrated space. The Zecia Sector was huge, and it turned out that less than 3% could actually be considered part of some force's domain. Most star systems might officially be within the domain of an empire or sect, but there was no way that they had the manpower or resources to keep a presence in the more remote zones.

The planet he had been sent to for his Sovereignty quest was a prime example of that situation. The planet was integrated and part of the Allbright Empire, but it was so weak and declined that the System only provided the barest of functions. Most unclaimed territories were just a bunch of junk planets with low potential, but millions of clans, sects, and mercenary groups traveled those zones in search of riches.

There was always some treasure hiding among the mountain of trash. You never knew when you might find an unclaimed Mystic Realm, precious remnants, or valuable treasures that had been left to grow for tens of thousands of years.

There were also the even more chaotic danger zones, such as the boundless area full of spatial anomalies close to the Allbright Empire. There were no doubt far more opportunities there compared to the unclaimed areas, but there were also far more dangers. Only the craziest mercenaries decided to risk their lives in such a place, contending not only with the pirates and unorthodox forces, but with the fickleness of space itself.

Zac still hadn't decided on his future course of action, but he instinctively felt unwilling to join a mercenary band or some army like Average. First of all, there was the risk of someone higher up in the organization becoming interested in digging out his secrets. But there was also the simple fact that Zac enjoyed his freedom.

His life had become a lot worse by most metrics since the integration, but one big plus was the huge degree of freedom he enjoyed.

"They're all through," Thea said through the crystal, waking Zac up from his dreams of the future.

"Do it." Zac nodded at Triv, and the ghost infused his Miasma into the jammer.

The array hummed into life, and Zac felt a weak pulse spreading out from where they stood. However, the wave turned invisible after less than ten meters, and Zac knew there was no way the Zhix would be able to find the source. He jumped up to sit on the branch of one of the taller trees, and it gave him a secluded vantage of the hive far in the distance.

Now it was up to the Zhix to deal with the rest.

Nonet walked at the forefront of the army, the warriors of Hive Kundevi following close behind. The chaos in the human settlement caused by their appearance had been cause for some amusement, but it couldn't shake the sense of heaviness that gripped the heart of the army. It wasn't natural. Using corruption to fight other Zhix because of their use of corruption.

Of course, the situation wasn't as simple as that, but that was still how it felt among some of the army. There were no doubt still many Zhix inside the enemy hives who believed in the old precepts as well, but it couldn't be helped. The corruption needed to be cleansed once and for all, and no roots of evil left behind.

"Get ready," Rhubat rumbled from his position at the vanguard, and Nonet looked up and saw the hive in the distance.

The walls were lined with soldiers standing in wait, but Nonet only needed a single glance to realize that the defenders were both outnumbered and lacking in power. This wouldn't be a battle, but a slaughter. A few warriors of Hive Kundevi seemed to have reached the same conclusion, as some struggle appeared on their faces.

"Remember the cause; remember the precepts," Nonet said with a heavy tone, and the warriors shook themselves free from any stray thoughts.

There were no negotiations and no posturing. Rhubat started increasing his steps as they came closer to the hive, and the Anointed lit up with corruption as the vast army behind them started running to keep up with their leaders.

Hundreds of Punishment Spears, each of them dozens of meters long, appeared in the sky, all of them shuddering with unbridled killing intent. A rumbling roar was finally unleashed from the hundreds of thousands of warriors who covered the vast plains, and the air shook as a red cloud spread across the area.

The haze was made from the congealed killing intent of the army, and it smoothly entered the fractal spears, empowering them with conviction. The Punishment Spears sucked in more and more, and the first group of attacks finally soared toward the hive as Rhubat, Vanexis, and Raha each launched their spears forward with a mental command.

Their power was far beyond that of the other Anointed, and they were able to carry the will of the Zhix with far greater grace than Nonet could ever dream of. The whole mountain vibrated as the spears soared toward the standing army, but a massive shield sprang up to block them out. It looked like someone had stolen a piece of the night sky, a vast cosmos that enclosed the whole mountain that held the Dominator hive.

It was them. It was the undeniable mark of the Dominators, the proof of their corruption. Only they had the ability to drown the world in night like this. However, the scene didn't deter the crusaders in the slightest. It only bolstered their conviction, and dozens of spears shot into the shield the next moment as the Anointed poured everything they had into the projectiles.

They all carried the momentum the Zhix had accumulated for millennia, the will to break free of the chains of the Dominators.

The shield barely managed to hold against the attacks, but they weren't done there. A ten-meter insignia depicting the seal of Hive Kundevi appeared behind Nonet, and similar scenes played out all across the front of the army. The seal shone down at Nonet, causing its frame to grow another meter as the regalia of the crusade covered its frame.

The power of the Anointment coursed through Nonet's veins, and all hesitation and worries were burnt out of its mind. The future didn't matter any longer. Only the crusade mattered. Nonet's feet turned to a blur as the leader shot toward the galactic shield, its ceremonial dagger already glowing with radiant luster.

A terrifying shockwave spread out as Nonet slammed into the wall, and small cracks spread out from where the dagger hit the barrier. The other Anointed had done the same, and the earth shook as one massive attack after another was launched. The shield finally couldn't take it any longer, and the night sky dissipated like it had just been a dream.

Nonet didn't need to give a signal on what to do next. The warriors of Hive Kundevi followed close behind as Nonet made its move. A squad of traitors was butchered with one swing of Nonet's dagger, and the Kundevi warriors made short work of the survivors. There were a lot of traitors still outside, but Nonet didn't focus on that as it pushed itself into the cramped entrance in front of it. Nonet had a mission to perform, and there would be others to deal with the warriors on the slopes.

The furious war machine of the Zhix had once again awoken to face the threat of the Dominators, and not a single soul would be spared.

38
MASSACRE

Zac looked on with both awe and horror at the carnage that was taking place in the distance. The Anointed were simply terrifying when working together, and Zac doubted that any local faction apart from his own would be able to survive their assault. He suddenly felt a presence to his side, and he looked over to a neighboring tree as he drew his axe.

"Hey," Thea said as she landed.

"Was I that easy to spot?" Zac grimaced as he put **[Verun's Bite]** away.

"Well, I knew the jammer would be placed in this area, and that you would spectate. It was only a matter of time," Thea said as she turned back to the battlefield. "It's a massacre."

There were no two ways about it. The Zhix crusaders were obviously not interested in taking prisoners or holding any trials to find the true culprits. Everyone in the hive received the same treatment: a swift death.

Only ten minutes had passed since the battle started, but less than 1% of the defending warriors remained. They were fighting desperately to prolong the inevitable, and Zac knew they fought for their honor, to prove their strength to their ancestors before they joined their ranks in the afterlife.

"A lot of them seem to have entered the hive, killing the civilians as well," Thea added after a brief pause.

"I know." Zac nodded.

"You could stop them. They would back down if you demanded it," she said.

"I think you underestimate the importance the Zhix put on this war. It's the very core of their society. Me telling them to stop would probably just give them two targets to fight rather than one," Zac said, and he added after some hesitation, "But I have no intention of finding out."

"How are we any different than our enemies if we go down this path?" Thea said as she turned to Zac.

There was no anger simmering in her eyes, nor was there reproach. There was only an almost disturbing tranquility.

"Who's to say we're any different?" Zac sighed. "We're just rival factions fighting in the mud. They must die so that we can live. We're not the good guys, and they aren't really the bad guys. At least not most of them. We just have opposing interests."

"Hmm," Thea only said, not commenting any further.

The silence stretched on, and Zac felt more and more suffocated as he looked at the increasingly silent mountain in the distance. Should he do something? Millions of lives would be extinguished just so that he could be sure that no Karmic threats were lurking on Earth. How could he be so calm while enabling a genocide?

"Someone's running," Thea suddenly said, and Zac saw what she was talking about.

A hidden door had appeared just a few hundred meters away from their location, and a group of Zhix was hurrying out through it. It looked to be mostly elders and clergymen, but they were guarded by a squad of elites. It was probably the leaders of the hive, the mouthpieces of the true Dominators. They were the true target, at least for Zac, and if these people managed to flee, then the crusade would lose most of its meaning.

The hidden exit was extremely far from the hive itself, and there was no way that their actions could be spotted by the Anointed. The squad of scouts wouldn't be able to stop these guys either, even if they put their lives on the line.

"I'll deal with it," Zac said and flashed away, each step taking him dozens of meters through the forest.

He appeared in front of the group of Zhix just a few seconds later, prompting the group to stop in their tracks. They first looked horrified upon being intercepted, but they soon breathed out in relief when they saw it wasn't an Anointed waiting for them, but rather a human.

"A human?!" one of the elders exclaimed as they took two steps forward. "Did your government send you? Hurry, help us get away from here. Our master is Void's Disciple, and we have a working cooperation with your kind. You will be richl–"

The old Zhix didn't get any further. Its body froze for an instant before it fell apart as blood spurted in every direction. A blue wave spread out the next moment, reaping the lives of more than half of the remaining escapees. Only those lucky enough to be standing far away survived the attack that seemingly came out of nowhere.

It was Thea, who had arrived as well, weaving a tapestry of death all around her. A few of the guards shot toward her with reckless abandon, releasing a terrifying killing intent. They all seemed to have the same class as well, some sort of earthen warrior. Stones grew to cover their whole bodies, and they quickly grew into three-meter golems with sharp spikes for arms.

Was this perhaps something devised to counter the towering Anointed?

Carrying around a ton of rock on their bodies did nothing to slow them down, and they tried to stab Thea from every direction. However, their rocky exterior was like paper in front of her, and each swing of her new weapon reaped a life. She weaved through the insectoids like a dancer, each of her strikes both beautiful and deadly.

Zac first felt her swordsmanship seemed a bit ostentatious, but he soon realized there was meaning behind every movement. Just slightly repositioning her shoulder or lifting her weapon a few degrees caused changes in the battlefield as the warriors instinctively responded. It was like she was a puppeteer who magically created openings in her opponents to deliver instant death.

The battle was over in less than thirty seconds, with Zac only killing two unlucky fellows who ran straight at him in their attempts to flee from Thea. The Marshall scion had done the rest, and her breath wasn't even labored, although Zac knew she wasn't in perfect condition at the moment. She looked over at Zac with a small smile before she shook her head and walked over.

"I've told you already, stupid. You're not alone in wanting to protect Earth," she said as she swung her sword in the air, causing all the blood on it to fly off its edge. "You don't have to carry this burden alone. And for what it's worth, I think you're one of the good guys."

Two Zhix scouts appeared the next moment ready for battle, but they froze when they saw the carnage. Zac briefly explained the situation, and one of them set off to fetch a regiment that could explore the escape tunnel. Zac and Thea walked back to the spot where the jammer was placed, and they found Triv nervously flitting back and forth until he spotted Zac.

The war was still raging, but there were no more breakouts, it seemed. Zac wordlessly watched as the last of the insurgent Zhix fell, his mind repeating Thea's words over and over. It helped him with his confusion a bit, but it was impossible to completely shrug off the weight of sin he had amassed today.

The four just needed to wait for another twenty minutes before one of the scouts returned to their hiding spot.

"It is done, Warmaster. You can release the lock," the scout said. "The Anointed asked for you."

"We'll be there in a minute." Zac nodded as he started to take out the Miasma Crystals from the array as Triv returned to his pagoda.

The group flew over to the fallen hive a second later, and they were shocked by the sight even if they had witnessed everything from a distance. It looked like the lone mountain was crying, as streams of blood covered its slopes. The smell was even worse, and Thea visibly paled before she bent over and puked.

Even Zac felt nauseated by the intense stench of death as he landed the leaf. There were thankfully almost no corpses around, but an enormous pyre was already burning some distance from the hive. Between the small mountain of corpses and how the world had been painted in blood, it really felt like they had entered the depths of hell.

Zac once more felt his conviction waver as he looked around. It felt like this whole mountain had become cursed from what had transpired. Ominous energies swirled around the mountain, visible only to his [Cosmic Gaze]. This was something that couldn't be created by a normal war as far as he could tell, but rather a mass genocide of an entire population.

"Warmaster," a bloodied Rhubat said as they walked over, "the purification is complete. The next target awaits."

"Alright." Zac sighed, forcibly pushing down all the confusion and hesitation. "Where to?"

"Come with us first," Rhubat said as they activated the teleporter and walked inside.

At least 90% of the Anointed followed Rhubat, but only a small part of the ordinary soldiers entered as well. It was around ten thousand normal warriors, all of them emitting a bloody aura. Zac guessed it was the captains and sergeants of the army, and he soon followed inside as well with Thea and Ibtep.

They found themselves in another subterranean chamber the next moment, and Zac's eyes widened when there was yet another identical army already waiting. Its size was even larger than the last one, probably approaching half a million warriors.

"We hope to be able to strike at least three hives before they realize what's going on," Rhubat said. "After that, we will join our forces, as we expect them to do the same. The next town is Gothenburg."

Zac nodded in understanding and turned to Thea, who activated the teleporter once more.

The same scene repeated itself as the vanguard stepped through the teleporter. Thea stayed behind as Zac set off with the advance scouts, and he looked around with marvel as they flew across the desolate landscape.

Roughly a year had passed since the integration, which meant that summer should be approaching once more. However, you wouldn't get that feeling at all in the northern reaches of Pangea where the Scandinavian cultivators had banded together and formed Asgard, an independent force allied to the Marshall Clan.

It was Zac's first time this far out on the reaches of the main continent. He had generally traveled within the heartlands, where most humans and incursions ended up, or to the southeast where the Dead Zone was located. This area didn't look like the old Scandinavia, but it would be more apt to say they had appeared in the Arctic Circle.

Thick layers of ice and snow had turned the world white, but that actually didn't mean that it was lifeless. He saw towering trees braving the extreme weather, seemingly unbothered by the permafrost. A massive pack of wolves consisting of thousands of hunters passed by beneath them as well, proving there was ample prey available as well.

It was the magical effect of Cosmic Energy. Zac guessed the temperature was minus 30 degrees or so, but he only felt a bit chilly in his normal robes. It would have to become a lot colder than this for him to be affected at all, so it was no wonder that beasts could deal with it just fine. There had probably been a lot of humans who succumbed to the harsh environment at the beginning of the integration.

They soon found their spot close to the hive and set up the jamming array, hidden by a mountain of ice. The same scene of carnage repeated itself an hour later. The snow-covered hive turned completely red as the merciless Zhix army slaughtered all the citizens of the hive. Zac started to feel numb to the carnage, but he still felt hollow inside as he gazed at the puddles of blood that had turned to ice all over the mountain.

The slaughter continued from there, but something suddenly changed when the army arrived at the fifth hive. This time, a full million Zhix marched across the wasteland, and Zac felt horrified at the amount of Nexus Coins the Zhix had spent to move around the armies like this. A war of this scale was probably only possible thanks to the wealth that the Zhix had gained from fighting the Zombies over the past months.

The last four assaults were essentially one-sided slaughters, but it looked like the Dominators were finally responding in kind. There was barely any free ground around the insurgent hive, as hundreds of thousands of warriors stood at the ready.

There were also unfamiliar towers that had been erected at the perimeter, seemingly a last-minute purchase from the Town Shop. They all radiated power, and Zac knew that there would be noticeable casualties to push past that line of defense. He even asked if they wanted him to act as a wall-breaker, but the Zhix War Council actually rejected it.

He could only shake his head in bemusement as he looked on, but he was relieved to see that the Zhix weren't completely incapable of resisting the fiery barrages that the towers launched. Those enormous seals that the Anointed summoned seemed to be a natural War Array of some kind, and the Zhix warriors infused it with power to create a sturdy shield that protected them from attacks coming from above.

However, the Array Towers were only the first counter that the defenders had prepared for them.

Hidden pathways suddenly opened up behind the Anointed army, and warriors flooded out of them. The War Council suddenly found themselves pincered as they dealt with the barriers and Array Towers to the front, and an all-out assault from the rear. Worse yet, almost all of the Anointed were on the other side of the army, acting as a vanguard, so the elite Zhix among the Dominators faced little resistance as they pushed into the rear guard.

Worry gripped Zac's heart as he looked at the scene, and he decisively started walking toward the army with a ruthless gleam. He had happily stayed out of the war until now as some sort of coping mechanism, but he couldn't allow this to go on. Their losses would be too big if he didn't turn things around.

"Are you really doing this? After standing back so long?" Thea asked from behind, and Zac only nodded in response.

However, he only managed to take a few steps before his mind screamed of danger. He tried to flash away, but he was shocked to find himself rooted in place as the whole world rapidly slowed to a crawl. One possibility immediately entered his mind.

Had the true Dominators finally made their appearance?

39
MONSTER

Zac's danger sense was screaming for him to watch out, but he didn't need a sixth sense to realize that he was in trouble. He activated **[Hatchetman's Spirit]** while the emerald leaves of **[Nature's Barrier]** exploded out from his body, covering him from every direction.

The spectral forest rose around him as well, but Zac's worries only intensified when he saw that the trees and leaves of his two skills were quickly stopped in their tracks as well. The leaves just froze in the air, utterly incapable of intercepting any attacks. He tried to look around in search of a threat, but he found himself stuck in position as well, no longer able to move at all.

The war was still raging in the distance, proving that time hadn't really stopped. It seemed that the effect only reached thirty meters or so judging by the movement of the grass on the ground. It was an extremely uncomfortable experience to somehow be out of sync with the world around him. It felt a bit like when the world froze from the Chaos Pattern's emergence inside the Tower, but he also got a similar feeling like when the Karmic Cultivator of the Hayner Clan had tried to control his movements.

Zac could at least be certain that it wasn't the System who was messing with him. A large hooded being had appeared in the sky, reaching over twenty meters into the air. Zac tried to discern its features, but it actually looked like it didn't have a face. In place of facial features, there was just a swirling void.

It held some weird brass contraption that seemed to contain the mysteries of the universe itself, and it felt like it was this item that was rooting him in place. Zac couldn't be sure, but he believed that the skill contained a hint of both Space and Karma. Zac guessed that it was the avatar of some sort of ultimate technique, and going by the types of energies, there was one clear suspect; the Dominators.

Zac was quickly proven right when he finally spotted the source of the restraints, an unassuming Zhix wearing the standard combat regalia of the Zhix War Council Army. However, instead of the short spears or daggers that the Zhix favored, they were instead wielding a pitch-black spear of full length that hummed with power.

The reason Zac knew this spear-wielding Zhix was his attacker was simple; he couldn't sense the warrior's aura. It was just like when he first met Inevitability; it was almost like there was no one standing in front of him. However, the Zhix warrior was very much alive, and they stepped into the locked zone and started making their way toward Zac.

Zac strained to rip himself free, but he couldn't even begin amassing any power in his limbs. It felt like he was trying to overturn the fundamental laws of the universe by moving; he glanced at the Zhix with some incredulity. How were they this strong? The strength of this restraining skill meant two things.

First of all, he could pretty much be sure that he was dealing with Harbinger, the last of the three elite Dominators. He had already met the other two, and the presumed Dominators beneath the three leaders were over fifteen levels behind. There was no way someone at level 85 would be able to unleash a force of this magnitude.

Secondly, the Dominator was likely burning their life force to deal with him. Zac knew that the Dominators were strong, but there shouldn't be such a disparity that he couldn't even lift his fingers in response. There was also a familiar aura on them, reminding him of that old warrior among the Berum Resistance who sacrificed his life to let them assault the Nenothep mountain.

Messing with life force wasn't something that people could do willy-nilly. First of all, you generally needed some sort of Berserker skill to tap into the core of your being. Using such a thing was equivalent to sacrificing eight hundred warriors to kill a thousand. It wasn't a tap you could turn on and off, but something that had a large risk of killing or crippling your cultivation. Zac knew he was an exception of sorts with how the Shard worked.

Harbinger was going a step further, putting everything on the line.

However, Zac didn't feel hopeless, as there were no doubt limitations to a skill or treasure as powerful as this. As expected, not only did Harbinger have some problems pushing through the spatial lock themselves, but the avatar was slowly dissipating in the sky.

A quick calculation proved that Zac would get skewered before the lock dissipated, and he frantically looked for a solution. A glance toward Thea showed that she was trapped as well, but she was thankfully at the edge of the sphere. There was no way that Harbinger would have time to target them both, as they could only move at a slow walk.

The Cosmic Energy felt like syrup in his body, and Zac wasn't really able to rotate it with the momentum needed to activate his skills. However, he had actually already activated two of them, and Zac gave a command to the divine tree stalwartly standing behind him.

The ceremonial band on the tree trunk snapped, and a shield started to form around him. However, just the edges had time to materialize before it was frozen as well, essentially looking like a hollow ring completely incapable of defending anyone. Zac wanted to swear when he saw the scene, but he was unable to form the words.

A defensive talisman fizzled the next moment as well, proving that the restrictions didn't only apply to his skills.

Harbinger seemed to have expected the failures, and a small smile crept up across their face as they closed in on Zac. Their spear moved in slow motion, but it slowly angled itself to begin a mighty jab aimed straight at his throat. The Dominator was going for an instant kill.

Real worry finally started to grip Zac's heart as one backup plan after another failed. He had initially believed that he would always be able to flee with the help of his newly acquired escape talismans, but he wasn't so sure any longer after seeing how nothing seemed to work inside this field.

However, a shudder in his mind suddenly made his eyes light up.

Most things were frozen in place, but there were exceptions. No matter what Daos and treasures were the basis for Harbinger's temporal bubble, how could they restrain the ancient slivers in his mind? The two Remnants were completely unaffected inside their prison, and the mysterious energies that had infiltrated his soul moved about as usual as well.

Wasn't this a perfect occasion to try out something he had been holding on to up until now?

Thea hovered frozen in the air, filled with a sense of impotence as she saw Zac in the same predicament. The terrifying Zhix pushed through the sealed space as though it were wading through water, and it was almost upon Zac. Its spear was already moving toward Zac's throat, and the weapon gained a stronger and stronger radiance.

The air around the weapon was cracking and splitting apart, which was very telling of its power. The Zhix was putting it all on the line with that one strike. Thea could even sense they were empowered by an offensive Dao Fragment, and she wasn't confident that even Zac's terrifying constitution would be able to withstand the attack.

She tried to figure out some way to help him out, just long enough for this seal to break, but she was coming up empty-handed. Her skills simply wouldn't activate, and she wasn't able to reach down toward her Cosmos Sack to take out any treasures. She felt her eyes were burning as she saw the spear point inching ever closer, passing straight beneath the incipient emerald shield that had failed to properly form.

Was this it? She had finally regained her momentum, and the two were almost walking in step again. Was it all about to be taken from her again?

A shocking aura suddenly slammed into the core of her being, and she looked with shock and horror at Zac. He looked the same as before, but Thea felt that she was gazing upon a natural calamity rather than a fellow cultivator. His eyes turned into metallic orbs as black runes slowly appeared across his face, creating tattoo pathways that led down toward his shoulders.

The runes looked simple enough, but they still contained a primordial power, something that Thea hadn't even encountered when dealing with Irei or his terrifying Sword Intent. Just what had Zac gotten himself mixed up in to have something so terrifying appearing on his body?

Unfortunately, it didn't seem as though the Zhix was deterred by Zac's outburst of power, but rather the opposite. Its mouth curved upward in a ruthless smile, and its until now subdued aura exploded outward, hitting Thea like a sledgehammer. How was this assassin so powerful? The aura was far stronger than that of Inevitability back during the Hunt!

Was it actually Void's Disciple, the leader of the Dominators?

Or had Inevitability perhaps actually been limited somehow inside the Hunt, making that chain-wielding lunatic unable to put forth their full potential. It didn't matter right now, though, as the spear was cutting through space itself as it finally reached Zac's throat.

However, no blood was actually drawn. The mysterious runes already covered much of Zac's throat, and they seemed able to resist the sharp point of the pitch-black spear. The Zhix didn't seem surprised, and a shimmering fractal halo made from inscrutable runes lit up behind them like they were a saint who had suddenly reached enlightenment.

The whole area was drowned in a shimmering dark-blue luster, and the spear gained newfound momentum as it was flooded with foreign but powerful energy. It allowed the spear to push even further into Zac's skin as it seemed to infuse the spear itself with some mysterious power. Zac's defenses couldn't stop the weapon, and the weapon finally started sliding into his throat. There were no groans of pain or gouts of blood, but Thea knew that was only because space was still frozen.

Despair flooded Thea's heart as she saw Zac's throat slowly being ripped open; the sickening sound of the spear digging deeper was the only thing she could hear in this frozen zone. How could this be the fate of Earth's savior? Was the defense of his mysterious tattoos really not enough to save him?

A terrifying change suddenly took place as Zac finally exploded with power. It was like that terrifying aura from before was congealed, and she looked on with incredulity as Zac's arms suddenly shot forward with impossible speed as a sphere of unadulterated power emerged from his hands.

It felt like Thea's brain stopped working as she looked at the pitch-black sphere. It was as big as a football, but it somehow felt as massive as a sun. Even odder, it felt like her memory and impressions were continuously being destroyed and renewed as she looked at it, making it impossible for her to form an opinion on what that thing was actually made from. It was Dao, but it wasn't Dao. It was Cosmic Energy, but it wasn't Cosmic Energy.

One thing was for sure: it wasn't restrained by the spatial cage they found themselves in, and it flew straight toward the chest of the Dominator. The Zhix saw the sphere shooting toward its body, but it completely ignored it and instead pushed its weapon even harder, seemingly fine with both of them going down to the underworld together.

But even that powerful Zhix couldn't have anticipated the scene that took place next.

There was no explosion and no shockwave as the ball hit the chest of the assassin, just an instantaneous expansion followed by utter annihilation. Thea couldn't see exactly how big the attack was, as there literally wasn't anything to see, but she could still sense what *didn't* exist. It felt like space and time had simply been removed from existence where the sphere exploded, and not even a vacuum remained.

The spatial lock was broken as the massive avatar in the sky fell apart, and the ground beneath Thea cracked as she shot away as quickly as her legs could move her. It wasn't a conscious decision, but a primal fear of whatever Zac had unleashed. To get too close was to die, where one's soul wouldn't even be able to remain. Only after running for hundreds of meters did she manage to stop herself, but her heart wouldn't stop hammering in her chest.

Only then did Thea see what had happened to the Zhix. Its torso and most of its legs were simply gone, leaving not so much as a scrap behind. Most of its arms had been annihilated as well, only hanging on to its neck by a thin ribbon of flesh. She knew there was no coming back from that, especially as she could sense a hint of that aura of annihilation in its remaining body parts as well.

Zac looked the same as before apart from the running blood that stained his chest red. The spear was still embedded in his throat, but he ripped it out without a care in the world. Thea's horror increased even further when the wound closed on itself with speed visible to the eyes, and there was only one thought in her head when she saw those terrifying lifeless eyes of his.

Monster.

40
WRATH

A wave of pain spread across Zac's body, shocking him awake from his trancelike state. He still felt under the influence of his skill, as the world was drowned in a metallic luster. He took a steadying breath as he looked around, and he finally spotted the remains of Harbinger.

Zac's brows rose when he realized that he actually hadn't gained any Cosmic Energy so far, and he pushed his exhausted body to walk over to the Zhix assassin. He was full of vigilance that it might release a final desperate attack, but he quickly realized that Harbinger was in no position to do so.

Cracks spread across the insectoid's remaining body parts before they crumbled to dust like his body was made from burnt-out wood rather than flesh and blood. There was also no energy remaining in its body according to [Cosmic Gaze]. The fact that the Zhix was still living was a miracle. There was no way that it would have the power to attack in this state.

"You sacrificed most of your life force to keep me trapped so long. Even if you succeeded, you wouldn't live much longer," Zac said with a hoarse voice. "All this for some insane cultivator who happened to visit your world thousands of years ago?"

"I... don't care... about him," the crumbling head actually managed to say with a whisper. "All... for... Father."

Harbinger died the next moment, and Zac felt a tremendous surge of Cosmic Energy entering his body. This was by far the greatest amount of energy he had ever gained from a single kill, with the possible exception of the dragon. However, he had been both level capped and unconscious that time around, so it didn't really count.

Cracking open the next node shouldn't be an issue with this much energy, even if he barely had worked on it so far. However, Zac wasn't as interested in a single node compared to the other things that were going on in his body, so he just trapped the energy before moving on.

This was the first time he had activated his **[Cyclic Strike]** to summon a bronze flash since his battle with the dragon, and he was a bit shocked how well things went, all things considered. There was no need to maim himself and almost no difficulty at all summoning the bronze flash, and he somehow even managed to shoot it out of his hands.

It really seemed that the forcibly redrawn pathways on his shoulders did exactly what he had hoped.

However, even if the result was good, there were undeniably some problems with how things went. First of all, he'd quickly lost control over the Remnants' energies, and he'd ended up using everything instead of just a portion. His soul was completely drained of the energy that had been slowly siphoned off the Splinter, and it would probably take weeks before he could even launch a weaker bronze flash.

He had also completely blacked out there for a second when the infused energies passed a certain threshold. He had felt a sharp stab in his soul and only woke up after he had finished the attack. However, he had not only launched the strike but even healed himself with the help of the Shard of Creation while unconscious, and there were fragmented memories of his actions.

Perhaps it would be more apt to say that he had entered some sort of autopilot or trancelike state, but it made him wonder if it was actually himself or the Remnants that were behind the wheel. In any case, it proved that he needed to keep grinding at the Soul Strengthening Array. He had been able to use his mind to slow down the flow of energy a little bit when activating **[Cyclic Strike]**, proving he might be able to freely control it in the future.

"Are… you okay?" a hesitant voice asked from the side, dragging Zac out of his thoughts.

Zac looked over, only to feel a searing pain on his shoulder. A couple of hairline cracks had appeared out of nowhere just as some sort of fractal pathway disappeared, looking just like the ones that had consumed the remains of Harbinger. Fear surged in Zac's chest, but he slowly calmed down when he realized that it didn't seem as though the cracks would spread any further.

Was this a side effect from unleashing a bronze flash of this magnitude? Was his body perhaps unable to bear the Dao of Oblivion, even if it was just a shadow of a corner of that high-tiered Dao?

In fact, his attack couldn't really be called a flash any longer. It was a proper sphere of unadulterated annihilation. It had disintegrated everything within a one-meter diameter. That was enough to pretty much kill any humanoid of normal size. Better yet, Zac doubted that there were too many things on Earth that could block those kinds of scary energies.

Space itself broke apart and was destroyed; how was some defensive talisman going to protect against that?

"I'm fine," Zac eventually answered, though that wasn't entirely true.

The cracks on his shoulders weren't the only thing ailing him. Zac felt weak all over, like he hadn't only overtaxed his mind but also his body. He still had an ample amount of Cosmic Energy remaining, but his Mental Energy was almost drained clean.

"What... was that?" Thea eventually asked as she kept her distance from Zac. "My mind has never screamed of danger like that before, not even when I was on the brink of dying. And I wasn't even the target."

"I guess you could say it was pure annihilation." Zac sighed. "Don't think about it too much. It involves some things that I can't talk about. Just consider it one of my hidden cards."

"Some card," Thea muttered as she looked down at the tragic remains of Harbinger.

Harbinger's face had cracked in two and collapsed into its skull, making it seem as though the head was just a broken sculpture. Zac sighed as he looked at the odd scene. Some card indeed. Only he knew there were still too many issues to resolve before it could really be called a hidden card though.

Apart from his lacking control, there was one more fundamental weakness to his Annihilation Sphere: it took too long to charge up. Who would let Zac stand still for a few seconds while he radiated that terrifying aura? He got lucky with Harbinger since it was willing to die to complete his strike, but most people didn't have that conviction.

They would either strike him from a distance or run for their lives if they encountered an attack imbued with oblivion. They wouldn't be trapped in a spatial lock like Thea or Harbinger. That meant he needed to learn how to create an opening so that he could get a chance to shoot out the blast without obstruction or interruption.

"Annihilation... Even its Cosmos Sack is gone," Thea muttered from the side.

Zac swore in surprise and hurried over to the corpse, no longer caring about the long-term implications of his situation.

It was true. There was simply nothing left between the insectoid's lower thighs and shoulders. Not even a scrap remained, meaning anything Harbinger carried on its belt or back was gone.

"Well, shit."

"OPEN IT!" Inevitability screamed as the air around her wailed from her unbridled bloodlust.

"We can't, Lady Inevitability! There's a–" an elder cried, but they didn't get any further before they were turned to meat paste from a lashing.

Over one hundred corpses were already strewn around her, but it did nothing to stymie the fury that was building in her chest. She had hoped to unleash it on her brother's killer, but these people were useless. She couldn't hold it in any longer, and she released a roar filled with her fury and madness.

The whole chamber quaked, and cracks spread along the walls, but Inevitability didn't care as she let the anger consume her. It rose with wave after wave until she barely remembered her name; it was all made inconsequential by the fiery wrath. Crackling sounds echoed out in the subterranean chamber as her skin ruptured and fell apart, but a new layer had already grown beneath it.

It was different from before. The skin was harder yet flexible, and there were streaks of red hidden right beneath the surface. Inevitability's remaining sliver of sanity knew it was a good thing, and she kept delving deeper and deeper into her madness as her power skyrocketed.

She felt she was filled with boundless power, and dozens of chains appeared around her, wildly flailing about in a mad dance of exuberance. Harbinger was almost completely forgotten as she drank the sweet nectar of strength.

Some of the already damaged walls couldn't take it any longer and collapsed, and screams echoed out across the hive. However, the screams ended as abruptly as they came, as the chains seemed to have a life of their own. They shot forward like a pack of frenzied beasts the moment they found something living.

Of course, it was Inevitability that was giving free rein to her bloodlust. It felt like a bottomless abyss, but each kill filled it a little bit. The moment the abyss had turned into a sea of blood, she would be made whole.

"Enough."

The calm voice was like a bucket of cold water that ripped Inevitability back to reality. She found herself standing in the middle of the ruins of her hive, over ten layers turned to rubble. Thousands of corpses and hacked-off body parts were strewn across the area, and a putrid stench made her nose curl.

What bad luck that she had damaged the air vents as well.

But most importantly, she saw that the teleportation array had just activated, and Void's Disciple had emerged. He was clearly furious, but he still seemed distracted by something as his gaze was trained on her.

"This is unexpected," Void's Disciple said as he looked her up and down, and Inevitability felt her heartbeat speed up.

But the gaze of her father-husband wasn't enough to make her forget what had happened just now.

"They killed him," Inevitability said with gritted teeth. "How could those abominations accomplish something like that?! We need to rip them to pieces."

"Your brother should have been able to kill at least a few dozen Anointed before safely escaping. His survivability is even higher than yours," Void's Disciple slowly said with his brows furrowed. "Something must have gone wrong. Did he encounter the remaining zealots or Super Brother-Man?"

He raised his hand the next moment, and a screen of light appeared, showing a grainy image of a human whose face was covered in weird markings. In front of him were just a head and a pitch-black spear. The man standing above her brother's remains looked a bit different, but how couldn't Inevitability recognize that cursed man?

"It's him! The human! I'LL KILL HIM!" Inevitability screamed as the red streaks across her body lit up.

"We might have a chance if we hurry," Void's Disciple muttered as his body exploded with power.

The teleportation array lit up the next moment, but it flickered ominously. Void's Disciple kept infusing more and more power, but he was suddenly pushed back by a spatial storm, and a couple of shallow wounds appeared on his face.

"Is it my fault? Did I damage it?" Inevitability asked with worry.

"No. I am unable to force my way through the disturbance," Void's Disciple grunted. "I have just touched the edge of the Dao of Space; it is not enough."

A killing intent that could easily match her own exploded out the next moment as Void's Disciple roared in fury and frustration, his face twisted into a mask of madness and murder. Inevitability's eyes lit up at the sight. This was the true face of Void's Disciple, and she was now the only one to have seen that visage and lived to tell the tale.

Void's Disciple punched down on the teleportation array the next moment, and it actually cracked.

Inevitability's eyes widened even further, as she knew just how sturdy the things provided by the System were. She had attacked the teleportation arrays multiple times before out of boredom and curiosity, but she had not even been able to leave a mark.

The second stage of Void's Disciple's **[Void Crusher]** was unleashed the next moment as thousands of spatial rifts shot out across the area. They dug into the earth or passed straight through a few of the lucky survivors, cutting anything into pieces until they formed a spherical pattern hundreds of meters wide.

"It looks like the Heavens doesn't want to provide today." Void's

Disciple sighed, his face once more turning expressionless. "But we will have our chance inside the Mystic Realm. Harbinger's death at least came with some good. Your anger reached a high enough level to awaken your implanted bloodline."

"Is that what this is?" Inevitability blurted as she looked down at her hands, a ruthless grin spreading across her face.

This was exactly what she needed to exact her revenge.

"You need to enter the machine once more. That way, you will be able to stabilize it and stop your body from rejecting it." Void's Disciple nodded.

Inevitability blanched when she thought back to that contraption that had tortured her in the darkness for weeks, but she knew better than to argue with her master. He might have outwardly calmed down, but she knew better than anyone that the fires were still burning beneath the surface. To question him now was to ask for death.

"Let's go," Void's Disciple said as he ripped open a tunnel in space. "This place will not last much longer."

The two stepped through the mid-range gate, leaving the wounded where they were. However, they only needed to suffer for a few seconds before the remaining spatial rifts congealed into a singular point.

The next moment, the whole hive imploded, leaving nothing but a perfectly spherical crater behind.

41
ADCARKAS

Harbinger's Cosmos Sack was gone, its contents probably lost in some unreachable spatial fold, but there was at least something for him to loot: the pitch-black spear that was lying in the grass, its shaft still in the grip of the Dominator. It was definitely valuable, probably a High-quality Spirit Tool, judging by the spirituality it emitted.

Zac lifted it and looked it over for a few seconds, but he couldn't figure out what it was made of. It was extremely hard and looked like some sort of stone, but it was pliable like a spear made from wood or metal. He was able to bend it almost 180 degrees when he exerted himself, and it sprang back to its original form the moment he let go.

It was a bit regretful, but it definitely looked like something that was a perfect fit for Ogras.

He didn't begrudge the demon finally getting his hands on a Spirit Tool. A boost in Ogras' combat strength was a direct benefit for Port Atwood. But Zac had been the one to almost get himself killed this time, yet he gained nothing, not even some trinkets. Perhaps he could squeeze some valuables out of the demon's paws in exchange for the weapon later.

"Warmaster, are you safe?" a rumbling voice suddenly echoed out as Rhubat came rushing over, closely followed by a score of Anointed and hundreds of elite warriors. "We sensed a massive spike in corruption and realized something was wrong."

Only then did Zac remember the ongoing war, but he breathed in relief when he saw that things weren't as bad as he had feared. The Anointed had spread out and reinforced the rear, and the front lines were stable enough to allow a contingent to freely head over to his location.

Larger numbers weren't enough to turn the tides when the opponents were life-force-burning Anointed.

"We got ambushed," Zac said as he pointed at the head on the ground. "I think it's Harbinger, but I can't tell for sure."

"It was truly one of the three!" another of the Anointed exclaimed. "The head releases such waves of corruption even in death."

"This is Karath… It's really them." Rhubat sighed as the giant knelt down to inspect the remains. "I met this one before the integration. To think such a promising scholar was hiding a secret like this. This must mean that Void's Disciple is Adcarkas; the Sage of the Grand Basin."

Zac's brows rose in interest. It sounded like the Dominators had actually been some sort of important people even before the integration. Their ability to mask their powers must have been shocking to be able to walk among the Zhix with their corruption-spotting antennae. He wanted to know more about their history, but there were more pressing matters at the moment.

"So what's our next move?" Zac asked. "It seems that the enemies have realized what we're doing here."

"Four hives were cleansed before this, and enough warriors to fill three more will be purified in this battle," Rhubat slowly said. "The numbers are now in our favor. We will try to keep going and take out more hives, but we expect the remaining heretics to have adapted by now. Our warriors need rest as well, so we will pause for reconnaissance after this battle."

"Good." Zac nodded with some relief. "I need to rest a bit as well. How long do you need?"

He had a huge amount of energy sloshing around his body at the moment, and he didn't want to waste it.

"Ten hours," Rhubat said after some thought before he turned toward Thea. "We'd like to keep the pathfinder in order to send out the scouts."

"That's fine with me." Thea nodded.

The Anointed returned to the war after seeing that everything was fine, but they still stayed close by so that they could come to Zac's aid at a moment's notice. Zac himself was about to sit down and rest up, but he suddenly saw an aquamarine stream of light shooting straight toward him. He wasn't worried as he saw the magical light, but rather amused.

It was Triv, who was using some sort of movement skill to return to him and the jammer.

"Young master, you are safe," the ghost said with relief as he congealed into a proper form.

"Just where did you go earlier?" Zac snorted. "I couldn't find you anywhere."

"I, ah... repositioned myself a bit. I did not want to become a burden during the young master's fight. That aura you released..." the ghost hesitantly said.

"Well, thank you for your assistance," Zac grunted, not seeing any reason to divulge the origins of his Annihilation Sphere. The lack of information might help keep the ghost in check even better. "I need to keep the energy inside my body for another hour while they finish up the battle. Look after the jammer for me."

He didn't dare break open the node right away in case one of the other Dominators showed up, so he could only focus on retaining the energy until he could go back to Port Atwood. The battle thankfully didn't last that long, and Zac hurried toward the teleportation array of the fallen hive after just forty minutes.

The deaths after this battle were staggering even compared to the previous ones, and Zac sighed when he heard that over one hundred thousand of their own had fallen over the last hour. It was still a great victory on paper considering how many enemies they'd faced, and a testament to how a small group of elites like the Anointed could keep fatalities down. But their losses were still large enough to populate a small town, making it hard to celebrate the win.

Zac soon appeared in his compound, and he found Joanna sitting in meditation just outside. She woke up when she sensed the fluctuations from the array and turned to Zac.

"I wasn't able to contact you, but Billy's returned as well," Joanna said with an odd face.

"Did he pass the trial?" Zac asked.

"I... don't know," Joanna said after some hesitation. "But I think so?"

"What's going on? Where is he?" Zac asked with a frown.

"He's just outside the Dao Repository. He's been sleeping for fourteen hours straight," Joanna said. "He isn't deeply wounded, but it looks like someone has been using him as a punching bag. He fell asleep the moment he emerged from the inheritance, and Brazla threw him out because of the snores. I tried to move him, but he almost bashed my head in without waking up."

Zac gazed at the Valkyrie with confusion before he flashed over to the Dao Repository once more. It didn't take a lot of effort to find where the giant was lying, as it sounded like someone was performing large-scale logging in his forest.

Billy was lying sprawled on his back just outside the tiled square of the Dao Repository, and Zac couldn't help but laugh when he saw Billy's face. It was completely swollen to the point that it looked like he just had an allergic reaction. However, the fact that his face also was almost purple from layers of bruises that looked like meaty fists indicated he had been repeatedly punched.

It seemed that the Titan's trial was a lot more straightforward than his own or Thea's.

Zac guessed that Billy's nose was broken as well, as it was completely congested, which caused the terrifying snore, and he shook his head as he prodded him from some distance with the help of his club.

"NO MORE!" Billy screamed as he shot up to his feet.

The giant wildly looked around for a few seconds with heaving breaths until he realized what was going on.

"Ah – it's you. Billy thought he was still stuck with the crazy one." Billy sighed in relief as he sat down.

"How did it go?" Zac smiled as he took out an ointment. "Your face is a bit swollen. This will help."

"Stupid crazy Titan said he wanted to teach Billy self-defense. But it only ended with Billy being punched in the face over and over," Billy cried. "But Billy is a lot better at defending now! Come, hit Billy."

"Uh, okay," Zac said before he moved forward; his club ripped through the air as he swung it toward Billy's chin with a decent amount of strength.

Billy's massive muscles suddenly tightened to the point that they looked like steel wires, and the hulking man turned to a blur the next instant. Zac's mind suddenly screamed of danger as the grotesque skull on Billy's club was bearing down on him with shocking speed.

The ground cracked all around Zac as he pushed himself back, narrowly avoiding the smash. He looked with surprise at the giant, feeling he was over twice as fast as before. Billy had neither excelled at defense nor speed before, making him an extremely lopsided meathead. However, one of those weaknesses had been shored up during the inheritance, it looked like.

But it seemed to be his speed rather than endurance that had been improved, so Zac didn't understand what Billy meant by self-defense.

"I thought you said that the Titan taught you how to protect yourself?" Zac asked with some confusion.

"Crazy man said that the best way not to get hit is to kill everyone before they can hit you," Billy sagely explained.

"Hard to argue with that logic," Joanna snorted from the side.

"Crazy man taught Billy a good skill that makes Billy quicker the stronger he gets. But it is very tiring." Billy sighed as he gulped down a couple of huge mouthfuls of water.

Zac believed he understood what Billy was talking about. It was either some sort of rare skill that increased Billy's Dexterity based on his Strength, or perhaps a movement skill that was based on Strength rather than Dexterity, as was the norm.

"I have to go." Zac sighed. "What are you doing next, Billy?"

"Billy is going to Billyville," Billy said after some thought. "Billy is tired and has not been home for a long time."

"That sounds good," Zac said and added after some thought, "Thea and I are going away in a few weeks. To a special place like the Hunt. We don't know how long we will be gone. Do you want to come as well?"

"Why are you going there?" Billy asked curiously.

"Find treasure and beat up bad guys." Zac smiled.

"Haha, you always do that. You need a hobby. But Billy will come help you." Billy grinned as he started walking away, heading toward the town.

Zac nodded at Joanna, who followed him to make sure he got home rather than kidnapped by some group of lovestruck demons. He was left alone in his private forest, and he entered his courtyard to finally absorb the massive amount of Cosmic Energy surging through his body.

However, he didn't immediately push the energy into his body, swapping over to his Draugr form first. He figured that if one of his pathways was going to be destroyed, then it might as well be the pathways in his undead form. His human pathways wouldn't be harmed this way, as they would be stored in his Specialty Core.

This allowed him to keep using his human form while recuperating while only bearing some of the detriments of node-breaking. He would still be weakened due to the shock to the system, but he would be able to use Cosmic Energy without getting a backlash like in the Dead Zone.

The process went quite smoothly, if you could consider a part of your body literally blowing up smooth. The energy from taking out the Dominator was easily able to crack open his eighth node, even though that node alone required about as much energy as the first three nodes combined. The energy was even enough to provide his Fetters of Desolation class with a level and set the foundation for his ninth node, meaning he was now level 83 in his undead form while his human side was still 82.

The next node was in an unfortunate spot, though. It was just between his right elbow and his bicep, making it a very precarious spot. He had already learned to somewhat decrease the degree to which he maimed himself with every node opening, but he needed to be careful now. His arms were pretty damn muscular compared to before the integration, but they were still far thinner compared to his legs.

One mishap and he might find himself in the same situation as Ogras, with only a stub for an arm. He wouldn't be able to grow it back before reaching D-grade at the earliest unless he managed to get his hands on a treasure with the same effect. Ogras had searched high and low for such a thing in the Base Town without any success, so items with that sort of effect seemed as rare as soul-mending treasures.

He needed to keep improving the process of node-opening with every level he gained. Pretty much all the nodes during Early E-grade were located in his extremities, but he would move on to more precarious placements in Middle E-grade. In Late E-grade, the nodes would all be located around his head and heart, and even cultivators could die from a single mistake at that point, let alone mortals.

A wave of exhaustion gripped him after the upgrade was complete, and he fell into a deep slumber as the Fragment of the Bodhi worked on both his node-related wound and the weird cracks that had appeared on his shoulders and neck.

Zac woke up only seven hours later, and he frowned when he saw that the tears from unleashing the Annihilation Sphere hadn't healed at all. They didn't really seem to cause any more problems than some random scars, but Zac knew it was important that he slowly healed the wounds. These kinds of injuries were a big problem to cultivators.

High-concept wounds from battles or overextending yourself was like spiritual sequela, and it could cause problems to one's future cultivation if left unchecked. What if some remnants of Oblivion hiding in his shoulders suddenly exploded when he opened a nearby node in the future? He might die then and there.

Zac's body was still feeling wrung out even after resting for such a long time, and something seemed to have changed at the war front while he was out. Nonet and Ibtep had actually appeared in Port Atwood as he was inspecting his body, and they were quickly ushered to his compound.

"What's going on?" Zac asked when he saw the two Zhix. "I thought I was supposed to meet up with you in two hours."

"There is no need. A challenge has been issued, and a final battle will take place in ten days," Nonet simply said.

4 2
SWAMP

"Ten days?" Zac frowned. "Why don't we just keep going?"

The New World Government's deadline for entering the Mystic Realm was inching closer, and he definitely couldn't get caught outside when the hidden world closed its doors. Besides, he wanted to be over with this bloody matter as quickly as possible.

"Our scouts returned a few hours ago. The hives are emptied except one that is utterly destroyed. Only the weak have been left behind, just like during a migration. The number of remaining Zhix is still in the millions, but we cannot locate them. A letter of challenge was issued just an hour ago. For the future of the Zhix," Ibtep explained.

Zac asked a bit more, and he learned that the challenge was something that occasionally happened before their integration. It was essentially an all-out war between two forces that competed for resources. The survivors would claim the hive and its land, and the losers would either be killed or assimilated.

This time, there would be no assimilation if the council won; only death awaited those who chose to follow the Dominators.

"So it's one all-out war. Do you think the Dominators will be there?" Zac asked.

"It is hard to say," Nonet said with a shake of their enormous head. "No Zhix would stay behind when the challenge is issued. However, the Dominators are Zhix, yet they are not. They might not care about the precepts and enter this hidden world you have mentioned. They might even try something before then."

Zac nodded with a frown. Retaliation from the Dominators was something he had been worrying about since slaying Harbinger. He knew all too well just how crazy Inevitability was, and he wouldn't put it past her to go slaughter everyone in his outpost. He had been half-expecting a notification in his communication crystal while cultivating, but he had thankfully been uninterrupted the whole time.

He didn't know why, but it looked like his people were safe for now. Void's Disciple seemed quite capable of moving about across Pangea freely, and he should have attacked one of his towns by now if he had decided to act. He still decided to pull back more of his forces to the island and his private continent just in case.

The two Zhix left a few minutes later, leaving Zac to ponder his next move. The break was honestly a relief to Zac, as he was not completely ready to meet another one of the Dominators. Fighting both of them simultaneously felt extremely risky as well, especially while Ogras was still in seclusion. The pause would give him some time to prepare his next move.

There was no way for him to prepare another Annihilation Sphere, even if the battle was delayed another ten days. The Splinter simply didn't produce enough energy for that. He would have to use some other means to deal with them instead.

The delay also threw about his plans a bit, as he needed to prepare himself for the Mystic Realm as well. He wanted to enter the Mystic Realm within two weeks if possible, as that would still give him some time to maneuver even if his sister proved unable to force open the broken pathway.

Zac hadn't heard any updates from his sister for a while, and he couldn't sit around any longer. He walked over to his own array and teleported over to Mystic Island. He needed to see how things were going.

It was quite some time since Zac was here last, but not much had changed. The base camp was a bit desolate, as most of the normal staff was stuck on the other side of the spatial tunnel. Now it was mostly demons and Valkyries staying here to protect Kenzie and a few scientists. A large number of the Sentry Golems were probably off wandering the island, making sure no one tried sneaking up on the camp.

"Oh, you're here?" Kenzie said with surprise as Zac entered her workshop. "Is the war over?"

"It's on hold for ten days." Zac smiled as he looked around. "How're things going here?"

"It's slow." Kenzie sighed. "The tunnel is still a mess; that bomb the zealots set up really did a number on space itself. The turbulence got better a lot faster in the beginning, but it has been slowing down lately. I'm not sure it will clear up before the deadline you set."

The deadline Zac set was ten days before the government's. Part of it was simply a precaution, but there was another important reason for the haste.

The other forces were frantically searching the Mystic Realm at this very moment, and he was already pretty far behind. He couldn't just enter at the last minute and expect everything to go his way. He definitely had a hidden ace with his familiar connection to the Mystic Realm along with his sister and Jeeves, but he wouldn't take anything for granted.

In a perfect world, he would already have started to explore the mysterious research base, but he wasn't ready to risk it all by trying to sneak into the New World Government's entrance. Seizing it was even riskier, as there were probably spies from both the cultists and the Dominators ready to blow up the spatial tunnel at a moment's notice.

"Can you crack it open early?" Zac asked.

"We can give it a try, but if we fail, it will make things a lot worse," Kenzie said. "If we wait another week or two, our chances will be better."

Zac slowly thought it over before he nodded in agreement.

"I want to try it in twelve days, after the battle is dealt with." Zac eventually decided. "If things fall apart, I'll just have to try my luck by sneaking inside some other way."

"You know you can just talk with the government officials, right?" Kenzie said.

"If they were ready to work together, they would have contacted us long ago," Zac said with a shake of his head. "They've had ample chances to extend an olive branch since I closed the last incursion. Even before then."

"Fine." Kenzie shrugged. "But remember not to kill a bunch of people willy-nilly."

"I know," Zac agreed.

Not killing weaklings was an unwritten rule of the Multiverse, and something Zac had to start taking note of now that he was at a higher grade than the rest of Earth. It was widely considered extremely vile to wantonly slaughter the weak, almost like killing innocent puppies. Of course, if that were the only problem, the blood-drenched cultivators of the Multiverse wouldn't have cared.

But there were a lot of signs pointing toward the fact that killing substantially weaker people went against the will of the Heavens and that it affected one's Karma negatively, almost like giving a hidden debuff to their Luck. It wasn't something that was visible on one's status screen, but through how the universe treated them.

After all, F-grade cultivators weren't useful to the System, but they represented seeds of potential. The System wouldn't care if a bunch of warriors killed each other in a war, as that might result in a few powerhouses emerging. But old monsters slaughtering substantially weaker cultivators was another matter altogether.

The strong didn't get stronger, and a lot of potential was snuffed out as the weak got culled. It was wasting resources and essentially working against the System. A few people dying here and there didn't really matter, but if you went too far, you would draw the ire of the System, and it would start treating you like an enemy of the Heavens like the Technocrats.

Voridis A'Heliophos was a prime example of this – his sacrificial path had angered the System enough for it to start giving out quests for his capture and execution.

There were even rumors of powerful cultivators who were actively hunted by the System for their actions, who were forced to hide from the eyes of the Heavens. That wasn't something that had any relation to a small corner like the Zecia Sector, as you needed to be much more powerful for something like that to happen, according to Triv.

"I'll be going away for a couple of days," Zac eventually said. "I need to keep improving as much as possible before we enter, so I have decided to head to one of the uncharted sectors of Pangea. It's the swamp."

"Really? The swamp?" Kenzie said with a scrunched-up nose. "That place seems pretty disgusting."

"There's a lot of putrefaction and death in the swamp, from what I understand," Zac said. "It might provide me with some sort of inspiration. Or there might be a lot of valuable plants."

It was the latter that was the biggest reason for Zac deciding to go. The integration of a new world led to the appearance of a bunch of valuable resources, like the Amanita and the Tree of Ascension. There were no doubt more that had appeared, but most had probably already been snatched up by the people around the world.

If there were any remaining natural treasures of that grade on Earth, then they were probably hidden in the unexplored pockets. The swamp seemed particularly dangerous, and Zac believed that no one should have properly explored its inner areas. Finding some valuable treasure was his last chance at gaining another power-up before heading into the Mystic Realm, and he could probably burst open another node while looking around.

It was a risky move considering that Void's Disciple might show up with a vengeance at a moment's notice, but he had the [Spatial Convergence Array] now. He could set an array up in ten minutes, and his town just had to defend that long for him to return. Ten minutes should definitely be doable even against Void's Disciple with the comprehensive upgrades to the defensive arrays of Port Atwood.

The value of a World Capital had quickly shown itself in the number of good things available in the Town Shop, and Abby and Adran had been busy squeezing as much benefit as possible out of the available arrays and fortifications.

Zac turned thoughts to action as he teleported to the array closest to the swamp, leaving just a small squad of Valkyries to act as a relay in case they needed to reach him through his communication crystal. He actually owned a town just on the edge of the swamp, a small base that was formerly one of the incursions he had closed. It had belonged to a humanoid race that somewhat reminded Zac of the Zhix, though they looked a lot more like humans.

It was most likely one of the demi-human Races of the Multiverse.

Humans were just too prolific, after all, and they had proven very compatible for procreation with most humanoid species. They were like blank canvases, and there were very few humanoids that didn't have a little bit of human in their genome.

What was human and what wasn't had already become blurred, but people essentially went by the Race in the status screen, which was dictated by the dominant Heritage. This was rarely the human side, especially not when matched against powerful races.

The ones who had controlled this former incursion were likely the result of a mix of some insectoid race and humans a long time ago, which might have been why they were placed so close to a swamp. It made Zac's life a lot easier anyway, as he didn't have to utilize the Marshall Clan for transportation this time, exposing his plans while doing so.

He was soon flying atop his treasure above the marsh, looking down with interest. After hearing the description of the place, he had first thought this might be where the Everglades ended up, but he soon realized that that wasn't exactly the case.

Zac was no botanical expert, but there were just too many unfamiliar trees and plants on the ground below for this to be a piece of Florida. At best, it might have combined the wetlands with some marshes and tropical forests of the other planets, most likely the Ishiate world, as it seemed to have been just one never-ending forest.

It had created a unique ecosystem with a forest floor that was mostly submerged like a mangrove system. However, there were smatterings of solid land with some regularity, though not quite to the point that you could freely walk on the ground.

However, the infusion of Cosmic Energy to the marshlands had helped the trees explode in size, which included their branches and roots. It had formed vast systems of bridges running along the rivers, and Zac saw one beast after another running along their length from tree to tree.

He just needed to travel above the marshland for a few minutes to realize the place was teeming with various species, just like the primordial jungle where he had spent a lot of time after dealing with the cultists. However, if the atmosphere over by the volcano was a boisterous cacophony, then this place held a subdued silence, with animal calls only occasionally breaking through the silence.

The whole area felt like it was full of adventure and mystery, and Zac wondered if this was how the explorers of old felt when they traveled along the rivers of the Mississippi or through the virgin jungles of Africa. Of course, he had the added safety net of being able to fly away, and a superhuman constitution that would protect him from most insect bites and poisons.

The place provided Zac with a sense of adventure, but more importantly, it provided him with solace. The bloody scenes over the past days had left him with a feeling of heaviness that reached deep into his soul, and this was an opportunity for him to not only regain a sense of balance but even work on his skills.

Of course, if he could find some treasure while doing so, all the better.

43
CONNECTEDNESS

The atmosphere of this unusual forest was fascinating, but the ambient energy was even more interesting. Zac was currently flying toward the center of the marshland at a leisurely pace that pretty much matched a speed that he would be able to keep on land as well. He hadn't noticed anything weird in the beginning, but he could now confirm that the energy density had increased a bit since he entered this place.

With this pace, it would only take him two days at the most to reach the core, but Zac eventually decided to land on top of a massive root that had grown over ten meters wide. The waters quickly turned chaotic as a group of oversized salamanders swam toward him, but they quickly fled for their lives when Zac unleashed a bit of his aura.

He took a deep breath, surprised that the smell was fresh and earthy rather than the expected foul odor of brackish water. Zac started walking along the roots toward the depths of the marshland, occasionally jumping up to instead use a bridge made from branches, following a somewhat meandering path.

Of course, he could always jump between trees in a straight line instead of using such a slow method of travel, but that would destroy the whole purpose of why he landed. He wanted to get a feel of the forest, to walk on top of the trees as he followed the natural paths formed by nature itself.

Zac had initially planned on using the primordial jungle as a means to evolving his nature-aspected skills. But large sections of the jungle were utterly ruined because of the battle against the cultists, or rather their emblem, and he had mainly tried to focus on gaining Blighted Cut during that week of recuperation. It had prevented him from working on his other class as much as he wanted.

But now was a perfect opportunity. It was just him and a boundless wilderness that had never been tread by man, from the looks of things. Zac kept emitting some of his latent killing intent, which essentially worked as not only a bug repellant but also a deterrent for any of the stronger beasts lurking in the depths of the wide rivers.

He occasionally stopped and sensed the various trees and gargantuan flowers in his path, trying to understand their role and path to survival in this place. The world of cultivation was a cut-throat place, but nature had always been just as competitive even before the integration. Everything needed a method to survive, along with the ability to adapt now that the atmosphere was chock-full of magic.

Some of the larger trees simply dominated their domain with size alone, stealing the sunlight for themselves. Other trees formed symbiotic relationships with other plants defending them in return for somewhere to grow. It wasn't all too different compared to before the integration, honestly, though it did feel like evolution was sped up by a huge degree.

Then again, there were quite a few new oddities that didn't exist before. He had been attacked no less than twenty times by the plant life itself after having just traveled for two hours. One tree moved its branches with surprising speed in an effort to spear him on a sharp point. Others tried to entangle him with their roots.

He had actually let one do it to see what would happen, and he was slowly dragged underwater, where he could see a bunch of rotting beast carcasses providing nutrients to the tree. Some plants had even formed hunting teams with the beasts. A huge flower had suddenly released a bunch of pollen in his face, and Zac felt some restrictions on his movement.

Not more than ten seconds passed before a swarm of mosquitoes appeared, hoping to bleed him dry while he was incapacitated. The pollen was only immobilizing, so the two groups had teamed up where the mosquitoes got the blood while the plant got the corpse.

It was both horrifying and extremely intriguing to see the hundreds of paths to survival, and Zac felt something click into place after walking along for half a day. He was delighted to see that **[Forester's Constitution]** finally reached Peak mastery. The upgrade had boosted his attribute bonus to 15% as expected.

But more importantly, he felt a sense of connectedness with the nature around him.

It wasn't like when he was using **[Hatchetman's Spirit]** and he essentially became omniscient within his conjured forest, but rather an innate sixth sense about the forest itself. It was like an inborn intuition had been implanted into his subconscious. He tried to make sense of the feeling, but he only found a use for it ten minutes later when he felt something attracting him from within a dense bush.

Zac decided to follow the hunch, and he pushed his way inside, his Endurance enough to avoid getting cut into ribbons by the extremely sharp barbs. He had expected the interior of the bush to be pretty dark, but there was actually a source of light inside: a small set of stalks that gave off a gentle green light.

He understood that this was some sort of Spiritual Herb hiding within the thorny bush, and his eyes lit up when he realized the use of Peak mastery of the skill. His hunch had actually led him to a hidden treasure that he never would have spotted before. He had essentially turned into a truffle-seeking pig that could find the hidden treasures of the forest.

It wasn't exactly that he could sense treasures, but rather that he had been given an instinctive understanding of the forests. He just felt that the brambles looked like a place that could contain some good things, and this feeling was in turn boosted by his massive pool of Luck.

Zac also noticed that his honed instincts worked with dangers as well within a few minutes. He somehow had a far better understanding of what parts of the rivers would hold aggressive beasts or which types of foliage could hide something lying in wait. This part of the skill wasn't as useful to someone like him, who already had his danger sense, but it would probably have been a huge boon for a normal cultivator who spent a lot of time in the forests.

Staying alive was the most important thing on the path of cultivation, after all.

The best thing was that the skill was passive too, meaning he could freely make use of his upgraded instincts without any ramifications. It allowed him to pick up one Spiritual Root after another as he walked through the marshes, each of them giving off impressive spiritual energy. However, he quickly realized that good herbs weren't like weeds, growing everywhere.

Less than a tenth of the spots his instincts told him about was actually home to something interesting; the rest were simply empty. However, he actually didn't need to dig or inspect every single one. As long as he got close enough, he would get a sense from his Luck as well, and he tried to understand this treasure sense just as well as he understood his danger sense.

This sense wasn't something new. He could always tell whether something he found in a Cosmos Sack was useless or something valuable by instinct, just like he could somewhat get a sense of the quality of Spiritual Tools. Part of it came from sensing the aura of the items, but part of it was simply instincts brought by his Luck. However, this sense hadn't really proven too useful while actually searching for treasures until now.

Zac soon concluded that his Luck was quite precise as long as he got within seven meters or so. He could tell there was something there with some certainty at such close proximity. The actual range was a bit odd, though, but he guessed that he might have been given one meter of detection range per effective 100 Luck.

Sometimes he could get a vague hint even further away than that, but it was to the point that Zac had a hard time discerning whether it was just his "gut" telling him something that might be completely fabricated, or if it was actually some supernatural phenomenon helping him out. In either case, it wasn't something he could put too much faith in.

A treasure sense of seven meters wasn't bad, but it wasn't life-changing either. It allowed him to pick up the occasional baubles that were strewn along his way, but it was a far cry from the examples Ogras had listed before. He didn't get any strong urge to suddenly make a turn only to find a divine treasure a few kilometers away or anything magical like that.

But it was far superior to what the general cultivator could enjoy.

The forest didn't look like it was full of treasures to the untrained eye, but **[Forester's Constitution]** had opened Zac up to the truth. His Luck then helped him make the best of the knowledge, which turned him into a moneymaking machine compared to most adventurers.

The number of plants Zac harvested as he explored was nothing compared to the vast fields his people grew back at Verdant Hills, but farmed Spirit Plants and wild ones couldn't be compared with each other. It was mainly weaker plants that could be freely farmed, whereas the more valuable ones resisted domestication.

There was also the issue of energy consumption. Most of the High-quality plants required quite a bit of energy, making it impossible to grow them in larger numbers. They needed a territory of their own, just like many beasts did. So a lot of spiritual roots and plants did not have a constant supply, which massively increased their value if they were needed for popular pill recipes.

That was one of the main fields of research for most Alchemy clans too. Any clan that managed to improve a recipe by changing a wild-grown plant with a farmed one stood to gain a tremendous amount of wealth. They could undercut the market while still maintaining huge profit margins thanks to using cheaper resources.

Zac had no idea if the roots, grasses, and flowers he picked up were anything valuable in high demand, but he still took a detour every time he sensed something in the vicinity. It wasn't like he was strapped for cash, but it went against every fiber in his body to leave money lying on the floor. He also wanted to nurture his instincts this way.

And who knew, some of the plants might be really effective in improving his Draugr Race. He was willing to do almost anything to swap out that terrifying dust for something less painful to use.

Constantly harvesting the low-grade Spiritual Plants gave him some insights as well. Spiritual Plants were essentially the equivalent of plants that had started on the path of cultivation, and it felt like exploring them helped him gain insight into his own nature-aspected Dao Fragment. He felt it might be even more conducive to his cultivation to travel through forests like this rather than sitting in his cultivation cave.

Zac kept going deeper and deeper into the swamp over the

following day, and his newfound intuition helped him avoid a lot of trouble. However, the energy in the atmosphere kept increasing, and the beasts both grew more numerous and more powerful. Most of them were just Late or Peak F-grade, though, with E-grade animals being very rare.

He would probably have to reach the core before he got an opportunity to see the real kings of the marshes.

Zac finally decided to stop for the day after having taken out a group of humongous E-grade crocodiles, each of them more than twenty meters long. It felt like going up against prehistoric dinosaurs when fighting them, but they were still ultimately just Early E-grade. Just a minute was needed to take out the whole pack, and he suddenly had eight more carcasses in his Cosmos Sack.

The stench of blood filled the air as the river ran red, so Zac quickly moved some distance away. The crocodiles should be the local rulers of this small section of the river, but the other animals could probably figure out that the blood meant there might be an opportunity for a sneak attack or even free food.

He soon found an enormous tree with a hollow large enough that he could rest for the day, perhaps the former resting place of some mutated squirrel. Zac blocked the entrance with one of his spare tower shields before he sat down and calmed his mind. The reason he moved away from the battle wasn't that he was worried that he would become embroiled in another battle, but it was rather that he didn't want a bunch of beasts interrupting him while redrawing his pathways.

He quickly changed to his Draugr form and once more started performing the arduous task.

The physical wound from breaking open the node was pretty much healed, though he had barely begun fixing the pathways. He estimated that his undead form was weakened roughly 30% or so, and even his human side wasn't in top shape, even though he looked fine on paper.

Zac guessed that the broken pathways in his inactive form counted like some sort of hidden wound even when he fought as a human, though the effect was limited. In either case, it meant he needed to work quickly so that the pathways were fixed before the war in eight days. He might need everything in his arsenal in case the remaining two showed up.

He kept working on the pathways for a few hours before he swapped back to his human form, at which point he simply closed his eyes and tried to sense the nature around him. He would normally have wanted to practice his Soul Strengthening Manual as well, but it was impossible while on the move. Setting up a teleportation array through his **[Spatial Convergence Array]** was technically possible, but they were temporary onetime consumables, so he wouldn't be able to return.

Going without the arrays for a few days wasn't a problem, and it freed up a lot of time to focus on other things, such as his Dao. It almost felt like the whole swamp was one enormous entity, and he tried to find some inspiration for the Fragment of the Bodhi by connecting to it. He spent the rest of the night in that sort of reverie before he once more set out at the break of dawn.

Today, he would explore the core of the wetlands.

44
RIVER

Zac had spent close to two days in the marshes already, and he would definitely reach what could be considered the core zone today. Of course, that wasn't saying much, as the core of such a vast forest was large enough that he could wander around for weeks without seeing the same tree twice.

As for what Zac considered the core area, it was where the Cosmic Energy was the densest. The Nexus Vein covered his whole island and then some back home, and he guessed it was a similar situation here in the forest. The core zone was equivalent to Port Atwood, and this was where the strongest beasts would reside, along with the most valuable herbs and minerals.

His hunch was quickly proven right over the following hours, as the number of E-grade beasts he encountered kept increasing. He even spotted a massive swarm of E-grade hornets far in the distance, each one of them as large as a Labrador. Even Zac felt a bit intimidated by the swarm, so he actually chose to hide inside the river so as not to draw their attention.

Beasts were weaker than cultivators in general, but they made up for it in numbers. He wasn't in any mood to be besieged by thousands of murderous hornets for no real return. Even if he emerged victorious, it would still be a pitched battle, and the risk didn't outweigh the rewards. There was no point in messing with a swarm like that unless they were guarding some great treasure.

He did fight the occasional E-grade beast, mostly overgrown bugs or river creatures. There was a large number of alien amphibians that looked like predatory catfish. Their maws were wide enough to swallow Zac in one bite, and there were over five rows of jagged teeth hiding within. They even had short, stubby legs like salamanders, and they could break into a surprisingly quick sprint on the ground.

Zac fought and harvested intermittently as he scoped the core zone, and his Cosmos Sack was gradually filling up with valuables. He didn't recognize the herbs he was picking at all, but each beast carcass was worth between 10,000 and 100,000 Nexus Coins depending on species and level.

The bountiful harvest went on for a few hours until there was a startling change in the atmosphere; it had become quiet.

The sounds of nature had always been a bit subdued in this swamp, but it had suddenly become completely silent after Zac passed an unseen threshold. He had never encountered this before, but it could only mean a few things. There were no beasts here, meaning they either had all been killed or scared away by something. Zac started to look around for clues, but there wasn't much to go by.

This section of the wetlands looked pretty much the same as the rest, with the exception that the river he was following along was a bit wider than the rest. It was over five kilometers across, which would have allowed it to compete with immense rivers like the Amazon River before the integration. Now it was just a tributary from some much larger source of water.

Zac's first instinct was to avoid this place just like the hornets earlier, but he eventually chose to stay. He was here for training and treasures, after all, and this felt like a place that could provide both. He kept going along the shoreline, but he concealed as much of his aura as he could. However, he only walked a few hundred meters before there was a change in his body.

His cells had all woken up and were screaming at him that there was something delicious nearby. This wasn't something coming from his recently upgraded **[Forester's Constitution]**, but rather the general feelings of desire that great treasures like the Fruit of Ascension elicited. Zac looked for any special energy signatures with **[Cosmic Gaze]**, though not without some hesitation.

There was something odd about the feeling, though he couldn't exactly place it.

It quickly became apparent that the treasure could be found on a small island in the middle of the river. There was a constant swirl of haze surrounding it, making it impossible for Zac to guess what was going on inside. He could only see the edges of the island sticking out, but he could at least make some deductions of what kind of situation might be waiting for him over there.

The island just had a diameter of a hundred meters or so, so the valuable item shouldn't be something huge like a crystal mine. It was also unlikely that there was some sort of hive with a huge number of beasts like a hornet hive or an ants' nest waiting on the other side of the fog. The island was too small, so there could either be just one big guy guarding the treasure, or a pack of medium-sized beasts.

As for the treasure, it was probably some sort of plant with a powerful energy signature.

However, Zac didn't immediately rush over to take the item. There was a constant buzz in the back of his head, alerting him of danger. It wasn't an acute sense of dread, but rather a pervasive sense of wrongness. He couldn't make heads or tails of the feeling, but he knew to take extra precautions.

Perhaps the feeling was simply because his subconscious believed a life-and-death struggle waited for him on the island. The most powerful animals always erected their lairs next to valuable herbs, as the aura the treasures released could help refine their bloodlines. There was no way that this island wasn't occupied since Zac's cells were screaming at him to eat whatever was hiding within the mists.

With the sheer number of hidden cards and advantages he had stacked up over the past year, Zac didn't feel all too worried about whatever was waiting for him. He was confident in dealing with pretty much anything Earth was able to throw at him this early into the integration. However, Zac still wanted to deal with this situation like a normal cultivator.

He needed to come up with a plan that would allow him to minimize the danger. He wouldn't always stay on Earth, where there were no real surprises. Cultivation on Earth was too orderly, as everyone had begun at the same time, and it provided him a false sense of security that wouldn't hold up out in the Multiverse. Even the Mystic Realm would contain unknown dangers that could threaten his life, by all accounts.

He needed to learn to do things the right way, or he would sooner or later be killed because he encountered something that couldn't be solved by swinging his axe extra hard.

His class and Dao thankfully enabled Zac to blend in with the surroundings, allowing him to spy on the island from his vantage hidden in a tree crown by the shore. However, Zac frowned when there was no change even after four hours. The mists didn't dissipate, and there were never any sounds that came from the island. No beast ever left the moat to hunt either, leaving Zac wondering if he was just being paranoid.

Was there actually no beast living there?

There was only so much time he had to spare, and he eventually decided to just go for it. He figured that he could either swap to his Draugr form and walk along the bottom of the river, or use his leaf as a boat. He eventually decided to move upstream a bit before he placed the leaf on the river. He infused himself with the Fragment of the Bodhi and simply allowed his flying treasure to drift toward the island like a normal piece of debris.

Zac didn't move in the slightest, and [Verun's Bite] was already in his hand in case of an ambush, but he drifted through the haze without issue until his flying treasure hit land. He disembarked and stowed away the treasure before he looked around the island with some confusion and desire. He had smelt an extremely enticing aroma since he'd entered the fog, and he couldn't wait to snatch whatever was the source.

The haze was actually not that thick on the island; one quick scan confirmed that there were no guarding beasts around. Not that they could fit with the tree that grew from the center of the island. The tree wasn't overly tall, just reaching twenty meters into the sky. However, it was shockingly wide, its trunk taking up the better part of the whole island.

Even the towering redwoods back then couldn't compete with this weird monstrosity in terms of girth.

Zac wasn't interested in the tree trunk, but rather the bulbous branches that spread out at its crown. There were only six branches in total on the whole tree, and each of them looked like a shrub with an enormous flower growing on it. It was no doubt these flowers that were the source of the smell, and Zac could sense how most of the energy gathered by the tree was infused into these six treasures.

The fact that there were no beasts around only made Zac more apprehensive as he stayed on the edge of the island. It was a bit disconcerting that he couldn't find the source of danger or wrongness, but he also couldn't just stand around doing nothing. He had already made his move, and delaying would just increase the danger he was in.

His Spirit Tool necklace transformed, and a chain shot out from his back and snaked around one of the stubby branches, and Zac shot toward it as he dragged himself up. The sudden movement was just in time as five sharp spikes punched through the ground and stabbed his previous location with enough force to make the air crackle. Zac looked back and saw that it was a group of roots, but they receded beneath the ground after they missed.

The scene wasn't very surprising to Zac. If there was no beast guardian around in this place, then it was most likely that the tree itself was a dangerous predator. And since there were no branches on this fatty tree, then it most likely had nimble roots to deal with its prey. A trunk of this width should be able to grow a massive root system, after all.

Zac wasted no time, as he didn't believe for a second that this probing attack was all the tree could muster, considering that the whole area was cleansed of animals. He moved to cut off the closest flower, but a weird shield actually appeared around it. Zac grunted in annoyance as he swung his axe down at the emerald barrier, and the collision made the whole tree shudder.

The shaking didn't subside, though, and Zac's eyes widened when the whole river exploded as thousands of roots, each one hundreds of meters long, rose into the sky. Zac had expected more roots to be waiting, but not to the point that the sky itself was almost blocked out. He hurriedly launched a barrage of strikes at the stalk connecting the flower to the branch, and the shield finally cracked.

But there was just enough time to harvest the one flower before his mind screamed of danger for real. Hundreds of roots shot toward him with a speed and agility that far surpassed any other plant he had encountered thus far, and he barely managed to dodge the strikes by moving over to the top of the trunk with **[Loamwalker]**.

The roots actually emitted a powerful killing intent as they froze in the air. However, they only wiggled in the air for a second before the tree seemed to have located him once more. Zac flashed toward the next flower as he cut apart roots by the score, but his eyes suddenly widened in alarm.

Two chains slammed into the top of the substantial trunk the next moment, dragging Zac right back where he came from.

It was just in time as well, as the flower released what looked like a plume of pollen that created a yellow haze that lingered just for an instant before it started spreading through the air. Zac thankfully evaded most of it, but some of it definitely made its way to him. A huge surge of desire and killing intent welled up in his heart, and his breaths started to become ragged as he looked at the remaining flowers.

His hunch had been right; that pollen was definitely not normal.

The other four flowers quickly followed suit and released their own clouds of pollen, and Zac was soon surrounded from all sides as he kept dancing back and forth while cutting off any incoming roots. He was only buying time, though, as the roots regrew within seconds and rejoined the battle.

However, there was nothing else he could do until those clouds of pollen dissipated enough for him to snatch the flowers. He was already in a bad state from just taking a whiff, and he might actually go insane if he stayed inside the clouds too long. It was a very weird feeling as two conflicting impulses fought inside his mind. One of the voices was telling him to stay away, as the increasingly large cloud of pollen was dangerous, while the other was screaming at him to jump into the cloud and push his face into the flower.

Was the thing a lure?

Roars suddenly echoed out across the area, as though in direct response to his hunch. Zac also saw a large number of Cosmic Energy clusters moving closer with the help of **[Cosmic Gaze]**, which probably meant that hundreds of beasts were pushing toward his location with their utmost speed. The quickest animals were all in E-grade, and the strongest ones actually managed to push through the forest of deadly roots to arrive at the small island.

The area had been devoid of life just a minute ago, but it suddenly looked as though a beast tide was forming all around him, madly fighting against the countless roots in the river. Something was clearly wrong with the animals, as many of them were frothing at the mouth as their eyes shone with madness.

They cared for nothing except their desire to reach the island. The water had already turned red, but the island had similarly grown to twice its original size thanks to the hundreds of snaking roots that had been cut or ripped off by Zac and the beasts. This was definitely the tree's doing.

It was orchestrating a bloodbath.

45
ROOTS

The chaotic scene made Zac's eyes widen with shock, but he quickly found his bearings as he started to prepare. A spectral forest rose on the small island, using the fallen roots as soil. He also summoned the unique blade of **[Chop]** and had it circle around him, which helped tremendously in dealing with the incessant attacks from roots.

The fat tree seemed infuriated that a bunch of other plants had sprung up in its private domain, and the water churned as even more roots rose to rip them apart. But how could normal roots destroy an incorporeal forest? They harmlessly passed straight through, which only angered the tree further. It was the drugged beasts that were forced to take the brunt of the tree's wrath in the end, though, as Zac was proving a tough nut to crack.

A slight vibration in the air was all the warning Zac got before he was suddenly attacked by a small bird, which flashed past him with such speed that it might as well have been a beam of light. Not even the additional sight afforded him by **[Hatchetman's Spirit]** was enough to avoid the strike. A small wound appeared on his right arm, but the small beast was thankfully not powerful enough to cause any more damage than that.

However, it seemed as though the bloodthirsty little swallow wasn't done there, and it veered in a wide arc around the tree before it shot toward him once more.

The emerald leaves of **[Nature's Barrier]** appeared to create a nigh impenetrable wall against the assailant, but it was like a blur completely unfettered by gravity or its own momentum, as it made seemingly impossible turns around the leaves and roots alike. Another bloody line was cut open on Zac's cheek, and he swore in annoyance when the autonomous fractal edge missed the bird for the second time.

The bird gave up on the kill after it realized Zac was barely affected at all. It instead shot toward one of the five remaining flowers, but Zac's eyes widened when the swallow suddenly just up and exploded just as it landed on the pistil. Was it the pollen or something else?

Zac was unsure what to do in either case. He wanted to loot the flowers without destroying the tree, as that would allow him to come back for more treasures in the future. But it looked extremely dangerous to get close. Zac eventually decided to test things out a bit, and he threw one of his beast carcasses at the closest branch.

The massive beast shot forward like a wrecking ball and ripped through multiple layers of roots that tried to stop its advance. It only got within a few meters of the flower before three extremely powerful roots appeared. They were pitch-black compared to the others, which were dark brown, and it looked like naturally formed fractals covered their length.

These were the real killing weapons of the tree.

The special roots effortlessly intercepted the carcass that weighed well over a tonne, and it was gored and flung away in an instant. However, Zac noted that the body didn't show any inclination to explode, meaning that the pollen probably only worked on living creatures. He tested things further and shot a few fractal blades at the special roots, but his eyes widened when he couldn't even cut them apart when he imbued [Chop] with Fragment of the Axe.

The three roots disappeared the next moment as they blended in with the thousands of normal roots, but Zac wouldn't be tricked now that he knew they existed. It might be hard to spot them with his normal sight, but the roots were almost lit up like beacons to his [Cosmic Gaze]. The normal roots contained a respectable amount of nature-aspected energy, but the three killing roots contained some sort of intense fiery power as well.

The vision of [Hatchetman's Spirit] also allowed him to keep track of the three roots, and it almost seemed as though the roots were observing him from a distance. However, danger screamed in his mind the next moment as one of the three shot straight toward him. The leaves of [Nature's Barrier] superimposed to create an extremely thick layer of protection, and Zac activated the first defensive charge of [Hatchetman's Spirit] for good measure.

A rippling shockwave spread out the next moment as the root slammed into his defenses with the force of a runaway train. Scores of roots around Zac were ripped apart from the chaotic swirls of energies, and his own defenses didn't fare much better. Over a dozen layers of leaves were ripped apart, and the emerald shield cracked as well.

The shield managed to absorb most of the remaining momentum from the strike, but Zac was still hurled hundreds of meters away from the impact. He groaned in pain from the punch as he fell into the river, but his brows furrowed when he saw a dark-brown sticky substance covered his chest where the root hit him. Only then did he somewhat realize that the tip of the root had been covered in some unknown compound.

Were the special roots venomous like actual snakes?

Thankfully, his defenses were powerful enough to prevent the root from drawing blood, which barely prevented Zac from being injected with this unknown liquid. He was filled with both dread and marvel as he looked at the three roots that acted just like beasts. It was amazing that a plant could evolve to such a degree in one short year. Or was this perhaps something that the System had planted here as a hidden opportunity?

In either case, it wasn't enough to deter him, and he swam back toward the island, slaughtering any beast that tried to get in his way. It was time to bring out the big guns. He didn't want to use his hidden cards for this fight, but that didn't mean that he couldn't even use his skills. A fractal woodcutter's axe appeared the next moment as Zac ran back toward the tree on top of floating carcasses.

Activating [Deforestation] was essentially effortless by now, and an extremely sharp wave of destruction rippled out the next moment.

Hundreds of roots were cut off and destroyed by that one swing, which once more exposed the bulbous tree within. The three special roots survived, though, which didn't really surprise Zac. But cleaning out the normal roots had fulfilled the purpose of the Axe of Felling, and Zac quickly threw out a fat stack of papers the moment he set his foot on the real part of the island.

The whole river shook, and a conflagration consumed the tree crown a second later, with a plume of flames rising over fifty meters into the air. The explosions came from the stack of over a hundred low-tiered fire talismans he activated as one, and it was Zac's best idea to disperse the barely visible pollen that had spread all over the area.

He figured that the flames would be able to clear out the toxin in the air, but he was worried that his Infernal Axe would not only destroy the pollen but even the tree itself. A bunch of low-tiered talismans shouldn't be able to harm a tree with vitality this strong, making them a better tool for this purpose. And if the tree was destroyed by something like this, it couldn't have been anything precious anyway.

Nothing ventured, nothing gained. That was what passed through his mind as Zac swallowed a handful of soul-soothing and general antidote pills. He shot toward the closest flower the next moment, and he could breathe out in relief when he didn't sense anything odd even after appearing right in front of it. Either the dangers of the pollen had been dealt with, or his body was simply strong enough to withstand it.

A few furious swings later, a second flower had entered his Cosmos Sack, and he was already moving toward the next. The Axe of Felling had contained a large amount of his Fragment of the Axe, and he could feel how it was still impacting the roots he'd cut earlier. The surging vitality of the tree tried to forcibly regrow the roots, but Zac was actively resisting using his latest insights into Dao control. His head hurt, but he refused to let his Mental Energy be dispersed.

It gave him enough breathing room to continue with his harvest. However, he only managed to pluck the third flower before a weird scene took place. The three special roots actually assaulted the remaining flowers themselves, stabbing straight into their cores before they absorbed the flowers' essence. Only a second passed before the flowers looked withered like they had been left to dry in the sun for weeks.

Cannibalism? Zac thought with wide eyes, and his eyes only got even wider when the roots suddenly doubled in size as their auras exploded with ferocity. He barely had time to think before he was slapped with a force that exceeded even the punch of Rhubat, but Zac wasn't even allowed to be thrown away in peace before he was attacked again.

The three roots had gained a massive spike in power from absorbing the three flowers, but the tree itself looked a bit wan. The normal roots didn't bother him any longer either, but they rather went after the huge number of beasts and dragged them underwater. It looked like it desperately needed some nourishment after losing all six of its treasures in one go.

But Zac was in no state to worry about the tree's situation, as he was being harried by those three roots. He had already gotten his hands on the treasure, so there was no point in staying here, but the three roots refused to let him leave. They were even a lot faster than he was since they'd grown in size, and he couldn't just saunter away.

His axe was a blur as he desperately countered the barrage of strikes, but he rapidly gained one wound after another even with his still active [Nature's Barrier] picking up some of the slack. This couldn't go on. His Endurance and Vitality were monstrous for an E-grade human, but how could it compare to that of a tree monster? It thankfully lacked the power to unleash a killing blow, but it was still a hassle to deal with.

It was a shame, but Zac saw no recourse but to launch the second strike of [Deforestation], Infernal Axe, and hope that he didn't accidentally burn up his treasure tree.

The second defensive charge of [Hatchetman's Spirit] provided enough time to activate the second swing, and a furious wave of cutting flames spread out across the river. It contained the fury of Mother Nature itself, and the attack incinerated everything from island to shore. Even the special roots were unable to resist the fiery wrath of Zac's ultimate skill, and they slunk away before they were ripped apart like everything else.

Zac saw his opportunity and flashed away, barely avoiding a large spurt of that odd liquid the roots were covered in. That final gout of venom had actually come from the tree trunk itself like it had opened a valve to shoot out a beam of poison at him. But Zac had already taken out his flying treasure at that point, and he was much too quick to be caught by now.

He found himself on the shore a second later, and he became one with the forest the next moment. Zac was certain he could feel the fury of that bloodthirsty tree in the distance, but Zac didn't care as he moved further away. The fight wasn't really finished, but there was no point to killing the goose that laid the golden eggs.

Three flowers had been reabsorbed by the tree itself, but getting at least half of them was decent enough. Better yet, he had managed to do so without permanently harming the tree and without using any of his cheats. Zac marked down the spot on his private map before he moved on, looking for other opportunities in the core region of the swamps.

Zac found a lot of precious herbs, but he also found himself in a constant struggle. He was actually assaulted by the hornets twice over the following day, and Zac finally couldn't take it any longer. He spent half a day looking for their hive before he mounted an assault on the small mountain. After thirty minutes of all-out carnage, he found himself in the depths of the hive.

There was a shocking monstrosity in the heart of the cave, a queen whose only job was to birth more soldiers. But it seemed as though the queen was unable to defend herself apart from a mental attack that couldn't harm Zac in the slightest. It reminded him of the queen he'd fought during the undead level at the Tower, though this hornet queen was a lot less evolved for war.

It allowed him to completely ignore the beast and ransack the place for treasures, but the only thing he found was lots of extremely energy-dense honey. Hornets shouldn't actually be producing honey as far as Zac knew, but perhaps these things were bees that had mutated into predators from the integration. In either case, the stuff was chock-full of Cosmic Energy, especially the Royal Jelly he found next to the queen.

It contained far more energy than even E-grade Nexus Crystals, and Zac actually gained a level in his human form just from eating a fifth of the Royal Jelly. It pushed him to level 83 in his human shape as well, catching up to his Draugr side. He quickly put the ten free points into Dexterity, just like he had with all other free points in the E-grade, before he moved on.

But he didn't find another real treasure like the fat tree and its flowers even after spending a total of six days in the vast forests. He still felt like the past week was well spent, as he'd made a lot of progress on his meditation, while even upgrading one of his skills. He had even gotten a better understanding of his Luck and how to make the most of it. But it was time to head home.

Zac eventually found a secluded cave and erected a teleportation array. It was a bit wasteful to burn almost 100 million Nexus Coins on a single-use array, but he didn't want to waste a whole day flying back to the settlement at the edge of the swamp. There were no messages waiting for him when returning, so he headed over to Calrin's place to get an estimate on his gains.

"You're back," Calrin said with curiosity as Zac sat down on a chair in the private meeting room of the Thayer Consortia. "Did you find anything interesting?"

"You tell me," Zac said as he took out one of the enormous flowers.

46

LIFE, DEATH, WAR

"My body is telling me that this should be good stuff, but its pollen also seemed pretty deadly," Zac said as he placed the flower on the merchant's inspection table.

"The energies condensed in the pistil are both strong and peculiar, but I don't recognize this species," the Sky Gnome said as he looked at the natural treasure with interest. "It should be something good. How did you find it?"

"It grew on a tree," Zac said as he described his encounter in the swamp.

"This reminds me of something," Calrin muttered as he took out one of his massive tomes.

A short moment later, a page depicting a similar tree to the one on the island appeared.

"It's a **[Rageroot Oak]**, a plant that can match your Tree of Ascension in rarity. It's lucky you didn't actually cut it down. Its trunk contains a sap that might even be able to drive you mad," Calrin read. "The sap and pollen are both valuable and can be continuously extracted. The flowers can take decades to form."

Zac felt some cold sweat running down his back when he saw the description. He remembered how something had dripped from those special roots; it turned out to be sap meant to turn him into a madman.

"What's it good for, though? Berserking pills?" Zac asked, not too enthused.

Power never came for free, no matter if you were talking about War Arrays or Berserking Pills. War Arrays would always force you to travel with weaker subordinates, each one of them a weak link. As for Berserking Pills, they generally had pretty gruesome side effects. The stronger the effect, the worse the drawback would be.

"The pollen can be made into a potent beast lure, which can be useful in all sorts of situations. You can both use it for yourself in case you need to refine yourself through battle, or you can use it to unleash a beast tide on your enemies. The sap is indeed a popular ingredient in Berserking Pills that allow warriors to unleash their potential during a battle," Calrin explained.

"And the flower itself? It should be the greatest treasure," Zac said.

"There is a core in the center of the flower," Calrin said. "It's a natural treasure that works as a Berserking Pill as well."

"That's it?" Zac asked with disappointment.

"Don't underestimate those cores. It will allow an E-grade warrior to increase their power by one step, and it will not have any major side effects, just extreme exhaustion afterward. These two combined make it extremely rare and valuable. A pill that gives such an impressive boost would carry severe long-term side effects, or might even lead to death," Calrin explained.

Zac finally realized that he really had picked up something good this time. He had researched this matter for a bit after getting his hands on the Cyborg corpse, which could be considered the epitome of a Berserking transformation. One step didn't refer to level, but stages of cultivation, meaning an Early E-grade warrior would be able to exhibit the power of a Middle E-grade warrior with the help of these flowers.

That was almost a doubling in power, and to be able to get such a boost without lasting detriments was amazing. The Cyborg might have gone all the way from Early E-grade to Half-step D-grade, but that also cut the Technocrat's life span down to less than a minute. These flower cores might save his life in the future, turning the tide in a tough battle.

"I also have some wild herbs here as well; see if there's anything valuable," Zac added as he threw over a Cosmos Sack.

There, unfortunately, wasn't anything too impressive, but his six-day haul was still worth over 300 million Nexus Coins. That was only the immediate value of the herbs he'd found thanks to [Forester's Constitution], and not including the mountains of E-grade carcasses that he had amassed in his Cosmos Sack.

It wasn't a huge sum for him any longer, but it proved how profitable even normal exploration could be. You needed both the skills to find the plants and the strength to survive the environment, which disqualified pretty much everyone on Earth apart from a select few. Besides, he had the advantage of being the first explorer, and future generations probably wouldn't be able to collect such a haul.

But it made him excited for the future. This was the gain from a random forest on his planet. How much wealth could one stand to profit by exploring a newly emerged Mystic Realm in the future, a world that was not only untouched but possibly held extremely rare or even previously unseen herbs?

Zac walked out of the consortium with a sense of excitement, but he didn't get far before he sensed a powerful presence close by.

"Hey," a voice said, and Zac looked over at the shadows with surprise.

"It's you?" Zac asked. "How do you keep finding me like this?"

"I just need to ask around. It's not like you're very circumspect," Ogras snorted.

"Well, is it done?" Zac asked.

"It's done." Ogras nodded as he stepped out into the light, and Zac could feel that the aura of the demon was a lot more condensed compared to before.

"What level are you now?" Zac asked with curiosity, as it was obvious the demon had gained a substantial amount of attributes.

"Eighty-three." Ogras shrugged, his mouth curving slightly upward. "A decent early push."

"Eighty-three? What the f–" Zac swore. "How have you already caught up to me? I had to fight multiple life-and-death battles to get here."

"Node-opening pills work as intended on me since I'm not a primordial beast," Ogras snorted. "You racked up a premature resistance by eating them by the handful."

"Well, it's good that you're out," Zac said. "I killed one of the Dominators while you broke through. I can use some backup soon."

"Oh? Which one?" Ogras said with surprise. "I thought they had already decided to follow the same strategy as the zealots."

Zac quickly recapped what had taken place while Ogras was in secluded cultivation.

"Well, it's good that one of them is dealt with, though it does make me worry a bit that there has been no response. Makes me think they are up to something," Ogras grunted. "Get anything useful from its body?"

"No, I accidentally broke his Cosmos Sack," Zac explained with a grimace. "I've saved the remains to cleanse of Karmic Ties later, but I want all three of them first. Oh, but I did get this."

Zac took out the pitch-black spear the next moment and threw it over to Ogras. The demon caught it effortlessly even though it weighed hundreds of kilos, and the weapon turned to a blur as Ogras started stabbing it into the air.

"It contains some material and insight related to Space," Ogras muttered with excitement. "It can even enter the shadows! I just need to find a decent Blacksmith to infuse some more shadow-related materials and it will be perfect for me! Are you giving this to me?"

"Sure, but you'll have to find some way to pay me back later." Zac smiled. "We both know how valuable this spear is. Some offhanded advice won't cut it."

"Fine, I'll figure something out." Ogras shrugged as he dripped his blood on the weapon. "Such a good thing."

"Get ready for the war in three days," Zac said as he started walking toward the closest teleporter. "We may have to deal with the other two Dominators there."

"I'll head out for a day or two to get used to my improved strength," Ogras said. "But I will arrange things."

Zac chose to stay behind in Port Atwood while the demon went away to hone himself through combat, spending his time either in his Soul Strengthening Array or pondering on the Dao. His most recent trips had given him a lot of insights, especially into the Fragment of the Bodhi, and he wanted to incorporate those snippets into his understanding of the Dao as quickly as possible. It wasn't enough to actually evolve any of the Fragments, but it was a step in the right direction.

The days flew by, and the morning of the challenge quickly arrived. Zac hadn't even left his cultivation cave during the three days, but he had gotten occasional reports from Triv. The ghost had availed himself as a sort of filter to save Zac time. Crystals full of reports were sent to his compound daily by Abby and others, and Triv sifted through them to categorize them by importance and urgency.

Of course, the most crucial reports were sealed so that only Zac could see them.

This time, Zac didn't set out to war with just Triv, but there was a whole squad waiting for him. Both Ogras and his two remaining generals were there, as was Joanna with a defensive squad of shield-bearing Valkyries and Emily. Triv was already resting inside his pagoda, ready to erect the jammers one final time.

Only his sister was missing from this group of core combatants of Port Atwood, with her being busy dealing with the Mystic Realm. Things were thankfully looking up over at Mystic Island, and Kenzie had indicated that there shouldn't be any problems with attempting a reopening in a few days.

"You know why we're here," Zac simply said as he looked around. "We're not going to participate in the war itself. Our only job is to deal with the real threat, the Dominators. There should still be two Karmic connections that can lead that man to Earth, but if we manage to destroy them, we'll be safe for a century."

"What if the insectoids want to deal with those guys by themselves?" Ilvere asked.

"Ignore them," Zac eventually said after giving it some thought. "This is a matter of survival for our planet. Taking out the Dominators takes precedence over anything else. I'll just apologize to the Anointed afterward if it comes to that."

The group nodded in understanding, each of them already well aware of their respective roles. Zac would be the main combatant, and Ogras would be backup, with the rest of the group offering assistance in different ways. Thea would take the same role as Ogras as well if she decided to join them this time as well.

Zac didn't feel safe with letting anyone else directly fight the Dominators, and he was only confident in those two thanks to their ability to escape if needed. Harbinger had both proven his power and conviction in the previous battle, and he was afraid that even elites like Billy would just find themselves to be cannon fodder in front of their strength.

The group set out just a few minutes later, and they appeared at an array at the foot of a mountain this time. Zac could sense a terrifying aura, and a breathtaking scene met his eyes when he turned his head.

Millions of Zhix stood armed and ready, an army many times larger than what he had witnessed so far. Not only that, one look was enough to tell that they hadn't thrown in random people to bolster the ranks. Each and every one was a hardened warrior who had seen battle before. The scene made him sigh with awe but also disappointment.

With an army like this in existence, why did he have to close all those incursions himself? It was living proof that the thing that made newly integrated planets fail was mostly lack of coordination and sacrificial will. The Zhix could have taken out a large number of incursions themselves, but they had been paralyzed by their complex relationship with Cosmic Energy.

"Warmaster, you are here." Rhubat nodded as they walked over. "You brought more people this time?"

"We will stay to the side as promised. I just want to take precautions in case the other two appear today," Zac explained.

The Grand Anointed slowly nodded in understanding, which Zac also took as a tacit agreement that his people could fight the Dominators in case they showed up.

There wasn't much else for them to do, and they set out just a few minutes later. Thea had already appeared before his group did, and it looked like the Anointed already had made their plans and preparations before this.

The vast army traveled for over six hours until they reached a secluded basin nestled in between towering mountains. There were no known human settlements within hours, according to Thea, which was one of the reasons this location was picked. Another reason was probably that the basin stretched far into the horizon, allowing it to accommodate two massive armies.

Zac didn't have to wait long for them to spot their enemies. An endless black snake was moving toward them from the distance, emerging from a canyon on the other side of the basin. The people in his group frowned when they saw that the enemy army was at least 30% larger than their own, but Zac wasn't as worried.

These people hadn't witnessed the power of the Anointed who had entered the crusade.

Their group found a small mountain not far from their own back lines. It rose about two hundred meters above the ground, which allowed them to be close enough to witness the action without risking being suddenly dragged into it.

"Activate the jammer," Zac finally said when the two armies had lined up with a kilometer's distance, and Triv adroitly activated the black pillar.

There was a subdued silence as the millions of Zhix stood ready for war; the War Council was betting everything to secure the future of their Race. The Dominators had been a shadow in the collective mind of the Zhix for millennia, and this was their final chance to fulfill the wish of their ancestors to completely cleanse it.

Conversely, if they failed, the Zhix would fall. The Dominators would seize control, which would be a short hegemony that would last until the Great Redeemer got here to cull the planet.

"So we just stand here?" Ogras muttered with a lazy expression.

"This is the struggle of the Zhix; our presence will only muddy the waters," Thea said from the side, only sparing the demon a glance before turning back toward the battlefield.

The stalemate only lasted for around ten minutes before a prolonged note was released from a horn somewhere. The call released the floodgates, and the two armies started rushing toward each other. There were no deft stratagems or tactics employed, but rather just brutal fervor as the armies clashed.

The warriors didn't even seem to utilize their classes or skills, but rather just infused their bodies and traditional weapons with Cosmic Energy. It was a bit like Zac before he figured out how his pathways worked, where he just pushed around the energy in his body to improve his power.

Was this a tacit agreement between the two sides? An oath to deal with their conflict following the ancient precepts?

The armies weren't thick, the rows only having a depth of a hundred warriors or so, but the war stretched all the way to the horizon. There were hundreds of thousands of simultaneous clashes, and even the sky was affected by the collective outburst of killing intent and Cosmic Energy. The whole sky glowed red as the Zhix fought tooth and nail with everything they had, and Zac started to enter a mystic state as he looked on from the mountaintop.

"This…!" Zac whispered, his eyes widening.

The others on the mountain looked at him with confusion, but he was no longer in any state to think about that as his aura exploded around him, forcing everyone to move away. His aura wasn't calm or condensed, but rather a chaotic mess of energies that tried to devour everything around them.

"Death," he muttered next, and order was imposed upon the chaos.

A massive sphere of darkness had been created, and the deathly energies inside it swirled in a vortex much like how his nodes looked. The enormous sphere took up almost half his vision, and perhaps by accident, it covered most of the enemy army. Zac didn't know if others could see what he saw, but it didn't matter. His mind was full of pictures flashing by, superimposing themselves over the gory bloodbath beneath him.

People died by the scores every second, and each death seemed to resonate with him. The two opposing armies were like two opposite energies clashing, and something new would be born from the struggle.

"Life," Zac whispered in a trance, and his aura was split in two.

The growing sphere of death was pushed aside, forced to share space with a vibrant ball of life. Inside it was a power-generating vortex as well, but it flowed in the opposite direction of the sphere of death. The two spheres brought order to the chaos, but they each struggled for dominance.

The space between the two turned into a delimiting line of constant conflict, perfectly mirroring the war of the Zhix. And just like something new would be born out of this carnage, so was something brewing in his own aura. The thing he had been searching for since he'd started looking for a truth of his own.

"War," Zac growled, and the world finally clicked in place.

Blood fell like rain under a crimson sky, and a Path was born.

47
TRINITY

Zac's robes fluttered as his burgeoning aura caused sharp winds to blanket the mountain peak. However, he wasn't in any state to notice the tumultuous state of the mountain he was sitting on. His full attention was split between the magical scene in the air that held the conceptualization of his path, and the all-out struggle below that resonated with him.

The two spheres seemed to hold the powers to both destroy the world and recreate it, but they were still bound and manipulated by the third force in the middle. If the two spheres were represented by the two armies below, then the war itself represented a third force that drew the two opposites toward each other, changing their energies through conflict.

Most of Zac's waking hours over the past months had gone into trying to understand the various moving components that comprised his unique situation, when he wasn't putting out fires left and right. On the most fundamental level, there were his two classes and their corresponding Daos, but that was just one aspect of his cultivation path.

There were also his weaponry and skills and even Port Atwood. Yrial and his guidance was also an important factor, and his master's own path had been the reason that Zac had so arduously tried to form a cycle of Life and Death until giving up during the Tower of Eternity. There was also the issue of the two Remnants in his head, and the powerful bloodline he suspected himself to have.

Not everything needed to necessarily be part of some sort of cultivation master plan, but the more the better. The more factors behind his success he managed to integrate into his path, the better and sturdier it would become. That would become even more important if he actually managed to take the step into Dual Arcane classes in the future.

Moving forward from that point on would be far more complicated, putting huge requirements on one's foundation. Certainly, no piddling E-grade warriors would be able to fathom a perfected path, but if their contradictions and mistakes were too large, then he might not be able to fix them further down the path.

The problem was that there had been a fundamental barrier to his improvements all this while: deciphering how all his unique points fit together. There was undeniably a theme of Life and Death, but he hadn't really figured out how to fuse that with his axe-work just yet. **[Rapturous Divide]** and **[Blighted Cut]** were a move in the right direction, but gaining scheduled skills couldn't be considered understanding one's cultivation path. He was still making isolated improvements without thinking of the whole, which was starting to become dangerous.

But that finally started to change.

He had completely lost any sense of time or his surroundings on the mountain by this point, as his whole being was consumed by his epiphany. The Dao always felt elusive and intangible, but it was so clear to him at this moment. It felt like one breath right now was as effective as hours of silent meditation. He suddenly understood everything with unprecedented clarity. Where he currently was, and where he needed to go.

Zac realized that he had looked at it all wrong until now. He had thought of his cultivation path as one of duality, where life and death were the main components. He had two Races and two classes and even two Remnants to match them. However, there were also triplets in the mix.

He had three sets of Daos, each distinct and unique, and he could produce three different "sparks" from the Remnants based on his Daos. However, he had been stuck in a mental trap even after discarding a cyclic path and the original purpose of **[Cyclic Strike]**.

He had still seen his future path as one of duality, even if it wasn't one of skill and balance but rather force.

But Life and Death weren't the concepts that defined him or his rise after the integration. It was his struggle.

His path was not one of cyclic dominance that used skilled control to seamlessly switch between states and concepts, and neither was it one of harmonic equilibrium. His path was one of struggle, where the flames of war would open the path of Life and Death. His path was one of a defiant struggle that would pave a bloody path all the way toward the peak.

One year ago, Zac had been stranded in the middle of nowhere with nothing but a hatchet in his hand. Now he was one of the most powerful people in the younger generation in the whole sector, and his name was known across whole galaxies. Was this thanks to his deep insight into Life and Death? Of course not.

The air screamed as [Verun's Bite] appeared in his hand, its blackish edge casting a deathly gleam. Zac's eyes turned down to the axe, the weapon that had followed him since the beast waves. His weapon had been a constant through his struggles, yet it had been relegated to being some sort of delivery method for his "more advanced" concepts.

But that was completely backward.

His weapon wasn't just a replaceable component, it was the catalyst to everything. Without it, his path was dead in the water, just like the two Remnants in his mind, which were stuck at an impasse that would only end when one of the two was defeated.

Zac's eyes flashed as he remembered the Stele and the vision it brought. The ancient plaque carried the essence of a primordial concept as it soared through space in search of new generals. It pushed the idea that without struggle there would be nothing. A universe could be born, only to never flourish. It would remain lifeless and slowly die to entropy over the countless eons if there was no catalyst for change and improvement.

It wasn't a duality he was looking to create, but a trinity with the axe in the center. The axe contained his struggle, his determination, and his undying will, and those things could even influence life and death itself as long as he became powerful enough. It would be the catalyst, the seed for change.

In the case of the sparks, "War" also represented his personal control. He had seen how things went once already when he excluded his Fragment of the Axe to create the Chaos Pattern. He had instantly lost control and conjured the System itself. He was just a cog rather than someone in control, and it was almost a miracle that he was still alive after doing something so foolhardy.

If his current ideas were correct, then the Fragment of the Axe was crucial when touching upon Creation and Oblivion. It was the fragment he was the most skilled with, and it was outside the purview of the two Remnants. It was truly his, and he could use this fact to draw in the opposing powers of both his two other Daos or the Remnants, and from there push their struggle to suit his goals by being the general in charge of the war.

That was why the Fragment of the Axe had been needed to create useable sparks. If you took that part out of the equation, you only had Oblivion and Creation to create Chaos, and those two were still exclusively the Heavens' Domain. He was only borrowing a small and simplified corner of the vast power of Oblivion and Creation through the Remnants, and there was no point in making it the core of his cultivation path.

That small insight made him realize something else. Was the ultimate spark perhaps not the combination of his Fragment of the Bodhi and Fragment of the Coffin, but rather a combination of all three of his Daos? Was that the key to activating both the Remnants at the same time? He had essentially become a vessel for the System the last time, but things might be different in the future if he managed to impose his will with the help of his Axe Dao.

Of course, he wasn't ready to test that any time soon. First of all, creating a spark with both Remnants and his Fragment of the Axe would require him to somehow modify **[Cyclic Strike]** to allow three simultaneous streams of energy. Besides, he didn't dare try something like that before his soul was much stronger.

It still wasn't certain that Zac would need to evolve his Fragment of the Axe into a Branch of War in the future to accommodate his most recent insights. He knew too little about those Daos. Of course, he knew too little about that powerful Dao, so taking that specific decision this early was pointless.

Besides, it wasn't like everything needed to revolve around the Remnants. They contained mysterious and incredible power, but the dangers were there to match. For now, he just needed to survive them. Controlling them would come later. Whether they would be truly integrated into his classes or remain as foreign objects that could be used to unleash ultimate strikes was still impossible to decide.

Who knew, as long as he followed this road, he might one day become powerful enough to control both Creation and Oblivion by himself without the need of any Remnants at all. At that time, he might be able to absorb them, or at least discard them, as they would be useless by that point.

Because, at that point, he would become an actual wielder of Creation and Oblivion, perhaps even able to conjure Primordial Chaos.

A sense of danger suddenly cut through his thoughts as the skies themselves rumbled in anger. Zac was forcibly snapped out of his reverie and finally regained the sense of his surroundings, prompting him to look around in confusion. The sky was still colored crimson from one of the suns setting, aptly matching the still ongoing carnage below.

However, there were mountains of Zhix corpses by this point, making Zac realize hours might have passed in his special state. There was no one around him either, and Zac saw that the others in his elite group sat a few hundred meters away from him, conversing with low voices or spectating the battle. None of them seemed to have heard the thunder crashing into his ears just now, as they didn't even glance toward the sky.

The fact that no one else seemed to have heard the thunder didn't relieve him, but it rather filled him with dread. He was pretty much a demigod by old-world standards; there was no way he was hearing things wrong.

A flash of lightning stretched across the whole sky the next moment. It was massive, drawing a line as thick as the smaller sun across the stratosphere. It looked to be extremely far off as well, which only magnified just how much lightning that arc contained. It might spear straight through the planet if it landed instead of just passing by Earth through the horizon.

Zac's eyes were wide as he witnessed the spectacle, and even the furious battle down below was utterly forgotten. The bolt looked absolutely terrifying, but it was also extraordinarily beautiful. It felt like it was condensed from the purest Dao, and Zac felt that limitless insights were just out of his reach.

If he could only absorb a little bit...

However, Zac immediately cursed his stray thoughts. An extremely small tendril suddenly appeared just a few thousand meters above him. It looked like a purple piece of string, but Zac didn't hesitate to start running away from his people even if they were hundreds of meters apart. His mind was screaming with horror, and it was not just his danger sense.

That purple lightning was far less mysterious and a lot more terrifying when it was bearing down on him. It felt like that seemingly insignificant tendril contained the wrath of the Heavens themselves, and just the thought of getting struck by that thing filled him with horror. His first instinct was that it was the System sending lightning at him a second time, but something told him that might not be the case.

The bolt looked completely different compared to the lightning that the System had conjured in the Tower of Eternity when he summoned the Chaos Pattern. For one, it was purple instead of blue and gold. Secondly, Zac had been able to sense a sort of presence that time, but now the feeling was completely different.

Before, it had felt like a vast and indifferent being had looked down at him from high above, but he couldn't sense a being this time. It was rather like the Dao itself was trying to kill him as he sensed a boundless, but inanimate, fury and killing intent in the bolt. It made him think that it might be less of a tribulation to withstand and more of an assassination attempt to survive.

It was futile. Zac was pushing **[Loamwalker]** to the limit, but it looked as though the tendril was affixed to the space right above his location no matter how far he moved. It snaked its way down with deceptive speed, and Zac barely had time to sit down and erect all his available layers of defenses.

However, some things were the same as during the tribulation. His skills, talismans, and even Daos seemed utterly incapable of impeding the bolt. The shields cracked and even his soul received a backlash as the thunderbolt struck straight between his eyebrows.

What followed next was a pain even greater than when he jumped into the Cosmic Pond.

48

HEAVEN'S MANDATE

Pain and pressure threatened to tear Zac's body apart in an instant as it swelled to uncomfortable proportions. Zac wasn't the same person as back when he had been flooded by Cosmic Water, and he forced himself to remain conscious as he looked for solutions.

Another thing that differed from similar situations was that Zac wasn't exactly being filled up with a terrifying amount of Cosmic Energy as he had been in the Cosmic Water or when forming his Duplicity Core in the Dead Zone. Whatever the purple bolt of lightning was made of seemed to be something different.

It would be more apt to call it a messy mix of countless different Daos.

Zac was almost delirious from pain, but he strove to actively combat the lightning bolt as well by utilizing his newest method of controlling his Mental Energy. Directly defending hadn't worked, so he instead tried to push it out of his body with Fragment of the Bodhi Mental Energy, essentially doing the opposite of when he had completed the quest for **[Blighted Cut]**. However, the mysterious lightning bolt was completely unmoved by Zac's efforts.

The odd and messy heterogeneity that Zac had never encountered before made it extremely hard to combat. His Daos were effective against some parts of the bolt but almost seemed to be making things worse on other parts. He was quickly reduced to passively enduring the lightning as he ground it down by exhausting his Mental Energy. However, it wasn't enough.

There was simply too much energy inside that bolt. And it was not only that; there were hints of high-tiered concepts beyond Zac's current understanding hidden in the chaotic mix, making it even more precarious to carry it around in his body. Even the Remnants seemed subdued in its presence, something he only had witnessed once before, trying to appear inconspicuous rather than railing against its prison due to the chaos.

Zac popped one pill after another into his mouth as he tried one thing after another to weather the storm, and the others had realized something was wrong by now. They rushed closer, but they didn't get too close after Zac arduously shook his head at them. They wouldn't be able to help him this time, but he was starting to despair, as the bolt seemed to have no intention of relenting in its efforts to rip his body apart. Bloody cracks had spread all over his body already, and a similar situation could be seen in his soul.

But a deep heartbeat suddenly echoed out across the area as **[Void Heart]** thumped.

Nothing Zac had done until now could even be considered a temporary relief against the bolt, but there was actually a change in the lightning that coursed through his body after his hidden node activated. Better yet, it didn't seem to be on an isolated part of his body either. The whole bolt was frozen after the first heartbeat. However, Zac also felt a sharp pain in his heart, seemingly a backlash from messing with the purple lightning. It looked like even his omnivorous hidden node had problems dealing with this.

The **[Void Heart]** didn't give up after just one try, and another beat, this one even heavier, made his whole body vibrate. This time, the foreign lightning didn't just stop, but the hidden node actually managed to rip off a small piece of the purple energy in the bolt before it swallowed it whole.

The stabbing pain that followed almost made him black out.

Zac started to worry for real as blood seeped from his mouth. He had only absorbed a few percent of the energy, but the backlash felt almost as dangerous as the lightning itself. He would be dead long before the node had absorbed it all, and Zac still hadn't found any way for him to control it. Zac was elated that something finally worked, but he was also worried about the implications.

He was pretty sure that this bolt was some sort of tribulation brought forth by the System. The timing was too spot-on, and what else would be able to conjure that endless bolt in the sky? Perhaps the tribulation came from forming a proper path, or perhaps there was something else behind its emergence.

In either case, it was something that should have been sent by the System. It felt extremely risky to try to steal that energy for himself, especially as the pain after the second beat almost knocked him unconscious. What if the System got angry and retaliated?

A third beat and another piece of the bolt was sucked into the vortex in his heart, disappearing into some unknown space of the **[Void Heart]**, and Zac was lying on the ground by this point. The rampaging energies lost their energy once again, freezing in place all over his body. It was extremely lucky as well, as the backlash this time actually did knock him out, though only for a few seconds.

Zac realized he had fallen down on the ground at some time, but he was too tired and in too much pain to sit up. He could only lay sprawled on the ground, panting and fearing for what would come next. Not a scrap of energy had been released back from the hidden node either, which was odd by itself.

The node instead started shaking more and more violently until Zac puked out a huge stream of blood that shot down the mountain and turned into a red mist. It was the trapped purple lightning that had actually managed to escape from his node, damaging it a bit while doing so. It did seem a bit changed, like he had spit it up mid-digestion.

A fourth beat echoed out, but it looked like the purple bolt had had enough of Zac's weird bloodline. It actually reabsorbed the regurgitated lightning and fled out of his pores, its tendrils seemingly destroying everything in his surroundings out of frustration. It created a magical scene where the whole mountain was illuminated in purple, and this time, it looked as though the lightning was visible to everyone.

The bolt in the sky disappeared the next moment after emitting a final burst of fury and murderousness. Zac looked like he had just lost ten battles in a row, but the lightning didn't get away completely unscathed either. The hidden node had actually managed to reabsorb a small part of the escaped energy before it left his body.

Zac weakly opened his eyes to see the group staying some distance away, seemingly afraid to approach without his go-ahead.

"Are you okay? What can we do?" Joanna shouted with worry in her eyes.

"It's over; it should be fine now," Zac said with a weak voice, but everyone on the mountain could easily hear it, as even the weakest among them were Late F-grade warriors by now.

The Valkyries and Triv rushed over while Ogras and Thea maintained their distance as they vigilantly looked at the surroundings. Zac snorted, as he knew that while Thea was looking for threats, the demon was simply afraid of getting hit by some surprise lightning. The Valkyries started to clean his wounds as they erected a series of arrays around him, hiding Zac's wretched state from any prying eyes.

The ghost flitted around as he seemed to be observing the air around Zac. It only took a few seconds before Triv's eyes widened as his head snapped toward Zac, who was still unable to get on his feet. He had clearly gleaned something from the remnant energy that had melded with the air and disappeared.

"This is Heavenly Lightning! Ancient Tribulation!" Triv said with horror in his eyes as he flew away from Zac once more. "What did you do to draw the wrath of the Heavens?!"

The Valkyries already looked utterly baffled as they looked at Zac's pathetic state, and that only intensified when they heard Triv's words.

"Just meditating," Zac said with a frown, his whole body feeling like it had been incinerated. "Why did I suddenly get blasted by another tribulation?"

The ghost seemed to be hesitating about something, his eyes darting toward the Valkyries, who were still inside the arrays.

"I have to rest a bit," Zac simply said. "Wake me up if something changes."

Zac spent over an hour in an almost fugue state where he completely focused on recuperation. He finally dared to move and circulate his energy a bit, and he was relieved to realize that his body wasn't as grievously wounded as he had feared. There were a huge number of both internal and external wounds, but that wasn't a problem for Zac.

The situation was similar with his soul, but it was thankfully far from fragmenting. His state more resembled having overextended himself in battle, which would be a lot quicker to recover from. Of course, there was always a risk that hidden threats were lurking in his body, waiting to explode.

"Thank you for your help. Give me and Triv a moment, please," Zac said with an exhausted voice as he opened his eyes. "No one comes in."

Joanna nodded and handed him a bottle of water before they exited the layers of arrays. However, they didn't go far, simply choosing to erect a perimeter around him.

"You know something," Zac evenly said.

"I... Ah..." the ghost said before his voice echoed out in Zac's mind.

'It's the punishment of the Heavens, the result of embarking on the Boundless Path,' Triv's voice said.

"WHAT?!" Zac exclaimed with shock before he quickly erected a sealing array and dragged the ghost inside. "When did I do something like that? Explain yourself."

"It is just what I heard," Triv said. "I might be wrong!"

"Just tell me what you know," Zac exhorted.

"Before the System, all cultivation went against the Heavens. It was to steal the essence of the Dao to attain immortality. But the universe wouldn't give in just like that, and it would send a tribulation down on the cultivators." Triv sighed. "This all changed with the arrival of the System.

"Cultivation no longer goes against the Heavens; it is now Heaven's Mandate. The only tribulations now are the trials that the System has envisioned to weed out the weak and train the strong. It is completely different from how it was before when the Heavens tried to smite those who stole its lifeblood."

"What does this have to do with me?" Zac asked with a sinking feeling.

"It seems young master has gained an insight that is either moving in an unrecognized direction or is outside the Heavens' Mandate altogether. You need to adjust your path to once more enter Heaven's Path."

Zac didn't understand what the ghost was talking about. How had he entered the Boundless Path? However, he suddenly remembered something. The last thing he had thought of before the lightning appeared was to personally take charge of Creation, Oblivion, and the Primordial Chaos itself. He only now realized how ballooned his ego was at that moment. This was something that not even the greatest masters of the universe could control, from what he had gathered.

More importantly, if he really took control of the Dao of Chaos, he would probably become one of the strongest beings in the universe, possibly even at the level of the Apostates. Was this what the System meant by "Beware the Terminus"? Did it think he was fomenting an insurrection when creating his cultivation path?

It was a bit odd, though; there shouldn't be any lack of people dreaming of seizing control of the Dao itself and becoming unparalleled across the Multiverse. In fact, it should be one of the most common goals among elite cultivators. Was the System really zapping people left and right for having ambition? It seemed completely contrary to its purpose. Or was there some other reason that the System actually felt threatened and took action? Something unique about him?

In either case, the ghost's words came at a really bad time. The vision he had seen during his epiphany earlier had already turned muddled and indistinct in his mind, but he still remembered how vast it was and how it encompassed his path of cultivation perfectly. How could he just part with it like that? He felt that he would never reach his full potential if he walked away from this.

"And if I don't change my path?" Zac asked with reluctance.

"The further you walk down this path, the greater the suppression of the Heavens. Not only will you be forced to withstand the true tribulations of the Heavens, the ones aimed at murder rather than training, but even the System will turn its back on you. I doubt the System would care about an E-grade or even D-grade warrior, but if you go too far, you might find yourself unable to freely walk in integrated space," Triv said fearfully. "However…"

"However what?" Zac asked with exhaustion.

He had somewhat understood where Triv was going with his explanation from the very beginning, but he had let him prattle on as he gathered his own thoughts. He truly didn't know what he should do even if the ghost was right. There was still a burning reluctance in his chest as he thought about giving up just as he began, but was it worth it to keep struggling?

He was not out to overthrow the Heavens or anything. He mainly wanted to get stronger so that he could protect those close to him. He had started to enjoy becoming stronger while uncovering the secrets of the universe, but it wasn't the main reason he pushed himself so hard. He would still be an elite even if he gave up on his envisioned path of cultivation; wasn't that enough?

"However, every single one of the Apostates walked the Boundless Path," Triv eventually said. "As did the Primo."

49

RETALIATION

The ghost was racked with pain after divulging information about the Primo, meaning Triv had once again been punished for breaking the laws branded onto his soul. He even turned mostly transparent this time, meaning that he might have been hurt pretty bad. Zac quickly threw a soul-mending pill he got from the Undead Kingdom into his incorporeal body as he considered the implications of what Triv had said.

Who would have thought that the big shots who had affected the Multiverse as a whole all stepped onto the Boundless Path? Perhaps that was even the only way to reach the greatest heights. He remembered his short conversation with the mysterious man who had married Be'Zi, who had spoken about the broken peaks of the System.

That wasn't to say that the System was useless though. It had drastically increased the average power of the elites of the Multiverse, and it had pushed the boundaries of what was possible. The Apostates were ultimately extreme outliers and not an indicator of the general situation of the average cultivator on the Boundless Path.

It did feel a bit like walking the Boundless Path was the way of the elite, from what Triv said, but he wasn't sure if it was for him. After all, most people seemed more than happy to stay on Heaven's Path, and it was still possible to reach C-grade and even greater heights.

Setting the issue of his path aside, there were some things that the ghost had said that he didn't quite understand.

"Are the System and the Heavens not the same thing?" Zac asked. "How can the Heavens send tribulations at me even if that's not how the System operates?"

"That is beyond me, perhaps beyond everyone in this sector. They are one but also separate, that's all I've heard on the matter. Digging too deep into taboo subjects like this is fraught with dangers as well. Heaven's secrets are not so easily divulged," Triv said as he looked up at the sky with some fear.

"That lightning bolt was extremely frightening. There is no way that normal cultivators would survive more than a second or two. How can whole factions possibly follow this path?" Zac asked next, hoping to find some sort of solution in case the lightning returned.

"I'm no expert on methods of unorthodox cultivation," Triv reiterated. "Though my impression was that both the F-grade and E-grades were safe from true tribulations."

"Guess I'm one lucky turkey, then," Zac snorted, but he suddenly thought of something and opened his title screen.

[Terminus – Gaze upon the Terminus.]

It was the first time in a long while he had looked at this odd title that neither appeared in his status screen nor provided any attributes. But Zac guessed that this actually might be the key as to why the Heavens had reacted to the creation of his path. If others thought about the Primordial Chaos and the Terminus, it was just wishful thinking and not something that the Heavens needed to waste its energy on.

But he had not only seen it, but he still lived to tell the tale. Perhaps this made him a real threat in the Heavens' eyes.

"That said," Triv added, though he seemed pretty reluctant at the idea of Zac continuing down this path, "I would guess that they either have methods to hide from or weaken the tribulation. You would probably have to visit unorthodox space to find out any real details. Taboo subjects are not freely spread in integrated space to avoid any repercussions."

Zac kept talking with the ghost for a while, but he really didn't know much about the subject. As for formalizing a path, he knew even less. It was the same with Ogras and the others. For one, creating a real cultivation path was something that a lot of weaker factions didn't have any organized intelligence on. They just muddled along, often focusing on lower-rarity cultivation to improve their odds.

He still didn't feel he really had a full handle on the situation with his cultivation, but he felt he should just stay the course for the time being.

The thing that muddied the waters was the opposing signals from the System. It seemed to want him to go down this path for some reason, but it also warned him of the "Terminus." Was this the name of the real Heavens perhaps? When the System told him to "beware the Terminus," was it perhaps warning him that the pre-System Heavens would try to stop him?

Zac eventually sighed and shook his head, deciding to focus on the present instead of worrying about these far-off things.

Hopefully, his previous experience was just a result of him wanting to take control of Chaos itself. If that was the case, he might be fine as long as he didn't become too greedy. He could simply focus on just Life, Death, and Struggle like he'd originally planned when pondering his path during the epiphany.

He deactivated the layers of defenses around him after letting Triv clean him up. The ghost had a skill called [Twilight Scrub] for this very purpose, true to his class. It was a convenient mix of a shower and a wash that just looked like a dense cloud, but it was unfortunately made for the unliving. The aquamarine haze that cleansed his body of both blood and grime felt like a touch of death itself. It wasn't harmful, though, so Zac didn't waste time changing into his Draugr form just to clean up.

The group outside breathed out in relief when they saw that Zac was really fine, at least outwardly.

"What the hell happened to you earlier?" Ogras asked with exasperation. "First you blast your aura at full power, then you sit around with the expression of a simpleton for hours until you suddenly start running like a maniac. And *what* was that lightning?! I've never seen anything like it."

Zac was exhausted, but seeing the demon so frazzled that he started prattling off did improve his mood a bit. It also looked like he didn't recognize the purple lightning as Triv did, once more proving the advantage of being part of a greater force. Then again, it might just be because Triv was a spirit being who was extremely sensitive to energies, as his body was made from them.

"Nothing much; I just had an epiphany." Zac shrugged, the corner of his mouth tugging slightly upward.

"What's with that smirk?" Ogras muttered, looking like he had swallowed a fly after hearing that Zac had taken yet another step forward.

Teasing aside, Zac still didn't really know if he had actually gained anything from his encounter apart from solidifying his path. The hidden node still hadn't spat out the energy it managed to reabsorb, and Zac started to think that the **[Void Heart]** had kept that tribulation lightning for itself. That might not be the worst thing, though, as it hopefully meant that the node would become stronger.

Zac also asked some questions about what had transpired while he was unconscious or mid-enlightenment, but the others hadn't really gained anything from witnessing the struggle below. They also hadn't shared his vision of the two massive spheres splitting the basin in two, and the vortex of struggle in the middle. Zac was relieved to hear it was for his eyes only, as that vision could be considered a core cultivation secret of his, almost on the level of his mutated Duplicity Core.

The shocking lightning field that had blasted out from his body earlier had apparently given pause to the bloodshed below, but the war had picked up its pace again as he focused on recuperation. Thankfully, it looked like the Dominators really weren't around. If they were, then they would definitely have attacked him during his moment of weakness.

He looked down at the battlefield once more. This time, he didn't see the scene as a representation of his cultivation path, but just as the gruesome war that it was. Hours had passed by this point, and the battle had reached its high point.

Over 90% of both sides were actively engaged in battle, with neither side retaining any spare combatants. The last 10% of Zhix were roving elite squads that shored up any weaknesses that appeared in the front lines, or who mounted assaults aimed at taking out leaders or Anointed. And it had worked with things being so chaotic.

It looked like a quarter of the Anointed had fallen by this point, and more joined their ranks by the minute. They resembled proud lions that were finally harried to death by a vast pack of hyenas. Vast swathes of destruction surrounded every fallen Anointed, and it took hundreds of strikes to finally bring one of the behemoths down.

Of course, the fall of a spiritual leader only led to further slaughter as the hive soldiers of the fallen Anointed turned insane in their desire for revenge.

The number of combatants was almost uncountable, but the ferocity of the war was also unmatched. Zac and his group once more found their spirits subdued by the bloodshed. Only a lunatic would be able to witness this much death without batting an eye. Even Triv looked downcast as he gazed upon the scene below, though his reasons were different than the rest.

"So many children… What a waste. Young master, why not…" Triv whispered by his side.

"I'm not going to raise an army of Zhix undead," Zac said without hesitation. "You've seen it. They cremate their fallen. I neither want nor need an army like this."

This wasn't the first time the ghost had brought forth the point of using the bodies of his enemies to create undead followers. Zac had staunchly refused until now, though he inwardly wasn't as confident. There were a lot of bodies of his fallen enemies stored in Cosmos Sacks. They had the potential to create a group of elites that might be able to rival all the geniuses in his force.

But the time wasn't right.

Triv had actually provided a large-scale array that would slowly infuse Miasma into bodies. The field of corpses he'd appeared on during the climb was one such Array of Awakening, as Triv called it. The problem was that anyone who was resurrected through that array would automatically be part of the Undead Empire. That was why Triv didn't even get a backlash from providing it. The Undead Empire was more than happy to let others raise more subjects for them.

Perhaps he could revisit the issue if the planet really gained a Life-Death attunement, and after he had visited Twilight Harbor and gathered intelligence on how unattached undead factions functioned.

Besides, he didn't have the resources to nurture unliving elites at the moment. He did have the [Corpsebloom Mantra] he'd looted from Mhal along with a few more random manuals and skills, but he was never able to unlock the manuals of the Lich King. Even if he managed to awaken a group of undead right now, he would just be wasting their potential.

The war raged on for a few more hours before there were just a few pockets of traitors on one side, with the Zhix War Council having more than enough steam to crush the last resistance in minutes.

Bloodied and ruthless Anointed pushed forward, their ceremonial knives continuously giving the last rites to those led astray, and finally, there was just deafening silence as the victors stood over the fallen. Zac looked down at the carnage with mixed emotions until he sighed and stood up. All in all, they had stayed in this basin for around eight hours, and Zac was eager to leave this cursed place and its intense stench of blood.

"Looks like it's over," Zac said as he turned to Triv. "You can turn off the jammer."

However, Zac got a sinking feeling when his communication crystal started vibrating just a few seconds after the black pillar stopped humming.

"Lord Atwood, settlements are under attack!"

Zac inwardly swore as his group gathered around him, looks of worry adorning their faces.

"Attacked? Who? Where?" Zac asked with anger. "Is it Port Atwood again?"

"No, it's thankfully just settlements on the mainland. We've first lost contact with Site 27 less than an hour after you activated the jammer. Four hours later, Bastion disappeared, and just now Site 2," the voice said on the other side of the crystal.

"Where are you?" Zac asked next, recognizing the owner to be one Sarah, one of the newer Valkyries. "How are you able to contact me?"

"We set out toward your location from the closest town when we lost contact with you. We've left relays to keep us updated. But we were unable to enter the mountain range where you are staying, so we could only warn you now. I'm sorry." Sarah sighed.

"That's okay. Are you able to get back by yourselves?" Zac asked. "I might need to move quickly."

"No problem. We'll be back in Port Atwood in a few hours," Sarah said without worry.

Zac sighed in relief as he muttered the list of towns with confusion. Those three settlements were nowhere near each other. Site 2 was the provisionary name of one of the first incursions he closed: the time he'd saved the Ishiate towns from the rockmen. Bastion was the location of another incursion, but it was given that name, as there were large numbers of humans actually living there.

The controlling faction there had been one of the better ones, all things considered, killing few natives and "only" enslaving them to gain a workforce. Finally, Site 27 was one of the last incursions, one he didn't actually fight against. It was one of the forces who gave up soon after Zac closed the undead incursion, leaving a ghost town between two secluded peaks behind.

Still, Zac couldn't completely understand why those three had been targeted. They were on different parts of Pangea, and they weren't of critical importance to him at all. None of them were all that easy to access, making it impossible they were random strikes. Either three forces would have to coordinate their efforts or a group that moved extremely quickly between the towns. Judging by the fact they were attacked in sequence, it was more likely it was the latter.

Was it Void's Disciple?

50
SHOWDOWN

Zac had been dreading a response from Void's Disciple since killing Harbinger, and this might be his opening move. He felt doubly thankful that he had already sent most people back to Port Atwood in case of an attack, minimizing loss of life. However, there were still skeleton crews stationed at every spot to keep operations going, and there had probably been losses.

"Did anyone manage to return from those places?" Zac asked with a sigh.

"Unfortunately, no," the answer came. "There were roughly twenty people stationed in each of those locations to maintain basic operations."

Zac and the others kept asking things through the crystal, but Sarah didn't know much. They didn't dare to roll out the army, as all the leaders of Port Atwood were currently away, so they could only look on with dismay as one settlement after another had disappeared from the screen. They had tried to send out a few squads to random settlements to look around, but they had all come back empty-handed.

Various thoughts swirled through Zac's head, but he eventually made his decision. He needed to get going, even if he had to pay the price to erect another teleportation array with his **[Spatial Transfer Array]**. But there was no point in rushing. He wasn't able to reach the three lost settlements in short order anyway, and heading there might allow even more of his towns to be attacked behind his back.

The problem was that he didn't know where this mystery attacker would strike next.

"Can anyone figure out why these three places were targeted?" Zac asked with a frown.

The Valkyries shook their heads, and Ogras didn't speak up either.

"Metals," Ilvere suddenly said, drawing the gazes of the others.

"What?" Zac asked.

"You know, I've been in charge of taking stock of the bases you've conquered. All three of those places you mentioned have Spiritual Metal deposits of pretty high quality. That's the only thing I can think of," the general said.

"Metals," Zac repeated thoughtfully. "But there shouldn't have been too much extracted, and it either left with the invaders or has been transferred to Port Atwood. I had already sent everyone back as well. It's not like they can extract the whole place in minutes or even hours."

"Either they want to stop you from extracting things, perhaps preventing us from properly preparing for the Mystic Realm," Ogras slowly said, "as the mines might be ruined. Or they are looking for an exotic piece of metal that might be found somewhere in their depths."

Zac nodded with a frown. Just like Nexus Crystal mines sometimes could produce Attuned Crystals or higher-grade ones, so could metal deposits contain small amounts of extremely valuable materials. It was on his radar to scan all his reserves for such items, but he sorely lacked the manpower for such a task.

He hadn't even fully mapped out his own crystal mine, as its tunnels stretched kilometer after kilometer below ground, seemingly never-ending pathways that kept turning and branching. He still only had an inkling of what all his conquered towns could provide.

The problem was how quickly things had transpired. It should take a few hours to reach those places from any other settlement even if you had some good movement method, and from there, you would have to enter the depths to extract that precious ore. Zac would have needed almost a whole day to travel to those three locations, even if he only gave himself an hour per mine and used the flying treasure.

"Do we have other places that fit the description?" he asked.

"There's just the one," Ilvere slowly said. "Site 16."

Zac somewhat remembered the place the demon was referring to. It was the incursion with the birdmen, the one placed on top of a mountain.

"Good. If the last town was lost just a few minutes ago, then we have a few hours if things progress as before," Zac muttered. "Traveling to that place will take time even if it's Void's Disciple. Stay here. I need to speak to the Zhix."

The others nodded, and Zac descended the mountain, walking straight toward the battlefield at a hundred meters per step. The war was over, but a subdued silence stretched across the whole basin. Groups of warriors walked across the fields to retrieve the fallen, but most simply sat down, many with tears streaming down their cheeks.

Those worst off were actually the Anointed, all of them sitting in prayer, tear-streaked blood covering their faces. Even the three great Anointed hadn't walked out of the war unscathed, and Vanexis had even lost a hand. It went to show how large groups of weaker cultivators could take out much stronger opponents if they were willing to sacrifice enough lives.

He found Rhubat sitting at the center of the army, and he was relieved to see a bloodied but living Nonet not far away. He had lost track of Nonet during his epiphany, but it appeared that Hive Kundevi thankfully was not one of the hives targeted by the elite executioner squads.

"Congratulations on your victory," Zac said as he turned back to Rhubat. "I'm sorry to interrupt; something urgent has come up."

"This is not a victory, Warmaster." Rhubat sighed, their enormous face a mask of pain and sorrow. "There are no victors today. We've lost half our children this day, yet the war is not over."

"That is why I've come. I won't be able to stay with you on the way back. Someone has attacked three of my settlements while you fought; it seems the person can move extremely quickly," Zac said. "I need to go before more of my towns are destroyed."

"Do you suspect the Dominators?" Rhubat said, and the other Anointed in the vicinity perked up from their desolate states.

"I do," Zac said. "Void seems to have some method to move about somewhat freely."

"What are you planning?"

"If it's really Void, I'm thinking we should launch an ambush. We need to hit hard and quick because he's so slippery," Zac said. "We have located the next place we believe he'll target. I'm heading there now."

"Good, agreed. Vanexis and Raha will oversee the rites," Rhubat said as the giant got to their feet. "Six councilors will come with me. Any more will likely just be a hindrance this time. Our old methods will not work in this scenario."

A few of the largest Zhix roused themselves and got to their feet with solemn expressions, joining Zac as they returned up the mountain. Zac wasted no time before he found a hidden cave large enough to house his group plus the Anointed. He erected an illusion array at the door before a pile of materials emerged from his Cosmos Sack.

His hands turned to a blur next as a crude but functional teleportation array was erected in minutes.

"How is this possible?" Thea muttered with incomprehension as she looked down at the newly created array. "There's no town for hours. Can you actually create arrays like this?"

"No. At least not that I know of. I was given this ability as a reward when the final incursion was closed." Zac shrugged. "Perhaps the System knew I would be running around all over. There are some limitations, though. Only I can activate it, and it is only usable once."

Zac didn't explain the other details of his array, letting them form their own hypotheses. He didn't even need to take out the bracelet hidden beneath his bracer for his **[Spatial Convergence Array]** to work. He just needed to infuse it with Cosmic Energy and a connection was formed between the bracelet and the array. Zac's best guess was that the bracelet contained some sort of spatial energy, and it infused it into Zac's previously dead array to give it enough power to work just once.

It was intentional that he did things this way. This meant that both the Zhix and the Marshall Clan would know that he could plop down an array at any time, anywhere. Such an ability was pretty scary and would make his force almost unassailable.

Port Atwood and these forces had a harmonious cooperation right now, and this display would hopefully help quash any contrary thoughts while he was off cultivating or looking for resources in the future.

"Can you place one inside the Mystic Realm later?" Thea suddenly asked. "In case we need to send out things or people?"

"Teleportation arrays don't work inside Mystic Realms," Ogras said with a lazy expression. "At least not conventional ones. Something about a different sort of space. Now, let's go before the next site disappears from the teleportation array."

Zac nodded, and the group flashed over, appearing at Site 16 a moment later. Their appearance caused some confusion among the stationed troops, and the confusion only increased when Joanna ordered them back to Port Atwood immediately.

After conferring with the Zhix for a bit, they quickly learned that if it really was Void's Disciple that was attacking them, then he should come from the south. An enemy hive was in that direction, and it was one of the closest settlements as well. The problem was whether they should set out from the town, or just sit around here while waiting for someone to show up.

In the end, only Zac, Ogras, the Anointed, and Janos stayed. They would form a squad that would patrol the area toward the south. The rest were sent back as well, as there simply wasn't enough room on the flying leaf. He was able to increase and decrease its size to some degree, but the Anointed would still be packed like sardines. It was clearly not a tool to transport armies, but rather a private treasure for a wealthy scion.

Thea wasn't all too happy about the arrangement, but Zac felt that Janos might be better to bring. There was already a lot of firepower between himself and the others, but Janos provided something unique. If he could trap or at least weaken the Dominators with illusions, his value would be extremely high in the battle.

Meanwhile, while Thea had gained a recent boost to her power through the Inheritance, she hadn't fully gained control of that strength just yet. She was also still at the F-grade, meaning she simply didn't have the attributes to join in on a fight of that level. It would have been a different matter if she had reached the same point as Ogras – getting that Early E-grade boost from leveling pills, but for now, she could only take a back seat.

The group flew back and forth at the foot of the mountain, looking for any sign of invaders. However, three hours passed without anything to show for it. Honestly, that was fine by Zac. Only seven hours had passed since he was sapped by that terrifying tribulation lightning, and the longer things dragged on, the more he would be able to recuperate. Certainly, he was in a good enough state to fight, but he wasn't in peak condition.

"Over there," Rhubat suddenly said as they pointed toward the forest. "An odd corruption suddenly appeared in that direction. It might be worth investigating."

Zac nodded and changed course, knowing already that the Zhix were able to sense Cosmic Energy to a far greater degree than humans. A few seconds later, he understood what the Anointed was talking about, as his [Cosmic Gaze] picked up something odd as well. A small spatial disturbance had appeared in the middle of a secluded glade, and it was steadily growing.

Zac landed right in front of it, and he quickly summoned Triv from his pagoda.

"Hide some distance away from here," Zac said as he took out the jammer. "Activate it the moment someone appears."

The ghost nodded and stowed away the jammer, immediately flying into the dense bushes and disappearing from sight.

The Anointed murmured in a mix of shock and disgust when they saw Triv, but they didn't comment on it, as their focus was all on the anomaly. They only needed to wait for ten more seconds before the gate rapidly changed, forming a proper portal, and Zac couldn't help his heartbeat speeding up when he saw a familiar figure emerging the next second.

"It's you after all," Zac said with a frown as he mentally prepared for one of the toughest battles of his life.

Shocking energies started to radiate from the bodies of the Anointed as well, and they glared at the much smaller Zhix that had appeared with seething hatred in their eyes.

"Betrayer, it turns out the deeds of your kin weren't even for yourselves in the end? We hear your kin betrayed the Zhix for an outsider? Why? Power? Power is available for everyone. There is no need to go so far," Rhubat rumbled as a dense killing intent blanketed the field.

"You were the Great Sage. You were supposed to help the Zhix move forward, not destroy us."

"And perhaps I would have if the integration waited for a few generations," Void's Disciple said with a hollow smile before he shot a dark look at Zac. "You killed my son."

"Death is unavoidable in war. Is that why you attacked some random settlements?" Zac retorted.

"Just releasing some tension before the real battle," Void's Disciple said as a savage grin spread across his face.

Zac had seen a glimpse of that madness once before, and he quickly activated [Hatchetman's Spirit] and [Nature's Barrier].

"Don't worry. There will be a reckoning, but not today." Void's Disciple laughed as his face returned to its original form. "You know where our fates will clash. Only one faction will gain the Dimensional Seed."

Dimensional Seed? That's the name of the treasure? Zac thought, but he still kept his face neutral.

"That is not up to you, betrayer," Rhubat rumbled, and the auras of the seven Anointed exploded out with enough power to even make the nearby trees sway.

Their life force shone like radiant beacons as crude patterns lit up across their bodies. Zac's eyes widened at the sight, guessing that this was the true form of the crusade. But if they would die in a year just from being in their normal state, how long would they be able to fight like this? And would they even be able to return?

"You lunatics have really entered the crusade, and you have even learned some new tricks since you embraced the truth of Cosmic Energy. However, it is still just a lamentable corruption of a true path," Void's Disciple said with a shake of his head, and Zac was almost certain he could see some pity in his eyes. "No matter."

"It's active," Triv whispered in his mind, meaning that the jammer was activated.

Zac inwardly nodded. This was an opportunity of sorts. An opportunity to see how Void's Disciple's mysterious skills worked, and what they could do to restrain them. He had personally seen Void's Disciple open tears in space twice now, simply disappearing or appearing where he wanted. Such a skill was even more annoying to deal with than his own **[Spatial Convergence Array]**. A lot of people had thought long and hard about how to combat such a skill, and the first idea that was brought forward was the jammer.

It worked on teleportation arrays, so why not on normal teleportation?

Four balls actually flew out of Void's Disciple's own shadow the next moment, and each of them exploded and caused intense spatial distortions. Zac recognized the items at a glance, as he had used that kind of offensive treasure before. They were not **[Void Balls]**, but rather the same sort of spatial disruption balls he'd used to block arrays in the Underworld.

Ogras had launched the first blow against the Dominator, and the rest were quick on the uptake. Zac's aura exploded outward as well, and determination shone in his eyes. **[Verun's Bite]** was already in his hand, and the Spirit Tool keened with bloodlust.

It was time to see whether he or Void's Disciple was the strongest warrior of Earth.

51
VOID

Hiring, or perhaps it was more accurate to say capturing, Smaug had proven extremely beneficial since Calrin was still unable to procure these types of offensive treasures, let alone more powerful ones like [**Void Balls**]. Void's Disciple frowned and seemed to prepare something to deal with the twisting air around him, but he suddenly got a blank look on his face as Janos fell down on his knees.

The illusionist had actually managed to trap the Dominator in an illusion or something similar, but the power gap between the two was just too great. The effect broke in less than a breath's time, and blood flowed out of Janos' ears and nose from the backlash. Zac frowned when he saw it, as he could quickly make some guesses from the way things had played out.

Void's Disciple didn't completely block the strike, which meant that he didn't have a top-tier mental protection treasure or skill. For example, Janos was able to break through [**Mental Fortress**] on his human side, but not [**Indomitable**] when Zac was a Draugr. But the fact that the Dominator was able to almost instantly break out of the mental trap meant that he likely had both a lot of Wisdom and an extremely strong mentality.

Then again, the latter was expected, considering his identity. Void's Disciple's very existence had been taboo most of his life, yet he had not only taken two disciples, but he had even made a name for himself in Zhix society. He had walked among his enemies for decades, not rousing any suspicion even though everyone was on the lookout for the slightest hint of corruption.

Such a feat shouldn't be possible without an extremely sturdy psyche.

However, Janos' attempt did slow Void's Disciple down long enough for the spatial chaos to envelop him completely before blending into the air and disappearing, which hopefully meant that the Dominator had been a bit restricted. But Zac also didn't dare to put all his hopes on these offensive treasures. They were essentially Array Breakers that targeted teleportation arrays, and there was no telling just how effective they were against a spatial warrior.

Of course, Zac and the Anointed weren't just sitting around either, and a probing fractal blade was already flying toward the Dominator, and **[Love's Bond]** had moved to his back. Two chains soundlessly slithered down his back and into the underbrush as they stealthily made their way toward the Zhix as well, while the seven Anointed were directly rushing toward Void's Disciple without any regard for their safety.

The Dominator didn't seem fazed by the situation at all. Their assault mostly seemed to infuriate Void's Disciple, and his visage once more turned into that of a frenzied murderer before it smoothed out again. However, Zac could still see the murder in his eyes as the Dominator stared back at him. A terrifying aura spread out, but he didn't lash out like some sort of berserker. He instead blocked Zac's Axe-infused fractal blade with just the palm of his left hand, and the edge actually shattered without even managing to draw blood.

Zac's eyes widened at the sight, unable to comprehend how he could avoid getting injured at all. The basic skill **[Chop]** couldn't really keep up with the latest improvements of **[Verun's Bite]**, but it still had a terrifying cutting power between the Fragment of the Axe and the skill itself. Even Zac would receive a deep cut if he hit himself with such a swing.

Just how sturdy was this guy?

The movements of Void's Disciple were short and concise, and he gave Zac the impression of a martial arts master who wasted no movement when delivering his strikes. Almost at the same time as he blocked Zac's attack, a parchment scroll appeared in his other hand,

and he unfurled it toward the two closest Anointed. Zac first thought it was a huge talisman, but it was oddly enough just painted black from top to bottom without any inscriptions or fractals at all.

However, a mysterious energy radiated from within the darkness. It was completely different from the darkness Zac conjured with **[Rapturous Divide]**, and Zac felt he was looking up at the night sky for some reason. His danger sense woke up by the scene even if he wasn't the target, which gave Zac an extremely bad feeling.

"Watch out!" Zac shouted, but it was too late.

The two Anointed seemed to sense the threat as well, but they showed no indication of backing down as the darkness of the scroll rippled forward until a star-studded barrier appeared right in front of them. It was like Void's Disciple had summoned a piece of the cosmos itself, and Zac could see both stars and nebulae in the depths of that wall.

A shockingly explosive power streamed into the ceremonial knives they each held, and they actually exploded into metallic shards that shot everywhere. However, a set of new golden energy blades had taken their place, and Zac shuddered when he felt the extremely condensed belief gathered within. It was just like the rune that the cultists had nurtured, only with a different flavor.

Each of them struck at the wall as the runes of their arms lit up, meaning the two were holding nothing back in their desire to break the first line of defenses and open a path for their allies. But Zac still hadn't expected what happened next as the two actually fell into darkness and disappeared. The night-sky receded back into the scroll in an instant, and the next moment, both the two Anointed and the darkness was gone.

Zac's eyes were wide in shock. He had seen over a hundred types of defensive barriers during his battles, everything from his emerald leaves to celestial deities appearing to block his strikes. They all worked essentially the same way, but this was something else entirely. Had Void's Disciple actually created a portal to space? However, that should be impossible, at least from what they had gathered.

Information on the Dao of Space was limited in the Zecia Sector, but they had managed to make some deductions from what they managed to find out. First of all, there was no Fragment of Space, meaning that Void's Disciple should be controlling some related subordinate fragment rather than the real thing. Just like Zac was currently in control of the Fragment of the Coffin rather than the Fragment of Death.

Secondly, there should be limits on distance. Zac could only move one hundred meters with **[Loamwalker]**, and Ogras a few times that distance if he pushed himself with his shadow warp skill. Void's Disciple was able to move a lot further through his portal skill, but it shouldn't be strong to the point that he could open a gate to outer space. An E-grade warrior simply didn't have the Cosmic Energy needed to create such a long-distance portal.

You would need at least a D-grade Hegemon's Cultivator Core to sustain that kind of massive drain.

"It's not teleportation. That scroll is some sort of trapping treasure," Ogras muttered with a frown from the side. "We might be able to get them back out again if we snatch it."

Zac's eyes turned to the scroll in the man's hand, also feeling that it was the most logical conclusion. The Dominator thankfully didn't activate the scroll again, but just punched out toward his next target. It was another one of the Anointed, and they roared in defiance as their whole body lit up, conjuring an enormous lance of fire that shot straight toward the much smaller Zhix.

The first looked like a simple training punch, but the air twisted and contracted as some invisible force pushed outward, shattering the beam of flames in instant before slamming into the gargantuan Zhix. Crushing sounds echoed out as the Anointed was shot backward, and Zac didn't know whether the warrior was alive or dead as they flew into the distance.

Rhubat roared in anger when they saw the exchange, and Zac almost fell off his feet when the giant stomped down on the ground with terrifying force. Trees were uprooted and thrown aside for over a hundred meters in each direction as the ground heaved. But Zac quickly realized that the stomp wasn't just an outburst of fury, as he saw dense brownish energies appear in the oddly symmetrical cracks around Rhubat's foot.

It was clearly some sort of earth-attuned Dao, and a Fragment at that. It looked like height wasn't the only way that Rhubat excelled if they had managed to reach such an accomplishment without either visiting the Tower of Eternity or partaking in opening the Dao Funnel.

Something shot out of the ground where the attuned energies were the densest the next moment, and it had such speed that even Zac could only see a blur as it hurtled toward the Dominator. Void's Disciple seemed ready, though, and what looked like a fisherman's net made from black silk appeared in his hands as he stretched it in front of him. A multicolored shimmer enveloped him, making Zac realize it was some sort of defensive treasure.

The projectile hit the net, and Zac subconsciously held his breath in anticipation to see if the greatest Anointed was enough to harm the most powerful Dominator. Zac could sense that Rhubat's attack held a force many times greater than what Ilvere could produce with his Dao of Momentum, even when using **[Cyclic Strike]** to push his force even further. Not only that, but Zac could also sense that the attack contained a terrifying amount of belief, far greater than what the two energy knives earlier contained.

The air itself seemed to cry before it exploded the instant the net and the projectile collided, but the black threads of the net actually held against the attack. The force in Rhubat's attack had been strong enough to rip apart the air as it shot out of the ground, but it looked like Void's Disciple managed to trap the projectile in one go, forcing it to a stop just a few centimeters away from his chest.

Only then did Zac see what the projectile actually was. It was a perfectly spherical stone that was absolutely covered in extremely dense fractals. It actually reminded Zac of his own Duplicity Core, though this stone was brownish gray. It had a diameter of around thirty centimeters, but the impression Zac got from it was that it was as heavy as a mountain. As for whether it was a skill or some sort of treasure, Zac actually had no idea.

It was instilled with a terrifying amount of energy, yet Void's Disciple had somehow managed to block it with the net. But it was not without effort, as he had been forced to take two steps back. Zac also noticed a minute tremor in his left hand, proving that he wasn't some invincible monster. The strike might not have been enough to harm him, but it had given a hint to the limits of his strength.

However, Rhubat was actually not done, as the energies inside the ball increased exponentially for an instant before it exploded in a terrifying eruption of stone splinters. Almost all of them shot toward Void's Disciple as though they were guided by the huge amount of faith within, but a few flew in Zac's direction as well. His arm turned to a blur as he blocked the three incoming shards with his axe, each of them looking like a ten-centimeter stone nail, and he was shocked at how much force they contained.

Even Zac felt some pain in his wrist after forcibly blocking the three strikes, which was all he needed to know about the power of the seemingly unassuming needles. Massive craters exploded all over the area, and a few sturdy tree trunks were turned to dust in an instant as the nails shot straight through them with the force of a rocket before continuing to wreak even more havoc upon the forest.

Zac was finally hopeful that something had worked against the immensely powerful Dominator. Even he had felt some pressure from three needles, but Void's Disciple had been drowned in over fifty of them at point-blank range while he was clearly the target of the zealous faith-based energy within. The situation was completely obfuscated by the chaotic energies in the air and the churning dust clouds, but Zac's brows furrowed when a wave of danger once more perked up in his mind.

A storm of emerald leaves infused with the Fragment of the Bodhi covered their whole side as Zac also activated [**Hatchetman's Spirit**]. Rhubat reacted almost as quickly as it knelt down and pushed both its hands against the ground, erecting ten sturdy walls that were covered in motifs of warriors holding different types of shields.

Zac only felt a shudder in the air as his mind screamed, and space split apart the next second. The consecutive walls fell apart like butter, and a terrifying slash almost bisected Rhubat while another councilor lost its legs. The dust and chaotic energies that had blocked Zac's sight was blown away as well, exposing a still-standing Void's Disciple within.

Over a dozen spikes were embedded in his small frame, and his face was covered in blood as he stood panting over twenty meters from his original position. Judging by the deep gouges in the ground, he had been unable to contain the strike and had been pushed backward. However, Zac frowned when he sensed that his aura was just as strong and stable as before. As for that invisible cut, it seemed to have been launched by a small, unassuming dagger in his hand. The attack had contained shocking power, but Zac knew it wouldn't impact the Dominator much.

Only a few seconds had passed since Ogras had thrown the spatial disruption spheres, but over half of the Anointed were already taken out of commission. They had already agreed that the group of Anointed launch the first strike if it really was the Dominators they were up against, but it didn't have the desired effect. They had hoped to at least wound him and make him expose some of his hidden cards.

Or at least anger him to the point that he was less likely to escape in case things turned dire.

It didn't really feel like Void's Disciple was going all out at all, but rather toying with the far larger targets. The chaos in space seemed to have barely affected him either, as both his offensive and defensive means seemed to carry a hint of space inside. He needed to do something before the Anointed were all killed, but he was still waiting for the right opportunity to burst out one final strike aimed to kill.

And that opportunity presented itself the next moment, as the two chains had finally made their way to their target.

52
PRESSURE

The two chains of **[Love's Bond]** had finally reached their target. However, Void's Disciple, or rather Adcarkas, only snorted as he swung his dagger at the two metallic snakes approaching him. Another invisible attack shot out, and an extremely deep scar appeared in the ground. The cut was laser sharp, but it exploded, and it created some sort of vacuum, causing dust and stones to shoot in all directions.

The power in the strike was shocking even when the Zhix clearly wasn't going all out, and Zac knew that most weapons would be ruined by such an attack. Then again, **[Love's Bond]** was no normal weapon. Not even Void's Disciple should be able to comprehend the value of the coffin on Zac's back, what kind of unique treasures and materials went into its creation.

White scars appeared on the two chains where Adcarkas struck, but they didn't even crack from the swing. Void's Disciple's eyes widened in surprise, as this was the first time in the battle things didn't go exactly his way. The Zhix reacted instantaneously though as he tried to move away, but the two chains gained a burst of speed, allowing one to catch his ankle before he got away.

This was exactly what Zac had been waiting for, and huge amounts of his corrosive Dao flooded the two chains as he stomped down onto the ground, flashing forward with **[Loamwalker]**.

He didn't actually think that the Dao Fragment would be able to harm the Dominator, but Zac hoped that it would restrict him like it did with Ogras when he tried to meld with the shadows. Even if that didn't work, they were still physically bound to each other. He didn't have access to **[Profane Seal]** in his current form, but this wasn't a bad substitute. There would be no escape, only a brutal melee, just what Zac excelled at.

But Zac had also seen just how powerful Void was and, more surprisingly, just how many treasures he possessed. Something unexpected could happen in a drawn-out fight, so he needed to go hard from the start. Exposing all his ultimate cards this early would spell disaster if he failed, but he knew that he needed to use some of his aces in this fight.

A storm was kicked up as Zac appeared right in front of Void's Disciple, and both he and his Tool Spirit were radiating a mesmerizing glow. He had activated not only the second rune on his axe, but also **[Hatchetman's Rage]** to push his power to the next level. Doing so essentially put a timer on the fight, but he didn't expect the battle to last very long with the intensity it had until now.

"So you found your courage after all. I might not be allowed to kill you, but I can make you suffer," the Dominator said as fury burned in his eyes, and he turned into a blur the next moment as his dagger shot straight toward Zac's kidneys.

Zac quickly pivoted while simultaneously swinging down his axe, and **[Verun's Bite]** fell in a vertical swoop toward Adcarkas. Zac also activated **[True Strike]**, trying to split the Dominator's attention by making him think someone was attacking him from behind, but the Dominator just snorted in derision at the ploy as he continued his stab. The chains of **[Love's Bond]** also made Void's Disciple lose his balance, but it was as though Zac were trying to move a mountain with the chain while Void's Disciple stood unmoving like a towering tree.

The dagger barely missed Zac's body, but he still felt a searing pain as a deep wound still opened up somehow, and blood streamed down his left leg. Just dodging that dagger wasn't enough; it had to be covered in some invisible energy. Zac was unfortunately completely incapable of spotting it. Was it because **[Cosmic Gaze]** was still stuck at Early proficiency? No matter how much he strained his eyes, he hadn't been able to see the attunement of any of the skills Void's Disciple used, only the destruction they caused.

Zac suddenly felt a pop as the strain on his eyes lessened, and hazy energies appeared around Void's Disciple the next moment. Zac felt a surge of confidence as he realized that his ocular skill had actually evolved mid-battle. Had he finally found the key to upgrading this skill: spotting invisible energies?

Improving his sight against someone who relied on invisible skills was huge, and it would hopefully allow Zac to gain an advantage. For example, just a first look at his enemy had exposed that the small dagger the Dominator held in his hand was just a decoy. There was also an invisible weapon that was attached to his fist, and Zac suspected that this was the real weapon Void's Disciple relied on.

Zac could only see a translucent outline, but it would appear that the weapon was some sort of bladed glove or a claw, something that a pugilist would use. Two edges stretched out on both sides of his arm, starting halfway down his forearm and ending fifteen centimeters in front of his fist, where they joined together into a rounded edge.

It was no wonder he had been cut even if he dodged the knife, as he had been well within reach of the much larger hidden blade. Zac couldn't see how the edge was attached to Void's Disciple's arm at all, making him believe that it might be an energy weapon like the fractal edges of his [Chop].

The wound in Zac's gut was deep, but with his berserking skill active, he barely registered it. The pain rather fueled his killing intent, and he growled in fury as he continued his own swing, trying to cut Void's Disciple in two. The Dominator's free hand rose to meet the blade, and Zac finally noticed that something was up with it.

There was a thin film covering the palm, and Zac barely could discern some sort of runes covering it. It turned out that it wasn't just his palm that had been able to block his [Chop], but there was some sort of defensive layer that Zac had been unable to spot until now. Adcarkas was trying to block Zac's attack the same way as before, probably thinking it would damage Zac's morale if his attacks were diverted by a simple palm.

However, a physical swing by a boosted Zac and a fractal edge were two completely different concepts.

A terrifying force slammed into the barely discernible barrier, and any remaining complacency in Void's Disciple's face was gone as cracks echoed out from his arm as bones broke. Zac's eyes lit up when he saw the scene, as this had been his goal all along. If he activated something like **[Deforestation]** or **[Rapturous Divide]**, then the Dominator would respond in kind. But Void's Disciple was clearly arrogant, using the bare minimum to fend off the assaults thus far, like it was an indignity for him to use proper skills against weaklings.

Zac was hoping to bank on this haughtiness to deliver a devastating blow with the help of the three superimposed boosts of his Dao and two berserking skills. But the Zhix reacted instantaneously and moved his body in a mysterious fashion, and Zac felt the force in his strike being slowly exhausted as the Dominator pushed his hands in a spiral while slowly bending further and further down toward the ground.

"Stellar Convergence," Adcarkas growled as his purple eyes stared into Zac's, and a miniature spiral galaxy sprang up around them the next moment.

It spread over a hundred meters around the two, and Zac could sense a shocking amount of destructive power in every single one of the stars. The others hurriedly scrambled out of the way, but Zac was caught in the heart of the galaxy, with Void's Disciple being the black hole. Zac frowned at the situation and thought to take a step back to regroup, but his mind screamed of danger.

Zac quickly understood that he would have to withstand the power inside the stars if he wanted to back away, and even he would be bloodied and battered if the hundreds of lights went off simultaneously. He could only push forward, but that was his desire anyway. It seemed as though Void was trying to steal or somehow convert the force in Zac's swing, but he would still be grievously wounded if Zac managed to cut through the defenses before he was done.

It was essentially a race, so he gritted his teeth as he tried to break the odd defense that Adcarkas' spinning hands continuously conjured. He could already see that the initial collision had caused fault lines to appear all over the Dominator's hand on top of the broken bones, and Zac felt that just a little more would be needed to break through. Besides, the stalemate also gave him a chance to maneuver **[Love's Bond]**, and the Dominator now had a fetter binding each of his limbs.

A pitch-black beam suddenly shot straight past next to Zac's leg, expertly avoiding the rotating stars all around him. It unerringly flew toward the Dominator's throat as he dealt with Zac's strike. It was Ogras, who had already turned into his ultimate form, but he actually had a second set of wings this time. As he pointed his newly acquired spear at the Zhix, he looked like a god of darkness, and multiple beams shot at weak spots of the Zhix in short order.

A bloody gash appeared on the Zhix's throat, but it was unfortunately not enough. Ogras' shadowlance simply wasn't strong enough to fatally wound someone like Void's Disciple in one go. However, Ogras was like a mobile turret, continuously shooting out more and more lances as Zac and Void's Disciple were locked in a stalemate where Zac couldn't retreat nor manage to push forward.

His arms were already shaking with strain, but the odd technique that the Zhix was using kept dissipating the impact, forcing Zac to instill more and more energy into the strike to keep going. Of course, it was just a swing that utilized his physical power and Dao rather than any skills, so Zac could keep going for a good while longer.

Ten shallow gashes appeared in an instant all across the Dominator's body thanks to the demon's efforts, most of them centered on weak spots. The other Anointed seemed to be preparing something similar, but it finally looked like Adcarkas had had enough, as a necklace cracked. A dome that locked everyone except Zac outside appeared in an instant, locking him, Adcarkas, and his swirling galaxy inside.

"Break it!" Zac heard Ogras roar from outside, but the voice was muted like he was extremely far away.

The Anointed had backed off when Rhubat was wounded, but their hulking bodies moved toward the glimmering barrier without hesitation. The runes on their body lit up as they punched the barrier, seemingly delighted that there was finally something they could do to assist Zac.

Unfortunately, Zac's brief break in his attention to see what was going on proved to be a fatal mistake, as a tremendous force surged within the Dominator's body. The palm blocking Zac's swing suddenly disappeared, and Zac lost his balance as he had been pushing with everything he had.

The Dominator had managed to slightly twist himself while

diffusing Zac's swing, and with Zac's lapse of concentration, he had swiveled to the point that his body wasn't even in the trajectory of the swing any longer. The blade of **[Verun's Bite]** harmlessly ripped apart the air right next to him, only cutting off a small piece of Void's Disciple's robes.

Zac knew he was in trouble, and the shield of **[Hatchetman's Spirit]** covered him as the emerald leaves completely ensconced him. He was even considering activating the first skill of **[Love's Bond]** to survive, but doing so would force him to transform the Spirit Tool to its shield form, which would free Void's Disciple of his four fetters.

He eventually decided to bet the house on him being able to withstand Void's Disciple's attack, at which point he would counter.

Void's Disciple was shockingly fast, and he had somehow transferred the force of Zac's downward swing into a rotating momentum that turned into a mighty roundhouse kick aimed at Zac's side. The kick broke the shield almost instantly, and Zac was thrown away, the pain even cutting through the haze of **[Hatchetman's Rage]**.

However, while the kick was mighty, it wasn't the real problem.

A series of explosions rocked Zac the next moment as one star after another in the galaxy exploded, each one of them containing the force of an Early E-grade warrior's full-powered attack. Zac desperately conjured more and more emerald leaves as they were disintegrated, and the spectral forest of **[Hatchetman's Spirit]** disintegrated before he even landed, as all the defensive charges were used up.

But he survived. A few of his ribs were definitely broken, and Zac looked like a bloodied corpse, but he was still alive and in fighting condition. The kick had thrown him straight through the galaxy until he hit the barrier from inside, and a coruscating series of explosions had detonated all the stars on this side of the galaxy.

The skill dissipated the next moment, leaving just Zac, Void's Disciple, and the four chains that connected them inside the dome.

Zac spat a mouthful of blood onto the ground, and he shot the Zhix a murderous look as the Cosmic Energy in his body surged. Space split apart the next moment as the massive wooden hand appeared above the dome, but that wasn't it. Zac himself was already rushing back toward Void's Disciple as a fractal blade grew out from his axe, its gleaming edge quickly turning golden.

Void's Disciple laughed as his body transformed. He only grew a head taller, but his body turned pitch black while his eyes became burning suns. His muscles grew in size as well, and he radiated a shocking pressure that made Zac think of the Cyborg. Void's Disciple seemed to have a class that mixed the concepts of space and pugilism, and this ought to be his true fighting form.

It looked like the Dominator was finally ready to show his real cards, but it remained to be seen whether they were greater than the combined force of both **[Nature's Punishment]** and **[Rapturous Divide]**.

53
LIAR

Void's Disciple emitted a terrifying aura in his changed form, and Zac briefly considered taking one of his newly acquired [**Rageroot Oak Seeds**] to push his power even further. However, he quickly decided against it and refocused on his two attacks.

The seeds belonged to the same category as [**Hatchetman's Rage**], both being berserking methods. Using multiple such means at the same was the height of foolhardiness, as the gain was far from multiplicative, while the dangers were exponential. He was somewhat confident that his uniquely sturdy body would allow him to survive using both at the same time, but that wasn't the only issue. He might even become weaker than his normal strength if the two rampant powers clashed. This was not the time to experiment.

That would put the whole group at risk, and the backlash might be so terrifying that he wouldn't be able to use his full power for months. After all, it was important to remember that while his longevity increased as he cultivated, so did the time required for recuperation. It wasn't unheard of for cultivators to enter seclusion for millennia in order to slowly deal with particularly nasty afflictions.

As he saw it, the item was better left for his Draugr side, which lacked such abilities on its own. Of course, there was also the issue of secrecy to consider. He didn't want to reveal cards like the seed or his second class unless he felt confident in taking out Adcarkas, and it still felt like he was peeling away one layer of another of his enemy.

His current combo wasn't far from his peak strength, and he was ready to make this one count. The enormous fractal appeared in the sky as the wooden hand was placed right above Void's Disciple; the pressure caused the Dominator to sink a few centimeters into the ground. However, his back was still ramrod straight, and he didn't try to extricate himself from either the chains or the pressure of [**Nature's Punishment**].

He seemed perfectly confident in being able to rebuff whatever Zac could bring forth.

A small branch started to descend from the fractal, as Zac didn't feel that any of the other punishments would have a particular advantage against the Zhix. The mountain would have a similar crushing effect, but it didn't benefit from his Fragment of the Bodhi nearly as much as the tree did.

However, the whole area was covered in darkness before the sapling had time to grow into a towering tree. It wasn't Void's Disciple who was conjuring a counter, but rather Ogras, who had drenched the whole area in shadows. A storm of attacks slammed into the Dominator's barrier the next moment as thousands of shadow spears rose out of the shade. The spears didn't contain a large amount of power on their own, but they were innumerable.

Ogras himself was enshrouded in extremely dense power, and he dove from the sky with shocking speed, his spear stabbing straight into the shield with enough force to cause the whole thing to wobble. It wasn't enough to completely break it, but his efforts should no doubt have pushed the barrier a lot closer to running out of steam, as it didn't have a source of energy.

Rhubat and his brethren had summoned their enormous sigils as well, and they slammed into the shield from different directions to overtax the defensive shield. The sigils were a lot smaller now that they weren't powered by the combined energy of the Zhix armies, but they were still nothing to scoff at, as they were powered by life force instead.

The shield shook and heaved, but Zac was shocked to see that it somehow managed to stay intact. Adcarkas' amulet must have been a real Peak defensive treasure to withstand such punishment, almost rivaling the ones Zac had lifted from the mentalist's pouch.

Zac still believed it should be a Peak E-grade talisman at best, even if Void's Disciple wasn't restricted like people were in the Tower of Eternity. The reason was simple; activating even a Low-quality D-grade talisman was as taxing as throwing out over a hundred E-grade talismans. Even Zac would be completely drained of Cosmic Energy before it was half-activated.

So it was with some confidence he instructed the branch to stab straight into the ceiling of the dome, and the barrier actually popped like a soap bubble. The desperate attacks of the others had exhausted the barrier enough to pave the way for Zac, and he intended to make the most of it.

The four chains grew taut as Zac tried to restrict the Zhix as much as possible, but the Dominator still managed to point his left hand toward the sky with a savage grin. Three small vortices appeared behind him the next moment, all of them hovering behind his head like a halo. They didn't look like galaxies though, but whirlpools with the core being a bottomless darkness like a black hole.

One of them flew up to Adcarkas' fist, and the vortex grew to over fifty meters in diameter in an instant. Zac frowned when a black pillar rose out of it, rising toward the rapidly growing branch that kept gaining momentum as it pushed downward.

What were the odds that his nemesis had such a similar skill to his own?

The massive pillar collided with the tip of the blooming tree branch, and the clouds in the sky were pushed away from the tremendous shockwave. It was like space itself cried as the two strikes tried to destroy the other, but it looked like neither Void's Disciple nor Zac could claim an advantage. Zac didn't bother about that as he rushed forward, and he was in front of the Dominator the next moment, both of them shrouded from the sun by the pillar above.

This close, Zac actually made a new discovery. It wasn't a black pillar that Void's Disciple had summoned, but it was actually a gargantuan finger over a hundred meters long. Even more shocking, not even the whole thing had emerged, making Zac wonder just how huge the being to whom the finger belonged was. But the good news was that it seemed as though Void's Disciple needed to match his finger with the skill, forcing him to keep pointing toward the sky.

The enormous branch was infused with the wrath of nature and his own Dao, so even this massive poke wasn't able to eradicate it. Cracks and explosions kept appearing across the trunk as the finger was infused with whatever Dao the Dominator utilized, but the branch quickly regrew and shot more and more branches into the finger to whittle it down. If **[Nature's Punishment]** actually broke through right now, Zac would harm himself as well, but he had a plan for that.

The radiant luster on both the wooden hand and the branch suddenly dimmed as Zac retracted the Fragment of the Bodhi, but his fractal edge lit up like a beacon instead. He had transferred his Dao infusion to his second strike, and the branch was quickly being dismantled as the finger pushed upward. That was fine by Zac, as **[Nature's Punishment]** was meant to create an opening and restrain the Zhix even further.

A puff of golden clouds swallowed them both as Zac slammed his axe in a downward motion aimed to cut the Zhix from shoulder to hip, but another of the vortices had appeared in front of Void's Disciple's free palm. It actually swallowed a good deal of the golden clouds, but Zac still knew he had succeeded, as his target was illuminated in a golden sheen. **[Rapturous Divide]** was his only E-grade skill in this class, and it wasn't as easy to counter.

However, Zac needed to get the second strike in as well, and fast. His skill in the sky was on the verge of falling apart, and Void's Disciple's other hand would be freed in a second. He activated **[True Strike]** a second time, pushing all of his killing intent into creating a believable illusion of a fatal attack. The Zhix had impeccable instincts and ignored the feeling, but both Zac and he were surprised to see a familiar spear stabbing the Dominator from behind.

It was obviously Ogras, who had taken the opportunity to launch a hidden strike from the large swathes of shadows that Void's Disciple had created with his finger.

The wound barely drew blood, but Adcarkas briefly lost his concentration from the surprise and pain, and Zac reacted by instinct. His fractal edge bloomed with the sinister power of both the second half of **[Rapturous Divide]** and the Fragment of the Coffin as Zac swung **[Verun's Bite]** with both urgency and force. Void's Disciple's eyes widened in alarm, and the last vortex started to expand with an explosive speed.

However, it was too late.

The two shrouds had come in contact, and the divide between Heaven and Hell was drawn. A smooth line appeared across Void's Disciple's torso before his body fell apart. The spatial divide had completely bisected the Dominator, and the angle should have destroyed lungs, heart, and most of his innards in one go.

Jubilation filled Zac's heart, but his mind suddenly screamed of mortal danger. There was no hesitation as he flashed away with [Loamwalker]. Ogras, true to form, had already receded into the shadows once more, which was lucky, as the three vortices simultaneously imploded. The eruption was similar to when he'd used his bronze flash on Harbinger, but not quite as final.

A huge crack in space appeared where they had fought, swallowing everything from Zac's branch to tons and tons of soil before the scar closed. Zac had no idea where that scar led, but his instincts told him that his odds of survival would have been zero if he had been caught up in that blast.

"Good attempt," a snort echoed out from every direction, and Zac's elation was quenched in an instant.

There had been no surge of Cosmic Energy when Zac killed the Dominator!

Void's Disciple had appeared once more, standing exactly where he stood earlier, or rather in the bottom of the crater he had created. Unscathed. The fatal wound was gone, and even the fetters of [Love's Bond] lay down on the ground, covered in cracks. His face wasn't a mask of fury either, but one of ridicule as he stomped down on the ground with a force that matched Rhubat's earlier efforts.

A wail echoed out the next moment as Ogras was somehow forced out of the shadows. The demon desperately tried to escape, but he was punched in his chest with enough force to be thrown over a hundred meters away. A huge amount of blood splashed in every direction until Ogras haplessly fell on the ground. He rolled for over a dozen meters more before he finally lay there, unmoving.

Horror and confusion plagued Zac's mind, but there was no time to see if his companion was alive.

"I have to admit, I underestimated you. It is no disgrace that my son fell to your hands," Adcarkas said as he surveyed the battlefield. "I can't help but wonder what else you have in store. But no matter. My intuition tells me we will have a chance to find out in the future, if you can make it to the heart of the Mystic Realm, that is."

A token appeared in his hand the next moment, and he crushed it before Zac had a chance to respond. A bright flash obscured the crater for an instant, and when the light disappeared, the Dominator was gone, not leaving a single clue as to where he had disappeared to.

They had failed.

Shock filled Zac's heart, and he flashed over to Ogras' unmoving form instead of trying to find the fleeing Dominator. Not that Zac felt he had any chance of catching up in either case. He didn't have a clue where the Zhix had gone. Even his upgraded [Cosmic Gaze] could only see a yellow glow at the spot he'd crushed the talisman.

It was some sort of escape treasure, but not one dependent on the Dao of Space.

But Zac didn't care about that right now as the demon released a racking cough before he weakly looked around. Zac's eyes were trained on Ogras, or rather the enormous hole in his torso where his heart should have been.

"Did we get him?" the demon weakly asked, his voice barely a whisper.

"We got him," Zac said with red-rimmed eyes.

"What a shitty liar." Ogras smiled as he closed his eyes.

54
BACK AGAIN

A deluge of sorrow and self-blame had turned Zac's mind into mush as he stared down at the unmoving form of Ogras. Countless what-ifs swirled in his mind, ways that he could have prevented this from happening. But he still couldn't comprehend how these latest events had come to be. He had seen Void's Disciple die; he just knew it wasn't some sort of illusion that he cut the man apart.

However, things had gotten out of hand too fast, even if he discounted the Dominator's miraculous recovery by the end. They had scrambled to get back in control since the moment two of the Anointed had been swallowed by that scroll, but things had only gotten worse instead. It wasn't completely unexpected, though; they had only learned of the situation less than an hour ago, and there had been no time for proper preparation.

The turbulence in his mind finally gave way to a bleak desolation. He had worked so hard, pushed himself beyond what he thought possible in his efforts to become stronger. Yet the ones he fought for kept falling one after another. First Alea, then Ogras. Would even more of his companions join the two when they set out for the Mystic Realm? The situation was almost as bad with the Anointed. The fight had lasted less than a minute, but Zac didn't doubt that the group of seven had burned a significant portion of their already limited life span.

Even more frustratingly, there was nothing he could do to remedy the situation. He still needed to enter the abandoned research base, and he still needed to fight Void's Disciple again, along with Inevitability and whoever else proved to be a threat to Earth. They had paid such a huge price just now, but they got almost nothing in return.

However, a sudden change startled Zac out of his self-reproach as the previously unmoving body of Ogras started to shudder and spasm. His skin turned pitch-black the next moment, and he instantaneously turned into shadows, only to be re-formed once more. His limbs twitched and kicked as well, but it didn't look like natural movements at all. It was more like a powerful electric current made him twitch uncontrollably.

Zac was aghast as he witnessed the macabre spectacle, but there was also a tinge of hope in the back of his mind.

If there was one thing that the demon excelled at, then it was keeping himself alive by any means. Had he actually found a way to defy death itself and bring himself back, just like Void's Disciple himself? However, Zac's anticipation was soon poisoned with suspicion. A minute passed while the cycle between demon and shadow kept repeating, and Zac could see that something was off.

The energy signatures the demon was emitting were wrong. They felt alien, sinister. Like a devil had taken the opportunity to possess Ogras' body when his own soul left it. However, Zac couldn't bring himself to nip this potential threat in the bud. He could only shake his head in an effort to clear his muddled thoughts, preparing for the worst.

If something really had possessed the demon, then he could only pray it wasn't a strong one, as he had already entered a weakened state after using **[Hatchetman's Rage]**.

The odd fluctuations finally ended, but Zac's heart was still hammering as he stood vigil in front of the body. He had clearly seen what the transformations had done. Ogras had cycled between shadow and flesh over and over, but a small change had taken place between each revolution.

The gaping hole in his chest grew a little smaller from each cycle, but not through flesh regrowing like how the Shard of Creation had healed his own mortal wounds. Missing flesh had instead been replaced with congealed shadows, shadows that had regrown the demon's missing organs bit by bit. An indistinct heart had formed from darkness itself, and Zac had felt its beat when it was fully formed.

The only sign of Ogras even being wounded in the end was the copious amount of blood around him, and the fact that the recreated skin on his chest was dark gray. Zac wasn't sure what to do, but the demon made the decision for him as he suddenly coughed and woke up, his eyes blearily looking around. Zac was relieved to see that Ogras' gaze looked the same, but he still could feel that sinister aura emanating from his body.

"Urh? Ah? I'm alive?" Ogras wheezed with confusion, but Zac wasn't in any state to answer him.

"What's the first thing you ever said to me?" Zac asked as **[Verun's Bite]** materialized in his right hand.

"What?" Ogras sputtered, clearly having some trouble understanding what was going on.

"Answer me," Zac said, the grip on his axe tightening. "What was the first thing you ever said to me?"

"I said 'You natives are barbarians, so aggressive.' You were wearing a dress at the time. Now what the hell is going on?" The demon sighed.

"You're emitting some pretty sinister energies," Zac said as he relaxed slightly, though not completely.

"Well, I can't seem to move. I need some healing," Ogras eventually said after a brief pause.

Zac hesitated for a second, but he ultimately took out one of his best healing pills and shoved it into Ogras' mouth as he infused the demon's body with the Fragment of the Bodhi. Only then did he realize how bad a state the demon was in, even after having re-formed the hole in his torso. His spiritual sense couldn't see what was going on in the shadow part of Ogras' body at all, but countless small scars covered the rest of his insides.

Worse yet, healing them with his Dao Fragment seemed to barely have any effect. The demon wasn't really at any risk of dying as far as Zac could tell, but it would no doubt be a long road of recovery, even provided that the demon's new heart worked as intended.

"What the hell happened at the end?" Ogras asked. "I remember escaping into the shadows when those vortices destabilized, and then waking up with your ugly face scowling down on me."

Zac sighed before he sat down himself, and he retold the final events without missing anything while simultaneously trying to gauge the demon's thoughts. However, the demon didn't let on anything; he just silently listened to the series of events with a small frown on his face.

"Well, people often say that I am heartless; I guess they were right," Ogras eventually said with a weak smile, but Zac felt that he could hear some confusion and perhaps even fear in his voice.

"It wasn't you who did this?" Zac asked. "I thought it might be the skill you got at E-grade or something."

"A skill that could allow me to walk away after getting a netherblasted hole in my chest? I wish. This must have been Leech. Can you take off my cast?" the demon said.

Zac nodded, and he gingerly took off the metal arm that usually held the congealed shadows. He was ready to blast out with [Verun's Bite] in case of an ambush, but his brows rose when the cast opened and nothing was there apart from Ogras' stump. He turned to Ogras, but he saw that the demon wasn't all that surprised by the disappearance of his shadow tentacle.

"I guess that I can't call that bast– I mean, little buddy, Leech any longer. How about Spare? If he's going to turn into spare organs for me in the future." Ogras grinned, still lying sprawled on the ground.

Zac wryly smiled, but there was still worry in his heart. Ogras seemed to want to pretend it was all under his control, but he had definitely cut it close just now. His face was completely pallid, and his hand shook noticeably. And who knew what the future ramifications would be for something like this? Getting possessed and having your body turned into a vessel wasn't unheard of in the Multiverse.

"Well, I'm glad you can laugh about this," Zac snorted as he glanced at the destruction around them.

It looked like Ogras had cheated death this time once more, but the others weren't so lucky. The two unscathed Anointed had just returned with the body of the one who was flung away, and he really had perished from the Dominator's strike. With Void's Disciple having escaped, there was probably no chance of saving the ones trapped in the scroll either, if that was even possible in the first place.

It was a poignant reminder of how cheap life was in the Multiverse.

"This was such a shitshow," Zac muttered with a shake of his head.

It looked like the universe agreed, as a massive explosion erupted far in the distance, in the direction of Site 16.

The displacement had caused more damage to Void's Disciple's already harried constitution, and waves of all-consuming pain buffeted him until he finally couldn't take it any longer. The only way for him to withstand the chaotic storm in his mind had been to unleash his might once more, destroying parts of the town around him.

Sweat trailed down his face as he started running, unhesitantly abandoning his original goal. It was regrettable, but he had already found most of what he needed. The enormous surplus of foul Karma gathered from the Zhix Wars would hopefully be able to substitute for what was missing. The notion made him start, and he quickly shook his head to refocus his straying thoughts.

He wasn't in the Mystic Realm right now; he couldn't let his mind wander so freely out here.

Fragment of the Vacuum helped remove the space in front of him, and he pushed himself as quickly as possible to get out of the range of whatever was preventing his [Cosmic Gate] from activating.

Void's Disciple's mind was filled with reproach as the surroundings flashed past him. To think that a moment of anger could cause such devastating results. He knew that he should have just left; what could those people have done to prevent it? But seeing the face of his son's murderer had made him lose control. How could he face Harbinger in the afterlife if he didn't exact at least a punishment that was within the bounds of his master's acceptance?

But the newly integrated sapling had grown into a towering tree, and Void's Disciple knew that he had barely gotten out of the situation alive.

At least he had managed to get back at that wretched demon for using [Skybreaker] right in front of him. There had been no energy forthcoming from his strike, but he should at least be crippled from the punch full of spatial tears. Void's Disciple kept moving for another hour until he finally sensed that the hidden dimensions were tranquil once more, and he arduously opened a gate toward the nearest hive.

However, he barely had time to walk through the portal before the pain erupted once more, and Void's Disciple helplessly fell over as he desperately clutched his head. The cost of subverting fate wasn't an insignificant one, at least not with the treasure that his master had provided. The timeline struggled to repair itself, and the wound spreading from his shoulder all the way to the hipbone on the opposite side deepened once more.

Having insight into a corner of space had driven home just how terrifying that final strike of Zachary Atwood had been. It had combined two opposing Daos to create an endlessly deep rift in space, and not even he would have survived normally. But it was also a testament to the greatness of space, the great delimiter.

The soul-shaking pain continued for a few more minutes until the bleeding finally stopped. The wounds managed to close a bit thanks to him having over 2,000 Vitality running at a tremendous efficiency, but he knew that it would keep getting worse almost no matter how high the attribute was. The threads of Karma surrounding the human progenitor were too strong, and subverting his deeds was far more difficult than normal.

Transferring all of it to the **[Karmic Subversion Effigy]** was impossible, and the effect would slowly weaken over time, the damage seeping back to him.

He popped a pill into his mouth as he got back on his feet, arduously opening a portal again. He needed to get back into the Mystic Realm, to enter the healing vats they had commandeered. He had been loath to use unknown technology thus far, especially since it required the assistance of those scheming natives, but now he didn't have too much of a choice. He would really end up bisected if he didn't increase his rate of healing.

Of course, the physical wound was just the most immediate concern.

The **[Karmic Subversion Effigy]** was a taboo item, and using something like that would have consequences even when not used against someone so loved by Karma as Super Brother-Man. It was one of his master's more successful experiments into harvesting Karma on a large scale, but it was ultimately a flawed item.

His master hadn't mentioned anything of the sort in the scriptures he left behind, but Void's Disciple had managed to make a few discoveries over the past centuries. Using it would allow you to live when you should have died, but that life would eventually become a curse. He could already feel the darkness spread in the depths of his mind, and he still hadn't figured out a method to counteract it.

Not yet.

He couldn't stop now. He had a goal to accomplish, and his daughter needed him to be strong for a while longer. The loss of his necklace was a shame, but the **[Scroll of the Depths]** would be able to be activated again as soon as it had absorbed enough energy from the stars. It should be finished well before the doors of the Mystic Realms closed.

Void's Disciple finally reached the hive, and he wordlessly activated the teleportation array before disappearing, his brooding aura quenching any questions from his followers. He appeared in a snow-blasted valley a minute later, the spatial tunnel just a few kilometers away. He entered the Mystic Realm after handing over the scroll to his trusted attendant, and he felt the sense of freedom once more as the darkness transferred him to a shielded subspace. Not even a brush with death and getting cursed could dampen the spirit of liberty after centuries of bondage.

Here, he was Adcarkas once more.

55
RETURN

Zac looked in the direction of Site 16 with incredulity. Void's Disciple hadn't fled as expected, but he actually went out of his way to blow up the town even when it was uninhabited. Was there some deeper meaning to his actions, or did he feel that he hadn't caused enough damage to their group before?

Zac personally wasn't really feeling ready for another battle, as he had already entered his weakened state. Swapping over to his Draugr form wouldn't help against that, and he would have to use one of his very limited **[Rageroot Oak Seeds]** just to regain his combat strength temporarily. The others looked just as worn out too, with only two of the Anointed maintaining full combat strength.

But could they just sit still, doing nothing?

"We are willing to set out if you are, Warmaster," Rhubat rumbled as the group of Anointed walked over. "We will ignite our life force to explode ourselves if need be."

"I'm sorry. I can't. I'm in no state to fight him again, and neither are these two," Zac eventually said as he nodded at the two demons.

Janos was sitting still not far away, his eyes closed in a slight frown. He had been knocked unconscious by the backlash, but his breathing was steady, and his aura was slowly stabilizing after having meditated for a while. Zac was confident that the illusionist simply needed rest to recover. But he still couldn't assist in another fight in this short a window. His soul might be irrevocably hurt if he did.

"Do not apologize, Warmaster. Without your efforts, all seven of us would have fallen," Rhubat said, and the other Anointed nodded in agreement. "Sacrificing one's life without a chance of victory isn't noble; it's foolishness. Especially now that doing so will empower our enemy."

"The Sage has grown so powerful. I couldn't sense any corruption even at such a close distance," another of the Anointed said with a forlorn expression. "Three councilors lost for nothing."

"Not for nothing," Ogras grunted as he finally managed to get up to a sitting position, though he had to lean against a rock to stay upright. "That asshole was a mystery until now. No one knew anything about him apart from his affiliation and his connection to the Dao of Space. But now we know quite a lot. We can use that next time."

Zac nodded in agreement. The mission was a failure, but not an abject one. They had gathered a lot of intelligence, and they had exhausted some of Adcarkas' aces. The scroll seemed very dangerous, but he'd still only used it once, meaning it was either a onetime thing or had other restrictions. He also shouldn't have too many Peak-grade defensive talismans, as those things simply had no supply on Earth.

Furthermore, now that Zac had calmed down from the heat of the battle, he realized something. Void's Disciple was definitely strong even though he only went all out toward the end, but his power wasn't insurmountable. Their attributes shouldn't be too far from each other judging by the stalemate from their clash, and Zac was probably even ahead in Strength and Endurance.

The cracks of bones had been heard when Zac launched his attacks, and Adcarkas had been slowly pushed down in their deadlock. Part of the reason was that the Dominator was taking the momentum for himself, but part of it was definitely because Zac was simply overpowering him with the help of [Hatchetman's Rage].

If he could make some improvements and perhaps even awaken a bloodline inside the Mystic Realm, then he would feel confident in clashing once more.

There was, however, the issue of the Zhix magically surviving getting bisected. It would be extremely difficult to finish off a person who not only was extremely strong but also had such a cheat-like skill. However, something so heaven-defying shouldn't come without a price. Zac had lost decades of his life span because of the Shard of Creation, and who knew what complications Ogras would be stuck with from getting his body fused with the shadow creature.

"Do you understand how he survived?" Zac asked as he turned back to Ogras. "I'm confident that it wasn't an illusion. He was really split apart by my attack. How the hell did he survive that?"

"Not illusion," Janos added from the side without opening his eyes, and Zac felt that he would know if anyone.

"I agree." Ogras nodded. "There are all kinds of odd techniques and treasures in the world, but it shouldn't have been a mirage. I was in the shadows right behind him when it happened. I saw blood rain down toward me; I could see his body splitting. I felt him die. Pretty scary skill of yours, by the way. What's it called?"

"Never mind that. Do you think it was a skill or a treasure he used?"

"I'm guessing treasure. I haven't heard of E-grade skills that can subvert life and death like that. I'm guessing that whatever you pulled off in the Base Town should be the same?" the demon said, his eyes boring into Zac's.

Zac slightly nodded in acquiescence, knowing that the demon was referring to the time that his chest had been blown apart in front of everyone, only to have it instantly regrow with the help of the last remnants of Creation Energy in his body. Zac still hadn't explained how he'd done that to the demon, not that Ogras had asked until now. He still wouldn't tell Ogras about the Shard of Creation, for both their sakes.

He had been reminded the hard way of the dangers of dealing with those things earlier today, and he didn't want to bring another tribulation down on the demon's head as well.

"Is that even possible, though? Where did he get something like this? He should mostly have stayed in secluded cultivation since the integration, apart from when he set out to cause some destruction," Zac said skeptically and turned to the Anointed to see if they knew anything else.

"Don't look at me, Warmaster," Rhubat said with embarrassment. "This is beyond our knowledge. The Dominators of old always followed one of three means of battle. Some controlled chains of enslavement. Others caused thousands of casualties with their spears. A few walked the path of pugilism, as Adcarkas did, rampaging through our ranks with their fists alone. There are no records of surviving something like this, and neither of the mystical skills of space we witnessed."

Zac nodded in understanding. They had already gotten an information package about ancient battles against the Dominators back on the Zhix homeworld. It wasn't much to go on, especially as those wars took place around two thousand years ago. The Medhin Royals seemed to have followed the spear Heritage as well, but Zac's best guess was that thousands of years had caused the Heritages to diverge.

"You called him the Sage of the Basin earlier," Zac asked instead, changing the topic. "What did you mean by that? What was his earlier identity?"

Zac didn't know much about the civilian identity of Void's Disciple from before. Even the Zhix War Council had only managed to confirm the real identities of the Dominators after Harbinger appeared. Adcarkas and his children had passed completely under the radar until the integration, and pretty much everyone who encountered them after was killed.

But perhaps they could find out some useful information by digging through their past.

"Adcarkas was a great scholar and artisan, to the point that his name was known across the world. He was an expert on all kinds of topics, from painting masterworks to perfecting superior smelting techniques to create stronger metals. The Sage also invented marvelous machines that would have made the lives of our kin easier if there had been time for them to spread and become adapted," Rhubat explained.

A few of the other Anointed had moved over by this point and added to Rhubat's explanation. He had been a "wanderer," a traveling Zhix whose hive had fallen in a war. He had taken up residence in a hive placed in the middle of an enormous basin, where he had mostly stayed to work on his projects. According to general knowledge, he should be around fifty years old, but he could be much older since he appeared out of nowhere.

It sort of sounded like Void's Disciple had been someone like the

Zhix world's Leonardo da Vinci, a great mind that could change the course of history. Then again, Zac suspected that Void's Disciple was quite a bit older than what was believed, and a few centuries was enough time to master all kinds of things.

He didn't have any proof on the last guess, but he trusted his intuition. Void's Disciple emitted a similar aura as the demon master he had fought during the Tower of Eternity. The aura of an old expert who had perfected his skills and combat techniques to the peak.

"All those treasures, though; where did he get them?" Zac muttered.

"He might have made them," Ogras ventured. "At least the weaker ones. Just think about it; he spent decades, possibly centuries, on an unintegrated world with very sparse Cosmic Energy. Cultivation would have to have been extremely slow. He might have built all those things in his search of improving his power in other ways."

Ogras' guess was as good as any theory they could come up with now, and the conversation eventually died out as everyone focused on recuperation. Only when an hour had passed did they begin to stir again, and Adcarkas was probably long gone by now.

"The crusade will truly move into the hidden world you spoke of after all." Rhubat eventually sighed.

Zac understood the giant's despondency. The Anointed were almost out of time, and who knew how long the visit to the Mystic Realm would last. The Anointed would perhaps never be able to return to their hives even if they won, provided that the supposed lockdown that Julia mentioned lasted longer than expected. No one would cherish the thought of dying in a foreign world.

"I'll look for more ways to restrain him until we set out. What will you do next?" Zac asked.

"We need to finish the rites for the fallen," Rhubat slowly said. "We will return to the hives for now, but we will follow you into the hidden world."

"Will you be done with everything in one week?" Zac asked, and he received a nod of confirmation. "Good. We'll try opening the pathway at that time. I'll send someone to discuss the details, but I need to focus on getting stronger myself. I'm not sure he'll back off next time, going by how much importance he places on the Spatial Artifact."

The group set out a few minutes later, and Ogras was able to walk again by the time they reached Site 16, albeit with the assistance of Janos. However, Ogras' aura was even weaker than a mortal's, and Zac wondered just how long it would take before he completely recovered.

The destruction of the outpost wasn't as bad as Zac had feared, but everything within a hundred meters of the mine entrance had been reduced to rubble, including the teleportation array. That wasn't a problem for Zac, as he could simply buy a new one, which made him even more confused as to why Void's Disciple had done something so pointless.

"We can sense remnants of the corruption," Rhubat said with some surprise. "We still don't understand how they managed to hide it, but perhaps he was unable to in his current state. There's a trail leading east from the epicenter of the attack."

"Look," Ogras added as he pointed to the left, and Zac's eyes lit up when he saw that one of the security cameras was still intact.

Port Atwood was still sorely lacking in personnel, but they had a huge amount of resources that they were able to use to get almost anything from the Marshall Clan. All outposts had been equipped with old-world security measures to shore up the lack of guards, so Void's Disciple's actions might actually have been caught on film.

They hurried toward a secluded guardhouse, and Zac turned on the monitors while the giants tried to peer inside through the doorway, their bulky frames much too big to fit inside. The latest hours started to flash by on the screen as Zac fast-forwarded the film until there finally was a change.

"It's him," Zac muttered when the familiar form appeared. "He's actually bleeding from the wound!"

There wasn't much else to see on the tape, but it was still good to see that Void's Disciple hadn't come out unscathed after all. It broke the illusion of them dealing with someone unkillable. And it also seemed as though he could confirm a suspicion: he was after the mine.

The Dominator had appeared within frame as he moved toward the mine with impressive speed, but he had suddenly stopped and grasped his head. A second later, the screen turned to static for a whole minute until the current scene outside appeared on the monitors, with the Dominator gone.

It seemed as though he had been planning on entering the mine, but changed his mind and left eastbound, if Rhubat's senses could be trusted.

"A backlash? Something else?" Zac muttered, his eyes glistening.

"Serves him right for killing me," Ogras muttered. "Though I wish he would have looked a bit more wretched than sporting some surface wound."

Zac grunted in agreement as he stepped out of the guardhouse and bought a new teleportation array. There was just a week left until his sister would rip open the portal to the Mystic Realm once more, not much time for his final preparations.

56
PRECIPICE

The following days passed quickly after Zac's group returned to Port Atwood. He sent Ibtep and Joanna with the Anointed to act as liaisons to iron out the logistics of the upcoming mission. As for himself, he had been planning on dealing with all kinds of things to prepare Port Atwood for the Mystic Realm. However, Zac was quickly shown the value of a proper support system, as everything was being taken care of better and more efficiently than if he had done it himself.

Triv and Abby were working in tandem to quash all sorts of issues, from designing a proper base that could hold everyone in Port Atwood, to figuring out what sorts of materials they needed to bring into the research base. The general plan was to set up a proper outpost in the garden on the other side of the portal and then build advance posts as they reached further and further inside the Mystic Realm. This freed up most of Zac's time, allowing him to spend most of his time inside his cultivation cave, nursing his wounds while looking for ways to improve his power.

The brush with death had increased his desire to become stronger even further, but time was limited. The best he could come up with was to solidify his gains from the battle while trying to figure out if there was any concrete gain from his epiphany. Unfortunately, no matter how he looked or experimented, he knew that he neither gained any affinity to his Daos, nor had he evolved any of them.

He had definitely taken a step in the right direction on the mountaintop, but he was still very lacking if he wanted to upgrade any of his Dao Fragments to High mastery. However, he did make one interesting discovery as he searched for clues inside his body. His [Void Heart] had turned inert since swallowing the tendril of Tribulation Lightning. It wouldn't activate no matter what he did or what energies he consumed.

Zac noticed the anomaly while dealing with the wounds from the fight. His broken ribs and flesh wounds would heal by themselves thanks to the atmosphere in his cave and his high Vitality, but there were extremely stubborn pieces of foreign Dao lodged in the wounds. Both the exploding stars and Void's Disciple's kick had been infused with Daos, and different ones at that.

The one in the kick was the strongest, and Zac guessed it might even be a High-tiered Dao. It was completely foreign as well, and not something that he had encountered in any of his other fights. The closest sensation to the stubborn Dao he'd felt before was when he had been thrown out of the Technocrat spaceship and found himself swirling in space for a bit. It wasn't surprising considering all of Adcarkas' skills seemed to be related to space.

The wounds from the stars instead contained an energy that made him think of the sun, a fire-aspected Dao that was distinctly different from neighboring Daos such as the Seed of Tinder. It wasn't as explosive, but it was still extremely stubborn as it smoldered in his wounds as though it would do so for billions of years. The Fragment of the Star did exist, according to Big Blue, though the space octopus had no idea how to form it.

These invasive Daos didn't really affect his combat readiness all too much after his bones had set and flesh healed, but it was still a hidden threat that he needed to deal with. Grinding them down with his own Daos was slow and arduous, which was why he thought of his [Void Heart]. If it could swallow tribulation lightning, it could surely eat a little bit of foreign Dao?

The problem was that it didn't act on the alien energies in his body, and he didn't have any control of the hidden node either. Since manually activating it was out of the question, he instead thought of another way to activate it. He once more absorbed some Miasma as a human to kickstart the node, but it ended with him being nauseated for thirty minutes until he managed to disperse the chill of death inside his body.

He still didn't know what to do with this information, but he hoped that he would get a huge surge of energy when the node was finally done digesting the purple lightning. Getting a free level or two wouldn't be enough to defeat Void's Disciple, but it was a start.

Ogras had entered seclusion as well when they returned, but the rest of Port Atwood exploded into action as every department worked around the clock to ready everything in time. His sister was one of the busiest people of all as she kept traveling between Mystic Island, Thea's Library, and the Towers of Myriad Dao to gather as much information as she could before trying to crack open the spatial tunnel.

The elites of his army were also recalled from the Zombie hunt to prepare and consolidate their gains over the following days, while the noncombatants prepared hundreds of different things that might be needed in the upcoming mission in the Mystic Realm. The settlements that Void's Disciple attacked were recaptured as well, but no one could figure out what Void's Disciple had done in those mines.

The New World Government had sent in over fifty thousand people, according to Julia, so there was definitely a use of manpower inside. Zac initially felt a bit reluctant to follow suit, as he had dealt with most threats either alone or with the help of a small group. He couldn't run around those endless tunnels by himself in search of the Spatial Treasure, so this time, he would bring a large chunk of his army. Besides, if it turned out that the excess personnel was superfluous, then he could always send them back at the last minute.

Julia tried to help out by gathering more intelligence from the New World Government, but it was slim pickings. Thomas Fischer had put in place a new set of extremely restrictive protocols to stop any further leaks, and anyone who entered the Mystic Realm had to sign a contract of confidentiality. A System-enforced contract, so there was no chance of shirking the agreement.

Ilvere suggested launching an assault, but Zac decided against it. He was afraid that the New World Government would do something drastic if he appeared at this juncture, like opening the pathways so that the natives of the Mystic Realm could escape and reach Earth. He couldn't let that happen; he didn't feel confident in leaving Earth exposed to a bunch of E-grade aliens while he was stuck inside the Mystic Realm.

It wasn't the end of the world, though, as Zac doubted there was much that Thomas Fischer knew that he couldn't figure out by himself in a few days. There was no way that these so-called native allies had given the government too much intelligence on the research base; the New World Government simply wasn't powerful enough to barter with high E-grade elders who might be over a thousand years old.

Kenzie arrived at the cultivation cave five days after Zac returned from Site 16, and Zac frowned when he saw her eyes were sunken from chronic sleep deprivation. Triv was with her as well, and the ghost bowed toward Zac before he started sprucing up the place.

"Don't overwork yourself." Zac sighed as he looked at his sister with worry.

"I'll be able to rest as soon as I pack things up here." Kenzie smiled.

"So it's done?" Zac asked with relief.

"It's done," Kenzie said, her smile turning into a grin. "You could start it up right now if you wanted, but it's better if you wait two days. The spatial turbulence grows weaker every day."

"That's amazing. Good job." Zac applauded. "Do you need any help here?"

"No, you'll just get in the way. Triv and I can handle this; you go deal with things in Port Atwood instead. Verana has been wanting to talk with you for a while," Kenzie said.

"Fine, I'll get out of your hair," Zac said as he stood up from his prayer mat. "What do the Tal-Eladar want?"

"They want to join us in the Mystic Realm, of course. No one should have told them outright, but it is impossible to keep an expedition of this magnitude secret." Kenzie shrugged.

"Is Ogras out yet?" Zac asked.

He liked having the demon with him when dealing with Clan Tir'Emarel. Ogras couldn't help himself when he saw the Beast Masters; he always started to annoy them by ruining their plans out of spite. That usually resulted in a better negotiation position for Zac, which was just what someone like him needed.

"No," Kenzie said with a shake of her head, her smile turning into a frown. "What happened back then? He doesn't even answer when I call."

"Void's Disciple is just as strong as we feared." Zac sighed. "None of us got off scot-free. He was wounded, and he might be a bit depressed after taking a loss right after evolving. He'll be out for the Mystic Realm, though."

Kenzie's eyes thinned a bit in suspicion, but Zac didn't want her to know just how close to dying Ogras got. He simply flashed away the next moment and teleported over to the Academy to deal with the Tal-Eladar. Zac eventually made a deal with Verana where she would send a squad of 150 experts into the Mystic Realm, focusing on cultivators excelling in scouting and healing.

Tylia was probably still the greatest healer on Earth, and having her join the mission might save a lot of lives. The keen senses of the Tal-Eladar war-beasts could be invaluable as well, so Zac relented on his stance against them for now. However, he did make sure to sign a contract with Verana that the Spatial Artifact and any D-grade or higher treasures would go to Port Atwood.

They would be given Merit Points for turning them in. This type of employer-employee contract was pretty common when exploring Mystic Realms, and she wasn't really surprised at all when Zac brought it up. As for E-grade resources and lower, it was up to luck. If you found it, it was yours. That was the simplest way of encouraging people to explore the depths of the research base.

The next two days were like a blur, and more and more powerful people appeared in Port Atwood by the minute. First it was Thea along with a hundred experts and five hundred support personnel of the Marshall Alliance. Then came Billy and Nigel, the latter looking less than enthused about entering such a dangerous place. However, Nigel had a rare buffing class similar to Emily's, and he would be able to singlehandedly bolster the defenses of any base.

The Underworld Council provided warriors of all four races as well, along with Gregor and five fellow councilors. The rest would stay to make sure nothing happened to their bases in their absence, just like the majority of the Port Atwood army. Finally, the Zhix arrived, and the appearance of over a hundred hulking Anointed caused quite the commotion among the citizens of Port Atwood.

In fact, a lot of people didn't even know about the existence of the Anointed since they mostly stayed in the hearts of their hives. It caused quite some chaos, and Zac was forced to send them to Mystic Island early so as not to cause a riot. Of course, it was only a day later that Zac and the others joined them.

Everyone had gathered in the central valley of Mystic Island, and Zac marveled as he looked back at the group of over five thousand people behind him. Most of them were normal Zhix warriors and the soldiers of Port Atwood, but this was still the greatest army that Earth had ever assembled. This group would probably be able to take out the New World Government in minutes even if he didn't personally get involved.

Zac eventually turned back and looked with anticipation at Kenzie and her group of craftsmen as they performed the finishing checks on the array they had drawn around the spatial tunnel. It would block out the turbulence from the Spatial Bomb that the cultists had detonated, allowing the old teleportation array to work once more.

Even Zac had some butterflies in his stomach as he looked at the still inactive array. There was so much hanging on this expedition. If they won, then Earth would finally be free of threats, at least for another ninety-nine years. It would give him and everyone else a breather, an opportunity to solidify their foundations and find their bearings.

Conversely, if they failed, then that was that. The Great Redeemer would come sooner or later, and Earth would be turned into a cultivation resource. Ogras and he had even discussed giving out some of his Teleportation Tokens beforehand just in case, but he knew it was kind of a moot point.

Coughing up between 1 and 10 billion Nexus Coins for the Nexus Hub activation wasn't something that average people could endure.

"Sometimes I don't know whether you're my lucky star or an ill omen," a voice echoed out from Zac's side as Ogras appeared out of nowhere. "A normal warrior would be given months to stabilize his foundation and get to understand their limits. I get time for a celebratory drink before I'm thrown at the big boss, and then I'm dragged here before I even have a chance to nurse my wounds."

"You can go on as long a vacation as you want after this is dealt with," Zac snorted.

"See, you say that, but how can that possibly be true while I am living next to a disaster magnet? If you run out of enemies, then the Ruthless Heavens will just conjure one for you," Ogras spat.

"Can't do much about that." Zac smiled before he turned serious again. "How's your situation?"

A shroud of shadows covered the two before Ogras spoke up.

"There's both good and bad news." The demon shrugged. "I won't be able to fight for at least a month, perhaps even longer. There are some complications on top of the wounds."

"Anything I can do to help?" Zac frowned. "I have a lot of pills."

"No, I think that I need to wait this out," Ogras said with a frown, and he hesitated a bit before he kept going. "Spare is redrawing my pathways."

"What?!" Zac blurted. "Is that even possible?"

"Apparently." The demon grimaced. "I don't think it's too bad, though. The changes are small, and they seem to be improvements. Even better, my affinity to the Dao of Shadows has taken a huge leap forward. I was a genius before, but now I'm simply a heaven-defying scion."

Zac only rolled his eyes in response, but he couldn't help but feel a pang of jealousy upon hearing about the affinity. Then again, Ogras had literally died to gain this lucky opportunity. And judging by the demon's face, it wasn't as simple as he let on. There were definitely dangers that accompanied this sudden windfall.

"Well, it's good that you're up and runn–" Zac responded, but he drifted off when he saw that Kenzie had stood up and waved at him.

Everything was ready.

"Do it." Zac nodded, his heart rapidly beating as he prepared for disaster.

57
CONVICTIONS

There was no time to lose now that everything was dealt with. They were already running behind the others who had spent weeks, even months inside the Mystic Realm already, and they needed to catch up.

Kenzie started drawing the final inscriptions that would complete the outer array since Zac had given the go-ahead. The assistants had already moved away just in case, with only Kenzie staying next to the array. The final touches only took a few minutes, and Zac saw the air all around them shudder for a few seconds before it returned to normal.

"It worked!" Kenzie exclaimed a few seconds later as the inner array lit up as well.

"Uh, it did?" Zac asked, feeling there was some lack of payoff.

He had almost expected a massive tear in space to appear, only for Kenzie's array to beat it back after a herculean effort. Zac obviously wasn't the only one feeling this way either. Ogras looked at the array with visible disappointment, and Thea was looking at Kenzie with confusion.

"That's it," Kenzie snorted, clearly miffed about everyone's reactions. "I can add some fireworks to the next array if you want."

"Just thought there would be some spatial rifts or something." Zac sheepishly smiled before he refocused. "I'll go first to make sure it's safe."

"I'm coming with. I know the place best, after all," Ogras said.

"I've also been inside enough to be able to tell if the array works as intended."

"What? In your condition?" Zac frowned as he asked with a low voice. "What's your goal? Last time, we almost had to drag you through the teleporter."

"I figure I'm better off on the other side in case this thing breaks down after one use." Ogras shrugged with a grin. "I'll just hide in your shadows and reap the rewards."

"Well, fine," Zac said as he turned to Thea and the other leaders. "I'll send a message back through the portal in a minute at most. You can begin the transfer as soon as I've done so, provided Kenzie gives the go-ahead."

Thea looked reluctant at being left behind, but Billy didn't care in the slightest. Nigel, on the other hand, looked like he was praying for the thing to fail so that he could stay behind. As for the Zhix, they stoically stood in vigil, their facial expressions unreadable.

"What should we do if this thing breaks after you enter, Warmaster?" Rhubat eventually rumbled. "The enemies of the Zhix are on the other side."

"If this thing really breaks down after we go through, have Kenzie fix it. If she's unable to… Enter through the New World Government's tunnel. Thea can show you the way," Zac said without hesitation.

This was something he had thought about before, and he eventually decided to sacrifice the New World Government if it came to that. The survival of Earth was more important than anything else, and they simply didn't have any other options. He had sent out dozens of squads in search of other tunnels, including to the uncharted continent. But they hadn't found anything, meaning the New World Government tunnel was the only other one remaining.

Of course, following the Dominators through their own tunnel would have been the best option, but no one had been able to figure out where it was. Void's Disciple must have tracked down a pathway as secluded as the one on Mystic Island.

"Be careful around the New World Government, though. The tunnel will be filled with traps. And be careful so as not to let anything dangerous reach Earth."

"You won't mind if we oust your kind?" Rhubat asked curiously.

"They're not my kind." Zac shrugged. "But try a nonviolent approach if possible, no matter if we meet them inside or outside. We're all part of this planet, after all."

The Anointed nodded in agreement, and Zac stepped onto the array with the demon following close behind. The darkness lasted just an instant until he appeared in a familiar room, a wave of relief washing over him when he could confirm that the array worked just fine. He didn't even realize that he had been holding his breath as he stepped through, and his hands were clammy as well.

Getting almost killed while teleporting once had undeniably left a shadow in his mind.

"Ah!" A scream echoed out the second Zac appeared, and he spotted a young woman grasping for a spear that stood balanced against the wall. "Intruders! Wait, Lord Atwood?"

"It's me. Tina, right?" Zac smiled as he recognized the Valkyrie. "I'm sorry it took so long to reopen the entrance. Is everyone okay here?"

Ogras appeared before Tina had a chance to answer, glancing around the building before walking up next to Zac.

"The array seems stable enough," Ogras muttered after he threw the Valkyrie a glance. "I didn't notice any differences compared to the last times. Should be fine, I think?"

"Good." Zac nodded as he sent back an information crystal to the other side, telling the others that it worked.

"More people are coming soon, so let's get out of the way," Zac said as he led the two out of the teleportation building.

The base camp outside looked pretty much the same as the last time Zac visited, except for a couple of new buildings having been added to the mix. The odd lines covered the sky, and the trees created a perimeter around the fields far off in the distance. Finally, there was the barely discernable wall, and Zac's heartbeat sped up at the thought of what awaited inside.

"Everything seems fine here. Have there been any problems?" Zac said as soon as he could confirm that there were no immediate threats.

"Nothing much has happened here apart from us going a bit stir-crazy," Tina said as she waved at the other castaways, who looked at Zac with relief in their eyes. "We have just explored the vicinity and cultivated. Those worm things don't attack as long as five of us travel together. We have encountered something odd, though."

"Odd? What's going on?" Zac asked as he looked around again, properly this time.

Only then did he realize that Ogras had stopped in his tracks after stepping outside the teleportation building, a deep frown adorning his face. Zac had only been here for a few short visits when he needed to talk with his sister, but he hadn't actually left the immediate vicinity of the entrance. However, it appeared as though the demon had figured something out.

"This world is growing," the demon finally blurted out, his eyes wide with shock.

"They are here," Leviala said, her milky-white eyes opening for the first time in weeks. "The door has been reopened."

"Sorry for having you do this, child." Uvek sighed as he hurriedly handed his granddaughter the extract before the backlash kicked in.

She drank the murky texture down with a slight frown, but she didn't complain about the astringent taste. She never did.

"It's not more horned beings," Leviala said. "Well, there are, but there are other races as well. Some I have never seen before."

"Any humans?" Tictus, the squirrely chief Datamancer, asked with worry in his eyes.

"Yes, most." Leviala nodded.

The eyes around the table lit up, but Uvek shook his head.

"Things outside are not like in here. Our races will not bring us together. Remember, it is our clan that needs to stand united, even against other humans," Uvek said.

The other elders soon remembered themselves, and low discussion as to what to do next started in the sealed Elders' Hall.

"How powerful are they?" Tictus eventually asked.

"I can't see," Leviala said with a shake of her head.

"How about…" another elder muttered.

"No! She cannot open the Eyes of Heaven again so soon. She has used her bloodline too much already to keep track of all the changes. It might kill her if we push even further. We need to remember our goal! These outsiders who keep pouring in are after that thing in the center, but what are we after?" Uvek said.

"Freedom," Tictus muttered.

"Exactly! We need to leave here, but then what?" Uvek said as he looked across the room.

"I have learned some things by speaking with Hekruv Vira of the True Sky Faction. They have had ample contact with the outsiders through their terminals. If he is speaking the truth, and I believe he is, then the planet outside has changed, and it will be thrown out into the universe in one hundred years. We need to have a D-grade warrior before then to protect us, and Leviala is our best hope! She is the first one since the ancestor to awaken [Heaven's Eyes] instead of [King's Eyes] or [Lord's Eyes]. We can't ruin her potential for short-term benefits!"

"Do not forget Yvian," the decrepit voice of the second elder spoke up, and Uvek forced himself to nod in acquiescence.

However, his inner thoughts weren't quite as agreeable. It would be a disaster for Clan Cartava if that impetuous man became the next patriarch. They had already been captured once due to their unique bloodline, and Uvek knew they needed to keep a low profile as they stepped out into the true universe. But Yvian carried dreams of grandeur, to lead the clan to the peak.

He didn't understand that they were just ants in the grand scheme of things. Their ancestral homelands had been like a fortress, and their echelon elders were renown for their prowess. But their sanctuary was reduced to ashes the moment the ancestor passed away, their elders slaughtered like chickens, proving they were just frogs in the bottom of the well.

Having wealth was a sin if you weren't powerful enough to protect it.

Even then, Yvian bore a deep desire for conquest. Before, he had wanted to conquer this accursed cage, but now he had turned his sights to the planet outside. He believed that it was ripe for the picking, as the outsiders were pathetically weak according to the True Sky Faction. But Uvek knew better. The real powerhouses hadn't made their moves yet, or they moved in the shadows.

"So what do we do?" Tictus asked.

"The storms are acting up again," Uvek muttered. "And we haven't found any terminals that can reach this new faction."

"The old patterns no longer hold, and some subsystems have completely shut down," Tictus said with a shake of his head. "A unit was caught unaware in Red-04; only three managed to return alive. We can't go to Section 8 at all at the moment."

"We left a message where the horned one appeared," Uvek eventually said. "We can't go there now, but we might soon meet in the inner sections."

"What if they're hostile?" the second elder asked with a rasping voice.

"We won't look for trouble, but we will not back away either. We will never be captives again," Uvek said, his eyes burning with determination.

"Never again," the others echoed.

"This is our edge. The outsiders are treating this as a treasure hunt. We are fighting for survival. Our convictions aren't the same."

"He's hurt," Yano whispered, the soulgems studding his head glimmering as his fury instilled them with power. "Another is missing, and the third is in the vat. This is our chance!"

"We can't." Helo sighed, his own, far grander gems instead spreading a soothing blue radiance. "Only three Masons remain, and they are badly wounded as well. And remember, they are not alone. Their armies outnumber us five to one. Those insectoids might be weaker in general, but you saw how they fought. We can't match that suicidal ferocity. Our kin is not meant for battle like that."

"But another opportunity like this won't come again!" Yano spat, though the red glow of his gems had clearly dimmed.

He knew the horror of their new masters better than anyone. He had seen his own parents getting ripped apart by the bare hands of the one called Void's Disciple, their soulgems being harvested the same way the old controllers did. What had their kin done to deserve a fate such as this? Captured and experimented on for thousands of years, and when they finally saw a chance at freedom, they were slaughtered and enslaved once more.

But Helo wouldn't give up. To many had fallen for him to give in to despair now.

"We need to be patient," Helo eventually said.

"You keep saying that, but our people are dying," Yano said, tears already streaming down his face. "Besides, if you help Void's Disciple to create that item... Even if you survive, you'll be cursed. The Heavens won't abide something like this. With the old Masons fallen, only you can lead us now."

"I will survive. I can't fall here," Helo said with determination, the soothing gems flashing a sanguine red for a second before he got a hold of himself. "We must endure for a little longer. Soon, the thing will be born. The elders believed that will bring about huge changes to our world, with previously inaccessible parts being forced open."

"How does that help us?" Yano asked. "Without our Masons, we are not powerful enough to compete for that thing."

"But we might be able to nudge events in our favor. Perhaps we might even be able to nudge those monsters right off a cliff. The Grand Mason told me something before he succumbed to his wounds, something that she only learned recently," Helo said, his voice growing even lower. "The Administrator is alive."

"What? How is that even possible? The Cataclysm back then–" Yano exclaimed, his gems turning gray out of fear.

"I don't understand either," Helo said, his gems shimmering yellow in confusion. "But if these insectoids want the item, they will have to enter the Administrator's domain. These interlopers are strong, but do you really believe they can survive such an encounter?"

58
LUNAR TRIBE

Hevastes rushed through the forest, his sharp nose all the guidance he needed to avoid his distant, and far less enlightened, cousins. A squad of silent killers followed in tow, ruthlessness gleaming in their eyes. They'd set out five days ago at the behest of Cervantes to find a new path to the weaklings of the Cartava Clan.

A century ago, this would have been considered a suicide mission, a way to discard unwanted members of the tribe. They would most likely perish to the environment, and if they somehow survived, they'd still have an impossible mission to complete.

However, things had changed. Hevastes looked up at the distant Skythreads, both excitement and trepidation filling his hearts. He remembered running through these woods just three hundred years ago as a fledgling member of his first hunting squad. The sky had been so much closer then, and the distances weren't so insurmountable. But the world had grown, just as Hevastes himself had.

It almost felt like he would leave part of himself behind when they finally left this place.

They finally reached their target location, a seemingly insignificant corner of the forest where the wall made a slight turn. There were no signs of anything special about this place, apart from a small grate in the Memorysteel close to the ceiling.

A century ago, this small vent just had a diameter of ten centimeters, but by now, it was over a meter across, effortlessly providing a new point of ingress for their kin. Similar weaknesses were appearing all over the base, with new ones being discovered every week. The sanctums of the Core Sector were still unreachable, meaning it was still impossible to reach the bloodline pools freely. But it was just a matter of time by now.

Of course, the dangers had increased just like the opportunities had.

"Isolating steps," Hevastes muttered, and one of his subordinates produced a series of spikes, each of them connected to a small dongle.

Hevastes took out his charger and poured some of the harvested Base Power into each spike. He couldn't help but grimace at the expenditure, especially now that it was so hard to harvest. But times had changed, and there was no point in hoarding things that would be useless in the outer world.

Seeing that the spikes had activated properly, he threw them into the wall with pinpoint precision, each of them hitting the wall with half a meter's distance, all the way up to the grate. The spikes embedded themselves in the Memorysteel as though the wall were made of mud, and a few seconds later, the fusion was complete.

The arrays on the Memorysteel surface had completely dimmed by the time that the spikes had become part of the wall, and Kato didn't need any prompting as he climbed up along the spikes. He took out a tablet from his backpack as he carved a small groove with his special tool, allowing him to connect to the local systems through a cable.

Hevastes saw the screen light up a second later, and the whole group tensed as they prepared themselves for retaliation. The seconds passed without either the wall awakening or the corruption appearing, allowing them to breathe out in relief. It wasn't that they didn't trust Kato - he was one of the most skilled Datamancers in the tribe, after all. But things had become too unpredictable as of late.

The grate swung up a few seconds later, and Kato jumped down to the others with a relieved look in his eyes. It wasn't surprising. It was usually the Datamancers who got the worst of it in case they were discovered.

"Excellent job. How long?" Hevastes asked.

"Sixteen hours under normal operations," Kato said before he hesitantly added, "But the risk of anomalies is high."

"Ten hours. Everyone needs to be back here by that time in case we get split up. Any latecomers will have to return by themselves," Hevastes eventually decided.

The rest of the squad nodded without hesitation, even though the implication was clear. Returning to the tribe without Hevastes' source of Base Power was a suicide mission, and they were better off staying in the forest, praying that some other squad would pass by before they were discovered by the beasts.

"Remember the goal. First of all, find a path to the Cartava Clan. Secondly, if an opportunity arises, capture the Grand Elder's granddaughter. Finding information about the interlopers would be a bonus, but other squads are working on that," Hevastes said as he looked across the group.

The group of veterans nodded, though they couldn't hide the confusion from their captain. After all, most of them had worked together for almost two centuries. They were elite warriors who were content to follow orders, which couldn't be said about the ever-curious Datamancer.

"Is that brat really worth the risk?" Kato hesitantly asked when no one else would speak up. "We have already spent such a large amount of our resources on this one objective."

"Are you questioning Cervantes' orders?" Hevastes asked coolly.

"N-No, absolutely not," Kato hurriedly said with a shake of his head, quickly realizing the folly of questioning the alpha's grandnephew. "I just hoped to understand the goal to better complete my mission."

"Very well. I don't know all the details either, but my uncle said one thing that might interest you. Leviala Cartava is the key to prolonging our life spans by many times over. Now tell me, is it worth snatching her?" Hevastes said with a cruel smile.

The eyes of even the veterans in the group widened in shock before a red tint spread in their eyes. Hevastes knew all too well what they were thinking. The bloodline of their tribe was unmatched and the only one in this realm solely focused on combat. Those gemlings far on the other side were only useful for creating living treasures, and the True Sky Faction had long lost their way by interbreeding.

Only the Titans and unique specimens were a match to their prowess, but the specimens were long gone, while the Titans had all perished when the Cataclysm turned their sector into the Wasteland. If it weren't for the unique environment, the werewolves would long have been able to dominate this whole realm.

But there was a downside to their power; it took them too long to cultivate. They were part-beast, which had provided them with superior bodies and power. But they still had the much shorter life span of humans, making it almost impossible to unleash their full potential before they grew old. But what if their life spans could be improved upon?

Hevastes could feel it. This was the era of the Lunar Tribe.

"You're right! This world is expanding!" Tina nodded with an odd face as she looked at Ogras. "It seems impossible, but this whole base seems to be growing like it was a living creature or something. It's already grown around ten percent since we were trapped here."

"Growing how?" Zac said with confusion.

The rest of the leaders had already arrived through the teleporter by this point, and they all looked at Ogras and Tina like they were crazy. How could a base grow by itself?

"We first noticed it with the keypad that allows us to enter the real base. It was rising higher and higher in the air, and now it's thirty centimeters further up than before," Tina said.

"Is it some sort of liquid metal?" Thea asked from the side, but the Valkyries shook their heads in response.

"I honestly feel like it's some sort of magic rather than something that can be explained rationally. We first assumed that the wall was rising from the ground, but we soon realized that this affects everything except for living things," Tina explained.

"I thought this place was made for giants, but what if the whole realm started growing around the same time the integration took place?" Ogras muttered as his eyes scanned the surroundings. "Or perhaps even sooner."

Zac looked over with confusion before he understood what Ogras was getting at. The demon was the first one to explore the Mystic

Realm, and he had already noted that he believed that this section was built to accommodate some sort of golem or giant species reaching five to six meters in height. But what if that wasn't the case, but rather the result of the place growing?

"A bunch of Cosmic Energy flooded Earth, and some of it was passed into this place?" Zac asked.

"Or the shock of integration kicked the Dimensional Seed into gear." Ogras shrugged.

"We found out some of the rules by studying the trees," another Valkyrie interjected. "They are the same as before, but they are now spaced further apart like the ground between them is expanding."

"Spatial expansion," Thea said with wonder as she looked around.

"But our people have only been trapped here for a few weeks and it's grown by ten percent? This base should be thousands of years old; it doesn't add up," Joanna countered with a frown as she looked at the Valkyries.

"The treasure is awakening," Zac said. "That is probably speeding up the process if it's the source."

"It's the most likely scenario," Ogras agreed. "But that means two things if true. First, these changes will probably only increase in severity as the treasure awakens. Second, we are just at the edge of the Mystic Realm. The effect might be far worse in the core, the closer we get to the treasure itself. We already knew this place is huge, but it might have turned into a continent overnight."

"We have tried mapping the growth rate, and it seems as though–" Tina said, but she forgot herself upon seeing the form of Rhubat breaking through the roof of the teleportation house like some sort of insectoid Godzilla.

"I forgot about those giants in all the excitement." Ogras looked over with a snort.

Zac sighed and flashed over and threw away the rubble of the teleportation house, the pieces of the building flying far out into the grassland.

"Amazing. Worlds within worlds," Rhubat said while looking around, ignoring the mayhem their appearance had caused.

"This place is extremely ancient, older than both your and our civilizations combined," Zac said. "There will be a lot of dangers inside. I'll be counting on you guys."

"The chief corruptor is still standing, so we will not stop either," Rhubat agreed and moved out of the way to make room for more Anointed to enter.

"Start setting everything up," Zac instructed the logistics crew before he flashed back to the core group. "I need some more details from the scientists who have stayed here."

The Valkyries who had been marooned in the Mystic Realm were not the only citizens caught inside when the cultists attacked. There was also a group of professors who were studying the Mystic Realm while Zac was busy dealing with other things.

The logistics officers got to work while Zac entered a warehouse to go over things in detail. There were proper meeting rooms as well, but they were too small to house the Anointed, and he wanted them represented.

The scientists seemed extremely uncomfortable at being stuck in a building with not only five-meter-tall giants who stared down at them as though they were snacks, but also with the most powerful people on the former ladder. But they quickly gathered their wits and started going over the measurements they had taken since they were stuck.

The biosphere had grown just like Tina and Ogras said, by 12% to be exact. This included everything that could be considered dead, such as stones, the metal walls, and the ground itself. The odd growth also affected organic materials that weren't alive, such as pieces of lumber. The people and the plants were completely unaffected, though.

Most of that growth had happened over the last sixteen days, and it seemed to be accelerating. As for the process of expansion, it couldn't be explained by science. The first guess of the scientists was that the spatial expansion acted on an atomic level, increasing the distance between molecules in materials. But it was quickly proven to be wrong.

Matter was literally appearing out of nowhere. A piece of lumber would keep growing in volume in this realm, but its density would remain constant, meaning that its weight increased. As for where the additional matter came from, the scientist had no idea. One conjecture was that it was being absorbed from subspace or neighboring dimensions, while some simply believed it to be magic no matter how unscientific that sounded.

"Isn't this a huge opportunity?" Ogras said from the side when he heard the explanation. "Can't we throw out everything of value and it will keep multiplying? What if we get a bunch of extremely valuable materials? Wouldn't we literally be growing money?"

59
EXPANSION

Zac's eyes lit up at the idea, and he could see himself throwing out his mountains of loot and watching them grow. This could be a game-changer for Port Atwood, and he turned toward the scientists with fire in his eyes.

"Unfortunately, no. It doesn't work that way," a scientist said, but he quickly shrank back when over ten angry glares were directed his way. "Ahem… That is… This change doesn't seem to affect items with a certain amount of energy. Nexus Crystals won't grow in size, for example, and neither will Spiritual Materials. However, we have only been able to test this on our limited supply of materials in this short while. There might be some materials we can grow this way to great effect."

Zac couldn't help but feel some disappointment at losing such a good moneymaking opportunity before it could even start. Being able to grow things like gold and steel might sound amazing, but mortal materials were essentially worthless in the Multiverse.

Even Zac could conjure a mountain out of nowhere with **[Nature's Punishment]**, and powerful beings could harvest whole planets with a wave of their hands. Some Mystic Realms also contained shocking amounts of certain elements. You could find a world containing hundreds of billions of tonnes of purest gold, ripe for the taking.

Of course, it was still worth growing some materials since it was free. There was a large demand for construction materials to build and expand the towns of his force, and normal materials were enough to build houses.

Zac already gave up on the idea, but the demon wasn't as easily convinced.

"What about the walls of this place?" Ogras said with a frown. "That metal can't be something common. I couldn't even leave a lasting mark when going all out last time I was here."

"That – we are not sure how to explain the walls, but we have a conjecture?" another scientist explained as she adjusted her glasses. "We believe that the material of the base itself, while extremely high technology, is not spiritual in nature. It is some sort of advanced metallurgy that we don't understand. Its regenerative properties are in turn powered by an external energy supply."

Zac nodded in agreement, remembering the Technocrat vessel he'd visited. It was the same there. The Technocrats seemed to use advanced techniques to somehow drain high-grade materials of their spirituality, while still retaining their strength. It seemed like a waste of time to Zac, but it might be required for the materials to work with the "Dao of Technology."

"We haven't been able to prove this, as we've been unable to take samples," she added.

They asked a few more questions about the mysterious growth, but there was only so much that the scientists had managed to find out. They neither had the tools nor the strength to get to the bottom of things, and most of what they knew was conjecture. Zac guessed that he would find out more as he ventured deeper into the Mystic Realm.

"Have you encountered any living beings?" Zac asked next. "Apart from the worms."

"No, but the amount of time we spent inside the actual construct is limited. Only three of us managed to get clearance," Tina said from the side. "We also never left the security door that protects this section, as we were afraid to open it and let the natives inside."

"It's good that you played it safe." Zac nodded before he asked with confusion, "But what do you mean not getting access? That console doesn't give access to everyone?"

"No," Tina said with a shake of her head. "I think it's bugged or something."

"Or it has some sort of requirements we don't fully grasp just yet," the head scientist added. "There seem to be some requirements, though, the main being a minimum power. All the people with access are over level 50."

"Anything else?" Zac asked.

"Two are mortals; one is a cultivator. So spirituality might not actually be a boon but a hindrance," a scientist hesitantly said. "It's too early to tell with such a small sample."

"Also, we only managed to get Tier 2 clearance, which only let us travel a very limited section outside. Only some doors opened for us. We might not even have been able to open that security door even if we tried," Tina said.

"Maybe I had beginner's luck? Or maybe I'm just that handsome?" Ogras grinned from the side, drawing multiple eye rolls in response.

It would be a problem if only Ogras could control that main exit from their position on the frontier. Would they have to station him like some sort of doorman just so they would be able to maintain their mobility? And what about further inside? There would no doubt be more barriers toward the core of the Mystic Realm.

"It might be looking for some specific genome that only a few in the Multiverse possess. It shouldn't be based on human anatomy, considering a demon has had the most success," Joanna ventured. "If this place is built by Technocrats, it shouldn't make its decision on something like constitution or levels, right?"

"Right." Zac nodded. "Anything else?"

"There has been seismic activity in the past two weeks. It might be related to the growth," another scientist said after some thought. "The earthquakes have been mild so far, but they could create issues down the line if they increase in severity. The walls might break apart from the vibrations, allowing outsiders to enter our secured area."

Zac nodded in understanding, a slight frown adorning his face. He had heard just how sturdy this place was from Ogras. Furthermore, it had managed to hold Peak E-grade warriors trapped for millennia. He probably wouldn't be able to open new pathways by punching his way through the walls even if he exhausted himself.

Then again, few things could contend against nature itself, and it wouldn't be too surprising if some cracks started to appear. Zac didn't feel that to be just a negative. There were obviously problems with mobility inside this place since the natives still hadn't managed to escape to Earth. That probably meant it would be difficult reaching either the Dominators or the Dimensional Seed as well.

"Thank you for your excellent work," Zac said as he looked around. "I know you guys are tired of this place, but we can't leave just yet. Some new intelligence has come to light since you were locked inside, and every faction on Earth is scrambling to get inside this place. We are already behind the others because of the cultists, so I will need to rely on your expertise a while longer."

The scientists nodded without hesitation, and Zac guessed that they were more than happy to stay now that there was a bunch of powerful people to protect them. After all, what scientist wouldn't be interested in researching a magical world in a hidden dimension that kept bending the laws of physics?

Everyone already knew what they were supposed to do, and they split up to lead their respective factions as one person after another emerged through the teleporter. The transportation of personnel took hours, as the teleporter couldn't stay active continuously. Kenzie shut it down on multiple occasions to make sure that her array wouldn't suddenly crack from overextension. It was important to maintain function as long as possible in case something unexpected happened.

They would probably need to order other things from Calrin as well as they kept figuring out the rules in this weird place. Besides, they were still able to spy on the other factions as long as the tunnel remained open, and Zac might also need to exit in the next few days depending on how things panned out.

Setting up a proper command center and barracks would take the better part of a day. They didn't know how long they would need to use this place for, so they did everything properly like they were building a whole town from the ground up. It felt extremely slow to Zac, but he also knew that something like this would be completely impossible without the aid of Cosmos Sacks and superhuman strength.

The large-scale expansion quickly angered the only other residents of the secluded biosphere enough to attack, and a hundred wormlike creatures suddenly burrowed out of the ground and struck the settlers to protect their domain. They were effortlessly cut into ribbons by Thea, who happened to be nearby.

Zac whistled in surprise at the efficiency with which she disposed of a bunch of Peak F-grade beasts. It looked like her gain had been pretty impressive after all. It might be a result of incorporating that Sword Intent she'd gained inside the inheritance, but Zac distinctly felt that her Dao was improving at a rapid pace.

"She's become more powerful," Ogras said as he emerged from the shadows. "You should either bed her or dispose of her while we're here. Either way, you'll have dealt with a potential threat."

"Whatever," Zac snorted. "I'm tired of standing around watching the construction. Let's go check out the base for a bit."

"What? Right now?" Ogras blanched. "I'm hurt over here."

"If you're well enough to run your mouth, then you're surely well enough to walk around a bit as well," Zac said as he started gathering people.

Soon enough, a preliminary scouting party was assembled, consisting of Zac, Kenzie, Ogras, Thea, and Ibtep. The insectoid acted as a representative to the Anointed, and it also had a scouting class, which might come in handy.

They weren't planning on going too far today, but just to see if they could get credentials and observe the changes inside the proper structure. There was also a hidden reason only known to Zac and Kenzie. Zac wanted to see if he or at least his sister could gain access to the main systems of this research base, either through their Heritage or through Jeeves.

That would give them a huge edge in the competition for the treasure. In fact, it might end the struggle altogether if they could simply lock everyone in place while they went and fetched the seed.

The group set out, leaving the massive Anointed to guard the base in case of another monster wave, but Zac felt it was unlikely. He had already scouted the biosphere from a high vantage with **[Cosmic Gaze]**, and he only found a few hundred markings of attuned energies. That last skirmish had probably wiped out over a third of all the so-called **[Ocodon Worms]**.

It didn't take long for Ogras to lead them to the gate he had used the last time he visited.

"It's really further up," Ogras said as he stabbed his spear into the ground to use as a foothold, and he had to jump up to touch the screen.

The door swung open without incident, displaying what looked like a storage room or perhaps a break room.

"Well, the arrays and technology seem to function just fine, even if this place is growing," Ogras muttered as he made to stride inside.

"Wait a bit," Kenzie said before she floated up to the screen herself, no doubt temporarily assisted by her Dao.

Zac looked on with anticipation, and his eyes lit up just like the screen the moment Kenzie touched the screen. A pleasant female voice spoke through some sort of hidden speaker, confirming that another credential had been handed out.

[Chief Caretaker Signature added. Tier-4 Access added.]

"What? Chief Caretaker? I only became a caretaker with worse access?" Ogras spat with jealousy written all over his face.

"The computer obviously felt you were meant for grunt work while I was leadership material. Or perhaps I'm just that handsome," Kenzie said with a grin, drawing a glare from the demon.

Everyone quickly followed suit to get their credentials, but the others weren't as lucky as Kenzie. Thea managed to at least get Tier-3 access like Ogras, but when it was Ibtep's turn, nothing happened. And worse yet, the same thing actually happened with Zac.

Zac looked at the screen with confusion, some intrusive thoughts gnawing at him in the back of his mind. He knew there was something odd about the timeline when he was a baby, and the visions of Leandra he had seen had hinted at some things that Zac didn't really want to think of. His sister had been given the best clearance right away, but he wasn't even accredited? How could that possibly happen when it was their family who built this place?

Unless his family tree wasn't as clear-cut as believed.

60
FIRST ENTRY

Not being welcomed like a long-lost son by the Technocrat console felt surprisingly distressing, but Zac pushed all errant thoughts to the back of his head. There was no way for him to get to the truth of the matter as things stood, and it wasn't like his biological heritage was all that important to him.

Besides, Zac wasn't actually worried about not getting any access even if the implications of his failure were troubling. He took out Leandra's talisman, and he jumped up to the console once more. He might not have gotten the reception he wanted, but he still held the key to the kingdom.

[Council Inspector identity confirmed. Tier-4 Access added.]

"What was that?" Thea asked with raised brows, looking up from the detritus she was studying.

"I got it in the Tower of Eternity," Zac lied, and he was relieved to see that the demon played along without causing trouble this time. "The enemies on one of the levels were Technocrats. I snatched this thing, and I just figured it might work here as well."

"What's a council inspector?" Ibtep asked curiously.

"No idea." Zac shrugged, and this time, he didn't need to lie. He really had no idea. "But this thing gave the same type of clearance at the Technocrat level in the Tower. Maybe they're Technocrat law enforcement, and this is their badge?"

"Can I try?" Thea asked, and Zac agreed after some thought.

She jumped up just like Zac did, but a scowl appeared on her face when nothing happened, and the scowl worsened into a glare when Ogras snickered to the side. Zac didn't know why, but he actually felt relieved to see nothing happen, and that feeling only increased when Ibtep similarly failed to gain any credentials with the help of the token.

"Perhaps it is bound to me because I was the first one to use it," Zac ventured. "It would be weird if multiple people could use the same identity."

"Well, let's just go," Thea muttered as she entered the base, with the others quickly following.

However, Zac held Kenzie back as he erected an isolation array. The others looked back at them curiously, but they soon walked further inside to not look like they were prying.

"Your clearance, was that by itself or something Jeeves did?" Zac asked when they were alone.

"It was Jeeves," Kenzie said, disappointment evident in her eyes. "I was supposed to get the same credentials as Ogras, but Jeeves made the System give me the highest clearance available to this terminal."

She still didn't look happy with the fact that she at least got a normal clearance, and Zac understood what she was thinking. This realm was supposed to be some sort of bridge between her and their mother, but she was only given the same treatment as an outsider. And even that was better than what Zac got.

It wasn't a good start.

"Don't worry about it," Zac said. "Just look at me. I was the same until I used Mom's token. The Technocrats are advanced, but they can't plan for every eventuality. The place was abandoned by Mom's family an incredibly long time ago, from the sounds of it, to the point that Mom planned on hiding out in this long-forgotten place. She was probably not even born when this place was created. It would be rather odd if we were suddenly given access."

"You're right." Kenzie nodded, her features easing up a bit.

"Besides, this is just some random terminal at the edge of the compound. The good stuff should be further inside. Or could Jeeves connect to some bigger system?" Zac asked.

"There wasn't anything interesting. Just thousands of years of automated reports on readings of the biosphere where we're staying inside. It seems that the terminal was mostly made for access and climate control. I can make it rain, I think, but that's about it," Kenzie said.

"Well, put a hold on that," Zac said with a small smile. "At least it's a good start that Jeeves can connect with these things. I doubt any of the other factions can get that much out of the systems in this place."

The two soon rejoined the rest of the expedition, and Ogras led them down the same paths as he had explored before. Zac had already read the reports, but he was still shocked at just how massive the place was. Some of it was probably due to the spatial expansion, but it was undeniable that this base was most likely bigger than his whole island even before it started to grow.

It was hard to grasp how a structure could have these kinds of dimensions. Port Atwood was roughly the size of Hawaii according to measurements taken by some geologists, and his mind had trouble computing such an undertaking. Then again, for the Technocrats, building something like this might be as easy as turning a page. They just needed to send out a few million robots to work around the clock for a couple of years.

They kept moving further and further inside, with Kenzie and Thea being responsible for most of the conversation. Zac and Ogras talked a bit as well, but Ibtep mostly walked in silence.

"You've been pretty quiet for a while," Kenzie finally said. "You don't think this is interesting?"

"A hive made of metal, large beyond comprehension. It makes one wonder about all the marvels out there in the universe," Ibtep said after some thought.

"You'll be able to see them sooner or later," Kenzie said with a smile.

"Perhaps…" Ibtep said with a sigh. "But Nonet will never get the chance, and neither will the rest of the Anointed. A lifetime of service to the Zhix, and only death is their reward. This is not cutting off weakness, it is cutting off our roots."

The Zhix suddenly turned to Zac, their eyes almost burning.

"Can you do something?"

"Save the Anointed?" Zac asked with surprise. "I have no idea how to do something like that."

"Here," Ibtep said as they took out a stone gourd from their massive backpack. "Please don't tell anyone I gave you this. Especially not Nonet."

"What's this?" Zac asked with a frown as he held the gourd. He could feel that there was some liquid inside, and he guessed that it wasn't something simple.

"It's the Elixir of Anointment," Ibtep said. "I figured you humans have all kinds of ideas and methods, so I... borrowed it from Rhubat's hive. Perhaps you can find a way to improve it, to cure the bad side effects of taking it. Perhaps even reverse the effect and allow the Anointed to cultivate as normal."

Zac looked at the odd Zhix with interest. It appeared as though this wasn't something they had come up with on the spur of the moment. The Elixir of Anointment was no doubt a highly controlled substance, and Zac had no idea how Ibtep had managed to abscond with it from one of the greatest hives in the world. Perhaps they had gained some unique advantages from their class?

Furthermore, it looked like their actions were highly sacrilegious among the Zhix, but they still went through with it to save the Anointed. It was a reminder that Ibtep's thoughts and actions were much more flexible compared to most Zhix, who were strictly bound by their precepts and conventions.

But could Zac do something, even if he had the elixir? Perhaps Jeeves could help once more?

"I'll be honest, Alchemy is one of the areas where our planet is especially lacking," Zac eventually said after he saw Kenzie surreptitiously shake her head. "We can't even make basic pills right now, let alone improve these types of formulae."

Ibtep only sighed and nodded their head, clearly not too surprised with the outcome.

"However... There might be a way," Zac said after some hesitation. "I made a connection with a very powerful faction while undertaking a trial. They are called the Zethaya Clan, and they specialize in Alchemy. If there is anyone who can help fix the Anointed's situation and these elixirs, it would be them," Zac said.

"Really?!" Ibtep said with shock.

"However, visiting them is extremely dangerous. They have not only D-grade Hegemons, but even C-grade Monarchs under their employ. They could destroy this whole planet without breaking a sweat," Zac said.

"Are you not friends? Did you not provide a proper gift?" Ibtep asked.

Zac blanched a bit before his face returned to normal. Blowing up their store and almost killing their direct descendant was more an act of war than a gift. However, that wasn't the only trouble with using the Teleportation Token.

"Well, my identity is a bit complicated for a number of reasons. I may be a wanted man in the whole sector, or I may be considered a promising youth worth nurturing."

The others were listening in on the conversation, their expressions ranging from shock to concern.

"Just what did you do in the Tower of Eternity?" Kenzie said. "Ogras said that you made a splash, but that's not it, is it?"

"I had a bit of a cultivation deviation," Zac said after some thought. "Things got a bit out of hand, and I had to kill a few hundred people."

"A few hundred scions of the most powerful clans around, including a prince of the most powerful empire of the whole Zecia Sector," Ogras said, almost looking like he had finally gotten rid of a huge burden, his smile growing wider and wider. "Your brother is probably a living legend by now, a bogeyman used to scare children."

"A deviation? Like that—" Thea whispered as her eyes turned to his neck, and Zac realized she was referring to his battle with Harbinger.

"Sometimes, strength comes at a cost," Zac wryly said, prompting Ogras' face to scrunch up as he nodded in agreement.

"Are you okay? Is there anything we can do to help? Perhaps Big Blue—" the Marshall scion ventured.

"I've luckily found a solution already," Zac said. "I'll slowly get better."

"These fallen princes and scions," Thea hesitated. "If they find Earth…"

"So what if it brings some trouble? Some bastards simply need to get cut down." Ogras snorted. "This planet would be long gone if not for him anyway."

"That's not what I—"

"It's alright." Zac sighed. "I didn't plan for things to get out of hand like that. The System was manipulating things from the shadows. It released something that made everyone lose their minds, and it was kill or be killed."

"Why would it do something like that?" Kenzie asked with confusion.

"To make the strong even stronger," Thea muttered as her fist clenched.

"Anyway," Zac said as he turned back to the eager Zhix, "I could send you or someone else to the Zethaya with this mixture, but they would still know you were related to me. They might catch you to get to me. And I won't be able to save you, no matter how much I would want to. They are simply too powerful."

"I would still be willing to go," Ibtep said without hesitation. "As would any number of Zhix, no doubt."

"The cost to activate this token is 2 billion Nexus Coins," Zac slowly said after having made his decision. "I can't fork out that much money right now. If you can cover half, I'll give you the token."

The main purpose of that particular token had been to concoct a pill for Alea as a last resort. Now that things turned out as they did, it didn't hold as much value to Zac. Certainly, having access to a D-grade Alchemist from a top-tier force would always be extremely convenient, but he wasn't in direct need of getting some item or pill completed.

Still, you never knew what would happen in the future, and he wasn't certain that giving it away would be the best move. They were onetime tokens, after all. So he decided to give a test of sorts to the Zhix. If he couldn't even scrounge up the money for transportation, how would he survive being sent to a C-grade continent?

Of course, Zac had to admit that he had a selfish reason for relenting as well. He was extremely anxious to know about what people were saying about him in the Multiverse. He needed to make some adjustments to his plans if it turned out that he had become a wanted man, and they would need to make preparations for Earth as well.

"I will do it! I am going right now," Ibtep said as they started running back toward the base, no longer caring the slightest about the Technocrat base, nor apparently about the fact that they never got any clearance to return through the security door.

The insectoid would have to wait a bit in the break room as the others kept going, since there still were sections to explore. They finally reached the door leading to the "outer section" that Ogras had mentioned, but they didn't immediately open it. For all they knew, there might be an army lying in wait on the other side.

"Do we keep going or head back?" Kenzie asked as she turned to Zac for a decision.

"You go back for now. Let me and Ogras sound things out first," Zac said.

"I'm coming as well," Thea said without hesitation.

"Like glue, this one," Ogras muttered from the side, drawing another glare from Thea.

"It's just a preliminary scouting mission to see if there are any threats nearby. Ogras and I'll go because we're already in the E-grade. You'll have plenty of time to get tired of this place over the coming weeks." Zac smiled. "We'll be back in a few hours."

"Fine," Thea eventually relented. "But I won't be left behind when the real missions start. Try to find a hunting ground like the ones you mentioned. If we just spend our days searching without cultivating, we might fall behind the other factions."

"I hear you looked like you just underwent a thousand-cut torture a few days ago, and you're already raring to get beaten up again?" Ogras snorted. "Did the inheritance turn you into a simpleton?"

"None of your business," Thea spat before turning to Zac. "Be careful, alright? Just ditch that guy if things get too dangerous."

"Alright." Zac grinned. "I know what you're thinking, but there's no need to worry. The distance between us is not that big. The moment you evolve, you'll be able to make a huge leap forward as you open the preliminary nodes."

"Hopefully, this place will give me enough time to reach that point." Thea sighed. "Alright, I'm going back."

With that, Thea turned into a gust of wind as she made her way back through the metallic pathways.

"Don't be like that to my sister-in-law," Kenzie admonished the demon, who clearly didn't take it to heart. "And you, blockhead. How hard would it be to take her with you? Just send that demon away on some mission and you're suddenly on a date. What a missed opportunity."

Ogras only snickered in response, clearly taking some pleasure in Zac's helpless expression. Kenzie gave them a reminder to be careful before she left as well.

"You know, the two of you might really be a pretty good match. She seems to have picked up a masochistic streak just like you. You can play around in beast tides for fun." Ogras laughed as he walked toward the console of the security door.

"Let's just go." Zac sighed as he readied himself in case of battle.

61
RIFTS

"Are you ready?" Ogras asked as he stopped next to the console. "You'll have to deal with any eventual threat by yourself, you know?"

"I'm fine." Zac nodded as a swirl of emerald leaves surrounded him. "Open it."

Ogras nodded and touched the panel, and he melded with the shadows as the door slid open. A fractal edge had already appeared on [Verun's Bite], but Zac could quickly breathe out in relief, as there was nothing on the other side. Ogras soon reappeared from Zac's shadow as well, though his eyes were fixed on the corridor outside, confusion evident in his eyes.

Zac was just as baffled, as the scenery definitely didn't match what he had pictured in his mind. Ogras had described the dilapidated state of the inner sectors in great detail for his report, but everything seemed to look the same as in their own private area. The hallway was devoid of life or activity, but it was clean and without damage. The fractals that ran along the wall shone with bright luster, and there was no dried blood to talk about.

"How is this possible?" Ogras muttered from behind Zac as he looked around in confusion.

Zac wouldn't immediately trust his eyes, and he carefully entered the inner sector, readying himself in case what they saw was an illusion. But if it was one, then it had to be a damn good one, as Zac couldn't feel anything amiss.

"Is the layout the same as before?" Zac asked after some thought.

"It should be." Ogras nodded after looking back and forth for some time. "The missing pieces have been replaced, but the general layout is the same."

Zac nodded in relief. He was afraid for a second that the Mystic Realm was able to move its corridors to rearrange its layout. That would have made it almost impossible to map the place out, and any progress would be random.

"I guess it's the arrays?" Zac ventured. "The walls slowly heal themselves, so there are probably even more maintenance functions. There might be repair puppets or machines running around and replacing broken things or something. Pretty convenient for the natives if the materials they scavenge actually get replaced somehow."

"That might explain why our sector is untouched," Ogras muttered. "No point in breaking past this door if they can keep mining their old tunnels. Perhaps they have already broken through to our place before, only to find the same empty corridors and barracks as us."

"Or they've already taken everything of value," Zac noted with a grimace. "We passed a lot of empty rooms back there."

"The simplest way to find out what's going on is by catching another native. The last one I took hostage actually went and died before I got a hold of anything interesting," Ogras spat as he looked around.

Zac nodded in agreement. It was a shame how things had panned out with Ogras' captive. He had only managed to confirm that the beastkin truly was a real-life werewolf and that they were of rival factions. A short time later, the human had shuddered and died, likely from suicide so as not to divulge any critical information. Perhaps he was afraid of leading a new unknown force to his faction's gates.

"So, where do you want to go?" the demon asked.

"Let's head in the direction where you saw those two fighting. Perhaps we can find some clues where the natives stay," Zac said after some thought. "No point in looking for the core areas at this stage."

"It's this way... I think," Ogras said as he led the way.

It was quite a distance between the door and the scene of the battle, and Zac only got increasingly baffled as they walked. He just couldn't make sense of the mental map of the compound. He understood that the Technocrats might not have the same sort of budgetary constraints as earthlings did, needing to make the most out of every square meter, but the winding pathways felt extremely suboptimized. It almost felt like this place was built just for the sake of it, and that it didn't really fill any objective.

"What do you think the purpose of these endless hallways is?" Zac finally asked after a while. "It would be one thing if there were a bunch of laboratories or office space, but the rooms we've looked into are just empty storerooms. Most of the space between these corridors doesn't even seem accessible."

"I guess millions worked in this place if this really was a research base," Ogras slowly said. "That is the same as a decent-sized clan. Any organization of that size would need a vast number of supportive functions. Perhaps this area is some sort of ancillary area, and arrays that run this place are hidden within the walls. These corridors might just be for Array Masters to make their way between the arrays."

"So service corridors." Zac nodded in agreement. "That might be it."

"It's also possible it's intentional," Ogras mused. "That these pathways form some sort of array themselves. Just think of those lines in the sky over the fields. They are not random, but rather form some sort of pattern."

"An array as large as a small country," Zac muttered. "It should be extremely powerful."

"We can't guess what's in the mind of some Technocrats," Ogras spat. "They're all insane. No offense."

Zac snorted, but he kept mapping the surroundings in his mind. It was a shame that the magical map that the Zhix owned couldn't be transferred over here, as it would have been a huge help. He had already checked his [**Automatic Map**] as well, but it didn't possess an indoor function. There was just one dot on the parchment, which called the base [**SGR-03**].

He guessed it was the abbreviation for the base, but he didn't know if it was the name given by Leandra's force or something decided by the force who took over after the Technocrats left.

"So, while we're on the subject, care to explain how the token from your mom could turn you into a council inspector?" Ogras said as he threw Zac a sideways glance.

"I don't know." Zac shrugged, and it was the truth. "I only found out about the credentials inside the Tower of Eternity. I didn't lie about that. Personally, I don't think it's real. I think it's something she prepared as some sort of Technocrat Array Breaker, something that would allow her to go where she pleased without divulging her real identity."

"You know what that means, right?" Ogras said with a calculating look. "You would have to be a real big shot to accomplish something like that. I can't imagine what kind of person would be able to create something that could bypass all the defenses of the Azh'Kir'Khat Horde. We would have been killed long ago by the Beast Master or some other enemy if it was that easy."

"Well, I'm still trying to figure out the truth as well. I'm hoping we'll be able to find more inside this place."

"You… don't think she's here, right?" Ogras hesitated, a flash of fear appearing in his eyes. "That could prove deadly."

"What are you worried about?" Zac snorted. "If she really is a big shot, she wouldn't be bothered with some E-grade people."

"Maybe she won't be happy about cultivators hanging around her Technocrat children and decides to purge us all," Ogras muttered.

"Well, I'm pretty sure she isn't here," Zac eventually said. "I'm almost positive she left Earth to heal and avoid pursuit."

"That would be for the best," Ogras muttered as he kept leading Zac down the hallways.

Ogras had no trouble remembering the path, provided that the sector truly hadn't changed, and it wasn't that far either, according to the demon. Zac suddenly felt a sharp spike of danger after they had walked for ten minutes. He immediately drew his weapon as he jumped back, not forgetting to drag the weakened demon along as well.

"What's going on?" the demon asked with confusion as he looked around for any threats. "I didn't sense anything."

"I suddenly felt a pang of danger," Zac said with a bit of confusion, as the surroundings were still the same sterile walls of metal.

"Well, go forward and test things out," Ogras said after a brief pause.

"You're really taking advantage of your wounds right now," Zac muttered, but he still went along with the arrangement.

"Well, it should work like this even if I were back in top condition. If I get hit by something in here, I might die, whereas you will get a flesh wound that might hurt for a couple of hours," Ogras said with an uncaring shrug. "If there's a trap, it's better you fall in it than me."

"Well, whatever," Zac snorted as he transformed [Love's Bond] to its shield form.

He also activated both [Nature's Barrier] and [Hatchetman's Spirit], the latter mostly to gain a better sense of the surroundings. However, nothing much changed. It was still an empty corridor in the middle of nowhere. Just what was it that made his mind scream of danger?

However, he only needed to take ten steps forward to find the answer.

The previously innocent-looking corridor transformed in an instant, and Zac found himself on a collision course with a spatial tear. There wasn't even any time for him to retreat, and his eyes looked on with horror as his coffin-shield hit the tear head-on. This was something he had been deadly afraid would happen, that his Spirit Tool, or rather Alea, would be damaged by something that it couldn't block.

However, the spatial tear didn't actually cut the thick black lid apart like it would with almost everything else. The coffin somehow managed to push back at it, destabilizing it enough to disappear. The clash did leave a mark on the lid, but something like that would heal by itself quickly enough, just like the chains that had cracked during his fight with Void's Disciple.

The scene was a huge source of relief, as not only were spatial tears one of the few things that could still cut him apart if he wasn't careful, but it was also something that Void's Disciple used when fighting. Seeing that [Love's Bond] was this durable gave him a lot more confidence for their next fight.

Seeing how limited the damage was essentially meant he could push his way out of the trap, but he didn't leave just yet. He instead swapped over to his Draugr form, and the fractal shield of

[Immutable Bulwark] infused with the Fragment of the Coffin appeared in front of the lid.

The mainstay defensive skill of his undead side was, unfortunately, suffering from the same fate as [Chop], where the skill couldn't quite keep up with his recent growth. The strength of the shield was based on the quality of his shield and his Endurance, but the increase in its durability had clearly not been linear lately. He would have to upgrade it to an E-grade skill for it to maintain its usefulness going forward.

However, while the skill wasn't able to completely block the spatial tears that came close, it did still manage to weaken them before they slammed into [Love's Bond]. It lessened the strain on his physical shield significantly, and Zac only needed to keep infusing more Miasma and Mental Energy into the skill to restore it.

Zac took one step after another as the buzzing sounds of void tears disintegrating echoed through the hallways. However, he didn't move back toward Ogras, but he kept going straight ahead.

A hidden spatial minefield had for some reason appeared to block their path, and Zac wanted to see if he could push through. Perhaps the anomaly only lasted for a few meters, allowing people to skip through if they were careful and skilled enough. Conversely, the whole area in this direction might be compromised, which would be valuable intelligence as well.

Zac didn't get far before new tears appeared out of nowhere, almost doubling the density of threats around him. Zac knew he was approaching his limits, as new cracks were forming almost as quickly on his shield as they healed up again. He kept pushing forward until there finally was a change to his surroundings.

A red barrier suddenly appeared five meters ahead, and Zac's eyes widened in recognition. It looked a lot like the barrier that Jeeves had conjured when he first met Kenzie in the border town. However, it was almost as though it was infected, with tinges of some unknown energy floating about within the shield. And it was from these corruptions that spatial tears kept spewing out one after another.

Some of the tears stayed put and hovered in front of the barrier, while others drifted about, some even disappearing out of sight. Zac's danger sense told him that they didn't actually disappear, but rather that they turned invisible somehow. Just as Zac noticed the barrier, it was as though the barrier noticed Zac. A spatial storm rippled out from the corruptions, pushing the previously static spatial tears in the tunnel toward him while simultaneously spewing out an endless number of new ones.

This time, there was no hesitation as Zac fled for his life, not even trying to break that barrier. He would be long dead before his attack landed. He spotted the demon in the distance, looking in his direction with a slight frown, but his face suddenly turned into a mask of terror as Zac closed in on him.

"Lunatic! Did you cause a crack in this dimension?!" Ogras shrieked in horror as he started running, but he only got a few steps before he was wrapped up by a chain as Zac flashed past him like some sort of nightmare spider.

There was no way for Zac to return to his human form without getting ripped apart by the spatial storm, so he had to use the chains of **[Love's Bond]** to drag himself and Ogras away. He tried to hamper the progress of the rapidly approaching storm by erecting one fractal bulwark after another, but they were cut apart without slowing the tears by more than a second.

"What's wrong with this place?!" Ogras screamed, tightly wrapped by a chain, and Zac wholeheartedly agreed.

It was one hell of a place his ancestors had built.

62

THE WORLD IS ENDING

The chains of [**Love's Bond**] slammed into the walls and floor of the research base with tremendous force, but they still barely managed to dig deep enough for Zac to propel himself forward. A swirling storm of spatial rifts was right on his tail, like a maw of a terrifying beast. If they caught up, they'd both be ripped apart in an instant.

"Left!" Ogras suddenly shouted, and Zac wordlessly changed course.

However, both Zac and Ogras couldn't believe what they were seeing when the spatial tears actually turned to continue the pursuit, though many of them didn't manage to pivot in time. There was no time for Zac to figure out why some dimensional rifts were seemingly alive, but the scene did give him an idea of what to do.

Zac kept turning back and forth in the endless tunnels, though he was careful not to stray too far from the pathway they came from. Each turn, they managed to shake off another group of tears until there only were a handful left. A small group was manageable, so Zac stopped in his tracks and let Ogras down before he changed [**Love's Bond**] to its shield form.

A second later, another group of scars covered the coffin's lid, but there was at least no threat any longer. They'd managed to escape unscathed, but a sheen of perspiration covered Zac's forehead as he looked at the demon.

"Since when did spatial tears get tracking capabilities?" he muttered, and Ogras snorted as he threw Zac a scathing look.

"What did you do back there? Everything was fine, then all hell broke loose," the demon said. "By the way, you'd better never use that movement technique in public. I'm not sure I'd be able to survive the secondhand shame."

"It's not stupid if it works," Zac muttered. "Did you find any clues to what was going on?"

"I suddenly saw you disappear into thin air, not even leaving a hint of energy behind. Thirty seconds later, a bunch of spatial tears appeared before you reappeared, looking like there were a dozen Rakefiends hot in pursuit," the demon said.

Zac was surprised to hear that he had disappeared from the demon's sight, just like some of the spatial tears seemingly appeared out of nowhere. It looked like the hallways were equipped with Technocrat cloaking technology just like what he'd encountered by the Battleroach King. That technology didn't release any energy either, at least not anything he could spot.

He still didn't know what to make of the encounter, so he told Ogras everything he'd seen in the booby-trapped corridor. Of course, he didn't mention that Kenzie, or rather Jeeves, could create shields that looked a lot like the one he saw. He instead likened it to the orange shields that the Technocrat incursion had used. Ogras frowned as he listened, but he didn't immediately offer an opinion.

"What do you think?" Zac finally asked. "Did you really pass through this way before?"

"I have never heard of something like this. But it sounds like something suddenly took control of those rifts if they originally were almost static as you said. My guess is that it's a security feature. Did you notice? Not one of the tears hit the walls. They either turned to follow us or gave up to avoid a collision," Ogras explained.

"It seems like a really weird security measure, though," Zac muttered. "It almost looked like the spatial tears seeped out of the Technocrat barrier like it was part of their energy source. Why make things so complicated instead of just adding some normal energy weaponry?"

"Perhaps it's not how things were originally designed." Ogras shrugged. "A powerful dimensional treasure is growing somewhere in the base. I've heard that grand treasures can affect whole planets. Perhaps spatial energies have somehow infiltrated whatever this place runs on."

Zac nodded in agreement. He remembered the vision of the cursed lotus in the Tower of Eternity all too well. A whole planet went insane with bloodlust because of its existence, and who knew what would have happened if that giant hadn't sealed it before it was too late. The implications were clear if this really was the case.

"If the treasure is powerful enough to cause something like this before it's even born, then just how powerful is it? It might even be greater than D-grade. The treasures I've found so far on Earth didn't have such a shocking effect on their surroundings at all."

"Well, the Tree of Ascension and that mushroom you found are not even true D-grade treasures. But I agree. Something like this should be Peak D-grade at a minimum. No wonder the cultists discarded everything for a chance at this treasure. It is likely worth more than your whole planet," Ogras said, the familiar tint of greed shining in his eyes.

"It's still odd that the tears only seem to be sporadically active," Zac muttered. "Unless the situation when you arrived the first time was out of the norm."

"Perhaps it was," Ogras ventured. "The blood and destruction wasn't fresh, but it wasn't too old either. Perhaps the defenses suddenly failed, allowing the natives to push further away from their bases than usual. Then the security measures recovered, and this sector became inaccessible again. We might be locked out of the rest of the base."

"But if that's the case, how will we ever be able to reach the core? If I can't survive pushing through in my Draugr form, I don't think any of us will," Zac said with a frown.

"If the defenses have been down once, then it might happen again. Or perhaps the spatial turbulence here is a result of the artifact awakening, and is completely random," Ogras ventured.

Zac nodded before he turned toward the way they came from.

"What are you doing?" Ogras asked with confusion as he followed in tow. "Ready for round two?"

"No," Zac said with a shake of his head. "But I want to see if the rifts are still there."

The chains of [**Love's Bond**] had moved them quite a distance in the minutes they'd fled, but they were soon back to the position where they'd stopped the last time. There wasn't a single spatial tear in sight the whole way, and everything looked exactly the same as before with not even a hint of a spatial storm having swept the hallways just a few minutes ago.

However, Zac still felt the same sense of palpitations from his danger sense from the area ahead of them, meaning that the tears no doubt still hid behind some sort of cloaking. He shot a second glance at the corridor just to make sure, but [**Cosmic Gaze**] still couldn't spot anything. Taking six steps forward took him to the outer layer of the spatial tears, and his vision lit up from the powerful energies they contained.

It really was the same sort of cloaking technology.

Zac eventually stepped back and placed a boulder to the side of the corridor at a safe distance from the trap before he left a communication crystal warning of the dangers ahead on top of it. He didn't know if it would be cleansed just like everything else, but it was worth trying out.

"And there really was nothing like this the last time?" Zac asked as he turned back to Ogras.

"No way; you think I'd forget to mention something like this in my report?" Ogras said with a roll of his eyes. "I wasn't attacked a single time while I entered here, not counting the werewolf."

"It's a bit weird we're being attacked at all," Zac muttered. "I have a Tier-4 clearance of a Council Inspector. It should be enough for me to not get attacked just for walking down an empty corridor. There were no warnings or anything."

"There might have been warnings," Ogras interjected. "Just that we don't have the equipment to hear it. So what do we do now?"

"Well, there's no lack of corridors," Zac eventually said. "Let's see if we can find an alternative route to the scene of the battle."

The demon nodded in agreement before he led Zac down another way. However, reaching their destination was quickly proving easier said than done, and they were forced to reroute by the very same type of spatial barriers as before another twenty-six times before Ogras finally declared they had arrived.

Altogether they had walked almost five times the distance as the direct route, and even Zac was starting to become a bit confused by this seemingly endless labyrinth. But coming here was definitely worth it since they had finally encountered something different. They weren't surprised that the bodies of the two fallen warriors were gone, but they didn't expect to see that something else was left in their stead.

A large steel board had been placed in the middle of the corridor, and two lines of words were written in an eye-catching red. The letters were penned in the general script of the Multiverse, which Zac had mostly mastered by this point.

We are Clan Cartava, we mean no harm.

The world is ending – Free us and gain an ally for life.

Beneath the words was an extremely intricate map that highlighted a certain path. It was a bit hard to judge, but it looked like it would take them up to half a day to follow the path indicated. As to where it led, the board didn't say.

"A bit bombastic message," Zac muttered before he thought of something. "Do you think it's true? Will the birth of the treasure actually destroy the Mystic Realm?"

"I doubt it," Ogras said, though not without hesitation. "The zealots are crazy, but they are not idiots. They wouldn't be so willing to move into this place if the treasure would blow up the whole Mystic Realm. Those guys clearly know what that thing is, and if it would break this place, they would find some other way to snatch it. It's easy to forget because of their antics, but that bunch of lunatics belongs to a proper B-grade force that spreads far beyond this sector."

"So they're lying?" Zac nodded at the signpost.

"They are either lying or they simply don't understand what's going on. We couldn't find out what a Dimensional Seed was even on the outside, so how can these people know? I'm more interested in the second line. 'Free us and gain an ally for life'? I guess that means the implicit meaning is 'Hinder us and gain an enemy for life'?"

"I feel they're trying to make first contact without divulging too much about themselves to either us or any other faction that might discover this thing. How did they know to leave this message here? It's clearly meant for us, or perhaps any outsiders, rather than some other native faction. Did you leave a note as well?" Zac asked.

"No, I tried to make it look like the two killed each other. I didn't want my presence to be known at all. Otherwise, I would have snatched the bodies for further study," Ogras said with a shake of his head. "I must have slipped up, or they have some means that could see through my actions. What do you want to do? Follow the map?"

"Not right now," Zac eventually said. "It will take us almost straight east for a huge distance. I'd rather get a better understanding of what we're dealing with before I head that far from our base."

A compass didn't work in this place, so directions were obviously a bit unclear here. However, they had a rough sketch of the Mystic Realm thanks to Julia's and Thea's efforts, and it looked a bit like a crude drawing of a sun or a star, where their secured area was located in one of the outer spikes.

The whole core section of the Mystic Realm formed a shockingly large circle, and the map essentially detailed a path that kept to a small part of the outer rim. The indicated path did have a huge amount of backtracking and twists and turns as well, making Zac believe that it took the spatial rifts into consideration.

They had already encountered a large number of barriers in their preliminary exploration, and it wasn't too out of field that there would be a lot more of them peppered throughout this place. This map might actually allow them to head over to the other camp while avoiding those spatial tears altogether.

"How is this thing still here?" Ogras suddenly muttered, making Zac start and look away from the map.

"What?" Zac asked with confusion.

"All debris has been removed; even bloodstains are scrubbed clean. Why is this thing left untouched?"

"It's made of metal that looks a lot like the walls," Zac slowly said. "Perhaps the cleaning arrays or whatever don't touch it because of that?"

"Perhaps," Ogras muttered as he tried to lift the foot that the sign was attached to, but both were surprised to see that Ogras couldn't budge it.

"Let me try," Zac said and gripped the signboard, and veins started appearing across his forehead as he strained to dislodge the thing from the ground.

A snap finally echoed through the corridor as the sign gave way, and Zac was thrown backward from the accumulated force.

"What kind of superglue was that?" Zac muttered as he rubbed the back of his head.

"Not glue," Ogras muttered as he pointed at the base of the sign. "Look."

63

BACKUP PLANS

Zac curiously looked where the demon pointed, and he realized that there were three thin spikes, each of them no more than five centimeters long, at the bottom of the sign. Just like the rest of the signpost, they seemed to be made from the very same material as the walls, though the spikes had intricate engravings covering their surface.

His eyes moved to the spot where the sign stood earlier, and he saw that three matching holes could be seen in the floor. However, the cavities were rapidly closing, and just a few seconds later, they were gone. It would have been impossible to know that something had been socketed there just a moment ago if they hadn't seen it themselves.

"Weird," Zac muttered, and he stabbed the sign down into the ground to see whether it would get stuck again.

A pinging sound echoed through the corridor, and three light marks on the floor were the only results of his attempt. Not even forcibly pushing it into the ground did any good, and neither did instilling the board with his Dao or Cosmic Energy.

"We're clearly missing something," Ogras eventually said after having watched Zac's failed attempts for half a minute.

Zac nodded in agreement and stowed away the sign, hoping that his sister or the scientists would be able to figure out what was going on with the help of that thing.

"You really don't want to follow the map?" Ogras asked.

"We've done what we came for," Zac said with a shake of his head after some thought. "Let's return."

The two started making their way back while simultaneously searching for other points of interest, but there was really not much going on. There were just more corridors and storage rooms, all of which were empty apart from the occasional crate full of worthless materials.

They also made a slight detour to see whether Zac's own leave-behind had survived like the signpost, but neither of them was really surprised to see that both boulder and communication crystal were gone. It wasn't a disappointment, as it cleared some things up for Zac. There really were secret rules that governed this place, as evidenced by the natives' ability to manipulate the floor and sign like that.

Was this perhaps the true message this Cartava Clan wanted to convey?

The message was short, but it had exposed a lot. First of all, Clan Cartava knew of their existence somehow. Secondly, they showed that the previously thought impervious metal was somehow possible to influence to great lengths. The map might lead to a third clue as well. All in all, it proved the value of the clan, and Zac leaned toward following the map as soon as possible.

They soon reached the security door leading to their area, and Zac used his credentials just to test that his unique title worked as well as the caretaker credentials. From there, they didn't immediately return to the settlement, as there was something Zac wanted to try first. They walked into one of the empty warehouses, and Zac took out **[Verun's Bite]**.

Ogras had already reported how sturdy the alloys the base was made from were, and seeing what had happened with the signpost had piqued Zac's interest even further. He wanted to cut off a piece and bring it back for further study.

Zac walked over to a wall and swung his axe in a precise arc, but he only ended up with a slight pain in his wrist, as the wall didn't budge at all. He frowned and infused the axe with the Fragment of the Axe, and his weapon finally cut into the wall without too much resistance. It reminded him of the early days of the integration, when he'd barely managed to cut into the extraordinarily hard walls of his Nexus Crystal mine.

Worse yet, the wall quickly healed itself the moment Zac prepared to swing again. A minute of furious swings later, he had managed to cut out a slab of metal that was as big as his fist, and it actually weighed over a hundred kilograms from the feel of it.

Ogras walked over curiously to take a look at the sample, but neither of them could make heads or tails of the situation. The alloy had definitely changed properties after Zac managed to cut it out, but not as they expected. He had almost thought that it would turn liquid from what they had seen, but it had only turned... worse.

It was definitely a solid like before, but Zac had no problem remolding it with his hands. It suddenly felt like it was barely as hard as gold, let alone steel. It was a far cry from the walls or the signpost, which seemed to be extraordinarily sturdy as well. However, they didn't have the opportunity to play around for long before Zac's senses prickled as previously unseen scripts appeared across the walls.

Zac had specifically chosen to enter a storeroom to cut out a sample since not one of the warehouses they had visited were booby-trapped with spatial rifts. However, it was quickly becoming clear that not even these side chambers were safe, as the whole room transformed in front of their very eyes. The walls turned into spears that shot toward them, and worse yet, a red barrier appeared across the exit, blocking their escape. A series of spatial tears emerged a second later, all of them heading for Zac.

"Give it back!" Ogras screamed as he dodged the incoming stabs, and Zac could only comply.

He tossed the slab of metal toward the wall where he took it, and they both breathed out in relief when the spears slowed down. However, Zac was still forced to block a series of attacks for half a minute before the room had calmed down again and the barrier disappeared.

"What a stingy building," Ogras muttered as he kicked one of the empty shelves, and Zac nodded as he glared at the walls.

It had billions of tonnes of this alloy, and it couldn't share just a handful of the stuff?

So it was mostly empty-handed that the two returned to the town, though the signpost caused some waves among the core members of the expedition. Some were worried that their activities had already been spotted, and a frantic search for hidden cameras began. The scientists were instead more curious about the spikes and the odd material that seemed to almost be alive.

Their first assessment was that their earlier assumptions were correct. It wasn't the material itself that was magical, it was either the script that covered the walls or some sort of energy that transformed it. Why the natives could build a sign made from the material and maintain its strength while Zac couldn't even harvest a single ingot still eluded them.

Zac left the sign with his sister, hoping that they could figure some things out. As for himself, he didn't head out again. There was no point in him running around in those endless corridors himself. Zac and Ogras had been walking around for hours, but they had only seen a fraction of the immediate area. It was more efficient to send out a hundred scouting units who could work together to map out the place and mark all the traps.

As for himself, he still had multiple things to work on, the most pressing being the intrusive Dao from Void's Disciple and pondering on the Dao.

This was both a way to save time and a way for him to relinquish some control. Zac knew he had a problem with delegating tasks he considered important since seeing Alea fall. He left the nitty-gritty to his people in Port Atwood while doing the rest himself. But his explorations had really driven home just how massive this base was, and the fact that he wouldn't be able to explore it by himself even if he was given months.

Things progressed quickly over the two following days. Kenzie's drone army was a huge help in mapping out the interiors of the base, which allowed the subsequent scouting squads to make rapid progress inside the Mystic Realm. The master map of the corridors was quickly expanded and improved upon without needing Zac to do much of the work himself.

There were a few issues that had quickly cropped up. The drones were unable to move too far in the tunnels, as Kenzie, or rather Jeeves, would lose control over them. This wasn't something unique to the Mystic Realm, but rather that the range of the AI was limited. Kenzie believed that this range would increase by a huge margin if Jeeves evolved, but there was no indication of that happening anytime soon.

Jeeves had only consumed a scant few items from the Technocrat incursion, and Zac doubted an item that magical would be easy to evolve. That was exactly how Zac liked things though, as an overpowered AI was not something he wanted to deal with. It was better if Kenzie focused on her own Strength, in Zac's opinion.

The real issue was the matter of the missing squad.

One hundred scouting units and ten elite squads had set out as soon as a strategy could be devised, and their goal was to find and map out the areas that the drones couldn't reach. The elite units consisted of powerful warriors of all factions, and they were supposed to take the vanguard in case one of the native factions showed up. They were all equipped with a lot of powerful talismans, both offensive and defensive, to the point that they would be able to blow up half a city if need be.

However, one of the ten squads, which included three Valkyries, had simply gone missing. There had been no sounds of struggle, and there were no clues left behind. They had vanished without a trace. Zac himself had set out to search for them, but there was simply nothing to go by, forcing him to return after a few hours.

Zac initially suspected Clan Cartava of kidnapping his people, but after thinking it through, he wasn't so sure. The map they provided seemed to indicate that the clan was located to the east, while the missing scouting unit had rather tried to move northbound in search of a way into the core sections of the base. That might mean that a second force in the area was responsible, or perhaps even some new type of trap.

The spatial barriers that blocked the corridors weren't actually that dangerous unless you forced your way inside as Zac had, so most were inclined to believe foul play was involved. They also had no idea whether Clan Cartava was the werewolves Ogras had encountered or the humans, or perhaps even a third force. In either case, it wouldn't be a surprise if there were both hostile and friendly factions inside the Mystic Realm.

However, the rest of the scouting units were making rapid progress, and the command center was bustling with activity as well.

A massive courtyard was already cordoned off for Zac in the original biosphere, which raised a few brows among the different forces. He already had a huge area for himself on his island, so people started to wonder whether he had turned agoraphobic or something. Of course, the real reason wasn't quite so exciting, though Zac still didn't want it to be known.

His compound needed to be pretty big to house not only his home, but also his Life-Death Array. Kenzie and Triv had dismantled it when they went to his cultivation cave a few days ago, though it only was a temporary measure until Kenzie was able to create an Array Disk able to match the death-attuned one in his possession.

Zac wasn't willing to let up on his soul cultivation, and who knew how long this place would be locked down when the Dimensional Seed awakened. This had become especially important after realizing that the array also kept his soul in check. Thankfully, he only caused some murmurs with his set of concealment and isolation arrays, and there was no lack of open space around.

In fact, people had already spread out across all the biospheres within the outer section they controlled. It allowed the various forces to keep to themselves a bit, and it was also necessary to deal with the limited amount of Cosmic Energy.

A surprising issue had cropped up while Zac and Ogras were off exploring. More and more people arrived in the Mystic Realm, and the supply of Cosmic Energy soon couldn't meet the demand. Thankfully, this issue was solved the moment they split up.

The tunnel to the real world also held steady, and according to Kenzie, it should definitely stay that way for at least another week, which incidentally was the deadline of the New World Government projects. It was Jeeves' opinion, based on data it extrapolated from analyzing the array that kept the pathway open. The cost of keeping it running kept increasing as the turbulence from the Mystic Realm's side slowly grew worse, and it believed the spatial chaos would reach a breaking point in around seven to twelve days.

After that point, the turbulence would be too strong for the natural pathway to remain open. The array Kenzie set up would be rendered useless, and the portal would naturally close. Zac was pretty impressed that AI had managed to extrapolate such critical information just from an array, but he was perhaps even more impressed that the New World Government seemed to have figured the same thing out somehow.

It was a valuable reminder that even a weak force like the New World Government had a lot of talents that he didn't even know about. A lot of the top scientists of the old world were probably part of the government as well, along with any next-gen technology that the governments had controlled before the integration. That might be what had allowed them to make such detailed plans for the Mystic Realm.

With things being a lot clearer, Zac finally decided to take the risk and go ahead with his backup plan. He had spent ten days in recuperation by now, and he was in peak condition apart from some remnant Dao that he still hadn't managed to completely rout. However, he sorely needed more tools to deal with Void's Disciple, along with the High E-grade elders who were apparently waiting for him.

He needed to break open the next floor of his Dao Repository.

64
FLAMES

Zac normally wouldn't have done something so risky as to challenge a Half-Step D-grade Golem, but he was running out of options. He had ambushed Void's Disciple with the strongest people he could muster, but he'd still walked away almost scot-free. Certainly, he had seemed to have been slightly worse for wear in the security feed, but their group was in a far worse condition.

He needed another power-up.

That was his greatest takeaway from the battle, and that feeling had only increased since arriving at the Mystic Realm. The influence that the Dao of Space had over this whole base was far greater than he had expected, and who knew whether that would bring Adcarkas even more advantages.

He had tried to come up with other ideas over the past ten days, but this was the only thing with a decent chance of success. His first hope had been to quickly find some way to awaken his bloodline; they hadn't found a single useful thing inside so far. There were a lot of signs pointing toward this being a bloodline research base, but the useful stuff might all be locked in the center of the research base. Furthermore, the portal would close in a couple of days, so it was now or never.

It didn't look like his Hidden Node was gearing up to provide him with pure Dao distilled from Tribulation Lightning either, so he would have to risk his life for power once more. If he could gain access to the E-grade skills, he would gain a large boost in power, and the same went for Ogras and the elite demons who had already evolved as well.

Besides, Zac wasn't doing anything he didn't have a certain confidence in succeeding at. Zac believed that he had found a path to victory, or at least a way to survive the attempt.

It became possible only when combining a few things that had changed over the past weeks. First of all was the discovery that [Blighted Cut] worked just as well on inanimate objects as it did on living beings. Even rocks would rot and lose their structural integrity when hit by the E-grade skill of his undead class.

Zac had also confirmed the same thing on the guarding puppets he got for closing the incursions. It was the most similar target to the trial of the Dao Repository, and his undead skill set was extremely efficient in taking them out. Even the captains were helpless against the combination of his extreme durability and high lethality.

Secondly, it was the fact that Triv had already confirmed that the [Rageroot Oak Seed] would work on his undead form. He had been worried before that he would encounter the same issue as with the Race-improving herbs. Luckily, there were surprisingly almost no life-attuned energies inside the seed, just a fiery power that would work even on the unliving.

Finally, he had visited Brazla five times over the past week, each time finagling a little bit of information about the trial, as he mainly focused on finding out about the Dimensional Seed. The takeaway was that berserking items such as the seed were allowed in the trial, whereas powerful arrays or talismans were not. The logic was that surviving using a powerful Berserker Treasure could be considered a strength of your own, and a unique perk of cultivators with high Vitality.

This meant that he could use his Draugr class, push it to the equivalent of Middle E-grade with the seed, and restrict and grind down the trial golem while staying safe with the toolkit of his Fetters of Desolation class. Zac quickly turned thoughts to action as he snuck back through the spatial tunnel, with only the guarding Valkyries knowing he had left the Mystic Realm.

Zac wasted no time back on Earth either, and he teleported back to his compound. Everything pointed to him having almost a week, but he still felt the risk of getting locked outside. He had already decided that he would stay in Port Atwood at most for an hour or two, even if he had to drag himself back to the Mystic Realm while half-dead.

"Oh? I thought you had left. I was looking forward to some peace and quiet," Brazla snorted as Zac entered the repository, but Zac still inwardly breathed out in relief when he saw that the Tool Spirit seemed to have one of his more amiable personalities today.

"I want to undergo the trial to unlock the E-grade skills," Zac said as **[Verun's Bite]** appeared in his hands.

"So you think you're infallible now that you've spent some time among the weaklings," Brazla said with disdain. "Well, no matter. It makes no difference to the Great Sage whether you live or die."

Brazla lazily waved the arms of his golden robes next, and a portal appeared in the middle of the hallway.

"Just step inside, and you'll be taken to the trial ground," Brazla said with disinterest.

Zac nodded, but he didn't immediately enter. He instead swapped over to his undead class while **[Love's Bond]** transformed into its shield form. Zac didn't stop there either, but he also activated **[Vanguard of Undeath]** along with **[Immutable Bulwark]**. This would be a trial conducted by Brazla himself, and Zac wouldn't take any chances. He might not get the opportunity to transform on the other side.

"So cautious," Brazla snorted, but Zac only ignored him as he stepped up to the teleporter.

"Any last-minute advice?" Zac asked.

"The faster you fail, the quicker I can return to my rest," Brazla said after some thought. "So don't dally."

"Great." Zac sighed as he stepped onto the teleporter.

The teleportation was immediate, but Zac didn't even have an opportunity to take stock of his surroundings before a stream of lava the thickness of his thighs almost hit his head. He barely had time to move his shield in time, but he was still pushed back over ten meters from the incredible force of the molten rock. If that wasn't enough,

Zac also was assailed by a terrifying heat until he finally managed to divert the stream in its entirety. He could feel a stinging sensation on his face, and he audibly groaned when he knew that he had become a monk once more.

However, he was still more concerned about the stream of molten rock, as it wasn't simple lava like the lava in the Underworld. This lava contained a fierce spirituality, and Zac actually guessed that it could be considered a powerful E-grade material. That fact alone made him gawk as he took stock of his surroundings. It was a huge sea of lava, with the only solid ground being the small island he was standing on.

Far in the distance, rocky walls could barely be discerned through the smoke rising from the fiery lake, and they reached toward the sky in all directions until he could spot a circle of red sky straight above him. It didn't take a genius to figure out that he had appeared inside a volcano, and a high-grade one at that.

Thankfully, Brazla had seen fit to let him out on the only safe spot, a circular plateau that rose a few meters above the sea of lava and spanned around five hundred meters across. It didn't seem to be a natural formation, as it was perfectly circular and flat. Even its surface consisted of beautiful tiles, each of them with a unique image engraved.

The platform was mostly empty apart from what looked like an enormous anvil placed in the middle. Next to it was what looked to be a small pool of lava no more than ten meters across. Zac guessed that it was connected to the massive lake, but he couldn't be certain, as the intense attuned energies that rose from that pond almost blinded him when using [Cosmic Gaze].

There were also several boulders studded across its surface along with a dozen slabs of unknown metals stacked to the side. The raw materials looked different from each other, but it was clear that all of them could withstand the intense heat without a problem, meaning they likely were spiritual metals.

At least Zac guessed anything that could survive in this harsh environment to be a valuable material.

Zac couldn't be certain, but it felt as though the sea of lava was at least a dozen miles across, which meant this monstrosity of a volcano completely dwarfed both the volcano in the underworld and the one that the Church of Everlasting Dao had controlled. It almost beggared comprehension how much lava would be required to fill it up.

There was one break in the lava right behind him, a single pathway leading across the whole ocean into a tunnel on the other side of the wall. But it was precariously narrow, just two meters across, and it was constantly being blasted by waves of magma or gouts of flames.

His first instinct was that his trial would take place on the other side, and Zac couldn't help but feel he had bitten off more than he could chew by taking on this trial. He wasn't confident in making it across that narrow bridge even when using his sturdier class. The power in that sea of lava was just too intense.

However, a voice soon dragged him out of his musings.

"This was my creator's smithy. Or, well, one of them," a grating voice echoed out, and Zac looked up to see Brazla floating in the air.

The Tool Spirit had changed getups since entering the trial ground, and he was currently gripping a grotesquely large hammer, its massive bulk even overshadowing Billy's club. It was golden just like everything else Brazla used, but this weapon actually had a palpable aura in contrast to the other weapons the Tool Spirit often conjured. A thought suddenly struck Zac, and he looked at the Tool Spirit with suspicion.

Was the guardian actually Brazla himself?

"A Celestial Craftsman such as Brazla wouldn't deign to lower himself to muck around in the mud with some child," Brazla snorted with disdain, clearly understanding what Zac was thinking. "Your opponent is over there. The Great Sage is only here to be amused."

Zac nodded in understanding as he turned in the direction the Tool Spirit was pointing.

A ten-meter rock was lying on the other side of the stone plateau, looking just like the other boulders that studded its surface. Zac had initially thought that those pieces of rubble were things that had been spit out by the lava and accidentally fallen onto the plateau, but the truth didn't seem so simple. Just as Zac looked over, a startling change took place as the rock itself exploded, causing the whole area to be shrouded in dust.

"Have fun." The Tool Spirit laughed as he floated higher in the air.

Zac wanted to swear at the cavalier attitude of Brazla, but he knew better than that. It was better to direct his ire toward the guardian than the Tool Spirit, as there was no telling what Brazla would do if he got annoyed. Zac couldn't see what was going on inside the dust cloud, but his [Cosmic Gaze] noticed that vast amounts of attuned energies radiated from its center.

Something illuminated the cloud in gray and a fiery orange, and Zac recognized both the Daos: Fire and Steel. Zac frowned when he felt the intense spiritual fluctuations, as they almost rivaled his own Dao Field. He had somewhat hoped that the trial guardian would be more like the Cyborg in the Underworld. It had possessed shockingly high attributes, but it didn't utilize the Dao at all, severely limiting the damage it did.

If the Cyborg had also been able to use a Peak seed rather than just its body, then Zac definitely wouldn't have survived the encounter.

However, he was clearly not as lucky this time around. An explosion erupted from within the cloud once more, and the blast forced Zac back a few steps. He quickly swallowed the [Rageroot Oak Seed], decidedly going all out from the start. His instincts told him that undergoing this trial without it would be nigh suicidal.

It was as though Zac swallowed the molten ocean itself as a shocking force spread through his limbs. It felt like every cell in his body suddenly had a heartbeat of its own, and all of them were beating like the drums of war. Even his soul had ballooned up to unprecedented proportions, and Zac almost believed he was the Heavens themselves for a moment before he found his bearings.

However, he couldn't sit still and wait to see what was going on in that ominous dust cloud. A surging momentum was building up in his chest, and it demanded release. A mighty roar escaped from his lips as he bent down toward the ground to rip out one of the intricate tiles. He would start this battle like he often did, with a pre-emptive throw containing all his bloodlust.

The stone refused to budge, and Zac felt a towering fury lambasting his mind, a fury directed at the creator of this place. How dare a mere tile setter subvert the will of a god? His arms shook with exertion, but it was to no avail. But Zac figured it might be for the best as he started running toward the cloud with purpose in his steps and death in his eyes.

After all, was there any better feeling than ripping apart your enemies with your bare hands?

65
ASH AND STEEL

Ash and steel swirled in Zac's eyes as he pushed forward, urged on by the call of battle. His muscles trembled in anticipation, and veins were popping out all across his body to accommodate the overflowing Miasma, and there was even a red haze rising from his very pores. It was no doubt weakness leaving his body, a miracle that the Zhix warriors could only dream of achieving.

The trial no longer mattered. The E-grade skills no longer mattered. The only thing of import was the thrill of the fight, to use this smithy as an opportunity to temper himself in the fires of war. His axe was already salivating corrosive venom across the floor, no doubt anxious to bite into their shrouded enemy.

A third explosion erupted from within the haze, but Zac's anticipation only grew as his arm swelled. His power was already enough to rival the firmament itself, but it wasn't enough. He pushed into the cloud, but he only took two steps before he sharply stepped to the right as his axe fell. The pincer of a metal tong suddenly appeared and barely missed his head, its size enough to grab Zac's whole torso even when he already had turned into his ultimate form that rose over three meters into the air.

Zac only sneered as his bardiche fell toward the exposed hand, his response already planned out. His soul was one with the Dao itself, so how could a paltry sneak attack ever work? However, he screamed in anger when his foe didn't have the decency to lose its hand from the transgression. What should have been a fountain of nurturing blood only turned into a reverberating clang that finally pushed all the dust out of the area, exposing his prey.

And it was big.

The target towered almost three meters above him, but Zac didn't care about the specifics. There were weapons to clash with and limbs to cut; what else was there to know? His first attack had only left a jagged scar on metal and a small festering wound, far from accomplishing his goal. But wasn't that great news? How boring would it be if one swing would have ended the fight? This way, he could keep tempering himself, keep reveling in the glory of slaughter.

The massive slab of a hand swiped out at him after being cut, and Zac laughed as he moved his shield to slam it out of the way. A faint voice whispered in the back of his head about a way to empower its defensive capabilities, but he couldn't abide such cowardice. An intractable force pushed into the core of his being as he was thrown away, and the sweet taste of Miasma appeared in his mouth as he slammed into the ground over thirty meters away.

But Zac had eaten the divine seed, making him invulnerable. He could be kicked down a million times, yet he would rise again to tear down his foes. Not even a second had passed before he was almost back at his target, launching a flurry of strikes aimed to maim and brutalize the big bastard in front of him. The tong kept slamming into him and throwing him away, but Zac was more than happy to go along with the cycle of destruction.

Every time he came back, he could see a few more scars on his enemy while he was just fine. The wounds were like a beautiful piece of art, and Zac an artisan using his axe as a paintbrush. A bit more and a masterpiece would be born. However, the coward in front of him seemed to finally have realized the futility of catching Zac with its tongs.

Zac was the incarnation of war, his technique and movements the peak of perfection. To catch him unaware was as impossible as catching the wind. The miscreant was clearly on its last legs as it reached for something attached to its back, no doubt another feeble attempt to take him out. Zac laughed uproariously as he gathered power in his fist to meet whatever his prey had in store. A punch felt like the right decision here.

Violence would be met with violence, and blood would be repaid with blood.

However, a piercing scream of danger finally managed to cut through the madness, and Zac's eyes widened in horror when he saw what was about to hit him. He barely managed to stop in his tracks and move his shield to block, but there was no time to activate [Immutable Bulwark]. He was also unable to completely dispel his accumulated momentum, so Zac was still caught by the edge of the enormous hammer and thrown to the other edge of the platform like a ragdoll.

His whole body hurt, but the pain was still muted and somehow distant thanks to the fierce killing intent still churning in his chest. However, his danger sense had allowed him to at least regain most of his rationality, though Zac couldn't be sure. He had felt completely lucid just a second ago as well, and that he had everything under control. But only now did he realize that he had acted like a raving lunatic, and worrying wounds covered his whole body.

Zac had severely overestimated his mental fortitude when planning this fight. He'd previously believed himself almost immune to the effects of taking a berserking item thanks to his experience dealing with this kind of affliction before. But it turned out that not even the Splinter of Oblivion had managed to prepare him for the insidious whispers of the [Rageroot Oak Seed].

Thankfully, he wasn't hurt to the point of no return, though it didn't look great. His shield arm was hurting quite a bit, and there were even some cracks in a few bones. He hadn't used his defensive skills at all when he'd fought like a rabid animal, and his body had paid the price. His internal wounds were too numerous to count, and black ichor leaked from the seams of his black armor. He would probably have to use one of his two remaining [Serene Flesh Pills] to quickly recover from this mess.

At least he still felt power coursing through his body, allowing him to fight far above his normal capability. No matter if it was speed or strength, it had nearly increased by 60% as far as he could tell. Besides, Zac wasn't the only one who had taken damage from his insane offensive, and he looked over at his target, who seemed content to maintain its distance.

Only after having woken up from his furor did Zac get a proper look at what he was dealing with. It was indeed a golem, but calling it a robot might be more appropriate going by its appearance. It was a bulky bipedal machine that reminded Zac of a five-meter-tall dwarf. It was roughly the height of the greatest Anointed, but its circumference was a few times wider than even Rhubat's. Its four limbs were short and stocky, with an almost spherical torso that was clad in a steel mesh apron. The apron was mostly in tatters by now, and Zac distinctly remembered having attacked it multiple times already.

Its head was attached straight on its torso without a neck, and in its right hand was an almost picture-perfect copy of the hammer that Brazla had had in his hands earlier. The only difference was that it was wrought from some black metal, and it emitted an extremely heavy aura. The array on its hammer face was a bit different too, and Zac almost got a bit dizzy when tracing the extremely intricate lines. This was the weapon the golem had finally grabbed from its back to deal with him.

The golem still held the same steel tong as before in its left hand, completing the look of a mechanical blacksmith. It looked far more like a proper craftsman when compared to the Creators over at Zac's shipyard. Perhaps it really was one too, an assistant who had helped the original Brazla in his work. That would explain why the hammer emitted such shocking pressure.

Anything that could be used in forging spiritual metals would have to be extremely durable so as not to break apart after a few days of hammering. The golem blacksmith was clearly made from some sort of attuned materials, making it exude an aura akin to Zac's own Dao Field. It wasn't quite at the same level, but it spoke volumes about the quality of the materials the golem was crafted with.

This was just further proven by his series of frenzied attacks earlier. Zac had maintained some sort of rationality earlier, or perhaps it would be fairer to call it a beast's instincts. He had primarily focused on cutting off the golem's limbs, and over a dozen strikes empowered by **[Blighted Cut]** and sometimes also **[Unholy Strike]** had reached their mark before he was thrown away. However, the golem clearly had its limbs, and they seemed to be in working order.

That wasn't to say that his efforts were completely ineffective. The colors of the metals around the axe scars were decidedly darker than the rest of its body, meaning that Zac had laid the foundation for victory. He was clear on how powerful his new E-grade skill was, and not even spiritual metals would be able to resist forever.

The golem might even have some problems, judging by the fact that it didn't move toward him. It just stood in the distance and stared at him. Zac needed to keep working on it, and it would sooner or later lose its limbs. However, now that he was awake, he would hopefully be able to do so without directly trading blows. After all, his body was sturdy, but not as sturdy as spiritual metals.

Zac really wanted to just sit down and rest up a bit first, but he forcibly pushed those ideas to the back of his mind. The timer had started the moment that he swallowed the berserking seed, and he had no idea how long it would retain its effect. He had turned a bit insane there for a moment, but its potency couldn't be denied.

Its boosting effect was far beyond what **[Hatchetman's Rage]** provided, a qualitative boost that pushed every aspect of his power to the next tier. Zac knew there was no way for him to break through this golem's defenses without it, especially not if he was suddenly forced to deal with a weakened state.

Calrin's book only described the general properties of the Rageroot Oak and its seeds, but it didn't provide any details. He didn't know exactly how bad the drawbacks were, and when they would kick in. He only knew that it would last longer than a skill, fifteen minutes at the minimum. That left ample time, but Zac was afraid that he would slide back into his delusions of being a god of war without notice. He needed to quickly finish this so that he could eat a soul-nurturing pill to calm down a bit.

Besides, the golem had finally started moving when it realized that Zac wasn't rushing back toward it, and it was already lumbering toward him.

Its step was slow and deliberate, and its weight caused tremors in the ground. Part of its slow speed could probably be attributed to the scars that covered its legs, but Zac also felt that the golem should have an attribute spread similar to his own, focusing on Endurance and Strength. It definitely wasn't something that excelled at speed, which was a shame, as his current class was particularly effective against those kinds of targets.

A power-based class was a lot trickier to deal with. That swing before had contained a ruthless finality that had warned him of death, and he didn't feel confident in trading a series of blows with the giant in front of him now that it didn't only use the restraining tongs and its fist. Not even with the seed empowering him to unprecedented heights.

Zac already had experienced dismantling an even bigger golem during the Hunt, and he knew how to deal with something like this. Zac released a deep breath as he started to walk back toward the golem, causing a storm of corrosive mists to spread across the whole platform. He didn't really expect the golem to be hurt by **[Winds of Decay]**, but he wanted to turn the battlefield more in his favor.

If some of the corrosive mists managed to enter the dozens of festering scars, then all the better.

The Miasmic mists of **[Fields of Despair]** soon billowed out as well, but it barely had time to spread out before the golem's chest expanded to the point that it almost doubled in size. A storm of fire spewed out of its mouth the next moment, spreading hundreds of meters in every direction and utterly destroying Zac's efforts in an instant.

Not a shred of his two skills remained, but the flames lingered on the floor, turning the plateau into an inferno as well. Zac stomped down with force, dispelling the flames in his immediate vicinity. But the temperature was definitely out of Zac's comfort zone, and he looked at the stoic golem with some trepidation. It looked like the golem had more abilities than just its physical prowess.

Zac had to admit that he might have taken on a bit more than he could chew this time.

66
DEATHWISH

Zac swore in annoyance when he saw the blacksmith effortlessly quash his attempts to putrefy the surroundings.

Turning a battlefield into one that favored you and restrained your enemy was a basic tactic that both his classes possessed. His human side had [Hatchetman's Spirit], while his Draugr side had multiple skills in this category. Zac was hoping to use these methods to counteract the blistering heat, but he was out of luck this time.

There was no time to formulate a plan either, as the hammer in the golem's meaty hand suddenly turned into a blur. The distance between the two was still over two hundred meters, but that wasn't much to E-grade beings. Zac conjured a fractal bulwark to meet whatever blow the guardian had prepared, but he frowned in consternation when the hammer slammed into the ground right in front of it rather than launching an attack in his direction.

It obviously wasn't a mistake, and Zac's first guess was that it had launched something through the ground, like an earthquake or metal spikes that would rise to stab him. Zac had still underestimated the advantage that the golem enjoyed in this place, and he was shocked to see a monstrous pillar of smoldering rocks rising out of the lava lake behind him.

It looked like a fiery dragon jumping out of the sea, and it reached almost a hundred meters in height before it started falling in a parabolic arc straight toward Zac. There was no hesitation as Zac started running as quickly as his legs could carry him. He would probably be able to block the pillar, as it only held the attunement of the lava sea itself, but doing so would fill no purpose.

The stream of lava slammed into the ground half a second after Zac got out of the way, causing a wave of magma to splatter in every direction. Even its fiery droplets were as large as small boulders, but it was far more manageable for Zac to control, and he easily blocked the ones that flew in his direction. However, the attack had left pools of magma across half the plateau, severely limiting Zac's mobility. Just the ambient heat was causing a constant drain on his Miasma, and this only made it worse.

Zac frowned at the scene, as he felt that the golem really was cheating. His **[Cosmic Gaze]** could clearly sense that there seemed to be some connection between the robot and the sea of lava surrounding them, which steadily supplied it with a stream of power. It all surged toward a spot roughly at the same place as his own Duplicity Core, which no doubt was the command core of the golem itself.

Destroying it would instantly end the battle, but it was easier said than done. Those kinds of cores were always the most heavily protected components of a puppet, and this blacksmith was no exception. Zac would have to cut his way through the extremely thick plating of its torso if he wanted to take out the golem that way.

Zac didn't know if he had the energy to keep fighting that long, especially when the golem was getting outside help. It was like the Dao Discourse all over again, and Zac was pretty certain that this thing would never run out of steam unless he somehow managed to break that connection.

He briefly considered erecting **[Profane Seal]** now that the lava pillar had already landed, but he eventually discarded the idea. The golem was still in peak condition, and Zac felt that he would have to wear the thing down a bit before trying to entrap it. He could only use the skill once, and it would be wasted if it immediately got destroyed by that huge hammer or another lava pillar.

First things first, he needed to sound out the power of this thing, this time while in control of his faculties. Zac made his way toward the robot, the black armor of **[Vanguard of Undeath]** at least somewhat protecting him from the scorching heat. He still couldn't quite match the golem in bulk even in this form, but the disparity wasn't nearly as bad as without it.

His fractal bulwark repositioned itself to the front of [**Love's Bond**], superimposing his defenses. Zac didn't have any movement skills to increase his speed, but the plateau was only so big. Each step forward increased his momentum, and he was in front of the golem in just a few seconds, his accumulated force already transferred to a mighty swing aimed to strike down its left leg.

His arm had already swollen up to a size that matched the golem's own as [**Unholy Strike**] was pushed to its limits once more. He needed to dig deeper and deeper with every swing, further increasing the amount of corrosion that could be left behind. However, the robot blacksmith responded with a speed that belied its stocky frame. Its hammer was somehow instantly moved to its left hand, and it pushed the massive hammerhead down toward the ground to block Zac's swing.

The clang of two metals clashing reverberated across the whole area, and the inner walls of the volcano bounced the sound back, making it sound like the tolling of church bells. Zac had no chance to appreciate the hauntingly beautiful sound as he looked at the hammer for signs of damage, only to come up empty-handed.

The first clash between weapons had ended without a victor.

[**Verun's Bite**] had reached new heights since its evolution, but the densely inscribed hammer was obviously a lovingly crafted treasure as well. A fractal had lit up on its side, completely protecting it from getting cut into by the furious swing of Zac's axe. He had managed to cause some damage to the metal plating on the golem itself during his earlier rampage, but it seemed that the hammer itself had reached a far greater level of durability. He didn't even have a chance to apply any corrosion with the array blocking the blackish liquid.

However, the power of Zac's swings wasn't anything to scoff at even for a Half-Step D-grade Golem. It contained layers of empowerment from multiple skills and the [**Rageroot Oak Seed**]. Its power was far beyond Zac's normal limits, and even the dragon wouldn't have been able to withstand its might. The enormous golem stumbled back a few steps, and the hammer was pushed away, exposing its legs once more.

Zac's eyes lit up at the opportunity, but the blacksmith managed to expertly make use of Zac's force to power a counter-swing before Zac had the chance to swing again. The enormous hammerhead moved in a precise arc, with Zac's head at the end of its trajectory.

There was no time to move away, so Zac forcibly stilled the whispers in his mind that told him to fight fire with fire. He instead readied himself to block the swing, moving to intercept it with his shield. Blocking a direct hit would activate **[Deathwish]**, and the distraction would hopefully create another opening to attack.

The array on the hammer lit up as it approached Zac's barrier, illuminating the pitch-black armor in gold. Zac's aura surged in anticipation of launching a counter of his own, but his abyssal eyes widened in shock when the golem's attack reached **[Immutable Bulwark]**. A weight that Zac had never felt before hit him, far surpassing any Gravity Array he had ever encountered.

It felt as though he were being crushed in the heart of a black hole as a soul-crushing pressure threatened to break every bone in his body. The furious energy of the **[Rageroot Oak Seed]** surged within his body to counteract the effect, but even the top-quality berserker item proved insufficient. It only took a fraction of a second to realize that his arm would break if he didn't back down.

He angled the shield to allow the hammer to slide down its side and slam into the ground instead. The shockwave would still wound him at such proximity, but it was far preferable to being brutalized by a direct hit. However, just as Zac tried to divert the attack, so did the golem try to keep the original trajectory. It somehow seemed to be able to anticipate and match Zac's actions, and small adjustments to its stance were all it required to keep the force pointing toward Zac.

A desperate push thankfully forced the golem a bit off-balance, allowing Zac to take a step to the side as he angled the shield even further. The hammer slid down its surface, the friction causing sparks across the whole coffin lid. But the huge slab of metal slammed into the ground instead of onto Zac's body, allowing him to breathe out in relief.

Zac still felt like he was being punched in the gut by the force from the shockwave, but he gritted his teeth and stood his ground, knowing he would have taken damage for nothing if he didn't respond in kind. The golem's reaction was quick as it tried to keep Zac at bay with its tongs, but he managed to push them aside with a swipe of his axe. His mind wasn't exactly on the tongs, but rather another realization.

It was [Deathwish]. He hadn't truly blocked the hammer's strike, but he had still absorbed some of the force from the swing while redirecting most of it. He didn't actually know if that was enough to activate the strike, and he quickly took the opportunity to conjure a spectral blacksmith that slammed down toward the back of the blacksmith's head.

The huge golem seemed to take the threat of the spectral hammer extremely seriously, perhaps thinking it would do as much damage as its own. It actually swiveled its torso 180 degrees to meet the attack while its legs stood rooted in place. Zac had no idea that its upper body could spin around like that, but he could spot an opportunity when he saw it.

The blacksmith's hammer rose to meet its spectral twin, and the whole ghost was obliterated in an instant as the true hammer ripped through the false one. Zac didn't care about that as he lunged for the closest leg. One, two, three swings bit into one of the deeper scars as Zac desperately tried to cut off its leg in one go. However, the metal was simply too hard, and Zac was beset by a counterforce almost strong enough to sprain his wrist.

The barrage was enough to deepen the wound at least, and this time, even more corrosive liquid empowered by the Fragment of the Coffin was left behind. The golem's response was quick, and it kept spinning its torso clockwise as it kept its hammer swing going. The two-meter-wide hammer once more ripped through the air as it moved straight toward Zac, but he was already moving away from the blacksmith.

The hammer ripped through the air just in front of Zac's face, a gust of fiery wind buffeting his face through the slits of his helmet. However, Zac didn't care, as it felt as though a new door had opened to him thanks to the latest exchange, and he realized that there was huge room for improvement in how he fought as a Draugr.

Zac had always been extremely confident of his Endurance since getting his second class, certain that he would be able to outlast anyone in a brutal melee. That had made his technique sloppy, where he relied on his body to be able to take the beating. There was no reason to take on unnecessary punishment, though; he needed to improve his efficiency.

Rather than blocking 100% of a strike, he could block 20% while diverting the rest of the force. This was just how many of the more experienced fighters had acted, like how Void's Disciple had somehow sapped the strength from his strikes. It would result in the same outcome, but with him wasting less Miasma and getting wounded less.

He needed to increase as much damage as possible while taking as little damage as possible. It was such a basic concept, but it was easier said than done to apply it in the heat of battle. The tongs were already coming for his head as the blacksmith advanced on him, but Zac took a step forward while angling his shield once more, allowing the pincers to push right past his head as he came close.

The corrosion from his previous strike along with his Dao was still lodged in the golem's leg, but it was quickly being eroded by a fiery heat emanating from the Puppet Core. He couldn't allow his earlier efforts to go to waste, and he swung twice in quick succession once more before a terrifying swing of the hammer forced him back.

Zac's mind screamed at him to keep going, to stop backing away from the battle, but he refused to give in to the battle lust again. He had already taken too much damage, so he needed to be measured in his approach. The golem kept pushing forward with an intractable momentum, like Zac was just a stubborn block of metal on the anvil.

Zac felt a slight flash of pain in his arm as he rerouted the hammer toward the ground, and another spectral blacksmith appeared. The golem froze from indecision for an instant, but Zac shook his head when it quickly chose to ignore the ghost.

The spectral hammer slammed into the golem's head with furious velocity, but Zac knew it was just a hollow strike. However, Zac's eyes widened in surprise when the hammer crashed into the golem with enough force to cause it to stumble, and a small but noticeable dent had appeared on its head. There was no earthly reason that his counter-skill could do enough damage for something like this to happen except one.

[**Deathwish**] had evolved to the next stage.

67
TEMPERING

Zac was elated to see that another one of his skills had evolved. It had become increasingly hard to push them forward lately, partly because of his lack of good targets to practice on. [Deathwish] was a mainstay of his class too, a skill that was a constant drain on his enemy and the bane of any Dexterity-based classes.

However, Zac knew that he couldn't expect too much from the skill in this fight, even if it had just reached Late proficiency. The spectral blacksmith's attack did cause a slight dent, but the golem quickly regained its footing. The small stumble did give Zac the opportunity to launch another barrage of axe swings before the tongs came for him, which was exactly what he needed.

He tried to repeat his earlier successes and block the pincers next, but he had underestimated the golem, and Zac suddenly had a meaty leg slam into his shield as the tong disappeared from sight. Zac was thrown away once more as pain racked his body. He had made some improvements to his fighting style just now, but it was too little, too late. This couldn't go on.

He was getting better, but the golem was also slowly adapting, and Zac would bleed out before he managed to completely dismantle that thing if he didn't change things up a bit. He eventually made a decision as [Love's Bond] turned into its offensive form, its four free chains hovering in the air around him like venomous snakes. Droplets of corrosive liquid fell down on the burning tiles beneath, causing a constant sizzling sound around him.

The fractal shield of [Immutable Bulwark] disappeared, as he no longer had a shield to base it on, but that was easily solved as Zac took out one of his backup shields. It wasn't anything special, but it was enough to conjure his defensive skills. The defensive capabilities of the skills were considerably worse when based on a normal shield, but it wasn't like Zac dared to take a direct hit in any case.

He rushed back to repeat the process, and the golem met his approach with a wide vertical arc of the hammer again. Zac had already expected this, and a new fractal bulwark had already appeared to divert the hammer. He quickly took a diagonal step as the four chains shot forward. Two of them moved to intercept the golem's left hand as the other two tried to poke holes in the golem's legs like spears.

Zac himself was in hot pursuit, though not without his own difficulties. His left arm hurt like hell, as the provisional shield had been turned to scrap metal that dug into his arm. Even blocking a portion of the hammer had completely destroyed both the fractal bulwark and the shield beneath. Zac could only throw the twisted shield to the ground and summon a new one from his Spatial Ring as he reached the golem's legs.

Metal clashed against metal, but the crisp sounds were slowly turning dull as the metal was steadily being deteriorated. Zac almost decided to go all-in then and there, but he quickly shook his head as he backed away. He had almost let his success go to his head, allowing the seed to take control once more.

But the two-meter-wide hammer was still a deadly threat. One hit and it would be game over. Zac couldn't help but briefly think of Ogras while he fought, moving back and forth to whittle down the golem while narrowly avoiding taking a lethal blow. Cold sweat would no doubt be running down his face and back if he were in his human form right now. Was this how fighting felt like for Dexterity-based cultivators, walking hand in hand with death?

It was just terrifying.

However, while the golem was mighty, it was ultimately not a sapient cultivator. It had some sort of battle algorithm that improved over the course of the fight, but Zac was able to figure out the preferred trajectories and fighting patterns soon enough. The swings that had felt life-threatening a few minutes ago no longer felt as dangerous as Zac and his chains swirled about.

The golem's attacks still contained the same power as before, but Zac was well aware of its reach and speed by now. He didn't take as much damage from his blocks either, as he slowly managed to lessen the force he forcibly had to block every time. In the beginning, he was taking on up to 30% before he managed to divert the strike, but after just a few minutes, that number had decreased to 20%.

His backup shields now managed to withstand two strikes before breaking apart, and his arm wasn't hurt every time either.

The chains of [Love's Bond] kept slamming into the scars with extreme force, and the ground was littered with metal plates and molten puddles from the disposable shields. It was like the chains lived their own lives as they targeted the weaknesses of the golem, and Zac could almost exclusively focus on creating as much damage as he could.

The golem, or rather its components, finally couldn't take it any longer after another five minutes of intense battering. It took a step toward Zac to launch its next swing, but a snap echoed out as its left leg shattered like it was made from brittle glass. The ceaseless attacks of [Blighted Cut] had finally permeated the whole leg, and Zac's eyes lit up as he saw his opportunity.

He stomped into the ground while the golem toppled over, and the cage of [Profane Seal] sprang up around them. The lava lake just outside the cage started to wear down the skill the moment it appeared, but Zac didn't care about that as he ordered the twenty spectral chains to shoot toward his prey. The four available chains of [Love's Bond] were even quicker as they wrapped around the golem multiple times before they slammed into the ground to pin it down, especially focusing on keeping the hammer-wielding arm in check.

The golem desperately tried to pry itself free with its tongs, but Zac was already upon the golem with his axe, and a frenzied series of swings destroyed the arm before the spectral chains had even reached him. Soon enough, the golem was barely visible beneath over a dozen chains, but Zac still felt a pang of danger as the whole golem burst into searing-hot flames.

Zac's eyes widened in alarm, knowing that his spectral chains wouldn't be able to last more than a second or two in this state. He still didn't back down. If the golem managed to break out, then it was over. He was running dangerously low on Miasma already, and just summoning **[Profane Seal]** had been a risk.

A bit more and his Specialty Core would activate by itself, and a three-second phase of weakness was enough for him to be turned into paste. The fires spread from the golem to the point that the pile of chains looked like a bonfire, and even Zac's armor had been ignited.

The golem was seemingly trying to bring Zac down with it to hell as it exuded more and more flames, but Zac ignored the scorching pain across his body as the fire danced in his eyes. He was waiting, each moment feeling like an eternity, but suddenly, there was a change in the skill fractal on his arm.

The real strike of **[Blighted Cut]** was finally ready.

Zac didn't hesitate, knowing his time was limited. The moment he felt the change in **[Blighted Cut]**, he immediately seized the opportunity. This was what he had worked so hard for, and he needed to make it count. Three black waves appeared around the golem, and they shot into its bulky frame in an instant, cutting through the flames like they weren't even there.

It was like the strike was both corporeal and a projection as it passed straight through the chains that held the golem in place, and the waves disappeared into the golem's torso, each of them aiming for the same spot. The robot blacksmith frenetically struggled for another few seconds, but it was futile. A subdued crack could be heard from within, and Zac breathed out in relief, knowing that the golem's core had been cut apart.

Without that, it was just a big hunk of metal, and it unsurprisingly stopped moving just a second later. There was no surge of energy entering his body to confirm the kill, but that was always the case with beings without sapience. The blacksmith was ultimately a puppet rather than a true golem cultivator like the Creators, and destroying it didn't award any Cosmic Energy at all.

It was as though the air left Zac's body after the golem stopped moving, and he barely managed to escape the flames before he helplessly fell down on the ground from exhaustion. He still felt the effects of the seed coursing through his body, but he knew his body wasn't in any state to take advantage of it any longer. Activating the final and ultimate strike of [Blighted Cut] had drained him of his last Miasma as well, and his Duplicity Core had already begun reverting him back to a human.

He would normally hold off on turning back to human considering the state his body was in, but Zac didn't have much choice at the moment. He could only prepare the [Serene Flesh Pill], and he popped it into his mouth the instant the transformation was complete. A surge of pain racked his body the moment he came alive, but it was thankfully quickly soothed by the High-quality Zethaya pill.

His body was still drained of energy, and he was content lying on the ground gasping for air a while longer.

"What a disgraceful display," a disgusted voice snorted, and Zac turned his bleary eyes toward the Tool Spirit, who had appeared next to him at an unknown time. "I knew you were talentless, but this was beyond the pale. What kind of craven backwater planet was I sent to if you're the best of the best?"

"Well, the golem is down, which means I passed, right?" Zac sighed, his voice barely recognizable.

"Luckily for you, my creator didn't add any base requirement of skill or grace, so you barely passed," the Tool Spirit said with a shake of his head. "As specified, you will be provided with a round of tempering for being the one to open the second floor of the Dao Repository. Considering your level, you would be given the full thirty minutes, but I'll go ahead and deduct ten minutes for cheating by using a berserking item."

"What tempering? And wait, I got a reduction for using the seed?! You never mentioned anything like this before," Zac said with a frown as he dragged himself up to his feet. "You said it was okay to use things like that!"

The fact that he had missed out on some rewards because the Tool Spirit wasn't doing his job was infuriating, and anger overcame his caution as he glared at Brazla.

"Well, you never asked." Brazla laughed, clearly delighted by

Zac's anger. "Besides, the Great Sage only said that you were allowed to use it. I never said that it wouldn't affect your grading."

Zac wanted to argue that it was clearly making things difficult for him, but his head was just a mush after the fight. He could only point at the Tool Spirit in righteous indignation, which only seemed to delight Brazla even further.

"Can't be wearing those rags during the tempering," Brazla muttered, and Zac found himself floating in front of the Tool Spirit the next moment.

"Wai–" Zac screamed, but it was to no avail as everything from his robes to his Spatial Ring was dragged off his body, leaving him stark naked.

"Now, off you go."

Zac's eyes widened in alarm, but the Tool Spirit was impossibly fast as his golden hammer turned into a blur. Zac wasn't even able to consider a response before the Tool Spirit had already attacked him. Zac was already exhausted from the battle, but he inwardly knew that he wouldn't have been able to block that strike even in peak condition. It was just on a completely different level than even the golem just now.

Thankfully, there was no painful sensation from being hit by the golden hammer, but alarm bells still went off in his head when he was launched into the air. Worse yet, he found himself completely restrained as his body became covered in dense golden fractals. He couldn't circulate his Cosmic Energy at all, and his mental connection to his Spirit Tools was severed as well.

He was utterly helpless, and he could only look on with trepidation as he flew closer and closer to the enormous anvil in the middle of the plateau. The battle before had caused shockwaves and fires to spread across the whole area, but the massive slab of metal still stood there completely unscathed.

Zac's flight got an abrupt end as he slammed into the anvil's side face-first, and the blinding pain almost made him pass out. He wanted to get away, or at least reset his broken nose, but he still couldn't move because of the runes covering his body.

So he could only mentally curse the Tool Spirit one last time as he started sliding down toward the pool of magma below.

68
PLUNGE

Zac struggled against the restraints that covered his body, but they bound him even tighter than the cultists' restrictive dust, and the only reason he didn't cry out in shock as he fell toward the red-hot magma was that he was physically unable to.

It was a poignant reminder of the true power of the annoying braggart who usually just messed around in the Towers of Myriad Dao. Brazla might not be a real cultivator, but he was definitely a top-tier D-grade Tool Spirit, perhaps even approaching C-grade. Going by how powerful Verun already was in E-grade, then Brazla was probably the most powerful entity in Port Atwood, with Karunthel being the only possible exception.

The lava in the small pond below him was definitely something far more dangerous than the lake surrounding the platform, and Zac was almost thankful that he couldn't activate [Cosmic Gaze] close to the pond. The shocking amounts of attuned energies below him made the hair on his arms stand on end, and looking straight at it with his skill might have blinded him.

However, Zac quickly calmed down even as he still fell. Suddenly being stripped naked and thrown into a metal anvil with enough force to break his nose had plunged his exhausted mind into chaos, but he quickly remembered what was going on. Brazla might be annoying and fond of causing trouble, but he always did what his creator had instructed him to.

The Tool Spirit's execution was definitely lacking, but this was no doubt an opportunity that Zac had to seize.

That notion only grew stronger as an extremely intricate script appeared on the pool of lava just before he dropped into it, and Zac realized how similar it was to the golden array that currently covered and restrained his body. He didn't get the chance to get a better look, as he was submerged in the lava the next moment, forcing him to quickly close his eyes.

His body instinctively strained to swim up to the surface, but he was still completely unable to move as he sank deeper and deeper into the depths. Thankfully, he quickly realized that the lava around him didn't hurt at all. The magma felt like a warm embrace, allowing Zac to breathe out in relief. That by itself confused Zac even further, as fresh air somehow entered his lungs even when he was supposed to be submerged.

Was the lava around him just an illusion?

The notion was so strong that he actually opened his eyes, but surrounding him was just an endless red, with the occasional wisp of white-hot fires. It definitely looked like lava, but his vision wasn't completely obfuscated, as he could actually see his body just fine, making him feel like he was submerged in water rather than molten rock.

The situation was extremely odd, but his attention was quickly seized by the small sparks of white flames that flitted about before they disappeared. There was something unique about those flames. It was definitely fire attunement, but also something more. It felt like he could only grasp the edge of it, similar to how he had been unable to understand even a corner of the Chaos Pattern back then.

It was pretty annoying that he couldn't activate **[Cosmic Gaze]** to get a better look, but he wasn't too sure it would do him any good against those small fires. They didn't feel as vast as the purple lightning or as domineering as the System's presence, but they were extremely pure. The impression they gave Zac was that all the attuned energies he had seen until now were fake, a hollow mimicry of energies truly touched by the Dao.

Was this perhaps what C-grade attuned energies looked like? Or was it something else entirely? It honestly didn't feel as powerful as something that could be considered C-grade, and it was more reminiscent of the Dao Intent that Thea had been imparted from the inheritance. In either case, it was definitely something valuable, and Zac's heartbeat sped up in anticipation.

The odd surroundings made it impossible to get a proper bearing, but it felt like he was being submerged deeper and deeper by the second, to the point that he had descended thousands of meters into the depths of the volcano. The pure energies around him only seemed to become even stronger as he sank deeper, and the surroundings quickly changed from red to a warm yellow until it was just a world of pure white.

When the color gradient stopped changing, so did Zac's impression of descending, and he knew that his opportunity was about to arrive. Brazla had said that he had gained twenty minutes of Body Tempering, and he guessed that the clock had already started ticking. The problem was that Zac had no idea what to do next.

He didn't own any bloodline tempering manual just yet, and the white fire around him didn't seem to do anything apart from heating his body. He wasn't a cultivator either, so he was unable to naturally absorb the energies from his surroundings. Not that he was sure it would be possible to circulate a Cultivation Manual when covered in a set of restraining runes.

However, tendrils of warmth finally started burrowing into his body, filling him with that mysterious force he had sensed earlier. Zac was initially worried that such a force would be dangerous to absorb when he was just E-grade, but the white fire was extremely gentle as the warmth spread across his body. The intensity kept increasing, but it didn't hurt at all.

It was as though his body could contain an endless amount of this force without issue, and that he could withstand the steadily increasing heat in his body. The exhaustion from the battle was soon forgotten, replaced with a state of complete relaxation. It was like he had returned to the womb, and his eyes were starting to get heavy.

Zac's eyes shot open just as they were about to close as he noticed a startling change across his body. His skin had started to change color, rapidly turning molten red. Zac couldn't believe what he was seeing as he looked down at his hands. It looked like he was made out of metal, and that this metal was heated in a furnace to a melting point. It didn't hurt at all, and Zac guessed this was the tempering that Brazla had mentioned.

Zac was about to close his eyes again and let the warmth wash his body clean, but a sudden force slammed into him, startling him awake. It felt startlingly similar to when the blacksmith golem had pummeled him with its hammer, and sharp pain radiated across Zac's torso. It wasn't quite at the level of the terrifying **[Bone-Forging Dust]** he had used a couple of times by now, but it was still extremely painful. However, he knew that he had to endure it to get the full benefits of whatever this tempering entailed.

One slam after another made Zac's body shudder, and the words of Brazla reappeared in the back of his mind. Less than a minute had passed, and it felt like he was about to pass out from the pain. How would he be able to withstand almost twenty more minutes of this? But Zac forcibly pushed those cowardly thoughts out of his mind, and he emptied his mind as he welcomed another hammering.

This was a god-given opportunity to empower himself, and he wouldn't waste it.

The hits kept increasing in both strength and frequency, and Zac's conviction was quickly starting to crack. He had essentially been turned into a piece of raw metal that was being worked over by this mysterious array, his flesh turned malleable by the heat around him. Were there even any benefits of doing this? He was just being pummeled over and over. What if this opportunity was meant for Peak E-grade warriors who had properly evolved their bodies to D-grade long ago? Was this perhaps even detrimental to him rather than beneficial?

However, those invasive thoughts were suddenly thrown away after a couple of minutes, as Zac suddenly could see palpable results, and his eyes lit up as he wished the hits could come even faster.

His body was still glowing red hot, but murky clouds were being expelled from his pores all across his body. They tainted the pure white of the surroundings for an instant before being incinerated to the point that they were utterly annihilated. These clouds were definitely impurities and various types of sequelae trapped in his body, and he could even recognize their sources with the help of the weak aura they emitted just before they were burnt away.

First to get expelled was the fiery energies of the **[Rageroot Oak Seed]**, and small explosions erupted as they came in contact with the magma. Next were the stubborn Dao energies left in his body from his fight with Void's Disciple. The sight made him widen his eyes, as there was a lot more stuck in his body than he had realized.

His pores kept spewing out the two foreign Daos, and by the time the slams no longer could extract any more, he had expelled even more than he had removed himself over the past ten days. The tempering didn't end there, though, and Zac's eyes were wide with marvel as impurities left from his **[Bone Forging Dust]**, node-breaking pills, and all other sorts of treasures spewed out one by one.

Every second, he felt as though his body was becoming lighter, and worry had long been exchanged with elation. Who would have known that such a huge boon was hidden within the Dao Repository? The magical molding even managed to find hidden remnants of the wound Mhal had left when implanting him with the Draugr samples so long ago, and the deathly energies were quashed in the lava lake.

Zac couldn't help but lament that his time in the lake was limited even though it felt like his body was being broken and remolded every second.

That feeling only grew when there was finally a reaction from his **[Void Heart]**. It had been utterly silent since swallowing the tribulation lightning, but it had suddenly started vibrating as it gobbled up a small part of the fiery energies in his body. Not only that, but Zac actually felt two more spots on his body vibrate in a similar fashion.

First was the same spot in his head as he had sensed before, the spot that Zac suspected to be another hidden node related to his soul or the Dao. The second vibration came from his spine down at the small of his back. It made him think of the **[Bloodline Marrow]** he had been awarded before, and he could only lament that it had been left in his Spatial Ring.

Unfortunately, the three spots only seemed to resonate with each other, with the two spots seeming unwilling to be opened. Zac tried everything he could to steer more of the mysterious energy into those two spots, but it was to no avail. Soon enough, there were only seconds left before twenty minutes had passed, and Zac knew that this opportunity wasn't enough to break open the two nodes.

He could only give up on breaking open those two nodes, but he also knew that just finding them was a huge step forward. Before, he had only suspected the spot in his head, but now he was 100% certain about the location of two hidden nodes. Forcibly opening them was just a matter of finding the right sort of treasure by now.

The time was running out, so Zac readied himself mentally in case he had to swim out by himself somehow, but a scene right at the end made him almost forget about the hidden node.

Not one, not two, but six small runes that clearly were of different origins suddenly shot out between his brows just before his vision blurred. The next moment, he found himself panting on the ground in the hallway of the Towers of Myriad Dao, and Zac was relieved to see his Spatial Ring and treasures lying next to him.

His mind was foggy and unfocused after having gone through both a tough battle and the subsequent tempering, but he forced himself to stay awake as he reached for his Spatial Ring and robes. Just getting dressed felt like an almost insurmountable task, but by the time he was clothed again, he actually felt a lot better.

The six runes he'd seen at the end were definitely cause for concern, but Zac couldn't stifle his curiosity as he quickly opened his status screen. His body had been thoroughly cleansed and tempered, and he hoped that the encounter had pushed him to D-grade Race. However, confusion rather than elation marred his face after opening the status screen. His status had changed, but definitely not as he had expected.

[E] Human – Void Emperor (Corrupted, Unawakened)

69
CORRUPTION

Zac mutely looked at the revised line in his status screen for a few seconds. There was only one way to interpret the addition even though it didn't exactly match the intelligence he had gathered so far. His lava bath had purified his constitution to the point that his previously unknown bloodline could be listed, even if it hadn't completely awakened yet.

And he had to admit that it sounded pretty damn powerful.

Zac almost ate his **[Bloodline Marrow]** then and there in hopes of properly awakening it, but he barely managed to restrain the impulse. First of all, his body was in a completely drained state after using the Berserking Pill even if the lava bath had managed to expel most of the toxins. Eating a treasure in this condition was essentially the same as flushing it down the toilet.

But more importantly, the fact that the status screen termed his bloodline "corrupted" gave him pause.

He had never heard of something like this before. Zac had bought a few general missives about bloodlines after realizing he might have one, but they didn't cover anything like this. The unawakened line was just as described, but the mention of corruption had never been brought up at all.

The most basic way to explain a bloodline was to call it a genetic mutation brought on by an extremely powerful ancestor. After reaching a certain stage, their bodies became vessels of their cultivation path, fundamentally affecting their genetics. The body of someone walking the path of fire would essentially turn into a being whose flesh could turn into flames at will. Even their convictions and beliefs were added into the bloodlines.

The rules of what was required to pass on a bloodline weren't exactly clear, but the general consensus was that one needed to reach Middle C-grade at the least for one's body to transform to the point that their cultivation path could be passed on. However, this actually happening was still extremely rare, which meant that there most likely were more requirements. Some posited that there was a requirement of affinity and understanding of the Dao, whereas others believed that great mental strength was required.

In either case, one needed to be beyond the norm for a bloodline to be born. It was also generally believed that the more powerful a cultivator became, the greater a bloodline they would leave behind. A C-grade Monarch's bloodline would probably be the lowest rung, to the point that it disappeared after a few short generations. Only the most powerful beings could leave behind bloodlines that could stay on generation after generation.

The effect of bloodlines was extremely varied as well, ranging from giving huge boosts to controlling specific Daos or calling upon the strength of your body, whereas others were essentially useless. Some might even become detrimental to the descendants if the ancestor practiced some cruel and unorthodox path.

Bloodlines started unawakened, but they could be awakened through either cultivating a Body Tempering Manual or some specific bloodline manual. Of course, some treasures could get the job done as well, such as the **[Bloodline Marrow]**. The average effect of the first awakening was generally set at around 15 to 25% provided the bloodline matched your path, and this boost could be anything from cultivation speed to power output in battle.

That meant that a mortal with a combat-oriented bloodline was almost equal to a cultivator without one, as one got a boost from their Heritage while the other got a similar boost from their Cultivation Manual. Of course, having both would provide multiplicative boosts, which was the situation most cultivators longed for. Higher-quality bloodlines could even provide unique skills, and Zac considered the devouring ability of **[Void Heart]** to belong to that category, even though he couldn't control it yet.

The line that said Corrupted on his status screen was actually the place that should display the rarity of the bloodline. Bloodlines shared the same rarity as classes, going from Common to Epic. Zac guessed there were even greater bloodlines, though that wasn't something that a cheap missive in the Zecia Sector would either cover or confirm.

Bloodline rarity was also fixed, according to the manuals, and not something that either training or treasures could impact. A higher rarity generally meant a more powerful bloodline that could be awakened more times. Of course, a higher-rarity bloodline was a lot harder to improve as well, just like how it went with classes. Furthermore, the number of awakenings you could perform depended on your bloodline's rarity to a large degree, but it could still be influenced by hard work and opportunities.

But what did corrupted mean? The line felt extremely ominous, to the point that Zac almost felt he was beset with an affliction rather than an opportunity. Nothing in the information missive had prepared him for that line, and Zac wasn't sure whether he should give up on his goal of awakening it.

Zac eventually decided to simply keep going. There were multiple possible explanations of why his bloodline was considered corrupted, with the most likely one being that it was affected by his Technocrat Heritage. Perhaps the System considered his body corrupted on that basis alone.

He had to admit there being a possibility of his condition being a result of his mother's experiments as well. But even if that was the case, it still shouldn't be something detrimental. Leandra should have been trying to make a powerful bloodline or modify an existing one to suit her needs better, which should mean that it wasn't a worthless constitution.

What was important was that it was useful and provided benefits, and Zac already felt that it was doing just that. For now, he had only one Hidden Node doing some work, but Zac believed it might prove extremely useful in the future. He still remembered the vision of that mysterious man passing by a sun, stealing its essence for his own cultivation.

That was exactly what he needed: an alternative method of cultivation that would help him move forward. Reaching the higher grades of cultivation as a mortal was already akin to defying the Heavens, and he was doing it with multiple high-rarity classes. Gaining the ability to break past bottlenecks might prove even more helpful than yet another power boost.

Zac could only put the matter aside for now, and he instead turned his attention to the state of his body. The tempering process had hurt to the point that he almost went insane, but it hadn't actually wounded him. The pain that he'd felt just a minute ago almost felt like a dream, and even the wounds from the battle with the golem had improved considerably. He still felt too tired to move at the moment, so he simply scrambled up to a sitting position for now.

It was a huge wake-up call for Zac to see the amount of impurities he had expelled during the tempering. He had thought himself almost in perfect condition based on looking at his interior with his spiritual sight, but there was actually so much gunk left behind without him noticing. Almost every life-threatening encounter seemed to have left a hidden wound, and who knew if the tempering even got it all.

However, the most worrying part wasn't the sequelae, but the small marks that had been expelled right at the end. Zac had barely had a chance to study them before he was returned to the repository, but he did manage to sense familiar auras from a few of them. The first, and perhaps the most worrying, definitely came from Faceless #13. The mark carried the same sinister aura as the spikes he still carried around in his Spatial Ring.

Zac couldn't imagine having a hidden mark left behind by that man was a good thing, no matter if it was meant to track or slowly kill him.

The second mark made him think of Rasuliel Tsarun for some reason. He didn't know how he had been marked by the Tsarun scion, but his eyes suddenly turned to the Spatial Ring on his finger. He had already swapped the ring he got from the Tsarun disciple for the much superior ring he'd looted from the Mentalist, but perhaps he had been branded when stealing Rasuliel's ring.

That would also explain why he didn't get a mark by taking the second ring, as he wasn't actually the one who killed the Mentalist or stole her ring. It was rather that squirrely thief who had tried to rob them while they both were out of commission.

The third mark, which was also the one that emitted the strongest energies, felt just like the cursed sword in his possession. He guessed that it was a hidden trap of using that accursed thing, a brand that would grow in power with every use. Nothing good could come from having that thing in his body, and he vowed not to use the sword again unless absolutely necessary.

Finally, there was one mark that had been created with Miasma, but Zac didn't get much more than that.

The fact that the mark was wrought from Miasma severely limited the number of suspects. Be'Zi, Catheya, Adriel, and perhaps Mhal were the main ones, though Be'Zi being the source felt like a long shot. Not because Zac implicitly trusted her, but rather that he didn't feel confident that an opportunity created by the original Brazla would be able to extract something that she had planted on him. Case in point, the Miasmic cage in his mind had been utterly unaffected by the tempering.

Be'Zi was definitely far stronger than Brazla ever was, sitting at B-grade cultivation at the minimum. That was a full two-stage difference, which should simply be too much to deal with for an opportunity left behind.

The last two marks Zac couldn't make heads or tails of, but that was perhaps because they were weaker than the first four. The other four marks were all far more intricate, which perhaps was what had allowed Zac to recognize them. His best guess was that they were left by people in the Base Town.

In either case, it was better to have them gone than remaining, but the experience made him wonder what else was hidden in his body. Unfortunately, there was not much he could do about the situation at the moment. Most cultivators had elders to turn to, far more powerful cultivators who could blast most hidden threats by circulating their own energies through their descendants' bodies.

Zac didn't have that advantage, meaning he would have to rely on other opportunities to purge himself of hidden threats. He knew there were cleansing arrays out there, and it was perhaps about time something like that was added to his cultivation cave.

"Are you done wallowing about? I can't have trash littering my floor," the all-too-familiar voice of Brazla echoed out from above, prompting Zac to reluctantly get up on his feet with a grunt.

"Thank you," Zac said, though he didn't feel all that grateful to the Tool Spirit itself, but rather its creator. "Is there any way for me to get back to the lava pool for another round of refinement?"

Zac wasn't thinking about going there right now, but rather when reaching Peak E-grade. He almost regretted partaking in such a good opportunity right now, as he probably would be saddled with another round of impurities by the time he was ready to form his Cultivation Core. He still remembered reading about Galvarion, the aquatic mortal who needed to spend over a century to remove all his impurities. Zac simply didn't have that kind of time.

He had made a huge splash in the Tower of Eternity, and there was also the issue of the Great Redeemer coming for revenge in a hundred years even if Zac managed to obscure Earth. Urgency pushed him forward, and his goal was to reach at least the middle stages of D-grade before Earth got integrated for real.

At that level, he should only have to worry about C-grade Monarchs, and those kinds of people generally wouldn't come for a tiny D-grade planet like Earth. There were only so many C-grade cultivators in a remote sector like Zecia, and they were either in perpetual secluded cultivation or exploring the most dangerous corners of the sector in hopes of progressing their cultivation.

But cultivating with that speed would be hard even for a genius cultivator, let alone a mortal. But this lava pool might be one of the keys to speeding up the process.

"Greedy little brat. Do you think such purification is something mundane that can be used as one wants? It was only possible thanks to the Earthen Fire seed that my master found in the bottom of that volcano, and it has a finite source of power. It had already been nurtured for tens of millions of years by the time my creator found it on an uninhabited world, and he kept purifying it for dozens of millennia as he turned the whole mountain into his forge. It was so limited that my creator couldn't even bear to use it for his own cultivation, so it was eventually left to future generations," Brazla said with a haughty voice.

"So it was something that magical?" Zac said with disappointment, though he wasn't too surprised.

Galau was the one who taught him about Pill Toxicity and how hard it was to get rid of it. If ridding your body of hidden threats was as easy as jumping into a pool of lava, then all volcanoes would have long become strategic resources of the Multiverse.

"Of course, why else would the System expend so much energy to cram my master's forge into a pocket dimension left in a corner of my body?" Brazla snorted.

70
SACRIFICES

"What? It was the System who created that trial?" Zac asked with confusion. "I thought it was Bra– ahem, your creator who put it there for his descendants?"

"Are you stupid?" Brazla sneered. "My creator didn't plan on being dead when his descendants would use the Towers of Myriad Dao. Why would there be restrictions and trials to visit the higher floors? It was the System that refitted my body a bit, perfecting the towers even further. Seems like a waste of effort to award the towers to someone like you, if you ask the Great Brazla, but here we are."

Zac was surprised to hear that the System was personally stepping in to modify its rewards, but he had to admit that he had never considered things from Brazla's perspective. Indeed, why would the original Brazla put forth such trials to access the skills? Most Dao Repositories were free to enter for the owning force, with the elders deciding who could get what skills. But Zac had to accomplish feats of strength to gain the same sort of access.

Furthermore, it was the same with Thea's library. She would also have to pass some sort of trial to gain access to higher-tiered intelligence. So it turned out that the System was refitting these quest rewards, both improving them and making them serve as motivational or training tools.

"Besides," Brazla said with a shake of his head, a hint of wistfulness flashing in his eyes, "that world is no more. Now that the final fragment was awakened, it will be lost forever, with the System taking the last energies."

"Then why couldn't you let me have it?" Zac muttered with some annoyance. "If the System was going to steal the rest anyways."

"Those were the rules that were put in place." Brazla shrugged. "It doesn't really matter in either case. You would only have gained the same amount of time even if you waited until reaching Middle E-grade for real. I guess it was a bad matchup. If you focused on Agility or Intelligence, you might have had a shot even without that treasure. That puppet was even dumber than you, after all."

Zac felt a bit disappointed he couldn't have his body forged inside the lava again, but he couldn't complain. It was a free bonus that he didn't even know existed, and while it hadn't directly improved his power, it did solve a lot of hidden issues for him. Besides, there was still the real reward to go for. However, Zac wanted to take advantage of the Tool Spirit's uncharacteristic mood to see if he could get some information.

"The tempering expelled something from my body I didn't know was there. Six marks, probably left by my enemies. Do you know what those are?"

"I saw; you really shouldn't let yourself get branded like that. Most of them were tracking marks, and one was a curse," Brazla snorted.

"Tracking marks? Are they heading for Earth now because of me?" Zac exclaimed. "Is it a Karmic Link?"

"Karmic Link? Don't get blinded by that one Karmic Cultivator who wants this desolate rock for some reason. Those methods are beyond rare. Isn't his family famous through this whole sector because of their extremely rare ability to touch upon that Dao?" Brazla snorted. "Even then, a small mark like those that got expelled isn't enough for something as great as intergalactic tracking. Perhaps if it was a supreme existence placing the mark. But why would someone like that turn his gaze toward you, or even this whole sector for that matter?"

"Then what is it?" Zac asked.

"The trees and bushes around my square—"

"I'll have someone beautify and prune the forest around you." Zac sighed without pause.

"I can't tell you about the curse, but the others are minor markers that would stay dormant until triggered," the Tool Spirit said as a satisfied grin spread across his face.

"Triggered? How?" Zac asked.

"The better ones could trigger upon entering an array covering a set area, usually a town. The worse ones would require a direct scan of your body specifically. It would essentially make it harder for you to stay hidden while traveling. Intelligence houses are notorious for placing such things on their clients if they think they can get away with it, but anyone with a portable array can do the same. Those runes are easily destroyed by purification methods, though, so they are generally useless against the wealthy." Brazla shrugged.

Zac sighed in relief, realizing it wasn't as bad as he had previously feared. The looming threat of the Great Redeemer had really made him a bit paranoid about the dangers of the Multiverse. But it was worth remembering that the plan of Voridis A'Heliophos was thousands of years in the making, and it still seemed easier said than done to even find Earth after all that effort.

It was a weight off his shoulders, and it allowed him to properly focus on the task at hand. As for plotting revenge for some random tracking mark, it wasn't really worth his time and effort. He had enough enemies as it was.

"I want to see the E-grade skills," Zac said as he slowly got to his feet.

Brazla shrugged with disinterest, and a set of stairs leading to a previously inaccessible section appeared to Zac's left. He looked over to see if Brazla was planning on joining him, but the Tool Spirit had already disappeared. It felt a bit like Brazla was depressed after visiting the lava world. It might have brought back memories of his creator, and the volcano was perhaps even Brazla's own birthplace.

Zac didn't mind the peace and quiet as he made his way toward the next floor. However, he actually had to stop and take a breath after just a couple of steps, his hands shaking with exhaustion. The lava bath had managed to cleanse him of the remnants of the **[Rageroot Oak Seed]**, but he was still completely wrung dry. He felt hungover, sick, and voraciously hungry at the same time.

He was really craving a proper dinner full of E-grade meat, but he wasn't sure he would be able to hold it down at the moment. He ate a couple of fasting pills instead, which somewhat relieved his symptoms and allowed him to walk up the rest of the stairs.

So he soon found himself in an austere chamber illuminated by only natural light. Gone were the opulent displays of the first floor, replaced with a display of pure craftsmanship. There were painstakingly engraved pictures covering the wall, and a quick look indicated that they were probably scenes out of the original Brazla's life.

It piqued Zac's curiosity, but he was ultimately more interested in the fourteen crystals that hovered in a semicircle on the other side of the room.

There were not a lot of crystals compared to the first floor, but Zac already knew that each and every one of them was a top-quality skill handpicked by Brazla himself, with the purpose of creating a foundation for his family. He could only pray that there was at least one or two that he could make use of.

Zac walked past the crystals one by one, touching a plaque in front of them to receive a stream of information about the skill stored within. After having gone through the whole set, he couldn't help but nod in appreciation at Brazla's foresight when preparing this set of skills.

There was an endless number of paths to take in cultivation, just like the name of the Dao Repository indicated. That meant that the odds of being a perfect match to a skill you randomly picked up was pretty slim. The first floor of the Dao Repository was a reflection of this, as the skills placed there were extremely varied, to the point that Zac barely had gained anything from it.

But seeing the selection on the second floor, Zac realized that the original Brazla probably had a purpose for arranging things like this. The first floor was available to anyone who had just set out on the path of cultivation. A new level one cultivator would be able to unlock a huge array of classes with the help of that set of skills.

That was how most people in the Tutorial started their cultivation journey, according to Thea. They were given a choice of skill after completing the first mini-mission, and that skill would become their main method of survival until reaching level 25. If someone picked **[Fireball]** and used it during the month-long Tutorial, then they would probably be able to choose some sort of mage class upon reaching level 25.

However, cultivators who had reached E-grade would generally be set in their own ways, with the more talented ones already having started forming their cultivation path. The Celestial Craftsman understood this fact and had therefore focused on skills that would be helpful for a wide array of people.

Six of the fourteen skills were heavily related to the six base attributes, without possessing a connection to a specific Dao. They also seemed to follow the concept of greatness from simplicity, which not only made them powerful but also easy to fuse with other skills down the line.

For example, the Dexterity-based skill was an offensive skill simply called **[Soaring Ocean]**, but it wasn't actually a water-based skill. It was rather a bit reminiscent of how Ogras fought with his shadow spears.

It was a speed-based attack that made use of a rapid series of strikes rather than one strong attack. The weapon could seemingly be almost anything from the looks of it, from hands to bladed weapons to even things like Ogras' shadows. The true power of the skill came from the fact that each consecutive strike would increase your speed by a bit, and your momentum would keep growing endlessly as long as you kept attacking.

Eventually, your speed would be far beyond your normal limits, and with increased speed came improved lethality. The enemy would be drowned in an endless sea of attacks until they succumbed.

It was a bit like a berserking skill, though. If you pushed your speed too far, your body would start to get hurt as well.

Meanwhile, both Endurance and Wisdom were defensive skills, while Vitality was a self-recuperating ability. Intelligence was surprisingly not a spell, but that was perhaps because most spells leaned toward a specific attunement. It instead was a mind-boosting spell that put your mind into overdrive, essentially slowing down the world around you.

That would allow you to use your other spells even faster, and from the sound of it, to the point that you would become a spell turret wreaking havoc on the battlefield. Zac was initially pretty interested in that skill even if it was meant for mages, but it clearly stated that it put high requirements on both calculating speed and affinities, so he would be completely unable to use it for things like rapid-fire [Chop].

As for the rest of the prepared skills, they were mainly ancillary skills that would come in handy for most adventurers.

The first one that piqued Zac's interest was actually an upgraded version of [Thousand Faces], aptly named [Million Faces]. It worked similarly to the F-graded skill, but it gave a greater influence on modifications.

With this skill, he would be able to completely change his build if need be, and even be able to pass off as other humanoid Races to a cursory glance. But most importantly, it allowed you to curtail and modify your aura to some degree. It could both bolster the aura you emitted, fooling others into thinking you were stronger than you were, or weaken it to make others underestimate you.

It would even be able to slightly change the "flavor" of your aura, which was even better. Your aura was like a fingerprint, and Zac could essentially identify anyone he knew in the base just by sensing their aura. There were a few exceptions to that, namely Billy and Kenzie.

Kenzie had help from her AI to completely mask her aura, while Billy could do so himself for some reason. Ogras was hard to spot as well, but that was because his shadows helped mute his aura a bit. Zac still could recognize the flavor as long as they were close enough.

The other ancillary skills were similarly impressive, and Zac felt like a child in a candy store as he looked at the varying options. However, his luck had finally caught up with him, as he, unfortunately, had spotted several clashes with his current skills. He only had so many slots for skills, and more than half of them were already used up.

If he wanted to learn these new skills, then he would have to sacrifice a few of his old ones.

71
VOID

Zac still hadn't fully gripped what he could and couldn't do with his future skill upgrades and skill fusions, so he couldn't help but worry about making a colossal mistake by removing some of his class skills to get a quick power-up. However, some choices weren't very hard to make, the first being his shape-shifting skill.

The upgraded version unsurprisingly commandeered the same skill slot as [Thousand Faces], and it was the first pick of Zac. A familiar screen appeared in front of him the next moment.

[Learning the skill Million Faces will result in the permanent loss of the skill Thousand Faces. Proceed?]

Following that was a simple **[YES/NO]** prompt.

Zac touched the "YES," prompting a stream of energy to enter his body. It made its way to his throat, and a stabbing pain spread across his neck as one skill fractal branded itself on top of the old one, supplanting its spot.

The discomfort was thankfully just at the level of redrawing one's pathways, and Zac had ample experience with that after breaking open a bunch of nodes. The pain soon abated, and the transfer was complete. He opened his skill screen, and Thousand Faces was gone as expected, replaced with a new line.

[Million Faces – Proficiency: -. A million faces, a million lives. Become an untraceable stream in the fabric of reality. Upgradeable.]

The prompt earlier was something that Alyn had already told him about, and Zac knew that he would only get it once like some sort of tutorial. There wouldn't be any warnings in case of skill clashes again, except when getting a new skill through one of his classes.

The skill was the same as the new one in the sense that it didn't have any proficiency, but its fractal was far more intricate compared to the old one. However, Zac saw the base pattern was pretty much the same, just with greater details and a couple of additions.

Zac also needed to add the skill in his undead form, but he would have to wait for an hour before he could swap over again.

In the meantime, there were more skills to learn as a human. The second one that Zac learned was [Primal Polyglot], a skill that was a superior E-grade alternative to [Book of Babel]. Zac had already learned that multiple skills had similar functions as [Book of Babel], but the better ones provided additional benefits as well.

This skill was one such example.

[Primal Polyglot] provided the same feature of breaking down language barriers, but it went one step further. It provided the user with an almost instinctual understanding of "Dao-based" language, according to the description. This applied to a lot of things, most notably inscriptions, formations, and even pathways.

The skill wouldn't allow him to understand any fractal he saw at a glance, but it would help him get a sense of what he was dealing with based on the fundamental characteristics of the fractal. The same went for inscriptions and even some written languages. It would help Zac with everything from deducing arrays to spotting hidden dangers, and it seemed like a skill that could go hand in hand with his [Cosmic Gaze].

[Primal Polyglot – Proficiency: -. To comprehend the Language of the Dao is to comprehend the universe.]

Zac hoped that this skill would not only help him catch up with cultivators who had properly learned to decipher fractals and pathways since they were young, but perhaps even bridge some of the gaps of having no Dao Affinities.

Another skill that he considered replacing was **[True Strike]**. The one that occupied the same slot was **[Surging Vitality]**, the skill unsurprisingly related to the Vitality attribute. The skill he'd gotten from the duplicitous demon during his Tower climb had proven useful in a couple of battles, but it wasn't a critical addition in his human form.

His Edge of Arcadia class rather excelled in large-scale battles, and **[True Strike]** couldn't help much there.

More importantly, its effect had proven somewhat limited on enemies with ample combat experience, such as Void's Disciple. They seemed able to intuit it was a feint with their honed battle instincts, making it a waste of effort. Replacing it with a skill that could boost his healing abilities drastically seemed like a worthy trade.

However, he held off on it for now, opting to wait to see whether he could add the skill in his Draugr class instead. His undead side was still superior for recuperation, as it didn't require his organs to function, and there was no skill occupying that specific slot in his second set of pathways.

The only issue was the fit on his undead side. The original Brazla had planned for a lot, but preparing for undead descendants wasn't one of his contingencies. Only the ancillary skills on the first floor had fit his Draugr side at all, and Zac wasn't sure he would fare any better this time around. But it was worth a try if it meant he could keep another skill.

Having gone through the options, he eventually sat down to rest, waiting for the cooldown of his Specialty Core to end. During that time, he kept absorbing Cosmic Energy from E-grade Nexus Crystals. It didn't really help him with his cultivation, but some of it was swallowed by the core to be converted to Miasma. He had been completely drained when he swapped over, and this way he wouldn't be hit by a severe state of weakness when turning undead again.

It was a bit stressful to stay outside the Mystic Realm this long, but he didn't have much of a choice. He needed to learn every skill that could be useful right now, and he was in a pretty wretched state in any case. He had joked about crawling back to the Mystic Realm if need be, but he might actually have been forced to do so if he didn't rest up while waiting for his Specialty Core cooldown.

Some of his weakened state could be traced to dozens of internal wounds he'd accumulated during his rampage, but most of it no doubt was an effect of the [Rageroot Oak Seed].

Zac had really underestimated that seed, no matter if you were talking about the influence it had had on his mind or the side effects of using it. Most of the toxins had been removed during the tempering, but he still felt almost like he had one foot in the grave. He didn't even dare to imagine what kind of state he would be in if he hadn't enjoyed the cleansing magma immediately after. More importantly, Zac understood that he never could use that item in front of people he couldn't trust 100%, as he would be utterly vulnerable afterward.

An hour quickly passed, and Zac reluctantly got back to his feet. One new skill after another was added to Zac's repertoire before he finally swapped to his Draugr form and went another round. The final tally was six skills in his human form and three skills in his Draugr side. His fears were unfortunately realized when it turned out that only the ancillary skills could be added to his undead side, which forced him to give up on [True Strike].

A top-tier E-grade healing skill simply trumped the utility that the misdirection skill provided.

Seeing that he was done with everything, he exited the repository, almost thankful that Brazla was nowhere in sight. Waves of exhaustion crashed against his mind, but he still made a last-minute decision to head over to the Thayer Consortium.

He had a lot of outstanding orders with the Sky Gnome at the moment, most of them for quite rare items. It felt prudent to check things out himself in case he needed to ask follow-up questions to whatever Calrin had managed to acquire.

But more importantly, he needed to see if the Sky Gnome could find out anything about corrupted bloodlines or the Void Emperor Bloodline. Hopefully, he would be able to get his hand on some missive explaining the situation before he was locked inside the Mystic Realm. That would allow him to sidestep a potential mistake down the line.

Each step felt like a workout, but he soon enough arrived at the Thayer Consortium, surprising Calrin, who was busy at work fielding the hundreds of work orders for everything from defensive talismans to cultivation resources to use in case they got stuck inside the research base.

"Lord Atwood, don't you look... Eh..." Calrin coughed, seemingly struggling to come up with a compliment that wasn't a blatant lie. "There's no need for you to come yourself next time. Those spear maidens of yours can bring the things you require next time."

"I was in the neighborhood. Have you found what I asked for?" Zac sighed as he collapsed into the closest chair.

"I have. It's only the box, though," Calrin said, a slight blush tinting his round cheeks. "I'm afraid that the rest were out of our grasp, even at a premium."

Zac had tried getting his hands on all kinds of items that could provide immediate power-ups, the most pressing being E-grade Dao Treasures. He hadn't eaten a single one since reaching E-grade, which meant that he would get the full benefit if he managed to secure one.

There was a decent chance that a High-quality Dao Treasure would propel him all the way to gaining a High-mastery Dao Fragment, which was why Zac had wanted to get one even if he had to pay ten times what they were worth. He was even ready to sell off most of his treasure stockpile if the Sky Gnome could make it happen. But it looked like money couldn't just solve everything.

Zac had also expended some efforts to figure out what the Spatial Artifact in the Mystic Realm was in case he needed to prepare something to snatch it. Void's Disciple had divulged the name, but neither Brazla nor Calrin could find anything out at all. Of course, Zac didn't dare to outright ask around about a "Dimensional Seed."

This treasure was something that the Church of Everlasting Dao were going all out to obtain, to the point that they gave up all their other objectives. If someone suddenly started inquiring about such an item to the intelligence-gathering houses, trouble might soon follow. Certainly, most such establishments prided themselves on their discretion, but that was just up to a point.

So they could only gather missives on spatial and dimensional treasures in general, hoping that one of them would detail what a Dimensional Seed was. But so far, there wasn't much.

"Oh! That reminds me," Calrin said as he took out a crystal. "This one didn't have any information on the Dimensional Seed, but it did actually have some information about the [Ferric Worldeater]."

"Oh, really?" Zac asked with surprise.

"There is a faction called the Void Gate led by a peak figure of the Zecia Sector, the Void Priestess. They are in control of a unique spatial anomaly, the Void Star. According to rumors, there have been sightings of [Ferric Voidwyrms] in its vicinity. The name sounded familiar, so I started looking into it. Apparently, [Ferric Voidwyrms] are the larval form of a [Ferric Worldeater]," Calrin said.

This was great news to Zac, and the excitement dispelled some of the exhaustion.

The [Ferric Worldeater] was one of the materials that Karunthel required to upgrade the shipyard. Zac already knew about the first two items, and it was just a matter of time before he could get his hands on them. The last two were trickier. But Zac believed he might be able to find out some more about the fourth item, [Daemonic Manastone], through Ogras.

Since it had the name Daemonic, it might perhaps be related to the demonic hordes. There were only two pure demonic factions in the whole Zecia Sector, with the Azh'Kir'Khat Horde being the stronger of the two. There were certainly more demonkin spread across the sector just like humans, but Azh'Kir'Khat was his best bet.

That left only the worldeaters, but there hadn't been much to go by. They were surprisingly hard to gather intelligence on, even after having such an ominous name. But it looked like the Sky Gnome had come through for him once more.

Better yet, Zac actually had an in with this particular force.

"They are still quite dangerous even in their larval form, but they will only evolve to their true state if they manage to devour a World Core. The better the World Core, the greater the potential of the critter. If it manages to gobble up a C-grade World Core, then the thing would eventually become unstoppable in a remote sector such as ours," Calrin said with some fear in his eyes.

"What kind of faction is the Void Gate?" Zac asked.

He knew that they were religious in nature based on the terminology, but he'd never had a chance to ask about it when he met Leyara in the Base Town. His curiosity had grown since getting the **[Void Heart]** node, and now it felt as though they were connected by fate.

The Void Gate might hold not only the solution to finishing Karunthel's quest, but it might even hold the key to his new bloodline.

72

GATE

It wasn't such a stretch to think that a faction that all seemed centered around the "Void" was related to his constitution. Someone called the Void Priestess living in the Void Monastery by the Void Star and lording over a faction called the Void Gate was a bit too on the nose for it all to be a complete coincidence.

Then again, there were no doubt quite a few Heritages containing the word "Void," just like there was an endless number of ones having the name Heavenly, Primordial, Divine, or Origin. These words conveyed a sense of profundity and vastness, a sense that was rarely justified. The only reason he had held back on researching Leyara's Heritage until now was the shocking cost of buying intelligence on a powerful C-grade faction.

But looking into it was worth the expense now, especially considering the **[Ferric Worldeaters]**.

"I can certainly buy the missive…" the Sky Gnome said, though he looked a bit troubled. "But… ah… our operational funds are currently a bit…"

"How much?" Zac asked, understanding what the Sky Gnome was getting at.

"Two point five billion." Calrin coughed, looking disgusted even if it wasn't his own money.

"Just send the report to the Mystic Realm before it closes. I'm especially curious whether they have a Void-related bloodline." Zac sighed as he transferred the funds. "Also, see if you can find out anything about abnormal bloodlines. Mutated, corrupted, and unique bloodlines."

"Mutated?" Calrin muttered before he quickly nodded. "I haven't heard of anything like it, but I will make some discreet inquiries."

"Great. Also, prepare for a flash sale of our stockpile of resources in case we need to flee in the future. I'm running a bit low on money," Zac added after some thought.

"Not to make young master's day worse, but the box came at a certain premium as well," the Sky Gnome said with a weak smile.

The box in question wasn't a treasure, but rather a treasure box that would hopefully house and isolate the Dimensional Seed when he managed to snag it.

It had cost 775 million Nexus Coins even though it wasn't even a Spirit Tool, and Zac felt almost physically ill when he had to fork out such an exorbitant sum for an empty box. The reason for the price was the same as with [Everlasting], the shield that had become a component of [Love's Bond]. The locker was almost exclusively made from some sort of treasure jade that was one of the best materials around for storing treasures.

Part of the cost also came from the meticulous arrays that covered both its inner and outer surfaces, inscriptions meant to boost the effectiveness of the materials even further. It might be a bit overkill, but Zac wouldn't take any chances with an item that was so valuable that both the Dominators and the cultists would stop at nothing to get it.

"Thank you," Zac said as he put away the box in his Spatial Ring. "If you manage to get your hands on anything else, send it directly into the Mystic Realm. I doubt I will exit again before the Mystic Realm closes."

"Certainly… And good luck," Calrin said. "Remember, wealth is important, but surviving even more so. My instincts are telling me that this treasure might cause more harm than good."

"I actually feel the same way," Zac grunted. "But someone is going to get it, and that someone might as well be me."

Zac made his way to the teleporter, and he could breathe out in relief when he passed through the tunnel to the Mystic Realm. Everything pointed toward the pathway lasting a few more days, but it had still been in the back of Zac's head the whole time he'd spent outside. He didn't know what he'd have done if he'd actually been closed out early by some freak accident.

The exhaustion from using the [Rageroot Oak Seed] was only growing in severity as he made his way toward his temporary compound. His surroundings were soon just a blur, and he simply fell down on the grass the moment he had entered his protective arrays, immediately entering a dreamless slumber. He had no idea how long he had slept when he finally roused himself, but the realization that he wasn't alone shocked him wide awake.

"I wish I had one of my cameras with me." A leering voice reached Zac's ears just as [Verun's Bite] appeared in his hands, causing him to sigh in exasperation and turn to Ogras, who was sitting by a table not far away.

"Wasn't it you who told me that entering others' arrays was the height of rudeness?" Zac muttered as he took out a bottle of water from his Spatial Ring.

He still felt drained even after having slept, but he didn't really feel weakened any longer. It felt like he would be ready to go again as long as he got something to eat.

"Well, that rule's for strangers, not good comrades. So, care to tell me what you've been up to? You look like you've been swallowed and spat out by a Govidar Mawbeast," Ogras asked as he took a swig of wine.

"Your home planet sounds like a real nightmare, going by all these monsters you've described," Zac snorted. "If you must know, I broke open the second floor of the Dao Repository, unlocking the skills within."

"WHAT?" Ogras exclaimed as he jumped to his feet. "How is that possible?! You shouldn't be that powerful!" the demon said, his eyes a chaotic mix of confusion, glee, and jealousy.

"I have my ways," Zac said with a smile as he took out a massive slab of meat.

Zac rarely felt hungry any longer, but he felt like his stomach was about to implode right now. He tore into the meat like a ravenous beast, and he only stopped when he had eaten over ten kilos of E-grade beast meat. He didn't understand the physics of it, but he didn't question it either, as every bite felt like quenching rain in the parched desert that was his body.

"So?" Ogras eventually asked, posture leaning forward.

"How about a pretty please?" Zac smiled.

"I'd rather get cut apart by those spatial storms," Ogras spat.

"I'm kidding," Zac snorted. "You can bring up to five of the evolved demons. Oh, and bring Verana."

"Why bother with her?" Ogras asked with confusion.

"The charges in the crystals are limited, but not to the point that we can't spare a couple of slots. It's all to improve our upcoming odds." Zac shrugged.

"Well, those beasts have been proven useful lately." Ogras thoughtfully nodded. "Might not hurt to keep them happy."

"What do you mean?" Zac asked as he looked at his watch, and he was shocked to find out that he had slept for thirty straight hours.

"Now you realize?" Ogras laughed. "The Beast Masters were getting anxious that no one really was overly interested in cooperating with them, so they volunteered to expand our maps. It turns out that their beasts can actually smell or somehow sense the spatial traps. Guess that's another thing you have in common with them."

Zac ignored the jab, but he understood what the demon was getting at. He was able to easily identify the hidden traps thanks to his danger sense, but others weren't as lucky. They had to tread carefully all the time, as moving too quickly could result in suddenly getting bisected by a hidden spatial tear. The scientists were working on some means to identify the tears ahead of time, but progress was slow for now.

However, these Beast Masters actually could keep a decent pace thanks to their companions. That would not only decrease the risk of getting hurt but also rapidly speed up the progress they were making. They might prove integral to dealing with the inner parts of the Mystic Realm, as Zac could only imagine that the spatial anomalies would get even worse in there.

"Have a Beast Master join every scouting unit. Take three Tal-Eladar to the repository instead," Zac eventually said. "Up to three skills per person."

"How about five for your good buddy?" Ogras asked. "I did just die helping you."

"Fine, but I honestly doubt that you can even benefit from that many. I only took six different skills myself, and that's for two classes," Zac said with a roll of his eyes. "So, what else happened while I slept?"

"Nothin' spec– oh, speak of the devil. Your little spear maiden is waiting outside. She might know more," Ogras said before he was swallowed by the shadows.

"Deal with the scouting parties before you leave!" Zac shouted with a roll of his eyes before he walked out to get Joanna.

Joanna understood what he was looking for, so she updated Zac on what had transpired while he was out of commission. Nothing urgent had happened apart from their people learning new things by the hour. Their internal map had rapidly expanded, but the most important realization might be that the Cosmic Energy seemed to grow denser the further inside the Mystic Realm you moved.

There were already murmurs of people wanting to move further into the base, to turn some of the larger warehouses into advance camps. Zac wasn't too surprised, as the ambient Cosmic Energy in the biospheres was pretty dismal, especially for the people of Port Atwood, who were accustomed to living on top of a Nexus Vein.

This area right here was the safest thanks to the meter-thick door that only Tier 3 access could open, but every cultivator felt as though they were being stifled by the lacking ambient energy.

The difference was already measurable in the abandoned halls, and people believed the inner sections of the Mystic Realm to be even better. However, moving to the core of the Mystic Realm was easier said than done, as they had discovered a troubling phenomenon. There didn't seem to be pathways leading further inside the Mystic Realm.

After they exited the massive door, they could walk for roughly an hour toward the center of the Mystic Realm. At that point, one could only turn left or right, forgoing exploring the inner reaches. This was partly because most of the corridors simply stopped, while the few remaining ones were all guarded by endless spatial barriers.

They had already termed the sector they explored the "Outer Band," endless corridors and service tunnels, and their current goal was to find a way to reach further inside.

"Are you really okay?" Joanna asked with worry after having

delivered the status update. "No one has seen you for almost two days; some people even believed you were hurt by a spatial storm."

"I'm just a bit exhausted. I had to go all out to upgrade the Dao Repository," Zac said with a tired sigh. "What about your mission? Did you make it?"

"Yes! We reached the end of the map." Joanna nodded.

Most of the activities had been focused on dealing with expanding their map while improving their understanding of this place. However, Joanna had put together a small squad of elites, and she had teamed up with Thea and Billy to follow the map to see where the Cartava Clan wanted to lead them. It was a test for his group of closest allies. It was a test for himself of sorts as well, to see if he could let go and let others handle important tasks.

The fact that Joanna seemed fine was ample proof that he hadn't misplaced his trust.

"We mostly followed the path, while also making sure we had a backup route in case of ambush. But there was nothing untoward through the path. At the end, there was an enormous gate, a lot bigger than the one leading into this biosphere. We, unfortunately, couldn't open it, which is why we returned. We figured that one of you two siblings might be able to open it with Tier-4 clearance," Joanna explained.

"A gate?" Zac mused. "Did you knock?"

"Well… Billy tried to break it open," Joanna said with a grimace. "We almost got ourselves killed then and there. The corridor came alive and tried to stab us."

"Sounds like Billy, alright," Zac snorted. "It's good that you're okay. Guess it's good to know what happens when you try to force these things open. Did you find out anything else?"

"No." Joanna sighed. "But the door is in the inner edge of the Outer Band. I think it's your best bet at reaching further inside the base."

"Good," Zac said with some excitement as he stood up. "I'll check it out myself. What credentials did Billy get?" Zac asked as he suddenly thought of something.

"Nothing," Joanna said with a shake of her head. "I did manage to get a Tier-3 clearance, though."

"Could it be... Bloodlines?" Zac mused.

"Excuse me?" Joanna asked with confusion.

"Nothing," Zac said as he passed through his arrays. "Are you rested enough to set out again? It would be best to bring someone who has already traveled that path."

"We're coming with." A familiar voice reached Zac's ears just as he exited his compound, and Zac looked over at Billy and Thea, who seemed to have been standing in wait for some time.

73
HUNGER

"Have you implanted me with a tracker or something?" Zac wryly smiled as he looked over at Thea. "I can't go five meters without you popping out of nowhere."

"Well, you do have a tendency to go off on your own and cause trouble. A tracker wouldn't be such a bad idea," Thea said with a small smile. "Do you not want me around?"

"No, I appreciate your company." Zac sighed. "You just seem… anxious. Is everything okay?"

"Well, I am a bit annoyed that you apparently went ahead and put a sector-wide bull's-eye on our planet when you went off-planet," Thea said with mock anger before she sighed. "But more than anything, I'm angry with myself. The inheritance… was a wake-up call. I thought I had done all I could to gain enough strength to protect those around me, but I was just comparing myself to the people of Earth.

"I feel I have wasted too much time playing politics already, so I need to grasp every opportunity that I can now. I can feel it. If I don't increase my momentum, I might not even make it past E-grade. My class rarity won't allow it."

Zac looked at Thea with wide eyes. He wasn't sure if he had ever heard her speak that much in one go, and Zac also noticed that Joanna had moved far away at some unknown time. It looked like she had already thought things over, and what she said made sense. You could never relent on the path of cultivation. He had gathered a huge advantage during his time in the F-grade, but he needed to keep at it if he wanted to stay relevant.

His titles and attributes would slowly lose their value as others gained more powerful cultivation manuals and improved their Dao control. According to his sister, the ability to braid two Dao Seeds into one attack almost had the same effect as boosting both seeds one stage. The sum became greater than its parts.

He could only imagine that Dao Arrays were even more powerful, and he would be left in the dust unless he came up with his own strengths. It was good that Thea also had come to understand this fundamental truth. That insight alone might be worth more than anything else she'd gained from that inheritance.

"Well, that's fine… But don't overextend yourself," Zac eventually said as he scratched his chin. "I only act like I do because I have layers and layers of defensive measures. I'm not really someone to take after."

"No, I've seen how you fight," Thea snorted. "I'm more interested in inheriting your bravado than your battle techniques."

"I'm sure you'd make an excellent axe warrior." Zac smiled before he turned to Billy, who was standing not far away with a contrite look. "What's wrong with you?"

"Billy made a mistake." Billy sighed with a blush. "Billy is so smart, but for some reason, the door was harder."

"Well, it's bad luck you didn't get any credentials to open it the normal way," Zac said, though he wasn't so sure.

The more he thought about it, the more sense it made. If Billy's titanic bloodline came from this place, then it made sense that he wouldn't be able to move about freely. What kind of security system would hand out clearance to research subjects?

If he really was correct on this, then it might even explain why he didn't get any credentials either, and why Ogras got one so effortlessly. He already knew that Clan Azh'Rezak didn't possess any hereditary bloodlines, and Ogras hadn't acquired a synthetic one either unless his fusion with a shadow creature could count.

The only hole in the theory was the fact that Kenzie got access while he didn't, unless he considered the very real possibility that Kenzie wasn't the only child that Leandra had experimented on. She'd given Jeeves to Kenzie, but she might have infused him with a bloodline instead for two separate experiments.

"Stupid door realized Billy was too powerful, tried to keep Billy away. But we'll see," Billy muttered, but he shrank back a bit after getting an even look from Thea.

"Don't thwonk any more doors," she simply said, and Billy nodded hurriedly in agreement.

"Well, let's go." Zac shrugged as they set out.

"I'm coming as well!" a youthful voice shouted, and Zac grimaced when he saw Emily run toward them.

"What happened to your face?" Zac asked with a frown, noticing the new scar that just barely missed her eye.

"My face? What about your head? Have you become addicted to being bald?" Emily said with a glare. "No scouting parties dared to take me with them because of you, so I've been fighting on Mystic Island to gain levels. Come on, let me come with you. I swear I'll be careful. And look at this!"

Cosmic Energy in her body suddenly surged as a five-meter-tall Totem Pole appeared in front of her.

"I've reached level 50 already, and this is my new skill," she said with a proud smile. "Not bad, right?"

"It looks good, but what does it–" Zac muttered, but he stopped when he felt the Cosmic Energy churn in the area.

Not only that, but it almost felt like he had turned into a cultivator, as the Cosmic Energy seemed to be actively burrowing into his body.

"That's not all!" Emily smiled as a fiery axe appeared in her hand.

She didn't use the buffing skill on Zac though, but threw it straight at the Totem Pole. This led to a startling transformation as the totem almost grew twice in size while its design changed. If the earlier version looked a bit like something you could find in Incan ruins to worship one's ancestors, then the new one was something made to worship a sun god.

Fiery energies radiated from the pillar, and a large flame radiated at its top.

"My Strength has increased," Thea exclaimed with surprise, while Billy almost drooled as he looked at the Totem Pole.

"It buffs everyone in an area this way?" Zac said with surprise, but he suddenly noticed something different compared to getting directly buffed by the axe.

It only gave half of the amount it normally did.

Still, a 5% area boost was huge if this thing was placed on a battlefield, and that number might even grow as the skill's proficiency increased. Coupled with the increased energy restoration, it could even turn the tides of a war.

"I don't get any buff when using it like this. But I can even detonate this thing in case an enemy tries to take it down," Emily whispered so that only Zac could hear. "Its explosion should hurt anyone that's not crazy durable like you."

"Alright, you can come with us." Zac eventually nodded. "Let's go see what's on the other side of that door."

It looked like Emily's face was about to split in two judging by her grin, but she quickly composed herself after getting stared down.

"This is a serious mission. No messing around," Zac said. "And if things look dangerous on the other side of the door, you need to back down immediately while I try to keep you safe. Understand?"

"I understand." Emily quickly nodded with a serious expression. "You can count on me. I'm not some kid any longer."

She put her hands on her hips and pushed out her chest to underscore her point, but the power pose didn't really inspire a lot of confidence. She still looked like a cosplaying child due to the combination of her oversized furs and diminutive frame. Even Thea could barely contain her smile, whereas Billy openly snickered.

"Where's the demon?" Thea suddenly asked as she looked around. "That guy is like bad weather, always appearing to ruin a good day."

"He's busy elsewhere." Zac smiled. "It's just us."

Zac considered bringing some more people, but these three and Joanna were enough. The rest would need to stay and guard the fort while he was away. Getting to the end of the map would take the better part of a day even if they didn't take any detours, so they immediately set out so as not to waste any time.

However, they only managed to get to the security door before Zac had to stop the group.

"Wait," Zac said as he took out a slab of grilled meat, digging into it like a voracious animal.

"What? You're hungry?" Emily asked with confusion. "You had grease on your face when you left your compound as well. Are you a pig or something?"

Thea looked on with confusion as well, whereas Billy's reaction was much more straightforward. He sat down himself and produced an even bigger slab of meat, happily joining Zac for a travel snack.

"I was forced to use a berserking item yesterday." Zac sighed after he had devoured another few kilos of meat. "It turns out that it left my body starving for nutrients. We might need to make a few extra pit stops."

"Should we cancel this mission?" Thea asked, and Joanna seemed to agree. "Someone told me that I shouldn't overextend myself earlier. I think that advice can apply to you as well."

"I'm fine," Zac said. "I'm already a lot better than I was yesterday. I'm sure I'll be back to normal by the time we reach that gate you mentioned."

It was true. Between his sleep and the E-grade meat, he felt a lot better. He was still feeling a bit drained, but he would be able to fight just fine, especially if he had time to digest some more energy-dense food over the following hours. Thea and Joanna eventually relented, and they set off again, though this time with a slightly slower speed to allow Zac to recuperate and restore his reserves.

His new skill, **[Surging Vitality]**, unfortunately didn't work at all against something like this either. The nourishing storm that swept through his body helped with the countless small wounds left from his battle with the golem blacksmith, but they weren't the real problem right now.

Emily also tried imbuing him with her Earthen axe, which improved Endurance and Vitality, but it didn't really help either, so Zac simply kept walking while almost constantly nibbling on something or another. The endless identical tunnels quickly turned into a blur, but having Emily and Billy around kept the atmosphere light. They quickly reached the inner part of the Outer Band, at which point they veered east.

They actually did pass a few corridors leading further inside, but they were blocked by spatial storms without exception. Not only that, the spatial tears were placed a lot more densely in these traps, and

Zac's danger sense seemed to think these pathways were a lot more dangerous than the first one he encountered.

He wasn't really confident in breaking through a normal spatial blockade, let alone these empowered versions.

"It's a bit odd," Thea eventually said after Zac had backed away from the third pathway that might lead out of the Outer Ring. "Have you looked at the layout on the other side of these storms? I'm not actually sure they lead to the inner reaches. These corridors seem to end in large empty rooms. There might not actually be any physical path leading further inside, which seems like a crazy design choice."

"Ogras and I guessed that these corridors might be an enormous array or something, forming massive arrays. Perhaps they wanted that stuff separate from the inner sections," Zac said, though he agreed with Thea's sentiment. "Those rooms on the other side might be teleportation rooms as well. The Technocrats have real teleporters that don't use Cosmic Energy. I saw something like that in the Tower of Eternity."

Of course, Zac wasn't really sure he would dare to use one of the ancient teleporters left behind by his mother's family. The research base had been abandoned for god knows how long, and it was now infected by a powerful Spatial Treasure. Using an unknown teleporter sounded like a surefire way to get ripped apart by spatial anomalies.

"Do you think it's worth it for me to go to the Tower of Eternity as well?" Thea suddenly asked, dragging Zac out of his thoughts.

"Absolutely," Zac said without hesitation. "My power almost doubled over there. It was the only reason I could take down the undead incursion in one go. Why, have you got your hands on a token?"

"Both Billy and I have; we have been thinking about going as soon as this Mystic Realm is dealt with," Thea said, and Zac noticed some hesitation on her face. "I have been thinking about rushing over there. We have a few days before this place is estimated to close."

"Honestly, I'm not sure if it's worth it," Zac said after some thought. "You're still missing the titles and ultimate skills from reaching level 75, and we don't have access to the array breakers needed to make the most out of a run. If not for Ogras joining me, I'd be pretty lost. Besides, would you be able to spend a hundred days inside the Tower, thinking about the situation here?"

"I guess you're right," Thea sighed. "I just want to be useful. I hate this sense of helplessness."

Zac could understand the sentiment. Who hadn't felt a sense of helplessness at times since the integration struck?

"I hate to say it, but this is just the beginning," Zac eventually said. "Even if we succeed here, new threats will keep cropping up sooner or later. That's simply how the Multiverse works. We can't keep rushing our cultivation, or we'll just harm ourselves and Earth in the long run. Besides, you're plenty strong as it is, and there might even be opportunities for you to get stronger in this weird place."

Thea only nodded in response, but there was a small smile on her face as they continued through the corridors.

The two kept moving forward, and Zac detailed most of his experiences in the Base Town and Tower of Eternity, sharing the lessons he'd learned the hard way. Thea in turn tried to teach him how to braid Daos to empower skills even further, though things quickly became a bit embarrassing, as Zac couldn't even finish the first step.

"So I guess I haven't completely fallen behind." Thea laughed when Zac eventually had to give up.

Zac only laughed in response as he went back to surveying the surroundings. It felt nice, almost like when the two had traveled together during the Hunt. A lot of the pressures of command could be put aside for a while, allowing Zac to just be himself. However, the journey eventually had to end.

It took them thirteen hours to reach their target, an enormous gate that reached over thirty meters into the air. In fact, even the tunnels were extra supersized the last kilometer or so, meaning that this area had probably been more spacious than the usual tunnels even before the spatial expansion began.

That fact alone made Zac believe they had finally reached something of value after running around in empty hallways for almost a week. Zac's heart beat rapidly as he walked up to the console to the side. His axe was already in his hand, while the others prepared themselves in case of battle.

"Here I go," Zac muttered as he activated the gate mechanism.

74
CONFORMATION OF SUPREMACY

The group released a collective sigh of relief when the gates slid open without issue, giving them a first look at what waited for them on the other side. It was definitely a change of pace, and the group walked inside curiously. It looked like they had actually entered a glasshouse in the middle of a forest.

The gate led them into a room over one hundred meters across, and it appeared to be some sort of holding room or stable for beasts, with metallic troughs and dozens of reinforced stalls. They could also spot all sorts of advanced equipment in a series of adjoining rooms, which was only possible because both the inner and outer walls were made from some transparent material.

Outside the building was an enormous forest completely different from the artificial biospheres they had arrived in. It felt wild and genuine, like something they might find on Earth if you discounted the fact that most of the foliage was either white, silver, or purple. The place was huge as well, and Zac could even spot a few mountains in the distance. Zac couldn't be sure from where he stood, but he guessed that it would take hours to traverse the whole thing even if he kept a high pace.

However, it didn't take long to realize that this enormous forest was still just another part of the research base, as the familiar lines ran across the sky, and the enormous alloy wall stretched into the distance. There was one odd addition, though, nine orbs in the sky that reminded Zac of the moon. Four of them seemed broken, but the other five radiated a silver glow.

The transparent building they found themselves in was installed like an extension of the wall, with the gate they passed through on one side and a large barn door on the opposite.

The glasshouse was just enormous, but Zac figured that it was probably only a few hundred square meters before the spatial expansion began. Furthermore, going by the current size of the stalls, the animals that had been housed here should be around the size of a rhinoceros, which wasn't that big for a Multiverse beast.

"I think it's a satellite base to perform field experiments," Thea eventually said as she looked across the building. "The original owners of this place were studying something inside this forest, and this place was used to take measurements."

Zac slowly nodded in agreement, feeling there was a lot of merit to that theory. It looked like there was room for about a dozen animals at a time, going by the number of stalls, whereas the forest outside was large enough to sustain a whole ecosystem.

"Ah!" Billy suddenly exclaimed from another room, and Zac swirled toward him with wide eyes, fearing that the giant had triggered another trap.

Zac breathed out in relief when he saw that Billy had actually managed to open the gates by pressing a large button on one of the closest consoles.

"Be careful," Zac quickly exhorted. "We have no idea what these things do. One of them might trigger an alarm and make the building attack us."

Billy quickly nodded and stepped away.

Still, it was good news to know that even someone without any clearance could open the door without assistance. As long as Zac placed a squad in this place in the future, they would be able to come and go as they pleased without having to rely on himself or Kenzie.

"Why would the Cartava Clan lead us here?" Zac muttered as he looked over the consoles.

Most of them seemed to be out of order or at least turned off. There were no new messages like another signpost either, leaving Zac a bit confused.

"This place definitely leads further inside the Mystic Realm than what we've accessed until now," Thea mused as she nodded to their left. "Look, we're right at the edge of the Outer Band, but the forest continues for god knows how much further in."

"Let's check it out," Zac said after some thought. "Not much any of us can gain from these machines anyway."

"Might have been a good idea to bring something more than a bunch of muscle-heads," Joanna muttered from the side, and Zac could only agree.

True, his expedition squad was a bit lopsided, with the three strongest humans along with a teenage shaman and a Valkyrie guide. Billy's disposition spoke for itself, and both Zac and Thea were only focused on getting stronger, to put it nicely. More accurately, they were both fighting idiots.

Billy was more than willing to get out of the boring stables, and he pushed open the barn doors with a grunt. The group walked outside, but they stopped after only a few meters, realizing the glasshouse had disappeared. More importantly, Zac felt a sense of impending doom, like he would die if he didn't get out of the way.

The only reason that he didn't start running was that the feeling was distinctly different from his danger sense, like it was a cheap mimicry of the real thing.

"Illusion array," Thea muttered as she looked around with some trepidation. "Do you feel the weird sensation of dread as well?"

"It might be something to keep beasts away," Emily ventured. "Like bug repellant."

"Probably." Thea nodded before she looked into the sky with a slight frown. "The ambient energy is so dense in here, and there is some attunement in it as well."

Zac needed a bit longer to properly sense the Cosmic Energy, but he could see what she meant with the help of **[Cosmic Gaze]**. The whole forest was shrouded in a silvery haze after he activated his ocular skill, and it seemed to radiate down from the moons like light summer rain.

"Should we head toward the closest mountain? The closest one isn't too far, and we might be able to spot other exits that way," Thea ventured. "It's either that or keep to the wall."

"Let's go to the mountain," Zac eventually said. "The wall looks the same far into the horizon. We will probably learn more if we head a bit further in."

They immediately set out, this time led by Zac, who was using his natural affinity with the forest that came from [Forester's Constitution]. There were occasional calls of beasts that reverberated through the forest, and Zac tried to keep them away from any potentially dangerous spot. It was worth remembering that this place wasn't like Earth or the Tower of Eternity, and even Zac felt some pressure as he walked through the woods.

There were no limits here, so the beasts could even be D-grade for all they knew.

The fact that the strongest cultivators were just High E-grade indicated that the beasts weren't that powerful, and neither did the howls contain that kind of power. But they couldn't be certain. So Zac's senses were pushed to their limits as he kept a vigil on the surroundings, and the others looked back and forth as they snuck through dense parts of the undergrowth.

However, they only had time to advance for fifteen minutes before Zac sensed a hint of killing intent to their left. He looked over with a frown, as he hadn't seen any actual threat, but Thea reacted even quicker as her sword both left and entered its sheath before Zac even had time to summon [Verun's Bite]. A thin sapphire blade shot out from her weapon, appearing to be a wind blade infused with some Dao.

The wind blade contained extremely sharp energy along with a hint of that mysterious force that Brazla had called Sword Intent. A muffled thud sounded out the next moment, and the group hurried over to see what had been the source of the killing intent.

It turned out to be a wolf with luxuriant white fur, with a gray marking on its forehead the only exception. It was about as large as a cow and seemingly just at the bottleneck of the E-grade, judging by the pressure the carcass emitted.

"Won't be too bad if the beasts are just at this level," Zac muttered. "But there could be stronger ones out there as well. Maybe we should–"

"We can't back down from seeing just one F-grade beast," Thea interjected. "We'll never reach the core of this Mystic Realm then. But we need to be careful; if there is one wolf, there are definitely more."

"Billy isn't afraid of any stupid dogs," Billy muttered as he gripped his club even tighter.

"Let's keep going, then," Zac said as he stowed away the carcass before spreading some corpse-removing powder across the grass to remove the scent of blood.

The group kept going, moving in a circuitous path toward the mountain ahead. Zac kept his eyes peeled for more wolves, but there were no odd energy movements in the air, nor were there any bloodthirsty howls of a pack on the prowl. A couple of minutes later, they started to relax again as they closed in on the mountain.

However, Zac's eyes widened in shock when hundreds of wolves materialized out of what looked like moonlight, each of them emitting an aura of an E-grade beast. Not only that, but Zac could tell with one glance that they weren't some average mutts. They should come from some powerful bloodline, as even the weakest E-grade wolves easily eclipsed the pressure that the Fiend Wolf of the Beast Tides had emitted.

He even sensed a few auras that were a match to his own.

"Run!" Zac unhesitantly shouted, but he froze upon turning around.

They were surrounded.

More and more wolves kept appearing out of thin air, and there were thousands of them encircling their small group before they had a chance to react. Zac didn't know if there were even more of them on the way, but he knew that dealing with just these ones would be difficult enough. They needed to get back to the glasshouse before they were overrun.

None of the wolves had made their move yet, but Zac wasn't above drawing first blood as a massive fractal blade appeared, stretching over a hundred meters and cutting dozens of trees apart from its aura alone. It shimmered in gold and black, and Zac launched two series of swings at the wolves that blocked their retreat.

Two wolves, each of them radiating an extremely condensed aura, were ready for the attack. The marks on their foreheads lit up as the two clouds of **[Rapturous Divide]** shot toward their rear guard, and the thousands of wolves released a unified howl. A huge moon appeared above them, and it drenched the whole battlefield in a silver radiance. The light contained an immense pressure as well, and it forced Emily to her knees.

The others were able to stand it, though Joanna was visibly pale from the effort.

More importantly, Zac frowned when he sensed the energies of his strike being continuously whittled down. He tried to counteract the effect by using his recently improved command of his Dao, but it felt like he was trying to hold back the tide with his bare hands. By the time the two energies of [Rapturous Divide] reached the wolves, they were all but hollowed out.

The familiar scene of the paradisial divide still appeared, but it almost felt like an illusion. A few dozen wolves were cut apart in an instant before one of the larger wolves literally bit the image with enough force to rip it apart, but there were more than enough beasts to fill up the holes in the ranks.

The two wolves that towered above the others howled again, and the previously orderly encirclement rippled as over a hundred wolves started rushing toward them.

"STAY AWAY FROM BILLY'S FRIENDS!" Billy roared as his body started growing, but the growth actually stopped when he reached just four meters.

His physique had transformed, his muscles turning inhumanly defined as a golden set of runes spread across his frame like a wildfire. Zac was mostly focused on the incoming wolves, but he could swear that the giant even gained at least twenty additional muscles that humans simply lacked. Even Billy's eyes radiated an immense primordial aura as the air exploded around him, and he was among the E-grade wolves before Zac had a chance to make his next move.

A coruscating shockwave erupted where Billy appeared, and five wolves were turned into paste before he had even swung his club. What followed was a tremendous horizontal swing that caused sixteen wolves to implode, and the whole area shook and heaved as the Titan remolded the area with his fury.

However, these wolves were far from ordinary prey, and a squad led by a grizzled alpha moved to intercept Billy's advance, and a wave of silver light actually managed to stop the giant's attack. It looked like the energy of his attack was whittled down just like Zac's had been just a few seconds ago.

Five wolves appeared out of silver light next to Billy the next moment, but it was as though the giant had eyes in his neck as the series of muscles in his shins generated a furious and instantaneous momentum, which allowed him to spin his club in a 360-degree arc, killing three and maiming another two.

"Help him carve a way out. I'll protect our backs," Zac said as he exploded into action as well, as a series of fractal blades shot out to hopefully cause some damage to the incoming beasts.

However, the incessant moonlight from above was still causing trouble, and the fractal blades couldn't even guarantee a single kill before they were drained and broke apart. It was like the environment itself was fighting against them, and the animals kept getting closer to the exposed backs of his squad. Thea and Joanna were already desperately pushing forward, and Emily's form was in constant motion as she sent out one buff or minor axe strike after another.

Zac frowned as he saw the incoming tide, and his eyes darted to the two leaders, which still kept their position on top of a rock in the center of the pack like generals overseeing their army. His wide-scale attacks were restrained by whatever that moon above was doing, so he would need to get closer if he wanted to kill them. But doing so would likely result in the death of at least one person in his squad.

The fighting had only started a few seconds ago, but everyone but Emily already sported wounds. If they also had to deal with the wolves coming from behind, they would be overrun in seconds. He needed to thin out the herd a bit before he dealt with the leaders. Using [Deforestation] or [Nature's Punishment] felt extremely risky as well, as long as the moon remained, so he needed to come up with another solution.

A huge amount of energy surged toward an intricate fractal at the lower end of his spine, and it quickly started to radiate a shocking amount of power.

There hadn't even been a chance to test the skill out, but Zac saw no option but to activate **[Conformation of Supremacy]**.

75
OVERRUN

A shockwave erupted from Zac's body, causing the closest wolves to be thrown away as their bodies twisted and deformed. Zac wasn't focused on that, but rather the three-meter halo that had appeared behind him. It was a circle that shone in silver, though the silver of a honed blade rather than the moonlight that drowned out the area.

It was covered in dense scripts, but the true core of the skill was the image in the middle of the halo.

It was the deceptively unadorned axe that Zac had witnessed in his very first Dao Vision, the weapon of the axe-man who had singlehandedly caused the death of both the divine faction and most likely a whole world. The axe looked almost exactly the same as how Zac remembered it when it had been stabbed into the ground next to the endless chasm, and the image infused the halo with an almost blinding sharpness.

"Supremacy," Zac muttered as he started running forward, each step causing cracks to spread for dozens of meters.

His momentum was rapidly growing as his spectral forest rose around him, giving him perfect vantage of the incoming wolves. He realized that there were as many invisible wolves approaching as visible ones, but he didn't worry. The heaviness and sharpness of the halo behind him coursed through his body, and it was ready to be released at a moment's notice.

Zac swung **[Verun's Bite]** toward the closest clump of wolves when they were just twenty meters away, and pained yowls cut through the incessant roars of the vast wolf pack. The mournful cries were cut short as a dozen E-grade wolves were flung away like they were pieces of trash, their bodies mangled almost beyond recognition. The ground itself was crushed and split apart as well, forming a deep chasm that stretched almost fifty meters before the power in Zac's swing lost its strength.

That was just the beginning, as one swing after another started reaping the lives of the vanguard of the wolves, to the point that his killing speed surpassed that of the other three combined. Waves of moonlight drowned him both from above and from the wolves themselves, but this new skill wasn't as easily worn down as [Chop]. The halo was connected to Zac himself and almost impervious to the effect while the strikes were instantaneous, not allowing for the slightest weakening before the damage was already done.

His targets weren't cleanly bisected as they would have been from [**Rapturous Divide**] or the final swing of [**Blighted Cut**], but they rather looked like they had been cut and bludgeoned simultaneously. Wherever Zac turned his attention, a wave of carnage would soon follow as long as the halo behind his back remained.

Each swing of his axe contained not only his own strength, but it also contained a fragment of the boundless conviction and power of the original wielder of the simple woodman's axe. The blood of the wolves was already dying the whole area red, and a shocking stream of Cosmic Energy was entering Zac's body from the kill.

There were simply too many wolves to stop them all from reaching Thea and the others, so he could only focus on the most powerful-looking squads. The others would be able to deal with the Peak F-grade wolves and their recently evolved brothers, but only Zac could kill the ones who were approaching Middle E-grade quickly enough.

Five packs was enough to almost open up his next node, and Zac was forced to trap the rest so as not to break open a node in the middle of the battle. It almost looked like he formed a sanguine cloud that rotated around him as he flashed back and forth among the trees, each jump with [**Loamwalker**] resulting in the death of even more wolves.

These elite wolves weren't dumb brutes that simply took Zac's attacks lying down, and his whole body was covered in wounds caused by razor-sharp claws and hundreds of energy attacks that they could launch from their foreheads. Their bodies were extremely sturdy as well, and if it weren't for the added sharpness of his swings, he would eventually have been overrun by their sheer numbers.

It was all thanks to his recently acquired skill, [Conformation of Supremacy], the skill in the Dao Repository that was linked to the Strength attribute. It didn't conjure a massive weapon like [Deforestation] or any fantastical sights like [Rapturous Divide]. It simply infused his normal swings with the power of the object depicted in the avatar.

The axe-man in his Dao Vision had almost split a whole world apart with a swing of his axe, but Zac obviously couldn't quite reach that level with his swings. But it still produced an effect far beyond the destruction he could cause with his most similar skill, [Unholy Strike], while also having a slew of other benefits.

First of all, [Conformation of Supremacy] didn't need to be charged for every attack like the skill he'd gotten from Mhal required. The halo did dim down a bit after every attack, but Zac could push more Cosmic Energy into it to reignite its power. The effect also wasn't limited to an increase in physical strength, but it rather imbued his swings with a mysterious energy based on the avatar, almost like it gained an additional Dao Seed.

The only downsides to the skill were the high energy consumption and the fact that the skill could be considered a mid-range attack at best since it didn't actually launch any projectiles. The damage caused by Zac's swings was rather just an outburst of the force contained in his attacks.

It had been a pretty big disappointment to see that the Endurance-based defensive skill clashed with [Deforestation], forcing him to give up on getting a new defensive skill now that [Nature's Barrier] was lagging behind. However, the fact that the Strength-based skill didn't clash with a single one of his skills felt like a huge windfall. It was the third skill he had picked up, and his only regret was that he couldn't get it in his Draugr side as well.

The skill was simple and direct, just how Zac liked it. He was only able to infuse it with his Fragment of the Axe at the moment, but some Dao limitations weren't that uncommon with Early proficiency skills.

The fact that the picture within the halo looked just like the axe in his Dao Vision obviously wasn't a coincidence, but the skill actually had no connection to that axe-wielding master at all. [Conformation of Supremacy] was rather a blank slate, where you could create your own avatar of supremacy.

The image was interchangeable, and it could be different every time the skill was activated. However, the better the image resonated with your current intent, the more power it would provide, albeit at a higher energy consumption.

Zac had chosen the image based on that Dao Vision, as it still held a huge position in his heart, and his thoughts often wandered back to the scene of that man's battle against the celestials and the gates of heaven. He had witnessed even more shocking sights and even more powerful beings since then, for example, the Grand Protector who defended his world against the death of a universe. But the axe-man was the first true supreme being Zac had seen, a testament of what was possible in this new world.

There was probably no avatar that was as defining of Zac's cultivation path as that lone axe, making it the optimal choice for an avatar. Choosing other avatars might bring out all kinds of interesting effects, but he needed every advantage he could eke out at the moment.

Another horizontal swing resulted in a wave of destruction rippling outward, but a solid silver crescent flew out to intercept the attack. It was one of the leading wolves, which had launched some sort of attack from its forehead, and Zac glanced at it with a frown. He tried another few attacks, but the wolves had caught on by now, and they spread out.

[Conformation of Supremacy] was able to boost the power of his attacks by a great degree, but its range was limited to around fifty meters, and it weakened the further away from Zac the strike was. He was forced to keep running back and forth, but each swing only managed to take out a couple of wolves after they started to adapt.

He was still keeping a decent pace, and the Cosmic Energy gathered in his body was starting to reach almost uncomfortable levels, but he knew that the situation wasn't really sustainable. Each swing empowered by his new skill cost a decent chunk of Cosmic Energy, even more than a dozen [Chop]s. That was fine when he killed over twenty powerful wolves with one strike, but he was killing fewer than five with each attack right now.

Zac appeared next to another elite wolf, and it bit straight at his throat the moment he appeared. Zac was ready for the attack thanks to **[Hatchetman's Spirit]**, and he simply pivoted his body a bit as **[Verun's Bite]** fell, cutting both its spine and lungs apart as a heavy wave of sharpness swallowed another three wolves before they had time to jump away.

Another surge of energy entered his body, and he was starting to feel bloated. However, his mind wasn't on slowing down his killing, but rather the opposite. He needed to change the current situation somehow. The moon in the sky was able to whittle down any long-range attacks from the looks of it, forcing both him and the others into a melee against the beasts.

The moon itself was hundreds of meters in the air, and there was no way for Zac to break it apart. He tried flashing toward the two leaders in an attempt to take them out, but two massive lunar crescents forced him into a defensive stance as the other wolves heedlessly started rushing toward the others.

He could only scramble back to protect the rear of the others, unable to leave as much as a flesh wound on the two alphas.

Zac growled in annoyance as he crushed the head of the closest wolf, and he was even considering taking out the cursed blade to deal with the moon above him. The curse that he had just managed to expel was a troubling hidden threat, but he didn't have a lot of options at the moment. He tried shooting a few fractal blades toward the sky, but the pressure that the moon emitted was clearly stronger the closer the blades got.

A sigh escaped his lips as he took out the rotting sword, but he froze when a sudden thud echoed out from his chest. The closest wolves staggered backward with bleeding ears, but Zac wasn't all that much better off as he stumbled to his knees. Another thud caused a wave of weakness to spread across his body, and he sensed how his accumulated energy was rapidly being stolen.

The **[Void Heart]** had finally woken up, and it was hungry.

The wolves clearly saw an opportunity when Zac fell down on his knees, but a sapphire sheen cut apart the two closest nearby wolves as Thea suddenly appeared next to him.

"Are you okay?" she shouted as she desperately fended off the elite wolves that were going in for the kill.

A wave of destruction rippled out to clear the area as Zac swung his axe from a kneeling position, but another heartbeat made him lose his balance, causing him to fall over. Even worse, he sensed that the hidden node was still voraciously hungry, and Zac was afraid that it would start feasting on his own Cosmic Energy if he didn't quickly kill some more beasts.

"Can you create an opening to the big ones? I might be able to take one out then," Thea whispered as she helped Zac to his feet.

Zac wordlessly nodded as he looked at the two wolves in the distance. Creating an opening didn't only mean occupying the two big bastards, but it meant also dealing with a huge number of the more powerful that were barring the path. He looked down at the tattered sword for a second, but he decidedly put it away.

The white arc that the sword produced was extremely powerful, but it wasn't that fast. He was afraid that the moonlight would have whittled it down before it even had a chance to pick up its pace, which would place a curse on him for nothing. More importantly, the cursed sword was considered an external tool, and kills with the weapon wouldn't count as his kills. Normally that wouldn't matter, but his hidden node was screaming for sustenance. **[Deforestation]** was also a risky move and something he wanted to save for later if possible.

Finally, there was only one thing that he could think of, and **[Love's Bond]** slithered across his body as it fastened itself to his back. He hadn't expected to waste any of the long-cooldown skills of his Spirit Tool at this juncture, but he saw no better option. He had one remaining card that might work even in these conditions, and it might even be able to destroy the foundations of the moon itself.

He needed to activate **[Fate's Obduracy]**.

76
STORM SURGE

The offensive skill of his Spirit Tool was extremely powerful, and it even had the unique feature of becoming stronger by being damaged. The moon would only assist him by forcing the chains to break and split apart like a hydra, and kills by his bound weapon obviously counted as his own. It was an attack of massive proportions as well, to the point that it might even destabilize the moon in the sky, killing two birds with one stone.

It was clear that the two leaders hadn't conjured the enormous moon by themselves. It was continuously bolstered by hundreds of streams of energy coming from the whole pack. The moon had already grown a bit dimmer from the mounting death tally, and Zac hoped there would be a critical point where the skill failed.

The two fractal lines on the lid lit up as the four chains of [Love's Bond] shot forward, and an eerie rattling sound echoed across the area as the fractals turned into two new chains wrought by pure darkness. A discordant sizzling sound entered Zac's ears as the moonlight started to break them apart, but Zac breathed out in relief when he saw that two chains turned into four as a result. Waves of silver light erupted from the wolves as well, and they slammed into the incoming chains to dispel the attack. But the result was simply even more chains.

The last time Zac had used this skill, he had focused it all on a small clump of targets, but this time, he spread the net wide. Most of the chains flew in the direction of the leaders to clear out all the beasts that were in the way, while the remainder turned in a parabolic ark in the opposite direction to assist his beleaguered squad. Billy was fighting valiantly, but his chest rose and fell like two bellows as sweat streamed down his face.

He was maintaining a speed that even Zac would have trouble matching, and Zac guessed it was the skill he had learned in the inheritance. There was no way that such a powerful technique didn't have a downside, and Zac guessed that its energy consumption was immense. Billy was still not even Peak F-grade, and he wouldn't be able to keep going indefinitely.

One wolf after another was gored by the chains, and the two leaders finally lost their patience as they roared in anger, each of them swiping at the chains from their position. A series of lunar blades shot out from their claws, and the air itself was ripped apart as they flew forward.

The chains of [Fate's Obduracy] were no match from the combined attacks of what no doubt were two Middle E-grade beasts with powerful bloodlines. But that was just what Zac had hoped to see, as the chains rapidly multiplied, turning into a sea of links that caused havoc across the battlefield.

A terrifying surge of Cosmic Energy soared into his body, almost immediately eclipsing what Zac could bear. But the [Void Heart] had turned into a black hole, unceasingly swallowing more and more pure Cosmic Energy. It was the exact opposite of how it usually worked, which was a bit concerning, but Zac figured that it was better than releasing it out into the atmosphere.

Over two hundred E-grade wolves had died from one single attack, and it was still going strong. This was no doubt Zac's largest harvest ever, and it had significantly lessened the pressure of the moon above. One of the leaders seemed to have entered a state of madness after witnessing the sea of corpses, and it could no longer hold back as it jumped forward, releasing a frenzied barrage of attacks on the chains of [Love's Bond].

Its whole body shone with lunar light, and the extremely durable links were like dried wood in front of its all-out offensive. The chains kept splitting and rejoining the fight, but they were steadily pushed back. Zac tried to cause as much damage to the wolf as possible, but he only managed to cause some minor wounds.

That was fine with Zac, as he intentionally retreated the chains further and further back, and he had soon created a distance of hundreds of meters between the two alpha wolves. The second leader seemed a lot more coolheaded, and it roared a warning to its companion. Only then did the leader seem to cool down a bit, but Zac had already achieved his purpose.

The wolves in the way were dead, and the leader was alone. It was just in time as well, as the sea of chains had reached a breaking point after taking on the whole wolf pack for half a minute, and all but four chains shattered and dissipated in an instant. It left a slightly wounded and disoriented wolf among a sea of corpses.

The chains didn't even have time to completely dispel before another form appeared right above the alpha wolf. It was Thea, and both her palms were pointed straight at the back of the wolf's head as terrifying energies surged around her body. The wolf was in a frenzied state, but its reactions were on point.

It lit up with lunar light as it tried to jump away, but four chains had unknowingly snaked around its legs, rooting it in place. It was the true chains of [**Love's Bond**], and Zac had snuck them next to the wolf among the skill he launched. The chains cracked in an instant from the pressure that the wolf emitted, but a fraction of a second was all that was needed.

A beam of pure energy that made Zac's hair stand on end slammed into the back of the alpha wolf's head before it had a chance to dodge, and Zac almost lost his footing as the beam passed straight through the skull and slammed into the ground with barely any loss of power. It was the very same skill that Thea had tried using against Inevitability during the Hunt, but this time, it was not only far more powerful, but it was also performed point-blank.

The attack was a success, but Thea didn't walk away unscathed. Her eyes rolled up in her head as she fell down on the ground after releasing the beam of destruction.

The concentrated power was perhaps only matched by Zac's final strike of [**Blighted Cut**], but it took everything of Thea to launch it. The other alpha wolf howled with rage and jumped off from the rock as well, but Zac's reaction was even quicker. He appeared next to the unmoving form of Thea and scooped her up before a barrage of attacks had a chance to kill her.

Such speed would have been impossible a second ago, but the combination of Zac's widespread killing and Thea assassinating one of the leaders was enough to break the moon lording in the sky. It dissipated into a cloud of chaotic energies that slowly started to dissipate.

The remaining wolves were utterly infuriated by seeing their leader being killed, but they still maintained their distance. Zac wasn't clear whether it was because they hadn't received any orders from the infuriated alpha, or if it was because of the hundreds of corpses that surrounded Zac's position.

But the air was almost vibrating from the incessant howls that came from every direction. There was a ruthless bloodlust in them, to the point that it was palpable. Their combined fury had essentially become a mental attack that caused even Zac to feel some shudders in his mind. And if he was in that state, then there was no need to explain the state of the others.

Thea woke up after just a second, but her face was pallid, and her hands were shaking badly.

"Billy! I need you to help the others! Take them and run back where we came from! I'll hold the rest off and lead them away from you. Can you do it?" Zac said as he started launching a barrage of fractal blades at the wolves.

Without the moon protecting them, [Chop] once more had a decent lethality, but that was just to a certain point. They still had only killed off less than 30 percent of the whole pack, and each fractal blade only managed to kill a few of the beasts before they lost their strength. Cutting through powerful E-grade beasts took a lot of energy, and [Chop] could only contain so much, being an F-grade skill.

These wolves were still a lot sturdier than most things Zac had encountered in the Tower of Eternity, and it probably wasn't a coincidence.

In fact, they reminded Zac more of Verun than any wolves he had seen thus far. They weren't similar in appearance, but rather the primal aura they emitted. Zac could only guess that it wasn't a coincidence that these beasts had been brought here. They were most likely former subjects for experimentation just like the groups of cultivators stuck in the research base.

"Billy will save them! Then Billy will come back and save you too!" the giant shouted before he gently scooped up an unconscious Emily in his free arm.

The teenager had constantly infused the others, including Zac, with buffs while also providing Cosmic Energy through her dance. But all of them were peak fighters with a lot of titles while Emily was just level 50. She had already overtaxed herself to the point she fell unconscious, with Joanna standing vigil over her.

Joanna herself wasn't much better off, as she was barely keeping upright with the help of her spear. Billy simply picked her up by the lapel of her battle suit and threw her across one of his shoulders. Billy was about to do the same with Thea as well, but she shook her head as she steadied her steps.

"I can walk by myself," Thea said before she turned to Zac. "I'm sorry. I keep letting you down."

"What are you talking about? Things would have been a lot worse if you didn't take out the big guy," Zac said. "Don't worry. I'll be fine now that the moon is gone. This might be an opportunity for me. You've already got your levels. I'll join you guys a bit later."

"That kill pushed me all the way to level 75. Next time, I won't be a burden," Thea said, and she led Billy away.

A group of wolves suddenly appeared out of nowhere to intercept them, but a blinding blue flash lit up the surroundings before they simply fell apart. Thea stumbled as blood poured from her ears, and she looked like she was teetering on the brink of collapse. However, she somehow managed to steady herself and start running, allowing Zac to finally breathe out in relief.

Unfortunately, the relief was short-lived, as over a hundred of the wolves split off from the main pack while the elites kept Zac busy. Thea was barely standing by this point, and Billy was carrying Joanna and Emily. There was no way they'd be able to fend off such a squad.

Zac growled in annoyance as he activated **[Hatchetman's Rage]**, and sharp pain spread across his body. He initially didn't want to use this skill while still dealing with some lingering effects of using the

[Rageroot Oak Seed]. However, he was out of options, and he needed to kill a lot of wolves quickly.

The fractal edge attached to his axe grew over a hundred meters and gained a golden sheen. **[Rapturous Divide]** had finally come off cooldown from his first attempt, and now was as good a time as any to use it. He didn't launch his enormous fractal edge at the hundreds of wolves that went for Billy, but rather toward the elites that were blocking his path.

His new skill was powerful, but the hides of these wolves were far too durable, and it wouldn't be able to take out all of them in one go.

That was not to say that he had abandoned his allies. Immense amounts of Cosmic Energy was already surging into his left forearm as he launched two swings toward the elite wolves with enough speed to turn his arm into a blur. The wolves shot out a barrage of crescent moons to stop the clouds, but **[Rapturous Divide]** wasn't possible to stop that way.

The alpha moved to intercept as well, but it was too slow. The hulking wolves were first covered in a layer of gold, which was followed by the darkness of the abyss. Zac didn't bother looking at the result, confident in the fact that most of the wolves should die from that attack. He instead activated **[Loamwalker]**, flashing right past the spatial divide.

He was more worried about the pack of wolves that were rapidly closing in on his allies. They thankfully didn't get far before a massive hand appeared in the air above them, and most of them were pushed down on their stomachs from the terrifying pressure it emitted thanks to **[Hatchetman's Rage]** and the Fragment of the Bodhi.

It was finally Zac who restrained the wolves, rather than the other way around.

A shocking amount of water spilled out of the fractal the next moment, drowning the whole area in water. A lot of wolves were crushed to death by the endless deluge while the survivors were swept up in a tsunami that started leveling this whole sector of the forest.

The water punishment wasn't as deadly as the wooden one, but it was able to cause more widespread chaos. He had essentially poured half a lake on top of the leader of the Underworld Golem incursion, and this time, there was no lava to turn the endless amount of water into steam.

A mighty howl reverberated through the air, and Zac frowned when he knew that the alpha wolf had made his move. This was only further evidenced by the fact that the whole area was drowned in a cold white luster. It was almost like the world had become monochrome, and Zac quickly turned back toward the alpha just in time to see an enormous beam shoot past him, aiming straight for the array in the sky.

Zac wanted to stop it, but there was no time. The speed of the beam was almost instantaneous, and it slammed into the emerald array the next moment. Zac grunted and staggered a step backward as the array cracked. Even the hand was pierced by the light, and Zac was forced to discard the skill.

Billy and Thea had already managed to flee by this point, but Zac knew his job was not over as he turned toward the remaining leader and the hundreds of wolves that were still standing.

77
ALPHA

The burning embers of **[Hatchetman's Rage]** kept Zac standing through the frenetic absorption from his **[Void Heart]** as scores of wolves were drowned or crushed by **[Nature's Punishment]** before the manmade calamity was ended prematurely. Each thump from the hidden node caused a bout of dizziness, but Zac forced his mind to focus as he gazed at the remaining wolves.

As for the wolves that had been swept away by the tsunami, he didn't really care. Almost half of them had died, judging by the streams of energy that still entered his body, and the survivors shouldn't be in any state to cause any more trouble. Billy and Thea were long out of sight, and Zac felt a huge weight had been lifted from his shoulders. He just needed to keep these rabid bastards at bay for a bit longer before he could retreat as well.

However, he would only escape if he really ran out of options, especially after having activated **[Hatchetman's Rage]**. He really didn't want to stop while his **[Void Heart]** was still absorbing energy. Something important was definitely happening inside the node, and Zac didn't want to ruin it at this juncture.

It might be evolving, or it might be fusing it with the extremely pure Dao Energy of the Tribulation Lightning to create something amazing.

Besides, Zac still had some cards up his sleeve, though the same could obviously be said about the alpha. A gibbous moon had appeared a hundred meters above its head, and it was no doubt the source of the earlier beam. The moon was different than the earlier one, as a single look with **[Cosmic Gaze]** indicated that it didn't draw any energy from the other wolves. Zac didn't feel any restrictions either, which hopefully meant that the moon wouldn't be able to whittle down his large-scale attacks.

The new moon might have been lacking some functionality, but it clearly had some other abilities to make up for it. Its luster gradually increased in intensity as the alpha howled, and Zac guessed that another beam was incoming. His mind raced as he tried to think of a solution. The last attack was just too fast, and he wasn't confident in countering its speed. The second skill of **[Love's Bond]** would no doubt be able to block it, but he had already wasted one of his aces for this fight.

It took a lot of resources and time to light up the two fractals of **[Fate's Obduracy]** after using it against the cultists, and he wasn't sure he'd be able to restore the skill again before he met his real enemies. He couldn't waste limited skills like his bronze spark or **[Death's Embrace]** against these wolves, as it was just a chance encounter with the wildlife.

Thankfully, there were some other options available now that the whole battlefield wasn't locked down.

Zac's arm strained as a massive axe appeared above his head, and the first swing of **[Deforestation]** was launched the moment that the second pulse of the moon shot toward him. The wave of destruction and the beam of lunar light clashed in the air between the two, and Zac's brows scrunched when he actually couldn't cut through the moonlight.

It was rather the beam that crushed his cutting wave, though it lost almost all its strength doing so. The rest was quickly dispersed by a swing of Zac's axe. The moon itself dimmed considerably, and it shrank from a gibbous moon to a half-moon. That no doubt meant that the conjuration had more charges in store. But so did Zac.

The Infernal Axe appeared while the shockwaves of the first clash had yet to ebb, and Zac launched it toward the wolf pack. If the Axe of

Felling barely fell short, then the second swing should get the trick done. Better yet, it appeared as though the moon needed a few more seconds to charge up its next attack. It gave Zac time to create some wholesale slaughter in the meantime.

A rippling wave of flames crashed toward the wolves, and there finally was a primal fear deep within their eyes. Not even the drowned shrubbery in the surroundings was spared as they were incinerated the moment the Infernal Axe crossed their path.

The alpha was obviously far smarter than a regular beast, and it seemed to understand that its pack was in a bad spot. It released another keening howl into the sky, and the scores of wolves around it quickly followed suit as their bodies started to radiate lunar light.

Zac's brows first scrunched at the scene, but his confusion was quickly replaced with shock as the howling wolves turned into pure light that was swallowed by the moon. Each infusion increased its luster by a noticeable degree, clearly cutting down on the time the skill needed to attack again. Zac couldn't believe what he was seeing.

Not only had the wolves activated what essentially was a War Array before, but they were even able to coordinate some sort of sacrificial skill now. The half-moon released a blinding wave of light the next moment, this time a widespread radiance that was a match to the incoming wildfire in width.

Fiery gouts and white flashes turned the battlefield into a blinding hellscape, and Zac was forced to close his eyes from the intensity. However, [Hatchetman's Spirit] was still active, allowing him to narrowly dodge a series of errant blasts of chaotic energies. A large number of the wolves weren't as lucky, and yet another dense stream of Cosmic Energy was gobbled up by the Hidden Node.

The last round of energy seemed to finally have satiated the [Void Heart], and Zac could finally breathe out in relief as the incessant beating stopped. However, the fact that the node didn't seem to demand any more energy wouldn't stop Zac from releasing the final axe. The last alpha wolf was looking a bit worse for wear, and it couldn't have too much energy left after unleashing these powerful attacks.

If Zac could kill it along with a last batch of elites, then he would get a round of energy just for himself, and it would definitely be enough for him to gain another level. Perhaps even two levels depending on how much the alpha provided. That would put him at level 85, and it wasn't completely unheard of to gain some sort of class quest at that point. Most got their second quests at level 90, but it wasn't an iron-clad rule.

The ominous Axe of Desolation took shape above his head even before the chaotic energies of the battlefield had abated, and his arm strained as he began the third and final swing. However, an extremely scary stream of almost impossibly condensed energies was suddenly spat out of the [Void Heart], and it started to rampage through Zac's body as though it was looking for something.

It felt like a stream of lava was burrowing through his body, and Zac was completely unable to maintain the skill because of the pain. A small gust of the ashen desolation shot out toward the wolves, but it was a far cry from the true power of the final swing of [Deforestation]. The alpha wolf quickly noticed Zac's wretched state, as he was lying on the ground spasming, and its eyes lit up as the remaining crescent moon actually shot straight toward him like a projectile.

"I think I need some help, buddy," Zac croaked as he looked at the army of remaining wolves.

An infuriated howl answered in his mind, and Verun appeared next to him in all its splendor. Its gaze was already trained on the incoming crescent, and bloodlust shone in its eyes. It released another mighty roar, this time for real rather than in Zac's head, and the forest shook from the power it contained.

The red streaks across Verun's hide shone with a sanguine luster as its mane danced in the wind. Swirls of blood floated around its paws, and Zac felt as though he was looking at a sea of death when gazing at the streams. The crescent was almost upon them, but Zac didn't worry even if he was barely able to remain conscious. His Tool Spirit emitted a haughty confidence even in front of the incoming attack.

Verun actually sent out a crescent of its own the next moment, a massive arc of condensed blood. It clashed with the crescent moon the next moment, but there was no explosion or shockwave. The blood was liquid, and it actually swallowed the moon whole as it continued its trajectory. The blood crescent quickly destabilized though, exploding into cascading streams of silvery blood that maimed any wolf it hit.

The Tool Spirit was clearly the one with the advantage, but Verun actually seemed enraged that it hadn't managed to hit the alpha wolf with its attack. It turned into a stream of sanguine energy as it flashed forward, heading straight for the core of the pack. A few wolves tried to block Verun's path, but they were quickly turned into dried husks that fell to the ground, causing Zac to be beset by another wave of Cosmic Energy.

A bloodthirsty aura exploded out from the alpha once more as it ran toward the Tool Spirit, and its eyes had turned into two silver moons.

A storm of red and silver erupted in middle of the pack as the two beasts fought for supremacy. Zac himself wanted to help, but he was in no state to even move. He could only make himself as inconspicuous as possible as he hid behind the carcasses of a couple of wolves, spectating the battle from his hidden spot.

Most of his concentration was still aimed at the situation inside his body, and he was starting to worry when he saw that the stream actually had glommed onto his [Axe Mastery] skill fractal. That skill wasn't all that important to him any longer, so losing it wouldn't be the end of the world. But if that odd stream of energy could destroy one skill, then it could destroy another.

A massive outburst of power forced Zac out of his introspection, just in time to see Verun bite down on the alpha wolf's neck with its oversized maw. Both combatants sported a series of wounds, but the wolf was clearly worse off. Not one of the other beasts helped their leader, though, and they just stood rooted in place as Verun started to fling its head back and forth until it managed to rip off most of the wolf's neck.

Blood poured out of the dying alpha wolf like a fountain, but it was quickly absorbed by Verun as the Tool Spirit roared victoriously toward the sky. Zac was completely inundated with Cosmic Energy as well a second later, to the point that he almost forgot the pain he was in. He was about to force himself back on his feet in case the wolf pack went berserk, but his eyes widened when he saw that the sea of wolves lay down on the ground in an act of submission, their heads pointing toward Verun.

Zac couldn't believe what he was seeing. Had these wolves actually accepted Verun as the new alpha after it killed the old one? A few of the more powerful wolves seemed to share Zac's skepticism, and they jumped the Tool Spirit as one. However, Verun had turned the far more powerful alpha wolf into a bloody mess, so how could these upstarts match its might?

They were ruthlessly slaughtered in seconds, and soon there was not a single wolf that dared to lift its head. Zac hesitated for a second before he started to make his way toward Verun, which still proudly stood on the hill overlooking its new subjects. His movement was immediately discovered, and dozens of wolves seemed ready to pounce.

A snarl from Verun stopped them in their tracks, but Zac could see that they were barely able to restrain themselves. The instinct of these animals was extremely strong, to the point that their muscles shuddered as they kept themselves at bay. Zac knew that just a hasty movement would be enough to set them off, no matter how much Verun ordered against it.

It was a shame, as thoughts of domestication had entered his mind when he saw the situation unfold. Who would say no to a powerful pack of E-grade wolves who could do their bidding? Having them would be far more effective than the barghest, which had essentially turned into training fodder for the young cultivators of Port Atwood.

His only hope was that the wolves were overly excited from the battle and all the blood, and that they would be easier to domesticate after things calmed down.

"Good job." Zac smiled as he patted the Tool Spirit, not caring at all about his hand being drenched in the blood of the alpha wolf. "Do you think you can keep these guys under contr–"

He didn't get any further as the sound of a tremendous heartbeat rippled out from his body. Verun yowled in surprise and took a step back, and the nearest wolves seemed to have been physically impacted from it, as blood started pouring out of their mouths and ears.

Zac himself was shocked to see that the terrifying stream of energy of before was just the first half, and the second part had just been expelled from the hidden node. He was barely standing upright with the original force in his body, and he felt the same sort of despair now as when he'd seen the Tribulation Lightning coming for him.

This was too much for him to handle.

"Protect me," Zac only had time to say before his Hidden Node beat again, causing the two streams to join up and slam into his soul.

78
DELAYED GRATIFICATION

The Bodhi had stood like a beacon in the arid badlands for centuries, its vitality in a constant struggle against the desolation around it. With each turn of the seasons, it was buffeted by the anguish of a dying world, but the onslaught only served to temper the purity of its conviction. The inscriptions on the golden leaves contained deeper truths every year, and its intention was clear: to bring life to this sea of suffering.

Another century passed before a wind picked up pace among the lifeless glaciers in the far east, and it met no resistance from the flat steppes as it pushed forward. The leaves of the Bodhi were once again dancing with delight from the ethereal caress, and a song of change echoed throughout the badlands. The proclamation of the Holy Sangha was hidden among the leaves, constantly consecrating its surroundings.

The world had been on the brink of death for untold ages, but life always finds a way. A stalk of grass pushed through parched dirt, heralding the new era.

A hundred hooded beings walked forward between the Fallen Hills, each step bringing forth the rattling of chains and clattering of bones. The sun was high in the sky, blasting an uncomfortable warmth that was rapidly dispelling the soothing haze. Now and then, a protector would emerge from his grave and charge at the procession, but their oath kept them bound to their graves. They finally reached their target, the Nameless Mountain.

The hooded beings knelt in obeisance, keeping in check their desire to gaze upon the Holy Coffin. The coffin in question was the only interment on the whole mountain, as nothing could encroach on its domain. One day, the black coffin had simply appeared there, and to this day, no one had been able to figure out its origin. They didn't even know who or what was inside.

But they knew it was powerful, akin to a god.

A thud echoed out from the coffin, a thud that made the whole clergy shake with excitement. The coffin had answered their call, meaning that their plight was over. A small crack opened in the chained-up coffin, and an endless tide of darkness and pestilence surged toward the sky to meet the punishing rays of the sun.

The whole world was covered in darkness a second later, and the land was at peace. The clergymen once more performed the rites of obeisance before they rose to their feet. The junior acolyte finally couldn't help himself as they started making their way out of the holy hills, and the skeleton snuck a glance at the peak of the mountain.

The coffin silently hung from its chains from the branch of a pitch-black tree, behind it a faltering sun; that was the last thing the novice Necromancer ever saw.

Zac finally remembered himself after being awash in the two visions, but his spiritual journey wasn't over there. He was shown one scene after another, not all of them from his own memories.

Many of the visions were all too familiar, each bringing with them a painful memory. They showcased his struggles and desperate battles, from the barghest that had found his campsite to the wolves that had surrendered just seconds ago. There were also visions of strange lands, of weird objects containing terrifying amounts of wild energies. They all beckoned to Zac, urging him to conquer the opposition and claim them as his price.

The visions were so quick that they almost turned to a blur, but he did notice one odd detail. In every single scene, there was one constant: the Stele of Conflict he had conjured during his climb. Sometimes it was placed right next to the action, and other times, it was discreetly placed in the background.

But it was always there.

Zac tried to make sense of the scenes, but something was just out of his grasp. He was instead swept up by the heat of the battles he witnessed, and it almost felt like he had eaten another berserking treasure as he saw one scene of bloodshed after another. Something was growing inside him. Each kill was another building block, each battle setting the foundation. He was building a bridge toward the Heavens with the corpses of his enemies.

The scenes were suddenly ripped apart by a shocking flash of blue lightning, throwing him into one final vision.

A cracked dome floated in space, an impossibly large structure broken and scorched beyond repair. An infant's cry echoed out toward the vast beyond, but it was overpowered by the roar of an endless sea of lightning. It should have ended then and there, but a hand pushed through Heaven's Wrath and brought him away, ignoring the sizzling sounds of molten flesh and metal.

Darkness.

Only then did Zac find himself back in his own body, and he took a ragged breath as he opened his eyes. Most of the wolves were gone, but a few new carcasses were strewn around him as Verun stood in vigil by his side. The streams of blood around its feet were mostly gone by this point, meaning that the Tool Spirit was running out of time.

Thankfully, Zac sensed that he would be able to keep Verun around for a few minutes longer as long as it didn't need to expend a bunch of energy fighting. Seeing that he was safe for the moment, Zac breathed out in relief before his mind turned to the scenes he had just witnessed. The last thing he remembered was the stream of power rushing straight for his mind, and then he had been swept up in a series of visions.

He was curious about his status screen, but the state of his body took precedence. Zac had seen how his skill had been attacked earlier by the initial stream of energy, and he definitely felt that something was different compared to before, prompting him to turn his sight inward. The moment he activated his spiritual sight, Zac realized that drastic changes had taken place, though he couldn't understand what the significance of the change was.

First of all, all three skill fractals that came with a Dao Vision had changed, not only [Axe Mastery]. The other two skills, [Forester's Constitution] and [Bulwark Mastery], had been transformed as well. Previously, they had resembled an axe, a tree, and a shield respectively, but they now looked like abstract skill fractals just like all the others.

Intuition fueled by [Primal Polyglot] told Zac that it wasn't an upgrade, but neither was it a devolution. The change probably came from the second difference that Zac spotted a second later. He could make out three objects in the middle of his soul.

His soul had looked like a slightly murky glass ball in his mind until now, with scars and lines crossing its surface. The cage for the Remnants was hidden in a subspace of its own, so it wasn't directly visible, but now actual objects were moving about in his mind.

In the absolute middle of his mind, Zac actually saw himself, or rather a small spiritual avatar in his likeness. He was holding [Verun's Bite] in his hand, and he kept swinging it as he dodged and pivoted in place. It looked like the small spirit copy was fighting an endless number of invisible enemies, and the constant battle was generating some sort of power that Zac could sense hidden within the avatar.

Pure streams of the Dao from the surroundings were steadily entering the avatar's body as well, like his miniature self was a black hole.

The energies didn't come from his soul, though, but rather the two other objects that were slowly orbiting his avatar. The first of them was the chained coffin hovering from the branch of a dead tree with a dying sun serving as its backdrop. The scene looked almost exactly like his vision earlier, and half of the energy that his avatar was absorbing was the deathly haze that escaped from within the coffin.

The final addition was unsurprisingly the Bodhi Tree that he had witnessed in two Dao Visions by now. Its canopy formed an almost perfect circle, and the leaves continuously radiated golden energy that slowly drifted toward avatar Zac. The energies of the two apparitions continuously clashed as they formed a black-and-gold nebula that swiveled around the avatar until they were swallowed.

It was obviously his three Dao Fragments given form, and Zac started to understand what was going on as he looked upon the scene. This was an actual embryonic representation of his cultivation path where the "core" of his Daos had moved from skill fractals to his soul. It seemed a lot more logical compared to before, though he didn't know if there were any real benefits of the change.

The odd thing was that neither Ogras nor anyone else on Port Atwood had ever mentioned anything like this. Zac had even asked if problems could arise when upgrading the skills or his Daos, but Ogras seemed to be of the understanding that it didn't matter. The fractal would upgrade to a better form that could keep housing the Dao, according to the demon.

The first reason for the change Zac could think of was the fact that he had taken the first steps toward a proper path worthy of an Arcane class. It wouldn't be too surprising if Ogras didn't know about that change, as Arcane classes simply didn't exist on his homeworld. Zac figured that the change could only be good if that was the case.

There might be hidden benefits of changing things up this way or even hidden pitfalls of keeping one's Daos inside the skill fractals.

However, what confused Zac a bit was where those energies were going. All three apparitions were steadily generating pure Dao, but it was all swallowed by the avatar. Zac tried to magnify the scene as much as he could until he suddenly froze in shock. He didn't hesitate this time as he took out what looked like a piece of coal, and he crammed it into his mouth like he was starving.

A prickling sensation spread through his body the next moment, like every cell in his body was undergoing some sort of acupuncture. A comfortable heat was also starting to accumulate in his spine. He was neither undergoing another round of tempering or acupuncture, but he had rather eaten the **[Bloodline Marrow]** because of what he sensed inside his avatar.

It was his second Hidden Node, nestled in the head of his spiritual avatar.

Zac had spotted this node a few times by now, but the latest burst of energy had almost completely opened it. He could feel that it was just on the verge of breaking open, but the burst from before wasn't quite enough to get the job done, causing it to slowly close again. The Dao Energies were trying to keep it open, but it was a losing battle.

He had saved the marrow all this time in hopes of using it to awaken his bloodline, but he couldn't give up on this opportunity. Breaking open Hidden Nodes was far more difficult than nurturing one's bloodline, and if his marrow could take him the final stretch, it would definitely be worth it. Zac thought of eating the spiritual **[Four Gates Pill]** as well, but he soon decided against it.

There was nothing that actually indicated that the pill would be able to help with Hidden Nodes, and his body was already chock-full of Cosmic Energy thanks to Verun's onslaught. Besides, he had already decided to eat it before reaching the core for a burst of levels in case he still hadn't gained enough power-ups by then.

This was no time to get distracted, though, and he stopped the energy from the marrow from burrowing into his bones, instead directing it toward his mind. He guessed that the **[Bloodline Marrow]** was trying to activate his bloodline, but he didn't change his mind as he staunchly pushed all of the energy into his spiritual avatar instead.

More and more power was crammed into the node hidden within his spiritual self until a ripple spread out from his glabella. It was his second Hidden Node that had properly been broken open, and Zac felt his Mental Energy surge and spread out like never before. For a moment, he felt connected with everything in the universe, where he was one with the Dao. But he lost the fantastical feeling as soon as he gained it, and Zac's mind was once again whisked away to yet another vision.

He was once more sitting next to his mysterious ancestor, hurtling through the vast space on top of a meteor.

79
PATHSTRIDER

It almost felt like Zac had never left the solitary rock hurtling through the boundless expanse. He felt the heat of the drained sun on his back, and the surface of the meteor was still illuminated by its rays. He soon realized that the meteor wasn't as simple as it seemed, though, as space and time seemed to bend to its will. It kept running into one energy-dense object after another at a rapid pace, the vast distances of outer space made inconsequential.

Everything from stars to mysterious meteors was sucked dry by the cultivator, turning him into a wandering calamity. But the world suddenly shuddered as the meteor was forced to a stop in the middle of nowhere, and Zac spotted a man standing in the void. He radiated terrifying killing intent, and he looked at the unmoving man on top of the meteor with greed in his eyes.

The man said something as a sword materialized in his hand, but Zac couldn't make out any sound at all. However, the sword alone spoke volumes, and its sharpness forced Zac to look away. Zac still couldn't see the features of his presumed ancestor from his vantage, but it looked like he didn't care all too much about the man who barred his path.

The ancestor didn't summon a weapon of his own, but he rather just pointed at the swordmaster with his left hand. Zac felt the world was ending the next moment as both space and time were ripped apart. An area spanning millions of kilometers was caught up in the storm of annihilation, and not even the vacuum of the void was unscathed.

Zac could somewhat spot the swordmaster struggling within the torrent for a few seconds, but he was soon drowned and obliterated. Neither his body nor his treasure sword survived, and the whole sector of space still hadn't restored its spatial integrity by the time the meteor started moving again.

The vision started to fade as soon as the "battle" ended, but it still replayed over and over in Zac's mind.

There was one thing that Zac was certain of: the attack hadn't contained even a shred of Cosmic Energy. It was a simple outburst of Dao and Mental Energy, a truly weaponized version of a Dao Field. That fact alone almost made Zac's mind short-circuit, and one thought remained even after Zac woke up in the silver forest.

Just how powerful was that man's soul to be able to utterly destroy an area far surpassing a planet with just his Dao?

Another screen appeared like when he'd opened his last node, but the text wasn't all that helpful this time around either.

[Spiritual Void – An omnivorous mind tempered by the primordial void.]

He quickly turned his sight inward once more, but not much had changed. The three apparitions still floated about in the center of his soul, and the Hidden Node inside his avatar was still slowly drawing on the energies of the three images. However, the node was properly opened this time around, and Zac figured that this behavior was one of the features of the node.

Part of him wanted to start experimenting with his Daos, but the time that Verun could maintain its corporeal form was quickly running out. He conveyed a couple of orders through the Tool Spirit, and he was relieved to see that most of the remaining wolves blended into the forest the next second.

He had only given two orders to the pack since he was afraid that they wouldn't be able to follow anything more complex than that. The first was to stay away from the wall at the side with the glasshouse. Secondly, he ordered all but six wolves to go away, to go about their business. The remaining six wolves were just at the Peak F-grade, and Zac alone could subdue their fighting spirit with his aura even after being afflicted by the weakness of **[Hatchetman's Rage]**.

Verun turned into a stream of blood that squeezed into the axe a minute later, leaving Zac and the wolves in an awkward stalemate. However, Zac was relieved to see that releasing his aura wasn't even necessary. The wolves were actually subdued by Verun even after it returned to the axe, and they even followed basic commands from Zac himself.

The group started to walk back the way Zac came from as soon as he had looted the corpses of both the alphas and most of the elites. Zac still held off on experimenting with his Daos, partly because he was afraid that he'd spook the wolves, and partly because he felt that his new hidden node hadn't completely stabilized yet.

But there were other things to check while he made his way back, and he opened his status screen to see if the recent experiences had changed anything there.

Name: Zachary Atwood
Level: 83
Class: [E-Epic] Edge of Arcadia
Race: [E] Human – Void Emperor (Corrupted, Unawakened)
Alignment: [Earth] Port Atwood – Lord

Titles: […] Fated, Peak Power, Sovereign-select, Frontrunner, Pathstrider
Limited Titles: Tower of Eternity Sector All-Star – 14th
Dao: Fragment of the Axe – High, Fragment of the Coffin – Middle, Fragment of the Bodhi – Middle
Core: [E] Duplicity

Strength: 2,756 [Increase: 91%. Efficiency: 228%]
Dexterity: 1,312 [Increase: 65%. Efficiency: 187%]
Endurance: 2,338 [Increase: 99%. Efficiency: 218%]
Vitality: 1,552 [Increase: 89%. Efficiency: 218%]
Intelligence: 584 [Increase: 65%. Efficiency: 187%]
Wisdom: 1,071 [Increase: 70%. Efficiency: 187%]

Luck: 359 [Increase: 91%. Efficiency: 197%]

Free Points: 0
Nexus Coins: [F] 1,839,996,020

Zac felt a surge of adrenaline course through his body when he saw how much his attributes had improved, almost completely making him forget how exhausted he felt from the backlash. The probable source was easily spotted as well, and Zac quickly opened up his Dao screen.

[Fragment of the Axe (High): All attributes +30, Strength +500, Dexterity +250, Endurance +30, Wisdom +110. Effectiveness of Strength +15%.]

He had initially been afraid that the series of Dao Visions wouldn't improve his Fragments, but it looked like it was an unfounded fear. The digested tribulation lightning had actually allowed him to push his main Dao to the next level just based on his insights back during the Zhix Wars. That was a huge windfall for Zac, and that improvement alone drastically increased his confidence for the upcoming battles. The attributes were a welcome boost, but the true gain was the improvement to the Dao's lethality in battle.

It was a bit of a disappointment that his earlier theory had been wrong, with neither the All Attributes nor Efficiency doubling at every upgrade. It rather looked like he gained 10 All Attributes and 5% Efficiency at every step. It meant that he would end up with 40 to all attributes at Peak mastery, as opposed to 80.

The total amount of gained attributes would still be the same, but the difference meant a loss of hundreds of points in Luck when including all three Fragments. This way it would possibly be easier for him to maintain his lead compared to others though, so Zac figured it might not be too bad. The other two Dao Fragments hadn't improved this time around, though Zac felt he had made some strides just by congealing those two apparitions.

That wasn't the only gain of the battle, as he had actually gotten a new title. Zac eagerly opened his Title screen to see what the Pathstrider title provided, but the prompt almost made him collapse in despair.

[Pathstrider: Form a cohesive Cultivation Path while still in E-grade. Reward: Marked for further training.]

This was the second title he got without an actual reward, but Zac inwardly groaned, as he felt that this one was even worse than the Terminus title. He knew all too well what the System considered "training." This title was essentially a trouble magnet, and the only thing that Zac felt was missing was the infuriating "congratulations" that the System extended.

Zac sighed and closed the status screen, which drew a few wary glances from the young wolves. At least the title brought some good news; his cultivation path had been given a passing mark by the System.

There was nothing else for him to do in this forest for the time being, and he increased his speed toward the glasshouse. The wolves followed in tow, though it looked like every step they took was full of reluctance as they ran further and further from the rest of the pack.

The return trip took him almost an hour thanks to his weakened condition, but he finally reached the area with the camouflaged glasshouse. Zac wasn't sure whether the others were still around or whether they were on the way back to the base, but his question was soon answered as Billy appeared out of nowhere with his club at the ready.

"Wait! I tamed these guys," Zac explained, but his voice rapidly lost its strength as the group of wolves pounced at the giant without hesitation.

The young wolves were clearly out for blood, and nothing Zac did with **[Verun's Bite]** could quell their bloodthirst. Zac could only sigh and flash forward, punching the closest one on the side of its head, instantly knocking it out. Billy grinned and followed suit as he bashed the closest one, and a few seconds later, all six wolves were lying unconscious on the ground.

"Ah, stupid dogs," Billy muttered. "Need to be trained."

"Exactly." Zac nodded as he turned to Thea, who had walked out from the illusion array while the two dealt with the wolves. "Are you okay?"

Billy was still looking a bit tired, but his wounds were mostly superficial. He would most likely be fine in a few days. However, Thea looked a lot worse for wear. Her face was completely pallid, and her eyes were sunken, and they even seemed to have lost some of their color. The skill she'd used, [Void Piercer], was able to display a completely shocking might, but something told him that the cost of using it was equally harsh.

She simply shouldn't be able to release such an amount of power as things currently stood, and Zac guessed that the skill could be considered a taboo skill like the escape method she possessed. It either had to cost life force or come with some other huge drawback, something far worse than his current state from using [Hatchetman's Rage].

For a moment, Zac had thought she'd rush off to the Tower of Eternity because of her sudden burst of levels, but it looked like that was out of the question going by her state.

"It's nothing," Thea said with a shake of her head. "I'll be better in a few days. It's good to see you're fine as well; the energy outbursts before were pretty intense."

"Be careful," Zac could only say, realizing that Thea didn't want him to worry. "How's Emily and Joanna?"

"They're both sleeping." Billy yawned. "Thea should be sleeping as well, but she refused."

"Emily overdrew her energy to the point that she even used a little bit of life force." Thea sighed. "She needs to rest, or it might harm her future cultivation."

Zac nodded with a grimace, feeling a wave of guilt coming over him. He knew that the teenager needed to spread her wings and join proper missions if she would have any chance of making it on the road of cultivation, but this was probably the wrong place to do so.

"Don't blame yourself. No one can predict everything, and she will be fine," Thea said. "More importantly, we were afraid you would be coming with a thousand wolves nipping at your heels, but you actually tamed a few of them? What's going on? Why didn't these guys attack you?"

"It's my Tool Spirit," Zac said after some thought as he looked down at the pitiable animals, explaining how Verun had become the alpha of the pack.

"It's that powerful?" Thea asked with glimmering eyes. "It seems I need to focus even more on my new companion."

"I was hoping they would stay docile even when I'm not around, but it looks like that might take some time. Perhaps the Beast Masters have some means to quickly domesticate them though," Zac muttered.

"The Tal-Eladar, can they be trusted?" Thea asked. "Your relations seem a bit strained."

"They are a business partner rather than an ally," Zac said after some thought. "They were pretty useless before, but they seem to have come around since they failed to assist during the undead incursion. Their ambiguous situation makes them work really hard as well."

"So what are you planning on doing next?" Thea asked, putting the matter of the wolves aside.

"I'm going to explore the forest a bit," Zac said without hesitation. "But I need to do something first."

As for what that was, it was simple. He still had a storm of Cosmic Energy rampaging about in his body, and he needed to break open some nodes now that he was safe within the glasshouse.

80
LUNAR FOREST

Zac had considered his next step on his way back, and he decided to take a tour of this place, taking advantage of the fact that his axe had somehow given him carte blanche of the forest. He had already sensed that there were a lot of valuable herbs in this forest, and only he could pass through these parts without becoming food for the wolves.

Everything pointed toward this place being created for bloodline research, so any plant that grew in this place might be useful for exactly that. Opening his second Hidden Node had been an unexpected gain, but it had also cost him one of his two bloodline treasures, leaving him only with the **[Bloodline Nucleus]** he'd gained during the Tower climb. It would be best if he could find some plants to make up for the loss.

The dimensional treasure wouldn't wake up for a few days in either case, and his sister seemed to believe that the spatial obstructions would be in place until it did. Now was his last chance to break open his nodes and do some simple exploration. He guessed there would be no time for that afterward.

He also wanted to set out on his own for a bit to get a better understanding of the changes in his body and to get accustomed to his new skills.

"So you're setting off alone again?" Thea asked with a frown.

"Bringing these guys was a test," Zac said as he pointed down at the unconscious wolves. "I can somewhat move among the wolves because I'm connected to my axe, but it looks like that protection doesn't extend to others. However, I still need your help."

"What are you thinking?" Thea asked, her brows relaxing a bit.

"We need to find the entrances to the inner reaches of the Mystic Realm, and we're running out of time. If we split up, we can cover more ground. I tried instructing the wolves to stay away, which hopefully will allow you to move along the wall toward in search of another path. It might still be extremely dangerous even without the wolves," Zac said. "Meanwhile, I'll cross the forest to take a look at the other side. Perhaps there's another structure like this one over there."

"Sounds like a plan. We'll go back and update the main group and bring Emily to a safer place to recuperate. Should we bring your sister back here?" Thea said before she gave Zac a pointed look. "She's the only other one who can open these doors. It's a bit odd that only the two of you managed to get Tier-4 clearance, by the way."

"I got my clearance through the Tower of Eternity. Kenzie might just be lucky. There can only be one chief caretaker, after all. Have Joanna stay in the glasshouse to open the gate for you instead. My sister has enough on her plate," Zac said after some thought before he looked down at the wolves. "Someone needs to look after these guys as well."

Billy and Zac carried the unconscious wolves into the oversized stalls next, and Zac was relieved to see that a barrier automatically sprang up, trapping them inside. Not only that, but water was also dispensed, and a few light bulbs started to emit the same lunar light as the moons outside. It saved Zac a lot of headache, allowing him to prepare to open his nodes.

It was over an hour since he'd gained the energy by this point, and he had already lost a third of the energy he'd gained from the battle. More and more energy seeped through the cracks of his energy trap, and if he didn't use the energy soon, it would all be lost.

"I need to break open a node. Give me an hour," Zac said as he walked toward one of the adjoining rooms.

"What? Break open? Are you crazy?" Thea blurted as she grabbed his arm. "I read that doing so is extremely harmful. It can even kill you!"

"I don't have a lot of options as a mortal," Zac explained with a grimace. "But I'm pretty sturdy. I'll be fine."

Thea reluctantly let him go, and Zac sat down as soon as the sliding doors closed. The next node was in his leg just like most of the previous ones, though it was a bit further up. It was just below his knee this time, forcing Zac to be extremely careful. He became a little bit more skilled every time he opened a node, but getting wounded was inevitable.

The only thing he could hope to accomplish was to try to avoid letting anything important get destroyed and rather sacrifice his muscles. It hurt just as much that way, but muscles seemed to be the easiest part to restore with healing pills and his Dao. So it was with extreme caution that he pushed more and more of his excess energy into the node until a surging force erupted twenty minutes later.

A stabbing pain almost made Zac black out, but he clenched his fist with enough force to draw blood from his palm to stay awake. His left leg had almost been blown clean off this time even with how careful he was, and it almost looked like one of the wolves from before had ripped out a part of his calf.

Blood drenched the whole floor, and some had even spattered on the glass walls, and Zac quickly ate a healing pill as he activated [Surging Vitality]. For a few seconds, there was no effect, but the maimed muscles on his legs started to wiggle and writhe a moment later, almost looking like a pack of snakes as they twisted about.

The pain intensified over twofold, but Zac held on, ignoring both the sweat that streamed down his leg and the large amount of Cosmic Energy that was drained. It turned out that [Surging Vitality] could actually utilize the energy he gathered from kills, and one stream after another entered the skill fractal by his Specialty Core.

The energy wasn't transformed into life-attuned energy or something nature-aspected like his Dao, but it rather reminded Zac of his [Bone-Forging Dust]. The energy was unattuned, or perhaps flesh-attuned if there was such a thing. The energy entered his mangled leg, and it boosted the natural healing ability of his body rather than traditional life-attuned healing. That was why his muscles were wriggling so much; they were being forcibly regrown.

Such a process was excruciating, though, a far cry from the warm and soothing streams of healing pills or the curing skills of people like Sui. It also only worked on his physical body and not his pathways, though that wasn't a surprise.

What was a bit surprising was how much energy it cost. Using the skill for just fifteen minutes had cost him almost as much Cosmic Energy as the pitched battle before, and it had cost him over half of the accumulated kill energy. The remaining energy was barely enough for him to push his human side to level 84 and start working on his next node.

On the bright side, it was very effective. Newly grown flesh had replaced the broken mess, and a process that would take even someone like Zac days had been shortened to fifteen minutes. His new muscles still felt a bit stiff and weakened, but he would no doubt get used to it soon enough.

This efficacy alone was reason enough to ditch [True Strike]. He would save so much time with the help of the skill in the future. The fact that the healing cost him around half a level was regrettable, but someone like Zac would always be fighting powerful enemies that provided huge amounts of energy.

Mending his flesh was quick, but his pathways were far harder to deal with. He spent another hour making basic repairs after his flesh was fixed, which should allow him to use his Cosmic Energy as long as he didn't use over 50% of his power. Any more than that and he would probably overtax himself like he had during the undead incursion. Falling unconscious was fine next to his sister and the Valkyries, but doing so in a foreign forest was another thing altogether.

He slowly got to his feet, causing a series of crackling and popping sounds as the dried blood that covered him started falling off. He saw Thea waiting just outside the transparent walls, staring at him with shock.

"How are you still standing? That room looks like something from a horror movie!" Thea exclaimed, her face completely pale as she looked at Zac with worry.

"Well, I'm used to it by now." Zac shrugged.

"Is this what you have to do every time to level up?" Thea said, her eyes fixed on the pool of blood on the floor. "I've read about it, but I had no idea…"

"Well, it's not like this when I use pills or treasures to gain levels," Zac said. "Sorry for making you worry."

"I…" Thea mumbled, but she eventually only shook her head with a sigh. "I can't join the squad you mentioned earlier. I need to rest after all. Should I get the demon instead? He's crafty enough."

"He should be back by now," Zac agreed. "Have him come over. I'll head out now."

Thea seemed inclined to stop him, but she eventually just walked next to Zac as he stepped out of the glasshouse again.

"The spatial tunnels might close while you're out. Anything you need to relay to the outside world?" Thea finally asked just as he was about to leave.

"I won't be that long. A day or two tops," Zac said. "Just let my sister and the other leaders know I'm okay. If some big changes take place and the gates close early, I'll hurry back as quickly as possible."

"Okay." Thea nodded. "Stay safe. There's no guarantee the wolves are the only threat in this place."

Zac set off, cutting a straight path through the enormous forest. His leg was hurting a bit, but he could maintain a good pace even with a slight limp. Only five minutes passed before he met a small family of wolves, but they quickly backed off when Zac waved Verun in their direction. It somewhat proved that they hadn't just forgotten about his Tool Spirit, at least not yet.

Thea's final warning echoed in his mind, but he eventually realized something odd after half an hour had passed. She seemed to be wrong about there being other threats than the wolves, almost impossibly wrong. He didn't encounter a single living being in this vast forest even after running for over an hour, except the occasional spotting of lunar wolves. Confusion marred his face as he looked back and forth, but he couldn't make sense of the situation.

Didn't these wolves need to eat?

He knew that it was possible to sustain yourself solely on Cosmic Energy further down the road, but that went for D-grade warriors and above. They still ate in general, though, as high-quality food could provide some benefits. But it wasn't necessary to survive. However, E-grade beings shouldn't have evolved to that point just yet.

Were these wolves perhaps an exception? Or were they rather

vegetarians? They definitely didn't look like animals that lived only on fruits or stalks of grass, so he was more inclined to believe they were able to find sustenance from energy alone. Perhaps that was the true purpose of those artificial moons in the sky, and even the reason why the wolves had been brought here.

The solitude also gave Zac a chance to try some things out, and he stopped in a secluded valley after having traveled for another hour. The aftermath of [Hatchetman's Rage] was completely gone by this point, and the halo of [Conformation of Supremacy] appeared behind his body once more. However, this time, the avatar didn't depict the unadorned axe of the axe-man, but rather the insanely powerful shield of the Grand Protector who had appeared in the Dao Vision for his second class.

A surge of power filled his body, and Zac could almost feel his mind connect with the ancient cultivator who had sacrificed his life to save his world. However, no fractal barrier appeared to protect his front as he swung [Verun's Bite]. He rather found his strikes gain a tremendous weight, like each of them carried the weight of a world. His attacks were heavy enough to cause scars in the air, but the damage to the ground looked completely different than the long scars before.

This time, it almost looked like a small meteor had hit the ground when he swung his axe, with a crater no more than five meters wide appearing. It was deep, reaching twice as far down as it was wide, and Zac accidentally fell into it when it appeared. A slight pain bloomed up when he face-planted on the ground, but a ten-meter drop couldn't hurt him any longer.

He was more interested in the soil itself. It had become almost impossibly dense, and it took some force for him to dig into it with his hands. It was as though the area had been subjected to a terrifying amount of gravity, packing the soil to the point that it had almost turned into solid matter. Zac jumped out of the pit before he looked back at his new skill with mixed emotions.

The effect of using the shield as a basis for the skill instead of the woodsman's axe was impressive, and it was perhaps a better avatar for a duel, but Zac was disappointed to find that it didn't work as he'd hoped. In his fight with the wolves, he used a weapon as an avatar, which increased his might. He had hoped that using a defensive treasure with **[Conformation of Supremacy]** would instead create some sort of defensive effect.

But his new skill was true to its nature as a pure Strength-based skill, and it looked like it just took the weight and power of the shield to use it as a bludgeon. It still opened a few new avenues of how he could use it, but it clearly wasn't a one-size-fits-all-type situation where he could use it as everything from a defensive to a movement skill.

The limitation was a bit of a letdown, but not overly so. Partly because Zac somewhat expected such a situation, but mostly because he felt that he finally could use his Dao again.

His new Hidden Node had finally stabilized, and it was time to see what it could do.

81
TRACKS

Zac's new Hidden Node had finally calmed down, and the somewhat erratic trajectories of the two circular apparitions had stabilized. The three now formed a stable system, and Zac's intuition told him that using his Mental Energy shouldn't pose a problem any longer. However, Zac still noted that his Hidden Node was still slowly eating the energies from the three Dao projections, though not nearly as frantically as before.

It felt like a small drain on his mind, but his soul was pretty strong by this point, and he was generating new Mental Energy a lot quicker than the speed of consumption of his hidden node. It would no doubt slow down his recuperation after a battle, but he still had a pile of Soul Crystals in case he was in a hurry.

He was about to infuse his skill, but a thought suddenly struck him as he activated **[Primal Polyglot]** first. The translation function worked passively just like the **[Book of Babel]**, but the active interpretation of the Dao-based language needed an infusion of Cosmic Energy. He had tried using it a few times before as they'd traveled through the endless tunnels, but it appeared as though the skill didn't really help with Technocrat materials.

His vision didn't change at all after activating the skill, but it still felt like he was looking at something different than before as he gazed at the halo hovering behind him. It felt a bit similar to how two different people could have completely different impressions of a painting or a poem; it gave Zac a completely new outlook as he gazed at the circular fractals.

The skill allowed him to gain a better understanding of how the halo and the apparition were connected, but he didn't gain any immediate insights into the limitations of his skill. Zac guessed he would have to experiment with one apparition after another to see what would be useful, and what would be inefficient.

Zac briefly considered using the Chaos Pattern or his Remnants for a huge destructive boost, but he quickly dispelled any such thoughts. He didn't want to call down the tribulation lightning again, even if things had turned out pretty good the last time around.

That scene with the endless sea of lightning might even have been a warning by the Heavens, so he instead focused on his Dao. He tried infusing [Conformation of Supremacy] with the Fragment of the Axe, seeing that everything seemed to be in order, but worry gripped his heart when nothing happened.

However, Zac calmed down when he found that he could infuse the skill with the Fragment of the Coffin just fine. It would appear that the choice of projection also impacted what Daos were infusible. The feeling he got from the shield was mostly one of imperviousness and hardness, and his Fragment of the Coffin was the Fragment that best represented that feeling.

A stream of Mental Energy made its way into the halo from his mind, and Zac noted with interest that the energies seeping out of the hanging coffin joined the Mental Energy flow, effectively turning it into Dao Energy. The infusion somehow felt a lot smoother than before, like the process had been streamlined. That by itself didn't really change its power or anything, though the speed of his infusion seemed to have somewhat sped up.

It was only a difference of a fraction of a second, but even such a small boost could prove vital in a pitched battle.

Another change made Zac's eyes glisten. A second stream was released from his avatar, or rather the Hidden Node lodged within his body. It was the same pitch-black energy as the one released from the coffin, and the two streams seamlessly merged just before they entered the skill fractal.

Zac initially didn't know whether this change held any significance, but he quickly realized what was going on. He hadn't used his new E-grade skill a lot, but he was almost certain that he was able to instill more of his Mental Energy compared to before.

Of course, that might be because he had changed the avatar to a shield that really matched the Fragment of the Coffin.

There was a simple way to make sure, and Zac quickly dispelled **[Conformation of Supremacy]** to instead conjure a fractal blade with **[Chop]**. It was the skill he was most used to, and he knew exactly how much Mental Energy he could infuse into the blade before it wouldn't work any longer.

Zac's eyes lit up as he infused more and more of his Dao into the blade, and he was still using the Fragment of the Coffin. A similar scene took place in his mind this time around as well, as two streams of energies fused just as they entered the skill fractal on his hand.

The fractal blade gained a sinister aura as it was filled with the putrefying part of his Dao Fragment, but the color kept increasing in intensity and power until it almost turned pitch-black.

It didn't take Zac long to figure out the difference from before. He could suddenly infuse around 20% more Mental Energy into his skills, which made his attacks around 10% more powerful compared to before if you contributed half his power to his Dao Fragments. It was an amazing boost that seemed to come with pretty much no downsides apart from a small but constant drain on his mind.

Of course, there was some bad news that came along with the good. Zac had hoped that the Hidden Node in his mind would be related to Dao control and affinity like the general Hidden Node **[Spirit Gate]**, but it rather looked like **[Spiritual Void]** was a combat-oriented node that replaced quality with quantity.

Zac experimented for a few minutes longer to make sure, but he could quickly confirm that he was still beyond incompetent when it came to things like Dao Braiding. He couldn't turn his Hidden Node on or off either, though he could somewhat reduce the amount of energy it expelled along with a Dao infusion.

Another change took place a few minutes later, as the additional infusion from his Hidden Node started to wane, leaving Zac with just his own Mental Energy. He wasn't too surprised about that. He had already guessed that the **[Spiritual Void]** acted like some sort of

Dao battery, storing excess energy until it would be released in battle.

The node was a bit unwieldy in the sense that he couldn't control when to use it and when his own Dao was enough, but his control would probably improve when his bloodline awakened. The boosting effect would probably become even greater in the future as well, and he couldn't help but think back to the scene where his presumed ancestor had crushed his enemy by simply releasing the floodgates in his mind.

Perhaps even more importantly, the node gave him an important glimpse into his Void Emperor bloodline. Things were finally starting to make sense, and the lack of affinities no longer felt as detrimental as they once did. His body might be "corrupted" with a complete lack of affinities, but it appeared that his bloodline was shoring up those weaknesses one by one.

The [Void Heart] was related to energy gathering, allowing him to eat all kinds of energies as an alternative form of cultivation. The second node in his soul allowed for an additional outburst of Mental Energy, replacing Dao Braiding or Dao Arrays with additional force.

It perfectly aligned with his insights back during the Dao Discourse to the point that it made him question whether that epiphany was actually just his bloodline telling his subconscious how to fight.

Zac did fell a few trees with his improved Fragment of the Axe as well, and it had taken a noticeable step forward in lethality. The Fragment hadn't really seemed to gain any new functionality as they sometimes did, but it had rather just become more powerful. It wasn't too surprising, as the upgrade had been based on war and conflict rather than adding something new like Mental Heaviness.

Seeing that everything was fine even after the drastic changes to his mind, Zac set out again, taking a circuitous route through the forest. It took almost twenty hours for him to reach the other side, but he had spent a few hours picking up energy-dense plants.

He didn't recognize a single one of them, but they all contained the energy of the moon. The combination of specific growth requirements and unique attributes was usually a recipe for a valuable treasure, so he had high hopes that the Sky Gnome could turn these things into piles of cash even if they proved useless in awakening his bloodline.

A few hours were spent on rest and redrawing his pathways as well. He ate a small hill of meat before he set out again, but he finally felt like he had rid himself of the last aftereffects of the [**Rageroot Oak Seed**]. His body was in pretty good condition all things considered, with only his pathways causing some issues now.

It was a bit of an annoyance, but Zac knew he couldn't complain. Most mortals would probably turn green with envy when hearing how quickly he pushed through levels.

Zac kept moving forward after resuming his exploration, and the silver forest finally gave way to the band of grass that ran along the wall. The opposite side of the forest was constructed pretty much the same way as the area they came from, with a thirty-meter-tall wall stretching across the horizon.

However, there was one startling difference; the wall was actually damaged, like it had just endured a siege. The scripts had lost their luster at multiple places, and there were hundreds of cracks. Zac even believed he would be able to cram himself through some of the larger fractures.

Zac's first guess was that another battle had taken place here just like the one that had taken place just before Ogras first arrived in the Mystic Realm, but he quickly discarded that thought. The damage was simply too widespread, going on for as far as he could see. If a battle had caused this kind of damage, they definitely weren't at the E-grade.

But more to the point, Zac sensed the same type of spatial energies in many of the cracks, making him believe that this was rather the result of spatial turbulence.

There were no spatial tears or other dangers for the moment though, so Zac started walking along the edge of the forest, parallel to the wall, keeping his form hidden among the shrubbery. He was looking for a natural exit like the glasshouse or a gate, but so far, there were no clues.

The cracks might provide ingress to the other side, but Zac wouldn't try that unless he really needed to. After all, the walls were alive, and he didn't want to get buried alive inside the Technocrat alloy. A sudden shudder from his forester's intuition made him turn his concentration to a patch of the forest ahead of him.

He at first didn't understand what **[Forester's Constitution]** was trying to tell him, as there were no herbs there, but his eyes widened when he noticed something.

There were footprints, and not something left by the wolves.

Zac bent down to get a closer look, and while he was no expert in tracking, he felt the trail was fresh. He hesitated for a second, but his curiosity quickly overcame his caution. He soon took out his axe, and he started to follow the tracks, taking great care not to create any sounds.

The tracks came from the depths of the forest before they made a turn at the edge. It looked like a group had taken a shortcut like him, but the droplets of blood on the grass indicated that their passage might not have been as carefree. The trail moved in the same direction as the one Zac already walked, keeping to the edge of the forest all the time.

There was no doubt that the owners of the footprints weren't far away, as the blood on the ground still hadn't dried, and it only took him fifteen minutes before he spotted some movement ahead. Zac had thought about how to make first contact with the natives a fair bit over the past weeks, but no planning had prepared him for the situation in front of him.

Five werewolves were standing not far from the wall, most of them sporting somewhat severe wounds. One of them even seemed to have lost an arm recently, and he swayed a bit where he stood. More importantly, one of them was carrying an unconscious human, a girl who looked no older than Zac himself.

How were you supposed to react to what looked like a straight-up kidnapping?

His first instinct was to help the captive out simply based on the fact they were both human, but he quickly discarded the thought. He had no idea what was going on, and getting involved might cause unnecessary trouble. His main goal was to kill the two remaining Dominators to cut off the last two Karmic Links leading to Earth.

Anything else was secondary.

However, a burst of annoyance made Zac grit his teeth when an all-too-familiar prompt appeared in front of him.

[Damsel in Distress (Training (1/10)): Rescue the Damsel in distress. Reward: Reward based on performance at the end of training regimen. (0/1) NOTE: Failure to comply with training regimen will result in loss of two random skills and 9 levels.]

82
LET'S TALK

Zac mutely looked at the quest prompt for a few seconds, realizing that his new Pathstrider title wasted no time in causing trouble for him. He had been free from any meddling by the System since the battle outside the Tower of Eternity, but it looked like his good days were over.

Not only did the System force him to take a side, but it even said that this was just the first of a series of quests. The failure penalty was almost of grotesque proportions as well. Losing nine levels would put him right back at the start of the E-grade, and this time, he wouldn't be able to gain most of the levels through pills.

Of course, the real threat was losing two of his skills, and it was something he couldn't allow to happen no matter what.

The one small blessing was that there was no time limit on the quest, which allowed Zac to stay hidden for a bit longer to spy on the werewolves. The beastkin actually felt a bit familiar to the lunar wolves in the forest with all of them emitting the same sort of lunar energy. Most of them had mottled fur in black and silver, but the one who emitted the strongest aura was almost completely silvery-white.

Zac guessed that the silver werewolf was the leader, and he even had a marking on his forehead. It pretty much confirmed Zac's earlier theory that the werewolves in this research base and the lunar wolves were somehow connected through bloodlines. The werewolves might even be normal humans who had the bloodline of the wolves transplanted into their bodies for all Zac knew.

The more pressing issue was how to deal with the situation.

The auras of the warriors weren't weak by any means, but neither did they make Zac feel a lot of pressure. He felt pretty confident in dealing with them without wasting any more of his aces, but that by itself made him a bit wary. The System wouldn't just give him a freebie, making him believe there was some catch to the quest.

So Zac wasn't in any rush to rush out, especially as the group was doing something that sparked Zac's curiosity.

They had been standing at a seemingly inconspicuous part of the wall, with one of the werewolves touching and prodding the smooth surface all this while. But it looked like he finally had found what he was looking for, and he took out one disk after another and pressed them against the metal. The disks stayed in place like they had suction cups, and the beastkin quickly formed two vertical lines with the help of twelve identical disks.

The werewolf wasn't finished there, but he actually took out a tablet next, and he connected it to one of the disks through a cable. It was a bit surreal watching a werewolf deftly using what seemed to be futuristic technology, but perhaps he shouldn't be surprised considering what kind of place this was.

There was still no sign of what they were up to even after the werewolf had been tapping away at the tablet with an almost dizzying speed for five minutes, but then there was finally a change. Zac couldn't believe what he was seeing as a gate started to take form in the wall with the disks acting as the frame.

It looked just like the gates they had passed through to get to this place, though it was only three meters high. It was also looking very rough, but it was gradually transforming into a proper door. Part of him wanted to stay and watch a while longer to see what else the tech-savvy werewolf had up his sleeve, but Zac knew that he couldn't wait longer if he wanted to intercept.

That door might disappear the moment they passed through it, locking Zac outside. There was no timer on the quest, but that didn't mean that he couldn't fail it. He slowly rose from his hidden position, but he had underestimated the senses of the werewolves, as even that small movement put them on edge.

Their bodies grew half a size as Zac prepared himself for battle, allowing them to tower over a meter above Zac. Their claws grew longer as well, and Zac felt that they could even match Low-quality E-grade Tool Spirits.

Zac's hypothesis that these beastkin were related to the lunar wolves was further confirmed as they started radiating a cold piercing light that turned the whole area into a blinding white.

Zac had already figured out the solution to this trick, though, so he activated [Cosmic Gaze] and [Hatchetman's Spirit], which immediately allowed him to spot the trio. They had discarded their captive on the ground and were now rushing straight toward him while the leader stayed behind to observe.

The auras of the warriors had grown since they transformed, but it was absolutely not to the point that Zac feared for his life. He still found himself in a tricky spot, as he didn't want to kill them in order not to ruin any potential cooperation with these people. After all, the quest had told him to save the girl, but nothing about killing these people.

"Wait, let's talk–" Zac said as he lifted a hand to indicate that he didn't want trouble, but he was quickly forced to move his hand away as a series of claws ripped through the air in an attempt to cut it clean off.

The werewolves seemed to have taken his words as a sign of weakness, as they looked at him with disdain. Zac was a bit confused about what gave these guys the guts to attack him even if his words were a bit defensive, but he suddenly realized that his aura was actually quite weak at the moment because of his broken pathways.

Not only that, but a lot of his excess spirituality was also swallowed by his [Spiritual Void] rather than being passively emitted from his body as an aura. He hadn't realized it before, but these two facts combined probably made him appear like a recently evolved cultivator at best. He still had a hard time deciding on a course of action, so he was put in a passive state as he started avoiding a furious barrage of claws infused with the power of the moon without trying to expose his real strength.

However, a single sentence quenched his hopes of a peaceful release of the human girl.

"Don't kill him. He's one of the outsiders," the leader growled as he spectated the battle. "The others we caught were even weaker than this one. Let's take him with us to the relay station as well."

Zac's pupils shrank as he realized what the werewolf was talking about. It turned out that it was these werewolves who were responsible for his missing squad. A thick killing intent roiled out from his body, far eclipsing his diminutive aura, causing the pupils of his enemies to shrink into pinpoints.

The outburst was so powerful that even the unconscious human on the ground stirred awake, and the werewolves quickly tried to back away and regroup. However, how could Zac allow something like that?

The closest werewolf was bisected as [Verun's Bite] emitted a sanguine glow, leaving just four alive. The other two werewolves barely had time to flash away by turning into moonlight before Zac's blade reached them as well, but he was immediately hot in pursuit.

"He must be one of their leaders!" the silver werewolf shouted from behind. "Restrain him!"

The silver light in the whole area transformed the next moment as the werewolves lit up like beacons, and the radiance was so powerful that the moonlight almost seemed to have turned into a liquid. It felt just like the restriction during his last fight, but perhaps even more powerful. Even worse, the pressure was steadily increasing, forcing him to flash forward with [Loamwalker], finally leaving the forest.

The light put some painful pressure on his still tender leg, but he knew that he simply needed to fight in melee range to almost completely circumvent its effect. Someone with less Strength than him might have been completely unable to move due to the pressure. He quickly targeted one of the soldiers at random, and while he seemed surprised at Zac's decisiveness, he still quickly responded by slashing at Zac's throat with his claws.

Zac blocked it with his axe before he rammed him straight on with his shoulder, but he was a bit surprised by the result. He had expected to send the werewolf flying with multiple broken bones, but he was actually just pushed back with a grunt. The bodies of these people were clearly extremely sturdy, making Zac wonder just what they had gone through to be in such a wretched state.

The attack had caused a shock to the werewolf's system, allowing Zac to follow up with a swing of **[Verun's Bite]** infused with the Fragment of the Axe.

A lunar barrier appeared to block the strike, but this was a High mastery Dao Fragment. The barrier was cut apart like it was made from paper, and the werewolf's head was lopped off the next moment. Zac didn't get any time to celebrate, as he felt a searing pain in his neck and back as a series of crescent moons hidden in the moonlight slammed into him, instantly drenching his body with blood.

Zac grunted with pain, but he was more surprised that the attacks had managed to hide from the omnipresence of **[Hatchetman's Spirit]**. He wildly looked around with **[Cosmic Gaze]** to spot the source of the attacks, and he realized that another werewolf had appeared from the forest. Zac was even more surprised to see that the newcomer was ignoring him after the first barrage, and instead was rushing straight toward the gate.

Not only that, but the others were doing the same, even leaving behind their tools and backpacks on the ground.

"Run! Run!" the leader shouted as he kicked the girl on the ground, which launched her body into the arms of one of the others. "Open that goddamn thing even if the algorithms are imperfect!"

Zac could sigh at how different these guys were compared to their frenzied cousins as he set out in pursuit.

Two combatants were already down, which left three more to go, not counting the werewolf who was still desperately working on opening the door. Zac was starting to feel a bit woozy from fighting in his current condition, but it wasn't like he had any option but to keep going.

It was a bit risky, but he started pushing energy into the skill fractal of **[Rapturous Divide]** as a fractal blade appeared in front of his axe-head. Zac knew he would need to take them out before they opened that door, so he wanted to catch them all in a close-range swipe. However, a series of spatial tears suddenly appeared out of nowhere, almost cutting him to ribbons.

Zac desperately jumped out of the way as he looked for the source of the attack. It was the backpack that one of the werewolves had discarded earlier. It was actually a booby trap, but Zac had ignored it because it didn't emit even a hint of Cosmic Energy, and his danger sense hadn't warned him either.

He quickly tried to find his footing and resume his pursuit, but a sense of foreboding suddenly came over him. However, he didn't even have time to make a move before a hand appeared from the moonlight and pressed a small mechanical item against his chest.

Terror filled Zac's heart when he thought he was about to get ripped apart by a bunch of spatial tears, but one fear was replaced with another as he found his body completely restrained. That little thing that looked like a toy had somehow taken control of the Cosmic Energy in his body, and his body had locked itself into place.

He tried to struggle free, but moving was completely impossible.

"Shit, the outsiders have some formidable people," the silver werewolf spat as he emerged out of the moonlight, and he lifted Zac by his neck before he started to walk toward the others. "But that's good. This one should know a lot more than those scouts."

Zac wasn't even able to respond, but he was suddenly filled with hope as he noticed something. His Specialty Core wasn't restrained at all by the odd item latched to his chest, and it had even started its transformation. The werewolf was thankfully completely oblivious to that fact, as he was more focused on the werewolf dealing with the gate.

He didn't get any further than ten meters as the massive cage of death sprang up around him, trapping all the remaining werewolves along with the human captive. The cable connecting the werewolf's tablet to the wall was ripped apart by the barrier of **[Profane Seal]** as well, effectively stopping his work.

The weird Technocrat restraining tool fell to the ground as Zac's hand punched through the chest of the werewolf leader. The bindings before had made him drop **[Verun's Bite]**, but his hand still had terrifying penetrating power since it was infused with his recently upgraded Dao Fragment.

The werewolf leader looked into Zac's abyssal eyes for a second before his head rolled over, and Zac felt a surge of energy entering his body. The pitch-black armor of **[Vanguard of Undeath]** covered him the next moment as he turned toward the remaining werewolves, and over a dozen chains stabbed toward the disbelieving targets as Zac started to advance on them.

The unexpected close call was enough for him to completely clear his head, and Zac started his customary grinding down of his targets with newfound zeal. The werewolves tried to turn into motes of light to escape again, but their moonlight was completely overpowered by the combination of [Winds of Decay] and [Fields of Despair].

Just a few seconds later, only one enemy was left alive, the werewolf who had been responsible for summoning the gate earlier. Zac figured that he would be able to answer some questions in case the human girl didn't know, for example, where that relay station was. He left the werewolf utterly restrained by his sets of chains, but he still felt a headache coming on as he turned his abyssal eyes toward the human.

She had been shocked awake by the kick earlier, and she had witnessed everything that came afterward. His getting locked down and then transforming to a Draugr. He knew that his unique situation would be exposed to the world sooner or later, but it was still too early. If this girl was allowed to return to her clan, then he would sooner or later be exposed. Not even a contract felt like a surefire way to protect the secrets, as Catheya had explained.

But could he really kill her to protect his secret? That would definitely be crossing a line.

"Don't kill me. I won't tell anyone, I swear on my clan's name," the girl hurriedly said, clearly understanding what kind of thoughts were running through Zac's mind.

"I won't harm you," Zac eventually said after some pause. "But I can't just let you go either. At least not for the time being. What you saw can get both me and my people in trouble if it spreads out. You will need to sign a contract and stay with me for a while."

"I understand your predicament, I really do." The girl sighed. "But I have too many people depending on me. I cannot let that happen. But don't worry. You risked your life to save me, so I'll keep my word."

Alarm bells went off in Zac's mind when he heard her response, and Zac immediately erected every defense he had while launching every single free chain at her. She was planning something, something dangerous. The feeling of alarm only intensified as the girl's eyes turned white, and Zac fought a strange feeling that enveloped his mind.

He tried to resist the feeling, but it was too late.

Zac desperately jumped out of the way as he looked for the source of the attack. It was the backpack that one of the werewolves had discarded earlier. It was actually a booby trap, but Zac had ignored it because it didn't emit even a hint of Cosmic Energy, and his danger sense hadn't warned him either.

He quickly tried to find his footing and resume his pursuit, but a weird mental nudge pushed him back a step.

"Behind you!" the human girl screamed in warning, and Zac's reaction was instantaneous.

83
THE HERO'S JOURNEY

Zac spun around just in time to see a hand materialize out of nowhere a meter away from him. It held some mechanism in its hand, but Zac slapped the thing out of the furry paw before he swung his axe twice in quick succession.

The clouds of **[Rapturous Divide]** spread in the area in front of him as a surprised-looking silvery werewolf was cut apart by the spatial divide. It was the werewolf leader who had been caught by surprise. He had somehow managed to hide completely in the moonlight, tricking both Zac's senses and his danger sense.

Thankfully, he had the tables turned on him because of the early warning, and the werewolf helplessly fell on the ground as his blood flowed like rivers. Zac didn't immediately target the other werewolves, but he rather stopped for a second and looked down at the dying warrior. He didn't know why, but Zac had felt an eerie sense of déjà vu as he saw the hand just now.

"It's you!" The werewolf coughed as he bled out, but his two blood-red eyes were actually staring at the girl fifty meters away rather than at Zac. "You weren't restrained!"

Zac looked over in confusion and was surprised to see that the young woman was in an extremely precarious condition for some reason, with blood freely running from her eyes, nose, and ears. She couldn't even respond to the werewolf's accusations, as she puked out both her dinner and a bucket of blood before she fell in a heap.

"You used the eyes of time to meddle! Don't think this will save you! You hold the key to immortality, and the Lunar Tribe will not be stopped! We will–" the werewolf raved until the light in his eyes died.

The dying words of the werewolf leader rekindled the feeling of wrongness, but he was more concerned about dealing with the remaining werewolves. He left the dead leader where he was and instead focused on the last two as he rushed toward the gate. However, he couldn't believe what he was seeing when the werewolves actually made a 180-degree turn, rushing straight toward him.

Did that werewolf leader hold such a big position in their hearts that they were ready to throw their lives away to avenge him? Zac's state was pretty bad from fighting so soon after node-breaking, but these remaining werewolves were absolutely not his match.

Zac prepared to meet their assault head-on, but he found himself swinging his axe through empty space as the werewolves suddenly disappeared. He sensed where they had appeared, though, right next to the girl and the fallen corpse of their leader.

A wave of anger surged in his mind when he thought of the wretched state of the former captive. She was clearly on the verge of death. Had the werewolves decided to retaliate against her instead of him when realizing they couldn't deal with him?

Rage bubbled in his heart when he saw her pitiable state, and he once more pushed himself beyond what was safe, instantly appearing next to the closest werewolf. The beastkin desperately reached for a pouch on his leader's waist as his body turned into moonlight, but the process was interrupted in the middle as Zac punched clean through his head with an Axe-infused jab.

The other werewolf actually appeared right next to him before his attack was even finished, snatching the satchel and disappearing. But his camouflage was nowhere near the level of his fallen leader, especially not when most of the moonlight in the area had dissipated by now. He might as well have skipped using the skill, as Zac could see his outline perfectly with the help of **[Cosmic Gaze]**.

Zac caught up with him with the help of **[Loamwalker]** and ended his life in one swing. He looted the stolen pouch without losing his momentum before he appeared right next to the smallest werewolf, who was still desperately typing on his tablet. Despair flooded his eyes when he saw Zac appear next to him, but a hint of ruthlessness flashed in his eyes as he pushed a button on the corner of his tablet.

A surge of danger screamed in Zac's mind, allowing him to barely dodge a metal spike as the wall came alive, ruthlessly stabbing at both himself and the werewolf. One attack after another was launched in quick succession like a crashing wave of liquid metal.

A painful wound was ripped open in Zac's side as the wall almost had turned into a terrifying maw that tried to swallow him whole, but he pushed through the pain as he ran for his life. The werewolf was even worse off, as he was killed by an alloy spike that pierced his head. Zac risked a look behind just in time to see the corpse being dragged inside the wall itself.

The scene only boosted Zac's desire to escape, but he still stopped for an instant to snatch up the wounded girl before he ran into the forest. He felt the spikes pierce into the ground right behind him even after reaching the edge of the forest, and only after running for another minute could he confirm that the wall wasn't hunting him any longer.

The girl was already unconscious again, and Zac sighed as he fed her some of his better healing pills for both the body and the soul before dealing with his own wounds. She was his ticket to learning about this base, and he couldn't let her die after going through all that trouble.

A sudden wave of dizziness threatened to push him into the embrace of unconsciousness just like the last time he'd fought while still overdoing it right after breaking open a node, but he couldn't risk it in this place. A burst of pain jolted him awake as he stabbed himself in the leg, and the shock to his system pushed the drowsiness away.

His body was still in a pretty pathetic state, but it slowly improved over the next two hours. The wound in his side was purely physical in its form, which allowed him to quickly heal it up with the help of [Surging Vitality]. It cost him most of the energy from his battle, but it wasn't all that much anyway.

Only the leader was powerful, but his aura had been pretty unstable even before the fight. The energy rewarded by the System took things like that into account, so he didn't get nearly as much energy from this battle as from the one against the wolves.

The whole fight made him wonder what the purpose of this

training session was. He hadn't really learned anything new from the battle, and it definitely hadn't pushed him beyond his limits to make some sort of breakthrough.

Was it more about setting a series of events in motion?

A second quest prompt quickly answered his question for him.

The Hero's Journey (Training (2/10)): Rescue your scouting squad before they are moved from the relay station. Reward: Reward based on performance at the end of training regimen. (0/7).
[04:34:22] NOTE: Three deaths count as failure. Failure to comply with training regimen will result in loss of two random skills and 7 levels.]

Zac quickly read the quest, and a sense of relief filled him when he saw that the punishment had lessened. However, the loss of skills was still there, meaning that he definitely couldn't skip it. Then again, he had no plans to do so anyway.

He had already decided to rescue his people the moment the werewolf leader opened his mouth, so the quest didn't really change anything this time around. The problem was that there was a time limit for this quest.

Four hours wasn't little, but it wasn't a lot either. The relay station was definitely on the other side of the wall, but the gate had disappeared when that smaller werewolf somehow triggered the defenses of the wall.

The encounter had also proved that there was even more about this place he didn't understand than he had anticipated. He took out a small trinket from his Spatial Ring, and he turned it over a few times before stowing it away again. It was the thing that the werewolf leader had tried to attack him with before he was killed, but Zac couldn't figure out how it worked or what it did at all.

Who knew what Technocrat weaponry and tricks these werewolves had? Zac was afraid that he would just get himself killed if he stormed the relay station blindly. Perhaps they could control the walls freely, easily trapping him in a corridor before flooding it with spatial tears. Not even he would be able to escape something like that.

Zac's eyes slowly turned to the unconscious girl lying next to him.

She was the key to this mission. He felt a bit bad about bringing her with him on a rescue mission in her wounded state, but he didn't have a lot of options. He couldn't risk failing the quest, and she would definitely increase the odds of success thanks to her knowledge of this place.

At least the girl's situation seemed to have stabilized thanks to his pills, though she was still unconscious. He looked down at her curiously, feeling for some reason that they had met before. But that was obviously impossible since she clearly wasn't someone from his force. She was wearing what looked like a Technocrat uniform, but she was definitely a cultivator judging by the aura she unconsciously emitted.

Zac couldn't be certain, but it felt like she had recently evolved to the E-grade, which was pretty impressive considering her young age and the somewhat lacking cultivation environment. Then again, the girl might look twenty, but she could be a hundred years old for all Zac knew.

Normally, Zac would have been happy to recuperate a while longer while waiting for the girl to come around, but the timer left him restless. He was in decent shape in any case, and he hadn't used any of his long-cooldown skills during the battle. It was time to start looking for a way to get to the other side of the wall.

He got up to his feet and slung the girl across his shoulder before he made his way back toward the wall as he kept vigil of the surroundings. There might be more werewolves lurking in the area, or some other hidden traps initiated by the werewolf technician. But it looked like the alloy had returned to normal, and an unmoving wall met his eyes when he reached the edge of the forest.

Even throwing anything from boulders to corpses at the wall elicited no response, and Zac finally dared to personally move closer. He let the girl down on a patch of grass before he started to prod the wall, but there was no sign of the gate at all. A quick survey of the immediate section of the wall exposed a pretty huge crack a few hundred meters away, but Zac was extremely hesitant to use it.

The werewolves hadn't even tried using those cracks as a means of escape when facing death, making Zac believe that the jagged scars in the walls were deathtraps. But he had no idea what to do next. He had found a few technological gadgets along with a spare tablet in the werewolf leader's Cosmos Sack, but he had no idea how to use it.

The tablet wouldn't turn on, and the disks wouldn't stick to the wall no matter how hard Zac pushed. Three minutes passed without him making any progress, and he finally couldn't wait any longer. He walked over to the unconscious girl as he took out a bottle of water. However, an idea struck him, and he released a burst of killing intent aimed at her. It actually worked. The girl groaned as her eyelids fluttered, and she woke up a second later.

Her bleary eyes peered back and forth until they finally found Zac. Her pupils constricted for a second, but she quickly calmed down as she slowly got up to a sitting position.

"Thank you for saving me. I'm Leviala Cartava," she said with a weak voice.

84

DATAMANCERS

Zac once more got a weird feeling when he looked into Leviala's eyes now that she had woken up. Of course, that might be because of the way they looked. The girl looked like a normal, albeit frail, Caucasian girl, with a both short and lithe frame. However, her eyes stopped Zac from mistaking her for some random earthling.

One of them was normal, though it seemed to contain impurities, small spots of darkness peppered about her sclera and green iris. But the other eye was completely white, to the point that it seemed that she was born without a pupil at all. In its place was an extremely dense fractal, and trying to understand it with **[Primal Polyglot]** could only provide him with one hint.

It was a curse, one aimed at the girl herself.

"I'm the one who should be thanking you for the warning before." Zac shrugged as he handed her the bottle of water, trying not to appear weirded out by the odd appearance of the eye. "Are you okay? I didn't know what was wrong with you, so I simply gave you a couple of different healing pills."

"My soul is wounded, but whatever you gave me is really helping. The outside is really full of marvelous things," she said with a weak smile.

"So I'm guessing you're from Clan Cartava?" Zac said. "How did you end up getting captured?"

"The Lunar Tribe have kept a lot of secrets over the years, it seems." Leviala sighed. "We've always thought them muscle-heads with limited understanding of how this world works. But they managed to sneak all the way to our domiciles without triggering any of our alarms. They used pathways that we had no idea existed, and killed my guards before the elders had a chance to react."

Zac slowly nodded. It wasn't too surprising if the native forces finally started to make use of hidden aces they had accumulated over the past millennia now that the world was changing. No matter if it was to get out of this place or to seize the treasures of this Mystic Realm, now was the time to go all out.

It was a bit odd that these werewolves had wasted this opportunity on this girl in front of him. It was almost a suicide mission to infiltrate a hostile faction like that, and he couldn't see anything on her that was worth the effort. He had already searched her for Cosmos Sacks or other spatial tools, and there simply wasn't anything on her.

The most likely reason was the parting words of the werewolf leader, but Zac had no time to worry about the key to immortality. He had a quest to complete. But there were some things he needed to understand before setting out.

"What is this thing?" Zac asked as he took out the small mechanism that he was almost struck by before. "A weapon?"

"No, they're called restraint modules," the girl said with a shake of her head as she took out an identical one from within her robes. "It locks your Cosmic Energy in place, which also restricts your movement. It was used to restrain research subjects long ago."

"So it was something like that." Zac whistled, though he wouldn't completely take her word for it. "Then how are you free?"

"They lose their efficacy over time as the body adapts. But my parents also implanted me with a hidden blocker at birth and only told me and my grandfather. It contains an algorithm to deactivate restraint modules and some other things, and enough Base Power to connect with items outside my body," Leviala said. "I was waiting for an opportunity to escape, but those werewolves were too vigilant. Luckily, you came along."

"Base Power? What's that?" Zac asked as he put away the small mechanism.

"It's the energy that this base runs on. All the tools we've looted in this world run on Base Power, and it's also required to interface with the base itself," Leviala explained.

"Is that why this tablet won't start up?" Zac said as he waved the thing he'd looted from the werewolf leader.

"Yes, these things require a fresh stream of Base Power to operate." Leviala nodded before she looked at the disks lying next to Zac with a frown. "What are you doing?"

"I need to get to the other side, but the door those werewolves summoned is gone. You should have heard them before; they have captured one of our squads. I want to get them back," Zac said. "How do I get that door to open again?"

"You shouldn't go there. The Wasteland is in that direction," Leviala said, her face turning a shade paler. "Besides, they should have been taken to the relay station. There are probably multiple squads waiting there to cross the Wasteland together. Not only that, the base might be protected by other means as well. I'm afraid that it's impossible to save your friends."

"Let me worry about that." Zac shrugged as he poured out everything from the werewolf's Cosmos Sack on the ground. "Where can I get this Base Power? Does anything among these items contain it?"

"Listen to me, it's a shame about your people, but we need to get out of this world. We are about to be trapped again in just a few days. The world is ending. Getting caught inside will only doom both our clans," she said as her odd eyes bored into his.

"We know," Zac said, ignoring the discomfort of the stare. "About the trapped thing, that is."

"You know? Why are you people still staying here, then? The space treasure? You don't understand the horror of that thing," the girl said with fear in her eyes, a fear that didn't seem faked to Zac. "Our clan is ready to form an alliance with your leaders provided that you help us out of this place. We left you a map to this forest before the storms returned. If you open a specific gate from your side, we can all–"

"I'm sorry, but we aren't going anywhere," Zac said with a shake of his head. "And neither are we letting anyone out. Now, these things, how do–"

"Why not?" Leviala blurted, and it was obvious she felt that Zac was a lunatic for wanting to stay in this place. "We know that your world is newly introduced to the world of cultivation, and we can help. There is much we have lost while locked in this place, but we can help each other to face the threat of outsiders."

"Various reasons. But the most important task our faction is dealing with is to hunt down a group of insectoid humanoids." Zac sighed, slightly annoyed at the delay.

He knew that he needed the help of this girl if he wanted to use these machines, as there was no time to go get his sister. So he quickly calmed down so that he could explain what was going on. He took out a picture of Void's Disciple that they had captured when the Dominator had entered Site 17.

"Unless this man dies, then everyone, including the people of your clan, will die. The same probably goes for a group of cultists who have entered this place. They need to be taken out as well. I don't really care about that treasure, but our enemies do. That's our way to hunt them down."

Blank incomprehension was written all over Leviala's face, but even more so despair. Zac guessed that she had expected to finally be able to leave this prison of theirs pretty soon, but that door had suddenly closed right in her face.

"I cannot speak for my elders… But if what you're saying is true, then Clan Cartava might be able to help you locate these threats. But can you explain what's going on? I'm willing to act as a liaison between our forces," she said after some thought.

Zac explained the threat of the Great Redeemer and the Church of Everlasting Dao in broad strokes, about the Karmic Ties that needed to be severed for their planet to remain hidden. This was not some secret intelligence, after all, but rather something that was generally disseminated by this point. Of course, a lot of people believed it was just a ruse by him and Port Atwood to seize control.

"A deviant Karmic Cultivator, at Peak D-grade at that?" Leviala blanched. "It seems the outside isn't all that safe either."

"We all have our problems," Zac said with a wry smile. "Now, the door?"

"A Datamancer is needed to open this thing, along with the specific key code. This whole world is full of hidden pathways like this, but we know of less than one percent of them. Forcing the gate protocol to activate is almost impossible without the prerequisite knowledge."

"A Datamancer? What?" Zac asked.

"That's what we call those who can interface with this base. Only they can rewrite protocols and bypass the restrictions. You should have people like this as well. Opening the gate to this forest was a test of sorts. Unless you have people extremely skilled in data manipulation, you wouldn't be able to pass that gate, let alone let us out," Leviala explained.

"Hackers?" Zac muttered. "I'm sorry, but that's not how we got here."

"What?" Leviala said with confusion. "Did you manage to break the door open? Do you possess such powerful means?"

"No. One of my friends almost got himself killed trying that," Zac snorted. "I have clearance high enough to open the door."

"Clearance? Wait… You're part of the Builders?!" she shrieked as she tried to get away.

Zac was a bit surprised at the strong reaction, but he couldn't let the girl get away. He instructed **[Love's Bond]** to snatch up the running girl, which wasn't too hard considering how weakened her current condition was. She didn't even get to her feet before she fell over again, only making it three meters in her escape.

Using the chains was as much to help her get up as to prevent her from escaping. It was a bit of a safety measure, though, as he was afraid Leviala possessed some sort of escape treasure or skill.

"Calm down. I'm not part of any builders," Zac said after Leviala had stopped struggling against the bindings. "The terminal where we arrived gives out clearances left and right. Most people got Tier-2 or Tier-3 clearance, but I managed to get Tier-4 clearance thanks to an item I acquired off-world. That's how I got in here."

Of course, Zac suspected that he tenuously could be considered part of the "builders," provided that Leviala was referring to his mother's clan. But he wasn't about to divulge that sort of information, seeing her strong reaction. Still, her reactions just now had divulged a lot. Not only did the natives completely lack clearances, but Clan

Cartava didn't seem to know as much about them as he'd feared after seeing the signpost left behind.

"What? Such a thing is possible? I've never heard of a terminal giving out clearances. Is it because you're outsiders, perhaps? It seems a lot of our assumptions about you were incorrect," Leviala mumbled with a slight frown before her eyes lit up. "You have traveled between worlds? How is it? What kinds of places exist out there?"

"I've been off-planet a few times, yes. There are all kinds of worlds out there, but I can't tell you about it right now. I'm a bit strapped for time," Zac said. "So, the Base Power? Anything among these things that has it? I want to activate the tablet."

It felt like Zac had over a hundred questions rattling around in his head, but he needed to prioritize his quest for now.

"These things are called chargers," Leviala eventually said as she pointed down at a cylindrical item. "Press the sheer side against the bottom of the tablet for a few seconds to instill it with power."

Zac followed her instructions, and it worked just as described. The tablet turned on after two seconds of charging, though that didn't help Zac much. Rows and boxes full of illegible text covered the screen, and Zac couldn't make heads or tails of it.

"Do you know how to work these things?" Zac asked.

"No," she said with a shake of her head. "I can read the language, but I don't know how these things work. It takes decades to learn these things, and only the Datamancers can make use of this information in any case. You would have to find the line for activating the door, and then bypass the security protocols."

Zac thought for a second before he showed her the tablet.

"Let me worry about the security checks. Can you tell me if one of these boxes is related to gate opening?

"It's either that or climbing through one of the cracks," Zac added.

"That's even more impossible!" Leviala said. "There are security protocols in place to trap research subjects. You're almost guaranteed to get trapped inside the Memorysteel if you try to enter through one of those places, and there are no Builders to let you out. Not a single one who has been caught inside a wall has ever made it out as far as I know."

Zac simply stared at her in response as he held the tablet toward her. She eventually sighed in defeat before her eyes started darting back and forth for almost a minute. She finally pointed at one of the boxes, though hesitation was written all over her face.

"Perhaps this one? It seems to mention something about a security check, which is always performed when opening a door. The other algorithms seem to be more related to the general operation of the wall itself," she said. "But just finding the right program isn't enough."

Zac nodded in thanks before he took the tablet. He honestly had no idea what to do from this point on, but he gained some confidence from the simple fact that he'd gotten the quest from the System. It seemed to believe he would have a chance to complete it, meaning he should be able to open the door.

He didn't even try to understand what he was looking at since it was too far beyond his understanding, and he simply pressed the box Leviala had indicated. However, he did take one precaution. He had taken out his mother's token from his Spatial Ring, and he held it against the same spot as the charger when he pressed the button.

"Wait, what are you doing?! You will alert the security protocols!" Leviala screamed when she saw Zac's impetuous actions, but her words got caught in her throat when the gate started forming without issue, and at a much greater speed than when the werewolf was trying to conjure it.

85

OLD FRIENDS

"I'm in," Zac said, his mouth tugging upward, as he felt like the lead in an '80s movie about hackers.

This was obviously lost on the Cartava scion, and she blankly looked back and forth between him and the gate.

"Wh– how?" she eventually sputtered, looking like a lifetime of common sense was rapidly being upended.

"I have my ways." Zac smiled as he stashed away the talisman again before the Cartava scion could spot it.

The talisman didn't contain any clear hints of its origins as far as Zac could tell, but it was obviously a Technocrat tool if you knew a bit about them. Even Ogras could discern the truth at a single glance, and someone like Leviala could probably glean even more. He obviously wouldn't divulge his secrets to this stranger, even if she was cooperative so far.

The door slid open a second later, exposing the interior. The state of the base on the other side was far worse than even the war-torn wall. The walls of the corridor had completely crumbled, and even the roof was missing in spots.

Only an endless black could be glimpsed through the cracks, making it seem as though the research base were hurtling through space. But the darkness that Zac could see through the cracks rather reminded Zac of the bleak blackness of the Abyss he could glimpse through **[Rapturous Divide]** rather than the empty darkness of outer space.

The truth probably wasn't quite that sinister. Mystic Realms were pocket sub-dimensions, and they had to have an end somewhere. What he saw was probably the void between dimensions, the place where one would end up if you fell through a spatial tear. However, he still got an oppressive feeling when he looked, so Zac's instincts told him there were other dangers lurking in the darkness.

The scene gave Zac some pause, but he quickly roused himself. There was no telling how long the door would last even if he'd used his mother's token.

"Okay, let's go." Zac nodded as he started walking, but Leviala looked at him like he was crazy.

"What? You want me to go?" Leviala almost screamed, her face a mix of horror and confusion. "I am no good to you. You've seen the state I'm in. I'll only be a burden. I'll rest up before returning to my clan instead. That way, I can warn them about those enemies of yours so that we can start prepar–"

"There'll be plenty of time for that later," Zac said as the chains of **[Love's Bond]** once more lifted the aghast Cartava scion into the air. "I'm sorry, but I'll need to bring you along as a guide. You've already proven you're essential to rescuing my people by helping me with the tablet."

"I've never been to this section of the base! I'll be of no use to you!" she exclaimed as she vehemently struggled against the restraints.

Zac ignored her complaints as he stepped through the gate, which soundlessly closed behind them. A few seconds later, it turned into another piece of broken wall that ran along the corridor. Strangely enough, there was no telling that a vast forest stood on the other side of the wall after passing through, not even after peering through the cracks. Only a murky haze could be seen on the other side, making Zac believe the cracks were actually filled with spatial anomalies.

No wonder the werewolves refused to take a shortcut.

"So much for not being captured. It was all for nothing," Leviala muttered with a hint of despair from her chain cocoon, and Zac could only apologetically smile in response.

She was right. She might have gone out of the ashes into the fire from her perspective, swapping a known captor to a more powerful unknown one. Not only that, but Zac was also fumbling in the dark in this dangerous place, which put them both at risk. But there was nothing to be done about the situation. The System gave him no choice in the matter.

"I really am sorry about all this." Zac coughed as he stepped further inside, dragging a clearly unwilling Leviala along with his chains. "You could say my hands are tied."

"Stop, STOP!" she screamed. "Alright, I'll help you. But stop walking ahead randomly, or you'll get us both killed!"

"What, really?" Zac said, but he still stopped in his tracks. "Help me with this matter, and I'll make it up to you. Is there anything you or your clan need? I can send for it before the pathways to this world close."

"Like what?" Leviala asked curiously as she stopped struggling against the restraints, confirming Zac's guess.

This girl was full of curiosity about the outside world and its marvels, which wasn't too surprising considering her situation. Hopefully, he would be able to use that to keep her cooperative.

"I have no idea what you guys are lacking in this world. Pills? Manuals? Attuned Crystals?"

"Land," Leviala said without hesitation. "I've heard that planets have spots with greater energy density compared to others, treasure lands where you can cultivate at twice the speed with half the effort. Can you provide us with such a thing?"

"There are a few such places on Earth." Zac slowly nodded. "But those places are extremely valuable strategic resources. Being my guide for a few hours isn't worth a Nexus Vein, no offense."

"I also saved you from being captured by werewolves by warning you, but fine. We'll revisit this matter later." Leviala sighed. "Our first priority should be staying alive in this place."

"Good. Now, how do I find that relay station?" Zac asked.

"I don't know where it is, but it shouldn't be too far in from this gate. Half an hour away at the most. Any further and the station would be inside the Wasteland itself, and no permanent structure can survive in there. But make no mistake, our lives are in peril every second even here at the edge."

"What's the Wasteland?" Zac asked with a frown. "Another biosphere like the forest before?"

"No," Leviala said with a shake of her head. "Something much more dangerous. It will take some time to explain, but you need to understand the dangers to not get us both killed."

"Give me the abridged version," Zac reluctantly agreed, though part of him just wanted to set out.

The windows into the void looked pretty unsettling, but the atmosphere was intact, and there was no suction dragging items out through the cracks. As for spatial tears, Zac figured his Luck had proven a pretty good early warning system. But seeing Leviala's exaggerated reactions, there were probably more dangers than what met the eye.

"Our people were taken here over fifteen thousand years ago and experimented on for millennia," Leviala began, but was interrupted by an impatient Zac.

"Is this really the short version?"

"Just listen," Leviala said with a glare. "We were taken here because of our bloodlines, but there was an incident that put an end to the experiments around five thousand years ago. A mystical item appeared out of nowhere, rippling through the spatial barriers like they didn't exist.

"It slammed into this base like a meteor, completely ripping apart a large section of it. It hit the base from the east, annihilating the subjects who were experimented on there. Only by digging through data did we find out that the subjects there were a clan of Titans, renowned for their physical prowess."

Zac's heartbeat sped up a bit when he heard the mention of Titans, although he had already been somewhat certain that this place was the source of Billy's Heritage. However, it seemed more likely that Billy's ancestor had somehow managed to reach Earth through a spatial tear or something, rather than the whole clan escaping.

"The object made its way into the core of the base, presumably killing all our captors as well," Leviala continued.

"Presumably? You don't know if they were killed?" Zac asked with confusion.

"What followed after the impact was over a hundred years of spatial chaos. We call the event the Cataclysm. You should have encountered those rifts by now, right? Those kinds of things raged across the whole base, wreaking havoc. We lost most of our people during those days. But one day, it just stopped, and the base woke up again. By that time, our captors were all gone, and we slowly managed to eke out a living here," Leviala said.

"Do you know who it was that captured you?" Zac asked curiously.

"They called themselves the Tsarun Clan," Leviala said.

"WHAT?!" Zac exclaimed. "Those guys?"

"You know of them? Are they still around? Do they know of your planet?" Leviala said, fear shining in her eyes. "Our elders were Peak D-grade, but they were all slaughtered by those people when they came for us. They are terrifying."

"They're around, and they are still extremely powerful. They have a pretty unsavory reputation as well, and no one wants to make an enemy out of them. There are also rumors of them working with unorthodox forces to become more powerful. So I guess it's not too surprising they started messing around with a Technocrat research base," Zac explained.

Leviala looked shaken that their captor was still around and living well.

"You don't need to worry about me selling you out," Zac added when he saw the fear in her eyes. "They probably are more interested in capturing me than they are in capturing you."

"What? Are you carrying a unique bloodline as well?" Leviala blurted.

"No, we are enemies for other reasons. A small disagreement ended up with them losing one of their main-branch descendants and being publicly embarrassed," Zac slowly said, his voice somewhat decreasing in strength after seeing the mounting horror in her eyes. "Anyway, I guess we have a common enemy? So what happened afterward?"

"When my ancestors realized they were left alone in this place, they started looking for a way to escape. But movement in this place is always highly restricted, and we never found a way out. However, we managed to find a few tablets left behind by the Tsarun Clan, and that's how we learned the methods of the Datamancers," Leviala said.

"Unfortunately, only a few of our people can become true Datamancers, as they can't be registered as research subjects by the AI of this place. Only one out of a thousand might have the ability to become a Datamancer, and even then, their degree of success is highly random," Leviala said.

"People without bloodlines," Zac muttered.

"Exactly." Leviala nodded. "Our clan was essentially bred and experimented on for millennia with the sole purpose of purifying and strengthening our bloodline, and it was the same with the other clans. For someone to be born without it after all that, it is extremely rare. I guess there are a lot more potential Datamancers among you outsiders.

"In either case, we found out about the fundamental rules of this base through reading the Tsarun Clan reports. As you mentioned, they didn't build this base. They rather stumbled upon it during an exploration trip outside of integrated space. They spent tens of thousands of years slowly gaining control over the basic functions, but we believe they never managed to get a hold on the core secrets of this place," Leviala continued.

"What do you know about the original creators?" Zac asked, straining to keep his face impassive.

"Not much," Leviala said with a shake of her head. "We know they were terrifyingly powerful, far greater than the Tsarun Clan. We think they finished their research, then left this base, though we don't know why they didn't repurpose this place. The Tsarun were only digging through the scraps for their own project."

Zac sighed and nodded. He wasn't sure if she was telling the truth or kept the secrets about his mother's clan to herself, but there was still ample time to find out the truth.

"This is all valuable information, but what does this have to do with the Wasteland?" Zac asked, returning to the main subject.

"I needed you to understand how dangerous it was during the age after the Cataclysm, where less than five percent of our clan survived. Because the Wasteland never healed. It is the sector where the dimensional treasure passed through before hitting the core of this base, and the laws of space are still in flux here. The rest of this world has found an equilibrium and is bound by the rules of the Builders, but the Wasteland is in a permanent state of turmoil." Leviala sighed.

"So what? If the werewolves can pass it, so can I," Zac said.

"We have spent millennia mapping the spatial storms, but that knowledge holds no sway in the Wasteland. A spatial storm can descend on you at a moment's notice, and that's not all. This area is full of spatial holes, and sometimes things fall out. Dangerous things," she said, her eyes inadvertently darting toward the ominous scars in the ceiling.

"Dangerous things?" Zac said with a frown.

"There are weird beasts hidden in the darkness. They can't survive in our environment for long, and they cause massive destruction in their attempts to return to the void. Encountering those things almost always results in death. But other things can fall out as well, like a mountain getting dropped on your head. You never know," Leviala said.

"Then how can the Lunar Tribe pass it?"

"They live the closest to the Wasteland, so they understand it the best. Their bodies are also very strong, and their lunar skills allow them to briefly pass through spatial storms unscathed. I've heard they also maintain routes where they have left protective measures, like small safe bubbles powered by Base Power," Leviala said.

"Doesn't your clan have something similar?" Zac asked with a frown.

"No. We never go here. Treasures sometimes fall out of the void, but the dangers far overshadow the potential gain. Besides, passing the Wasteland only leads to the Lunar Tribe, and you've seen how our relationship is," Leviala said.

"So, the relay station?" Zac asked.

"It's probably a base where the scouting units gather to cross the Wasteland together. Powering those safe bubbles requires a lot of Base Power, and each squad can't pass alone. Besides, there is safety in numbers. I've also heard that they make the troublemakers and the elderly take the vanguard, so they'll somewhat block the spatial storms with their bodies if one arrives unnoticed," Leviala said.

"Okay, we hopefully won't need to worry about that. Which way? If you don't know, just follow your instincts," Zac said.

Leviala looked into the eyes of Zac for a few seconds before she sighed as a small glimmer activated in her eyes. Her one remaining good eye turned milky white the next moment, eliciting a strong sense of unease in Zac's mind. However, it soon returned to normal, though Leviala looked even more sickly than before.

"That way," she said as she nodded at a route as blood started to flow from her nose again. "Now, can you rearrange these chains to something more comfortable?"

86

BUBBLES

Zac frowned when he saw that Leviala's condition seemed to have worsened even further, instead simply nodding in thanks. He went down the corridor that Leviala indicated, maintaining a pace just slow enough so that his danger sense would be able to pick up any hints of spatial tears in time.

He would have preferred to transform **[Love's Bond]** to its defensive form as well, but it turned out that was impossible because of Leviala. She could barely stand at the moment, let alone keep up with him. He instead had to fashion some sort of chair out of two of his chains, allowing him to carry her to his side. Carrying her on his back would have been a lot more convenient, but he definitely wasn't about to let a complete stranger have her arms around his neck. That was a good way to get yourself killed or captured.

The path they followed looked very much the same as the area where they'd entered, with a state of decay that far exceeded anything Ogras had described in his report. Occasional flickering in the scripts on the wall indicated that the area wasn't completely disconnected from the base, but it apparently wasn't in any state to repair this place. Or perhaps the Base AI had simply deemed it too costly what with the spatial turbulence.

They continued down the corridor for a few minutes before they reached a huge crack in the wall. It was wide enough for five people to enter together, and it seemed to be heading in the direction of the

Wasteland. Zac tried to peer inside, but it was completely pitch black apart from some light at the end of the tunnel, making it a possible shortcut.

"Do you think they entered here?"

"I can't activate my eyes again. I will end up in a coma," she said as she peered into the darkness. "But it's doubtful. I don't think the Lunar Tribe would use these kinds of paths unless absolutely necessary. The corridors are still connected to the base, and they follow most of the rules, but anything can happen in a crack like this. I think we should continue down the road."

Zac nodded and kept walking without hesitation. He felt a vague sense of threat from that dark ingress anyway, and he probably wouldn't have entered even if he'd traveled alone. Something dangerous waited inside.

A minute later, they reached a crossing, with a proper path heading the same way as the eerie crack from before. Zac looked at his reluctant guide again, but she still shook her head.

"No, not that way either," Leviala said. "That corridor is the start of a looping spiral, a dead end. Cracks might have created a new path in there, but perhaps not. We would waste almost an hour going this way."

"A looping spiral?" Zac asked.

"These endless corridors follow certain patterns, and we have learned to somewhat intuit some of them after living in them all our lives. I'm almost certain that this corridor is a dead end, but I can't actually explain how I know it. It's a vague sense based on the direction we're walking, proximity to the forest, previous corridors, and so on."

"Is it your ocular bloodline?" Zac asked.

"No, everyone born in this place can somewhat do this," Leviala explained.

Zac guessed that it was a naturally nurtured equivalent to his recently gained sense from **[Forester's Constitution]** unless she was hiding something. Perhaps she could tell based on the inscriptions on the wall or some other small sign that Zac couldn't notice. Either way, he felt it was better to go with her instincts unless his own Danger Sense started to rail against them.

The state of the base gradually worsened even further as they proceeded until Zac suddenly froze before he activated [Loamwalker], moving himself and Leviala back where they came from. Not even a half a second passed before an extremely dense storm of spatial tears passed right through the corridor, seemingly both exiting and entering through the Memorysteel walls.

"You see?" Leviala sighed, her face ghastly white. "We were lucky this time, but things will only get worse from here on out. You can't sense these sudden storms either, so it's imposs–"

She didn't get any further before Zac moved again, once more narrowly avoiding a weird fluctuation that appeared from one of the cracks in the roof. It almost felt like the spatial tears from before had summoned something.

"–ible to completely avoid. Wait, how are you doing that?" Leviala asked as she looked down at Zac with confusion.

Zac didn't immediately answer, but rather kept his eyes peeled at the situation ahead. The thing that had appeared was clearly of a spatial nature, but it was something other than a tear. It almost looked like a soap bubble, but it actually reflected a blue sun rather than the surroundings. The bubble was almost two meters across, and much smaller spheres surrounded it like satellites.

It only remained a few seconds before it destabilized with a pop, causing an extremely powerful implosion that made Zac's hair stand on end. There was no way that he would have survived it if he hadn't moved away in time.

"What was that?"

"We call them void bubbles," Leviala said with a sigh. "It's actually a pretty rare sight. We don't really know what they are. Some believe that they are the result of the dimensional layers temporarily weakening, giving a glimpse of the outside. More than one desperate cultivator has jumped into those bubbles in hopes of escaping this place, but I doubt anyone actually survived."

Zac nodded in agreement. He could somewhat sense the power brewing in the center of that bubble, and it was definitely not something any random E-grade cultivator could survive. However, he suddenly froze with realization. Triv seemed certain that quite a few people had escaped from this base because there were so many high-quality corpses on Earth. Was this the method they used?

"Is it always that blue sun?" Zac asked to make sure.

"No, the scene is always different. Most of them picture outer space, though," Leviala said. "Seeing one depicting land is very rare."

Zac nodded, feeling that his theory wasn't completely without merit, but something she said piqued his curiosity.

"You guys know what space is?" Zac asked curiously.

"You know, we've lost much, but we've only been in this place for a couple of millennia. My great-grandfather was born in the Zecia Sector," she said with a scathing glance.

"Alright then." Zac coughed and started walking.

He felt a bit stupid hearing her explanation, and his plans for exchanging information about the outside for information on the inside died in its cradle. She might know even more than himself about the Zecia Sector for all he knew since the Cartava Clan was seemingly a proper cultivation clan before they were captured.

They kept going further from their starting point, and the spatial anomalies only grew more and more common. Zac's Danger Sense kept doing wonders, and seeing that Zac really was able to somewhat predict the spatial tears made Leviala calm down a bit. It allowed her to relax before she started explaining the base patterns in greater detail.

Zac felt he learned a lot, though he knew that he simply couldn't gain an intuitive feel for the place just by hearing about patterns such as "Downstream Wing" and "Fierce Otodon." But it did give him a glimpse into how these native forces functioned, which might be even more valuable.

"We should turn here," Leviala eventually said as they reached another crossing. "This should be the main path leading toward the Wasteland, and if we go any further without turning, we'll reach the Outer Divide. I doubt that the Outer Divide is breached even this close to the Wasteland, so going there is a waste of time."

Zac nodded in agreement, but they only proceeded a hundred meters before Zac's mind once more screamed of danger. This time, it was to the point that Zac almost fell over from the shock to his mind, with only thoughts of escape remaining. He scrambled out of the way like his life depended on it, completely forgetting about Leviala.

The Cartava scion was dragged along thanks to the chains of **[Love's Bond]**, barely missing a massive claw that suddenly appeared from one of the cracks in the roof. It slammed into the ground with devastating force, shredding the sturdy alloy like it was nothing. Zac desperately scrambled to his feet to keep backing away, and he looked at the hand with fear. He didn't even dare to think about attacking that thing out of fear that it would sense his killing intent.

The hand emitted energy waves almost at the level of Greatest, meaning that the beast should be somewhere in the Late D-grade.

The hand looked both corporeal and energy-based, and it twisted and distorted as it tried to grab hold of something in the corridor. It almost looked like a hologram if not for the deep scars that were caused in the walls. However, the runes on the walls suddenly lit up, and dozens of Memorysteel spears stabbed into the hand.

But seeing the result only made Zac even more certain of the power of the creature. He had been on the receiving end of those things, and the still tender flesh in his side was a poignant reminder of how powerful they were. But the spears were actually completely unable to harm the claw, and it easily crushed them like they were made out of paper.

The claw had its own problems, and it kept distorting more and more until it was barely recognizable any longer. Only then did the hand recede into the void again, leaving an utterly decimated hallway that seemed unable to restore its previous form.

"It's a Void Creature, the things I warned you of," Leviala whispered, her face pallid. "I never expected to see one in person. We're lucky to be alive."

"Where the hell did it come from?" Zac muttered as he peered into the darkness.

"We believe they live in the void, hence the name. But I have no idea how that's possible," Leviala said.

"Why did it attack?" Zac muttered.

"They are drawn here by the dimensional treasure, but they can't enter this type of dimension freely. So they skulk around the cracks in space, sometimes reaching in to attack people. A few of the smaller ones sometimes fall through completely, but that only happens in the Wasteland and the core region where the cracks are larger," Leviala said.

Zac grimaced when he heard the mention about the core section where the Dimensional Seed was located. It sounded like the sector itself was just as dangerous as the Wasteland, perhaps even more so. Void's Disciple and the zealots might be the least of his worries when he reached that place.

"What now?" Zac muttered. "Is there an alternative path?"

"The beast should go away if we wait a few minutes. But be careful," Leviala said. "I already overdid it by activating my bloodline twice. You're on your own now. I can't warn you again as I did during the battle against the werewolves."

"That's no problem," Zac said. "But while we're on the subject, just how did you manage to warn me before? You've seen how sharp my senses are, but I didn't sense a thing. More to the point, you shouted out before Hevastes had even reached me. Are your clan members Karmic Cultivators?"

Leviala's warning was as good an opening as any, and Zac finally couldn't hold back his curiosity after having walked these broken hallways for almost an hour. He had replayed that battle over and over in his mind, and Karma was the only explanation he could think of. He still remembered that odd feeling of déjà vu, and it made him think of his battle with the Hayner patriarch more than anything.

He knew that Karmic Cultivators were exceedingly rare, but it really looked like she had divined the future before, warning him of something that was about to take place. The backlash also matched with what he knew of divination. There was always a price to pay to peer into the future, and even a powerful monk like Lord 84th wasn't an exception.

Perhaps the Tsarun Clan wanted the power of precognition for themselves and had tried to extract that capability from the Cartava Clan. Or perhaps they wanted to breed a bunch of seers, forcing them to write divinations day in and day out until they were killed by the Heavens. There was no doubt that such a power would prove immensely beneficial for a power-hungry man like the Tsarun patriarch.

"No," she hurriedly said as she shook her head with such force that she almost fell out of her chair made out of chains. "Our clan has nothing to do with Divination or Karma."

"Then why such a strong reaction?" Zac said as a frown spread across his face. "Our planet does have a grudge against a Karmic Cultivator, but that doesn't mean we're enemies with all of them. But let me be clear; if I find out that you're lying, then your clan will have to find another way out of this place than through me. I can't have another group of people manipulating Karma against me or my people. You'd better tell me right now what's going on."

87

KARMA AND TIME

"No, I swear I'm not lying!" Leviala exclaimed with a pale face. "You're not the first one to make that deduction. Our clan was constantly harassed because a lot of forces believed us to manipulate Karma for our profit. I only reacted strongly because our clan suffered a lot of harassment because of this."

"If not Karma, then what?" Zac asked.

"You have probably realized that my clan has an eye-based bloodline after seeing me," Leviala eventually said. "That's why we were caught and brought here."

"Really? Just because of that?" Zac asked, skepticism written all over his face. "There's no way the Tsarun Clan would capture you because of that."

It wasn't without reason Zac had that sort of reaction. He had learned a thing or two about bloodlines from gathering missives by now, and he wasn't completely clueless any longer. The most common types of bloodlines were combat-oriented, with the second most common being affinity-related, either boosting cultivation speed or skill control.

Ocular bloodlines were a lot rarer than those types, but not to the point that it was exceedingly rare. But more importantly, they were generally not seen as too useful since they mainly focused on scouting or helping with things like inscriptions and crafting.

There was no way that the power-hungry Tsarun Clan would waste so much effort on something useless. Those werewolves had gained a pretty decent boost to their combat strength when their bloodlines awakened, surpassing the general estimates of common bloodlines. There had to be something special about Clan Cartava to warrant their capture.

"Our clan has nothing to do with Karma, really. Our bloodlines provide us with scouting abilities and some suppression," Leviala repeated once more.

"Then why did that guy say that you're the key to immortality?" Zac asked with a frown, feeling he was being taken for a ride.

Zac's gut told him that the werewolf had thrown out that last line with his dying breath to cause trouble, but that didn't mean that he was lying. These werewolves had fought in the Outer Ring against the humans, and now they had managed to somehow capture one of them. The fact that the werewolves worked so hard against the humans rather than trying to escape meant they possessed something even more valuable than freedom.

Immortality was one such thing. Even a pig would become an overlord given enough time, so it was definitely an alluring concept for most cultivators. Perhaps the werewolf believed Zac would feel the same and torture the girl for her secrets. However, Zac wasn't personally all that interested in the prospect of immortality.

He grew up expecting to live around eighty years, so his current life span approaching the thousands was already shocking enough. Who would want to walk the universe until the end of time? It sounded torturous more than anything. The girl seemed reluctant to say anything more as she looked around back and forth. Zac had an idea of what she was worried about, and he took out and activated an isolation array.

"No one can hear us now," Zac said. "I normally wouldn't pressure someone like this, but you're simply acting too suspiciously. I can't have anything going wrong in this place. Billions of lives depend on it."

"Fine." Leviala eventually sighed. "You have to swear on your path of cultivation to not divulge what I'm about to say, and not to experiment on me or my clansmen."

"I swear not to divulge anything as long as you don't move against me or my force." Zac nodded. "And I would never experiment on people."

Leviala looked at Zac for a while longer before she eventually nodded.

"Our bloodline really isn't anything more than a decent ocular Heritage. But that wasn't always the case. Our founding ancestor's eyes were different from ours. They contained the power of time itself. Not only did he live five times longer than a normal cultivator at his stage, but he was able to glimpse into both the past and present to some degree," Leviala said. "His children never inherited his gift, though, but the ancestor's actions started the rumors about us being a Karmic Clan.

"Eventually, the rumors died down, and our lives started to return to normal. However, the Tsarun Clan found out about the true nature of our founding ancestor's eyes through a traitor. They wanted that power of time for themselves. I don't know why, but I think it was for the same reason as the Lunar Tribe. They want to extract the power in our eyes to increase their longevity," Leviala said.

"And you have the same types of eyes as your ancestor," Zac deduced before he looked at her with exasperation. "All that talk, and it's still related to Karma after all?"

"You seem to have a flawed understanding of the Dao of Karma. Karma and Divination are completely separate from the Dao of Time. Karma is an understanding of the interconnectedness of everything in the universe. It's understanding causality, and in some cases deliberately influencing the future by taking some seemingly inscrutable actions," Leviala explained.

"They are unable to see the whole picture as normal cultivators, so they connect with the omnipresent Heavens for a short moment to borrow its omniscience, all the Karmic Ties and relations. But ultimately, they are still not actually peering into the future or the past," she continued. "Furthermore, Karma is just one type of Divination. There's also the Numerology of the Dao of Order, and some oracles even enter contracts with strange beings of other dimensions who can show them glimpses of the unknown. I'm sure there are even more types out there."

"So they aren't actually able to see the future. But you are?" Zac said with a frown.

Timeline altering seemed extremely overpowered, especially for someone in the E-grade. Getting your soul wounded and a bleeding nose could barely be considered a backlash for something so heaven-defying. The brand on her eye looked a lot more worrisome, but how could that compare to altering the past?

"No. I can just glimpse fragmented images and generally just from the past. When I chose a direction before, I looked into the past and saw werewolves coming from this corridor," Leviala explained. "But during your battle, I felt a sudden urge to peek into the future, and I saw a hand holding a restraint module behind you. I knew that we both would be in trouble if that really happened, so I called out.

"As you saw, looking into the future is a lot more dangerous than the past, because even just looking will invariably change the future. Besides, I can only see a short image, but there's no guarantee that I would understand what I saw. This time, I was lucky, since I knew that you getting sealed would be bad for me, but the risk of receiving the backlash and gaining nothing in return is high," Leviala said. "The backlash is also extremely harsh; every usage comes with a permanent cost."

Zac slowly nodded. He couldn't pinpoint what, but he felt that there was something odd with her description of the events. Perhaps it was the "sudden urge" to peek into the future that was the most suspect. Then again, he often got those sorts of urges thanks to his high Luck, and perhaps she had a similar ability.

"So you got a glimpse of a bad future and warned me to prevent it? Can everyone in your clan do this?" Zac asked.

"No," Leviala said. "Just a select few."

"Thank you for letting me know. And don't worry, I have no interest in your time eyes," Zac said as he picked up the isolation disk. "I don't want to be hunted down by the old monsters in the sector for holding a key to increased longevity."

Leviala could only weakly smile in response, and the two set out a few minutes later after there was no sign of the Void Creature returning. Zac wasn't joking when he said that he would keep the secret to himself. Part of it was the reason he just said. He didn't want to live a life where he was hunted by powerful factions, like Yrial or the Eveningtide Asura.

But part of it was definitely because of her situation. She hadn't said it outright, but warning him had definitely come at a cost. He had noticed that Leviala had repeatedly reached for her branded eye as they traveled along the corridors, and he guessed that the curse was a direct result of peering into the future.

After all, if meddling with the strings of Karma came at a sharp price, then the same would probably hold for meddling with time. The System or the real Heavens protected the fundamental rules of the universe, it seemed. Otherwise things would turn extremely chaotic with people jumping back and forth through timelines as they pleased.

The minutes turned into two hours as they progressed further and further from their starting position, though they had to backtrack a few times after encountering completely crumbled sections of the corridors. Perennial spatial storms were swirling about in these places, making it completely impossible to pass through.

But finally, there was a change as they heard a loud argument in the distance. They had moved in complete silence after the first thirty minutes out of fear of alerting the sensitive werewolves, with Leviala only giving directions with her hands. Two gruff voices echoed through the corridors, making the two freeze in position. Zac once more took out the isolation array, hoping that the energy fluctuations wouldn't alert anyone.

The two listened for a bit, and it quickly became apparent it was an argument between two squad leaders. One of them wanted to set out already since he believed something had gone wrong. The other wanted to wait for Hevastes, as he carried a lot of the Base Power required to power the safe bubbles placed in the Wasteland.

They couldn't hear everything, though, and the voices stopped after a minute.

"It should be just up ahead," Zac said with a low voice. "Stay here."

"You'll come pick me up, right?" Leviala said with worry. "I don't think I can get back alone. I should tell you, I hold some weight in my clan; things will get a lot easier for you if you have me assisting you from the inside. I doubt my people would be ready to head for the depths of this place rather than the exit if my grandpa doesn't tell them to."

"Of course I'll help you," Zac assured her as silvery tufts of hair started to grow from his face.

A blinding agony spread through Zac's body the next moment as he activated **[Million Faces]** for the first time. The fit with his pathways wasn't any better with the upgraded skill, which meant that every minor adjustment was accompanied by the feeling of his bones being crushed and re-formed. And Zac wasn't planning on a minor adjustment.

His face elongated while his body grew a few decimeters as he donned a hunched-over posture with his arms hanging low. Sharp claws grew out from his hands, and he felt his teeth growing sharp as well.

"How do I look?" Zac grunted a minute later, though he had some problems forming words properly with a canine snout.

"Just what are you? Can you turn into anything?" Leviala whispered in shock.

"It's a transformation skill," Zac snorted. "Do I look like a werewolf?"

"Honestly, you look like a failed miscreation," Leviala said, and she clearly had problems looking in his direction.

Zac sighed when he saw her disgusted face, and a wave of disgust hit him as well when he took out a mirror. The only way he would be mistaken for a werewolf was if the werewolf not only suffered from a severe case of mange but also a series of birth defects.

The extent he could change his body was a lot greater with his new skill, but turning into a werewolf was clearly overreaching. But he still wanted to get a small advantage this way. Leviala believed that the relay station was in what she called a chokepoint chamber, a large warehouse with one entrance and one exit.

It would be the only path to get to the other side, and it was easily defended. Most settlements in the Mystic Realm were built in these kinds of chambers, or a series of such warehouses, and sometimes they could even control the barriers leading in and out. Leviala guessed that they wouldn't have too great a control of a base this far from their real domain, but she couldn't be sure.

The Lunar Tribe had already provided her with plenty of surprises.

He thought for a second before he had an idea to improve the disguise. He took out a couple of bandages next and covered over half his face and hands, with the uneven tufts of silver hair sticking out between. He took out the dead werewolf leader next and pushed his bisected body against the bandages, drenching them with blood.

Leviala seemed ready to vomit at the macabre display, but Zac had long turned numb to these kinds of grotesque actions. What did it matter if he got a little bloodied if he could complete his quest and save his people? Next, he put on a spare set of the clothes he found in Hevastes' Cosmos Sack, finishing the makeshift transformation.

"What about now?" Zac said as he spun around.

"I guess you can pass as Hevastes from a distance, but you won't be able to infiltrate them this way," Leviala said.

"That's fine. I just need to get through the door," Zac muttered.

"You know, Hevastes and the others were weakened after they killed my guard, but I don't think the other squads are in that bad a shape. And there might be quite a few of them," she exhorted. "You might not–"

"I have to do this," Zac said as he stood up and cracked his neck. "Wait here. I'll be back in a few minutes."

Zac started making his way toward the source of the argument earlier, and he took on a shuffling walk to make it look like he was wounded. He wanted to create the illusion of Hevastes returning alone in defeat after failing his mission. He soon enough reached a proper arch that was blocked with a familiar red barrier.

"Lord Hevastes, is that you?" A hesitant voice emerged from the other side as a werewolf stepped forward, looking at Zac's appearance with shock.

"Get the fuck out of the way," Zac growled, trying to make his voice mimic the gruff timbre of the werewolf leader.

A surge of relief hit Zac a second later as the barrier flickered out, and Zac wasted no time.

"Wh–" the werewolf said with wide eyes, but he didn't get any further before Zac's hand snapped forward, gripping the werewolf by the throat and cracking his neck.

A surge of Cosmic Energy confirmed the kill, and **[Verun's Bite]** appeared in his hand as he started to transform back to normal.

"We're under attack!" another guard screamed just before Zac managed to end his life as well.

Zac had never expected to enter the open space unnoticed with his wretched disguise. Cosmic Energy churned through his body, as he was primed for an all-out assault.

88
HANDS

"Who are you?!" a bulky werewolf roared as he produced a large spear that seemed to be made from the same material as the walls, and a quick estimate by Zac indicated there were around fifty werewolves in the emptied-out storeroom.

It was a bit more than Zac had hoped, but he knew that he couldn't back down now. Zac's only response to the inquiry was unleashing a roar at the top of his lungs, reinforced with his aura and billowing killing intent. The very air in the room vibrated, and two large screens that displayed some unintelligible data actually cracked from the pressure.

The sudden outburst made the werewolves freeze for an instant like they were faced with a dangerous predator, giving Zac a brief window to scan the large warehouse that had been outfitted into what looked a bit like a campsite. He soon found what he was looking for: a group of dirty and bloodied humans and one demon huddled in a corner, chained to the wall.

All of them carried somewhat serious wounds, with two apparently being unconscious. The pathetic state of his people ignited another surge of fury in his heart, and any hesitation flew out of his head as he threw out over a hundred items while activating **[Nature's Punishment]**.

The werewolves had already regained their bearings after the surprising outburst, and they started to radiate lunar light one by one.

The room was over two hundred meters across, but it was still a lot more confined compared to the earlier battles in the forests. More importantly, the walls were reflective, and Zac worried what would happen if they were allowed to completely unleash their Bloodline War Array.

However, the cold moonlight was overpowered before it even had a chance to stabilize as the whole area erupted in an unceasing cascade of elemental eruptions.

Huge flowers wrought from flame bloomed as icicles as long as five meters fell from the sky. Lakes of thunder covered the ground, and torrential winds full of hidden blades cut at the flustered werewolves. It was as though an army of elementalists had descended upon the relay station, intent on ripping it apart.

There obviously were no mages assisting Zac in his rescue attempt, but the commotion was rather the result of throwing out a full stack of low- and medium-grade talismans at the cost of a decent chunk of his Cosmic Energy. These low-quality offensive talismans would normally not be able to kill even a Peak F-grade warrior, let alone these werewolves with powerful constitutions.

But packed together in a confined space like this, they could cause some serious harm. More importantly, they emitted almost blinding light while the explosions made any attempts of organization impossible.

A storm of spatial tears erupted the next second as Zac's hidden ace, a [Void Ball], detonated right where the most powerful-looking werewolves were fending off blasts from every direction. A few werewolves were cut into ribbons, but most of them suddenly turned into light, allowing the tears to pass right through their intangible forms.

Zac had already learned about this bloodline ability, so he wasn't surprised to see them materializing almost immediately with various degrees of wounds. There were still a lot of chaotic spatial tears around them, forcing the werewolves to find another way to protect themselves. Most of them were suddenly enclosed in red barriers as they jumped out of the way.

The shields were obviously of the same source as the ones he had seen in this base before, but the werewolves had managed to construct portable defensive mechanisms.

However, it looked like the barriers shared one inconvenient trait with the barriers of the base itself. The spatial tears seamlessly entered the shields themselves, melding with them into one entity. Zac couldn't be sure, but he felt there was no way that some portable device would be able to lock in and contain a spatial tear.

As expected, the leaders quickly grabbed small machines hidden their pockets and threw them far away, and a series of small explosions erupted soon after as the machines broke apart into what looked like weakened copies of the [Void Ball] itself. The werewolf leaders had managed to save their hides, but Zac had already achieved his purpose.

The chaos caused by the [Void Ball] and explosive talismans had caused complete disorder amongst the ranks of the werewolves, and their Lunar War Array had almost completely fallen apart.

Zac knew they would be able to restore order soon enough, but the confusion had given him just enough time to conjure the enormous wooden hand hovering by the ceiling fifty meters up in the air. Zac didn't waste even a second before the large emerald array appeared, and a small branch started to descend the moment it appeared.

"Above!" a werewolf shouted, but it was too late.

The branch rapidly grew as innumerable branches sprouted, each of them shooting for a werewolf. Transcendent lights rose to meet their descent, and smoke rose from Zac's hand as the damage was transmitted from the avatar in the sky. However, the wooden punishment contained an almost boundless vitality, and that effect was only boosted even further thanks to the Fragment of the Bodhi and his newly acquired [Spiritual Void].

His strike was chock-full of Dao, and bark rained down from the sky as it was ripped off and regrew in a rapid cycle of growth and withering. Zac's consumption of energy was enormous to withstand the hastily erected War Array, but their defense had one fatal weakness: it didn't actually provide any physical defenses.

A massive surge of Cosmic Energy filled his body as one werewolf after another was speared through. Over ten branches were aiming for each werewolf, and they could only maintain their intangible form for a short while. Over half the werewolves died from the blitz attack before the War Array finally managed to exhaust

[Nature's Punishment] to the point that Zac could no longer maintain it.

Just under twenty werewolves remained at this point, some of them maimed or even grievously wounded from fending off the branches of the bloody tree that now stood in the center of the relay station like a cursed effigy adorned with carcasses for offerings. Surrounding it was the spectral forest of [Hatchetman's Spirit], and together they had turned the sci-fi interior into a fey forest.

The attack was a huge success, but Zac still couldn't help but worry as he glanced at the enormous cracks that had appeared in the walls. The powerful Memorysteel normally wouldn't have been damaged to this point from the battle, but the metal in this section clearly wasn't being provided enough Base Power to recover. He knew that he would have to end this quickly unless he wanted to bring the whole roof down on his head.

"Join together!" one of the leaders desperately screamed, but Zac was relieved to see that six of the remaining warriors completely ignored the call as they fled through the gate on the other side.

There were still twelve werewolves to deal with, each of them powerful enough to withstand the strike of [Nature's Punishment]. Certainly, none of them came out of the clash unscathed, but they still carried a great fighting spirit as they moved together. A radiant silver moon had already appeared behind their backs as they howled toward Zac, causing dense lunar energies to stream out of their bodies.

The moonlight congealed into an enormous lunar wolf that lunged at Zac, and he felt a huge pressure bearing down on him. He didn't hesitate to activate the defensive charge of [Hatchetman's Spirit], but the shimmering barrier was quickly whittled down by an extremely piercing radiance that radiated from the spectral wolf's forehead.

Four chains shot out from the coffin that had appeared on Zac's back, and they launched forward like black spears full of corrosion as Zac flooded them with the Fragment of the Coffin. They pierced into the intangible wolf with enormous momentum, but it was like he was hitting a cloud. However, the radiant luster of the wolf somewhat dimmed from the black gases that spread from the chains, and the invasion caused a slight pause in the beast's advance.

The reprieve was enough for Zac to charge up his next ultimate skill, and a golden cloud spread out in a wave as a fifty-meter fractal blade swept out. The wave was rapidly diminished by the moonlight, but a second wave came crashing into the first just as the four chains slid out of the way. The two opposites of **[Rapturous Divide]** emerged in the warehouse the next moment, and both gold and black started competing with the silver for dominance.

The collision caused the whole room to shake, and cracks in the wall grew even further as Zac's newly erected corpse tree was cut in half and fell onto the ground with a deep thud. A few pieces of the wall and roof were actually completely dislodged from the shockwave, but they didn't fall down as Zac expected.

They instead were sucked up into the Void, leaving gaping holes just like the ones that were everywhere in the corridors. The scene intensified Zac's worries, but it seemed to have a far more profound impact on the few remaining werewolves, as over half of them started running for their lives even if the spectral wolf managed to cancel out most of Zac's attack.

That left just four beastkin, who seemed to be in a state of conflict between duty and fear, but Zac felt no such turmoil as he pushed forward. A brutal melee where **[Verun's Bite]** and the chains of **[Love's Bond]** turned into a dizzying blur resulted in the last of the werewolves, including the leader who had spoken up at the start, lying dead on the ground.

Zac sported some minor wounds and a nasty scar across his throat, but he was still in decent shape. His victory was all thanks to his initial blitz this time around. Zac had thought about the battle on the way over here, and he realized something while talking with Leviala. These natives had a lot of weird items that Zac didn't understand, but that worked the other way as well.

The fat stack of talismans and the **[Void Ball]** had essentially put them in a reactive position while breaking their Lunar War Array, the greatest threat to Zac's large-scale attacks. After that, it was just a matter of time before Zac was the last man standing. The werewolves weren't even given a chance to launch any of the technological weapons or traps they should have prepared in this place.

This wasn't the time to wallow in self-congratulatory revelry, though, and he quickly snatched up the closest corpses of the werewolf leaders before he rushed over to his scouting squad. The walls of the room were all creaking ominously by this point, and Zac got a bad feeling when he remembered the fear in the eyes of the werewolves as they'd fled.

He had thought the fear was directed at himself in the heat of the battle, but he now had a feeling that he was overestimating his importance.

"Are you guys okay?" Zac panted as he started ripping apart the bindings that held the group in place.

The scouts were bound by Memorysteel chains that were fused with the walls themselves, but they definitely didn't contain the same restraining capabilities as the odd gizmo in his possession. Then again, the material was extremely sturdy by itself, and even Zac had to strain a bit to break the chains.

"We're fine. We knew that you'd come for us," one of the two Valkyries said as she got to her feet.

Zac could only weakly smile in response, too shamefaced to admit that he'd only found out about their situation by a coincidence. He could only redouble his efforts in freeing everyone, urged on both embarrassment and a mounting fear as the cracks in the walls kept spreading.

"We should hunt the last ones down before they bring back more people!" a man Zac didn't recognize huffed as Zac broke apart his fetters. "Better yet, we should invade them… right… back."

The man had begun speaking with surging momentum, but he barely managed to squeeze the last words out as Zac silenced him with a glare. The others looked at Zac with confusion, but there was no time to explain the mounting danger he felt.

"Wha–" the man stuttered.

"Just shut up and run," Zac said as he freed the last scout, the demon warrior.

However, it was too late.

A series of odd explosions erupted all along the roof, and Zac guessed it was the remaining Base Power in the wall that had been become unstable as the chamber had lost the last of its structural integrity. The blasts were the straw that broke the camel's back, and the roof was ripped clean off and swallowed by the void. The atmosphere was still intact, but Zac didn't care about that, as he felt a very familiar dread gripping his heart.

Not only that, but an immense pressure weighed down on him like a restrictive array had been activated.

"Run!" Zac screamed as he grabbed one of the scouts with his free arm while his chains grabbed another four.

Only the demon warrior was able to stand, and he carried the last scout on his back. However, the two only managed to take a few steps before a horrifying scene entered their eyes. Two tentacles reached down from the void, making their way toward Zac and the demon warrior. The scene was scary enough by itself in conjuncture with the immense aura the appendages emitted, but Zac's terror reached even greater heights when he realized what the vines were made of.

Hands. Thousands of hands stitched together.

89
THE COLLECTOR

Zac felt like his brain was about to short-circuit when he saw what he was dealing with. It was one thing to see the distorting claw of the Void Creature before, but just what kind of eldritch horror would have these kinds of appendages? The sinister aura of this thing was far beyond the earlier creature as well, and Zac believed the only reason he could even stand was that the being was greatly restrained when entering the dimension of the Mystic Realm.

But there was no time to ponder what he was dealing with, as the ropes made of hands were extremely quick and nimble. He desperately activated **[Loamwalker]** to flash out of the way of one of the two appendages, but he could see that the demon wouldn't be able to do the same.

The ground cracked under Zac's feet as he hurriedly changed direction, forcibly tackling the demon from behind. The demon coughed up a mouthful of blood, and the Valkyrie's wounds seemed to worsen, but the push was enough to throw the two away, allowing them to avoid the first grab.

The demon's face was pallid, but he understood what was at stake. He gritted his teeth as he got up to his feet, and Cosmic Energy surged through his body as he sprinted toward the red barrier. This was Zac's only hope, that the base would block this thing as a security measure. He had already learned from Leviala that the barriers worked just like normal defensive arrays, usually just blocking passage from one direction. But hopefully, it would detect the Void Creature passing through the barrier and move to intercept it.

Zac activated [Loamwalker] once more to follow in the demon's footsteps, but horror gripped his heart when his skill was forcibly deactivated mid-step. One of the appendages had managed to grab hold of one of the unconscious scouts hanging from one of [Love's Bond's] chains, and Zac shuddered when he realized that the hands could actually move like normal as they grabbed the scout's legs and arms.

Desperation welled in his heart as Zac tried to drag him free only to find himself completely unable to match the power of the being still hidden in the void. He quickly found himself being lifted off the ground, utterly incapable of resisting. Guilt welled up in Zac's heart, but he could only release the scout before it was too late, and dropping toward the ground barely allowed him to dodge the second appendage.

The poor unconscious scout was quickly being hoisted into the darkness as the hands passed him along, but Zac resolutely looked forward as he activated [Loamwalker] again. The demon had already managed to escape through the barrier with one of the Valkyries, and the appendages completely ignored him after that.

The scene somewhat confirmed Zac's guess, and not having to worry about the demon gave Zac at least some reprieve. If he could only make it through the barrier, he would be safe as well.

However, Zac was gripped by despair when a third rope of hands suddenly descended from the sky, barring Zac's escape. He was forced to stop, as another step with his movement skill would put him right in range of the outreached hands. He frantically ran in a different direction as he started charging up his most powerful remaining skill, [Deforestation]. If he couldn't run out, then he would need to fight his way out.

The brief pause caused by the appearance of a third appendage was all that the eldritch horror needed, and it effortlessly snatched up a second scout. This time, it simply yanked him free, causing cracks to spread all over the links of [Love's Bond]. The body of the scout obviously couldn't withstand such force either, and just the upper body of the poor man was taken away while his legs fell on the floor.

The only consolation was that the scout had already been severely wounded before, and losing both his legs was just too much to endure. The shock instantly killed him, sparing him from being alive for whatever the Void Creature had in store.

Sweat beads streamed down Zac's face as he desperately dodged the lightning-quick vines as he prepared his Hail Mary attempt to get out of the relay station. He definitely feared for his life, but now there was yet another reason for him to worry: his training quest still hadn't been completed.

Two people had been lost to the horrifying appendages in an instant. Losing a third one meant the failure of his quest, and he couldn't let that happen no matter what. He moved the Valkyrie under his arm into one of his chains to free up his movement, and he kept the three scouts tight on his back to avoid another snatching.

But whatever the thing was on the other side of the Void, it still didn't seem satiated, and the three vines reached for him as he dodged back and forth in the refitted warehouse in an attempt to find an opening. Zac could sense a palpable hunger coming from the void even if he couldn't see the main body of the creature.

[Deforestation] was finally charged up, and the woodsman's axe emerged before it released a wave of destruction toward the sky. Zac didn't even pause to see the result as he rushed for the exit, but he found himself blocked again. The vines were only pushed back a bit from the strike as shallow wounds that looked like spatial tears appeared on the hands, but they were still able to move around freely in the room.

An odd undulation rocked Zac's mind for an instant, but he shook his head and followed up with the second swing. The Axe of Felling had not really hurt the creature, but it had at least stopped it for a second. Perhaps an opening would show itself if he kept pushing, so Zac unhesitantly unleashed a fiery wave of Axe-infused destruction toward the void.

The flames were unfortunately restrained, as the air was almost nonexistent in the chamber by this point, and it didn't seem like this creature was weak to fire either like one could have hoped. The cutting fire glommed onto the vines like napalm, but it was as though the hands absorbed its energy, quickly extinguishing it before they shot out toward Zac again.

Zac didn't completely give up hope, as he saw that the appendages had started distorting just like the claw from before. It seemed like his attacks had increased the pace at which the Void Creature was expelled from the Mystic Realm, and if he could cause enough damage, he might be able to flee. Luckily, there was one final card up Zac's sleeve, and the ominous Axe of Desolation made its entry.

A wave of darkness almost completely filled the relay station, engulfing all three appendages in a darkness that seemed a shade blacker than even the Void itself. A series of powerful implosions could be heard within, and Zac's eyes lit up as he started rushing for the exit again. However, a scream of danger made him stop in his tracks, allowing him to barely dodge a badly mangled hand that grabbed for his throat.

An instant later, the full tentacle emerged through the desolation, proving that even his strongest strike had failed to take out the tentacles.

The hands on the appendage had turned completely pitch-black from the attack, and a large number of them had their fingers turn into ash that drifted toward the void. Its form was rapidly distorting back and forth as well, and it was clearly about to be booted out of this space. However, a weird rune suddenly lit up on the back of all the hands, and the tentacle flashed forward with unprecedented speed and snatched Zac up by his waist.

A crushing pressure threatened to grind his pelvic bone to dust, but Zac ignored the pain as he desperately cut into the hands with everything he had. The sanguine glow of the first rune on [Verun's Bite] had already been activated again, quickly burning through the small amount of E-grade blood he had managed to gather since the battle with the lunar wolves.

Every swing contained enough force to turn a Middle E-grade warrior into paste, but the only effect was small scars like the earlier ones appearing across the hands. But the barrage also increased the speed the appendage destabilized, and Zac suddenly found his axe striking air as the appendage disappeared with a pop, just like the void bubble from before.

The implosion made Zac helplessly hover in the air for a short moment before a huge force exploded outward, slamming Zac into the

Memorysteel wall. However, luck was on Zac's side one final time, as he had been thrown right next to the gate. He quickly crawled through the barrier while dragging the chains with him.

It was just in time, since the last two tentacles finally managed to break through the cloud of desolation just as Zac passed through the red barrier. His whole body was hurting, but he arduously got up to his feet in case the hands tried to force their way through the gate. He didn't want to use it, but he still had the second skill of [Love's Bond] to block the path in case that happened.

But the tentacles stopped right outside the barrier before they started to retreat into the void again.

A surge of relief almost made Zac pass out, but his eyes suddenly widened in shock when he saw that none of the three scouts he had carried in his chains was moving. Blood was streaming down his mouth because of internal injuries, but he ignored his own state as he frantically reached for the people on the ground.

Thankfully, it turned out that none of them were dead, but they had rather been rendered unconscious sometime during the battle. It was no wonder, considering the speed Zac had moved around to avoid the grasping hands. Just the g-force alone would probably have been enough to kill a normal human.

Add to that the scouts' conditions, the sparse oxygen, and intense pressure from the Void Creature, and it was almost a miracle they were still alive. The demon and the Valkyrie he'd carried outside were sitting just a few meters away, and he was blankly staring at the Void through the barrier like his soul had left his body.

Zac threw a Cosmos Sack full of first-aid items to the demon, dragging him out of his blank state before he quickly fed all the unconscious scouts healing pills himself. Their complexions quickly improved, and a few of them even started to stir like they were about to wake up. A prompt appeared the next moment, allowing Zac to breathe out in relief.

He had passed the quest, albeit barely.

It seemed like the Void Creature really didn't dare pass through the red barrier for some reason. Of course, the terrifying tentacles were on their last legs because of the Axe of Desolation, and it was possible that the creature simply didn't want to lose two more appendages and cut its losses.

Seeing that he had escaped death once more, Zac simply slumped down on the ground, a wave of exhaustion hitting him like a punch to the face. However, he knew that he still was at the edge of the Wasteland, and a new horror could appear at a moment's notice, quest or no quest. He quickly took out a healing pill and two D-grade Nexus Crystals to restore his energy as quickly as possible.

The first of the unconscious scouts roused themselves a few minutes later, prompting Zac to open his eyes again. It was the man who had spoken up just before the Void Creature appeared. He blankly looked around like he was surprised to be alive for a few seconds before he spotted Zac seated against the wall.

"I – ah, I'm Jonas, Jonas Marshall," the man said with a hoarse voice. "Thank you for saving us from the wolves and that... thing. I didn't mean to order you about earlier. I –"

"It's fine." Zac shrugged, his voice equally hoarse. "I simply sensed something was wrong."

Of course, that was only part of the story. Another reason for the scathing glare was the fear this guy had put him in harm's way. He'd thought the training quest finished at that point and was afraid that the call for revenge would trigger the third part of his training regimen.

But no prompt had appeared as a result of the man's words, which was a huge relief.

The next logical step would have been to enter the Wasteland, and Zac was in no mood to risk his life against spatial storms and Void Creatures. He knew the System's preferences, and he wouldn't have been surprised if it kept escalating the conflict through quests until he had eradicated the whole Lunar Tribe before it turned him toward the Core Sector.

"And we can't follow those werewolves as we are, even if that monster weren't around," Zac added as he got to his feet with a grunt. "A place called the Wasteland is in that direction, and we don't have the equipment or understanding to cross it. It's apparently full of the things we just encountered."

The others visibly paled at that as they threw a few fearful glances toward the barrier. The horrifying appendages were gone for now, but that didn't mean there were even more of them waiting in the darkness.

"Let's go," Zac said. "We can't stay here any longer. We're returning to our base camp."

The scouts were more than willing to comply, and they got themselves ready to travel even in their pitiable states. The demon wordlessly kept carrying one of the unconscious scouts on his back, while Zac carried another one in his chains. The last two managed to walk by themselves, albeit barely.

None of them were in any mood to talk, and neither was Zac. This encounter had been much too close for comfort. Worse yet, this was just the second of ten quests. He didn't even dare to think what fresh hell the System would put him through next. So it was in an oppressive silence the group scurried away from the relay station, following the same route that Zac took on the way in.

They quickly reached the alcove where Zac had left Leviala, and the Cartava scion was still sitting there, fretfully peering around the corner. When she saw Zac's and the others' states, her eyes widened in shock as she got up to her feet.

"What happened?" Leviala hesitantly asked as her eyes peered at the group behind Zac.

"I managed to catch them off guard, and things worked out against the werewolves. A weird creature made from thousands of hands popped up, and we lost two of our people." Zac sighed as he formed the chain-chair again. "Let's go."

However, Leviala didn't move, but simply looked at Zac with horror.

"Thousands of hands? You met the Collector?" Leviala said, her voice barely a whisper.

"What? The Collector? I don't know. It had tentacles made from thousands of hands sewn together. I managed to destroy one of the tentacles, allowing us to escape," Zac said.

"YOU HARMED IT?!" Leviala shrieked as she scrambled onto the chair. "We need to go! *NOW!*"

90

THE HERO'S BURDEN

The Hero's Burden (Training (3/10)): Avoid the Collector while leading your followers to safety. Reward: Reward based on performance at the end of training regimen. (0/1)

[NOTE: Failure to comply with training regimen will result in loss of two random skills and 5 levels.]

Zac barely had time to take in Leviala's exaggerated reaction before the prompt in front of him appeared. Zac quickly scanned the quest with some exhaustion. He wasn't completely wrung dry just yet, but he was also far from an optimal condition. But the quest acted as a warning of sorts, and Zac knew there wasn't anything he could do except keep going.

The quest didn't have a timer, and neither did it have any restrictions. But that might actually not be a good thing, since it might mean that a single death would result in failure. The punishment for failing had decreased once more at least, though the punishment was still far too rich for Zac's tastes.

"Let's keep moving. If you're unable to move any longer, tell me, and I'll carry you," Zac said before he turned to Leviala, who was already sitting on her chair. "Is it safe to talk?"

"It can't hear us, but it can sense us," Leviala whispered with fear in her eyes as she gazed at the cracks in the ceiling. "It'll pounce if we stop for just a moment."

Zac nodded in understanding as he set out, keeping as high a pace as he dared in this chaotic place.

"What do you know about that thing?" Zac asked.

"The Collector is said to be the second greatest source of deaths during the Cataclysm, only lacking compared to the spatial storms themselves. It's not necessarily the strongest Void Creature, but it's definitely one of the weirdest. More importantly, it's unusually resilient to our dimension. You saw the claw before. It deformed by itself in seconds. But the Collector's hands can stay for hours as long as they're not attacked," Leviala said.

"The Collector is also extremely crafty, and it's even able to enter the research base through spatial tears. There have been reports of people being snatched all over the base, even in sectors thought to be safe," she said as she held her hands against her chest. "But I don't understand. It's been gone for thousands of years. It left a few centuries after the Cataclysm, and there have been no sightings since."

"Well, I guess it came back now that the treasure is maturing." Zac sighed. "Why do you call it the Collector? Does it actually collect hands?"

"That's our guess, at least. We think it somehow attaches them to itself to better withstand this dimension. That's why it's so dangerous to attack it. It really treasures its collection, and it will hunt you down if you harm the hands," Leviala said, looking almost ready to cry. "And now we're in a sector full of breaches."

"Uh, well," Zac muttered, but he didn't get any further before a sense of dread filled him. "RUN!"

The others didn't hesitate at all as Cosmic Energy surged in their bodies as they rushed down the corridor. It was just in time as well, as a tentacle suddenly rushed out of a crack in the ceiling just behind them.

"It's really the Collector," Leviala said. "We're doomed. We're doomed. It's either the Collector or getting bisected by spatial tears."

"Shut up, or I'll use you as a shield," Zac growled as he kept running.

Another sense of danger filled his mind the next moment, and he stopped just in time to avoid running straight into a spatial tear. A piece of his robes was cut apart, telling him just how close he had come to getting split open like a melon. The others quickly stopped in their tracks as well, barely avoiding the spatial storm that emerged from the void the next second.

Zac's nerves were as taut as a bowstring, but there was no way to force himself through the storm. Waiting for the spatial storm to pass was obviously not an option either with the Collector in pursuit.

"Left!" Leviala screamed, and Zac turned down another corridor, the others desperately following in tow.

The hands were too close, though, and the slower Valkyrie was about to get snatched up.

"Shit!" Zac growled as he stopped in his tracks before he shot forward like a cannonball as his free chains slammed into the Memorysteel in the opposite direction.

A barrage of five-meter fractal edges slammed into the hands of the Collector the next second, each carrying a tremendous force. Small scars appeared on the hands, but Zac's normal F-grade [Chop] could barely slow the tentacle down as it grasped for the deathly pale Valkyrie. Zac saw no option but to go in himself, and he appeared right behind his follower just as a hand was about to grasp her neck.

A tremendous shockwave caused cracks to spread across the whole corridor as [Verun's Bite] collided with the palm of the slightly larger hand at the end of the tentacle. A weird scar appeared on the skin as the fingers on the closest hands spasmed and bent at impossible angles, perhaps an indication of pain.

Zac wasn't much better off, though; a weird, sinister energy had entered his body the moment the two opposites clashed. Zac felt his vision blur for a second, but a thud from his chest woke him right up, just in time to avoid getting snatched up by a second grab. Whatever energy had entered his body just now, his [Void Heart] had swallowed it. If that was a good or a bad thing, only time would tell.

The all-out Axe-Infused swing had only left a flesh wound, but Zac didn't care as he fled, dragged away by two of the chains he had embedded in the wall before rushing back. The collision had fulfilled its purpose, as the Valkyrie had already moved a hundred meters away, and Zac sighed in relief when he saw the Collector retracting its appendage.

Those things were only so long, so if Zac could obstruct it a second or two, he would be able to keep his people safe.

"Argh!" the demon suddenly screamed from the vanguard, immediately proving Zac wrong.

The group had kept running while Zac stalled the tentacle, and this time, they didn't have Zac's Luck to keep them safe from a spatial tear.

A huge wound had opened up in the demon's side, and blood already pooled on the floor beneath him.

"Eat this," Zac said as he threw out one of his top-quality private healing pills.

"Thank you," the demon said as he swallowed the pill, but Zac's eyes widened when a flame appeared in his hands.

However, the demon wasn't targeting him or anyone else, but rather used a fireball spell to quickly cauterize the wound, leaving a nasty burn instead.

"I can keep going," the demon said with a ragged breath, but Zac saw that his whole body shook.

Zac nodded, but he still took the unconscious Valkyrie the demon had been carrying. The demon actually stretched out his hand to take her back, but he reluctantly stopped himself after looking down at his wound.

"You can carry her when the pill has restored you a bit more," Zac said as he started running.

"Thank you... Jana is... my wife," the demon said. "Save her first if it comes down to that."

Zac's brows rose, but now wasn't the time to ask for details. The group kept running down the unknown corridor, led by Leviala's expertise and guesswork. It was clear their speed wasn't enough to avoid detection, as the tentacles of the Collector kept appearing through the cracks in the walls or ceilings. It felt like they were one bad turn away from disaster at every moment.

They thankfully weren't all that far from the gate, and Zac knew that he would only need to keep it up for another fifteen minutes if they kept this pace. He could do it.

However, disaster finally struck after they had been forced down yet another unknown corridor by the emergence of another tentacle. What should have been a normal pathway had turned into a dead end because of a collapsed wall some distance in, with an endless number of spatial anomalies making it impossible to climb across the rubble.

The Collector's tentacle was actually still around as well, like it knew that they were trapped.

"It's over," Leviala said as tears streamed down her face, her eyes slowly turning toward the spatial tears. "Better the tears…"

"I told you to stop talking like that," Zac muttered as a terrifying aura exploded out from his body, and he felt how a series of black fractals appeared across his face.

He was out of options, so he could only blast his way out. And the only card he had that could deal with this monstrosity was his Annihilation Sphere. A surge of destruction coursed through his body as the energy of Oblivion seeped out of his soul like steam on a cold day. His avatar had stopped fighting as well and instead stretched out its two hands in front of it as a surging river of Dao was released from it.

The coffin was the same, releasing a small amount of Coffin Dao that blended with the energy of the Splinter of Oblivion, though the amount it released was somewhat lower because of the infusion of Oblivion. The streams entered his pathways, and Zac started to feel his mind blur, but he couldn't let himself go into a trance in a place like this, against an enemy like this.

He desperately held on to his sanity as he pushed his two hands forward, meeting the outreached hands of the Collector head-on.

The world froze for an instant before the tip of the tentacle simply disappeared, taking dozens of hands with it. A half-meter sphere of nothingness replaced the tip, and Zac looked at it with wonder as he was thrown back. He didn't know why, but that small ball of Annihilation was infinitely beautiful, like it contained the ultimate truth of the universe.

The sphere only existed for a fraction of a second before it disappeared, leaving a frozen and maimed tentacle behind. However, the tentacle didn't remain unmoving for long, and a series of shudders spread through its hands. One implosion after another erupted next as the whole tentacle seemed to fall apart.

A single Annihilation Sphere had done more harm to the creature than all of [Deforestation's] swings combined, and the thing lost its ability to stay in this dimension. Leviala looked at Zac with blank incomprehension, and the others in the group weren't any better. Even the Valkyries looked at Zac with a mix of awe and horror, like Zac suddenly had become even more terrifying than the eldritch horror hunting them.

"Are you okay?" one of the Valkyries asked, but she didn't dare to walk over.

"I'm fine," Zac lied as he got back to his feet with some difficulty.

It wasn't completely true, though. Using the Annihilation Sphere so soon after having gone through a heated battle had put an immense strain on his mind, and he was barely holding on to his consciousness. He could also feel that the cracks that ran down his neck had worsened this time around, making Zac feel some helplessness.

The cracks had never really healed since the last time he'd used his Annihilation Sphere. His flesh had mended, but the odd energies had stayed on like hidden tendrils lodged in his body. Not even the lava bath had managed to expel them like the rest of his impurities, and neither was his [Void Heart] able to gobble them up.

He had no idea what the long-term ramification was of using the bronze flash over and over, and he could only pray that he would find some solution sooner rather than later. Because it wasn't like he could stop using the Remnants even if he wanted to. They were his final card when everything was hopeless, when it was either do or die.

"Wh–" Leviala wheezed, seemingly struggling to form a coherent sentence.

"Looks like I had to go all out again." Zac wryly smiled in response as he started running back down the path they'd come from now that the tentacle was gone.

"What kind of –" the Cartava scion stuttered, but she was interrupted as a massive earthquake rocked the whole corridor with such force that she fell out of her chair.

Zac tried to make his mind focus as he turned around, but he realized that he wouldn't be able to do anything against what was coming, even if he were in perfect condition.

At least twenty tentacles had forced their way out of the rubble of the collapsed corridor, and they madly pushed toward them, destroying everything in their path. The Memorysteel walls were ripped apart and deformed, exposing a series of worn-down tubes and contraptions hidden inside the walls.

It looked like a tide of hands was coming for them, no longer caring about playing it safe.

No orders were needed this time around as the group ran for their lives, not caring about anything but moving as quickly as possible. But the tentacles were too quick, especially since they didn't bother taking the same winding path as Zac's group. They rather just crushed the walls in the way, forming a new path for themselves.

Zac was out of ideas. He was exhausted and out of aces. He still had [**Love's Bond**], but he didn't believe for a second that his Spirit Tool's skill would be able to block the Collector's path. It would probably just end with his Spirit Tool being damaged and Alea's soul being wounded even further.

A radiant light suddenly filled the corridor as the decrepit scripts on the walls flared into life. An endless series of clanking sounds echoed from within the walls the next moment, like someone had turned on the machines inside. Dozens of red barriers sprang up next, the closest one right in front of Zac's group.

Zac and the others passed through effortlessly, allowing them to breathe out in a collective sigh of relief. Of course, one single barrier wasn't enough for Zac to feel safe considering that the sounds of destruction from behind hadn't abated at all. The group kept running through one barrier after another, barely maintaining their footing.

"The base is intervening!" Leviala suddenly cried with joy. "Is the Administrator really alive?!"

A huge surge of power made Zac's hair stand on end the next moment, and he quickly looked back to see what was going on. He could quickly determine there was no immediate threat, but what he saw still made him want to run for the hills.

Was this the true form of the Collector?

91
HORROR

Seeing the scene behind them almost made Zac forget the primal fear the tide of hands had elicited just a few seconds ago. The whole base had simply disappeared just a hundred meters behind them, replaced by a void that stretched into infinity. It looked like the series of red barriers had been erected to maintain atmospheric pressure to the base.

There were no stars or nebulae in the void, yet it wasn't completely dark. A thin strand of light stretched across the horizon, like a beam of light that had squeezed through a crack. Zac had no idea what that crack was, but he figured that it perhaps was a path to a real space-time rather than the void between dimensions.

The scene was pretty shocking, but it was nothing compared to the appearance of the Collector.

The disgusting hand-tentacles were horrifying enough, but its main body easily topped it. Zac had imagined some sort of Lovecraftian horror after seeing the tentacles, but he wasn't sure whether the real Collector was better or worse. It almost looked like an ashy-gray blob of yarn floating in space, but the more he looked, the more horrific it became.

Its form was a slightly uneven sphere that spanned thousands of meters across, making it a creature far larger than anything Zac had ever encountered before. He initially thought it was covered with coarse skin or short-haired fur, but a second glance actually revealed that they were just more body parts sewn onto its real form. However, it wasn't just hands on its main body, but everything from legs to whole torsos and heads.

Worse yet, the body parts moved in everything from lackluster swaying to frantic clawing. Zac even spotted a head-and-handless torso desperately clawing at its midriff with its two stumps, probably trying to rip itself off of the Collector's body. The scene made him gape in horror, and an intrusive thought pushed away everything else.

Were the collected bodies still alive?

There weren't only humans attached to the body either, but Zac quickly spotted hundreds of werewolves as well. That wasn't the extent of it, as he could easily discern at least thirty different Races in short order. It looked like the research base wasn't the Collector's only hunting ground, which would explain why it had disappeared for so long.

As for the tentacles, there were hundreds, most of them randomly swaying about in the void like strands that had come loose from the ball of yarn. Only a few of them actually had body parts covering them, with the rest appearing to be made from something that looked like an oily liquid. In fact, there were large patches of bare parts on the main body as well, meaning that the Collector wasn't done with its horrifying undertaking.

The Collector only had one additional feature, a weird hole in the middle of its body that seemed endless, like it led into a dimension of its own. Just looking into the depths made Zac's soul shudder and forced him to look away. He had actually felt a pull on his soul, like the maw of the Collector had some sort of spiritual pull.

A clanking sound dragged Zac out of his muddled state as a series of enormous metal rings floated out in the void. There were over a hundred of them, each covered in dense scripts and thrumming with power. Zac quickly realized that the rings were made out of Memorysteel, and it was likely this "Administrator," who had chosen to completely transform a section of the base to defend against the Collector's attacks.

The rings were of varying sizes, with the smallest ones being just ten meters in diameter and the largest ones being at least a few hundred meters across. The rings moved themselves to form a series of uneven tubes aimed at the creature before they started spinning with increasing velocity. The rings had turned into a blur in almost an instant, easily having reached tens of thousands of rpm.

Radiant motes of light soon appeared out of nowhere in the center of the tubes, likely somehow generated by the spinning. It was hard to tell whether the lights were made from extremely condensed energy or if they were an actual liquid, and it made Zac think of the experiments on plasma he had read about years ago.

However, this definitely wasn't something that would have been possible to create in some Earth lab, but rather some high-tiered energy that definitely exceeded anything he had seen aboard the *Little Bean*. Zac knew that he would instantly be turned to ash if he even got close to those things, and he kept backing away as he gazed at the accumulating lights with trepidation.

Suddenly, one of the blobs of light turned into a ten-meter-wide streak, hitting the Collector's main body like the discharge of a rail gun. Cascading lights illuminated the void, and Zac felt a series of small wounds appearing on his soul from just looking at the spectacle. The Collector shuddered from the collision, but it clearly wasn't dead, as dozens of tentacles shot toward the still-accumulating energy weapons.

"Run! Just being witness to a fight like this is a death sentence," Leviala screamed, blood streaming from her nose.

Zac wordlessly nodded, no longer daring to stay on to watch the result of the clash between the Void Creature and the base itself. He snatched up the scouts, who had all fallen unconscious, as he rushed back where they'd come from, barely keeping himself upright after a series of shockwaves that meant that the battle had started in earnest.

The base was at least occupying the Collector's attention now, allowing Zac to only worry about the spatial tears as he ran for his life. However, that was easier said than done since the epic struggle was causing serious damage to the already weakened section. It looked like the whole place could collapse at a moment's notice, with pieces of wall and ceiling falling all around them.

The spatial tears constantly poured through the cracks, and Zac was forced to jump back and forth like a monkey to avoid getting himself and his people cut into ribbons. On top of that, there was the constant threat that the Collector would return full of vengeance after having been blasted by the base's energy weapons.

Zac's heart was beating like a drum when they finally reached the inconspicuous part of the wall that led back to the forest, and he quickly took out the tablet, his shaky hands barely able to maintain a grip on it.

The gate was conjured the same way as last time, with Leviala being much too distracted to even care about how he did it. She kept a constant vigil to their back in case the tentacles returned, and she only turned back when she heard the sound of the gate sliding open. Zac didn't wait for even a second as he rushed out.

Seeing the lush forest felt like a stay of execution, and he unceremoniously fell down in a heap on the grass as he dumped his followers on the ground. He didn't know why, but it felt like the enormous wall would be able to keep the monster at bay, and the System apparently agreed, as he suddenly got a prompt that he had completed the third part of his training regimen.

A wave of exhaustion hit him the second he saw the prompt, but he barely managed to keep himself from falling unconscious. His pumping adrenaline had kept him going even after unleashing the power of Oblivion, but his debts had come back to haunt him as a searing pain spread from his head down to his shoulders.

He quickly ate a series of pills, ranging from soul-mending to fasting pills to provide nutrients, and he took out both a Soul Crystal and a D-grade Nexus Crystal to start restoring his condition. The scouts started to come to one after another as well, and they quickly sat down and focused on recuperation as well after having taken in their surroundings.

Three hours passed before Zac sighed and opened his eyes again, having barely reached a combat-ready state. New flesh had once more covered the cracks formed from unleashing the Annihilation Sphere, and his mind didn't feel like it was full of cotton any longer. However, he knew that he was spreading himself too thin at the moment, and he wasn't sure how many more training quests he had in him.

It felt like the difficulty had taken a sharp spike after the first one, but he didn't know if that was just because he was unlucky enough to run into the Collector. It was hard to tell whether the System created its quests as things progressed, or whether it had foreseen everything that would happen. If it was the former, then he could only blame his bad luck and pray that his hardships would be taken into account when he finished the quest chain.

If it was the latter, he could only once again chalk it up to the System being a real asshole.

He suddenly heard some shuffling next to him, and he looked over to see Leviala getting to her feet to stretch. It looked like she finally had regained some of her strength after using her taboo bloodline skill.

"I don't know whether to call you lucky or unlucky," she muttered as she glanced at Zac with a complicated look. "Getting attacked by two different Void Creatures is some misfortune; they're not *that* common. But we still managed to survive somehow, even being saved by the base itself."

"Well, I often find myself asking that as well. Luck and misfortune seem to be two sides of the same coin in the Multiverse," Zac said with a wry smile.

"What happened there at the end, though?" Leviala asked with a frown. "Why did the Collector become so angry that it directly attacked the base? Did you do something? I must have blacked out for a second."

"I just damaged one of its tentacles a bit again." Zac shrugged. "Perhaps it got angry because it happened for a second time."

"Hmm," Leviala said, suspicion written all over her face.

Actually, Zac wasn't surprised at her reaction. He had learned something peculiar from talking with Thea some time ago. She was actually unable to remember exactly what Zac had done when he'd killed Harbinger back during the Zhix Wars. She only remembered him stretching out his arms, then seeing the Zhix lying destroyed on the ground while he stood above it covered in weird runes. Everything in between was just a blank.

It turned out that his Annihilation Sphere actually messed with the minds of others, somehow deleting or destroying any memory of witnessing it. He didn't know if it was because of the System's meddling, or rather if it was because normal people couldn't withstand that kind of high-tiered concept.

Zac was actually leaning toward the latter, as the oddity reminded him of him seeing the Chaos Pattern during his battle with the dragon. He could still somewhat remember a sense of complete understanding of the universe for an instant, just like how he had felt when seeing his Annihilation Sphere just now.

But any actual understanding had gradually disappeared, and he couldn't remember a single feature of the Chaos Pattern by the time he left the Tower of Eternity. This weird phenomenon was partly why he dared to use the Annihilation Sphere in front of others. He even believed that the only thing awaiting Leviala if she used her bloodline skill to see what had happened would be a shocking backlash, especially considering the Collector had been involved as well.

"Well, now what?" Leviala asked, the leading question making Zac freeze in fear.

But it looked like the System was giving him a breather this time around, with no new prompt appearing.

"None of us are in great shape," Zac eventually said as he took out the backpacks of the werewolves. "Let's rest a bit longer before we get going."

He had only managed to snatch one Cosmos Sack and two backpacks back at the relay station, but all three belonged to squad leaders, meaning they should hold the best stuff. Now was as good a time as any to see if there actually were any returns from almost getting killed a dozen times over.

However, Zac's face scrunched up when he noticed the sacks were mostly full of food and first-aid items, along with some gadgets that mostly looked like more of the same as what he had looted off of Hevastes. He noted with interest that there was not a single pill or Nexus Crystal among their possessions, and it was the same with Hevastes' bag.

Instead, there were a few vials of a milky liquid that had healing properties according to Leviala, but the effect was a lot worse compared to his healing pills. That wasn't to say that his mother's family was unable to create proper remedies. The problem was rather that these vials essentially contained runoff of the real thing, siphoned off the base by the natives.

Seeing there was not much of interest, he turned his attention to the gadgets. There were two chargers similar to the one he'd looted from Hevastes, but they both were not only smaller, but they also looked homemade. His best guess was that Hevastes' charger had been looted somewhere on the base, while the other two had been created in its likeness to the best of the werewolves' abilities.

Still, it was an impressive feat to reverse-engineer a piece of equipment like this, and it proved that the natives weren't simply scavengers in this place.

There were also two tablets identical to the one in his possession, and Zac simply put them aside as he honed in on a tablet that looked a bit different compared to the others.

"What's this?" Zac asked as he turned to the Cartava scion.

"A mapper," Leviala said as she leaned over, and Zac could see some desire in her good eye. "It's used to record safe paths. You can also add comments about security measures, spatial traps in it, creating detailed maps."

Zac's eyes lit up as he looked down at the smaller tablet in his hands. Wasn't this exactly what he needed right now?

92
MAPPER

Zac looked down at the rough tablet in his hands like it was a priceless treasure, and he infused it with some Base Energy as he kept Leandra's token hidden in his palm. It hummed a second later as the screen lit up, making Zac feel a surge of success. No matter what the true intentions of his mother were, it was undeniable that she had provided him with a huge advantage by leaving behind the token.

It was starting to look like it was some sort of ghost key in this place, working on almost everything. Of course, the thing was clearly not infallible, as the walls held no compunctions about attacking him, and neither did it remove the barriers in the corridors.

"It's unlocked!" Leviala said with wide eyes, and it almost looked like she would drag the tablet out of his hands. "How could this intelligence be unsecured?! This is top-secret information for a faction. Look, this! It's their route through the Wasteland. And these paths, they're completely new! They're taking advantage of the spatial expansion to find new routes through vents and even some pipes."

Zac let her keep talking, as it helped him a lot as well. The maps Leviala browsed through almost looked like schematics for circuitry to him, and he had a hard time understanding all of them. His sister or the scientists would probably be able to figure the thing out, but learning from a native would save a lot of time and effort.

"Look at these ones! They're circumventing so many natural blockades. A few of them might even be able to reach the inner labs!

Just what is the Lunar Tribe planning?" Leviala added with grudging respect mixed with a hint of confusion. "And why are they going in that direction? All the pathways out of here seem to be at the edges of the realm. Aren't they trying to escape?"

Zac was about to ask a few questions, but he froze as the dreaded prompt appeared once again. He threw Leviala an exasperated look even though he knew it wasn't really her fault before he focused on the blue screens that had appeared this time.

[Man Versus Nature (Training (4/10)): Reach the heart of the Wasteland before Dimensional Seed matures. Reward: Reward based on performance at the end of training regimen. (0/1)]

[Man Versus Machine (Training (4/9)): Enter "Inner Lab 16" before Dimensional Seed matures. Reward: Reward based on performance at the end of training regimen. (0/1)]

[NOTE: Failure to comply with training regimen will result in loss of one random skill and 4 levels. Choosing second option will disqualify trainee from highest reward tier.]

It turned out that Zac had been given a branching quest this time, likely based on the large number of maps in his new mapper. Zac was about to discard the one that would lead him into the Wasteland, but he stopped himself. At first glance, it felt like the first option was suicidal, but perhaps that wasn't the case.

As long as the Collector had been pushed back from the direct vicinity of the base, then he had everything he needed to succeed. He had the map and a lot of Base Power and the ability to discern spatial tears before they appeared. Meanwhile, the second quest indicated that he might come in direct conflict with the base itself, which could complicate things when trying to deal with the Dominators.

It wasn't that Zac wanted to enter a place like the Wasteland, but the note at the end gave him pause. Judging by the difficulty of the training session so far, the reward would probably be at the level of the eighth floor of the Tower of Eternity or even higher. Getting a customized top-tier reward at this stage would be huge, considering that all Zac's greatest assets, from **[Love's Bond]** to the Creator Shipyard and the Dao Repository, came from these kinds of rewards.

This difference was further exemplified by the fact that the Man Versus Machine quest decreased the quest chain to nine total quests. The punishment had decreased as well, and it looked like completing six quests essentially was a "passing grade," with every subsequent quest improving the reward.

Stopping at the ninth quest instead of the tenth might be a massive blow, like how huge Zac's loss would have been if he had stopped at the seventh floor instead of the eighth in the Tower of Eternity.

But Zac also had to think of the big picture. He wasn't here to gain rewards, but to complete a specific task. He wasn't sure whether passing through the Wasteland or heading to these laboratories was the best course of action to deal with the Dominators.

"What's the inner labs?" Zac asked, turning to the Cartava descendant for guidance.

"What? Well, that's…" Leviala said, hesitation clearly written all over her face.

"I should tell you that Port Atwood controls more than half of the world outside, including almost all the top-quality cultivation sites and high-value resources. If Clan Cartava wants a good domain to rebuild your clan on the outside, you need to give something in return," Zac said.

Jonas and the other scout who weren't from Port Atwood looked a bit miffed at the domineering proclamation, but they held their tongues. Zac's words were a bit boastful, but they were essentially true if you counted the whole second continent as his own. There were certainly a lot of Nexus Crystal mines and other resources strewn across the planet, but most of the really valuable deposits had received an incursion next to them, meaning they now belonged to Port Atwood.

"Well, it's not really secret knowledge among the people in here," Leviala said after some hesitation. "Each faction in here has managed to take control of some laboratories or unique technology in their area, and each of them provides something valuable. For example, Clan Cartava owns a series of unique greenhouses with various valuable fruits for Race upgrades and even upgrading your constitution."

Zac's eyes lit up when he heard about Race upgrades. Perhaps they even had some herb that worked on his undead constitution, allowing him to keep working on his Draugr Race now that he had almost run out of **[Bone-Forging Dust]**.

"The most valuable of the outer laboratories are arguably controlled by the gemlings on the opposite side of the base," Leviala continued after some thought. "They contain something called bloodline vats. I hear that bathing in that stuff can help forcibly awaken a bloodline. The bloodlines of the gemlings are apparently notoriously hard to awaken naturally, but thanks to these vats, they are able to have as many bloodline warriors as the rest of us."

"Then what about the inner laboratories?" Zac asked curiously.

"The outer laboratories contain great things, but they were ultimately used for large-scale experiments. The materials are helpful, but not without limits or side effects. However, the inner laboratories were made for more valuable experiments. The number of resources that can be found there is much scarcer, but their quality is conversely higher. Quite a few skirmishes have erupted for the things that can be found there over the past millennia." Leviala sighed.

"Who controls the inner laboratories now, then?" Zac asked.

"No one. Or perhaps the Administrator, if you can believe the rumors," Leviala said. "The inner laboratories are normally not accessible, but every few decades, a lot of the barriers in this place disappear. We believe it's the base that shuts down some functions for routine maintenance or energy conservation. That always gave us a brief window to rush to the inner areas and loot the valuables.

"However, no one who has chosen to stay behind when the barriers reappeared has ever been found alive again. We think the Administrator kills them when it wakes up," she continued. "But it usually gave us a month of searching for opportunities and trading or fighting with the other factions."

"So the Lunar Tribe wants to snatch the good things in this base before escaping," Zac muttered. "What can be found in the inner labs that the werewolves have targeted here?"

"I don't know," Leviala said. "It's actually random. The core of the base is running as though it was never abandoned by the Builders. The base itself prepares all kinds of experiments and scenarios, completely changing the layouts of the inner labs between gatherings. I... managed to enhance my bloodline in an inner lab fifteen years ago."

Zac's eyes lit up at the piece of news. His mouth was almost frothing at the mention of bloodline vats and Races upgrades, but it sounded like there were even more valuable things waiting in the inner labs. He was first a bit hesitant when the System mentioned better rewards by heading to the Wasteland, but it sounded like these labs provided a different set of opportunities instead.

Of course, he understood that the quest wasn't a complete freebie, and he had just been given a glimpse of the base's defensive powers just a few hours ago. Still, the second quest seemed to take him in the direction he needed to go, whereas going through the Wasteland was a gamble that might or might not result in better rewards.

A weak gust of wind ruffled Zac's robes as he turned his head in the direction of the heart of the base. It was there the true treasures of this place waited, where the final challenge of the integration remained. Between the mapper and his recent breakthroughs, everything he needed for his true mission was in place.

This would be the final battle for Earth's future, and this time, he wouldn't allow Void's Disciple to slink away.

THANK YOU FOR READING
DEFIANCE OF THE FALL,
BOOK SIX.

We hope you enjoyed it as much as we enjoyed bringing it to you. We just wanted to take a moment to encourage you to review the book. Follow this link: Defiance of the Fall 6 to be directed to the book's Amazon product page to leave your review.

Every review helps further the author's reach and, ultimately, helps them continue writing fantastic books for us all to enjoy.

DEFIANCE OF THE FALL
BOOK ONE
BOOK TWO
BOOK THREE
BOOK FOUR
BOOK FIVE
BOOK SIX
BOOK SEVEN

You can also join our non-spam mailing list by visiting www.subscribepage.com/AethonReadersGroup and never miss out on future releases. You'll also receive three full books completely Free as our thanks to you.

Facebook | Instagram | Twitter | Website (www.aethonbooks.com)

Want to discuss our books with other readers and even the authors? Join our Discord server today and be a part of the Aethon community.

Looking for more great books?

Qube was designed to die...

As the cheerful childhood NPC companion who helps the [Player] learn the world during the start of the game, it was only natural that the big bad would kill her at the end of the tutorial, kick-starting the [Player] on a quest for vengeance.

The only thing is, no one told her that...

And this particular [Player] doesn't like to play by the rules. Being a chaos-loving gremlin, he glitches her out of her programming loop and drags her on various adventures. They'll grapple with friendly sharktopuses, Evil Emperors, and what it means to be a person.

On the way, they pick up equally unlikely party members, with Qube breaking the world in increasingly strange ways as she seeks to be the very best companion ever.

All the while, Qube herself slowly realizes that her reality is not quite what it seems...

Get The Chosen One

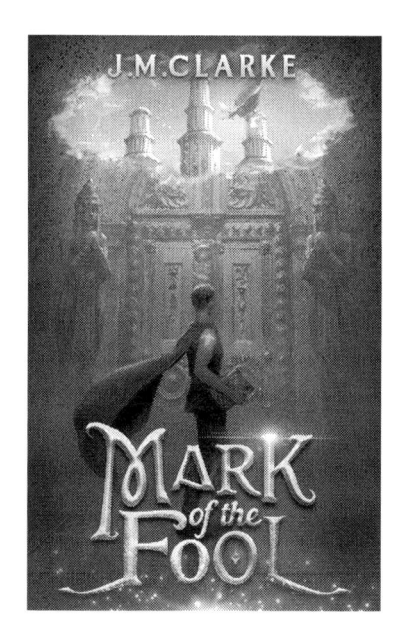

The gods chose him. He said no.
After his parents died, Alex Roth had one desire: become a wizard. Through hard work, he was accepted into the University of Generasi, the world's greatest academy of wizardry...

Fate, however, had other plans.

On his eighteenth birthday, he is Marked by prophecy as one of his kingdom's five Heroes, chosen to fight the Ravener, his land's great enemy. But his brand is 'The Fool'. Worst of the marks.

Rather than die or serve other Heroes like past Fools, he takes a stand, rejects divine decree…and leaves. With his little sister, his childhood friend, and her cerberus, Alex flees for the university, hoping to research the mystery of the Ravener. He'll make lifelong friends, learn magic from mad wizards, practice alchemy, fight mana vampires and try to pay tuition.

There's one small problem. The Mark insists on preventing the Fool from learning and casting spells, while enhancing skills outside of divinity, combat, and spellcraft…
…that is, unless he learns to exploit the hell out of it.

Get Mark of the Fool now!

Damien nearly ended the world. Now, his mistake might be the only thing that can save it.

Good things come to those who wait. Damien Vale didn't, and he ended up bound to an Eldritch creature from beyond the reaches of space. It has lived since the dawn of time, seen the world born and destroyed countless times, and wants to be called Henry.

Unusual companion or not, Damien was still determined to go to a mage college and study magic. He wants nothing more than to live normal life as a researcher, but if Henry's true nature is revealed, he'll be killed.

To top it all off, Damien's teacher is a madman from the front lines of war, his alcoholic dean suspects something is awry with his companion, and Blackmist might possibly be the worst school in history. Damien has to prevent the end of the world, but he isn't even sure he's going to make it through Year One at Blackmist.

Get My Best Friend is an Eldritch Horror

For all our LitRPG books, visit our website.